The Mandarins

SIMONE DE BEAUVOIR, Europe's leading woman novelist, was born in Paris in 1909. A close friend of the late writer and philosopher Jean-Paul Sartre, and well known as a leader of the existentialist movement in Paris, her novels have won wide acclaim throughout the world. Her famous work, *The Second Sex*, was hailed as a classic study of women and *The Mandarins*, her brilliant survey of post-war intellectualism in France, won the coveted Prix Goncourt. She died in 1986.

'There are a few, a very few novels that have what one can only call a climate of their own; they are usually long but they are rewarding, for in them are the seeds of greatness; one comes away from them with the feeling of having travelled, experienced, learned, of being enlarged in understanding. Such a book is *The Mandarins*.'
Rumer Godden, *The Bookman*

Simone de Beauvoir

The
Mandarins

Translated by
Leonard M. Friedman

Published by Fontana Paperbacks

First published in Paris by Librairie
Gallimard under the title *Les Mandarins* 1954
First English translation published in Great
Britain by William Collins Sons & Co. Ltd 1957
First issued in Fontana Paperbacks 1960
Fourteenth impression May 1982

This Flamingo edition first published
in 1984 by Fontana Paperbacks,
8 Grafton Street, London W1X 3LA
Second impression 1986

Made and printed in Great Britain by
William Collins Sons & Co. Ltd, Glasgow

To Nelson Algreen

CHAPTER ONE

HENRI FOUND himself looking at the sky again—a clear, black crystal dome overhead. It was difficult for the mind to conceive of hundreds of planes shattering that black, crystalling silence! And suddenly, words began tumbling through his head with a joyous sound—the offensive was halted . . . the German collapse had begun . . . at last he would be able to leave. He turned the corner of the quay. The streets would smell again of oil and orange blossoms, in the evening there would be light, people would sit and chat in outdoor cafés, and he would drink real coffee to the sound of guitars. His eyes, his hands, his skin were hungry. It had been a long fast!

Slowly, he climbed the icy stairs. "At last!" Paula exclaimed, hugging him tightly, as if they had just found each other again after a long, danger-filled separation. Over her shoulder, he looked at the tinselled Christmas tree, reflected to infinity in the large mirrors. The table was covered with plates, glasses, and bottles; bunches of holly and mistletoe lay scattered at the foot of a step-stool. He freed himself and threw his overcoat on the couch.

"Have you heard the wireless?" he asked. "The news is wonderful."

"Is it?" Paula said. "Tell me, quickly!" She never listened to the wireless; she wanted to hear the news only from Henri's mouth.

"Haven't you noticed how clear the sky is to-night? They say there are a thousand planes smashing the rear of von Rundstedt's armies."

"Thank God! They won't come back, then."

"There never was any question of their coming back," he said. But the same thought had crossed his mind, too.

Paula smiled mysteriously. "I took precautions, just in case."

"What precautions?"

"There's a tiny room no bigger than a cupboard in the back of the cellar. I asked the concierge to clear it out for me. You could have used it as a hiding place."

9

" You shouldn't have spoken to the concierge about a thing like that ; that's how panics are started."

She clutched the ends of her shawl tightly in her left hand, as if she were protecting her heart. " They would have shot you," she said. " Every night I hear them ; they knock, I open the door, I see them standing there." Motionless, her eyes half closed, she seemed actually to be hearing voices.

" Don't worry," Henri said cheerfully, " it will not happen now."

She opened her eyes and let her hands fall to her sides. " Is the war really over?"

" Well, it won't last much longer," Henri replied, placing the stool under one of the heavy beams that crossed the ceiling. " Want me to help you?" he asked.

" The Dubreuilhs are coming over early to give me a hand."

" Why wait for them?" he said, picking up a hammer.

Paula put her hand on his arm. " Aren't you going to do any work?" she asked.

" Not to-night."

" But you say that every night. You haven't written a thing for more than a year now."

" Don't worry," he said, " I *feel* like writing now, and that's what counts."

" That newspaper of yours takes up too much of your time ; just look at how late you get home. Besides, I'm sure you haven't eaten a thing since noon. Aren't you hungry?"

" No, not now."

" Aren't you even tired?"

" Not at all."

Those searching eyes of hers, so constantly devouring him with solicitude, made him feel like an unwieldy and fragile treasure. And it was that feeling which wearied him. He stepped up on the stool and with light, careful blows—the house had long since passed its youth—began driving a nail into the beam.

" I can even tell you what I'm going to write," he said. " A light novel."

" What do you mean?" Paula asked, her voice suddenly uneasy.

" Exactly what I said. I feel like writing a light novel."

Given even the slightest encouragement, he would have

made up the story then and there, would have enjoyed thinking it out aloud. But Paula was looking at him so intensely that he kept quiet.

"Hand me that big bunch of mistletoe," he said instead.

Cautiously, he hung the green ball, studded with small white berry eyes, while Paula held out another nail to him. Yes, he thought, the war was really over. At least it was for him. This evening was going to be a real celebration. Peace would begin, everything would begin again—holidays, leisure trips, pleasure—maybe even happiness, but certainly freedom. He finished hanging the mistletoe, the holly, and the puffs of white cotton along the beam.

"How does it look?" he asked, stepping off the stool.

"Perfect." She went over to the tree and straightened one of the candles. "If it's no longer dangerous," she said quietly, "you'll be going to Portugal now?"

"Naturally."

"And you won't do any work during the trip?"

"I don't suppose so."

She stood nervously tapping one of the golden balls hanging from a branch of the tree, waiting for the words she had long been expecting.

"I'm terribly sorry I can't take you with me," he said finally.

"You needn't feel sorry," she said. "I know it's not your fault. And anyhow, I feel less and less these days like traipsing about. What for?" She smiled. "I'll wait for you. Waiting, when you know what you're waiting for, isn't too bad."

Henri felt like laughing aloud. What for? All those wonderful names—Lisbon, Oporto, Cintra, Coimbra—came alive in his mind. He didn't even have to speak them to feel happy; it was enough to say to himself, "I won't be here any more; I'll be somewhere else." Somewhere else! Those words were more wonderful than even the most wonderful names.

"Aren't you going to get dressed?" he asked.

"I'm going," she said.

Paula climbed the stairway to the bedroom and Henri went over to the table. Suddenly he realised that he had been hungry. But he knew that whenever he admitted it a worried look would come over Paula's face. He spread himself some pâté on a slice of bread and bit into it. Resolutely he told himself, " As soon as I get back from Portugal, I'll move to a hotel. What a wonderful feeling it will be to return at night to a room where no one is waiting for you!" Even when he was still in love with Paula, he had always insisted on having his own private four walls. But in '39 and '40, while he was in the army, Paula had had constant nightmares about falling dead on his horribly mutilated body, and when at last he was returned to her, how could he possibly refuse her anything? And then, what with the curfew, the arrangement turned out to be rather convenient, after all. " You can leave whenever you like," she would say. But up to now he hadn't been able to. He took a bottle and twisted a corkscrew into the squeaking cork. Paula would get used to doing without him in less than a month. And if she didn't, it would be just too damn bad! France was no longer a prison, the borders were opening up again, and life shouldn't be a prison either. Four years of austerity, four years of working only for others—that was a lot, that was too much. It was time now for him to think a little about himself. And for that, he had to be alone, alone and free. It wouldn't be easy to find himself again after four years ; there were so many things that had to be clarified in his mind. What, for instance? Well, he wasn't quite sure yet, but there, in Portugal, strolling through the narrow streets which smelled of oil, he would try to bring things into focus. Again he felt his heart leap. The sky would be blue, laundry would be airing at open windows ; his hands in his pockets, he would wander about as a tourist among people whose language he didn't speak and whose troubles didn't concern him.

He would let himself live, would *feel* himself living, and perhaps that alone would be enough to make everything come clear.

Paula came down the stairs with soft, silken steps. " You uncorked all the bottles!" she exclaimed. " That was sweet of you."

" You're so positively dedicated to violet!" he said, smiling.

" But you adore violet!" she said.

He had been adoring violet for the past ten years ; ten years was a long time.

" You don't like this dress?" Paula asked.

" Yes, of course," he said hastily. " It's very pretty. I just

thought that there were some other colours which might
become you. Green, for example," he ventured, picking the
first colour that came to mind.

She looked at herself in one of the mirrors. " Green?" she
said, and there was bewilderment in her voice. " You really
think I'd look well in green?"

It was all so useless, he told himself. In green or yellow he
would never again see in her the woman who, that day ten
years earlier, he had desired so much when she had nonchalantly held out her long violet gloves to him.

Henri smiled at her gently. " Dance with me," he said.

" Yes, let's dance," she replied in a voice so ardent that it
made him freeze up. Their life together had been so dismal
during the past year that Paula herself had seemed to be losing
her taste for it. But at the beginning of September, she
changed abruptly ; now, in her every word, every kiss, every
look, there was a passionate quivering. When he took her in
his arms she moved herself hard against him, murmuring,
" Do you remember the first time we danced together?"

" Yes, at the Pagoda. You told me I danced very badly."

" That was the day I took you to the Musée Grévin. You
did not know about it. You did not know about anything,"
she said tenderly. She pressed her forehead against his cheek.
" I can see us the way we were then."

And so could he. They had stood together on a pedestal
in the middle of the Palais des Mirages and everywhere around
them they had seen themselves endlessly multiplied in a forest
of mirrored columns. *Tell me I'm the most beautiful of all
women. . . . You're the most beautiful of all women. . . .
And you'll be the most glorious man in the world . . .*

Now he turned his eyes towards one of the large mirrors.
Their entwined dancing bodies were infinitely repeated alongside an endless row of Christmas trees, and Paula was smiling
at him blissfully. Didn't she realise, he asked himself, that
they were no longer the same couple?

" Someone just knocked," Henri said, and he rushed to the
door. It was the Dubreuilhs, heavily laden with shopping bags
and baskets. Anne held a bunch of roses in her arms, and
slung over Dubreuilh's shoulder were huge bunches of red
pimentos. Nadine followed them in, a sullen look on her
face.

" Merry Christmas!"

"Merry Christmas!"

"Did you hear the news? The air force was able to deliver at last."

"Yes, a thousand planes!"

"They wiped them out."

"It's all over."

Dubreuilh dumped the load of red fruit on the couch. "Here's something to decorate your little brothel."

"Thanks," Paula said coolly. It annoyed her when Dubreuilh called her studio a brothel—because of all the mirrors and those red draperies, he said.

He surveyed the room. "The centre beam is the only place for them; they'll look a lot better up there than that mistletoe."

"I like the mistletoe," Paula said firmly.

"Mistletoe is stupid; it's round, it's traditional. And moreover it's a parasite."

"Why not string the pimentos along the railing at the head of the stairs," Anne suggested.

"It would look much better up here," Dubreuilh replied.

"I'm sticking to my holly and my mistletoe," Paula insisted.

"All right, all right, it's your home," Dubreuilh conceded. He beckoned to Nadine. "Come and help me," he said.

Anne unpacked a pork pâté, butter, cheese, cakes. "And this is for the punch," she said, setting two bottles of rum on the table. She placed a package in Paula's hands. "Here, that's your present. And here's something for you," she said, handing Henri a clay pipe, the bowl shaped like a bird's claw clutching a small egg. It was the same kind of pipe that Louis used to smoke fifteen years before.

"Remarkable," said Henri. "How did you ever guess that I've been wanting a pipe like this for the past fifteen years?"

"Simple," said Anne. "You told me."

"Two pounds of tea!" Paula exclaimed. "You've saved my life! And does it smell good! Real tea!"

Henri began cutting slices of bread which Anne smeared with butter and Paula with the pork pâté. At the same time, Paula kept an anxious eye on Dubreuilh, who was hammering nails into the railing with heavy blows.

"Do you know what's missing here?" he cried out to Paula. "A big crystal chandelier. I'll dig one up for you."

" Don't bother. I don't want one."

Dubreuilh finished hanging the clusters of pimentos and came down the stairs.

" Not bad!" he said, examining his work with a critical eye. He went over to the table and opened a small bag of spices ; for years, on the slightest excuse, he had been concocting that same punch, the recipe for which he had learned in Haiti. Leaning against the railing, Nadine was chewing one of the pimentos ; at eighteen, in spite of her experiences in the various French and American beds, she still seemed in the middle of the awkward age.

" Don't eat the scenery," Dubreuilh shouted at her. He emptied a bottle of rum into a salad bowl and turned towards Henri. " I met Samazelle the day before yesterday and I'm glad to say that he seems inclined to go along with us. Are you free to-morrow night?"

" I can't get away from the paper before eleven," Henri replied.

" Then stop by at eleven," Dubreuilh said. " We have to go over the whole deal, and I'd very much like you to be there."

Henri smiled. " I don't quite see why."

" I told him that you work with me, but your actually being there will carry more weight."

" I doubt if it would mean very much to someone like Samazelle," Henri said, still smiling. " He must know I'm not a politician."

" But, like myself, he thinks that politics should never again be left to politicians," Dubreuilh said. " Come over, even if it's only for a few minutes. Samazelle has an interesting group behind him. Young fellows ; we need them."

" Now listen," Paula said angrily, " you're not going to start talking politics again! To-night's a holiday."

" So?" Dubreuilh said. " Is there a law against talking about things that interest you on holidays?"

" Why do you insist on dragging Henri into this thing?" Paula asked. " He knocks himself out enough already. And he's told you again and again that politics bore him."

" I know," Dubreuilh said with a smile, " you think I'm an old reprobate trying to debauch his little friends. But politics isn't a vice, my beauty, nor a parlour game. If a new war were to break out three years from now, you'd be the first to howl."

"That's blackmail," Paula said. "When *this* war finally ends its coming to an end, no one is going to feel like starting a new one."

"Do you think that what people *feel* like doing means anything at all?" Dubreuilh asked.

Paula started to answer, but Henri cut her off. "Look," he said. "It's not that I don't want to. It's just that I haven't got the time."

"There's always time," Dubreuilh countered.

"For you, yes," Henri said, laughing. "But me, I'm just a normal human being; I can't work twenty hours at a stretch or go without sleep for a month."

"And neither can I!" Dubreuilh said. "I'm not eighteen any more. No one is asking that much of you," he added, tasting the punch with a worried look.

Henri looked at him cheerfully. Eighteen or eighty, Dubreuilh, with his huge, laughing eyes that consumed everything in sight, would always look just as young. What a zealot! By comparison, Henri was often tempted to think of himself as dissipated, lazy, weak. But it was useless to drive himself. At twenty, he had had so great an admiration for Dubreuilh that he felt himself compelled to ape him. The result was that he was constantly sleepy, loaded himself with medicines, sank almost into a stupor. Now he had to make up his mind once and for all. With no time for himself he had lost his taste for life and the desire to write. He had become a machine. For four years he had been a machine, and now he was determined above all else to become a man again.

"I wonder just how my inexperience could help you," he said.

"Oh, inexperience has its advantages," Dubreuilh replied with a wry smile. "Besides, just now you have a name that means a lot to a lot of people." His smile broadened. "Before the war, Samazelle was in and out of every political faction and all the factions of factions. But that's not why I want him; I want him because he's a hero of the Maquis. His name carries a lot of weight."

Henri began to laugh. Dubreuilh never seemed more ingenuous to him than when he tried being cynical. Paula was right, of course, to accuse him of blackmail; if he really

believed in the imminence of a third world war, he would not
have been in so good a mood. The truth of the matter was
that he saw possibilities for action opening before him and he
was burning to exploit them. Henri, however, felt less enthusiastic. Clearly, he had changed since '39. Before then, he
had been on the left because the bourgeoisie disgusted him,
because injustice roused his indignation, because he considered
all men his brothers—fine, generous sentiments which involved
him in absolutely nothing. Now he knew that if he really
wanted to break away from his class, he would have to risk
some personal loss. Malefilatre, Bourgoin, Picard had taken
the risk and lost at the edge of the little woods, but he would
always think of them as living men. He had sat with them at a
table in front of a rabbit stew, and they drank white wine and
spoke of the future without much believing in what they were
saying. Four of a kind, they were then. But with the war
over they would once again have become a bourgeois, a
farmer, and two mill hands. At that moment, sitting with
them, Henri understood that in the eyes of the three others,
and in his own eyes as well, he was one of the privileged
classes, more or less disreputable, even if well-intentioned.
And he knew there was only one way of remaining their
friend: by continuing to do things with them. He understood this even more clearly when, in '41, he worked with the
Bois Colombes group. At the beginning things didn't go very
well. Flamand exasperated him by incessantly repeating,
" Me, I'm a worker, you know; I think like a worker." But
thanks to him Henri became aware of something he knew
nothing about before, something which, from that time on, he
would always feel menacing him. Hate. He had taken the bite
out of it; in their common struggle, they had accepted him as
a comrade. But if ever he should become an indifferent
bourgeois again, the hatred would come to life, and with
good reason. Unless he showed proof to the contrary, he was
the enemy of several hundred million men, an enemy of
humanity. And that he did not want at any price.

Now he had to prove himself. The trouble was that the
struggle had shifted its form. The Resistance was one thing,
politics another. And Henri had no great passion for politics.
He knew what a movement such as Dubreuilh had in mind
would mean: committees, conferences, congresses, meetings,
talk, and still more talk. And it meant endless manœuvring,

patching up of differences, accepting crippling compromises, lost time, infuriating concessions, sombre boredom. Nothing could be more repulsive to him. Running a newspaper, that was the kind of work he enjoyed. But, of course, one thing did not preclude the other, and as a matter of fact they even complemented each other. It was impossible to use his paper as an excuse. Henri did not feel he had the right to look for an out ; he would only try to limit his commitments.

" Look," he said, " I can't refuse you my name. I'll put in a few appearances, too. But you mustn't ask much more of me."

" I'll certainly ask more of you than that," Dubreuilh replied.

" Well, at any rate, not straight away. From now until I leave, I'll be up to my ears in work."

Dubreuilh looked Henri straight in the eyes. " The trip still on?" he asked.

" More than ever. Three weeks from now, at the latest, I'll be gone."

" You're not serious!" Dubreuilh said angrily.

" Now I've heard everything!" Anne exclaimed, giving Dubreuilh a bantering look. " If *you* suddenly got an urge to go somewhere, you'd just pick yourself up and go, and you'd tell people it's the only intelligent thing to do."

" But I don't get those urges," Dubreuilh replied, " and that's precisely wherein my superiority lies."

" I must say that the pleasures of travelling seem to me pretty much overrated," Paula said. She smiled at Anne. " A rose you bring me gives me more pleasure than the gardens of the Alhambra after a fifteen-hour train journey."

" Travel can be exciting enough," Dubreuilh said. " But just now it's much more exciting being here."

" Well, as for me," Henri said, " I've got so strong an urge to be somewhere else that I'd go by foot if I had to. And with my shoes full of pebbles!"

" And what about *L'Espoir*? You'll just take off and leave it to itself for a whole month?"

" Luc will get along quite well without me," Henri replied.

He looked at the three of them in amazement. " They don't understand," he said to himself. " Always the same faces, the same surroundings, the same conversations, the same

THE MANDARINS   19

problems. The more it changes, the more it repeats itself. In
the end, you feel as if you're dying alive." Friendship, the
great traditional emotions—he had valued them all for what
they were worth. But now he needed something else, and the
need was so violent that it would have been ridiculous even
to attempt an explanation.

" Merry Christmas! "
The door opened. Vincent, Lambert, Sézenac, Chancel, the
whole gang from the newspaper, their cheeks pink from the
cold. They had brought along bottles and records, and at the
top of their voices they were singing the old refrain they had
so often sung together during the feverish August days:

> We've seen the last of the hun,
> The bastards are all on the run.

Henri smiled at them cheerfully. He felt as young as they,
and yet at the same time he also felt as if he had had a small
hand in creating them. He joined in the chorus. Suddenly
the lights went out, the punch flamed up, sparklers flared and
Lambert and Vincent showered Henri with sparks. Paula lit
the tiny candles on the Christmas tree.

" Merry Christmas! "
Couples and small groups continued to arrive. They listened to Django Reinhardt's guitar, danced, drank; everyone was laughing. Henri took Anne in his arms. In a voice
filled with emotion she said, " It's just like the night of the
invasion ; the same place, the same people."

" And now it's all over."

" For us, it's over," she corrected.
He knew what she was thinking. At that very moment
Belgian villages were ablaze, the sea was foaming over the
Dutch countryside. And yet here in Paris, it was a night
of festivities, the first Christmas of the peace. There had
to be festivities, sometimes. Because, if there weren't, what
good were victories? This was a holiday ; he recognised that
familiar smell of alcohol, of tobacco, of perfume and face
powder, that smell of long nights. A thousand rainbow-
tinted fountains danced in his memory. Before the war there
had been so many nights—in the Montparnasse café where
they all used to get drunk on coffee and conversation, in the

old studio that smelled of still-wet oil paintings, in the little dance halls where he had held the most beautiful of all women, Paula, tightly in his arms. And always at dawn, accompanying the metallic sounds of morning, a gentle ecstatic voice inside him would whisper that the book he was writing would be good and that nothing in the world was more important.

"You know," he said, "I've decided to write a light novel."

"You?" Anne looked at him in amusement. "When do you begin?"

"To-morrow."

Suddenly there was in him the urgent hurry to become again what he had once been, what he had always wanted to be—a writer. Deep inside him he knew again that uneasy joy that came with "I'm starting a new book." He would write of all those things that were just now being born again: the dawns, the long nights, the trips, happiness.

"You're in fine fettle to-night, aren't you?" Anne said.

"I am. I feel as if I've just come out of a long dark tunnel. Don't you?"

She paused a moment and then answered, "I don't know. In spite of everything, there were some good moments in that tunnel."

"Yes, I suppose there were, at that."

He smiled at her. She was looking pretty to-night, and he found her appealing in her severely tailored suit. If she hadn't been an old friend—as well as Dubreuilh's wife—he would willingly have tried his chances. He danced with Anne several times in succession and then with Claudie de Belzunce who, in plunging neckline and bedecked with the family jewels, had come slumming among the intellectual élite. Next time he danced with Jeanette Cange, then Lucie Lenoir. He knew them all too well, those women; but there would be other parties, other women.

Henri smiled at Preston who, somewhat unsteadily, was walking towards him across the room. He was the first American acquaintance Henri had come upon during the liberation of Paris in August, and they had fallen happily into each other's arms.

"Had to come and celebrate with you," Preston said.

"Then let's celebrate," said Henri.

They drank and then Preston began speaking sentimentally

about New York nights. He was quite drunk and he leaned heavily on Henri's shoulder. " You must come to New York," he said, and it sounded like a command. " I guarantee that you'll be a huge success."

" Wonderful," said Henri. " I'll come to New York."

" As soon as you get over, rent yourself a small plane," said Preston. " Best possible way to see the country."

" But I don't know how to fly."

" Nothing to it. Easier than driving a car."

" Then I'll learn to fly," said Henri.

Yes, decidedly, Portugal would be only a beginning. After that, there would be America, Mexico, Brazil, and maybe even Russia and China. In every place in the world Henri would drive cars again, would fly planes. The blue-grey air was great with promises ; the future stretched away to infinity.

Suddenly a silence fell over the room. Henri saw with surprise that Paula was sitting down at the piano. She began to sing. It had been a very long time since that had happened. Henri tried to listen to her with an impartial ear ; he had never been able to form a true opinion as to the value of that voice. Certainly it wasn't mediocre ; at times it even sounded like the echo of a bronze bell, muffled in velvet. Once again he asked himself why, exactly, she had given up singing. At the time, he had looked upon it as a sacrifice, an overpowering proof of her love for him. Later he was surprised to find that Paula continually avoided every opportunity that would have challenged her, and he had often wondered if she hadn't used their love simply as a pretext to escape the test.

There was a burst of applause ; Henri applauded with the others.

" Her voice is still as beautiful as ever," Anne said quietly. " If she appeared in public again, I'm certain she'd be well received."

" Do you really think so?" Henri asked. " Isn't it a little late?"

" Why? A few lessons . . ." Anne looked hesitantly at Henri. " You know, I think it would do her good. You ought to encourage it."

" Perhaps you're right," he said.

He studied Paula, who was smiling and listening to Claudie de Belzunce's gushing compliments. No doubt about it, he thought. It would change her life. Being without anything to

do was not doing her any good. And wouldn't it just simplify
things for him. And, after all, why not? To-night everything
seemed possible. Paula would become famous, she would
devote herself to her career. And he would be free, would
travel wherever he liked, would have brief, happy affairs here
and there. Why not? He smiled and walked over to Nadine ;
she was standing next to the heater, gloomily chewing gum.

" Why aren't you dancing?"

She shrugged her shoulders. " With whom?" she asked.

" With me, if you like."

She was not pretty. She looked too much like her
father, and it was disturbing to see that surly face on the body
of a young girl. Her eyes, like Anne's, were blue, but so cold
they seemed at once both worn-out and infantile. And yet,
under her woollen dress, her body was more supple, her breasts
more firm, than Henri had thought they would be.

" This is the first time we've danced together," he said.

" Yes," she replied. " You dance well, you know."

" And that surprises you?"

" Not particularly. But not one of these little snot-noses
here knows how to dance."

" They hardly had the chance to learn."

" I know," she said. " We never had a chance to do anything."

He smiled at her. A young woman is a woman, even if she
is ugly. He liked her astringent smell of eau de Cologne, of
fresh linen. She danced badly, but it didn't really matter ;
there were the youthful voices, the laughter, the trumpet
taking the chorus, the taste of the punch, the evergreens with
their flaming, sparkling blossoms reflected in the depths of the
mirrors, and, behind the curtains, a pure black sky. Dubreuilh
was performing a trick ; he had cut a newspaper into small
pieces and had just put it together again with a sweep of his
hand ; Lambert and Vincent were duelling with empty bottles ;
Anne and Lachaume were singing grand opera ; trains, ships,
planes were circling the earth, and they could be boarded.

" You dance pretty well yourself," he said politely.

" I dance like a cow. But I don't give a damn ; I hate dancing." She looked at him suspiciously. " Jitterbugs, jazz, those
cellars that stink of tobacco and sweat, do you find that sort
of thing entertaining?"

" From time to time," he replied. " Why? What do *you* find entertaining?"

" Nothing."

She spoke the word so fiercely that he looked at her with growing curiosity. He wondered if it was pleasure or disappointment that had thrown her into so many arms. Would true passion soften the hard structure of her face? And what would Dubreuilh's head on a pillow look like?

" When I think that you're going to Portugal . . . well, all I can say is that you have all the luck," she said bitterly.

" It won't be long before it's easy for everyone to travel again," he said.

" It won't be long! You mean a year, *two* years! How did *you* ever manage it?"

" The French Propaganda Service asked me to give a few lectures."

" Obviously no one would ever ask *me* to give lectures," she muttered. " How many?"

" Five or six."

" And you'll be roaming around for a month!"

" Well," he said gaily, " old people have to have *some* rewards."

" And what if you're young?" Nadine asked. She heaved a loud sigh. " If something would only happen . . ."

" What, for instance?"

" We've been in this so-called revolutionary era for ages. And yet nothing ever seems to change."

" Well, things did change a little in August, at any rate," Henri replied.

" As I remember it, in August there was a lot of talk about *everything* changing. And it's just the same as ever. It's still the ones who work the most who eat the least, and everyone goes right on thinking that's just marvellous."

" No one here thinks that's marvellous," Henri protested.

" Well, anyhow, they all learn to live with it," Nadine said irritably. " Having to waste your time working is lousy enough, and then on top of it if you can't eat your fill . . . well, personally, I'd rather be a gangster."

" I agree wholeheartedly ; we all agree with you," Henri said. " But wait a while ; you're in too much of a hurry."

Nadine interrupted him. "Look," she said, "the virtues of waiting have been explained to me at home at great length and in great detail. But I don't trust explanations." She shrugged her shoulders. "Honestly, no one ever really tries to *do* anything."

"And what about you?" Henri asked with a smile. "Do *you* ever try to do anything?"

"Me? I'm not old enough," Nadine answered. "I'm just another butter ration."

Henri burst out laughing. "Don't get discouraged; you'll soon be old enough. All too soon!"

"Too soon! There are three hundred and sixty-five days in a year!" Nadine said. "Count them." She lowered her head and thought silently for a moment. Then, abruptly, she raised her eyes. "Take me with you," she said.

"Where?" Henri asked.

"To Portugal."

He smiled. "That doesn't seem too feasible."

"Just a little bit feasible will do fine," she said. Henri said nothing and Nadine continued in an insistent voice, "But why can't it be done?"

"In the first place, they wouldn't give me two travel orders to leave the country."

"Oh, go on! You know everyone. Say that I'm your secretary." Nadine's mouth was smiling, but her eyes were deadly serious.

"If I took anyone," he said, "it would have to be Paula."

"But she doesn't *like* travelling."

"Yes, but she'd be happy being with me."

"She's seen you every single day for the last ten years, and there's a lot more to come. One month more or less, what earthly difference could that make to her?"

Henri smiled at her. "I'll bring you back some oranges," he said.

Nadine glowered at him, and suddenly Henri saw before him Dubreuilh's intimidating mask. "I'm not eight years old any more, you know."

"I know."

"You don't! To you I'll always be the little brat who used to kick the logs in the fireplace."

" You're completely wrong, and the proof of it is that I asked you to dance."

" Oh, this thing's just a family affair. I'll bet you'd never ask me to go out with you, though."

He looked at her sympathetically. Here, at least, was one person who was longing for a change of air. Yes, she wanted a great many things, different things. Poor kid! It was true she had never had a chance to do anything. A bicycle tour of the suburbs: that was about the sum total of her travelling. It was certainly a rough way to spend one's youth. And then there was that boy who had died; she seemed to have got over it quickly enough, but nevertheless it must have left a bad scar.

" You're wrong," he said. " I'm inviting you."

" Do you mean it?" Nadine's eyes shone. She was much easier to look at when her face brightened.

" I don't go back to the newspaper on Saturday nights. Let's meet at the Bar Rouge at eight o'clock."

" And what will we do?"

" That will be up to you."

" I don't have any ideas."

" Well, don't worry, I'll get one by then. Come and have a drink."

" I don't drink. I wouldn't mind another sandwich though."

They went over to the buffet. Lenoir and Julien were engaged in a heated discussion; it was chronic with them. Each reproached the other for having betrayed his youth—in the wrong way. At one time, having found the excesses of surrealism too tame, they jointly founded the " para-human " movement. Lenoir had since become a professor of Sanskrit and he spent his free time writing obscure poetry. Julien, who was now a librarian, had stopped writing altogether, perhaps because he feared becoming a mature mediocrity after his precocious beginnings.

" What do you think?" Lenoir asked, turning to Henri. " We ought to take some kind of action against the collaborationist writers, shouldn't we?"

" I've stopped thinking for to-night," Henri answered cheerfully.

" It's poor strategy to keep them from being published," Julien said. " While you're using up all your strength prepar-

ing cases against them, they'll have all the time in the world to
write good books."

A heavy hand came down on Henri's shoulder: Scriassine.
" Take a look at what I brought back. American whisky!
I managed to slip two bottles into the country, and I can't
think of a better occasion than this to finish them off."

" Wonderful!" said Henri. He filled a glass with bourbon
and held it out to Nadine.

" I don't drink," she said in an offended voice, turning
abruptly and walking off.

Henri raised the glass to his mouth. He had completely
forgotten what bourbon tasted like ; he did remember, though,
that his preference used to be Scotch, but since he had also
forgotten what Scotch tasted like, it made no difference to
him.

" Who wants a shot of real whisky?"

Luc came over, dragging his large, gouty feet ; Lambert and
Vincent followed close behind. They all filled their glasses.

" I like a good cognac better," said Vincent.

" This isn't bad," Lambert said without conviction. He gave
Scriassine a questioning look. " Do they really drink a dozen
of these a day in America?"

" *They? Who are *they*?" Scriassine asked. " There are a
hundred and fifty million Americans, and, believe it or not,
not all of them are like Hemingway heroes." His voice was
harsh and disagreeable ; he seldom made any effort to be
friendly to people younger than himself. Deliberately, he
turned to Henri. " I came over here to-night to have a serious
talk with Dubreuilh. I'm quite worried."

He looked preoccupied—his usual expression. He always
created the impression that everything happening where he
chanced to be and even where he chanced not to be—was his
personal concern. Henri had no desire to share his worries.
Offhandedly, he asked, " What's worrying you so much?"

" This movement he's forming. I thought its principal objective was to draw the proletariat away from the Communist
Party. But that's not at all what Dubreuilh seems to have in
mind," Scriassine said gloomily.

" No, not at all," Henri replied.

Dejectedly, he thought, " This is just the kind of conversation I'll be letting myself in for for days on end, if I get mixed

up with Dubreuilh." From his head to his toes, he again felt an overpowering desire to be somewhere else.

Scriassine looked him straight in the eyes. " Are you going along with him?"

" Only a little way," Henri answered. " Politics isn't exactly my meat."

" You probably don't understand what Dubreuilh is brewing," Scriassine said, giving Henri a reproachful look. " He's trying to build up a so-called independent left-wing group, a group that approves of a united front with the Communists."

" Yes," Henri said. " I know that. So?"

" Don't you see? He's playing right into their hands. There are a lot of people who are afraid of Communism ; by winning them over to his movement, in effect he'll be throwing their support to the Communists."

" Don't tell me you're against a united front," Henri said. " It would be a fine thing if the left started splitting up!"

" A left dominated by the Communists would be nothing but a sham," Scriassine said. " If you've decided to go along with Dubreuilh, why not join the Communist Party? That would be a lot more honest."

" Completely out of the question. We disagree with them on quite a few points," Henri answered.

Scriassine shrugged his shoulders. " If you really do disagree with them, then three months from now the Stalinists will denounce you as traitors to the working class."

" We'll see," Henri said.

He had no desire to continue the discussion, but Scriassine fixed him insistently with his eyes. " I've been told that L'Espoir has a lot of readers among the working people. Is that true?"

" Yes."

" Which means you have in your hands the only non-Communist paper in France that reaches the proletariat. Do you realise the grave responsibility you have?"

" I realise it."

" If you put L'Espoir at Dubreuilh's service, you'll be acting as an accomplice in a thoroughly disgusting manœuvre," Scriassine said. " Dubreuilh's friendship doesn't matter here," he added, " you've got to go the other way."

" Listen, as far as the paper is concerned, it will never

be at anyone's service. Neither Dubreuilh's nor yours," Henri said emphatically.

" One of these days, you know, *L'Espoir* is going to have to define its political programme," Scriassine said.

" No. I refuse to have any predetermined programme," said Henri. " I want to go on saying exactly what I think when I think it. And I'll never let myself become regimented."

" That kind of policy won't stand up," Scriassine said.

Luc's normally placid voice suddenly broke in. " We don't want any political programme ; we want to preserve the unity of the Resistance."

Henri poured himself a glass of bourbon. " That's all a lot of crap!" he grumbled. Old, worn-out clichés were all that Luc ever mouthed—The Spirit of the Resistance! The Unity of the Resistance! And Scriassine saw red whenever anyone mentioned Russia to him. It would be better if they each had a corner somewhere where they could rave by themselves! Henri emptied his glass. He needed no advice from anyone ; he had his own ideas about what a newspaper should be. Obviously, *L'Espoir* would eventually be forced to take a political stand—but it would do it entirely independently. Henri hadn't kept the paper going all this time only to see it turn into something like those pre-war rags. Then, the whole press had been dedicated to fooling the public ; the knack of presenting one-sided views in a convincing, authoritative manner had become an art. And the result soon became apparent : deprived of their daily oracle, the people were lost. To-day, everyone agreed more or less on the essentials ; the polemics and the partisan campaigns were out. Now was the time to educate the readers instead of cramming things down their throats. No more dictating opinions to them ; rather teach them to judge for themselves. It wasn't simple. Often they insisted on answers, and he had to be constantly on his guard lest he gave them an impression of ignorance, doubt, or incoherence. But that was precisely the challenge—meriting their confidence rather than robbing them of it. And the fact that *L'Espoir* sold almost everywhere in France was proof enough that the method worked. " No point in damning the Communists for their sectarianism if you're going to be just as dogmatic as they are," Henri said to himself.

" Don't you think we could put this discussion off to some other time?" Henri asked, interrupting Scriassine.

" All right," Scriassine answered. " Let's make a date." He pulled a note-book from his pocket. " I think it's important for us to talk over our differences."

" Let's wait until I get back from my trip," Henri said.

" You're going on a trip? News-hawking?"

" No, just for pleasure."

" Leaving soon?"

" Very soon," Henri answered.

" Wouldn't you call that deserting?" Scriassine asked.

" Deserting?" Henri said with a smile. " I'm not in the army, you know." With his chin, he pointed to Claudie de Belzunce. " You ought to ask Claudie for a dance. Over there . . . the half-naked one dripping with jewellery. She's a real woman of the world, and, confidentially, she admires you a lot."

" Women of the world are one of my weaknesses," Scriassine said with a little smile. He shook his head. " I have to admit I don't understand why."

He moved off towards Claudie. Nadine was dancing with Lachaume, and Dubreuilh and Paula were circling around the Christmas tree. Paula did not like Dubreuilh, but he often succeeded in amusing her.

" You really shocked Scriassine!" Vincent said cheerfully.

" My going on a trip seems to shock damned near everyone," Henri said. " And Dubreuilh most of all."

" That really beats me!" Lambert said. " You did a lot more than any of them ever did. You're entitled to a little holiday, aren't you?"

" There's no doubt about it," Henri said to himself. " I have a lot more in common with the youngsters." Nadine envied him, Vincent and Lambert understood him.. They, too, as soon as they could, had rushed off to see what was happening elsewhere in the world. When assignments as war correspondents were offered them, they had accepted without hesitation. Now he stayed with them as for the hundredth time they spoke of the exciting days when they had first moved into the offices of the newspaper, when they had sold *L'Espoir* right under the noses of the Germans while Henri was busy writing his editorials, a revolver in his desk drawer. To-night, because he was hearing them as if from a distance, he found new charm in those old stories. In his imagination he was lying on a beach of soft, white sand, looking out upon the blue sea and calmly thinking of times gone by, of faraway friends. He was delighted at being alone and free. He was completely happy.

At four in the morning, he once again found himself in the red living-room. Many of the guests had already gone and the rest were preparing to leave. In a few moments he would be alone with Paula, would have to speak to her, caress her.

"Darling, your party was a masterpiece," Claudie said, giving Paula a kiss. "And you have a magnificent voice. If you wanted to, you could easily be one of the sensations of the post-war era."

"Oh," Paula said gaily, "I'm not asking for that much."

No, she didn't have any ambition for that sort of thing. He knew exactly what she wanted: to be once more the most beautiful of women in the arms of the most glorious man in the world. It wasn't going to be easy to make her change her dream. The last guests left; the studio was suddenly empty. A final shuffling on the stairway, and then steps clicking in the silent street. Paula began gathering up the glasses that had been left on the floor.

"Claudie's right," Henri said. "Your voice is still as beautiful as ever. It's been so long since I last heard you sing! Why don't you ever sing any more?"

Paula's face lit up. "Do you still like my voice? Would you like me to sing for you sometimes?"

"Certainly," he answered with a smile. "Do you know what Anne told me? She said you ought to begin singing in public again."

Paula looked shocked. "Oh, no!" she said. "Don't speak to me about that. That was all settled a long time ago."

"Well, why not?" Henri asked. "You heard how they applauded; they were all deeply moved. A lot of clubs are beginning to open up now, and people want to see new personalities."

Paula interrupted him. "No! Please! Don't insist. It horrifies me to think of displaying myself in public. Please don't insist," she repeated pleadingly.

"It horrifies you?" he said, and his voice sounded perplexed. "I'm afraid I don't understand. It never used to horrify you. And you don't look any older, you know; in fact, you've grown even more beautiful."

"That was a different period of my life," Paula said, "a period that's buried forever. I'll sing for you and for no one else," she added with such fervour that Henri felt compelled to remain silent. But he promised himself to take up the subject again at the first opportunity.

There was a moment of silence, and then Paula spoke.

"Shall we go upstairs?" she asked.

Henri nodded. "Yes," he said.

Paula sat down on the bed, removed her ear-rings, and slipped her rings off her fingers. "You know," she said, and her voice was calm now, "I'm sorry if I seemed to disapprove of your trip."

"Don't be silly! You certainly have the right not to like travelling, and to say so," Henri replied. The fact that she had scrupulously stifled her remorse all through the evening made him feel ill at ease.

"I understand perfectly your wanting to leave," she said. "I even understand your wanting to go without me."

"It's not that I want to."

She cut him off with a gesture. "You don't have to be polite." She put her hands flat on her knees and, with her eyes staring straight ahead and her back very straight, she looked like one of the infinitely calm priestesses of Apollo. "I never had any intention of imprisoning you in our love. You wouldn't be you if you weren't always looking for new horizons, new nourishment." She leaned forward and looked Henri squarely in the face. "It's quite enough for me simply to be necessary to you."

Henri did not answer. He wanted neither to dishearten nor encourage her. "If only I had something against her," he thought. But no, not a single grievance, not a complaint.

Paula stood up and smiled; her face became human again. She put her hands on Henri's shoulders, her cheek against his. "Could you get along without me?"

"You know very well I couldn't."

"Yes, I know," she said happily. "Even if you said you could, I wouldn't believe you."

She walked towards the bathroom. It was impossible not to weaken from time to time and speak a few kind words to her, smile gently at her. She stored those treasured relics in her heart and extracted miracles from them whenever she felt her faith wavering. "But in spite of everything, she knows I

don't love her any more," he said to himself for reassurance.
He undressed and put on his pyjamas. She knew it, yes, but
as long as she didn't admit it to herself it meant nothing. He
heard a rustle of silk, then the sound of running water
and the clinking of glass, those sounds which once used to
make his heart pound. " No, not to-night, not to-night," he
said to himself uneasily. Paula appeared in the doorway, grave
and nude, her hair tumbling over her shoulders. She was
nearly as perfect as ever, but for Henri all her splendid beauty
no longer meant anything. She slipped in between the sheets
and without uttering a word, pressed her body to his. Paula
withdrew her lips slightly, and, embarrassed, he heard her
murmuring old endearments he never spoke to her now.

" Am I still your beautiful wisteria vine?"

" Now and always."

" And do you love me? Do you really still love me?"

He did not have the courage at that moment to provoke a
scene, he was resigned to avow anything—and Paula knew it.
" Yes, I do."

" Do you belong to me?"

" To you alone."

" Tell me you love me, say it."

" I love you."

She uttered a long moan of satisfaction. He embraced her
violently, smothered her mouth with his lips, and to get it over
with as quickly as possible immediately penetrated her.

When finally he fell limp on Paula, he heard a triumphant
moan.

" Are you happy?" she murmured.

" Of course."

" I'm so terribly happy!" Paula exclaimed, looking at him
through shining tear-brimmed eyes. He hid her unbearably
bright face against his shoulder. " The almond trees will be in
bloom . . ." he said to himself, closing his eyes. " And there'll
be oranges hanging from the orange trees."

II

No, I shan't meet death to-day. Not to-day or any other day.
I'll be dead for others and yet I'll never have known death.

I closed my eyes again, but I couldn't sleep. Why had
death entered my dreams once more? It is prowling inside
me; I can feel it prowling there. Why?

I hadn't always been aware that one day I would die. As a
child, I believed in God. A white robe and two shimmering
wings were awaiting me in heaven's vestry and I wanted so
much to break through the clouds and try them on. I would
often lie down on my quilt, my hands clasped, and abandon
myself to the delights of the hereafter. Sometimes in my sleep
I would say to myself, " I'm dead," and the voice watching
over me guaranteed me eternity. I was horrified when I first
discovered the silence of death. A mermaid had died on a
deserted beach. She had renounced her immortal soul for
the love of a young man and all that remained of her was a bit
of white foam without memory and without voice. " It's only
a fairy tale," I would say to myself for reassurance.

But it wasn't a fairy tale. I was the mermaid. God became
an abstract idea in the depths of the sky, and one evening I
blotted it out altogether. I've never felt sorry about losing
God, for He had robbed me of the earth. But one day I came
to realise that in renouncing Him I had condemned myself to
death. I was fifteen, and I cried out in fear in the empty house.
When I regained my senses, I asked myself, " What do other
people do? What will I do? Will I always live with this
fear inside me?"

From the moment I fell in love with Robert, I never again
felt fear, of anything. I had only to speak his name and I
would feel safe and secure: he's working in the next room . . .
I can get up and open the door . . . But I remain in bed; I'm
not sure any more that he too doesn't hear that little, gnawing
sound. The earth splits open under our feet, and above our
heads there is an infinite abyss. I no longer know who we are,
nor what awaits us.

Suddenly, I sat bolt upright, opened my eyes. How could I
possibly admit to myself that Robert was in danger? How
could I ever bear it? He hadn't told me anything really dis-

turbing, nothing really new. I'm tired, I drank too much; just a little four-o'clock-in-the-morning frenzy. But who's to decide at what hour one sees things clearest? Wasn't it precisely when I believed myself most secure that I used to awaken in frenzies? And did I ever really believe it?

I can't quite remember. We didn't pay very much attention to ourselves, Robert and I. Only events counted: the flight from Paris, the return, the sirens, the bombs, the standing in lines, our reunions, the first issues of *L'Espoir*. A brown candle was sputtering in Paula's apartment. With a couple of tin cans, we had built a stove in which we used to burn scraps of paper. The smoke would sting our eyes. Outside, puddles of blood, the whistling of bullets, the rumbling of artillery and tanks. In all of us, the same silence, the same hunger, the same hope. Every morning we would awaken asking ourselves the same question: Is the swastika still flying above the Senate? And in August, when we danced around blazing bonfires in the streets of Montparnasse, the same joy was in all our hearts. Then the autumn slipped by, and only a few hours ago, while we were completing the task of forgetting our dead by the lights of a Christmas tree, I realised that we were beginning to exist again, each for himself. " Do you think it's possible to bring back the past?" Paula had asked. And Henri had said, " I feel like writing a light novel." They could once again speak in their normal voices, have their books published ; they could argue again, organise political groups, make plans. That's why they were all so happy. Well, almost all. Anyhow, this isn't the time for me to be tormenting myself. To-night's a holiday, the first Christmas of peace, the last Christmas at Buchenwald, the last Christmas on earth, the first Christmas Diego hasn't lived through. We were dancing, we were kissing each other around the tree sparkling with promises, and there were many, oh, so many, who weren't there. No one had heard their last words ; they were buried nowhere, swallowed up in emptiness. Two days after the liberation, Geneviève had placed her hand on a coffin. Was it the right one? Jacques' body had never been found ; a friend claimed he had buried his note-books under a tree. What note-books? Which tree? Sonia had asked for a sweater and silk stockings, and then she never again asked for anything. Where were Rachel's bones and the lovely Rosa's? In the arms that had so often clasped Rosa's soft body, Lambert was now holding Nadine and Nadine was laughing the way she used to laugh when Diego held her in his arms. I looked down the row of Christmas trees reflected in the large mirrors and I thought, " There are the candles and the holly and the mistletoe they'll never see. Everything that's been given me, I stole from them." They were killed. Which one first? he or his father? Death didn't enter into his plans. Did he know he was going to die? Did he rebel at the end or was he resigned to it? How will I ever know? And now that he's dead, what difference does it make?

No tombstone, no date of death. That's why I've been groping for him through that life he loved so tumultuously. I hold out my hand towards the light switch and hesitantly withdraw it. In my desk is a picture of Diego, but even though I looked at it for hours I would never find again under that head of bushy hair, his real face of flesh and bones, that face in which everything was too large—his eyes, nose, ears, mouth. He was sitting in the study and Robert had asked, " What will you do if the Nazis win?" And he had answered, " A Nazi victory doesn't enter into my plans." His plans consisted of marrying Nadine and becoming a great poet. And he might have made it, too. At sixteen he already knew how to turn words into hot, glowing embers. He might have needed only a very little time—five years, four years ; he lived his life so fast. Huddled with the others around the electric heater, I used to enjoy watching him devour Hegel or Kant ; he would turn the pages as rapidly as if he were skimming through a murder mystery. And the fact of the matter is that he understood perfectly everything he read. Only his dreams were slow.

He had come one day to show Robert his poems, which was how we first got to know him. His father was a Spanish Jew who was stubbornly determined to continue making money in business even during the Occupation. He claimed the Spanish consul was protecting him. Diego reproached him for his luxurious style of living and his opulent blonde mistress ; he preferred our austerity and spent almost all his time with us. Besides, he was at the hero-worshipping age ; and he worshipped Robert. The moment he met Nadine, he impetuously gave her his love, his first, his only love. For the first time she had a feeling of being needed ; it overwhelmed her. She immediately made room in the house for Diego and invited him to live with us. He had a great deal of affection

for me as well, even though he found me much too rational.
At night, Nadine insisted upon my tucking her in, the way I
used to when she was a child. Lying next to her, he would
ask me, " And me? Don't I get a kiss?" And I would kiss
him. That year, we had been friends, my daughter and I.
I was grateful to her for being capable of a sincere love and
she was thankful to me for not opposing her deepest desire.
Why should I have? She was only seventeen, but both Robert
and I felt that it's never too early to be happy.

And they knew how to be happy with so much fire! When
we were together, I would rediscover my youth. " Come and
have dinner with us. Come on, to-night's a holiday," they
would say, each one pulling me by an arm. Diego had filched
a gold piece from his father. He preferred to take rather than
to receive ; it was the way of his generation. He had no
trouble in changing his treasure into negotiable money and he
spent the afternoon with Nadine on the roller coaster at an
amusement park. When I met them on the street that evening, they were devouring a huge pie they had bought in the
back room of a near-by bakery ; it was their way of working
up an appetite. They called up Robert and asked him to come
along too, but he refused to leave his work. I went with them.
Their faces were smeared with jam, their hands black with
the grime of the fair grounds, and in their eyes was the arrogant look of happy criminals. The maître d'hôtel must have
surely believed we had come there with the intention of squan-
dering some ill-gotten gains. He showed us to a table far in
the rear of the room and asked Diego with chilly politeness,
" Monsieur has no jacket?" Nadine threw her jacket over
Diego's threadbare sweater, revealing her own soiled, wrinkled
blouse. But in spite of it all, we were served. They ordered
ice cream first, and sardines, and then steaks, fried potatoes,
oysters, and still more ice cream. " It all gets mixed up inside
anyhow," they explained to me, stuffing the food into their
mouths. They were so happy to be able for once to eat their
fill! No matter how hard I tried to get enough food to go
around, we were always more or less hungry. " Eat up," they
said to me commandingly, as they slipped slices of pâté into
their pockets for Robert.

It wasn't long after this that the Germans one morning
knocked at Mr. Serra's door. No one had informed him that
the Spanish consul had been transferred. Diego, as luck would

have it, had slept at his father's that night. They didn't take the blonde. " Tell Nadine not to worry about me," Diego said. " I'll come back, because I want to come back." Those were the last words we ever heard from him ; all his other words were drowned out forever, he who loved so much to talk.

It was springtime and the sky was very blue, the peach trees a pastel pink. When we would ride our bicycles, Nadine and I, through the flag-decked parks of Paris, the fragrant joy of peacetime week-ends filled our lungs. But the tall buildings of Drancy, where the prisoners were kept, brutally crushed that lie. The blonde had handed over three million francs to a German named Felix who transmitted messages from the prisoners and who had promised to help them escape. Twice, peering through binoculars, we were able to pick out Diego standing at a distant window. They had shaved off his woolly hair and it was no longer entirely he who smiled back at us ; his mutilated head seemed even then to belong to another world.

One afternoon in May we found the huge barracks deserted ; straw mattresses were being aired at the open windows of empty rooms. At the café where we had parked our bicycles, they told us that three trains had left the station during the night. Standing by the barbed-wire fence, we watched and waited for a long time. And then suddenly, very far off, very high up, we made out two solitary silhouettes leaning out of a window. The younger one waved his beret triumphantly. Felix had spoken the truth: Diego had not been deported. Choked with joy, we rode back to Paris.

" They're in a camp with American prisoners," the blonde told us. " They're doing fine, taking lots of sun baths." But she hadn't actually seen them. We sent them sweaters and chocolate, and they thanked us for the gifts through the mouth of Felix. But we stopped receiving written messages. Nadine insisted upon some sort of sign to prove they were still alive— Diego's ring, a lock of his hair. But it was just then that they changed camps again, were sent somewhere far from Paris. It became increasingly difficult to locate them in any particular place ; they were gone, that was all. To be nowhere or not to be at all isn't very different. Nothing really changed when at last Felix said irritably, " They killed them a long time ago."

Nadine wept frantically night after night, and I held her

in my arms from evening till morning. Then she found sleep once more. At first Diego appeared every night in her dreams, a wretched look on his face. Later even his spectre vanished. She was right; I can't really blame her. What can you do with a corpse? Yes, I know. They serve as excuses for making flags, heroic statues, guns, medals, speeches, and even souvenirs for decorating the home. It would be far better to leave their ashes in peace. Monuments or dust. And they had been our brothers. But after all, we had no choice in the matter. Why did they leave us? If only they would leave us in peace! Let's forget them, I say. Let's think a little about ourselves now. We've more than enough to do remaking our own lives. The dead are dead; for them there are no more problems. But after this night of festivity, we, the living, will awaken again. And then how shall we live?

Nadine and Lambert were laughing together, a record was playing loudly, the floor was trembling under our feet, the blue flames of the candles were flickering. I looked at Sézenac who was lying on the rug, thinking no doubt of those glorious days when he strutted down the boulevards of Paris with a rifle slung over his shoulder. I looked at Chancel who had been condemned to death by the Germans and at the last moment exchanged for one of their prisoners. And Lambert whose father had denounced his fiancée, and Vincent who had killed a dozen of our home-grown Nazi militiamen with his own hands. What will they all do with those pasts of theirs, so grievous and so brief? And what will they do with their shapeless futures? Will I know how to help them? Helping people is my job; I make them lie down on a couch and pour out their dreams to me. But I can't bring Rosa back to life, nor the twelve Nazis Vincent killed. And even if I were somehow able to neutralise their pasts, what kind of future could I offer them? I quiet fears, harness dreams, restrain desires; I make them adjust themselves. But to what? I can no longer see anything around me that makes sense.

No question about it, I had too much to drink. After all, it wasn't I who created heaven and earth; no one's asking me to give an accounting of myself. Why must I forever be worrying about others? I'd do better to worry a little about myself for a change. I press my cheek against the pillow; I'm here, it's I. The trouble is there's nothing about me worth giving much thought to. Oh, if someone asks who I am, I can always show him my case history; to become an analyst, I had to be analysed. It was found that I had a rather pronounced Oedipus complex, which explains my marriage to a man twenty years my elder, a clear aggressiveness towards my mother, and some slight homosexual tendencies which conveniently disappeared. To my Catholic upbringing I owe a highly developed super ego—the reason for my puritanism and my lack of narcissism. The ambivalent feelings I have in regard to my daughter stem from my aversion to my mother as much as to my indifference concerning myself. My case is one of the most classic types; its segments fall neatly into a predictable pattern. From a Catholic point of view, it's also quite banal: in their eyes I stopped believing in God when I discovered the temptations of the flesh, and my marriage to an unbeliever completed my downfall. Politically and socially, Robert and I were left-wing intellectuals. Nothing in all this is entirely inexact. There I am then, clearly catalogued and willing to be so, adjusted to my husband, to my profession, to life, to death, to the world and all its horrors; me, precisely me, that is to say, no one.

To be no one, all things considered, is something of a privilege. I watched them coming and going in the room, all of them with their important names, and I didn't envy them. For Robert it was all right; he was predestined to be what he was. But the others, how do they dare? How can anyone be so arrogant or so rash as to serve himself up as prey to a pack of strangers? Their names are dirtied in thousands of mouths; the curious rob them of their thoughts, their hearts, their lives. If I too were subjected to the cupidity of that ferocious mob of rag-pickers, I would certainly end up by considering myself nothing but a pile of garbage. I congratulated myself for not being someone.

I went over to Paula. The war had not affected her aggressive elegance. She was wearing a long, silk, violet-coloured gown, and from her ears hung clusters of amethysts.

" You're very lovely to-night," I said.

She looked at herself quickly in one of the large mirrors. " Yes, I know," she said sadly. " I'm lovely."

She was indeed beautiful, but under her eyes there were deep circles that matched the colour of her dress. At heart she knew very well that Henri could have taken her to Portugal. She knew much more than she pretended to know.

" You must be very happy ; your party's a great success."

" Henri loves parties so much," Paula said, her hands, heavy with rings, mechanically smoothing her shimmering silk dress.

" Won't you sing something for us? I'd so much like to hear you sing again."

" Sing?" she said, surprised.

" Yes, sing," I replied laughingly. " Have you forgotten that you used to sing once upon a time?"

" Once—but that was long ago." she answered.

" Not any more it isn't. Now it's like old times again."

" Do you really think so?" Paula asked, staring intently into my eyes. She seemed to be peering into a crystal ball somewhere beyond my face. " Do you think it's possible to bring back the past?"

I knew how she wanted me to answer that question, but with a slightly embarrassed laugh I said only, " I don't know; I'm not an oracle."

" I must get Robert to explain the meaning of time to me," she said meditatively.

She was ready to deny the existence of space and time rather than admit that love might not be eternal. I was afraid for her. She had been well aware during these past four years that Henri no longer felt anything more than a wearied affection for her. But ever since the liberation, I don't know what insane hope had awakened in her heart.

" Do you remember the Negro spiritual I used to like so much? Won't you sing it for us?"

She walked over to the piano and lifted the keyboard cover. Her voice seemed slightly hollow, but it was just as moving as ever. " You know, she ought to appear in public again," I said to Henri, who greeted my words with a look of astonishment. When the applause died down, he went over to Nadine and began dancing with her. I didn't like the way she was looking at him. There was nothing I could do to help *her*, either. I had given her my only decent dress and lent her my prettiest necklace ; that was all I had the power to do. I knew it would be useless to probe her dreams ; all she needed was the love Lambert was so anxious to give her. But how could I prevent her from destroying it, as I knew she ultimately would? And yet when Lambert entered the room, she raced down the little stairway from the top of which she had been surveying us with a look of disapproval. She stopped dead on the last step, embarrassed by her too-open display of affection.

Lambert walked over to her and smiled gravely. " I'm glad you came," he said.

" The only reason I came was to see you," she said brusquely.

He looked handsome this evening in his dark, well-cut suit. He always dresses with the studied severity of a person much older than himself; he has ceremonious ways, a sober voice, and he exercises a very careful control over his smiles. But his confused look and the softness of his mouth betray his youthfulness. Nadine, obviously, is at once flattered by his seriousness and reassured by his weakness.

" Did you have a good time?" she asked, looking at him with an affable, somewhat silly expression. " I hear that Alsace is very beautiful."

" Once a place is militarised, you know, it becomes utterly dismal."

They sat down on one of the steps of the stairway, chatted, danced, and laughed together for quite a long while. And then they began to argue. With Nadine it always ended like that. Lambert, a sullen look on his face, was now sitting next to the heater, and Nadine was standing by the stairway. Bringing them together from opposite ends of the room and joining their hands was completely out of the question.

I walked over to the buffet and poured myself a brandy. My eyes glanced down along my black skirt and stopped at my legs. It was funny to think I had legs; no one ever noticed them, not even myself. They were slender and well-shaped in their beige stockings, certainly no less well-shaped than many another pair. And yet one day they'd be buried in the earth without ever having existed. It seemed unfair. I was still absorbed in contemplating them when Scriassine came over to me.

" You don't seem to be having a very good time," he said.

" Well, I'm doing the best I can."

" Too many young people here. Young people are never gay. And far too many writers." He pointed his chin towards

Lenoir, Pelletier, and Cange. "They're all writers, aren't they?"

"Every one of them."

"And you, do you write, too?"

"God, no!" I said, laughing.

I liked his brusque manner. Like everyone else, I had read his famous book, *The Red Paradise*. But I had been especially moved by his book on Austria under the Nazis. It was something much more than a mere journalistic account; it was an impassioned testimony. He had fled Austria after having fled Russia and finally became a naturalised French citizen. But he had spent the last four years in America and we had met him for the first time only this autumn. Almost immediately he began calling Robert and Henri by their first names, but he never seemed to notice that I existed.

"I wonder what's going to become of them," he said, turning his eyes from me.

"Who?"

"The French in general and these people here in particular."

I studied his triangular face with its prominent cheekbones, its hard, fiery eyes, its thin, almost feminine mouth. It wasn't at all the face of a Frenchman. To him Russia was an enemy nation, and he did not have any great love for the United States. There wasn't a place on earth where he really felt at home.

"I returned from New York on an English boat," he said with a slight smile. "One day the steward said to me, ' The poor French! They don't know if they won the war or lost it.' It seems to me that that sums up the situation rather well."

There was an irritating complacency in his voice. "I don't think it matters much what kind of tag you put on things that happened in the past," I said. "What does matter is the future."

"That's just it," he said spiritedly. "To make something good of the future, you have to look the present in the face. And I get the distinct impression that these people here aren't doing that at all. Dubreuilh talks to me of a literary review, Perron of a pleasure trip. They all seem to feel they'll be able to go on living just like before the war."

"And of course, you were sent from heaven to open their eyes," I said dryly.

Scriassine smiled. " Do you know how to play chess?"
" Very poorly."
He continued to smile and all trace of pedantry vanished
from his face—we were intimate friends, accomplices, had
known each other since childhood. " He's working his Slavic
charm on me," I thought. And as a matter of fact, the charm
worked ; I smiled back at him.
" When I'm just watching chess, I can spot good moves
more clearly than the players themselves, even if I'm not as
good at the game as they are. Well, that's the way it is here ;
I'm an outsider, an onlooker, so I can pretty well see what's in
store for you people."
" What?"
" An impasse."
" An impasse? What do you mean by that?"
Suddenly, I found myself anxiously awaiting his reply. We
had all been living together in such a tightly sealed circle for
so long a time, with no intrusions by outsiders, any witnesses,
that this man from without troubled me.
" French intellectuals are facing an impasse. It's their turn
now," he added with a kind of satisfaction. " Their art, their
philosophies can continue to have meaning only within the
framework of a certain kind of civilisation. And if they want
to save that civilisation, they'll have no time or energy left
over to give to art or philosophy."
" This isn't the first time Robert's been active in politics,"
I said. " And it never before stopped him from writing."
" Yes, in '34 Dubreuilh gave a great deal of his time to the
struggle against fascism," Scriassine said in his suave voice.
" But to him, that struggle seemed morally reconcilable with
literary preoccupations." With a slight trace of anger, he
added, " In France, the pressure of history has never been
felt in all its urgency. But in Russia, in Austria, in Germany, it
was impossible to escape it. That's why I, for example, was
never able to write."
" But you have written."
" Don't you think I dreamed of writing other kinds of books,
too? But it was out of the question." He shrugged his
shoulders. " To be able to continue taking an interest in things
cultural in the face of Stalin and Hitler, you have to have one
hell of a humanistic tradition behind you. But, of course," he
went on, " in the country of Diderot, Victor Hugo, Jaurès, it's

easy to believe that culture and politics go hand in hand. Paris has thought of itself as Athens. But Athens no longer exists ; it's dead."

" As far as feeling the pressure of history is concerned," I said, " I think Robert could give you a few pointers."

" I'm not attacking your husband," Scriassine said, with a little smile that reduced my heated words to nothing more than an expression of conjugal loyalty. " As a matter of fact," he continued, " I consider Robert Dubreuilh and Thomas Mann to be the two greatest minds of this age. But that's precisely it ; if I predict that he'll give up literature, it's only because I have confidence in his lucidity."

I shrugged my shoulders. If he was trying to soften me up, he was certainly going about it the wrong way. I detest Thomas Mann.

" Robert will never give up writing," I said.

" The remarkable thing in all of Dubreuilh's works," said Scriassine, " is that he was able to reconcile high æsthetic standards with revolutionary inspiration. And in his own life, he attained an analogous equilibrium : he was organising vigilance committees at the same time he was writing novels. But it's precisely that beautiful equilibrium that's now becoming impossible."

" You can count on Robert to devise some new kind of equilibrium," I said.

" He's bound to sacrifice his æsthetic standards," Scriassine said. Suddenly his face lit up and he asked in a triumphant voice, " Do you know anything about prehistoric times?"

" Not much more than I do about chess."

" But perhaps you know this : that for a vast period of time the wall paintings and objects found in caves and excavations bear witness to a continuous artistic progress. Abruptly, both drawings and sculptures disappear ; there's an eclipse lasting several centuries which coincides with the development of new techniques. Well, just now we're at the edge of a new era in which, for different reasons, humanity will have to grapple with all sorts of difficult problems, leaving us no time for the luxury of expressing ourselves artistically."

" Reasoning by analogy doesn't prove very much," I said.

" All right then, let's forget that comparison," Scriassine said patiently. " You've probably been too close to this war we've gone through to properly understand it. Actually, it was something entirely different from a war—the liquidation of a society, and even of a world, or rather the beginning of their liquidation. The progress that science and engineering have made, the economic changes that have come about, will convulse the earth to such an extent that even our ways of thinking and feeling will be revolutionised. We'll even have difficulty remembering just who and what we had once been. And among other things art and literature will become nothing more than peripheral divertissements."

I shook my head and Scriassine resumed heatedly: " Don't you see? What weight will the message of French writers have when the earth is ruled by either Russia or the United States? No one will understand them any more; very few will even speak their language."

" From the way you talk, it would seem you're rather enjoying the prospect," I said.

He shrugged his shoulders. " Now isn't it just like a woman to say a thing like that! They're simply incapable of being objective."

"Well, let's be objective then," I said. " Objectively, it's never been proved that the world *must* become either American or Russian."

" In the long run, give or take a few years, it's bound to happen." With a gesture of his hand, he stopped me from interrupting him and then gave me one of his charming Slavic smiles. " I think I understand you. The liberation is still fresh in your mind. All of you are wading shoulder deep in euphoria. For four years you suffered a great deal and now you think you've paid enough. Well, you never can pay enough," he said with a sudden harshness. He looked me squarely in the eyes. " Do you know there's a very powerful faction in Washington that would like to see the German campaign continued right up to Moscow? And from their point of view they're right. American imperialism, like Russian totalitarianism requires unlimited expansion. In the end, one or the other has to win." A note of sadness entered his voice. " You think you're celebrating the German defeat, but what you're actually witnessing is the beginning of World War Three."

" Those are *your* prognostications," I said.

" I know Dubreuilh believes in peace and in the possibility of maintaining a free and independent Europe," Scriassine said.

" But even brilliant minds can sometimes be mistaken," he added with an indulgent smile. " We'll be annexed by Russia or colonised by America, of that you can be sure."

" Well, if that's the case, then there's no impasse," I said gaily. " If it's inevitable, what's the sense of worrying about it? Those who enjoy writing will just go right on writing."

" What an idiotic game that would be! To write when there's no one to read what you've written."

" When everything has gone to hell, there's nothing to do but to play idiotic games."

Scriassine remained silent for a moment and then a half-smile crossed his face. " Nevertheless, certain conditions would be less unfavourable than others," he said confidently. " If Russia wins, there's no problem: it's the end of civilisation and the end of all of us. But if America should win, the disaster wouldn't be quite so bad. If we were able to give her certain values while maintaining some of our own ideas, there'd be some hope that future generations would one day re-establish the ties with our own culture and traditions. But to succeed in that would require the total mobilisation of all our potential."

" Don't tell me that in case of a war you'd hope for an American victory!" I said.

" No matter what happens, history must inevitably lead to a classless society," Sriassine said in reply. " It's a matter of two or three centuries. But for the happiness of those men who'll be living during the interval, I ardently hope that the revolution takes place in a world dominated by America and not by Russia."

" In a world dominated by America," I said, " I have a sneaking suspicion that the revolution will cool its heels a good long time."

" And you think that it should be a Stalinist revolution? The idea of revolution had quite an appeal in France, around 1930. But let me tell you, in Russia it wasn't quite so appealing." He shrugged his shoulders. " You're preparing a big surprise for yourselves! The day the Russians occupy France you'll begin to realise what I mean. Unfortunately, it'll be too late then."

" You yourself don't believe in a Russian occupation," I said.

Scriassine sighed. " So be it," he said. " Let's be optimists. Let's admit that Europe has a chance of remaining independent. But we can't keep her that way except by waging a constant, interminable battle. Working for oneself will be entirely out of the question."

I did not attempt to answer him. All that Scriassine wanted was to reduce French writers to silence, and I clearly understood why. There was nothing really convincing in his prophecies, and yet his tragic voice awakened an echo in me. " How shall we live?" The question had been painfully pricking me all evening and for God knows how many days and weeks.

Scriassine looked at me intently. " One of two things can happen. If men like Dubreuilh and Perron look the situation square in the face, they'll become involved in things that will demand all their time, all their energies. Or if they cheat and obstinately continue to write, their works will be cut off from reality, and deprived of any future; they'll be like the works of blind people, as distressing as Alexandrine poetry."

It's difficult to engage in a discussion with someone who, while talking of the world and of others, talks constantly of himself. I was unable to speak my mind without hurting him. Nevertheless I said, " It's useless trying to imprison people in dilemmas; life always causes them to break out."

" Not in this case. Alexandria or Sparta, there's no other choice. It's far better to admit a thing like that to-day than to put it off," he said rather gently. " Sacrifices are no longer painful when they're behind you."

" I'm sure Robert won't sacrifice anything."

" We'll talk about it again a year from now," Scriassine said. " A year from now he'll either have deserted politics or he'll have stopped writing. I don't think he'll desert."

" And he won't stop writing, either."

Scriassine's face grew animated. " What would you like to bet? A bottle of champagne?"

" I'm not betting anything at all."

He smiled. " You're the same as all women; you need fixed stars in the heavens and milestones on the highways."

" You know," I said, shrugging my shoulders, " those

fixed stars did quite a lot of dancing around during the last four years."

"Yes, and nevertheless you're still convinced that France will always be France, and Robert Dubreuilh, Robert Dubreuilh. If not, you'd be lost."

"Listen," I said cheerfully. "Your objectivity begins to seem rather doubtful."

"I'm forced to follow you on your grounds; you oppose me with nothing but subjective convictions," Scriassine said. A smile warmed his inquisitive eyes. "You take things very seriously, don't you?"

"That depends."

"I was warned about that," he said. "But I like serious women."

"Who warned you?"

With a vague gesture, he indicated every one and no one. "People."

"What did they tell you?"

"That you were distant and austere. But I don't really think so."

I pressed my lips together, hoping it would prevent me from asking further questions. I've always been able to avoid being caught by the snare of mirrors. But the glances, the looks, the stares of other people, who can resist that dizzying pit? I dress in black, speak little, write not at all; together, all these things form a certain picture which others see. I'm no one. It's easy of course to say " I am I." But who am I? Where find myself? I would have to be on the other side of every door, but when it's I who knock the others grow silent. Suddenly I felt my face burning; I felt like ripping it off.

"Why don't you write?" Scriassine asked.

"There are enough books in the world."

"That's not the only reason," he said, staring at me through small, prying eyes. "The truth is you don't want to expose yourself."

"Expose myself to what?"

"On the surface, you seem very sure of yourself, but basically you're extremely timid. You're one of those people who pride themselves on not doing things."

I interrupted him. "Don't try analysing me; I know every dark recess of myself. I'm a psychiatrist, you know."

"I know," he said smiling. "Do you think we could have dinner together one evening? I feel lost in this blacked-out Paris; I don't seem to know anyone any more."

Suddenly, I thought, "Well, well! At least for him I have legs!" I took out my note-book; I had no reason for refusing.

"All right, let's have dinner together," I said. "Can you make it the third of January?"

"It's a date. Eight o'clock at the Ritz bar. Does that suit you?"

"Fine."

I felt ill at ease. Oh, it isn't that I cared much what he thought of me. No, not that. When I see my own likeness in the depths of someone else's consciousness, I always experience a moment of panic. But it doesn't last very long; I snap right out of it. What did bother me was having glimpsed Robert through eyes that weren't mine. Had he really reached an impasse? I looked over at him and saw him take Paula by the waist and spin her around; with his other hand, he was drawing God only knows what in the air. Perhaps he was explaining something about the flow of time to her. In any case, they were both laughing; he didn't give the least impression of being in danger. Were he in danger, he would surely have known it; Robert isn't often mistaken and he never lies to himself. I went to the bay window and hid myself behind the red draperies. Scriassine had spoken quite a bit of nonsense, but he had posed certain questions I was unable to brush off so easily. During all these weeks, I had fled from questions. We'd been waiting so long for this moment—the liberation, victory—that I wanted to get all I could out of it. There would always be time enough to-morrow to think of the next day. Well, now I had thought of it, and I wondered what Robert thought. His doubts never produced a diminishing of activity, but on the contrary they stimulated him to excesses. Didn't those long-drawn-out conversations, those letters, those telephone calls, those nocturnal debauches of work cover up a deep disturbance? He never hides anything from me, but sometimes he keeps certain worries temporarily to himself. And besides, I thought remorsefully, to-night he again repeated to Paula. "We're at the crossroads." He said it often, and through cowardice I avoided giving those words their true weight.

The crossroads. Therefore, in Robert's eyes, the world *was* in danger. And he is the world for me. *He* was in danger! He spoke volubly as we were returning home, arm in arm, through the familiar darkness along the quays. But to-night his voice wasn't enough to reassure me. He was bursting with what he had seen and heard, and he was very gay; when he has remained shut in for days and nights on end, the least occasion to go out becomes an event. When he spoke of the party, it seemed to me as if I had spent the evening with my eyes blindfolded and my ears stuffed with cotton. *He* had eyes all around his head and a dozen pairs of ears. I listened to him, but at the same time I continued questioning myself. He was never going to complete that journal he had kept so conscientiously all during the war. Why not? Was that a symptom? Of what?

"Poor, unhappy Paula! It's a catastrophe for a woman to be loved by a writer," Robert was saying. "She believed everything Perron told her about herself."

I tried to concentrate on Paula. "I'm afraid the liberation went to her head," I said. "Last year she had practically wiped out all her illusions. And now she's beginning to play at being madly in love again. But she's only playing."

"She wanted absolutely to make me say that time doesn't exist," Robert said. "The best part of her life is behind ner, and now that the war's over she's hoping to relive the past."

"Isn't that what we were all hoping for?" I asked. I thought I had spoken the words lightly, but Robert's hand tightened around my arm.

"What's wrong?" he asked.

"Not a thing; everything's perfect," I said flippantly.

"Come now! I know what it means when you start speaking in your worldly woman's voice," Robert said. "I'm sure something's churning in that little head of yours. How many glasses of punch did you have?"

"Certainly less than you. And anyhow, the punch has nothing to do with it."

"Ah! You admit it!" Robert said triumphantly. "Something *is* the matter and the punch has nothing to do with it. What is it then?"

"Scriassine," I answered, laughing. "He explained to me why French intellectuals are done for."

" He'd like that!"

" I know, but he frightened me anyhow."

" A great big girl like you who lets herself be frightened by the first prophet who comes along! I get a big kick out of Scriassine; he's restless, he rambles on, boils up, makes you know he's there. But you shouldn't take him seriously."

" He said that politics will eat you up, that you'll stop writing."

" And you believed him?" Robert said gaily.

" Well, it *is* true you're not showing any sign of finishing your memoirs," I replied.

Robert paused for a second and then said, " That's a special case."

" But why?"

" There are too many weapons in those memoirs that can be used against me."

" That's precisely why the thing is worth what it's worth," I said spiritedly. " It's so rare to find a man who dares to come out in the open! And when he *does* accept the dare, he invariably wins in the end."

" Yes," Robert said, " after he's dead." He shrugged his shoulders. " Now that I'm back in politics I have a lot of enemies. Do you realise how delighted they'd be the day those memoirs appeared in print?"

" Your enemies will always find weapons to use against you, the ones in the journal or others," I said.

" Just imagine those memoirs in the hands of Lafaurie, or Lachaume, or young Lambert. Or in the hands of any journalist, for that matter," Robert said.

Cut off completely from politics, from the future, from the public, not even knowing whether his journal would ever be published, Robert had rediscovered in its writing the adventure of the explorer venturing into an unnamed wilderness at random, without a trail to follow, without signs to warn him of its dangers. In my opinion, he had never written anything better. " If you become involved in politics," I said impatiently, " then you no longer have the right to write sincere books. Is that it?"

" No, you can write sincere books but not scandalous ones," Robert replied. " And you know very well that nowadays there are a thousand things a man can't speak about without causing a scandal." He smiled. " To tell the truth

there isn't much about any individual that doesn't lend itself
to scandal."

We walked a few steps in silence and then I said, " You
spent three years writing those memoirs. Doesn't it bother
you to leave them lying in the bottom of a drawer?"

" I've stopped thinking about them. I have another book
on my mind now."

" What's it about?"

" I'll tell you all about it in a few days."

I looked at Robert suspiciously. " And do you really
believe you'll find enough time to write?"

" Of course."

" It doesn't seem that certain to me. At the moment you
don't have a minute to yourself."

" In politics, it's the beginning that's the hardest. Afterwards you can take it easier."

His voice sounded too confident. " And what if it doesn't
become easier?" I persisted. " Would you get out of politics
or would you stop writing?"

" You know, it really wouldn't be a great tragedy if I
stopped writing for a little while," Robert answered with a
smile. " I've scribbled a lot of words on a lot of paper in my
life!"

I felt a wrench at my heart. " Just the other day you were
saying your best works are still ahead of you."

" And I still think so. But they can wait a while."

" How long? A month? A year? Ten years?" I asked.

" Listen," Robert said in a conciliatory tone of voice,
" one book more or less on earth isn't as important as all
that. And the political situation at present is extremely stimu-
lating; I hope you realise that. This is the first time the left
has ever held its fate in its own hands, the first chance to
try to organise a group independent of the Communists
without running the risk of serving the cause of the right.
I'm not going to let this opportunity slip by! I've been
waiting for it all my life."

" For my part, I think your books are more important," I
said. " They bring people something unique and different.
But when it comes to politics, you're not the only one about
who can become involved in it."

" But I'm the only one who can steer things in the
direction I want them to take," Robert said cheerfully. " You

of all people ought to understand me. The vigilance committees and the Resistance were useful, all right, but they
were negative things. To-day, it's a question of building, and
that's much more interesting."

" I understand you very well, but your writing interests me
more."

" Haven't we always agreed that one doesn't write just for
the sake of writing?" Robert said. " At certain times, other
forms of action become more urgent."

" Not for you," I replied. " First and foremost, you're a
writer."

" You know that's not true," Robert said reproachfully.
" For me, the revolution comes first."

" Yes," I said, " but you can best serve the revolution by
writing your books."

Robert shook his head. " That depends on the circumstances. We're at a critical moment of history just now ; first we
have to win the political battle."

" And what happens if we don't win it?" I asked. " Do
you really believe there's a chance of a new war?"

" I don't believe a new war is going to start to-morrow,"
Robert replied. " But what has to be avoided at all cost is
the creation of a situation in the world which might easily
lead to war. If that happens, then we'll sooner or later come
to blows again. And we also have to prevent this victory
from being exploited by capitalism." He shrugged his
shoulders. " There are a lot of things that have to be prevented before one can afford to amuse oneself writing books
that no one might ever read."

I stopped dead in the middle of the street. " What? Do
you believe that too? That people will lose interest in
literature?"

" Believe me, they'll have a lot of other things to keep
themselves busy with," Robert said in a voice that again
seemed to me too reassuring.

" The prospect doesn't seem to bother you at all," I said
indignantly. " But a world without literature and art would
be horribly sad."

" In any event, there are millions of men at this very
moment to whom literature means absolutely nothing,"
Robert replied.

" Yes, but you always expected that to change."

" I still expect it to. What makes you think I don't?"
Robert asked. " But that's precisely it," he went on without
waiting for me to answer. " If the world decides to change,
there's no doubt we'll go through a period in which literature
will be almost completely out of the picture."

We went into the study and I sat down on the arm of one
of the leather chairs. Yes, I had certainly drunk too much
punch ; the walls were spinning crazily. I looked at the table
on which Robert had been writing night and day for twenty
years. He was sixty now, and if this period of political up-
heaval dragged on for very long he ran the risk of never
seeing the end of it. He couldn't possibly be as indifferent
to such a prospect as he tried to appear.

" Let's look into this thing a little," I said. " You believe
your major works are still ahead of you and just five minutes
ago you said you were going to begin a new book. That
implies that you believe there are people around who want to
read what you've written . . ."

" Oh, I suppose that's more than likely," Robert said.
" But the opposite view can't be rejected out of hand."
He sat down next to me in the chair. " It's not really as
horrible as you might think," he added cheerfully. " Literature is created for men and not men for literature."

" It would be sad for you," I said. " You wouldn't be
happy if you stopped writing."

" I don't know," Robert replied with a grin. " I have no
imagination."

But he has. I remember how worried he was the night he
said to me, " My major works are still ahead of me!" He's
determined that those works shall have weight, permanence.
It's useless for him to protest ; above all else he's a writer.
At first perhaps he had dreamed only of serving the revolution ; literature was just a means. But it soon became an
end ; he loved it for itself and all his books prove it, especially those memoirs he doesn't want published. He wrote
them purely for the pleasure of writing. No, the truth is that
he simply doesn't want to talk about himself, and that reluctance isn't a good sign.

" As for me," I said, " I have plenty of imagination."
The walls were spinning, but I was thinking very lucidly,
much more lucidly than I do in the morning before breakfast.

In the morning before eating, you're on the defensive, you manage somehow not to know things you really do know. Suddenly I saw everything with perfect clarity. The war was ending and a new history in which nothing was guaranteed was beginning. And Robert's future wasn't guaranteed; it was perfectly possible for him to stop writing and even for all his published works to be swallowed up into nothingness.

"What do you really think?" I asked. "Do you think things will turn out good or bad?"

Robert began to laugh. "I'm not a prophet! But one thing is certain," he added. "We're holding a lot of trumps."

"But what are the chances of winning?"

"Shall I look into my crystal ball? Or would you like me to read your tea leaves?"

"You don't have to make fun of me," I said. "I have a right to ask a few questions from time to time."

"I ask myself a few, too, you know," Robert said.

Yes, he does ask himself questions, and graver ones than I do. Personally, I rarely act on my beliefs; that's why I so easily become unhappy. I realise I'm wrong being that way, but with Robert it costs so little to be wrong.

"But you only ask yourself those questions you're able to answer," I said.

He laughed again. "Preferably, yes. The others don't serve much purpose."

"That's no reason not to ask them," I said. My voice was rising, but I wasn't angry with Robert. I was angry with myself, with my blindness during these past weeks. "I'd still like to have some idea of what's going to happen to us," I persisted.

"Don't you think it's rather late?" Robert asked. "We've both had a lot of punch to drink, and our minds will be a lot clearer to-morrow morning."

To-morrow morning the walls will stop spinning, the furniture and books will be in their proper places, always the same places. And my ideas, too, will fall back into place, and I'll begin to live again from day to day, without turning my head, looking just so far and no farther into the future. I'll stop paying attention to that discordant clatter in my heart. I'm tired of that diet. I looked at the cushion by the fireplace on which Diego used to sit. "A Nazi victory doesn't enter into my plans," he had said. And then they had killed him.

"Ideas are always too definite!" I said. "The war is won. There's a definite idea for you. Well, in my opinion we went to a very peculiar party to-night, with all the dead who weren't there."

"There's quite a difference between saying that their deaths served some purpose and none at all," Robert said.

"Diego's served no purpose at all," I retorted. "And what if it had?" I added irritably. "It's fine for the living, this system by which everything leads to something else. But the dead stay dead and we're constantly betraying them; they don't lead to anything."

"We don't betray them by choice," Robert protested.

"We betray them when we forget them and when we use them," I said. "Regret has to be useless or else it's not really regret."

Robert thought for a moment and then, with a perplexed look on his face, said, "I suppose I've no great talent for regretting. I don't bother myself much with questions I can't answer, things I can't change." He paused a moment and added, "I don't say I'm right about that."

"And I don't say you're wrong. In any case, the dead are dead and we go on living. All the regretting in the world won't change that."

Robert took my hand. "Don't go looking for things to make you remorseful," he said. "We'll also die, you know; that brings us very close to them, doesn't it?"

I withdrew my hand; at that moment I was the enemy of all friendly feelings. I didn't want to be consoled, not yet.

"Your damned punch has really gone to my head," I said. "I'm going to bed."

"Yes, go to bed now. And to-morrow we'll ask each other all the questions you want, even those that serve no purpose," Robert said.

"And you? Aren't you coming to bed?"

"No, I think I'll have a shower and do some work."

"There's no doubt Robert is better armed than I against regrets," I thought, getting into bed. He works, acts; the future is more real to him than the past. And he writes. All the things that fall outside his normal course of life—mis-

fortune, defeat, death—he puts into his books and considers
himself rid of them. But I have no recourse; whatever I lose
I can never regain, and there's nothing to redeem my infidelities. Suddenly I began to weep. "These are *my* eyes
that are weeping," I thought. "He sees everything, but not
through my eyes." I was weeping, and for the first time in
twenty years I was alone, alone with my remorse, my fear.
I fell asleep and dreamed I was dead. I woke up with a
start, and the fear was still there. And death continues to
prowl silently in the room. I switch on the lights, turn them
off; if Robert sees the ray of light under my door, he'll
worry. It's useless; to-night he can't help me. When I
wanted to talk to him about himself, he evaded my questions. He knows he's in danger; I'm afraid for him. Up
to now I've always had the fullest confidence in him; I've
never tried to measure him. For me the measure of all things
was Robert. I've lived with him as I've lived with myself, no
distance separating us. But, suddenly, I've lost all confidence
—in everything. No fixed stars, no milestones. Robert is a
man, a fallible, vulnerable man of sixty whom the past no
longer protects and the future menaces. I lean back against
the pillow, my eyes wide open. To see him better I've got to
step backwards, far enough back to blot out the view of those
twenty years of unquestioning love I'd given him.

It's not easy. There was a time I did see him from a distance, but I was too young. I looked at him from too far off.
Friends had pointed him out to me at the Sorbonne; they
spoke of him a great deal, with a mixture of admiration and
disapproval. It was whispered that he drank and frequented
brothels. If that had been true, I think it would have
attracted rather than repelled me; I was still rebelling against
my pious childhood. In my mind, sin was a touching
manifestation of the absence of God, and if someone had
told me that Dubreuilh raped little girls I'd have taken him
for a saint of sorts. But his vices were minor and his too-
well-established fame irritated me. When I began taking his
courses, I had already made up my mind that the "great
man" was a charlatan. Of course, he was different from all
the other professors. He would come rushing into the room
like a gust of wind; he was always four or five minutes
late. He would survey us for a moment with his large, crafty

eyes, and then he would begin speaking in either a very amiable or a very aggressive voice. There was something provocative in his surly face, his violent voice, his bursts of laughter which sometimes seemed to us a little insane. He wore very white shirts, his hands were always carefully manicured, and he was impeccably shaven; it was impossible, therefore, to attribute to negligence his zipper jackets, his pullovers, his clumsy shoes. He preferred comfort to decency with such an obvious lack of restraint that I thought it affected. I had read his novels and didn't like them at all; I expected them to bring to me some inspiring message, and all they ever spoke to me of were indifferent people, frivolous sentiments, and a lot of other things that didn't seem to me the least bit essential. As for his courses, they were interesting all right, but he never really said anything worthy of a genius. And he was always so cocksure of being right that I had an irresistible desire to contradict him. Oh, I was convinced, too, that the truth was to the left; ever since my childhood I had sniffed an odour of stupidity and lies in bourgeois thinking, a very foul-smelling odour. And then I had learned from the Gospel that all men are equal, are brothers; that's one thing I continue to believe in with an unshakable faith. But spiritually, after I had been for so long crammed full of absolutes, the void left in the heavens made a mockery of all morality I had been taught. But Dubreuilh believed there could be salvation here on earth. I let him know where I stood in my first essay. "Revolution, fine," I said, "but what then?" When he gave me back my paper a week later as we were leaving the classroom, he ridiculed my efforts. According to him, my absolute was the abstract dream of a petty bourgeoise incapable of facing reality. Of course I couldn't hold my own against him, and he won every round. But that didn't prove anything, and I told him as much. We resumed our discussion the following week and this time he tried to convince me, rather than overwhelm me. I had to admit that in private discussion he didn't at all seem to feel that he was a great man. He began chatting with me, rather often after classes, sometimes he walked home with me occasionally taking a longer route than was necessary. And then we began going out together in the afternoons, the evenings. We stopped talking about morality and politics and other lofty subjects. He told me about the people he knew and the things he did, and most of all he would take me for walks, show me streets, squares, quays, canals, cemeteries, suburbs, warehouses, vacant sites, little cafés, and a hundred corners of Paris that were completely new to me. And I began to realise that I had never really seen things I believed I had always known; with him everything took on a thousand meanings—faces, voices, people's clothing, a tree poster, a neon sign, no matter what. I reread all his novels. And I soon realised I had completely misunderstood them for the first time. Dubreuilh gave the impression of writing capriciously, for his own pleasure, completely without motivation. And yet on closing the book, you felt yourself overwhelmed with anger, disgust, revolt; you wanted things to change. To read certain passages from his works, you would take him for a pure æsthete; he has a feeling for words, and he's interested in things for themselves, in rain and clear skies, in the games of love and chance, in everything. Only he doesn't stop there; suddenly you find yourself thrown in among people, and all their problems become your concern. That's why I'm so determined for him to continue writing; I know through my own experience what he can bring to his readers. There's no gap between his political ideas and his poetic emotions. Because he himself loves life so much, he wants all men to be able to share it abundantly. And because he loves people, everything that's part of their lives interests him deeply.

I reread his books, listened to him, questioned him; I was so taken up with this new life of mine that I didn't even think of asking myself why, exactly, he enjoyed being with me. I was already so involved that I had no time to discover what was happening inside my own heart. When one night he took me in his arms in the middle of the Jardins du Carrousel, I was offended. " I will only kiss a man I love," I said coldly. " But you do love me!" he answered calmly. And when he said it, I knew it was true. I hadn't been aware of it; it had all happened too fast. With Robert, everything happened so fast! In fact, that was precisely the quality in him that had captivated me at first. Other people were so slow, life was so slow. He burned up time and pushed everything out of his way. From the moment I knew I loved him, I followed him eagerly from surprise to surprise. I learned that one could live without furniture and without schedules, skip lunches, not go to bed at night, sleep in the afternoon, make love in a wood as well as in bed. It seemed a simple and joyous thing to me to become a woman in his arms; when the pleasure was frightening, his smile would reassure me. A single shadow lay over my heart—term was nearly over and the thought of being separated from him terrified me. Robert obviously realised that. Was that why he suggested we get married? The idea had never even crossed my mind; at nineteen, it seems as natural to be loved by the man with whom you're in love as by doting parents or all-powerful God.

" But I really did love you!" Robert told me much later. Coming from him, what precisely did those words mean? Would he have loved me a year earlier when he was still taken up body and soul in political battles? And the year I came to know him, couldn't he have chosen someone else as consolation for his inactivity? That's the kind of question that serves no purpose whatsoever. Let's drop it. One thing was definitely certain: he was determined to make me happy, and he did not fail. Up to then I hadn't been unhappy, but neither had I been happy. I was always in good health and occasionally I had moments which I enjoyed. But most of the time I was plainly and simply disconsolate. Foolishness, lies, injustice, suffering; all around me a deep, black chaos. And how absurd it all was! Those days which repeated themselves from week to week, from century to century, without ever getting anywhere. Living was simply a matter of waiting some forty or sixty years for death to come, trudging along through emptiness. That was why I studied so avidly: only books and ideas were able to hold their own; they alone seemed real to me.

Thanks to Robert, ideas were brought down to earth and the earth became coherent, like a book, a book that begins badly but will finish well. Humanity was going somewhere; history had meaning, and so did my own existence. Oppression and misery contained within themselves the promise of their disappearance; evil had already been conquered, shame swept away. The sky closed above my head and the old fears left me. Robert hadn't freed me with theories; he simply showed me that to live was sufficient unto life. He didn't give a damn about death, and his activities weren't merely diversions; he liked what he liked, wanted what he wanted, and ran from nothing. Quite simply, all I wanted was to be like him. If I had questioned life, it was mostly because I was bored at home. And now I was no longer bored. From chaos, Robert had drawn a full, orderly world, cleansed by the future he was helping to produce. And that world was mine. I had to make my own place in it. Being Robert's wife wasn't enough; before marrying him I had never pictured myself making a career of being a wife. On the other hand, I never for a moment dreamed of taking an active part in politics. In that domain, theories can interest me deeply and I harbour a few strong feelings, but practical politics aren't for me. I have to admit that I lack patience; the revolution is on the march, but it's marching so slowly, with such tiny, uncertain steps! For Robert, if one solution is better than another, that's the correct one; a lesser evil he considers a good. He's right, of course, but no doubt I haven't completely buried my old dreams of the absolute. It does not satisfy me. And then the future seems so very far off; I find it hard to become interested in men who aren't born yet. I would much rather help those who are alive at this very moment. That's why my profession attracted me. Oh, I never believed that you could, from the outside, supply people with a prefabricated salvation. But sometimes only trifles separate them from happiness, and I felt I could at least sweep away those trifles. Robert encouraged me. In that respect he differs from orthodox Communists; he believes that psychoanalysis can play a useful role in bourgeois society and that it might still be of use even in a classless society. And the possibility of rethinking classical psychoanalysis in terms of Marxist ideology struck him as a fascinating idea. The fact of the matter is that my work did interest me, and very deeply. My days were as full as the earth around me. Every morning I awakened more joyously than the day before and every evening I found myself enriched with a thousand new discoveries. It's an incredible stroke of luck, when you're only twenty years old, to be given the world by the hand you love. And it's equally lucky to find your exact place in that world. Robert also accomplished another feat; he guarded me against isolation without depriving me of privacy. We shared everything in common; and yet I had my own friendships, my own pleasures, my work, my worries. If I wanted to, I could spend the night nestled against a tender shoulder. Or, like to-night, I could

remain alone and chaste in my room. I look at the four
walls and the rays of light under the door; how many times
have I known the sweetness of falling asleep while he was
working within earshot. It's been years since we lost our
desire for each other, but we were too closely bound in
other ways to attach any great importance to the union of our
bodies. Therefore we had, so to speak, lost nothing. It seems
almost like a pre-war night to-night. Even this worrying that's
been keeping me awake isn't new; the future of the world has
often seemed very black. What is it, then, that's different?
Why has death come prowling again in my room? It continues
to prowl. Why?

What stupid obstinacy! I'm ashamed. During these past
four years, in spite of all that's happened, I somehow managed to persuade myself that everything would be the same
after the war as it was before. In fact, only a little while
ago I was saying to Paula, " It's just like it used to be, isn't
it?" This is what I am trying to say to myself: the way it
is now is exactly the way it used to be. But no, I'm lying
to myself; it's not and it never again will be the same. Up
to now, I always knew in my heart that we would somehow pull out of the gravest crises. Certainly Robert *had*
to pull out of them; his destiny guaranteed that of the
world, and vice versa. But with the horrifying past behind
us, how can anyone have any faith in the future? Diego
is dead, too many others have died; shame has returned
to the earth, the word " happiness " has lost all meaning.
All around me, nothing but chaos again. Maybe the world
will pull out of it. But when? Two or three centuries are
much too long; our own days are numbered. If Robert's
life ends in defeat, in doubt, in despair, nothing will ever
make up for it.

I hear a slight movement in his study; he's reading,
thinking, planning. Will he succeed? And if not, what
then? No need to think of the worst; until now, no one
has ever eaten us up. We just go on existing, following
the whim of a story that isn't ours at all. And Robert
has been reduced to the rôle of a passive witness. What
will he do with himself? I know how much the revolution
means to him; it's his absolute. The experiences of his
youth left an indelible mark upon him; during all those

years he spent growing up among soot-coloured houses
and lives, socialism was his only hope. And it wasn't
because of generosity or logic that he believed in it, but
because of necessity. For him, becoming a man meant
only one thing: becoming a militant partisan, like his
father. It took quite a lot to make him withdraw from
politics—the infuriating disillusionment of '14, his rupture
with Cachin two years after Tours, his inability to awaken
the old revolutionary flame in the Socialist Party. At the
first opportunity, he leaped eagerly into the political arena
again, and now he's more excited about it than ever. To
reassure myself I tell myself that he has all manner of
resources at his command. After our marriage, during the
years he spent away from active politics, he wrote a great
deal and was happy. But was he? I chose to believe it,
and until to-night I never dared pry into what really went
on inside him. I no longer feel very certain about our
past. If he wanted a child so soon, it was probably
because I alone wasn't enough to justify his existence. Or
perhaps he was trying to take revenge against that future
which he could no longer control. Yes, that desire of his
to become a father seems rather significant now that I
look back upon it. And the sadness of our pilgrimage to
Bruay is significant, too. We walked through the streets
of his childhood and he showed me the school where his
father had taught, the sombre building in which, at the
age of nine, he had heard Jaurès. He told me about his
first encounters with daily routine and disappointment
with pointless work; he was speaking very fast, he sounded
very uninterested, and then suddenly he said heatedly,
" Nothing has changed. But I write novels!" I wanted to
believe it was only a fleeting emotion; Robert was much
too lighthearted for me to imagine that he had any serious
regrets. But after the Congress of Amsterdam, during that
whole period when he was busily organising vigilance committees, I saw him as he acted when he was really happy,
and I had to admit the truth to myself: before then, he had
been straining at the leash. If now he finds himself condemned once more to impotence, to solitude, everything
will seem useless to him, even writing. Especially writing.
Between '25 and '32, when he was holding himself in

check, he wrote, yes. But it was a lot different then. He still had close ties with the Communists and some of the Socialists; he nourished the hope of a united workers' front and of a final victory. I know by heart that phrase of Jaurès' he used to repeat at every opportunity: "The man of to-morrow will be the most complex, the richest in life, that history has ever known." He was convinced his books would help to build the future and that the man of to-morrow would read them. That being the case, he wrote. But faced with a sealed future, writing becomes meaningless. If his contemporaries stop listening to him, if posterity no longer understands him, there's nothing left but to be silent.

And what then? What will become of him? It's awful to think of a living creature turning into foam, but there's an even worse fate: that of a paralysed man who can't move his tongue. It's far better to be dead. Will I find myself some day hoping for Robert's death? No. That's unthinkable. He's had hard blows before and he's always got over them. He'll get over them again. I don't know how, but he'll surely think of something. It's not entirely impossible, for example, that one day he'll become a member of the Communist Party. Now, of course, he wouldn't dream of doing it; his criticisms of their policies are too violent. But suppose the party line changes, suppose there comes a day when, excepting for the Communists, there is no coherence left. If that ever happens I wonder if Robert won't end up by joining them rather than remaining inactive. I don't like that idea. It would be much harder for him than for anyone else to take orders with which he didn't agree; he's always had his own definite opinions on what tactics to use. And it would be useless for him to attempt to be cynical; I know he'll always remain faithful to his old principles. The idealism of others makes him smile; he has his own, and there are certain Communist methods he would never accept. No, that's no solution. There are far too many things that keep them apart; his humanism isn't the same as theirs. Not only would he be unable to write anything sincere, but he would be forced to reject his whole past.

"Too bad," he'll tell me. Just a little while ago he said, "One book more or less isn't very important." But does he really believe that? As for me, I value books greatly, too much perhaps. When I was an adolescent, I preferred books to the world of reality, and something of that has remained with me—a slight taste for eternity. Yes, that's one of the reasons why I take Robert's writings so much to heart. If they perish, both of us will once more become perishable ; the future will be nothing but the grave. Robert doesn't see things that way, but neither is he the perfect militant completely un-concerned with himself. He definitely hopes to leave a name behind him, a name that will mean a great deal to a great many people. And after all, writing is the thing he loves most in the world ; it's his joy, his necessity ; it's he, himself. Re-nouncing writing would be suicide for him.

Well, all he would have to do is resign himself to writing to order. Others do it. Others, but not Robert. If I had to, I could imagine him working actively for a cause halfheartedly. But writing is something else again ; if he were no longer able to express himself freely, the pen would fall from his hand.

Now I see the impasse. Robert believes completely in cer-tain ideas, and before the war we were positive that one day they would be realised. His whole life has been devoted to en-riching them and preparing for their birth. But suppose they're never born? Suppose the revolution takes a different tack, turns against the humanism Robert has always defen-ded? What can he do? If he helps build a future hostile to all the values in which he believes, his struggle becomes absurd. But if he stubbornly insists on maintaining values that will never come down to earth, he becomes one of those old dreamers whom, above all, he has always wanted not to emulate. No, between those alternatives, no choice is pos-sible. In either case, it would mean defeat, impotence ; and for Robert that would be a living death. That's why he's thrown himself so energetically into the fight. He tells me the present situation offers an opportunity he's been waiting for all his life. All right. But it also carries with it a graver danger than any he has ever experienced, and he knows it. Yes, I'm sure he's already told himself everything I've been thinking. He's told himself that his future might be nothing but the grave, that he'll be buried without leaving any more trace of himself than Rosa and Diego. And it's even worse: perhaps the men of to-morrow will look upon him as a dunderhead, a fool, a charlatan, a drone, a complete failure.

It may even be that one day he'll be tempted to look upon *himself* through their mean, cruel eyes. In that case, he'll live out the rest of his life in disillusionment. Robert disillusioned! That would be an even more intolerable horror than death itself. I can accept my death and his, but never his disillusionment. No. To think of waking up to-morrow, and the next day, and all the days that follow, with that monstrous menace on the horizon! I won't stand for it. No. But I can say no, no, no ; I can say it a hundred times, and it won't change a thing. I'll wake up facing that menace to-morrow and all the days after that. When you're faced with an inescapable fact, you can at least choose to die. But when it's nothing more than a baseless fear, you have to go on living with it.

CHAPTER TWO

THE NEXT morning the radio confirmed the German collapse. " It's really the beginning of peace," Henri repeated to himself, sitting down at his desk. " At last I can start writing again!" He would, he assured himself, write every day from now on. But what exactly would he write? He didn't know and he was perfectly content not to know ; always before he had known only too well. Now he would attempt to talk to the reader without premeditation, as one writes to a friend. And perhaps he would at last succeed in saying all those things for which he had never found room enough in his too carefully constructed books. There are so many things one would like to preserve with words but which are forever lost. He raised his head and looked through the window at the cold sky. What a pity to think that this winter morning would be lost ; everything seemed so precious: the white, virginal paper, the smell of alcohol and stale cigarette ends, the Arab music drifting up from the café next door. Notre Dame was as cold as the sky, a tramp with a huge collar of bluish chicken feathers was dancing in the middle of the street, and two girls in their Sunday clothes were watching him and laughing. It was Christmas, it was the German collapse, and life was beginning again. Yes, all those mornings, all those evenings, that he had let slip through his fingers in the last four years, he was determined to make up for them during the next thirty. You can't say everything, that's true enough. But nevertheless you can try to get across the real flavour of your life. Every life has a flavour, a flavour all its own, and if you can't describe it, there's no point in writing. " I've got to tell about what I liked, what I like, what I am," he said to himself as he finished sketching a cluster of flowers on a scrap of paper. Who was he? What manner of man would he discover after that long absence? It's difficult, working from within, for a person to define himself, to set limits on himself. He wasn't a political fanatic, nor a literary æsthete, nor a dedicated man in any sense. Rather, he felt quite ordinary, and the feeling didn't upset him in the least. A man like everyone else, who spoke sincerely of himself, would speak in the name of everyone, for everyone. Complete sincerity: that was the only distinctive thing he felt he had to aim for, the only restriction he would have to impose upon himself. He added another flower to the cluster. But it isn't easy to be sincere. First of all, he had no intention of making an open confession. And secondly, whosoever says novel, says lie. Well, he would think about that later. For the moment, he had above all else to keep himself from becoming burdened with too many problems. Say anything, begin anywhere—beneath the moon in the gardens of El Oued. The paper was bare; he had to take advantage of it.

"Did you start your light novel?" Paula asked.

"I don't know."

"What do you mean, you don't know? Don't you know what you're writing?"

"I'm planning to surprise myself," he said with a laugh.

Paula shrugged her shoulders. As a matter of fact, what he said was quite true; he really didn't want to know. Without any semblance of order, any basic plan, he jotted down odds and ends of his life, and it amused and pleased him, and he could ask for nothing more.

The evening he went to meet Nadine, he left his writing regretfully. He had told Paula he was going out with Scriassine; during the last year he had learned to be more discreet. To have said "I'm going out with Nadine" would have brought on so many questions, so many misinterpretations, that he chose not to say it. But it was really absurd to hide the fact that he was meeting that awkward girl whom he had always looked upon as a sort of niece. It was even more absurd to have made the appointment in the first place. He pushed open the door to the Bar Rouge and walked over to her table. She was sitting between Lachaume and Vincent.

"No fights to-night?"

"No," Vincent said peevishly.

Young men and women crowded into that red cellar not primarily to be among friends, but rather to confront adversaries. Every conceivable shade of political opinion was represented there, and Henri often came there to spend a few pleasant moments talking with his friends. He would have liked to sit down now and chat casually with Lachaume and Vincent while he watched the crowd in the room. But Nadine got up at once.

" Are you taking me to dinner?"

" That's what I'm here for."

Outside, it was dark; the sidewalk was covered with dirty slush. What in the world, he wondered, would he be able to do with Nadine?

" Where would you like to go?" he asked. " To the Italian place?"

" To the Italian place."

She wasn't difficult to please. She let him choose the table and ordered the same things as he—peperoni and ossobuco. She approved of everything he said with a delighted air which somehow seemed rather suspect to Henri. The truth was that she wasn't listening to him; she was eating greedily and quietly, smiling into her plate. He let the conversation lapse and Nadine appeared not to notice it. Having swallowed the last mouthful, she wiped her lips with a broad gesture.

" And now where do you plan to take me?"

" You don't like jazz and you don't like dancing?"

" No."

" Well, we can try the Tropic of Cancer."

" Can we have any fun there?"

" Why? Do you know some place we can have some fun? The Tropic isn't a bad place for a quiet talk."

She shrugged her shoulders. " Public benches are all right, too, for talking." Her face lit up. " As a matter of fact, there are some places I do like—the ones where you see those naked women."

" Really? That sort of thing amuses you?"

" Oh, yes. Of course, the Turkish baths are better, but the cabarets aren't bad."

" You .ouldn't by any chance be just a little bit perverted, would you?" Henri asked, laughing.

" It's possible," she said dryly. " Have you anything better to suggest?"

It was impossible to imagine anything more incongruous than going to see naked women with this tall, awkward girl who was neither a virgin nor yet a woman. But Henri had taken it upon himself to entertain her and he had no idea of how to go about it. They went to Chez Astarte and sat down at a table in front of a champagne bucket. The room was still empty; at the bar, the house girls were chattering to each other. Nadine studied them carefully.

" If I were a man," she said, " I'd take a different woman home with me every night."

" If you had a different woman every night, they'd all seem the same after a while."

" You're wrong. Take that little brunette over there, and the redhead with those pretty falsies, for example. You wouldn't find the same thing at all under their dresses." She rested her chin in the palm of her hand and looked steadily at Henri. " Aren't you interested in women?"

" Not in that way."

" How then?"

" Well, I like looking at them when they're pretty, dancing with them when they're graceful, or talking to them when they're intelligent."

" For talk men are better," Nadine said. She looked at him suspiciously. " Look," she said, " why did you ask me to go out with you? I'm not pretty, I dance badly, and I'm a poor conversationalist."

Henri smiled. " Don't you remember? You were reproaching me for not asking you?"

" And I suppose every time someone reproaches you for not doing something, you immediately do it?"

" All right," Henri asked, " why did you accept my invitation?"

She gave him such a naïve and inviting look that he was suddenly upset. Was it true, as Paula claimed, that she couldn't see a man without offering herself to him?

" One must never refuse anything," she said sententiously.

For a moment she silently stirred her champagne. Then they started to talk idly again. But from time to time Nadine would abruptly stop talking to stare insistently at Henri, a look of astonished reproof on her face. " One thing is sure," he told himself. " I can't very well make a pass at her." She only half-appealed to him; he knew her too well; she was too easy; and besides, it would have embarrassed him because of the Dubreuilhs. He tried to fill the silences, but twice she yawned deliberately in his face. He, too, found that time passed slowly. A few couples were dancing, mostly Americans and their girls, and one or two pairs of lovers from the provinces. He decided to leave as soon as the dancers had done their number and he felt relieved when they finally came on. There were six of them, in sequin-studded panties and brassieres, wearing top hats on which the French tricolor or the American stars and stripes were painted. They danced neither well nor badly, they were homely but not excessively so. It was an uninteresting show, a show that never got off the ground. What was it then that made Nadine look so delighted? When the girls took off their brassières, uncovering their wax-firmed breasts, she cast a sly glance at Henri and asked, " Which one do you like best?"

" They're all the same."

Nadine silently examined the women with an expert, rather blasé look. After they had backed out of the room, waving their panties in one hand, and holding their red-white-and-blue hats over their genitals with the other, Nadine asked, " Do you think it's more important to have a pretty face or a good figure?"

" That depends."

" On what?"

" On the woman, on your taste."

" Well, how do you rate me?"

" I'll tell you in three or four years," he said, looking her over carefully. " You're still unfinished."

" You're never finished until you're dead," she said angrily. Her eyes wandered around the room and came to rest on the blonde dancer, who was now wearing a tight black dress and sitting at the bar. " You know, she really does look sad. Why don't you ask her to dance?"

" That certainly won't cheer her up much."

" All her friends have men. She looks like a leftover. Ask her ; what can it cost you?" she said with a sudden burst of vehemence. Then her voice softened, and pleadingly she added, " Just once."

" If it means that much to you," he said.

The blonde followed him unenthusiastically on to the dance floor. She was a silly, ordinary-looking thing ; he couldn't see why Nadine took such an interest in her. To tell the truth, Nadine's whims were beginning to get on his nerves. When he returned to the table, he noticed she had filled two champagne glasses and was looking at them meditatively.

"You're nice," she said, looking at him tenderly. Suddenly she smiled and asked, "Do you get funny when you're drunk?"

"When I'm drunk I always think I'm very funny."

"And other people, what do they think?"

"When I'm drunk, I don't worry very much about what other people think."

She pointed to the bottle. "Let's see you get drunk."

"Champagne isn't what'll do it."

"How many glasses can you drink without getting drunk?"

"Quite a few."

"More than three?"

"Of course."

She looked at him doubtfully. "That's something I'd like to see! Do you mean to say you could gulp these two glasses down and it wouldn't do anything to you?"

"Not a thing."

"Let's see you try."

"Why?"

"People are always bragging; sometimes you have to call their bluff."

"After that, I suppose you'll ask me to stand on my head," Henri said.

"After that, you can go home and go to bed. Drink up; one after the other."

He swallowed the contents of one of the glasses and felt a sudden shock in the pit of his stomach.

"Now the second," Nadine said, handing him the other glass.

He drank it down.

He woke up stretched out on a bed, naked, alongside a naked woman who was holding him by the hair and shaking his head.

"Who are you?" he mumbled.

"Nadine. Wake up, it's late."

He opened his eyes; the lights were on. He was in a strange room, a hotel room. Yes, he remembered the desk clerk, the stairway. Before that, he had been drinking champagne. His head ached.

"What happened? I don't understand."

" That champagne you drank was spiked with brandy,"
Nadine replied, laughing.

" You spiked my champagne with brandy?"

" I did. It's a little trick I often play on the Americans when
I have to get them drunk. Anyhow," she said, still smiling,
" it was the only way to have you."

He carefully touched his head. " I don't remember a
thing."

" Oh, there was nothing much to it."

She got out of bed, took a comb from her purse, and, standing nude before a full-length mirror, began combing her hair.
How youthful her body was! Had he really held that lithe,
slender form, with its softly rounded shoulders and small
breasts, against him? Suddenly she realised that he was studying her. " Don't look at me like that!" she said. She grabbed
her slip and hastily put it on.

" You're very pretty!"

" Don't be silly!" she said haughtily.

" Why are you getting dressed? Come over here."

She shook her head and Henri, suddenly worried, asked,
" Did I do something I shouldn't have? I was drunk, you
know."

She walked over to the bed and kissed him on the cheek.
" You were very nice," she told him. " But I don't like starting
all over again," she added, walking away. " Not the same
day, anyhow."

It was annoying not being able to remember anything. He
watched her putting on her socks and suddenly he felt uneasy,
lying there naked between the sheets. " I'm getting up. Turn
round."

" You want me to turn round?"

" Please."

She stood in a corner, her nose to the wall and her hand
behind her back, like a schoolgirl being punished. In a
moment, she asked mockingly, " Time enough?"

" Ready," he answered, buckling his belt.

Nadine looked at him critically. " You are complicated!"

" Me?"

" You make quite a fuss about getting into bed and about
getting out of it."

" What a head you've given me!" Henri said.

They left the hotel, walked towards the Gare Montparnasse, and went into a little café which was just opening up for the morning. They sat down at a table and ordered two ersatz coffees.

" I'd like to know why you were so set on sleeping with me," he said lightly.

" I wanted to get to know you."

" Is that always the way you get to know people?"

" When you sleep with someone, it breaks the ice. It's better being together now, isn't it?"

" The ice is certainly broken," Henri said, laughing. " But why is it so important for you to know me?"

" I want you to like me."

" But I do like you."

She gave him a look that was both malicious and embarrassed. " I want you to like me enough to take me to Portugal with you."

" Oh, so that's it!" He put his hand on her arm. " I've already told you it's impossible."

" Because of Paula? But since she's not going with you anyhow, there's no reason why I can't."

" No, you just can't. It would make her very unhappy."

" Don't tell her."

" That would be too big a lie." He smiled and added, " Besides, she'd know about it anyhow."

" So just to spare her a little pain, you'd deprive me of something I want more than anything in the world."

" Do you really want to go that much?"

" A country where there's sun and plenty to eat? I'd sell my soul to go."

" You were hungry during the war?"

" Hungry? And bear in mind that when it came to scrounging for food, no one could beat Mother. She'd ride her bike fifty miles out into the country just to bring us back a couple of pounds of mushrooms or a chunk of meat. But that still didn't keep us from being hungry. I literally went mad over the first American who plunked his rations in my arms."

" Is that what made you like Americans so much?"

" That, and at first they used to amuse me." She shrugged her shoulders. " Now, they're too well organised ; it's not fun

any more. Paris has become sinister again." She gave Henri
an imploring look. "Take me with you."

He would have enjoyed giving her that pleasure; nothing
could be more gratifying than to make someone truly happy.
But how could he ever convince Paula to accept a thing like
that?

"You've had affairs before," Nadine said, "and Paula put
up with them."

"Who told you that?"

Nadine smiled slyly. "When a woman talks about her
love affairs to another woman, it gets about pretty fast."

Yes, Henri had admitted to a few infidelities, for which
Paula had magnanimously forgiven him. But the difficulty
now was that an explanation would inexorably lead him
either to an entanglement of lies—and he wanted no more
lies—or to abruptly demanding his freedom. And he had no
stomach for that.

"But going away together for a whole month," he murmured, "is something else again."

"But we'll leave each other as soon as we get back. I don't
want to take you away from Paula," Nadine said with an
insolent laugh. "All I want to do is get away from here for a
while."

Henri hesitated. To wander through strange streets and
sit in outdoor cafés with a woman who laughed in your face,
to find her warm, young body in a hotel room at night,
yes, it was tempting. And since he had already decided to
break off with Paula, what did he gain by waiting? Time
would never patch things up; just the opposite.

"Listen," he said, "I can't promise you anything. Just
remember, this isn't a promise. But I'm going to try talking
to Paula, and if it seems possible to take you, well . . . I
will."

II

I looked at the little sketch, and I was discouraged. Two months earlier I had said to the child, " Draw a house," and he had drawn a cottage with a roof, a chimney, smoke ; but not a window, not a door, and surrounding the house was a tall black fence with pointed bars. " Now, draw a family," and he had drawn a man holding a little boy by the hand. And to-day again he had sketched a house without a door, surrounded by pointed black bars. We were getting nowhere. Was it a particularly difficult case, or was it I who didn't know how to handle it? I put the drawing into his file. Didn't I know how? Or didn't I want to? Perhaps the child's resistance merely reflected the resistance I felt in myself. It horrified me to have to drive that stranger, who had died two years earlier at Dachau, from his son's heart. " If that's the way it is, I ought to give up the case," I said to myself, standing silently beside my desk. I had two full hours ahead of me which I could have used to sort and file my notes, but I couldn't make up my mind to get down to it. It's true I've always been the kind to ask myself a lot of questions. Why does healing so often mean mutilating? What value does personal adjustment have in an unjust society? But nevertheless, it has always fascinated me to devise solutions for each new case. My objective isn't to give my patients a false feeling of inner peace ; if I seek to deliver them from their personal nightmares, it's only to make them better able to face the real problems of life. And each time I succeeded, I felt I had accomplished something useful. The task is huge, it requires everyone's co-operation. That's what I thought yesterday. But it's all based on the premise that every intelligent being has a part to play in a history that is steadily leading the world towards happiness. To-day I no longer believe in that beautiful harmony. The future escapes us ; it will shape itself without us. Well then, if we have to be content with the present, what difference does it make whether little Ferdinand once more becomes carefree and happy like other children? " I shouldn't be thinking such things," I told myself. " If I go on like this, it won't be long before I'll have to close up my office." I went into the bathroom and brought back a bowl of water and an armful of old newspapers. In the fireplace, balls of paper were burning dully; I knelt down, moistened the printed sheets, and began crumpling them up. This sort of task was less distasteful to me than it used to be; with Nadine's help and an occasional hand from the concierge's wife, I kept the apartment in fairly good shape. At least while I was crumpling those old newspapers, I knew that I was doing something useful. The trouble was that it kept only my hands busy. I did succeed in driving little Ferdinand, as well as all thoughts of my profession, from my mind. But I gained little by it—once more the record began turning insistently in my head: *There aren't enough coffins left in Stavelot to bury all the children murdered by the S.S.* We had escaped; but elsewhere it had happened. They had hastily hidden the flags, buried their guns; the men had fled into the fields, the women had barricaded themselves behind their doors. And in the streets abandoned to the rain, the sound of their raucous voices could be heard. This time they hadn't come as magnanimous conquerors; they had returned with hate and death in their hearts. And then they went off again, leaving nothing behind of the festive village but burned-out houses and heaps of little bodies.

A sudden gust of cold air made me shiver; Nadine had opened the door.

" Why didn't you ask me to help you?"

" I thought you were getting dressed."

" I finished dressing long ago," she said. She knelt beside me and grabbed a newspaper. " Are you afraid I don't know how to do this? Don't worry; it's not beyond me."

The fact is that she really wasn't very good at it; she wet the paper too much, didn't wad it enough. But nevertheless I should have asked her to help. I examined her critically. " Let me dress you up a little," I said.

" For whom? Lambert?"

I took a shawl and an antique brooch from my dresser and put them on her. Then I handed her a pair of pumps with leather soles, a present from a patient who believed herself cured.

Nadine hesitated. " But you're going out to-night, too. What are you going to wear?"

" No one ever looks at my feet," I said laughing.

She took the shoes and grumbled, "Thanks." I almost answered, "You're welcome," as one would to a stranger. My attentions, my generosity made her feel uncomfortable, for she wasn't really grateful and she reproached herself for not being so. I felt her wavering between gratitude and suspicion as she awkwardly crumpled the newspaper. And after all, she was right in distrusting me; my devotion, my generosity were the most unfair of my wiles: I was seeking to escape remorse at the expense of making her feel guilty. Remorse because Diego was dead, because Nadine didn't have any pretty dresses, because sullenness made her ugly; remorse because I didn't know how to make her obey me and because I didn't love her enough. It would have been more honest of me not to smother her with kindness. Perhaps I might have been able to comfort her if I simply took her in my arms and said, "My poor little daughter, forgive me for not loving you more." If I had held her in my arms, perhaps it would have protected me against those little bodies which had gone unburied.

Nadine raised her head. "Have you spoken to Father again about that secretarial job?"

"No, not since the day before yesterday," I answered, hastily adding: "The magazine doesn't come out until April. There's still plenty of time."

"But I want to know now," Nadine said, throwing a ball of paper into the fire. "I really don't understand why he's against it."

"He told you; he thinks you'd be wasting your time." A job, adult responsibilities—I personally thought it would be good for Nadine. But Robert had more ambitious plans for her.

"And chemistry, don't you think I'm wasting time with that?" she said, shrugging her shoulders.

"No one's forcing you to study chemistry."

Nadine had chosen chemistry for the sole purpose of upsetting us; she succeeded only in punishing herself.

"It isn't so much chemistry that bores the hell out of me," she said. "It's just being a student. Father doesn't seem to realise it, but I'm much older than you were when you were my age. I want to do something real."

"I agree with you," I replied. "You know that. But just

be patient. If your father sees you're not going to change your mind he'll end up by saying yes."

"He may say yes, but you can bet he'll say it grudgingly," Nadine replied sulkily.

"We'll convince him," I said. "Do you know what I'd do if I were you? I'd learn to type at once."

"I can't start now," Nadine replied. She paused, gave me a rather defiant look, and added, "Henri is taking me to Portugal with him."

I was taken by surprise. "Did you decide that yesterday?" I asked in a voice which didn't hide my disapproval.

"My decision was made a long time ago," Nadine said. Aggressively she added, "Naturally, you disapprove, don't you? You disapprove because of Paula. Isn't that right?"

I rolled one of the moist paper balls between the palms of my hands. "I think you're going to make yourself very unhappy."

"That's my business."

"Yes," I said. "I suppose it is."

I tried to force myself to hold my tongue. I knew my silence annoyed her, but she provokes me when, in that biting voice of hers, she spurns the very explanations she is anxious to hear. She wants me to force her hand, but I do not like to play her game. Nevertheless, I gave it a try. "Henri doesn't love you," I said. "He's in no mood just now to fall in love."

"But Lambert, Lambert would be a dumb enough idiot to marry me, is that it?" she said angrily.

"I've never tried to push you into marriage," I answered. "But the fact of the matter is that Lambert does love you."

"That's not true," she said, interrupting me. "He doesn't love me. Not only has he never asked me to sleep with him, but the other night at the party, when I practically came right out and asked him, he turned me down flat."

"That's because he wants other things from you."

"If I don't appeal to him, that's his business. Besides, I can understand someone being difficult to please after having had a girl like Rosa. Believe me when I tell you I try to make allowances for that. Just don't keep telling me he's so completely gone on me," Nadine said, her voice rising.

" Do whatever you like!" I said. " You're free to do as you please. What more can you ask for?"

She cleared her throat, as she always did when she was nervous. " As far as Henri and myself is concerned, it's only a matter of a little adventure. As soon as we get back, we stop seeing each other."

" Honestly, Nadine, do you believe that?"

" Yes, I do believe it," she said with too much conviction.

" After you've spent a month with Henri you'll want to hold on to him."

" You're wrong." Again a look of defiance appeared in her eyes. " If you want to know, I slept with him last night and it did absolutely nothing to me."

I turned my eyes away; I would rather not have known about it. " That doesn't mean anything," I said, trying not to reveal my embarrassment. " I'm sure that when you get back you won't want to leave him—and he'll have other ideas about it."

" That remains to be seen," she said.

" Ah! So you admit it; you are hoping to hold him. But you're only deceiving yourself, you know. All he wants at the moment is his freedom."

" There's a game to be played. I enjoy it."

" Calculating, manœuvring, watching, waiting—is that the kind of thing you enjoy? And you don't even love him!"

" I may not love him," she said, " but I want him." She threw a handful of paper balls into the fireplace. " With him at least I'll live. Can't you understand that?"

" To live, you need no one but yourself," I said angrily. She looked around the room. " Do you call this living! Frankly, my poor mother, do you believe you ever lived? What an existence! talking to Father half the day and treating crackpots the other half." She stood up and brushed off her knees. " I do foolish things sometimes," she continued in an exasperated tone of voice, " I don't deny it. But I'd rather end my days in a whorehouse than go through life wearing immaculate kid gloves like a good little bourgeoise. You never take off these gloves of yours, do you? You spend your time giving people advice, but what do you know about men? And I'm damned certain you never look at yourself in the mirror and never have nightmares."

Attacking me was the tactic she always employed when she felt guilty or had doubts about herself. When she saw I didn't intend to answer, she walked towards the door, stopped, hesitated a moment, and then turned around and asked in a calmer voice, " Will you come and have tea with us?"

" Just call me whenever you're ready."

I stood up. I lit a cigarette. What could I do? I didn't dare do anything. When Nadine first began seeking and fleeing Diego in bed after bed, I tried to do something about it. But she had discovered unhappiness too brutally; it had left her too bewildered with revolt and despair for anyone to exercise any control over her. When I tried to talk to her, she stopped her ears, she cried, she ran away. She didn't return to the flat until the next morning. Robert, at my request, tried to reason with her. That evening, she didn't go out to meet her American captain; she stayed at home alone in her room. But the next day she disappeared, leaving a note which said, " I am leaving." Robert searched for her all that night, all the next day, and all of another night, while I waited at home. The waiting was agonising. At four o'clock in the morning a bartender in one of the Montparnasse cafés telephoned. I found Nadine, dead drunk and with a black eye, stretched out on a seat on one of the booths of the bar. " Let her have her freedom. It will only be worse if we try to restrain her," Robert said to me. I had no choice. If I had continued to fight her, Nadine would have begun to hate me and would purposely have defied me. But she knows I disapprove of her conduct and that I gave in against my will. She knows and she holds it against me. And maybe she's not entirely wrong. Had I loved her more, our relationship might have been different. Perhaps I would have known how to stop her from leading a life of which I disapprove. For a long while I stood there looking at the flames, repeating to myself, " I don't love her enough."

I hadn't wanted her; it was Robert who wanted to have a child right away. I've always held it against Nadine that she upset my life alone with Robert. I loved Robert too much and I wasn't interested enough in myself to be moved by the discovery of his features or mine on the face of that little intruder. Without feeling any particular affection, I took notice of her blue eyes, her hair, her nose. I scolded her as little as possible, but she was well aware of my reticence; to her, I've always been suspect. No little girl has ever fought more tenaciously to triumph over her rival for her father's heart. And she's never resigned herself to belonging to the same species as I. When I told her she would soon begin menstruating and explained the meaning of it to her, she listened attentively, but with a fierce trapped look in her eyes. Then she violently threw her favourite vase to the floor, shattering it to bits. After her first period, her anger was so powerful that she didn't bleed again for another eighteen months.

Diego had created a new climate between us; at last she owned a treasure which belonged to her alone. She felt herself my equal, and a friendship was born between us. But afterwards, everything grew even worse. Just now, everything is worse.

" Mother."

Nadine was calling me. As I walked down the corridor, I thought to myself, " If I stay too long, she'll say I monopolise her friends; but if I leave too soon, she'll think I'm insulting them." I opened the door. In the room were Lambert, Sézenac, Vincent, and Lachaume. There were no women; Nadine had no girl friends. They were sitting around the electric heater, drinking ersatz-coffee. Nadine handed me a cup of black, bitter water.

" Chancel was killed," she said abruptly.

I hadn't known Chancel very well, but ten days earlier I had seen him laughing with the others around the Christmas tree. Maybe Robert was right; the distance between the living and the dead really isn't very great. And yet, like myself, those future corpses who were drinking their coffee in silence appeared ashamed to be so alive. Sézenac's eyes were even more blank than usual; he looked like a Rimbaud without brains.

" How did it happen?" I asked.

" Nobody knows," Sézenac replied. " His brother got a note saying he died on the field of honour."

" Do you think there's any chance he did it on purpose?" Sézenac shrugged his shoulders. " Maybe."

" And maybe no one asked him for his advice," Vincent said. " They're far from stingy with human material, our generals. They're great and generous lords, you know." In his sallow face, his bloodshot eyes looked like two gashes;

his mouth was a thin scar. One failed to notice at first that his features were actually fine and regular.

Lachaume's face, on the other hand, was at once calm and tormented, like a craggy rock. " It's all a question of prestige," Lachaume said. " If we still want to play at being a great power, we must have a respectable number of dead."

" Besides," Vincent said, " disarming the members of the Resistance was a neat trick. But let's face it. If they could be quietly liquidated, that'd suit the great lords even better," Vincent added, his scar opening into a sort of smile.

" What are you trying to insinuate?" Lambert asked severely, looking Vincent straight in the eyes. " De Gaulle ordered De Lattre to get rid of all the Communists? If that's what you want to say, say it. At least have that much courage."

" No need for any order," Vincent replied. " They understand each other well enough without exchanging words."

Lambert shrugged his shoulders. " You don't believe that yourself."

" Maybe it's true," Nadine said aggressively.

" Don't be silly. Of course it's not true."

" What's there to prove it isn't?" she asked.

" Ah, ha! So you've finally picked up the technique!" Lambert said. " You make up a fact out of whole cloth, and then you ask someone to prove it's false! Obviously I can't swear to the fact that Chancel wasn't killed by a bullet in the back."

Lauchaume smiled. " That's not what Vincent said."

That was the way it always went. Sézenac would hold his tongue, Vincent and Lambert would engage in a squabble, and then at the right moment Lachaume would intervene. Usually, he would chide Vincent for his leftist views and Lambert for his petit-bourgeois prejudices. Nadine would side with one camp or the other, depending upon her mood. I avoided getting entangled in their argument; it was more vehement to-day than usually, probably because Chancel's death had more or less unnerved them. In any case, Vincent and Lambert weren't made to get along with each other. Lambert had an aura of gentlemanliness about him, while Vincent, with his fur-collared jacket and his thin unhealthy face, looked rather like a hoodlum. There was a disturbing coldness in his eyes, but nevertheless I couldn't bring myself to believe that he had killed real men with a real revolver. Every time I saw him I thought of it, but I could never actually bring myself to believe it. As for Lachaume, he, too, may have killed, but if he did, he hadn't told anyone and it hadn't left any visible mark.

Lambert turned towards me. " You can't even have a talk with friends any more," he said. " It's no fun living in Paris, the way it is now. Sometimes I wonder if Chancel wasn't right. I don't mean getting yourself shot up, but going off and doing some fighting."

Nadine gave him an angry look. " But you're hardly ever in Paris as it is!"

" I'm here enough to find it a lot too grim for my taste. And even when I'm at the front, believe me, I don't feel especially proud of what I'm doing."

" But you did everything you could to become a war correspondent," she said bitterly.

" I liked it better than staying back here, but it's still a half measure."

" If you're fed up with Paris, no one's holding you here," Nadine said, her face twisted with rage. " Go on and play the hero."

" It's no better and no worse than some other games I know of," Lambert grumbled, giving her a look heavy with meaning.

Nadine eyed him up and down for a moment. " You know, you wouldn't look bad as a stretcher case, with bandages all over you." Sneeringly, she added, " Only don't count on me to come visiting you in the hospital. Two weeks from now I'll be in Portugal."

" Portugal?"

" Perron is taking me along as his secretary," she replied casually.

" Well, well! Isn't he the lucky one," Lambert said. " He'll have you all to himself for a whole month!"

" I'm not as repulsive to everyone as I am to you," Nadine retorted.

" Yes, nowadays men are easy," Lambert muttered between his teeth. " As easy as women."

" You're a boor!" Nadine shouted.

Irritably, I wondered how they could let themselves be

carried away by their childish manœuvres. I felt certain they could have helped each other to live again; together they could have succeeded in conquering those memories that both united and separated them. But perhaps that was precisely why they tore each other apart: each saw his own faithlessness in the other, and they hated themselves for it. In any event, interfering would have been the worst possible blunder. I let them continue their squabble and quietly left the room. Sézenac followed me into the hall.

"May I have a word with you?" he asked.

"Go ahead."

"There's a favour," he said, "a favour I'd like to ask of you."

I remember how impressive he looked on the twenty-fifth of August, with his full beard, his rifle, his red sash—a true soldier of 1848. Now his blue eyes were dead, his face puffy; when I shook his hand, I had noticed that his palm was moist.

"I haven't been sleeping well," he said haltingly. "I have . . . I have pains. A friend of mine once gave me an opium suppository and it helped a lot. Only the pharmacists won't sell it without a prescription . . ." He looked at me pleadingly.

"What kind of pains?"

"Oh, everywhere. In my head. And worst of all I have nightmares . . ."

"You can't cure nightmares with opium."

His forehead, like his hands, grew moist. "I'll be honest with you. I have a girl friend, a girl I like a lot. In fact, I'm thinking of marrying her. But I . . . I can't do anything with her without taking opiates."

"Opium is a narcotic, you know. Do you use it often?" I asked.

He pretended to be shocked by my question. "Oh, no! Only once in a while, when I spend the night with Lucie."

"Well, that's not too bad then. You know it's very easy to become addicted to those things."

He looked at me pleadingly, sweat beading his brow.

"Come see me to-morrow morning," I said. "I'll see if I can give you that prescription."

I went back to my room. He was obviously pretty much an addict already. When had he begun drugging himself? Why?

I sighed. Another one I could stretch out on the couch and try to empty. At times, they got on my nerves, all those recliners. Outside, in the world, standing on their own two feet, they did the best they could to play at being adults. But here, in my office, they again became infants with dirty behinds, and it was up to me to wash their childhood away. And yet I spoke to them in an impersonal voice, the voice of reason, of health. Their real lives were elsewhere; mine too. It wasn't surprising that I was tired of them—and of myself.

I was tired. "Immaculate kid gloves," Nadine had said. "Distant, intimidating," were Scriassine's words. Is that how I appear to them? Is that how I am? I recalled my childhood rages, the pounding of my adolescent heart, the feverish days of that month of August. But all that was now of the past. The fact is that nothing was stirring inside me any more. I combed my hair and touched up my make-up. You can't go on living indefinitely in fear; it's too tiring. Robert had begun a new book, and he was in high spirits. I no longer awakened at night in a cold sweat. Nevertheless, I was depressed. I could see no reason for being sad. It's just that it makes me unhappy not to feel happy; I must have been badly spoiled. I took my purse and gloves and knocked at Robert's door. I hadn't the least desire to go out.

"Aren't you cold?" I asked. "Wouldn't you like me to build a little fire?"

He pushed back his chair and smiled at me. "I'm fine," he said.

Naturally. Robert always felt fine. For two years, he happily sustained himself on sauerkraut and rutabagas. He was never cold; it seemed almost as if he produced his own warmth, like a yogi. When I return around midnight, he'll still be writing, wrapped in his plaid blanket. And he'll be surprised: "What time is it, anyhow?" Up to now, he had spoken to me only vaguely of his new book, but I gathered he was satisfied with the way it was going. I sat down.

"Nadine just told me something pretty surprising," I said. "She's going to Portugal with Perron."

He looked up at me quickly. "Does it upset you?"

"Yes. Perron isn't the kind of person you pick up and drop as you please. She's going to become much too attached to him."

Robert placed his hand on mine. "Don't worry about Nadine. First of all, I'd be very surprised if she became attached to Perron. But in any case, it won't take her long to console herself if she does."

"I hope she isn't going to spend her whole life consoling herself!" I said.

Robert laughed. "There you go again! You're always shocked when you think of your daughter sleeping around, like a boy. I did exactly the same thing at her age."

Robert refused to face the fact that Nadine wasn't a boy. "It's different," I said. "The reason Nadine grabs one man after another is that she doesn't feel she's alive when she's alone. That's what worries me."

"Listen, we know why she hates to be alone. She can still see Diego too clearly."

I shook my head. "It's not only because of Diego."

"I know. You think it's partially our fault," he said sceptically. He shrugged his shoulders. "Don't worry," he said, "she'll change; she has lots of time to change."

"Let's hope so." I looked at Robert pleadingly. "It's very important to her to have something to do that really interests her. Give her that secretarial job. She spoke to me about it again just now. She wants it badly."

"It's not very exciting," Robert said. "Typing envelopes and filing all day long. It's a crime to waste her intelligence on a thing like that."

"But she'll feel she's being useful; it will give her confidence," I said.

"She could do so much better! She could continue to study."

"Just now what she needs is to do something. And she'd make a good secretary." I paused a moment and then added, "You mustn't ask too much of people."

For me, Robert's demands had always been a stimulant, but they only succeeded in discouraging Nadine. He gave her no orders; rather, he confided in her, expected things of her, and she played along with him. She had read too many heavy books when she was too young; she had been too precociously part of adult conversations. And so, after a while, she tired of that severe routine. At first, she was disappointed in herself, and now she seemed to enjoy avenging herself by disappointing Robert.

He looked perplexed, as he always did whenever he detected a note of reproach in my voice.

"If you really believe that's what she wants . . . Well, you know best."

"I do believe it," I said.

"All right," he said. "Consider it done."

He had given in too easily. That proved that Nadine had succeeded only too well in disappointing him. When he can no longer give himself without reserve to something that means much to him, Robert wastes no time in losing all interest in it.

"Of course, a job that would make her completely independent of us would be even better," I said.

"But that isn't what she really wants; she simply wants to play at being independent," Robert said sharply. He no longer felt like speaking of Nadine, and I was unable to kindle his enthusiasm for a project of which he disapproved. I let it drop.

"I really can't understand Perron going on that trip," he said in a livelier tone.

"He wants a holiday," I replied. "After all," I added spiritedly, "he has the right to enjoy himself a little. He certainly did enough . . ."

"He did more than I did," Robert said. "But that's not the question." He looked at me intently. "In order for the S.R.L. to get going, we've got to have a newspaper."

"I know," I said. Then I added hesitantly, "I wonder . . ."

"What?"

"If Henri will ever turn his paper over to you. It means so much to him."

"It isn't a question of his turning it over to us," Robert replied.

"But it is a question of his submitting to the orders of the S.R.L."

"He's already a member. And it would certainly be to his advantage to adopt a clearly defined programme; a newspaper without a political programme just doesn't make sense."

"But that's their idea."

"You call that an idea?" Robert said, shrugging his shoulders. "To perpetuate the spirit of the Resistance without taking sides! That sort of jargon is fine for some idiot

like Luc. The spirit of the Resistance! It makes me think
of the spirit of Locarno. But I'm not worried; Perron
isn't the kind to go in for spiritualism. He'll end up by
going along with us. But meanwhile we're losing valuable
time."

I was afraid Robert was due for quite a surprise. When
he's deeply involved in a project, he thinks of people as mere
tools. But Henri had given himself body and soul to that
paper; it was his personal achievement and he wasn't going
to be casual about letting anyone dictate policy to him.

"Why haven't you spoken to him about it yet?" I asked.

"All Henri has on his mind these days is that trip of
his."

Robert looked so unhappy that I suggested, "Try to make
him stay."

For Nadine's sake, it would have made me happy to see
him give up the trip. But I'd have felt sorry for Henri; he
was counting on it so much.

"You know how he is," Robert said. "When he's stubborn, he's stubborn. I'd better wait until he gets back." He
drew the blanket over his knees. "I'm not saying this to
chase you out," he added cheerfully, "but usually you hate to
be late . . ."

I got up. "You're right; I should leave now. Are you sure
you don't want to come?"

"Oh, no! I haven't the least desire to talk politics with
Scriassine. Maybe he'll spare you, though."

"Let's hope so," I said.

During those long periods when Robert shut himself in
with his work, I often went out without him. But that evening, as I hurried into the cold, into the dark, I was sorry
that I had accepted Scriassine's invitation. I understood
perfectly well why I hadn't declined: I knew my friends
much too well and I was tired of always seeing the same
faces. For four years we had all lived side by side; it kept
one warm. But now, our intimacy had grown cold. It smelled
musty and it benefited no one. I had reacted to the appeal of
something new. But what would we find to say to each
other? Like Robert, I didn't feel like talking politics.

I stopped in the lobby of the Ritz and looked at myself in
a mirror. What with clothes rationing, to be well dressed took
a lot of doing. I had chosen not to bother myself about it at

all. In my threadbare coat and wooden-soled shoes, I didn't look very exciting. My friends accepted me as I was, but Scriassine had just come from America where the women always seem to be so well groomed. He would surely notice my shoes. "I shouldn't have let myself go like this," I thought.

Naturally, Scriassine's smile didn't betray him. He kissed my hand, something I hate. A hand is even more naked than a face; it embarrasses me when someone looks at it too closely.

"What will you have?" he asked. "A martini?"

"A martini will do."

The bar was filled with American officers and well-dressed women. The heat, the smell of cigarettes, and the strong taste of the gin went to my head immediately, and I was glad to be there. Scriassine had spent four years in America, the great liberating nation, the nation in which fountains spout streams of fruit juices and ice cream. I questioned him avidly and he patiently answered all my questions. We had a second round of martinis and then we had dinner in a little restaurant where I gorged myself without restraint on rare roast beef and cream puffs. Scriassine, in turn, interrogated me; it was difficult to answer his too-precise questions. If I tried to recapture the taste of my daily existence—the smell of cabbage soup in the curfew-barricaded house, the ache in my heart whenever Robert was late in returning from a clandestine meeting—he would sharply interrupt me. He was a very good listener; he made you feel as if he were carefully weighing each of your words. But you had to speak for him, not for yourself. He wanted practical information: How did we go about making up false papers, printing L'Espoir, distributing it? And he also asked me to paint vast frescoes for him: What was the moral climate in which we had lived? I tried my best to satisfy him, but I'm afraid I didn't succeed very well; everything had been either worse or more bearable than he imagined. The real tragedies hadn't happened to me, and yet they haunted my life. How could I speak to him of Diego's death? The words were too sad for my mouth, too dry for Diego's memory. I wouldn't have wanted to relive those past four years for anything in the world. And yet from a distance they seemed to take on a sombre sweetness. I could easily understand why Lambert was bored with this peace which gave us back our lives without giving us back our reasons for living. When we left the restaurant and stepped out into the pitch-black cold, I remembered how proudly we used to face the nights. Now, I longed for light, warmth; I, too, wanted something else. Without provocation, Scriassine plunged into a long diatribe; I wished he would change the subject. He was furiously upbraiding De Gaulle for his trip to Moscow. "The thing that's really serious," he said to me accusingly, "is that the whole country seems to approve of it. Look at Perron and Dubreuilh, honest men both, walking hand in hand with the Communists. It's heartbreaking for someone who knows."

"But Robert isn't with the Communists," I said, attempting to calm him down. "He's trying to create an independent movement."

"Yes, I know; he spoke to me about it. But he made it perfectly clear that he doesn't intend working against the Stalinists. Beside them, but not against them!" Scriassine said crushingly.

"You really wouldn't want him to be anti-Communist, would you?" I asked.

Scriassine looked at me severely. "Did you read my book *The Red Paradise*?"

"Of course."

"Then you must have some idea of what would happen to us if we made Stalin a present of Europe."

"But there's no question of giving Europe to Stalin," I said.

"That's precisely the question."

"Nonsense! The question is how to win the struggle against reaction. And if the left begins to split up, we won't have a ghost of a chance."

"The left!" Scriassine said ironically. "Let's not talk politics," he added with an abrupt gesture of finality. "I hate talking politics with a woman."

"I didn't start it," I said.

"You're absolutely right," he replied with unexpected gravity. "Please excuse me."

We went back to the Ritz bar and Scriassine ordered two whiskies. I liked the taste; it was something different. And as for Scriassine, he, too, had the advantage of being new to me. The whole evening had been unexpected, and it seemed to emit an ancient fragrance of youth. Long ago there had been nights that were unlike others; you would meet unknown people who would say unexpected things. And, occasionally, something would happen. So many things had happened in the last five years—to the world,—to France, to Paris, to others. But not to me. Would nothing ever happen to me again?

"It's odd being here," I said.

"Why?"

"The heat, the whisky, the noise, and those uniforms . . ." Scriassine glanced around him. "I hate this place. They requisitioned a room for me here because I'm a reporter for a Franco-American magazine," he explained. "Fortunately, it won't be long before it becomes too expensive for me. And then I'll be forced to get out," he added with a smile.

"Can't you leave without being forced?"

"No. That's why I find money such a corrupting influence." A burst of laughter brightened his face. "As soon as I get hold of some, I can't wait to get rid of it."

A bald-headed little man with mild and gentle eyes stopped at our table. "Aren't you Victor Scriassine?" he asked.

"Yes," Scriassine answered. I caught a mistrustful look in his eyes—and at the same time a gleam of hope.

"Don't you recognise me? Manès Goldman. I've aged a lot since Vienna. I promised myself that if I ever met you again I would say thank you, thank you for your book."

"Manès Goldman! Of course!" Scriassine said warmly. "Are you living in France now?"

"Since '35. I spent a year in the camp at Gurs, but I got out just in time . . ." His voice was even more gentle than his eyes, so gentle in fact that it seemed almost dead. "I don't want to disturb you any longer; I just want to say I'm very happy to have shaken the hand of the man who wrote *Vienna in Brown*."

"Nice seeing you again," Scriassine said.

The little Austrian walked quietly away and went out the glass door behind an American officer. Scriassine followed him with his eyes.

"Another defeat!" he said abruptly.

"A defeat?"

"I should have asked him to sit down, should have spoken

to him. He wanted something and I don't even know his address, didn't think to give him mine," Scriassine said, his voice choked with anger.

" If he wants to see you again, he'll surely come here."

" He wouldn't dare. It was up to me to make the first move, to make him sit down and question him. And the thing that really hurts is that it would have been so easy! A year at Gurs! And I suppose he spent the other four hiding. He's my age, and he looks like an old man. He was hoping I could do something for him. And I just let him walk away!"

" He didn't seem disappointed. Maybe he did only want to thank you."

" That was just an excuse," Scriassine said, emptying his glass. " It would have been so simple to ask him to sit down. God! when you think of all the things you could do and yet somehow never do! All the opportunities you let slip by! The idea, the inspiration just doesn't come fast enough. Instead of being open, you're closed up tight. That's the worst sin of all—the sin of omission." He spoke as if I weren't present, in an agonising monologue of remorse. " And during those four years, I was in America, warm, safe, well-fed."

" You couldn't have stayed here," I said.

" I could have gone into hiding too."

" I really don't see what good that would have done."

" When my friends were exiled to Siberia, I was in Vienna ; when others were being slaughtered by the Brown Shirts in Vienna, I was in New York. What's so damned important about staying alive? That's the question that needs answering."

I found myself moved by Scriassine's voice. We, too, felt ashamed whenever we thought of the deportees. No, we had nothing to blame ourselves for ; it was just that we hadn't suffered enough.

" The misfortunes you don't actually share . . . well, it's as if you were to blame for them," I said. " And it's a horrible thing to feel guilty."

Suddenly Scriassine smiled at me with a look of secret connivance. " That depends," he said.

For a moment I studied his crafty, tormented face. " Do

you mean there are certain feelings of remorse that shield us from others?"

Scriassine studied me in turn. "You're not so dumb, you know. Generally, I dislike intelligent women, maybe because they're not intelligent enough. They always want to prove to themselves, and to everyone else, how terribly clever they are. So all they do is talk and never understand anything. What struck me the first time I saw you was that way you have of keeping quiet."

I laughed. "I didn't have much choice."

"All of us were doing a lot of talking—Dubreuilh, Perron and myself. You just stood there calmly and listened."

"Listening is my job," I said.

"Yes, I know, but you have a certain way with you." He nodded his head. "You must be an excellent psychiatrist. If I were ten years younger, I'd put myself in your hands."

"Are you tempted to have yourself analysed?"

"It's too late now. A fully developed man who's used his defects and blemishes to piece himself together. You can ruin him but you can't cure him."

"That depends on the sickness."

"There's only one sickness that really amounts to anything —being yourself, just you." An almost unbearable sincerity suddenly softened his face, and I was deeply touched by the confiding sadness in his voice.

"There are people a lot sicker than you," I said briskly.

"In what way?"

"There are some people who make you wonder when you look at them, how they can possibly live with themselves. Unless they're complete idiots, they should horrify themselves. You don't seem like that at all."

Scriassine's face remained grave. "Do you ever horrify yourself?"

"No," I said. "But I'm not very introspective," I added with a smile.

"That's why you're so relaxing," Scriassine said. "The moment I met you I found you relaxing. You gave the impression of being a well-brought-up young girl who always listens quietly while the grown-ups are talking."

"I have an eighteen-year-old daughter, you know."

"That doesn't mean anything. Besides, I find young girls

insufferable. But a woman who looks like a young girl—that I find charming!" He examined me very closely. "It's a funny thing. The women in the crowd you go around with are all quite free. But you—one wonders if you've ever deceived your husband."

" Deceived! What a horrid word! Robert and I are completely free to do as we please ; we hide nothing from each other."

" But have you ever made use of that freedom?"

"Occasionally," I said. I finished my drink, trying to conceal my embarrassment. There really weren't very many occasions ; in that respect, I was quite different from Robert. Picking up a good-looking girl in a bar and spending an hour with her seemed perfectly normal to him. As for me, I could never have accepted a man for a lover if I didn't feel I could become friends with him—and my requirements for friendship are quite exacting. I had lived the last five years in chastity, with no regrets, and I believed I would go on that way forever. It seemed natural to me for my life as a woman to be ended ; there were so many things that had ended, forever . . .

Scriassine silently studied me for a moment and then said, " In any case, I'll bet there haven't been many men in your life."

" That's true," I replied.

" Why not?"

" I suppose the right ones just didn't come along."

" If the right ones didn't come along, that's simply because you never looked very hard."

" Everyone knows me as Dubreuilh's wife, or as Doctor Anne Dubreuilh. Both inspire nothing but respect."

" Well, I for one don't feel any special respect for you," Scriassine said, smiling.

There was a brief silence and then I asked, " Why should a woman who's free to do as she pleases sleep with everyone on earth?"

He looked at me severely. " If a man, a man for whom you might have a little liking, asked you straight out to spend the night with him, would you do it?"

" That depends."

" On what?"

" On him, on me, on the circumstances."

" Let's suppose that I asked you now. What then?"

" I don't know."

I had seen it coming ever since we broached the subject but, nevertheless I was taken by surprise.

" I am asking you. Which is it—yes or no?"

" You're going a little too fast," I said.

" I hate a lot of beating around the bush. Paying court to a woman is degrading for both oneself and for the woman. I don't suppose you go for all that sentimental nonsense, either."

" No, but I like to think things over before I make a decision."

" Think it over then."

He ordered two more whiskies. No, I had no desire to sleep with him, or with any other man. My body had too long been steeped in a sort of selfish torpor. What perverse turn of mind could have made me want to disturb its repose? Besides, it seemed impossible. It always amazed me that Nadine could give herself so easily to total strangers. Between my solitary flesh and the solitary man seated beside me drinking his whisky, not the slightest bond existed. To think of myself naked in his naked arms was as incongruous as imagining him embracing my old mother.

" Let's wait and see how the evening turns out," I said.

" That's ridiculous," he replied. " How can you expect us to talk politics or psychology with that question bothering us? You must know already what you're going to decide. Tell me now."

His impatience seemed to assure me that, after all, I wasn't my old mother. Since he desired me, I was forced to believe I was desirable, if only for an hour. Nadine claimed she was as indifferent about getting into bed as sitting down at table. Maybe she had the right idea. She accused me of approaching life with white kid gloves. Was it true? What would happen if for once I took off my gloves? If I didn't take them off to-night, would I ever? Reason said to me, " My life is over." But against all reason, I still had a good many years to kill.

" All right," I said abruptly, " the answer is yes."

" Ah! now there's a good answer," he said in the encouraging voice of a doctor or professor. He wanted to take my hand, but I declined that reward.

" I'd like a cup of coffee. I'm afraid I've had a little too much to drink."

" An American woman would ask for another whisky," he said with a smile. " But you're right ; it'd be a damn shame if either of us were under the weather."

He ordered two coffees which we drank in embarrassed silence. I had said yes mainly because I had come to feel a certain affection for him, because of the precarious intimacy he had created between us. But now that yes was beginning to chill my affection.

No sooner had we emptied our cups than he said, " Let's go up to my room."

" Right away?"

" Why not? It's obvious we have nothing more to say to each other."

I could have wished for more time to get accustomed to my decision ; I had hoped our pact would generate, little by little, a feeling of complicity. But as a matter of fact, I really didn't have anything more to say.

Suitcases were scattered everywhere about the room. There were two brass beds, one of which was covered with clothing and papers, and on a round coffee table stood several empty champagne bottles. He took me in his arms and I felt a hard yet gentle mouth pressing against my lips. Yes, it was possible, it was easy. Something was happening to me, something different. I closed my eyes and stepped into a dream as lifelike as reality itself, a dream from which I felt I would awaken at dawn, carefree and lighthearted. And then I heard his voice: " The little girl seems frightened." Those words, which hardly had anything to do with me, rudely brought me out of my dream. I pushed myself free.

" Wait a moment," I said.

I went into the bathroom and hastily freshened up, pushing aside all thoughts ; it was too late now to think. He joined me in bed before there was time for any questions to arise in me. I clung tightly to him ; at that moment he was my only hope.

At last he said commandingly, " Open your eyes."

I raised my eyelids, but they weighed heavily and closed

quickly against the light which hurt them. " Open your eyes,"
he was saying. " It's just you and I." He was right; I didn't
really want to escape, but first I had to grow accustomed to
that strange presence. Becoming aware of my flesh, seeing his
unfamiliar face, and under his gaze losing myself within myself—it was too much all at once. But since he insisted, I
opened my eyes and I looked at him. I looked at him and
was halted midway in my inner turmoil, in a region without
light and without darkness, where I was neither body nor
spirit. He threw off the sheet, and at the same moment it occurred to me that the room was poorly heated and that I
no longer had the belly of a young girl. The mutilated flower
burst suddenly into bloom, and lost its petals, while he muttered words to himself, for himself, words I tried not to hear.
But I . . . I had lost interest. He came back close to me and
for a moment the warmth of his body aroused me again.

" How could I ever feel any tenderness for this man?" I
thought. There was a discouraging hostility in his eyes, but I
didn't feel guilty towards him, not even by omission.

" Don't worry so much about me. Just let me . . ."

" You're not really cold," he said angrily. " You're resisting with your head. But I'll force you . . ."

" No," I said. " No . . ."

It would have been too difficult to explain my feeling.
There was a look of hate in his eyes and I was ashamed to
have let myself be taken in by the mirage of carnal pleasure.
A man, I discovered, isn't a Turkish bath.

" You don't want to!" he was saying. " You don't want
to! Stubborn mule!" He struck me lightly on the chin; I was
too weary to escape into anger. I began to tremble. A beating fist, thousands of fists . . . " Violence is everywhere," I
thought. I trembled and tears began running down my
cheeks.

Now he was kissing my eyes, murmuring, " I'm drinking
your tears," and a conquering tenderness appeared in his face,
a childlike tenderness, and I had pity as much for him as for
myself. Both of us were equally lost, equally disillusioned. I
smoothed his hair; I asked, " Why do you hate me?"

" It has to be," he said regretfully. " It just has to be."

" But I don't hate you, you know. In fact I like being in
your arms."

" Do you really mean that?"

" Yes, I do."

In a sense I did mean it ; something was happening. True, it had missed the mark, was sad, ridiculous even, but it was real.

" It's been a strange night," I said with a smile. " I've never spent a night like this before."

" Never? Not even with younger men? You're not lying to me, are you?"

The words had lied for me. I endorsed their lie. " Never." He crushed me ardently against him. " All right?"

I knew my pleasure found no echo in his heart, and if I impatiently awaited his it was only to be done with it. And yet I had been subdued, was willing to sigh, to moan. But not very convincingly, I imagine.

He, too, had been subdued, for he didn't insist. Almost immediately, he fell asleep against me ; I also dozed off. The weight of his arm across my chest awakened me.

" You're here! Thank God!" he exclaimed, opening his eyes. " I was having a nightmare ; I always have nightmares." He seemed to be speaking from very far off, from the darkest depths of night. " Don't you have a place where you can hide me?"

" Hide you?"

" Yes. It would be so wonderful to just disappear. Can't we disappear for a few days?"

" I have no place. And I can't get away myself."

" What a shame!" he said, and then asked, " Don't you ever have nightmares?"

" Not very often."

" I envy you! I always have someone near me at night."

" I have to leave soon, you know," I said.

" Not right away. Don't go. Don't leave me!" He grabbed me by the shoulders. I was a life preserver. But in what shipwreck?

" I'll wait till you fall asleep," I said. " Would you like to meet me again to-morrow?"

" Yes, certainly. I'll be at the café next door to your place at noon. Is that all right with you?"

" Fine. Now try to sleep quietly."

As soon as his breathing grew heavy, I slipped out of bed. It was hard for me to tear myself from the night which clung so tenaciously to my skin. But I didn't want to arouse

Nadine's suspicions. Each of us had her own way of duping the other: she told me everything; I told her nothing. As I stood before the mirror, transforming my face into a mask of decency, I realised Nadine had been one of the main reasons for my decision to say yes to Scriassine, and I couldn't help myself from holding it against her. Yet I really hadn't the least regret for what I had done. You learn so many things about a man when you're in bed with him, much more than when you have him maunder for weeks on a couch. Only I was far too vulnerable for this sort of experiment.

I was kept very busy all morning. Sézenac didn't come, but I had quite a few other patients. I had only a vague impression of Scriassine, and I needed to see him again. Our night together was resting heavily on my heart, incomplete, absurd. I hoped that in talking to him we would be able to bring it to a conclusion, to save it perhaps. I was the first to arrive at the café, a small place, painted bright red, with highly polished tables. I had often bought cigarettes there, but I had never sat down. Couples were sitting in booths and talking quietly. A waiter appeared and I ordered a glass of ersatz port. I felt as if I were in a strange city; I no longer seemed to know what I was waiting for. Suddenly Scriassine burst into the café and walked hurriedly over to my table.

"Sorry I'm late. I had a dozen appointments this morning."

"That makes it all the nicer of you to have come."

He smiled at me. "Sleep well?"

"Very well."

He, too, ordered a glass of ersatz port and then leaned towards me. There was no longer any trace of hostility in his face. "I'd like to ask you a question."

"Go ahead."

"Why did you agree so readily to go up to my room with me?"

I smiled. "I suppose it's because I like you a little," I replied.

"You weren't drunk?"

"Not at all."

"And you weren't sorry afterwards?"

"No."

He hesitated. I gathered he was anxious to obtain a detailed commentary for his most intimate catalogue. "There's one thing I'd like to know. You said you'd never spent a night like that before. Is that true?"

"Yes and no," I answered with a slightly embarrassed laugh.

"That's what I thought," he said, disappointed. "It's never really true."

"It's true at the moment; less so the next day."

He swallowed the sticky wine in a single gulp.

"You know what chilled me?" I said. "There were moments when you looked so terribly hostile."

He shrugged his shoulders. "That couldn't be helped."

"Why? The struggle between the sexes?"

"We're not on the same side. I mean, politically."

For a moment I was stupefied. "But politics has so little place in my life!"

"Indifference is also a stand," he said sharply. "You see, in politics if you're not completely with me you're very far from me."

"Then you shouldn't have asked me to go up to your room," I said reproachfully.

A sly smile wrinkled his eyes. "If I really want a woman, it's all the same to me whether she agrees with my politics or not. I wouldn't even have any qualms about sleeping with a fascist."

"But apparently it isn't all the same to you, since you were hostile."

He smiled again. "In bed, it's not bad to hate each other a little."

"That's horrible," I said, staring at him. "You're quite an introvert, aren't you? You can pity people and feel remorse for them, but I doubt if you could ever really like anyone."

"Ah! so you're the one who's doing the analysing to-day," he said. "Go on; I love being analysed."

In his eyes I saw the same look of maniacal greed I had noticed the night before when he looked down at my naked body. I could not have tolerated it except in a child or a sick person.

"You believe loneliness can be cured by force; but in making love, there's no greater blunder."

He got the point. "What you're saying is that last night was a failure. Is that right?"

" More or less."

" Would you be willing to begin all over again?"

I hesitated. " Yes. I don't like to stop at a failure."

His face hardened. " That's a pretty poor reason," he said, shrugging his shoulders. " You don't make love with your head."

That was precisely my opinion. If his words and desires had wounded me, it was because they came from his head. " I think both of us do things too much with our heads," I said.

" In that case, I suppose it'd be better if we didn't try again," he said.

" Yes, I suppose so."

Yes, a second failure would have been even more disastrous than the first, and a happy outcome was inconceivable. We had absolutely no love at all for each other. Even talk was useless ; there had been nothing worth saving and the whole affair, in any case, didn't lend itself to a conclusion. We politely exchanged a few idle words and then I went home.

I hold nothing against him, and I hold hardly anything against myself. Besides, as Robert told me immediately, the whole thing was quite unimportant—nothing but a distasteful remembrance lingering in our minds and concerning no one but ourselves. But when I went up to my room, I promised myself I would never again attempt to remove my kid gloves. " It's too late," I murmured, looking into the mirror. " My gloves are grafted to my flesh now ; they'd have to skin me alive to get them off." No, it wasn't only Scriassine's fault that things turned out the way they did ; it was my fault too. I had slept with him out of curiosity, out of defiance, out of weariness, to prove to myself God only knows what. Well, whatever it was, I certainly proved the contrary. I thought casually that my life might have been different. I might have dressed more elegantly, gone out more often, known the little pleasures of vanity or the burning fevers of the senses. But it was too late. And then all at once I understood why my past sometimes seemed to me to be someone else's. Because now I am someone else, a woman of thirty-nine, a woman who's aware of her age!

" Thirty-nine years!" I said aloud. Before the war I was too young for the years to have weighed upon me. And then for five years, I forgot myself completely. And now I've found myself again, only to learn that I'm condemned. Old age is awaiting me; there's no escaping it. Even now I can see its beginnings in the depths of the mirror. Oh, I'm still a woman, I still bleed every month. Nothing's really changed, except that now I know. I ran my fingers through my hair. Those white streaks are no longer a curiosity, a sign; they're the beginning. In a few years, my head will be the colour of my bones. My face still seems smooth and firm, but overnight the mask will melt, laying bare the rheumy eyes of an old woman. Each year the seasons repeat themselves; wounds are healed. But there's no way in the world to halt the infirmities of age. "There isn't even any time left to worry about it," I thought, turning away from my reflection. "It's even too late for regrets. There's nothing left to do but to keep going."

CHAPTER THREE

NADINE WENT to meet Henri several evenings in a row at the offices of the newspaper. One night, in fact, they even took a room in a hotel again, but it didn't amount to much. For Nadine, making love was clearly a tedious occupation and Henri, too, tired quickly of it. But he enjoyed going out with her, watching her eat, hearing her laugh, talking to her. She was blind to a great many things, but she reacted strongly to those she did see—and without ever cheating. He was convinced she would make a pleasant travelling companion, was touched by her eagerness. Each time she saw him she would ask, "Did you talk to her about it yet?" And he would answer, "No, not yet." She would lower her head in such utter desolation that it made him feel guilty, made him feel as if he were depriving her of all those things she had for so long gone without: sun, plenty of food, a real trip. Since he had decided in any case to break off with Paula, why not let Nadine profit from it? Besides, it would be a lot better for Paula's sake if he explained things to her before leaving, rather than let her ruin herself with hope while he was gone. When he was away from her, he felt he was in the right; he had rarely acted falsely towards her and she was only lying to herself when she pretended to believe in the resurrection of a dead and buried past. But when he was with her, it often occurred to him that he, too, might be at fault. "Am I a bastard for not loving her any more?" he would ask himself, watching her come and go in the apartment. "Or was I wrong ever to love her in the first place?"

He had been at the Dôme with Julien and Louis and seated at the next table, making a great show of reading *The Accident,* was a woman of extraordinary beauty, dressed from head to foot in mauve. She had placed her long violet gloves on the table and, as Henri arose to leave, he remarked, "What beautiful gloves!"

"Do you like them? Take them, they're yours."

"And just what, may I ask, would I do with them?"

"You can keep them as a souvenir of our first meeting."

They exchanged a soft, lingering look. A few hours later he was holding her naked body in his arms and saying, " You're too beautiful, much too beautiful." No, he really couldn't blame himself. How could he have helped but be captivated by Paula's beauty, by her voice, by the mystery of her words, by the distant wisdom in her smile? She was slightly older than he, knew many things of which he was ignorant and which seemed at that time much more important to him than the bigger things. What he admired in her above all was her complete disdain for worldly goods ; she soared in some supernatural region, and he despaired of ever joining her there. He was amazed that she permitted herself to become flesh in his arms. " Naturally, it went to my head a little," he admitted to himself. And she, for her part, had believed in his declarations of eternal love and in the miracle of being herself. Therein no doubt was where he had been guilty— by first exalting Paula immoderately and then too lucidly taking her true measure. Yes, they had both made mistakes. But that wasn't the question ; the question now was to break it off. He turned over words in his mind. Did she have any suspicion of what was about to come? Generally, when he remained silent for any length of time, she was quick to question him.

" Why are you moving things around?" he asked.

" Don't you think the room looks nicer this way?"

" Would you mind sitting down for just a minute?"

" Why? Am I annoying you?"

" No, not at all. But I'd like to have a talk with you."

She let out a choked little laugh. " How solemn you look! You aren't going to tell me you don't love me any more, are you?"

" No."

" Then anything else does not matter." She sat down, leaning towards him with a patient, slightly mocking expression. " Go ahead, darling, I'm listening."

" Loving or not loving each other isn't the only thing in the world," he said.

" To me, it's all that matters."

" But not to me ; I'm sure you know that. There are other things that count, too."

" Yes, I know—your work, travelling. I've never tried to dissuade you from them."

" There's another thing that's important to me, and I've told you this often—my freedom."

She smiled again. " Now don't tell me I haven't given you enough freedom!"

" As much as living together permits, I suppose. But for me, freedom means first of all solitude. Do you remember when I first came here to stay? We agreed then it would only be till the end of the war."

" I didn't think I was a burden on you," she said, no longer smiling.

" No one could be less of a burden than you. But I do think it was better when we lived apart."

Paula smiled. " You used to come here every night. You used to say you couldn't sleep without me."

True, he had told her that, but only during the first year, not after. He didn't, however, contest the point. " All right," he said, " but at least I used to work in my room at the hotel . . ."

" That room was just one of your youthful whims," she replied in an indulgent voice. " No promiscuity, no living together—you must admit your code was rather abstract. I really can't believe you still take it seriously."

" But it's not at all abstract. When two people live together, you can't avoid building up tensions on the one hand and becoming negligent on the other. I realise I'm often disagreeable and negligent, and I know it hurts you. It would be much better for us not to see each other except when we really felt like it."

" But I always feel like seeing you," she said reprovingly.

" When I'm tired, or out of sorts, or when I'm working, I prefer being alone," Henri said coldly.

Again Paula smiled. " You're going to be alone for a whole month. When you get back, we'll see whether or not you've changed your mind."

" No," he said firmly, " it won't change."

Suddenly, Paula's smile vanished and a look of fear appeared on her face. " Promise me one thing," she murmured.

" What?"

" That you'll never live with another woman."

" What an idiotic notion! Don't be a fool! Of course I promise."

"Then I suppose you can go back to your cherished old habits," she said with resignation.

He studied her curiously. "Why did you make me promise that?"

Again a look of panic appeared in Paula's eyes. She was silent for a moment. "Oh, I know that no other woman could ever take my place in your life," she finally said. There was a false calmness in her voice. "But I cling to symbols, you know." She started to get up, as if she dreaded hearing any more. He stopped her.

"Wait," he said. "I want to be completely frank with you. I'll never live with another woman. Never. But I have an urge to do things, meet new people, have a few little affairs. I think it's because of these four years of austerity we've just gone through."

"But you are having an affair now, aren't you?" Paula said calmly. "With Nadine."

"How do you know?"

"You don't lie very well."

At times she was so completely blind—and at times so clear-sighted! He was disconcerted. "I was an idiot not to talk to you about it," he said embarrassed. "I was afraid of hurting you. But there's absolutely no reason for you to feel hurt; practically nothing has happened, and it won't last long, in any case."

"Don't let it upset you. I'm not one to be jealous of a child, especially Nadine!" She walked over to Henri and sat down on the arm of his chair. "On Christmas Eve I told you a man like you isn't subject to the same laws as other men. I still believe that. There's a commonplace form of faithfulness that I'll never demand of you. Have a good time with Nadine, and anyone else you like." She ruffled Henri's hair. "You see how much I respect your freedom!"

"Yes," he said. He was both relieved and disappointed; his too-easy victory led him nowhere. He felt he had to carry it at least to its conclusion. "As a matter of fact, Nadine doesn't have a shadow of feeling for me. All she wants is for me to take her along. But it's completely understood that we'll stop seeing each other just as soon as we get back."

"Take her with you?"

" Yes, she's going to Portugal with me."

" No!" Paula exclaimed. Suddenly her serene mask shattered into a thousand pieces and Henri saw before him a face of flesh and bones, with trembling lips and eyes glistening with tears. " You said you couldn't take me!"

" You didn't seem anxious to go, so I didn't try very hard."

" I wasn't anxious! I'd have given an arm to go with you! Only I thought you wanted to be alone. I'm perfectly willing to sacrifice myself to your beloved solitude," she cried out in revolt, " but not to Nadine! No!"

" It doesn't make much difference whether I take Nadine or whether I go alone, since you say you're not jealous of her," he said bitingly.

" It makes all the difference in the world!" she replied, her voice breaking with emotion. " Alone, I would still be with you, in a way; we would still be together. The first trip since the war! You haven't any right to take someone else."

" Listen," he said, " if you see any sort of symbolism in this trip, you're completely wrong. Nadine simply wants to see something of the world. She's just an unhappy kid who's never had a chance to see anything, and it would make me feel good to give her this pleasure. And that's all there is to it."

" If that is really all there is to it," Paula said slowly, " then don't take her." She looked at Henri pleadingly. " I ask it of you in the name of our love."

They looked at each other silently for a moment. Paula's whole face was a longing plea. But suddenly Henri grew stubborn. He felt as if he were facing an armed torturer rather than a woman at her wits' end. " You have just told me that you respected my freedom," he said.

" Yes," she replied fiercely. " But if you wanted to destroy yourself I'd try to stop you. And I'm not going to let you betray our love."

" In other words, I'm free to do as you please," he said ironically.

" How can you be so unfair!" she said, sobbing. " I'd take anything from you, anything! But I know inside me I mustn't take this. No one but I should be going with you."

" That's your opinion," he said.

" But it's obvious!"

" Not to me."

" Because you're blind, because you want to be blind. Listen," she said, forcing her voice to be calm, " you're really interested in that girl, and you see how much you're hurting me. Please don't take her."

Henri was silent for a moment. There wasn't very much he could say in answer to that argument, and he resented it as much as if Paula had used physical force to stop him.

" All right," he said finally, " I won't take her!" He got up and walked towards the stairway. " Only don't talk to me any more about freedom!"

Paula followed him and put her hand on his shoulder. " Does your freedom have to make me suffer?"

He shook off her hand. " If you suffer when I do what I want to, then I'll have to choose between you and my freedom."

He took a step away from Paula, and she cried out to him anxiously. There was panic in her eyes. " Henri," she pleaded, " what do you mean by that?"

" Just what I said."

" You're not going to destroy our love on purpose, are you?"

He turned and faced her. " All right!" he said. " Since you insist on it, let's have it out once and for all!" He was irritated enough by now to want to get to the very heart of the matter. " There's a basic misunderstanding between us. We don't have the same conception of love . . ."

" There's no misunderstanding," Paula said quickly. " I know what you're going to say—my love is my whole life and you want it to be only a part of yours. I know, and I agree."

" Yes, but with that as a start, there are other questions that have to be answered," Henri said.

" Oh, no," Paula said. " It's all so stupid," she added in an agitated voice. " You're not going to question our love just because I've asked you not to take Nadine!"

" I'm not taking her. That part is settled. But there's something entirely different involved."

" Listen," Paula said abruptly, " let's get it over with. If you absolutely must take her with you to prove you're free, then take her with you. I don't want you to think of me as a tyrant."

" I certainly will not take her if you're going to eat your heart out the whole time I'm away."

" I'd eat my heart out even more if you chose to destroy our love out of spite." She shrugged her shoulders. " You're capable of doing it too. Your least little whims are so important to you!"

She looked at him imploringly, hopefully waiting for him to say, " I hold no grudge against you." She could wait a long time for him to say it. She sighed. " You love me," she said, " but you're never willing to sacrifice anything for our love. It always has to be me who gives everything."

" Paula," he said amicably, " if I make that trip with Nadine, I repeat to you again that when we get back I'll stop seeing her, and nothing will be changed between you and me."

Paula remained silent. " I'm blackmailing her, that's just what it amounts to," Henri thought. " It's rather disgraceful." And the ugliest part of it was that Paula was aware of it, and would play at being the generous one, knowing all the time that she was accepting a rather sordid bargain. But what of it! You want what you want. And what he wanted was to take Nadine.

" Do as you please," Paula said with a sigh. " I suppose I give too much importance to symbols. Really, it makes hardly any difference whether the girl goes with you or not."

" It makes no difference whatsoever," Henri said emphatically.

During the days that followed, Paula didn't mention the matter again. Except that with each of her gestures, with her every silence, she was saying, " I'm defenceless, and you're taking advantage of it." It was true she had no weapons to fight back with, not even the most ineffectual. But her defencelessness was itself a trap; it left Henri no choice but to become either the hangman or the hanged. He had no desire to play the hanged, but the trouble was that neither was he a hangman.

The night he met Nadine on one of the platforms of the Gare d'Austerlitz, he had a gnawing, uneasy feeling inside him.

" You're not early," she grumbled.

" I'm not late, either."

" Let's hurry and get on. If the train should leave . . ."

" It won't leave ahead of schedule."

" You never can tell."

They boarded the train and chose an empty compartment. With a perplexed look on her face, Nadine stood motionless for a long moment between the two seats. Then she sat down next to the window, her back to the locomotive. After a moment, she opened her suitcase and began preparing for the night with the meticulous care of an old maid. She slipped on a bathrobe and slippers, wrapped a blanket around her legs, and propped a pillow under her head. From a small basket that served her as a purse, she took a stick of chewing gum. Then she remembered that Henri was present and smiled at him engagingly.

" Did she moan very much when she saw you were dead set on taking me?"

Henri shrugged his shoulders. " Naturally, she wasn't overjoyed."

" What did she say?"

" It's none of your business," he said dryly.

" But I'd really like to know."

" And I really don't want to tell you about it."

She took a garnet-coloured piece of knitting from her basket and began clicking the needles together while chewing her gum. " She's laying it on too thick," Henri thought peevishly. Perhaps she was annoying him on purpose because she suspected his remorse and felt that he was still, in spirit, in the red apartment. Actually Paula had kissed him good-bye without tears. " Have a nice trip," she had said. But at this very moment, he knew she would be weeping. " I'll write to her as soon as I get there," he promised himself.

The train got under way and sped through the sad dusk of the Parisian suburbs. Henri opened a detective story and glanced quickly at the sullen face opposite him. At the moment, he could do nothing about Paula's unhappiness, but there was no point in spoiling Nadine's pleasure, too. He made an effort and said cheerfully, " To-morrow at this time we'll be passing through Spain."

" Yes."

" They're not expecting me so soon in Lisbon. We'll have two whole days all to ourselves."

Nadine did not answer. For a moment or so, she continued to knit diligently, and then she stretched herself out on the seat, stuffed a ball of wax in each ear, tied a kerchief around her eyes and turned her back on Henri. "And I was hoping Nadine's smiles would make up for Paula's tears!" he said to himself. He closed the book and turned out the lights. The blue paint that had covered the train windows during the war had been scraped off, but the fields outside were completely black under the starless sky. Inside the compartment, it was cold. Why, he wondered, was he in this train, opposite that almost total stranger who was breathing heavily in her sleep? Suddenly, it seemed impossible that the past would really be waiting for him in Lisbon.

"She could at least be a little more agreeable!" he said to himself angrily the next morning as the train made its way towards the border. When they had changed trains at Hendaye, where a light breeze and the warm sun played against their skins, Nadine hadn't so much as smiled; instead, she yawned unrestrainedly while their passports were being checked. Now she was walking in front of him with her long boyish strides as he struggled with their two heavy suitcases, growing hotter by the minute under the unaccustomed sun. He looked with distaste at her strong, rather hairy legs; her socks underlined their ungracious bareness. Behind them, a barrier closed; for the first time in six years he was walking on soil that wasn't French. Another barrier rose before them and he heard Nadine cry out unbelievingly: "Oh!" It was an impassioned sound, a sound he had tried in vain to wring from her with his caresses.

"Oh! Look!"

Alongside the road next to a burned-out house was a stand covered with oranges, bananas, chocolate. Nadine rushed over to it, grabbed two oranges, and handed one to Henri. At sight of this carefree joy, so completely cut off from France by only a little over a mile, he felt that hard black thing inside his chest, that thing which for four years had taken the place of his heart, suddenly become soft wax. He had looked unflinchingly at pictures of Dutch children starving to death; now, at the sight of that sudden burst of joy, he felt like sitting down at the edge of the road, his head in his hands, and never moving again.

Nadine's good humour came back. She gorged herself on fruits and candies all across the Basque countryside and the Castilian desert, looked smilingly at the clear Spanish skies. They spent one more night stretched out on the dusty seats. In the morning they followed the course of a pale blue stream which wound its way among countless olive groves. Gradually the stream turned into a river and finally a lake. And then the train stopped. They were in Lisbon.

"All those taxis!" Nadine exclaimed.

A line of taxis was waiting in the driveway of the station. Henri checked the suitcases in the baggage room, got into a cab with Nadine, and said to the chauffeur, "Drive us around." Nadine gripped his arm and cried out in terror as they plummeted down steep streets at a speed that seemed dizzying to them; they had forgotten what it was like to ride in a car. Henri laughed along with Nadine and held her arm tightly. He turned his head rapidly from side to side, joyful and yet incredulous. The past was there to meet him; he recognised it. A southern city, a fresh, hot city with its ancient clanking streetcars, and on the horizon the promise of salty winds and the sea beating against high walls. Yes, he recognised it, and yet it astonished him more than ever had Marseilles, Athens, Naples, Barcelona. Because now everything new, everything unknown, was a thing to be marvelled at. It was beautiful, that capital, with its quiet heart, its unruly hills, its houses with pastel-coloured icing, its huge white ships.

"Let us off somewhere in the centre of town," Henri said. The taxi stopped at a large square surrounded by cinemas and cafés. Seated at tables in front of the cafés were men in dark suits. No women sat there. The women were busily moving along the shop-lined street which led down to the estuary. Suddenly Henri and Nadine stopped dead simultaneously.

"Will you please look at that!"

Leather! real thick, supple leather! You could almost smell it through the shop window. Cowhide suitcases, pigskin gloves, tawny-coloured shoes you could walk in without squeaking, without getting your feet wet. Real silk, real wool, flannel suits, poplin shirts! It suddenly occurred to Henri that he looked rather seedy in his suit of ersatz cloth and his cracked shoes with their upturned tips. And alongside the women in their furs and their silk stockings and hand-made pumps, Nadine looked like a rag picker.

"To-morrow we're going to buy things," he said. "A lot of things!"

"It just doesn't seem real!" Nadine exclaimed. "I wonder what everyone in Paris would say if they saw all this!"

"Exactly what we're saying," Henri replied, laughing.

They stopped before a pastry shop, and this time it wasn't a look of greed, but rather one of shock which appeared on Nadine's face. Henri, too, stood there for a moment, frozen in unbelief. Then, "Let's go in," he said, nudging Nadine.

Except for an old man and a little boy, there were only women seated around the tables, women with oily hair, weighed down with furs, jewels, and fat, religiously performing their daily gorging. Two little girls with black braided hair, wearing blue sashes across their chests and a lot of religious medallions around their necks, were sitting quietly at a table casually sipping thick hot chocolate overflowing with whipped cream.

"Do you want one?" Henri asked.

Nadine nodded. A few minutes later, a waitress placed a cup of chocolate before her, but when Nadine brought it to her lips the blood drained from her face. "I can't," she said. "My stomach just isn't used to it any more," she added apologetically. But it wasn't her stomach that had rebelled; she had suddenly thought of something—or someone. He did not question her.

Crisp, fresh cretonne curtains hung in their hotel room; in the bathroom there was hot water, real soap, and soft, fluffy terry-cloth robes. All of Nadine's gayness came back to her. She insisted upon rubbing Henri with a rough bath-glove, and when his skin was red and burning from head to foot she laughingly tumbled him on to the bed. And she made love with such high spirits that it seemed as if she actually enjoyed it. The next morning they went to the shopping district, and her eyes shone as she fingered the rich silks and wools with her rough hands.

"Were there ever such beautiful shops in Paris?"

"Much more beautiful. Don't you remember?"

"I never went to the expensive shops. I was too young."

She looked hopefully at Henri. "Do you think we'll have them again some day?"

"Some day, maybe."

"But how are they so rich here? I thought Portugal was a poor country."

"It's a poor country, with some very rich people."

For themselves and for their friends in Paris, they bought materials, stockings, underclothes, shoes, sweaters. They lunched in a basement restaurant the walls of which were covered with colourful posters of mounted picadors defying furious bulls. "Meat or fish—even they have their shortages!" Nadine said laughingly, as they ate steaks the colour of cinders. Afterwards, in their supple, thick-soled, blatant yellow shoes, they wandered along cobblestoned streets which rose towards the working-class quarters. At one street corner barefoot children were solemnly watching a faded puppet show. The sidewalks became narrow, the fronts of the houses scaly.

A shadow darkened Nadine's face. "It's disgusting, this street. Are there many like this?"

"There are."

"It doesn't seem to upset you."

He was in no mood for indignation. In fact, it even gave him a twinge of pleasure to see again the multi-coloured wash drying at sun-drenched windows above the streets' shadowy crevasses. They walked down a passageway in silence. Suddenly, Nadine stopped in the middle of the greasy, stone stairway. "It's disgusting!" she repeated. "Let's get out of it."

"Let's go on just a little farther," Henri said.

In Marseilles, Naples, Piraeus, in Chinatowns of many cities, he had spent hours wandering through these same squalid streets. Of course, then as now, he wished that all this misery could be done away with. But the wish remained an abstract thing. He had never felt like running away, and the overpowering human odour of these streets went to his head. From the top of the hill to the bottom, the same swarming multitudes, the same blue sky burning above the roof tops. It seemed to Henri that from one moment to the next he would rediscover his old joy in all its intensity. That was what he sought from street to street. But it wouldn't come back.

Barefooted women—everyone here went barefooted—were squatting before their doors frying sardines over charcoal fires, and the stench of stale fish mingled in the air with the smell of hot oil. In cellar apartments opening on to the street, not a bed, not a piece of furniture, not a picture; nothing but straw mats, children covered with rashes, and from time to time a goat. Outside, no happy voices, no laughter; only sombre dead eyes. Was misery more hopeless here than in the other cities? Or instead of becoming hardened to misfortune, does one grow more sensitive to it? The blue of the sky seemed cruel above the unhealthy shadows; he began to share Nadine's silent dismay. They passed a haggard-looking woman dressed in black rags who was scurrying through the street with a child clinging to her bare breast, and Henri said abruptly, " You're right; let's get out."

But the next day, at a cocktail party given at the French Consulate, Henri found that it was useless to have tried to flee from that wretched hill. The table was laden with sandwiches and rich cakes, the women were wearing dresses in colours he had long ago forgotten, every face was smiling, all were speaking French, and the Hill of Grace, for a time, seemed far off, in a completely foreign country whose misfortunes were no concern of his. He was laughing politely with the others when old Mendoz das Viernas came and led him off to a corner of the drawing-room. He was wearing a stiff collar and a black tie; before Salazar's dictatorship, he had been a cabinet minister. He looked at Henri suspiciously.

" What is your impression of Lisbon?" he asked.

" It's a very beautiful city," Henri answered. He saw das Viernas' face darken and he hastily added with a smile, " I must say, though, I haven't seen very much of it."

" Usually, the French who come here somehow manage to see nothing at all," das Viernas said bitterly. " Your Valéry, for example. He admired the sea, the gardens, but for the rest—a blind man." The old man paused a moment. " And you? Do you also intend to blindfold yourself?"

" On the contrary!" Henri said. " I intend to keep my eyes as wide open as I can."

" Ah! From what they have told me of you, that is what I had hoped," das Viernas said, his voice gentler now. " We shall make an appointment for to-morrow and I shall then show you Lisbon. A beautiful façade, isn't it? But you will see what is behind it!"

" I've already taken a walk on the Hill of Grace," Henri said.

" But you did not go into the houses! I want you to see for yourself what the people eat, how they live. You would not believe me if I told you." Das Viernas shrugged his shoulders. " All that writing about the melancholy of the Portuguese and how mysterious it is. Actually it's ridiculously simple: of seven million Portuguese, there are only seventy thousand who have enough to eat."

It was impossible to get out of it. Henri spent the following morning visiting a series of wretched hovels. At the end of the afternoon, the former cabinet minister gathered his friends for the sole purpose of having them meet him. It was impossible to refuse. All of them were wearing dark suits, stiff collars, and bowlers ; they spoke ceremoniously but every now and then a look of hatred crossed their sensitive faces. They were mostly former cabinet members, former journalists, former professors who had been crushed because of their obstinate refusal to rally to the new régime. All of them were poor and trapped, many had relatives in France who had been deported. Those who stubbornly continued to take what action they could knew that the Island of Hell awaited them. A doctor who treated poverty-stricken people without remuneration, who tried to open a clinic or introduce a little hygiene into the hospitals, was immediately suspect. Whosoever dared organise an evening course, whosoever made a generous gesture, or simply a charitable one, was branded enemy of both Church and State. And yet they doggedly persisted. They wanted to believe that the destruction of Nazism would somehow bring to an end this hypocritical fascism, and they dreamed constantly of overthrowing Salazar and creating a National Front like the one which had been formed in France. But they knew they were alone: the English capitalists had large interests in Portugal and the Americans were negotiating with the government for the purchase of air bases in the Azores. " France is our only hope," they repeated over and over. " Tell the people of France the truth," they begged. " They do not know; if they knew they would come to our rescue."

They imposed daily meetings on Henri, overwhelmed him with facts, figures, statistics, took him for walks through the starving villages surrounding Lisbon. It wasn't exactly the kind of holiday he had dreamed of, but he had no choice. He promised that he would wage a campaign in the press in order to get the facts to the people. Political tyranny, economic exploitation, police terror, the systematic brutalisation of the masses, the clergy's shameful complicity—he would tell everything. "If Carmona knew that France was willing to support us, he would join our ranks," das Viernas said. Years ago he had known Bidault, and he was thinking of suggesting to him a kind of secret treaty: in exchange for France's backing, the future Portuguese government would be able to offer advantageous trade concessions in connection with the African colonies. It would have been difficult to explain to him, without being brutal, how completely fantastic his project was!

"I'll see Tournelle, his administrative assistant," Henri promised on the eve of his departure for Algarve. "He was a friend of mine in the Resistance."

"I shall map out a precise plan and entrust it to you when you return," das Viernas said.

Henri was glad to get out of Lisbon. For greater convenience in making his round of lectures, the French Consulate loaned him a car and told him to keep it as long as he wanted. At last he would have a real holiday! Unfortunately, his new-found friends were counting on his spending his last week in Portugal conspiring with them. While he was away, they were going to assemble exhaustive documentation and also arrange for meetings with certain Communists from the Zamora dockyards. Turning them down was unthinkable.

"That means we have exactly two weeks and no more to see the country," Nadine said sulkily.

They dined that night at a roadside inn on the opposite bank of the Tagus. A waitress served them slices of fried codfish and a bottle of cloudy pink wine. Through the window they could see the lights of Lisbon rising tier upon tier between the water and the sky.

"With a car, you can cover an awful lot of ground in two weeks!" Henri said. "Do you realise what a stroke of luck that was!"

"Exactly. And it's a shame we can't take more advantage of it."

"Those men are all counting on me; I'd really be a louse to disappoint them, wouldn't I?"

She shrugged her shoulders. "There's nothing you can do for them."

"I can speak for them. That's my job. If I can't at least do that, there's no point in my being a newspaperman."

"Maybe there isn't."

"Don't start thinking already about going back," he said soothingly. "Just think of the wonderful trip ahead of us. Look at those little lights along the water; they're pretty, aren't they?"

"What's so pretty about them?" Nadine asked. It was just the sort of irritating question she enjoyed asking. "No, seriously," she added, "what makes you think they're pretty?"

Henri shrugged his shoulders. "They're pretty, that's all."

She pressed her forehead against the window. "They might be pretty if you didn't know what's behind them. But once you know, it's . . . it's just another fraud," she concluded bitterly. "I hate that filthy city."

It was a fraud, no doubt of it. And yet he was unable to keep from seeing a certain beauty in those lights. No longer did he fool himself about the hot stench of poverty, the colourfulness of rags and tatters, but those little flames twinkling along the edge of the dark waters moved him in spite of everything. Perhaps it was because they made him recall a time when he was unaware of the reality hiding behind appearances, or perhaps it was nothing but the memory of an illusion that made him like them. He looked at Nadine—eighteen years old and not a single illusion to remember! He at least had a past. "And a present, and a future," he said to himself. "Fortunately, there are still some things left in the world to like."

And there were, fortunately. What a joy to have a wheel in your hands again! And those roads stretching out before you as far as the eye can reach! The first day out, after all those years of not having driven, Henri felt unsure of himself. The car seemed endowed with a life of its own, and so much the more so since it was heavy, had bad springs, was noisy and rather erratic. And yet it soon began obeying him as spontaneously as his own hand.

"It's really got speed! It's terrific!" Nadine exclaimed.

"You've driven in cars before, haven't you?"

"In Paris, in jeeps. But I never went this fast."

That, too, was a lie—the old illusion of freedom and power. But she gave into it without a qualm. She lowered all the windows and greedily drank in the wind and dust. If Henri had listend to her they would never have got out of the car. The thing she seemed to enjoy most was driving as fast as they could towards the horizon. She hardly took any interest at all in the scenery. And yet how beautiful it was! Hillsides covered with golden mimosas; endless groves of round-topped orange trees which brought to mind calm, primitive paradises; the twisted, frenzied rocks of Battaglia, the majestic pair of stairways which rose crisscrossing to a white-and-black church, the streets of Beja through which echoed the ancient cries of a lovesick nun. In the south, with its African atmosphere, little donkeys moved in endless circles to force a trickle of water from the arid ground. At distant intervals, half-hidden among blue century plants rising from the red earth, they came across the false freshness of smooth, milky white houses. They began driving back towards the north through country in which stones and rocks seemed to have stolen their intense colours from the most brilliant flowers—reds, ochres, violets. And then, on the gentle hills of Minho, the colours once more became flowers. Yes, a beautiful setting, a setting that flashed by so rapidly that there was no time to think of what lurked behind it. Along these granite shores, as on the burning roads of Algarve, the peasants they saw all went barefooted. But they did not see many of them.

The holiday ended at red Oporto, where even the filth was blood-coloured. On the walls of hovels darker and danker than those of Lisbon and teeming with naked children, notices had been pasted up, reading: "Unhealthy! It is forbidden to live in this house." Little girls of four or five, clad in torn sacks, were rummaging about in garbage pails. For lunch, Henri and Nadine sought refuge in a dark corner of a restaurant, but all through the meal they had the uneasy feeling that, outside, faces were glued to the windows. "I hate cities!" Nadine said furiously. She stayed in her room the whole day, and the following day on the road she hardly unclenched her teeth enough to speak. Henri made no attempt to cheer her up.

The day they were to return to Lisbon, they stopped to eat in a little port town three hours from the city. They left the car in front of the inn and climbed one of the hills overlooking the sea. At the summit stood a white windmill with a roof shingled in green tile. Small, narrow-necked, terra-cotta jars were attached to its vanes, and the wind sang through them. Henri and Nadine ran down the hill past leafy olive trees, past blossoming almond trees, and the childish music followed them. They dropped down on the sandy beach of the cove. Boats with rust-coloured sails were moving lazily on the pale sea.

" Let's stay here a while; it's pleasant," Henri said.

" All right," Nadine replied sullenly. " I'm dying of hunger," she added.

" Naturally. You didn't eat a thing."

" I ask for soft-boiled eggs and they bring me a bowl of lukewarm water and raw eggs."

" Well, the cod was good, and so were the beans."

" Another drop of oil and I'd have been sick," she said, spitting angrily. " There's even oil in my saliva."

Suddenly and calmly she pulled off her blouse.

" What are you doing?"

" Can't you see?"

She was wearing no brassière. Lying on her back, she offered up to the sun the nakedness of her firm, small breasts.

" Nadine! No! Suppose someone should come . . ."

" No one'll come."

" How do you know?"

" Anyhow, I don't give a damn. I just want to feel the sun on my body." Her breasts exposed to the wind and sun, her hair spread out on the sand, she looked up at the sky and said reproachfully, " It's our last day; we've got to take advantage of it."

Henri said nothing.

" Must we really go back to Lisbon to-night?" she asked in a whining voice.

" You know very well they're expecting us."

" We haven't even seen the mountains yet. And everyone

says they're beautiful. With a whole week left, we could see a lot of them."

"Nevertheless, as I've already told you a dozen times. I've got to see those people."

"Your old gentlemen in stiff collars? They might look pretty good in the showcases of the Musée de l'Homme. But as revolutionaries . . . don't make me laugh."

"Well, they affect me differently," Henri said. "And they do take big risks."

"They talk a lot," Nadine said, sifting the sand between her fingers. "Words, nothing but a lot of words."

"It's always so easy to feel superior to people who are trying to accomplish something," he said, slightly annoyed.

"What I have against them is that they're really not trying to accomplish anything at all," she replied irritably. "Instead of gabbling so much, I'd blow Salazar's brains out."

"That wouldn't help much."

"He'd be dead, and that would help. Like Vincent says, at least death doesn't forgive." She looked meditatively at the sea. "If you're willing to be killed with him, you could certainly get rid of him."

"Don't you try it!" Henri said with a smile. He placed his hand on Nadine's sand-encrusted arm. "That'd be quite a spot you'd put me in."

"It would be quite an exit," Nadine said.

"Are you in such a hurry to make yours?" he asked.

She yawned. "Do you enjoy living?"

"I'm not bored," he said cheerfully.

She raised herself on one elbow and studied him curiously. "Tell me. Scribbling from morning to night the way you do, does that really fill your life?"

"Yes," he said. "When I'm writing my life is full. In fact, I'm damned anxious to get back to it."

"What made you want to become a writer?"

"Oh, that goes a long way back," Henri replied. Yes, it went very far back into the past, but he couldn't decide how reliable his memories of the beginning were. "When I was a young boy," he said, "a book seemed like a magic thing to me."

"But I like books, too," Nadine said spiritedly. "Only there are so many of them already! What good will it do to add one more?"

" We all have different things to say. Every writer has his own life, his own way of seeing things, his own way of writing about them."

" And it doesn't upset you to realise that things have been written that are far above anything you'll ever pound out?" Nadine asked in a vaguely irritated voice.

" At first I didn't think that was true," Henri replied, smiling. " You're very arrogant when you haven't done anything. And then, once you get into it, you're too interested in what you're writing to waste time comparing."

" Naturally," she said sullenly. " You can always justify yourself." She let herself fall back on the sand and stretched out lazily, at full length.

He didn't know how to answer her. It's hard to explain the joys of writing to someone who doesn't enjoy it. Besides, was he capable of explaining it even to himself? He didn't for a moment imagine he would be read forever and yet while he was writing, he felt as if he were secrely settled in eternity. Whatever ideas he was able to shape into words on paper seemed to him to be preserved, fully rescued from oblivion. But how much truth was there in that feeling? How much of that also was only an illusion? That was one of the things he should have figured out during his vacation, but as a matter of fact he had figured out nothing at all. One thing was certain: he felt an almost agonising pity for all who did not even attempt to express themselves—Paula, Anne, Nadine. Suddenly he remembered that this was the day on which his book was to be published. It had been a long time since he had last faced the public and it frightened him a bit to think that at that very moment people were reading his novel and talking about it.

" Everything all right?" he asked, bending over Nadine and smiling at her gently.

" Yes, it's nice here," she said a little peevishly.

" It is, isn't it?"

He lay back on the warm sand and laced his fingers in Nadine's. Between the listless, sun-faded sea and the stark blue of the sky, happiness hung lazily in the air; a single smile from Nadine and he might have been able to grasp some of that happiness. She was almost pretty when she smiled, but now her lightly freckled face remained impassive.

" Poor Nadine!" he said.

She bolted upright. "Why poor?"

Certainly, she was an object of pity, but he wasn't quite sure why. "Because you're disappointed in the trip."

"Oh, I didn't really expect too much out of it, you know."

"But you have to admit we had some pleasant moments, anyhow."

"And there could still be more," she said, the cold blue of her eyes growing warmer. "Why don't you just forget those old dreamers? They're not what we came here for. Let's keep on the move ; let's enjoy ourselves while we can, while we still have flesh on our bones."

He shrugged his shoulders. "It's not so easy to enjoy one-self."

"Well, let's try, anyhow. Let's drive through the mountains! Wouldn't that be wonderful? You like driving so much. But those meetings and investigations, all they ever do is bore you."

"Yes, that's true."

"Well, why do you always have to be doing things that bore you? That's no way to live."

"Try to understand. Can I tell those poor old men that no one's interested in their misfortunes, that Portugal is too small, that no one gives a damn what happens to her?" Henri leaned over Nadine and smiled gently. "Can I?"

"You could ring them up and tell them you're sick, and then we could head for Evora."

"It would break their hearts," Henri replied. "No, I just can't."

"Say instead that you don't want to," Nadine retorted bitterly.

"All right," he answered impatiently. "I don't want to."

"You're even worse than my mother," she grumbled, turning her face to the sand.

Henri fell back and stretched out alongside Nadine. "Let's enjoy ourselves!" Years ago, he had known how to enjoy himself ; yes, he would unhesitatingly have sacrificed the dreams of those old conspirators for the pleasures he had known then. He closed his eyes. He was lying on another beach beside a golden-skinned woman clad in a flowered sarong—Paula, the loveliest of all women. Palm trees were swaying lazily above their heads, and through the reeds he was watching three plump, laughing Jewish women inching their way into the sea, encumbered by their dresses, veils, and jewels. Sometimes at night they would sit together on the beach and watch Arab women, wrapped in their long garments, venturing into the water. And afterwards, in a tavern in an ancient Roman basement, they would sip syrupy coffee. Or they would sit in the market place and Henri would smoke a narghile while chatting with Amur Harsin. And then they would come back to their room and tumble happily on the bed. But what Henri remembered most nostalgically now were those mornings spent on the terrace of the hotel beneath the blue sky, amid the exciting fragrance of flowers. In the freshness of the newborn day, in the intense heat of noon, he would write; he would write, and under his feet the cement was burning hot. And then, dizzy from the sun and from words, he would go down to the shaded patio and drink a tall, cool anisette. The sky, the pink laurel bushes, Djerba's violent waters, the gay talk of idle nights, and especially the freshness and excitement of the mornings—these were the things he had come here to recapture. Why hadn't he recaptured that burning, sweet taste his life had once had? He had wanted so much to take this trip; for days he had thought of nothing else, for days he had dreamed of lying on the sand under the sun. And now he was here, stretched out on a sandy b.ach, beneath a hot sun. Only something was missing, missing from inside himself. Happiness, pleasure—he was no longer quite sure what those old, familiar words really meant. We have only five senses, and they become satiated so quickly. Even now his eyes were growing weary of looking out on that endless blue which never ceased being blue. He felt like ripping apart that smooth, satiny surface, felt like tearing Nadine's tender skin.

" It's getting cool," he said.

" Yes," she replied. Suddenly she pressed her whole body tight against him, and through his shirt he could feel her naked young breasts against his chest. " Warm me," she said.

He gently pushed her away. " Get dressed. Let's get back to the village."

" Afraid someone will see us?" Nadine's eyes were gleaming, her cheeks were slightly flushed. But he knew her mouth would still be cold. " What do you think they'd do to us? Do you think they'd stone us?" she asked, as if the prospect appealed to her.

" Get up. It's time to start back now."

She pressed the whole weight of her body against him; he was barely able to resist the desire that was sweeping through him, numbing his arms and legs. He liked her young breasts, her limpid skin; if only she would let herself be gently lulled by pleasure instead of romping about in bed with determined shamelessness ... She looked at him, her eyes half closed, and her hand crept down to his linen trousers.

" Let me ... won't you let me?"

Her mouth and hands were adroit, but he hated that look of triumphant assurance he saw in her eyes every time he gave in to her. " No," he said, " No, not here. Not like this."

He freed himself and stood up. Nadine's blouse was lying on the sand; he threw it over her shoulders.

" Why not?" she asked resentfully. " Maybe it would be a bit more fun out here in the open," she added languidly.

He dusted the sand off his clothes. " I wonder if you'll ever grow up to be a woman," he murmured in a falsely indulgent voice.

" I'll bet there isn't one woman in a hundred who enjoys getting laid. Most of them are just putting on an act, trying to be sophisticated."

" Let's go; let's not argue," he said, taking her arm. " Come on, we'll buy you some cakes and chocolate to eat in the car."

" You're treating me like a child," she said.

" No, I know you're not a child. I understand you a lot better than you think."

She looked at him suspiciously, and then a little smile formed on her lips. " You know, I don't always hate you," she said.

He squeezed her arm a little harder, and they walked silently together towards the village. The light of day was growing soft; boats were returning to the port and oxen were pulling them towards the beach. The villagers, standing or sitting together in small groups, watched silently. The men's shirts and the women's full skirts were brightly checkered, but the joyousness of those vivid colours was congealed in dismal immobility. Their stony faces were framed by black kerchiefs; their eyes, staring blankly at the horizon, were drained of hope. Not a gesture, nor a word; it was as if a curse had withered all their tongues.

" They make me want to scream," Nadine said.

" I doubt if they'd even hear you."

" What are they waiting for?"

" Nothing. And they know they're waiting for nothing."

In the main square, life sputtered feebly. The widows of fishermen who had drowned at sea were sitting at the edge of the sidewalk, begging; children were bawling noisily. At first Henri and Nadine had detested those rich women with their thick furs, whose majestic reply to all beggars was a curt, " Have patience!" But now, they, too, fled like thieves when the hands were held out to them; there were just too many.

" Buy yourself something," Henri said, stopping before a pastry shop.

She went in. Two children with shaven heads were pressing their noses against the window pane. When she came out again, her arms laden with paper bags, the children began squalling. She stopped.

" What are they saying?"

Henri hesitated. " They say you're lucky to be able to eat when you're hungry."

" Oh!"

With a furious gesture, she threw the swollen bags in their arms.

" No, I'll give them some money instead," Henri said.

She pulled him away. " Forget it; I've lost my appetite. Those filthy urchins!"

" But you said you were hungry."

" I told you I lost my appetite."

They got into the car and drove for a while in silence. Then, " We should have gone to some other country," Nadine muttered in a choked-up voice.

" Where?"

" I don't know. But you must know."

" As a matter of fact, I don't know," he replied.

" Well, there must be some country in the world where people live decently," she said.

Suddenly, Nadine burst into tears. Henri looked at her incredulously; Paula's tears were as natural as rain, but to see Nadine weeping was as disturbing as if he had stumbled on

Dubreuilh sobbing. He put his arm around her shoulders and drew her close to him.

"Don't cry," he said, stroking her rough hair. "Don't cry." Why had he been unable to make her smile? Why was his heart so heavy?

Nadine wiped her eyes and noisily blew her nose. "Were you happy when you were young?" she asked.

"Yes, I was happy."

"You see."

"Some day you'll be happy, too," he said.

He should have held her tightly, should have told her: "I'll make you happy, Nadine." At that instant, he felt like saying it—a momentary desire to pledge her his whole life. But he said nothing. "The past doesn't repeat itself; the past won't repeat itself," he thought.

"Vincent!" Nadine cried out, racing towards the exit.

Clad in his war correspondent's uniform, Vincent was waving his hand and smiling broadly. Nadine slipped on her crêpe-soled shoes and caught herself by grabbing Vincent's arm.

"Greetings!" she said.

"Greetings to the travellers!" Vincent said cheerfully. He looked Nadine over and whistled admiringly. "That's quite a get-up!"

"A real lady, huh!" Nadine said, spinning around. She looked elegant and almost feminine in her fur coat, her nylon stockings, her soft leather shoes.

"Here, let me take that," Vincent offered, relieving Henri of a large duffle bag he was dragging behind him. "What've you got in here? A body?"

"One hundred pounds of food!" Henri replied. "Nadine's going to restock the family cupboard. The problem now is how to get it over to Quai Voltaire."

"No problem," Vincent said triumphantly.

"You stole a jeep?" Nadine asked.

"I stole nothing," he replied. He crossed the driveway and stopped in front of a small black car. "She's all right, isn't she?"

"She's ours?" Henri asked.

"Ours," Vincent said. "Luc finally managed to wangle a deal. What do you think of her?"

" Very small," Nadine said.

" Well, it's going to be damned useful to us." Henri said, opening the door. They piled the baggage in the back as best they could.

" Will you take me driving?" Nadine asked.

" Are you nuts?" Vincent said. " This car's a working tool." He sat down at the wheel, and the car started off with a painful sputtering. " With all your cargo in here, it's a little crowded," he conceded.

" Are you sure you know how to drive?" Nadine asked.

" If you'd seen me the other night zipping along over mined roads in a jeep without headlights, you wouldn't insult me so gratuitously." Vincent turned to Henri. " I'll drop Nadine and take you to the paper," he said.

" Fine. How's *L'Espoir* been doing? I didn't get to see a single copy in that blasted country. Are we still using the postage-stamp format?"

" We are. They just authorised two new dailies, but for us they can't seem to find enough paper. But Luc'll fill you in a lot better than I can ; I've just got back from the front."

" Circulation hasn't fallen off, has it?"

" I don't believe so."

Henri was anxious to get back to the paper. Only Paula must surely have telephoned the station, must know that the train was on time. She would be sitting there waiting, her eyes riveted to the clock, listening attentively to every sound.

After they had left Nadine in the lift surrounded by her baggage, Henri said, " On second thoughts, I think I'll go home first."

" But the boys are waiting for you," Vincent protested.

" Tell them I'll be over in an hour."

" All right. I'll leave the Rolls to you," Vincent said. He stopped the car in front of the house. " Should I take the bags out?" he asked.

" Just that small one, thanks."

Unhappily, Henri pushed open the downstairs door, which banged noisily against a garbage pail ; the concierge's dog began barking. Before he even had a chance to knock, Paula had flung open the door to the flat.

" It's you! It's really you!" For a moment she remained motionless in his arms, and then she stepped back. " You

look wonderful. You're all sunburned! Was the trip back
tiring?" She smiled, but a little muscle in the corner of her
mouth was quivering spasmodically.

" Not at all," he replied, setting the suitcase down on the
couch. " Here are some things for you."

" How sweet of you!"

" Open it."

She opened the suitcase. Silk stockings, doeskin sandals and
a handbag to match, lengths of material, scarfs, gloves. He
had chosen every article with anxious care and he was a little
disappointed when, moved and yet vaguely indulgent, she only
looked down at them, without touching them, without even
bending over to examine them closely.

" How really sweet of you!" she repeated. And then, suddenly turning towards him, she exclaimed. " Your suitcases!
Where are they?"

" Downstairs in the car. Did you hear that *L'Espoir* got a
car? Vincent picked me up in it," he said animatedly.

" I'll call the concierge and get him to bring them up,"
Paula said.

" Don't bother," Henri said, adding very quickly, " How
did you spend the month? The weather wasn't too bad, was
it? Did you get out a little?"

" A little," she replied evasively, her face cold and expressionless.

" Who did you see? What did you do? Tell me all about
it."

" Oh, nothing very interesting happened," she replied.
" Let's not talk about me." Quickly, but in a listless voice, she
added, " Your book is a sensation, you know."

" I haven't heard a thing yet. Do they really like it?"

" Oh, the critics really didn't understand anything, of
course. But even so, they scented a masterpiece in it."

" It's good to hear that," he said with a reserved smile. He
would have liked to ask her a few questions, but he found
Paula's manner of speaking insufferable. He changed the
subject. " Did you see the Dubreuilhs? How are they?"

" I saw Anne for a moment one day; she's up to her ears
in work."

She answered his questions reluctantly, tight-lipped. And
he, he was burning with impatience to get back to his
life!

" Did you keep the back issues of *l'Espoir*?" he asked.

" I didn't read them."

" No?"

" There was nothing of yours in them. And I had other things to think about." She sought his eyes and suddenly her face came to life. " I've been doing a lot of thinking this past month and I've come to understand a great many things. I'm sorry about that scene I made before you left. I'm sincerely sorry."

" Oh, let's not talk about that!" he said. " First of all, you didn't make a scene."

" Yes," she insisted, " I did. And I repeat, I'm truly sorry. I've known for a long time that a woman can't be everything to a man like you. Not even all the women in the world. But I never really accepted it ; I'm prepared now to love you with complete generosity, to love you for what you are and not for what I want. You have your mission and that has to come above all else."

" What mission?"

She forced a smile. " I've come to realise that often I must have been a burden to you ; I can understand your wanting a little solitude. Well, you need not worry any more. I promise you your solitude, your freedom." She looked intensely at Henri. " You're free, my love, and I want you to know this and believe it. Besides, you've just finished proving it, haven't you?"

" Yes," he said, adding feebly, " But as I explained to you . . ."

" I remember," she said. " But with the change that's taken place in me, I can assure you you no longer have any reason to move to a hotel. Listen, you want independence, adventures ; but you want me, too, don't you?"

" Of course."

" Then stay here. I swear you won't have any reason to regret it. You'll see for yourself how much I've changed and how little I'll get in your way from now on." She stood up and reached for the telephone. " The concierge's nephew will bring your things up."

Henri rose and walked towards the stairway leading to the bedroom. " Later," he said to himself. He couldn't after all, begin torturing her again the moment he came back. " I'm going to clean up a little," he said. " They're waiting for me at the office. I just stopped off to give you a kiss."

" I understand perfectly," she replied tenderly.

" She's going to bend backwards to prove to me I'm free," he thought unhappily as he got into the little black car. " But it won't last. I won't stay there indefinitely," he said to himself bitterly. " I'll start taking care of that little matter tomorrow." But for the moment, he no longer wanted to think about Paula ; all he wanted was to luxuriate in his happiness at being back in Paris. The streets were grey and the people had been cold and hungry that winter ; but here, at least, everyone wore shoes. And then, you could speak to them, speak for them. In Portugal, the thing that was so depressing was the feeling of being a completely impotent witness to a totally foreign disaster.

Getting out of the car, he looked affectionately at the façade of the building. How had things gone at the paper while he was away? Was it true his novel was a success? He climbed the stairs quickly and when he reached the top he was greeted with cheers. A streamer hanging across the hallway read " Welcome Home!" Standing with their backs to the walls, his colleagues formed a military arch, but in place of swords, they held their fountain pens. They began singing an unintelligible couplet in which " Salazar " rhymed with " gal and car." Only Lambert was missing. Why?

" Everyone to the bar!" Luc cried out, giving Henri a hearty slap on the back. " How did it go?"

" What a sunburn!"

" Look at those clodhoppers."

" Are you going to do an article on Portugal?"

" Hey! Look at that shirt!"

They fingered his suit, his tie ; they shouted and joked and asked question after question while the bartender filled and refilled their glasses. Henri in turn questioned them. Circulation had dropped off a little, but the paper would soon be going back to a larger format, which would help make up the loss ; there had been some trouble with the censor—nothing very serious ; everyone had nothing but praise for his book, and he had received a tremendous amount of mail ; on his desk, he would find every issue of *L'Espoir* for the month he had been away. Preston, the Yank, was trying to arrange

for a larger allotment of paper, enabling them to put out a
Sunday magazine supplement. And there were a great many
other things to discuss. But all this noise, the voices, the
laughter, the problems, added to three nights of fitful sleeping,
made him dizzy—dizzy and happy. What a silly idea to have
gone to Portugal in search of a past that was dead and buried,
when the present was so joyfully alive!

" All I can say is I'm damned happy to be back!" he
exclaimed, his face beaming.

" And we're not exactly unhappy to have you back, you
know," Luc said. " In fact we were even beginning to need
you. I warn you, though, you're going to have a hell of a lot
of work to catch up on."

" Well, I hope so!"

The typewriters were clicking away. They separated in the
hallway after a few more jokes and bursts of laughter. How
young they seemed after coming from a country in which
everyone was ageless! Henri opened the door to his office
and sat down in his chair with the satisfaction of an old
bureaucrat. He spread out the latest issues of *L'Espoir* before
him. The usual by-lines, the same careful lay-out—not a
fraction of an inch of space wasted. He jumped back one
month and began leafing through the issues, one after another.
They had got along wonderfully without him, and that, of
course, was the surest proof of his success. *L'Espoir* wasn't
merely a wartime adventure; it was a solid enterprise.
Vincent's articles on Holland were excellent, and Lambert's on
the concentration camps even more so. No question about it,
they had hit precisely the right note—no nonsense, no lies, no
humbug. Because of its scrupulous honesty, *L'Espoir* appealed to the intellectuals, and it attracted the masses because
it was so alive. There was only one weak point: Sézenac's
articles were rather thin.

" Can I come in?" Lambert asked, standing in the doorway
and smiling timidly.

" Of course! Where've you been hiding? You could at
least have come to the station, you lazy bum."

" I didn't think there'd be enough room for four," Lambert
explained. " And their little party . . ." he added with a grimace. " Am I disturbing you?"

" Not at all. Pull up a chair."

" Was it a good trip?" Lambert asked. " I guess you've been asked that question twenty times already," he added, with a shrug of his shoulders.

" Good and bad. A beautiful setting, and seven million people starving to death."

" They certainly have excellent cloth," Lambert remarked, examining Henri approvingly. He smiled. " Is that the style there, orange shoes?"

" Orange or lemon. But it's good leather. There's plenty of everything for the rich ; that's the lousiest part of it. I'll tell you all about it later, but first fill me in on what's been happening here. I've just finished reading some of your articles ; they're damned good, you know."

" I felt as if I were back in school writing a composition : Describe your impressions while visiting a concentration camp," he said ironically. " I think there were more than twenty of us there writing on the same subject." Suddenly his face brightened. " Do you want to know something that's really good? Your book. I started it after driving a whole night and day without sleep, and believe me I was really beat. But I read it straight through, couldn't go to sleep until I finished it."

" You make me happy," Henri said.

Compliments always embarrassed him. Yet what Lambert said gave him real pleasure. It was precisely the way he had dreamed of being read—straight through in a single night by an impatient young man. That alone made writing worthwhile. Especially that.

" I thought maybe you'd like to see the reviews," Lambert said, tossing a thick yellow envelope on the desk. " You'll find my two cents' worth in there, too."

" You're damned right I'd like to see them. Thanks," Henri said.

Lambert looked at him questioningly. " Did you do any writing there?"

" An article on how I found things."

" And now you'll be starting another novel?"

" I'll get to it as soon as I have the time."

" Find the time ! " Lambert said. " While you were away, I was thinking . . ." he began, his face colouring. " You have to defend yourself."

" Against whom?" Henri asked with a smile.

Lambert hesitated again. " It seems that Dubreuilh has been waiting impatiently for you to get back. Don't let your-self get involved in his schemes . . ."

" I'm already more or less involved in them," Henri said.

" Well, if I were you, I'd get myself disinvolved fast!"

" No," Henri replied, smiling. " It just isn't possible nowa-days to stay apolitical."

Lambert's face grew sombre. " I suppose that means you disapprove of me, doesn't it?"

" Not at all. What I mean is that it's impossible for me. We're not the same age, you know."

" What's age got to do with it?" Lambert asked.

" You'll find out. You change, you begin to understand a lot of things when you get older." Henri smiled and added, " But I promise you I'll find time enough to continue writing."

" You have to," Lambert said.

" I just remembered something, my sermonising friend! What happened to those short stories you were telling me about?"

" They aren't worth a damn," Lambert replied.

" Let me have them. And then we'll have dinner together some evening and talk about them."

" Right," Lambert said. He got up. " I don't suppose you'll want to see her, but little Marie-Ange Bizet is dead set on interviewing you. She's been waiting for two hours. What'll I tell her?"

" That I never give interviews and that I'm up to my ears in work."

Lambert closed the door behind him and Henri emptied the contents of the yellow envelope on his desk. On a bulging folder, his secretary had written: " Correspondence—Novel." He hesitated a moment. He had written the novel during the war without ever having given any thought to what the future might hold for him; he hadn't even been sure that the future would hold anything at all for him. And now the book had been published, people had already read it. All at once, Henri found himself judged, discussed, classified, as he him-self had so often judged and discussed others. He spread out the clippings and began going through them one at a time. " A sensation," Paula had said, and he had thought she was exaggerating. But, as a matter of fact, the critics also used

some pretty impressive words. Lambert, of course, was prejudiced; Lachaume, too. And all those young critics who had
just come into their own had a natural predisposition for the
writers of the Resistance. But it was the admiring letters
sent by both friends and strangers that confirmed the verdict
of the press. Really, without getting a swelled head about it,
it was certainly enough to make any man happy. His pages,
written with deep feeling, had actually stirred people! Henri
stretched happily. In a way, it was miraculous—what had
just happened. Two years earlier, thick curtains had veiled
blue-painted windows; he had been completely shut off from
the black city, from the whole earth; his pen would pause
hesitantly over the paper. Now those unformed sounds in his
throat had become a living voice in the world; the secret
stirrings in his heart had been transformed into truths for
other hearts. " I should have tried explaining it to Nadine,"
he said to himself. " If others don't count, it's meaningless to
write. But if they do count, it's wonderful to gain their friendship and their confidence with words; it's magnificent to hear
your own thoughts echoed in them." He raised his eyes;
someone was opening the door.

" I've been waiting for you for two hours," said a plaintive
voice. " You could at least give me fifteen minutes." Marie-
Ange planted herself solidly in front of his desk. " It's for
Lendemain. A big front-page spread, with pictures."

" Look, I never give interviews."

" Exactly. That's why mine will be worth its weight in
gold."

Henri shook his head, and Marie-Ange said indignantly,
" You wouldn't ruin my whole career just because of a
principle?"

He smiled. Fifteen minutes meant so very much to her, and
it would cost him so very little! To tell the truth, he even felt
like talking about himself. Among the people who liked his
book, there were certainly some who wanted to know the
author better. And he felt like telling them about himself,
telling them so that their approval would really be directed at
him.

" You win," he said. " What do you want me to tell you?"

" First of all, where do you come from?"

" My father was a pharmacist in Tulle."

" And?"

Henri hesitated. It isn't easy to begin talking about yourself out of a clear sky.

"Go ahead," Marie-Ange prodded. "Tell me a few things about your childhood."

Like everyone else, he had memories enough, only they didn't seem very important to him. Except for that dinner, in the Henri II dining-room, when he finally delivered himself of his fear.

"All right, here's one for you," he said. "Actually, it's nothing, but for me it was the beginning of a great many things."

Her pencil poised above her note-book, Marie-Ange gave him an encouraging look.

"The major subject of conversation between my parents," he began, "was the disasters that were menacing the world— the red peril, the yellow peril, barbarism, decadence, revolution, bolshevism. And I imagined them all as horrible monsters who were going to swallow up all humanity. Well, at dinner one evening, my father was doing his usual prophesying—the revolution was imminent, civilisation was foundering. And my mother was nodding agreement, a look of terror on her face. And then suddenly I thought, ' But no matter what happens, the winners will still be men.' Maybe those aren't exactly the words I used, but that's the gist of it." Henri smiled. "The effect was miraculous. No more monsters. It was all here on earth, among human creatures, among ourselves."

"And then?" Marie-Ange asked.

"So, ever since then I've been hunting down monsters," he replied.

Marie-Ange looked perplexed. "But your story?" she asked. "How does it end?"

"What story?"

"The one you just began," she replied impatiently.

"It's finished; there is no other ending," Henri answered.

"Oh," Marie-Ange said, disappointed. "I was hoping for something picturesque," she added plaintively.

"There was nothing picturesque about my childhood," Henri said. "The pharmacy bored me to death and living out in the country was annoying. Fortunately, I had an uncle in Paris who managed to get me a job with *Vendredi*."

He hesitated. There were a great many things he could say

about his first years in Paris, but he didn't know which ones
to choose.

"*Vendredi* was a leftist paper?" Marie-Ange said. "You
had leftist ideas even then?"

"Let's say I loathed all rightist ideas."

"Why?"

Henri thought for a moment. "I was very ambitious when
I was twenty, and that's precisely why I was a democrat. I
wanted to be the best—but the best among equals. If the race
is fixed from the start, there's no point betting."

Marie-Ange scribbled in her note-book. She didn't look
too intelligent, and Henri tried to think of simple words with
which to express himself. "Between a chimpanzee and the
lowliest of men," he thought to himself, "there's an enormously greater difference than between that man and an
Einstein! A consciousness that gives evidence that it exists is
one of the absolutes." He was about to open his mouth, but
Marie-Ange spoke first.

"Tell me about your start."

"What start?"

"Your start in literature."

"I've always scribbled a bit."

"How old were you when *The Accident* was published?"

"Twenty-five."

"Dubreuilh was the one who gave you your start, wasn't
he?"

"Yes, he helped me a lot."

"How did you get to know him?"

"They sent me over to interview him once, and he made
me do the talking. He asked me to come back and see him
again, and I did . . ."

"Give me more details," Marie-Ange said plaintively.
"You're not very good at explaining things." She looked at
him. "What do you talk about when you're together?"

He shrugged his shoulders. "Everything and nothing, like
everyone else."

"Did he encourage you to write?"

"Yes. And when I finished *The Accident*, he got Mauvanes
to read it, and Mauvanes accepted it at once."

"Was it successful?"

"Call it a *succès d'estime*. You know, it's funny . . ."

"Yes, tell me something funny!" she said eagerly.

Henri hesitated. " It's funny how you begin by having big dreams of glory. And then, with the first little success, you're completely happy . . ."

Marie-Ange sighed. " I already have the titles and dates of your other books. Were you in the service?"

" In the infantry. Ordinary private. I never wanted to be an officer. Wounded the ninth of May at Mont Dieu near Vouziers ; evacuated to Montélimar ; back in Paris in September."

" What exactly did you do in the Resistance?"

" Luc and I founded *L'Espoir* in 1941."

" You did other things, too, didn't you?"

" Nothing very interesting. Skip it."

" Right. Exactly when did you write your last book?"

" Between '41 and '43."

" Have you started a new one?"

" No, but I'm going to."

" What'll it be? A novel?"

" A novel. But it's still very vague."

" I've heard some talk about a magazine."

" That's right. Dubreuilh and I are going to put out a monthly called *Vigilance*. It'll be published by Mauvanes."

" What's this political party Dubreuilh's founding?"

" It'd take much too long to explain."

" In a few words, then."

" Ask him."

" You can't get near him." Marie-Ange sighed. " You're funny, you know. If I were famous, I'd be getting myself interviewed all the time."

" Then you'd have no time left to do anything and you'd stop being famous. Now, you're going to be a nice little girl and let me get back to my work."

" But I still have a lot of questions. What did you think of Portugal?"

Henri shrugged his shoulders. " It stinks."

" What stinks?"

" Everything."

" Make that a little clearer. I can't just say to my readers: It stinks."

" Well, tell them that Salazar's paternalism is nothing but an unspeakable dictatorship, and that the Americans ought to get rid of him in a hurry," Henri said rapidly. " Unfortunately, it won't happen to-morrow; he's going to sell them air bases in the Azores."

Marie-Ange frowned, and Henri added, " If that upsets you, don't use it. I'm going to break it soon in *L'Espoir*, anyhow."

" Of course I'll use it!" Marie-Ange said emphatically. She studied Henri seriously. " What inner motives made you take that trip?"

" Listen, you don't have to ask idiotic questions to be a success as a newspaperwoman. And I repeat again that that's enough. Be a nice girl and leave quietly."

" I'd have liked a few anecdotes."

" I don't have any."

Marie-Ange minced out. Henri felt a sense of disappointment; Marie-Ange hadn't asked the right questions, and he had said none of the things he had had to say. But after all, just what did he have to say? " I'd like my readers to know who I am, but the trouble is I'm not quite sure myself." At any rate, in a few days he would get back to his book and he would try to define himself systematically.

He began going through his correspondence again, and he was staggered by the number of telegrams and clippings there were to be read, the letters to answer, the people to see! Luc had warned him; he had his work cut out for him. The following days he spent shut away in his office; he went home to Paula's only to sleep. He had just barely enough time to prepare his article and the printers grabbed it from him page by page. But after his too-long holiday, he was happy to get back to this excess of activity.

Without enthusiasm, he recognised Scriassine's voice on the telephone. " Listen here, you quitter, you've been back four days now, and nobody's seen you. Come over to the Isba right away. Rue Balzac."

" I'm sorry but I've got work to do."

" Stop feeling sorry and come over. We're all waiting to drink a champagne toast to you."

" Who's we?" Henri asked cheerfully.

" I, among others," said Dubreuilh's voice. " And Anne, and Julien. I've got a thousand things to tell you. What in hell are you doing over there anyhow? Can't you crawl out of your hole for an hour or two?"

"I was planning to come over to see you to-morrow," Henri said.

"Well, come over to the Isba now."

"All right! All right! I'm on my way."

Henri hung up the telephone and smiled; he was really looking forward to seeing Dubreuilh again. He picked up the telephone and called Paula. "It's me. The Dubreuilhs and Scriassine are waiting for us at the Isba . . . Yes, the Isba . . . I don't know any more about it than you. I'll come and pick you up in the car."

A half hour later they went down a stairway flanked on either side by magnificently dressed Cossacks. Paula was wearing a new evening gown and he realised that green did not, as a matter of fact, become her.

"What a peculiar place!" she murmured.

"With Scriassine, you can expect just about anything."

Outside, the night had been so empty, so quiet, that the Isba's lush luxury was disturbing; it made one think of a perverse ante-chamber to a torture dungeon. The quilted walls were blood-red, the folds of the draperies dripped blood, and the gypsy musicians' shirts were made of crimson satin.

"There you are! Did you slip by them?" Anne asked.

"They look safe and sound to me," Julien said.

"We were just attacked by a mob of reporters," Dubreuilh explained.

"Armed with cameras," Anne added.

"Dubreuilh was wonderful," Julien exclaimed, stammering with enthusiasm. "He said . . . Well, I forget exactly what he said, but anyhow it was damned well put. A couple of questions more, and he'd have sailed right into them."

They were all speaking at once, except for Scriassine, who was smiling and wearing a slightly superior look.

"I really did think Robert was going to start swinging," Anne said.

"He said: 'We're not a bunch of trained monkeys,'" Julien quoted, beaming broadly.

"I've always considered my face my own personal property," Dubreuilh remarked with dignity.

"The trouble is," Anne said, "that for people like you nudity begins with the face. Just showing your nose and eyes is exhibitionism."

"They don't take pictures of exhibitionists," Dubreuilh replied.

"That's a shame," said Julien.

"Drink up," Henri said, handing Paula a glass of vodka. "Drink up; we're way behind." He emptied his glass, and asked, "But how did they know you were here?"

"Yes," Julien said, looking at the others in surprise. "How did they know?"

"I imagine the *maître d'hôtel* telephoned," Scriassine said.

"But he doesn't know us," Anne said.

"He knows me," Scriassine said. He bit his lower lip, looking like a woman caught in the act. "I wanted him to give you the kind of attention you deserve, so I told him who you were."

"Well, it looks as if you succeeded," Henri said. Scriassine's childish vanity never failed to astonish him.

Dubreuilh burst out laughing. "So it was he who betrayed us! Now I've heard everything!" He turned abruptly towards Henri. "Well, what about that trip? Instead of playing, it would seem as if you spent your entire time attending conferences and conducting investigations."

"Oh, I managed to get in a lot of sight-seeing, too," Henri said.

"Your articles make one want to do one's sight-seeing somewhere else. It's a sad country!"

"It was sad, but it was beautiful too," Henri said cheerfully. "It's primarily sad for the Portuguese."

"I don't know whether you do it on purpose," Dubreuilh said, "but when you say that the sea is blue, blue somehow becomes a sinister colour."

"And at times it was. But not always," Henri smiled. "You know how it is when you write."

"Yes," said Julien, "you have to lie to avoid telling the truth."

"Anyhow, I'm happy to be back," Henri said.

"But you didn't seem to be in much of a hurry to see your friends again."

"You're wrong; I was," Henri replied. "Every morning I've been telling myself that I'd drop over to see you. And then, all of a sudden it was after midnight."

"Well, keep a sharper eye on your watch to-morrow," Dubreuilh said grumpily. "There's a pack of things I have to bring you up to date on." He smiled. " I think we're getting off to a good start."

" You're beginning to recruit? Has Samazelle decided to go along?" Henri asked.

" He doesn't agree on all points, but I'm sure we'll be able to compromise," Dubreuilh answered.

" No serious talk to-night!" Scriassine said, motioning to the monocled *maître d'hôtel.* " Two bottles of Mumm's, brute."

" Is that absolutely necessary?" Henri asked.

" Yes. Strict orders!" Scriassine followed the *maître d'hôtel* with his eyes. " He's really come down a notch or two since '39. Used to be a colonel."

" Do you come to this joint often?" Henri asked.

" Whenever I feel like breaking my heart, I come here and listen to the music."

" But there are so many less expensive ways of doing it," Julien said. " Besides, all hearts were broken long ago," he concluded vaguely.

" Well, my heart breaks only to jazz," Henri said. " All your gypsies do to me is ruin my feet."

" Oh!" Anne exclaimed.

" Jazz," Scriassine said musingly. " I wrote several definitive pages on jazz in *The Son of Abel.*"

" Do you really believe it's possible to write something definitive?" Paula said haughtily.

" I won't discuss it; you'll be reading the book soon," Scriassine said. " The French edition will be out any day now." He shrugged his shoulders. " Five thousand copies! It's ridiculous! They ought to make exceptions for worthwhile books. How many did they allow you?"

" The same. Five thousand," Henri replied.

" Absurd! After all, what you've written is *the* book on the Occupation. A book like that should have a printing of at least a hundred thousand copies."

" Fight it out with the Minister of Information," Henri said. Scriassine's overbearing enthusiasm irritated him. Among friends, one avoids speaking of one's books; it embarrasses everyone and amuses no one.

" We're bringing out a magazine next month," Dubreuilh said. " Well, let me tell you, getting paper was one hell of a job!"

"That's because the Minister doesn't know his business." Scriassine said. "Paper? I'll find him all he wants!"

Once he began attacking a technical problem in his didactic voice, Scriassine was inexhaustible. While he was complacently flooding France with paper, Anne said quietly to Henri, "You know, I don't think there's been a book in the last twenty years that's affected me as much as yours. It's a book . . . Well, exactly the kind of book you'd want to read after these last four years. Some parts moved me so much that I had to put it aside and take a walk in the streets to calm myself down." Suddenly she blushed. "You feel idiotic when you say things like that, but it's just as idiotic not to say them. Anyhow, it can't do any harm."

"In fact, it even gives pleasure," Henri said.

"You moved a great many people," Anne continued. "All those who don't want to forget," she added with passion.

He smiled at her gratefully. To-night she was wearing a Scotch-plaid dress which made her look years younger, and she had applied her make-up with care. In one way, she looked much younger than Nadine. Nadine never blushed.

Scriassine raised his voice, "That magazine could be a very powerful instrument of culture and action, but only on condition that it expresses more than the opinions of a tight little coterie. I maintain that a man like Louis Volange ought to be a member of your team."

"Out of the question," Dubreuilh stated flatly.

"An intellectual's lapse isn't that serious," Scriassine said. "Name me the intellectual who has never made a mistake." Gravely he added, "Should a man be made to bear the weight of his mistakes all his life?"

"To have been a Party member in Russia in 1930 wasn't a mistake," Dubreuilh said.

"If you have no right to make a mistake, it was a crime."

"It's not a question of right," Dubreuilh replied.

"How dare you set yourselves up as judges?" Scriassine said, without listening to him. "Do you know Volange's reasons, his explanations? Are you sure that all the people you accept on your team are better men than he?"

"We don't judge," Henri said. "We choose sides. There's a big difference."

Volange had been clever enough not to compromise himself too seriously, but Henri had sworn that he would never shake hands with him again. When he read the articles Louis wrote in the Free French Zone, he hadn't been the least bit surprised by what they said. From the moment they left college, their friendship had gradually become an almost open enmity.

With a blasé air, Scriassine shrugged his shoulders and motioned to the *maître d'hôtel*. "Another bottle!" Again, he stealthily studied the old *émigré*. "A striking head, isn't it? The bags under the eyes, the droop of the mouth, all the symptoms of decay. Before the war you could still find a trace of arrogance on his face. But the weakness, the dissoluteness of their caste gnaws at them. And their treachery. . . ." He stared in fascination at the man.

"Scriassine's serf!" Henri thought. He, too, had fled his country, and there they called him a traitor. That probably was the reason for his immense vanity: since he had no homeland, no one to stand up for him but himself, he needed always to reassure himself that somewhere in the world his name meant something.

"Anne!" Paula exclaimed. "How horrible!"

Anne was emptying her glass of vodka into her champagne glass. "It livens it up," she explained. "Why don't you try it? It's good."

Paula shook her head.

"Why aren't you drinking?" Anne asked. "Things are gayer when you drink."

"Drinking makes me drunk," Paula answered.

Julien began to laugh. "You make me think of that girl— a charming young thing I met on the Rue Montparnasse in front of a little hotel—who said to me, ' As far as I'm concerned, living kills me.' "

"She didn't say that," said Anne.

"She could have said it."

"Anyhow, she was right," Anne said in a drunk's sententious voice. "To live is to die a little."

"For God's sake, shut up!" Scriassine half shouted. "If you don't want to listen, at least let me listen!" The orchestra had begun an enthusiastic attack on *Dark Eyes*.

"Let him break his heart," Anne said.

"In the breaking surf a broken heart . . ." Julien murmured.

" Will you *please* shut up!"

Everyone fell silent. Scriassine's eyes were fixed on the violinists' dancing fingers; a dazed look on his face, he was listening to a memory of time long past. He thought it manful to impose his whims on others, but they gave in to him as they would to a neurotic woman. Their very docility should have made him suspicious, as it did. Henri smiled as he watched Dubreuilh tapping his fingers on the table; his courtesy seemed infinite—if you didn't put it too long to the test. You then learned soon enough that it had its limits. Henri felt like having a quiet talk with him, but he was not impatient. He didn't care for champagne, or gypsy music, or all this false luxury; nevertheless, simply to be sitting in a public place at two o'clock in the morning was cause for celebration. " We're home again," he said to himself. " Anne, Paula, Julien, Scriassine, Dubreuilh—my friends!" The word crackled in his heart with all the joyfulness of a Christmas sparkler.

While Scriassine was furiously applauding, Julien led Paula on to the dance floor. Dubreuilh turned towards Henri. " All those old codgers you met in Portugal, are they really hoping for a revolution?"

" They hope. Unfortunately Salazar won't fall before Franco goes, and the Americans don't seem to be in a hurry."

Scriassine shrugged his shoulders. " I can understand their not being anxious to create Communist bases in the Mediterranean."

" Do you mean to say that out of fear of Communism you'd go so far as to endorse Franco?" Henri asked incredulously.

" I'm afraid you don't understand the situation," Scriassine replied.

" Don't worry," Dubreuilh said cheerfully. " We understand it very well." Scriassine opened his mouth, but Dubreuilh cut him off with a laugh. " Yes, you're farseeing all right, but you're still no Nostradamus. Your crystal ball is no clearer than ours when it comes to predicting things that'll happen fifty years from now. One thing is sure right now though, and that is that the Stalinist menace is purely an American invention."

Scriassine looked at Dubreuilh suspiciously. " You talk exactly like a Communist."

" Do you think a Communist would ever say aloud what I just said?" Dubreuilh asked. " When you attack America, they accuse you of playing into the hands of the fifth column."

" The line'll change soon enough," Scriassine replied. " You're just anticipating it by a few weeks, that's all." He knitted his brow. " I've often been asked in what ways you differ from the Communists. And I have to admit I'm always at a loss for an answer."

Dubreuilh laughed. " Well, don't answer then."

" Hey!" Henri said. " I thought serious talk was out of order to-night."

With an irritated shrug of his shoulders, Scriassine indicated that it was frivolity that was now out of order. " Is that a way of getting out of it?" he asked, looking at Dubreuilh accusingly.

" Now look," Dubreuilh answered. " I'm no Communist, and you know it."

" I'm not so sure of that." Scriassine's face underwent a sudden transformation; he gave Dubreuilh his most charming smile. " Really, I'd like to learn more about your point of view."

" I believe the Communists are backing the wrong horse just now," Dubreuilh said. " I know why they're supporting Yalta; they want to give Russia enough time to get on her feet again. But as a result, the world is going to find itself divided into two camps with every reason to pounce on each other."

" Is that the only thing you have against them? An error of judgment?" Scriassine asked severely.

" What I have against them is not being able to see farther than the end of their noses," Dubreuilh shrugged his shoulders. " Reconstruction is all very well and good, but not when it's done without considering the means. They go on accepting American aid, but one of these days they're going to be sorry. One thing will lead to another, and eventually France will find herself completely under America's thumb."

Scriassine emptied his glass and banged it down on the table. " Now that's what I call an optimistic prediction!" In a serious voice, he continued rapidly, " I don't like America and I don't believe in the Atlantic community. But I sincerely hope America predominates, because the important question in this day and age is one of abundance. And only America can give it to us."

" Abundance? " Dubreuilh said. " For whom? And at what price? That would be a pretty picture, to be colonised by America! " he added indignantly.

" Would you rather Russia annexed us? " Scriassine asked. He stopped Dubreuilh with a sharp gesture. " I know. You're dreaming of a united, autonomous, socialist Europe. But if Europe refuses the protection of the United States, she'll inevitably fall into the hands of Stalin."

Dubreuilh shrugged his shoulders. " Russia has no intention of annexing anything at all."

" In any case, that Europe you dream so much about will never come about," Scriassine said.

" That's what you say! " Dubreuilh protested. " Anyhow," he continued heatedly, " here in France we have a clear-cut objective—to achieve a real popular front government. And for that, we need a non-Communist left that's able to hold its own." He turned towards Henri. " We mustn't lose any more time. At the moment people feel that the future is wide open. Let's not wait until they become discouraged."

Scriassine downed a glass of vodka and lost himself in contemplating the *maître d'hôtel*. He had given up talking sense to fools.

" You say you've got off to a good start? " Henri asked Dubreuilh.

" We've started, but now we have to continue. I'd like you to see Samazelle as soon as possible. There's going to be a committee meeting on Saturday and I'm counting on your being there."

" Let me have a little time to catch my breath," Henri said, giving Dubreuilh a slightly worried look. It wasn't going to be easy defending himself against that nice, imperative smile.

" I purposely delayed the meeting so that you could be there," Dubreuilh said reprovingly.

" You shouldn't have," Henri replied. " I assure you you're overestimating my qualifications."

" And you your lack of them," Dubreuilh said. He looked at Henri severely. " You've got a pretty good picture these last four days of what's been happening; things have been moving along at a damned rapid pace. You must have realised by now that neutrality is no longer possible."

"But I've never been neutral!" Henri protested. "I've always agreed to go along with the S.R.L."

"Is that right? Well, let's see now . . . Your name and a few appearances—that's all you ever promised me."

"Don't forget I have a newspaper on my hands," Henri replied.

"Precisely. It's the paper I have in mind more than anything else. It can't remain neutral any more."

"But it never was!" Henri said, surprised.

"How can I get it through your thick skull?" Dubreuilh said, shrugging his shoulders. "Being on the side of the Resistance doesn't constitute a political programme nowadays."

"No, I don't have a programme," Henri admitted. "But whenever the occasion demands it, L'Espoir does choose sides."

"No, it doesn't, not any more so than all the other papers. You argue about trifles, but when it comes to the big things, all of you somehow manage to agree on covering up the truth." There was anger in Dubreuilh's voice. "From Figaro to L'Humanité, you're all nothing but a bunch of humbugs. You say yes to De Gaulle, yes to Yalta, yes to everything; you act as if you believe there's still a Resistance and that we're heading steadily towards socialism. Your friend Luc has really been going to town with that hogwash in his recent editorials. All we're doing, really, is marking time; in fact, we're even beginning to retreat. And not a one of you has the guts to tell the truth!"

"I always thought you agreed with L'Espoir," Henri said. He was stunned; his heart began beating rapidly. During the past four days, he had meshed with that paper as one meshes with one's own life. And then all of a sudden L'Espoir was being indicted. And by Dubreuilh!

"Agree with what?" Dubreuilh asked. "L'Espoir has no line. You're constantly complaining that nothing's been nationalised. And what do you do about it? Nothing. Now what would be interesting would be to tell who's putting on the brakes, and why."

"I don't want to take a stand for or against any particular

class," Henri said. " Reforms will come about when public opinion demands them, and what I'm trying to do is arouse opinion. I can't very well do that if I'm going to set half my readers against me, can I?"

" You can't possibly believe that the class struggle is outmoded, can you?" Dubreuilh asked suspiciously.

" No."

" Then don't come telling me about public opinion," Dubreuilh said. " On one side, you have the proletariat which wants reforms, and on the other, the bourgeoisie which doesn't. The middle classes are treading water because they don't know where their true interests lie any more. But don't get the idea you can influence them; it's the situation that will do the deciding."

Henri hesitated. No, the class struggle wasn't outmoded. All right. But did that automatically doom any appeal to people's good intentions, to their common sense? " Their interests are quite complex," he replied. " I'm not at all convinced you can't influence them."

Dubreuilh was about to say something, but Henri cut him off. " Another thing," he said spiritedly. " The workers who read *L'Espoir* read it because it gives them a change from *L'Humanité*; it gives them a breath of fresh air. If I take a class stand, I'll either repeat what the Communist papers are saying, or I'll take issue with them. And either way, the workers will drop me." In a conciliatory voice, he added, " I reach a lot more people than you do, you know. That means I have to have a much broader platform."

" Yes, you do reach a lot of people," Dubreuilh said. " But you yourself just gave the reason why. If your paper pleases everybody, it's because it disturbs nobody. It attacks nothing, defends nothing, evades every problem. It simply makes for pleasant reading, like a local sheet."

Dubreuilh's outburst was followed by a brief silence. Paula had returned to the table and was sitting next to Anne; she seemed outraged, and even Anne was quite embarrassed. Julien had disappeared. Scriassine, awakened from his meditations, looked back and forth from Henri to Dubreuilh as if he were watching a tennis match. But it was a strictly one-sided match; Henri had been overwhelmed by the sudden violence of the attack.

" What are you getting at?" he asked.

"Stop shilly-shallying," Dubreuilh answered. "Take the bit in your teeth and define your position in relation to the Communist Party."

Henri looked at Dubreuilh suspiciously. It often happened that Dubreuilh would heatedly involve himself in the affairs of others, and, just as often, you came to realise that he had in fact made them his own affairs. "In short, what you're proposing is that I accept the S.R.L.'s entire programme."

"Yes," Dubreuilh replied.

"But you don't really expect L'Espoir to become the official organ of the movement, do you?"

"It would be perfectly natural," Dubreuilh said. "L'Espoir's weakness stems from the fact that it doesn't represent anything. Besides, without a newspaper the movement has almost no chance of getting anywhere. Since our goals are the same . . ."

"Our goals, but not our methods," Henri interrupted. Regretfully, he thought, "So that's why Dubreuilh was so impatient to see me!" The good spirits with which he began the evening had, in the course of the last few minutes, completely deserted him. "Isn't it ever possible to spend an evening among friends without talking politics?" he asked himself. There was nothing in their conversation so terribly urgent that Dubreuilh couldn't have put it off for another day or two. He had become as much a crank as Scriassine.

"Precisely. And take my word for it, it would be to your advantage to change your methods," Dubreuilh said.

Henri shook his head. "I'll show you letters I receive every day, letters from intellectuals especially—teachers, students. What they all like about L'Espoir is its fairness. If I tack on a programme, I lose their trust."

"Of course. Intellectuals are delighted when you encourage them to be neither fish, flesh, nor fowl," Dubreuilh replied. "Their trust? Who needs it?"

"Give me two or three years and I'll lead them by the hand to the S.R.L."

"If you really believe that, then all I can say is you're a starry-eyed idealist!" Dubreuilh said.

"Possibly," Henri replied with a slight show of annoyance. "But in '41 they branded me an idealist too." Firmly, he added, "I have my own ideas about what a newspaper should be."

Dubreuilh gestured evasively. "We'll talk about it again. But believe me, six months from now either *L'Espoir* aligns itself with our politics or it's all washed up."

"All right, we'll talk about it again in six months," Henri said.

Suddenly, he felt tired and at a loss. Dubreuilh's proposition had taken him by surprise, but he was absolutely resolved to do nothing about it. He felt a desperate need to be alone in order to clear his mind. "I have to be getting home," he said.

Paula remained silent on the way home, but they were no sooner in the apartment than she began her attack. "Are you going to give him the paper?"

"Of course not," Henri said.

"Are you really sure?" she asked. "Dubreuilh wants it, and he is stubborn."

"I'm pretty stubborn myself."

"But you always end up by giving in to him," Paula said, her voice suddenly exploding. "Why did you ever agree to join the S.R.L.? As if you didn't have enough to do already! You've been back for four days now, and we haven't had five minutes together. And you haven't written a line of your novel!"

"I'll get back to it to-morrow. Things are beginning to settle down at the paper."

"That's no reason to burden yourself with new loads," Paula said, her voice rising. "Dubreuilh did you a favour ten years ago; he can't expect you to repay him for it for the rest of your life."

"But I'm not working with him simply to repay a favour, Paula. The thing interests me."

She shrugged her shoulders. "Don't give me that!"

"I mean it," he said.

"Do you believe all that talk about a new war?" she asked with a worried look.

"No," Henri replied. "There may be a few firebrands in America, but they don't like war over there. One thing you can be sure of—there's going to be a radical change in the world for better or for worse. What we've got to do is to try to make it a change for the better."

"The world is always changing. But before the war you let it change without getting yourself involved," Paula said.

Henri started up the stairway. " It isn't before the war any more," he replied, yawning.

" But why can't we go back to living like we did then?"

" Circumstances are different—and so am I." He yawned again. " I'm tired."

Yes, he was tired, but when he lay down in bed beside Paula he couldn't sleep. The champagne, the vodka, Dubreuilh, all conspired to keep him awake. No, he wouldn't give him *L'Espoir*. That was so clear to him that it needed no justifying. Nevertheless, he wished he could find a few good reasons for his stand. Was he really an idealist? And exactly what did that mean? Naturally, and to a certain extent, he believed in people's freedom, in their basic good will, in the power of ideas. *You can't possibly believe that the class struggle is outmoded, can you?* No, he couldn't believe it, but what, after all, did that mean? He turned over on his back. He felt like lighting a cigarette, but he was afraid of awakening Paula, who would have been only too happy to distract him in his sleeplessness. He didn't move. " My God!" he said to himself with a sharp feeling of anxiety. " How ignorant we really are!" He read a great deal, but he had little real knowledge excepting in the field of literature. And even in literature . . . Until now it hadn't bothered him—no need for any specialised knowledge to fight in the Resistance or to found a clandestine newspaper. He had believed that that was the way it would continue to be. Obviously he had been wrong. What is an opinion? What is an idea? What power do words have? On whom? And under what circumstances? If you publish a newspaper, you have to be able to answer those questions. And what with one thing leading to another, you eventually question everything. " You have to decide in ignorance," Henri said to himself. " Even Dubreuilh often acts blindly—Dubreuilh, with all his learning." Henri sighed; he was unable to resign himself to this defeat. There are degrees of ignorance, and the simple fact was that he was particularly ill-equipped for the political life. " Well, I'll just have to start working at it," he said to himself. But if he really wanted to extend his knowledge, it would require years of study. Economics, history, philosophy —he would never be done with it! What a job! And all that just to come to terms with Marxism! Writing would be completely out of the question, and he wanted to write. Well?

Whatever happened, one thing was sure: he wasn't going to let *L'Espoir* fail simply because he wasn't an expert on all the fine points of historical materialism. He closed his eyes. There was something unfair in this whole thing. He felt obliged, like everyone else, to take an active interest in politics. That being the case, it shouldn't require a specialised apprenticeship; if politics was a field reserved for technicians, then they shouldn't be asking him to get mixed up in it.

"What I need is time!" Henri thought as he awakened the next morning. "The only problem is finding enough time." The living-room door opened and closed again. Paula had already gone out; now, back again, she was tiptoeing about the room. He threw back the covers. "If I lived alone, I'd save hours." No more idle conversations, no more formal meals. While drinking his coffee in the little Café Biard on the corner, he would read the morning papers, would work right up to the moment when he would have to leave for the office; a sandwich would do for lunch, and his day's work over, he would have a quick dinner and read late into the night. That way, he would be able to keep everything going at once—*L'Espoir*, his novel, his reading. "I'll speak to Paula this morning," he told himself firmly.

"Did you sleep well?" Paula asked cheerfully.

"Very well."

She was arranging flowers in a vase on one of the tables and humming cheerfully to herself. Ever since Henri's return, she made a point of being always cheerful, ostentatiously cheerful. "I made you some real coffee. And we still have a little fresh butter left."

He sat down and spread a piece of toast with butter. "Did you eat?"

"I'm not hungry."

"You're never hungry."

"Oh, don't worry about me. I eat; in fact I eat quite well."

He bit into the toast. What could he do if she didn't want to eat? After all, he couldn't very well force-feed her. "You were up very early this morning," he said.

"Yes, I couldn't sleep." She placed a thick album with gilt-edged pages on the table. "I've been putting in the pictures you took in Portugal." She opened the album and pointed to the stairway of Braga. Nadine, smiling, was sitting on one of the steps. " You see, I'm not trying to escape the truth," she said.

" Yes, I know." .

No, she wasn't escaping the truth but, much more disconcerting, she saw through it. She turned back several pages. " Even in these old snapshots of you as a child you had that same distrustful sort of smile. How little you've changed!" Before, he had enjoyed helping her collect and arrange his souvenirs; to-day it all seemed so futile. He was annoyed by Paula's stubborn determination to exhume and embalm him.

" Here you are when I first met you!"

" I don't look very bright, do I?" he said, pushing away the album.

'" You were young; you were very demanding," she said. She stood in front of Henri and, in a sudden burst of anger, asked, " Why did you give an interview to *Lendemain*?"

" Oh! Is the new issue out?"

" Yes, I just bought a copy." She went to get the magazine at the other end of the living-room, brought it back, and threw it on the table. " I thought we'd decided you'd never grant any interviews."

" If you stick to all the decisions you make . . ."

" But this was an important one. You used to say that when you start smiling at reporters, you're ripe for the Académie Française."

" I used to say a lot of things."

" It really pained me when I saw pictures of you spread all over the cover," she said.

" But you're always so delighted when you see my name in print."

" First of all, I'm not delighted. And secondly, that's quite different."

Paula was not one to stop at a contradiction, but this particular one irritated Henri. She wanted him to be the " most glorious of all men," and yet she affected a disdain for glory. She insisted upon dreaming of herself as long ago he had dreamed of her—proud, sublime. But all the while, of course, she was living on earth, like everyone else. " It's not a very good life she has," he thought with a twinge of pity. " It's only natural for her to need some sort of compensation."

" I wanted to help the kid out," he said in a conciliatory voice. " She's just getting started and doesn't know her way around yet."

Paula smiled at him tenderly. " And you don't know how to say no."

There was no double meaning hidden behind her smile. He smiled. " You're right. I don't know how to say no."

He placed the weekly on the table. On the front page, his picture smiled back at him. " Interview with Henri Perron." He wasn't the slightest bit interested in what Marie-Ange thought of him. Yet reading those printed words, he felt a little of the naïve faith of a peasant reading the Bible. It was as if he had succeeded at last in discovering himself through words he himself had fathered. " In the shadows of the pharmacy in Tulle, the magic of red and blue jars . . . But the quiet child hated the medicinal smells, the restricted life, the shabby streets of his birthplace . . . As he grew up the call of the big city became more and more pressing . . . He swore to raise himself above the bleak greyness of mediocrity ; in a secret corner of his heart, he even hoped some day to rise higher than all others . . . A providential meeting with Robert Dubreuilh . . . Dazzled, disconcerted, torn between admiration and defiance, Henri Perron trades his adolescent dreams for the true ambitions of a man ; he begins to work furiously . . . At twenty-five, a small book is enough to bring glory into his life. Brown hair, commanding eyes, a serious mouth, direct, open, and yet secret . . ." He tossed the paper aside. Marie-Ange was no idiot ; she knew him pretty well. And yet to titillate the working girls, she had made him into a small-time opportunist.

" You're right," he said. " There's no sense in talking to reporters. All a life means to them is a career ; work is nothing but the path to success. And what they mean by success is making a big splash and piling up a lot of money. You just can't get them to think any other way."

Paula smiled indulgently. " Did you notice the nice things she said about your book? Only she's like all the others— they admire but don't understand."

" As a matter of fact, they don't admire as much as all that, you know. It's the first novel published since the liberation ; they're practically forced to praise it."

In the long run, the symphony of eulogies became annoying. It amply demonstrated the timeliness of his novel, but in no way said anything about its merits. Henri finally even came to the conclusion that the book owed its success to misunderstandings. Lambert believed he had meant to exalt individualism through collective action, and Lachaume on the other hand, believed it preached the sacrifice of the individual to collectivism. Everyone emphasised the book's moral character. And yet Henri had set the story in the Resistance almost by pure chance. He had thought of a man and of a situation, of a certain relationship between man's past life and the crisis through which he was passing, and of a great many other things which none of the critics mentioned. Was it his fault or the readers'? The public, Henri was forced to conclude, had liked a completely different book from the one he believed he was offering them.

" What are you planning to do to-day?" he asked affectionately.

" Nothing special."

" But what?"

Paula considered. " Well, I think I'll ring up my dressmaker and get her to take a look at those beautiful materials you brought back."

" And after that?"

" Oh, I always manage to find something to do," she said gaily.

" By that you mean you have nothing at all to do," Henri said. He looked at Paula severely. " I've been doing a lot of thinking about you during the last month. I think it's a crime for you to spend your days vegetating inside these four walls."

" You call this vegetating!" Paula said. She smiled gently, the way she used to long ago, and there was all the wisdom of the world in that smile. " When you love someone, you're not vegetating."

" But loving isn't a vocation."

She interrupted him. " You're wrong. For me, it is a vocation."

" I've been thinking over what I said to you Christmas Eve," he said, " and I'm sure I was right. You've got to take up singing again."

" For years I've been living exactly the same way I do now," Paula said, " Why are you suddenly so concerned?"

" During the war it was possible to be satisfied to just kill

time. But the war is over now. Listen to me," he said authoritatively, " you're going to tell old man Grépin that you want
to go back to work. I'll help you choose your songs; I'll even
try to write a few for you, and I'll ask the boys if they'd care
to try their hand at it, too. Come to think of it, that would be
right up Julien's alley! I'm sure he'd be able to write a few
charming ballads for you, and Brugère could put them to
music. Just wait and see the repertoire we'll put together!
Whenever you're ready, Sabriro'll give you an audition, and
I guarantee he'll get you star booking at the 45 Club. After
that, you're made!"

He realised he had spoken too volubly, with too much
enthusiasm. Paula gave him a look of startled reproach.
" And then what?" she said. " Will I mean any more to you
if you see my name on posters?"

He shrugged his shoulders. " Don't be foolish! Of course
not. But it's better to be doing something than to do nothing.
I try to write, and you ought to sing because you've got a real
gift for it."

" I'm alive and I love you. To me, that's not nothing."

" You're playing with words," he said impatiently. " Why
don't you want to give it a try? Have you become so lazy?
Or are you afraid? Or what?"

" Listen," she said in a voice suddenly grown hard, " even if
all those vanities—success, fame—still meant something to
me, I wouldn't start out on a second-rate career at the ripe
age of thirty-seven. When I sacrificed that tour in Brazil
for you, it was a final retirement. I have no regrets. Let's just
forget the whole thing."

Henri opened his mouth to protest. Without consulting
him, she had only too willingly decided to make that sacrifice, and now she seemed to be holding him responsible for
it! He held his tongue and gave Paula a perplexed look.
He had never been able to decide whether she really scorned
fame or whether she was afraid of not being able to attain
it.

" Your voice is as beautiful as ever," he said. " And so are
you."

" Not quite," she replied impatiently, shrugging her
shoulders. " I know exactly how it would turn out. To make
you happy, a handful of intellectuals would proclaim my
genius for a few months. And then—good-bye. I might have

been a Damia or a Piaf, but I missed my chance. Well, it's too bad! Let's drop it."

She could never become a great star now, no doubt about that. But it would take only some small success to make her lower her sights. In any event, her life would certainly be less wretched if only she took an active interest in something. "And it would be ideal for me!" he said to himself. He knew only too well that the problem concerned his own life even more than Paula's.

"Even if you can't take the world by storm, it would still be worth it," he said. "You have your voice, your special talent. Don't you think it would be interesting to try to get all you can out of it? I'm certain you'd find life a lot more satisfying."

"But I find it satisfying enough as it is," she replied, a look of exaltation brightening her face. "You don't seem to understand what my love for you means to me."

"I do understand! But," he continued cuttingly, "you won't do, for love of me, what I ask you to do."

"If you had good reasons for asking, I'd do it," she said gravely.

"Actually, of course, you prefer your reasons to mine."

"Yes," she said calmly. "Because they're better. You've been giving me a purely superficial point of view, worldly reasons that aren't really your own."

"Well, as for your point of view, I honestly don't see what it is!" he said peevishly. He stood up; it was useless to continue the discussion. He would try instead to confront her with a *fait accompli*—bring her songs, make appointments for her. "All right, let's drop it. But I'm telling you, you're wrong."

She hesitated a moment, smiled, and then asked, "Are you going to go to work now?"

"Yes."

"On your novel?"

"Yes."

"Good," she said.

He climbed the stairs. He was anxious to get back to his writing, and he was happy at the thought that his novel, at least, wasn't going to be the slightest bit edifying. He still had no exact idea of what he was going to do; the only assignment he had set himself was to enjoy himself fully in being sincere. He spread his notes in front of him—almost a hundred pages. It was good to have put them away for a month; now he would be able to reread them with a fresh eye. He plunged into them joyfully, happy to rediscover memories and impressions formed into careful and smooth-flowing sentences. But after a while he began to worry. What was he going to do with all this stuff? These scribblings had neither head nor tail, even though they did have something in common—a certain feeling, a climate, the climate of the pre-war era. And that suddenly bothered him. He had thought vaguely, " I shall try to give the flavour of my life." As if such a thing were a perfume, labelled, trade-mark-registered, always the same, year after year. But the things he had to say about travelling, for example, were all in terms of a young man of twenty-five, the young man he had been in 1935; they had nothing at all to do with what he had experienced in Portugal. The story of his affair with Paula was equally dated; neither Lambert, nor Vincent, nor any of the boys he knew would have any similar reactions to-day. And besides, with five years of living under the German occupation behind her, a young woman of twenty-seven would be very different from Paula. There was one solution: deliberately to place the book around 1935. But he had no desire to write a " period " novel recreating a world that no longer was. On the contrary, what he had hoped for in jotting down those lines was to throw himself life and whole on to paper. Well then, he would have to write the story in the present, transposing the characters and events. " Transpose—what an annoying word! what a stupid word!" he said to himself. " It's preposterous, the liberties one takes with the characters in a novel. They're transported from one century to the next, pulled out of one country and pushed into another, the present of one person is glued to the past of a second. And all of it is larded with personal fantasies. If you look closely enough, every character in a novel is a monster, and all art consists in preventing the reader from looking too closely. All right then, let's not transpose. Let's make up characters out of whole cloth, characters who have nothing at all in common with Paula, with Louis, with myself. I've done it before. Only this time it was the truth about my own experiences that I wanted to tell . . ." He pushed aside the stack of notes. Yes, it was a bad idea, this setting things down hap-

hazardly. The best way was to proceed as usual, to begin
with an outline, with a precise purpose. " But what purpose?
What truth do I want to express? *My* truth. But what
does that really mean?" He looked dully at the blank page.
" It's frightening, plunging into empty space with nothing to
clutch at. Maybe I have nothing more to say," he thought.
But instead it seemed to him that he had never really said
anything at all. He had everything to say, like everyone else,
always. But everything is too much. He remembered an old
couplet painted on a plate: " We enter, we cry, and that is
life; we cry, we leave, and that is death." What more was
there to add? " We all live on the same planet, we are born
from a womb, and one day we'll serve to fatten worms. Yes,
we all have the same story. Why then should I consider it
mine alone and decide that it's up to me to tell it?" He
yawned; he had had too little sleep, and that blank page
made him feel dizzy. He was sunk in apathy. You can't
write anything apathetically; you've got to climb back to the
surface of life where the moments and individuals count,
individually. But if he shook off that torpor all he would find
was worry. " *L'Espoir*—a local sheet. Was it true? When I
try to influence opinion, am I simply being an idealist?
Instead of sitting here dreaming in front of this piece of paper,
I'd do a lot better to start studying Marx seriously." Yes, it
had become urgent now. He had to set up a schedule and
stick to it. He should really have done it long ago. His
excuse to himself had been that he was caught up in the tide
of events and was forced to give his attention to more pressing
problems. But he had also wasted time; ever since the liberation he had been in a state of euphoria, a totally unjustified
euphoria. He got up. He was incapable of concentrating on
anything at all this morning; his conversation with Dubreuilh
the night before had shaken him too much. Besides, he had
correspondence to catch up on; he was anxious to find out
from Sézenac whether Preston would be able to get them the
paper they wanted; and he still hadn't gone to the Quai
d'Orsay to deliver das Viernas' letter. " I'll take care of that
straight away," he decided.

" May I see Monsieur Tournelle for a moment? My name
is Henri Perron. I have a message for him."

The secretary handed Henri a printed form. " Please write
your name and the reason for your visit," she said.

He took out his fountain pen. What possible reason could he give? Interest in a wild dream? He knew how futile the whole business was. He wrote: "Confidential."

"There you are," he said.

With an indulgent air, the secretary took the form and walked towards the door. Her smile and her dignified walk made it very clear that the administrative assistant to a cabinet minister was a person much too important to barge in on without an appointment. Henri looked pityingly at the thick white envelope he was holding in his hand. He had played out the comedy, and now it was no longer possible to escape reality. Poor das Viernas would soon find himself the victim of a cruel reply, or of silence.

The secretary reappeared. "Monsier Tournelle will be happy to see you as soon as he has a moment. In the meantime you can leave your message with me and I'll see that he gets it at once!"

"Thank you," Henri said, handing her the envelope. Never had it seemed more absurd to him than in the hands of that competent young woman. All right, that was it. He had done what he had been asked to do; whatever happened after that no longer concerned him. He decided to stop off at the Bar Rouge. It was a few minutes past noon and Lachaume would surely be there; Henri wanted to thank him for his review. Opening the door, he caught sight of Nadine seated with Lachaume and Vincent.

"Where have you been hiding?" she said in a sulky voice.

"I've been working." He sat down beside her and ordered a drink.

"We were just talking about you," Lachaume said cheerfully. "About your interview in *Lendemain*. You did right in bringing things out in the open. I mean about allied policy in Spain."

"Why don't you do it?" Vincent asked.

"We can't. At least not just now. But it's good someone did it."

"That's really funny!" Vincent said.

"You just don't want to understand anything," Lachaume said.

"I understand only too damned well."

"No, you don't, not at all."

Henri sipped his drink and listened idly. Lachaume never let an opportunity slip by to explain the present, the past, and the future as reviewed and revised by the Party. But this couldn't be held against him. At twenty, in the Maquis, he had discovered adventure, comradeship, and Communism. And that was excuse enough for his fanaticism. " I like him because I did him a favour," Henri thought ironically. He had hidden him in Paula's studio for three months, had obtained false papers for him, and in parting had made him a present of his only overcoat.

" By the way," Henri said abruptly, " I'd like to thank you for your review. It was really wonderful."

" I said exactly what I thought," Lachaume replied. " Besides, everyone agrees with me—it's one hell of a book."

" Yes, it's funny," Nadine said. " For once all the critics agree. It's as if they were burying someone or awarding a prize for virtue."

" You might have something there!" Henri said. " The little viper," he thought with amused bitterness, " she found just the words I didn't want to say, not even to myself." He smiled at Lachaume. " You're dead wrong on one point, though. My man will never become a Communist."

" What else do you expect him to become?"

Henri laughed. " Just what I've become!" he said.

Lachaume laughed in turn. " Precisely!" He looked Henri in the eyes. " In less than six months, the S.R.L. will no longer exist and you'll have realised that individualism doesn't pay. You'll join the Communist Party."

Henri shook his head. " But I do more for you as I am. You're delighted I brought the Spanish thing out in the open instead of your having to do it. And what good would it do if *L'Espoir* rehashed the same stuff *L'Humanité* prints? I'm doing much more useful work trying to make people think, asking questions that you don't ask, telling certain truths that you don't tell."

" But you ought to be doing that work as a Communist," Lachaume said.

" They wouldn't let me!"

" Of course they would. It's true there's too much factionalism in the Party just now, but that's because of circumstances. It won't last forever." Lachaume paused a moment and then said, " Don't repeat this, but some of my friends and I are hoping to start a magazine of our own pretty soon, a magazine with a little scope, in which everything will be discussed with complete freedom."

"First of all, a magazine isn't a daily," Henri said. "And as for being free, I'd have to see it to believe it." He gave Lachaume a friendly look. "Anyhow, it would be a good thing if you could have a magazine of your own. Do you think it'll go through?"

"There's a good chance of it."

Vincent leaned forward and looked at Lachaume defiantly. "If you get your sheet I hope you'll make sure that you'll explain to the comrades what a lousy stinking thing it is to open your arms wide to all those so-called ' repentant ' sons-of-bitches."

"We? Accepting collaborators with open arms? Tell that to the readers of *Figaro*. It'll cheer them up a little."

"Don't tell me you're not quietly clearing a lot of those lousy bastards."

"Don't confuse the issue," Lachaume said. "When we decide to clear one of them, it means we think he can be regenerated."

"Well, if that's the way you look at it, how do you know the guys we shot down couldn't be regenerated?"

"At the time it was out of the question; they had to be shot."

"At the time! But I've killed them all my life!" Vincent smiled maliciously. "Let me tell you something. They're all nothing but shits—all of them, without any exceptions. And what we ought to do now is to get rid of all those we missed."

"What do you mean by that?" Nadine asked.

"I mean we ought to organise," Vincent replied, his eyes trying to catch Henri's attention.

"Organise what? Punitive expeditions?" Henri said, laughing.

"Do you know that in Marseilles they're throwing everyone who belonged to the Maquis in jail, just as if they were a bunch of common criminals?" Vincent said. "Are we going to let them get away with it?"

"Terrorism is no solution," Lachaume said.

"No," Henri said. He looked at Vincent. "I've heard talk

about gangs who enjoyed playing at being judges. Now if it's
a question of settling a personal account, I can understand.
But guys who think they're saving France by killing a few
collaborators here and there are either sick men or stupid
bastards."

"Yes, I know. The sound thing is to join the Communist
Party or the S.R.L.!" Vincent said. He shook his head. "You
won't get me."

"I guess we'll just have to do without you!" Henri replied
amiably.

He got up; Nadine followed his example. "I'll go with
you," she said.

She seemed to enjoy trying to look like a woman; she had
even made an attempt to use make-up. But her eyelashes
looked like a sea urchin's spiny bristles and there were black
smudges under her eyes. As soon as they got outside she
asked, "Are you having lunch with me?"

"No, I have some work to do at the paper."

"At this time of day?"

"At all times of the day."

"Well, let's have dinner together then."

"No again. I plan to work very late. And afterwards, I'm
going to see your father."

"Oh! That paper! Can't you ever talk about anything
else? After all, you know, it's not the centre of the world!"

"I never said it was."

"No, but that's what you think." She shrugged her
shoulders. "Well, when will we see each other?"

He hesitated. "Honestly, Nadine, I haven't a minute to
spare these days."

"You do sit down at a table and eat occasionally, don't
you? I really don't see why I can't sit down opposite you."
She looked Henri squarely in the face. "Unless I give you a
pain in the neck."

"Of course you don't."

"Well?"

"All right. Meet me at the office to-morrow between nine
and ten."

"I'll be there."

He was quite fond of Nadine and seeing her didn't, as she
put it, give him a pain in the neck. But that wasn't the point.

The thing was that he had to organise his life as efficiently as possible. And there was simply no place in it for Nadine.

"Why were you so hard on Vincent?" Nadine asked. "You really shouldn't have been."

"I'm afraid he'll do something foolish."

"Something foolish! Whenever anyone wants to do something, you call it foolishness. Don't you think writing books is the most goddamned foolish thing of all? Everyone applauds you and for a while you're all puffed up. But afterwards they all stick your book in a corner and no one gives it another thought."

"That's my profession," he said.

"It's a funny profession!"

They continued walking in silence. When they arrived at the door to the newspaper Nadine said dryly, "I'm going home. See you to-morrow."

"So long."

"Hesitantly, she turned back and stood before him. "Between nine and ten—that's rather late, isn't it? We won't have much time to do anything. Can't we begin the evening a little earlier?"

"I won't be free before then."

She shrugged her shoulders. "All right then, at nine-thirty. But what's the use of being famous and everything if you don't take any time out to live?"

"To live!" he thought as she turned on her heels and walked briskly away. "To them that always means only one thing; to spend your time with them. But there's more than one way of living!"

He liked that familiar smell of stale dust and fresh ink that greeted him as he entered the building. The offices were still empty, the basement silent. But soon a whole world would rise from this stillness, a world which was his creation. "No one will ever lay his hands on *L'Espoir*," he repeated to himself. He sat down at his desk and stretched out his legs. There was, he told himself, no sense in getting upset. He would not give up the paper; somehow you always manage to find time for things you want to do; and after a good night's sleep his work would move along much more smoothly.

He went through his mail quickly and looked at his watch. He had an appointment with Preston in half an hour, which

left him ample time to have it out with Sézenac. " Ask
Sézenac to come to my office," he said to his secretary. He
went back to his desk and sat down. It's all well and good to
have confidence in people, but there were a lot of guys
who would jump at the chance of taking Sézenac's place and
who deserved it more than he did. When you stubbornly
decide to give one man a chance, you arbitrarily deny it to
another one. And that was not right. " Too bad!" Henri
said to himself. He recalled how promising Sézenac had
seemed when Chancel had first brought them together. For a
year he had been the most zealous of the liaison agents;
maybe he needed extraordinary circumstances to bring out his
best. But now, pale, puffy, glassy-eyed, he constantly trailed
in Vincent's wake and he was no longer able to write a
coherent sentence.

" Ah! There you are! Sit down."

Sézenac sat down without saying a word. Henri suddenly
realised that he had been working with him a whole year and
that he knew him not at all. He was more or less familiar
with the lives of the others, their tastes, their ideas. But
Sézenac kept things to himself.

" When are you going to turn in something better than the
junk you've been giving us lately?" Henri said much more
sharply than he had intended to.

Sézenac shrugged his shoulders helplessly.

" What's wrong?" Henri asked. " Not getting laid enough?
Got yourself in a jam?"

Sézenac sat quietly, rolling a handkerchief between his
hands and staring stubbornly at the floor. It was really
difficult to get through to him.

" What's wrong?" Henri repeated. " I'm willing to give you
another chance."

" No," Sèzenac said. " Journalism just isn't my dish."

" At first you were doing all right."

Sèzenac smiled vaguely. " Chancel helped me a little."

" He didn't write your articles for you, did he?"

" No," Sézenac replied without assurance. He shook his
head. " No use in pressing the matter. It's not the kind of
work I like."

" You could have told me sooner," Henri said with a trace
of annoyance. Again there was a brief silence, and then
Henri asked, " What would you like to do?"

" Don't worry about me. I'll get along."

" How?"

" I'm giving English lessons. And I've been promised some translations." He stood up. " It's really been good of you to keep me on so long."

" If you ever feel like sending us something . . ."

" If I get round to it."

" Can I do anything for you?"

" You can lend me a thousand francs," Sézenac said.

" Here's two thousand," Henri said. " But that's no solution."

Sézenac shoved his handkerchief and the money into his pocket and then, for the first time, he smiled. " It's a temporary solution; they're the surest." He opened the door. " Thanks."

" Good luck," Henri called after him. He was disturbed. It seemed almost as if all Sézenac had been waiting for was a chance to escape. " I'll get news of him through Vincent," he thought in order to reassure himself. But it bothered him a little not to have been able to make him talk.

He took out his fountain pen and placed a sheet of writing paper in front of him. Preston would be along in fifteen minutes. He didn't want to think too much about the magazine before he was sure, but his head was full of plans. The weeklies that were being published since the end of the Occupation were all rather pitiful; that would make it all the more fun to put out something really good.

Henri's secretary poked her head in the door. " Mr. Preston is here."

" Ask him to come in."

In his civilian clothes, Preston didn't look at all like an American. The very perfection of his French, however, made him somewhat suspect. He came to the point almost immediately.

" Your friend Luc must have told you that we saw each other several times during your absence," he said. " Both of us deplored the state of the French press; it's really sad. It would be a very great pleasure for me to help your paper by furnishing you with additional newsprint."

" Yes, that would fix us up fine!" said Henri. " Of course, we couldn't think of changing our format," he added. " The agreement with the other papers is still in effect. But there's nothing to stop us from bringing out a Sunday magazine supplement, and that would open up a whole new area."

Preston smiled reassuringly. "As far as the newsprint is concerned," he said, "there's no problem. You could have it to-morrow." He slowly lit a cigarette with his black enamelled lighter. "I have to ask you a very blunt question. *L'Espoir's* political line is not going to change, is it?"

"No," Henri replied. "Why?"

"To my way of thinking, *L'Espoir* represents precisely the guide your country needs," Preston said. "That's why my friends and I want to help it. We admire your independent mind, your courage, your lucidity . . ."

He stopped speaking, but his voice hung in the air.

"Well?" said Henri.

"I followed the beginning of your series on Portugal with great interest. But this morning, I was a bit surprised to read in an interview you recently gave that you intend—in regard to the Salazar régime—to criticise American policy in the Mediterranean area."

"As a matter of fact, I do find this policy unfortunate," Henri said rather sharply. "Both Franco and Salazar should have been booted out a long time ago."

"Things aren't that simple, as you know very well," Preston said. "It goes without saying that we have every intention of helping the Spanish and Portuguese to regain their democratic freedoms—but at the right moment."

"The right moment is immediately," Henri said. "There are people in Madrid's prisons who have been sentenced to death. Every day counts."

"That's my opinion, too," Preston said. "And I'm certain that the State Department will take the same position." He smiled. "That's why it seems to me especially inopportune to turn French opinion against us now."

Henri smiled in turn. "Politicians are never in a hurry; the best thing just now, it seems to me, is to back them into a corner."

"Don't fool yourself," Preston said amiably. "Your paper is well thought of in American political circles. But don't expect to influence Washington."

"I don't expect to," Henri said. "I say what I think, that's all," he added heatedly. "You were just congratulating me on my independence . . ."

" And it's exactly that independence which you are going
to jeopardise," Preston said. He looked at Henri reproachfully. " In opening that campaign, you play directly into the
hands of those who want to picture us as imperialists." He
paused a moment and added, " You take a humanitarian position with which I fully agree, but one which is not politically
sound. Give us a year, and the republic will be re-established
in Spain—and under the most favourable conditions."

" I have no intention of opening a campaign," Henri said.
" All I want to do is point out certain facts."

" But those facts will be used against us," Preston said.

Henri shrugged his shoulders. " That's not my business.
I'm a journalist. My job is to tell the truth."

Preston looked Henri firmly in the eyes. " If you knew
that printing certain truths would have unfortunate consequences, would you print them?"

" If I were absolutely certain that truth would be harmful,
then I could see only one solution: I'd resign; I'd give up
journalism."

Preston smiled engagingly. " Isn't that a rather rigid
ethical concept?"

" I have Communist friends who've asked me exactly the
same question," Henri replied. " But it's not so much the
truth I respect; it's my readers. I admit that under certain
conditions telling the truth can be a luxury. That may well
be the case in Russia," he said, smiling. " But in France,
to-day, I don't recognise anyone's right to suppress the
truth. Maybe it isn't so simple for a politician, but I'm not on
the side of those who are doing the manœuvring; I'm with the
ones they are trying to manœuvre. They count on me to keep
them informed of what's happening as well as I can, and if I
remain silent or if I lie I'd be betraying them."

He stopped, a little embarrassed by his lengthy speech. He
hadn't addressed it only to Preston; he had a vague feeling of
being cornered and he was striking out haphazardly against
everyone.

Preston shook his head. " We come back to the same
basic misunderstanding: you say you simply want to keep
them informed, but I call that a form of action. I'm afraid
you're a victim of French intellectualism. As for me, I'm a
pragmatist. Do you know the works of John Dewey?"

" No."

" That's a pity. We pragmatists aren't very well known in France. Dewey is a very great philosopher." Preston paused a moment, and then continued, " Mark you, we have no objections at all to being criticised. No one is more open to constructive criticism than an American. Explain to us how to keep the affection of the French and we'll listen to you with rapt attention. But France is in no position to judge our Mediterranean policies."

" I speak in my name only," Henri said irritably. " Whether you're in a good position or a bad one, you still have the right to speak your mind."

There was a brief silence, and then Preston said, " You understand of course that if L'Espoir takes a position against America I can no longer continue to sympathise with it."

" I understand," Henri said sharply. " And I imagine that you, for your part, can easily understand how unthinkable it would be for me to subject L'Espoir to your censorship."

" But who said anything about censorship! " Preston replied in shocked surprise. " All I want is for you to remain faithful to your guiding principle. I mean your neutrality."

" Exactly. I have every intention of remaining faithful to it," Henri said with a sudden flash of anger. " L'Espoir can't be bought for a few pounds of newsprint."

" Well, if that's the way you're going to take it . . ." Preston said. He got up. " Believe me, I'm sorry," he said.

" Well, I'm not," Henri replied.

All day long he had felt vaguely angry. But he had certainly chosen a fine time to blow up. He had been a fool to imagine that Preston would play Santa Claus. He was, after all, an agent of the State Department and Henri had been inexcusably naïve in talking to him as a friend. He stood up and walked towards the editorial room.

" Luc, old boy, it looks like we're going to have to do without a magazine supplement," he said, sitting down on the edge of the conference table.

" No! " Luc said. " Why? " His face looked puffy and old, like a dwarf's. When his plans were thwarted, he seemed to be on the verge of tears.

" Because that Yank wants to keep us from opening our mouths about America. He practically offered me a deal."

" That's hard to believe. He seemed to be such a decent chap."

" In a way, it's flattering," Henri said. " We're really being courted. Do you know what Dubreuilh suggested last night? That *L'Espoir* become the official organ of the S.R.L."

Luc looked dismayed. " Did you refuse?"

" Of course."

" All those parties that are coming to life again, the factions, the movements—we have to stay clear of all those things," Luc said pleadingly.

Luc's convictions were so strong that even when you agreed with them you were sometimes tempted to harry him a little. " But it is true that the unity of the Resistance is nothing more than words now," Henri said. " And we are going to have to state our position clearly one of these days."

" They're the ones who're sabotaging unity!" Luc said with a sudden burst of emotion. " They call the S.R.L. a ' regrouping,' but all they're doing is to create a new schism."

" No, it's the bourgeoisie who are creating the schism. And when you try to place yourself above the class struggle, you run the risk of playing right into their hands."

" Listen," Luc said, " as far as the paper's political position goes, you're the one who makes the decisions ; you've got more brains than I. But hooking up with the S.R.L. is another story. I'm absolutely opposed to that." His face hardened. " I've spared you the details of our troubles— financial matters and such—but I did warn you that things weren't going too well. If we get hooked up with a movement that means damned little to damned near everyone, that's not going to help things."

" Do you think we'd lose more readers?" Henri asked.

" Obviously! And then we're done for."

" Yes," Henri said. " I suppose you're right."

Circulation had dropped appreciably, for as long as people were forced to buy minuscule tabloids the non-Parisians preferred their local papers to the Parisian dailies. But even if they could go back to the regular-sized format, he wasn't at all sure that *L'Espoir* would regain its readers. In any case, he couldn't afford the luxury of a crisis. " I suppose I am just an idealist!" Henri thought. In arguing with Dubreuilh, he had raised the issues of confidence, influence, rôles to be played. And all the while the real answer was plainly written

In figures: they would go broke. It was one of those solid arguments that neither sophisms nor ethics could alter. He was anxious to use it.

Henri arrived at Dubreuilh's apartment on the Quai Voltaire, at ten o'clock, but the launching of his planned attack was delayed for a while. As usual Anne produced a light supper: Portuguese sausages, ham, a rice salad, and, to celebrate Henri's return, a bottle of Meursault. They exchanged stories about their travelling experiences and shared the latest Paris gossip. To tell the truth, Henri did not feel very aggressive. He was happy to be back once more in Dubreuilh's study, among those well-worn books, most of them inscribed by their authors, among the unpurchased paintings signed with well-known names, among the exotic curios acquired over the years in many travels. As an observer from the outside Henri could truly appreciate the value of that whole discreetly privileged life, and at the same time he felt those rooms were his real home. In the most intimate reaches of his own life, he was warm and comfortable there.

" It's really cosy here," he said to Anne.

" Isn't it? Whenever I go out, I feel lost," she said cheerfully.

" I must say Scriassine picked a weird place to take us," Dubreuilh said.

" What a dive! But all in all, it turned out to be a pretty good evening," Henri said. " Except for the end," he added with a smile.

" The end? No, not the end. The moment I found particularly difficult was when they played Dark Eyes," Dubreuilh said with an innocent air.

Henri hesitated. Perhaps Dubreuilh had decided against bringing it up again so soon. It certainly would be a shame to spoil this moment; why not profit from his discretion? But Henri was impatient to confirm his secret victory.

" You certainly did a good job of dragging L'Espoir through the mud," he said lightly.

" Not at all," Dubreuilh replied with a smile.

" Anne is my witness! Anyhow, I'll admit that not all of what you had to say was wrong," Henri conceded. " And I do want to say that I've been thinking seriously about your proposition to tie L'Espoir in with the S.R.L.; in fact, I even spoke to Luc about it. But it's completely out of the question."

Dubreuilh's smile vanished. "I hope that isn't your last word," he said. "Because without a paper, the S.R.L. will never amount to anything. And don't go telling me there are other papers; none of them really share our ideas completely. If you refuse, who'll accept?"

"I know," Henri said. "But let me tell you something: at the moment *L'Espoir* is in a financial crisis, like most of the other papers. I believe we'll come out of it all right, but for a good long while we're going to have a hard time making ends meet. Now the day we decide to become an organ of a political party, circulation will drop at once. And we just won't be able to take it."

"The S.R.L. isn't a party," Dubreuilh said. "It's a movement, a movement with a broad enough base so that your readers won't be shocked by the change."

"Party or movement, practically speaking it's the same thing," Henri replied. "All those Communist workers and Communist sympathisers I spoke about, they'll willingly buy an informative paper along with *L'Humanité*, but they wouldn't touch another political sheet. Even if the S.R.L. walked hand in hand with the Communist Party, it wouldn't change a thing. Stick a label on *L'Espoir*, and it immediately becomes suspect." Henri shrugged his shoulders. "The day we're read only by the members of the S.R.L., we may just as well close up shop."

"But membership would increase enormously if we had the help of a paper."

"In the meantime, though, we'd have to ride out a long storm," Henri said. "It would be more than enough to sink us. And obviously, that wouldn't help anyone."

"No . . . no, that certainly wouldn't help anyone," Dubreuilh conceded. He remained silent for a moment, drummed on his blotter with the tips of his fingers. "Obviously there's a certain risk," he said.

"A risk we just can't allow ourselves to take," Henri added.

Dubreuilh reflected again and then said with a sigh, "What we need is money."

"Exactly. And we haven't got any."

" No," Dubreuilh repeated in a subdued voice. " We haven't got any."

Naturally, Dubreuilh would never admit defeat that easily ; he still had hopes that it would somehow work out. But the argument had carried weight, and although Henri saw him frequently during the following week Dubreuilh did not broach the subject again. Henri, for his part, was determined to show proof of his good will ; he kept two appointments with Samazelle, attended the meetings of the committee, and promised to publish the movement's manifesto in *L'Espoir*. " Do as you like," Luc constantly repeated. " As long as we stay independent."

Yes, they would stay independent ; that at least was settled. But now the question was what to do with that hard-earned independence. In September, everything had seemed so simple : a little common sense, a little good will, and that was all that was needed ; they would be all right. Now, however, there was an endless stream of new problems, and each one posed a new question. Lachaume had been so effusive in his praise of Henri's series on Portugal that there was a good chance *L'Espoir* might be taken for an instrument of the Communist Party. Should he deny that? Henri didn't want to lose the intellectuals who liked *L'Espoir* because of its impartiality, and neither did he want to antagonise his Communist readers. But in trying to please everyone, he merely condemned himself to vacuity, and thereby helped to lull people back to sleep. What to do then? As he walked over to the Scribe where Lambert was awaiting him for dinner, he kept turning the question over in his mind. Whatever he decided, he'd be letting himself be swayed by a mood rather than by any concrete evidence. Despite all his resolve, he was still back where he started from ; he didn't know enough, he didn't know anything. " It would certainly be more logical to learn first, and to talk afterwards," he said to himself. But that's not the way things happen. First, you've got to speak, because the matter is urgent ; afterwards, events prove you right or wrong. " And that's precisely what's known as bluffing," he said to himself unhappily. " Yes, even I bluff my readers." He had promised himself to speak the truth, to tell his readers things that would enlighten them, that would help them think. And now he was bluffing them. What to do? He couldn't shut down the newspaper, fire everyone, lock himself up in a room for a year with his books. The paper had to live, and to keep it alive Henri was forced to give himself to it completely, day after day. He stopped in front of the Scribe. He was glad he was dining with Lambert, but it disturbed him a little to have to speak to him about his short stories. He hoped Lambert didn't take them too seriously. He pushed through the revolving door; once inside, it seemed to him as if he had suddenly been transported to another continent. It was warm here, the men and the women wore American uniforms, the air smelled of mild tobacco, luxurious trinkets were on display in glass show cases. Lambert, smiling and dressed in a lieutenant's uniform, came to meet him. In the dining-room, reserved for the use of war correspondents, butter and very white bread were on every table.

" You know, you can get French wine in this drugstore," Lambert said cheerfully. " To-night we'll eat as well as a German prisoner-of-war."

" Do you resent the fact that the Yanks feed their prisoners well?"

" No, not especially. But as for the average Frenchman who's living on air—it makes him sick. It's just that the whole thing stinks—the way they handle the Fritzes, including the Nazis, with such consideration, and the way they treat the concentration camp prisoners."

" I'd like to know if it's true that they're keeping the French Red Cross from going into the camps," Henri said.

" That's the first thing I intend to look into," Lambert replied.

" We're not very hot on America these days," Henri said as he filled his plate with tinned meat and noodles.

" And there's no good reason to be!" Lambert knitted his brow. " It's just too bad it makes Lachaume so damned happy."

" I was thinking about that as I was walking over here," Henri said. " You say a word against the Communist Party, and you're playing into the hands of the reactionaries! You criticise Washington, and you're a Communist. Unless they suspect you of being a fifth columnist."

" Fortunately, two truths balance each other out," Lambert said.

Henri shrugged his shoulders. "Don't count on that too much. Do you remember how at the Christmas party we were saying we shouldn't allow *L'Espoir* to become regimented? Well, that's a whole lot easier said than done."

"It's just a question of speaking as our consciences dictate!" Lambert said.

"Did you ever stop to think what that means?" Henri asked. "Every morning I tell a hundred thousand people how they ought to think. And what do I guide myself by? The voice of my conscience!" He poured himself a glass of wine. "It's a gigantic swindle!"

Lambert smiled. "Show me a journalist who's more scrupulous than you," he said affectionately. "You personally open every telegram, you keep your eyes on everything."

"I always try to be honest," Henri said. "But that's the trouble; it doesn't give me the time to really study the things I talk about."

"Nonsense! Your readers are more than happy with what you give them," Lambert said. "I know a hell of a lot of students who swear by *L'Espoir*."

"That only makes me feel more guilty!" Henri replied.

Lambert gave him a worried look. "You're not going to start studying statistics all day long, I hope."

"That's just what I ought to do." There was a brief silence and then suddenly Henri decided the moment had come to unburden himself. "I brought back your stories," he said. He smiled at Lambert. "It's funny, you've had lots of interesting experiences, you've lived them hard, and I've often been fascinated hearing you tell about them. Your articles are always full of meat. And yet in these stories nothing seems to happen. I've been wondering why."

"You don't think they're any good, do you?" Lambert said. He shrugged his shoulders. "Well, I warned you."

"The trouble is you haven't put anything of yourself into them," Henri said.

Lambert hesitated. "The things that really affect me wouldn't be interesting to anyone else."

Henri smiled. "But it's all too obvious that the ones you do talk about don't affect you at all. You get the feeling that you wrote these stories as if you were writing a hundred lines for punishment."

" I never really did believe I had any talent," Lambert said.

The forced smile which Lambert somehow managed only confirmed Henri's feeling that these stories were actually very important to him. " Who's talented and who isn't?" he said. " It's hard to say what that really means. No, you simply made a mistake in picking subjects that mean so little to you. That's all. Next time try putting more of yourself into your writing."

" I wouldn't know how," Lambert said. He laughed. " I'm the perfect example of the poor little intellectual who's utterly incapable of ever being creative."

" Don't be an ass!" Henri said. " These stories don't prove a thing. It's natural to miss the target the first time."

Lambert shook his head. " I know myself. I'll never accomplish anything worth while. And an intellectual who accomplishes nothing is pretty pitiful."

" You'll do something if you're really determined to. And besides, being an intellectual is no disgrace!"

" It's nothing much to be proud of either," Lambert replied.

" Well, I'm one, and you seem to have a pretty high opinion of me."

" With you, it's different," Lambert said.

" Not at all. I'm an intellectual, period. And it annoys hell out of me when they make that word an insult."

He sought Lambert's eyes, but Lambert was looking obstinately at his plate. " I wonder what I'll do when the war's over," he said.

" You don't want to stay in journalism?"

" Being a war correspondent is more or less defensible. But a ' peace ' correspondent—I can't see it," Lambert said, adding spiritedly, " Yes, it's well worth it, being the kind of journalist you are ; it's a real adventure. But being an editor, even with *L'Espoir*, wouldn't mean anything to me unless I had to earn my living by it. On the other hand, living off my income would give me a bad conscience." He hesitated and then continued, " My Mother left me too damned much money ; no matter what, I'll have a bad conscience."

" And so does everyone else," Henri said.

" But everything you have, you earn. There's no question about that."

" No one ever has a perfectly clear conscience," Henri said.
" For example, it's utterly childish for me to be eating here
when I refuse to go to black-market restaurants. All of us
have our little tricks. Dubreuilh pretends to look upon money
as a natural element. He has a hell of a lot of it, but he does
nothing to earn it, never refuses anyone a loan, and leaves it
up to Anne to manage it. And as for Anne, she puts her mind
at rest by not considering it as her own ; she tells herself she's
spending it for her husband and her daughter, making a
comfortable life for them which she, by chance, happens to
profit from. The thing that helps me is that I have a devil of
a time balancing my budget ; it gives me the feeling that I
don't have anything to spare. But that's just another way of
cheating, too."

" Still there's a difference."

Henri shook his head. " When conditions are unfair, you
can't very well live a blameless life. And that's the real
reason for going into politics—to try to change conditions."

" I sometimes wonder if I shouldn't give away that money,"
Lambert said. " But what good would that do?" He hesitated. " Besides, I have to admit that the prospect of being poor
frightens me."

" Why don't you try to use it effectively?"

" That's just it! How? What can I do with it?"

" There must be some things that interest you?"

" I wonder . . ." Lambert replied.

" There are things you enjoy, aren't there? Don't tell me
there isn't anything in the world you enjoy!" Henri said a
trifle impatiently.

" Yes, I enjoy having friends, but ever since the liberation
we do nothing but argue. Women? Either they're idiots or
they're unbearable. Books? I've got so many now I don't
know what to do with them. And as for travelling, the world
is too sad. And then, for some time now, I've not been able to
distinguish good from evil," he concluded.

" What do you mean by that?"

" A year ago, everything seemed as simple as a kid's painting book. But now you begin to realise that the Americans
are beasts as racialist as the Nazis, and that they don't give a
damn if people go on dying in concentration camps. And
speaking of concentration camps, it seems as if they've got a

few in Russia that aren't very pretty, either. Here they shoot
some of the collaborators. And some of the other bastards,
who were just as bad, get garlanded with flowers."

" If you can get angry, that means that you still do believe
in certain things."

" No, frankly, when you begin asking yourself questions,
nothing stands up. There are a lot of values you're supposed
to take as fundamental facts. In the name of what? When
you get right down to it, why freedom? Why equality? Does
justice have any meaning? Why give a damn about other
people? A man who wants nothing else but to enjoy life, like
my father, is he so wrong?" Lambert gave Henri a worried
look. " Am I shocking you?"

" Not at all. Sometimes you have to ask yourself questions."

" More than that, there has to be someone to answer them,"
Lambert said, his voice growing heated. " They beat us over
the head with politics, but why side with one party rather
than another? First of all, we need a set of principles, an
approach to life." With a trace of defiance in his eyes, Lambert looked steadily at Henri. " That's what you ought to give
us ; it would be a damned sight more worth-while than helping Dubreuilh write manifestos."

" A set of principles necessarily includes a political attitude," Henri said. " And on the other hand, politics is itself a
living thing."

" I don't think so," Lambert replied. " In politics, all you're
concerned with are abstract things that don't exist—the future,
masses of people. But what is really concrete is the actual
present moment, and people as separate and single individuals."

" But each individual is affected by collective history,"
Henri said.

" The trouble is that in politics you never come down from
the high plateau of history to the problem of the lowly
individual," Lambert said. " You get lost in generalities and
no one gives a damn about particular cases."

Lambert's voice as he spoke these words was so determined
that Henri looked at him curiously. " For example?" he
said.

" Well, for example, take the question of guilt. Politically,
abstractly, people who worked with the Germans are no-good

bastards not fit to spit upon. No problem, right? But now, when you look at one of them all by himself, close up, it isn't at all the same any more."

"You're thinking of your father?" Henri asked.

"Yes. I've been wanting to ask your advice about that for some time now. Should I really continue to turn my back on him so stubbornly?"

"But my God! The way you were talking about him last year!" Henri said, surprised.

"Because at that time, I thought he had denounced Rosa. But he convinced me he had no part in it; everybody knew she was Jewish. No, my father was involved in 'economic' collaboration, which is bad enough. But after all, he's getting old, and they're going to make him stand trial, and it's almost certain he'll be convicted . . ."

"You've seen him again?"

"Once. And since then he's sent me several letters, letters that rather upset me, I must admit."

"If you feel like making up with him, you're perfectly free to do so," Henri said. "But I always thought you got along so badly?" he added.

"When I first met you, yes." Lambert paused a moment and then continued with some effort. "He raised me, you know. I believe that in his own way he liked me a lot; only you could never disobey him."

"Before you got to know Rosa, you'd never disobeyed him?" Henri asked.

"No. That's what made him furious; it was the first time I ever went against him," Lambert said. He shrugged his shoulders. "I suppose it suited me to believe he denounced her; that way, there wasn't any problem. I'd have killed him with my own hands at the time."

"But what made you suspect him?"

"Some friends of mine put the idea in my head—Vincent among others. But I talked to Vincent about it again; he has absolutely no proof, not a shred. My father swore on the grave of my mother that it was a lie. Now that I've cooled off and can look at things objectively again I'm convinced he could never have done a thing like that. Never."

"It would have been a ghastly thing to do," Henri said. He hesitated for a moment. Now Lambert hoped that his father was innocent, just as two years earlier, without any proof, he had hoped he was guilty. And there was probably no way of ever knowing the truth. "Vincent likes to think of himself as a cloak-and-dagger character," Henri said. "Listen, if you no longer have any reason to suspect your father, if personally you don't bear him any grudge, it's not for you to act as his judge. Go and see him, do as you see fit, and don't worry about what anyone else has to say."

"Do you really think I can?" Lambert asked.

"Who's to stop you?"

"Don't you think it would be a sign of infantilism?"

Henri gave Lambert a surprised look. "Infantilism?"

Lambert blushed. "I suppose I mean cowardice."

"Not in the least. It's not cowardly to live as you see fit."

"Yes," Lambert said, "you're right. I'll write to him." Gratefully, he added, "I'm glad I talked to you about it." He dipped his spoon into the small saucer of pink, shimmering gelatine. "You could really help us so much," he murmured. "Not only myself, but a lot of other young people who are in the same boat."

"Help you in what way?" Henri asked.

"You have a sense of what is real. You ought to teach us how to live for the moment."

Henri smiled. "Formulating a set of principles, an approach to life, doesn't exactly enter into my plans."

His eyes shining, Lambert looked up at Henri. "Oh, I stated that badly. I wasn't thinking of a theoretical treatise. But there are things that you consider important, there are values you believe in. You ought to show us the pleasant things on earth. And you could also make it a little more livable by writing beautiful books. It seems to me that that is what literature should do."

Lambert delivered his little speech in a single breath. It seemed to Henri that he had prepared it in advance and that for days he had been waiting for the right moment to get it off his chest.

"Literature isn't necessarily pleasant," he said.

"But it is!" Lambert said. "Even things that are sad become pleasant when they're done artistically." He hesitated. "Maybe pleasant isn't exactly the right word, but it'll do." He paused again and blushed. "I'm not trying to dictate to you what you should write. Only you mustn't forget that you are first and foremost a writer, an artist."

" I never do forget it," Henri said.

" I know, but . . ." Once more Lambert paused, seemed embarrassed. " For example, your series on Portugal is very good, but I remember those pages you once wrote on Sicily. It makes you feel a little sad not to find anything like them in what you're writing now."

" If you ever go to Portugal, you won't feel very much like describing pomegranates in bloom," Henri said.

" I wish you'd feel that way again," Lambert said urgently. " Why not? You certainly have the right to stroll along the seaside without worrying about the price of sardines."

" But the fact is that I couldn't," Henri replied.

" After all," Lambert continued vehemently, " we fought in the Resistance to defend the individual, to defend his right to be himself and to be happy. It's time now to reap what we sowed."

" The trouble is that there are several hundred million individuals for whom that right still doesn't exist," Henri said, shrugging his shoulders. " I think it's precisely because we began to take notice of them that we can no longer stop."

" Then everybody has to wait for the whole world to be happy before trying to be happy?" Lambert said. " And art and literature must be put off until that golden age? It's now, right now, that we need them!"

" I don't say one has to stop writing," Henri replied. He paused; Lambert's reproach had touched a sore spot. Yes, there were a great many other things to be said about Portugal, and it was with no little regret that he had pushed them aside. An artist, a writer—that's what he wanted to be, that's what he had to keep in mind at all times. Long ago he had made great promises to himself; now was the time to keep them. Precocious triumphs, a too-opportune book, too highly praised—he wanted something else more than that. " As a matter of fact," he resumed, " I've just got started on the kind of novel you'll like. Just a story, in which I'll write what I please for my own pleasure."

" Really?" Lambert said, his face brightening. " Have you done very much? Is it going well?"

" Beginnings, you know, are always thankless. But it's coming along!" Henri replied.

" You don't know how happy I am to hear that!" Lambert

said. " It would be a damned shame if you let yourself be eaten up!"

" I won't let myself be eaten up," Henri said.

" How's your light novel coming along?" Paula asked.

" It's coming," Henri replied.

She stretched herself out on the bed behind him, and he felt her eyes studying the back of his neck. She made him feel uneasy, but it would have been unkind of him to chase her out. After all eyes make no noise. He tried to concentrate on the novel. During the past month, he had made several decisions and had finally resigned himself to setting the story in 1935. Perhaps it was a mistake—for days now, sentences had been withering at the tip of his pen.

" Yes, it is a mistake," he said to himself decisively. He had wanted to write about himself. Well, he had nothing in common with the person he had been in 1935. His political indifference, his curiosity, his ambition, all that stubborn insistence on individualism—how quickly it passed, how foolish it was! It presupposed a future without obstacles, with guaranteed progress, the immediate brotherhood of man, and peace everlasting. Above all it presupposed selfishness and thoughtlessness. Oh, he would no doubt have been able to find excuses enough. But he was writing this book in order to try to tell the truth about his life, not to explain away its faults. " It has to be written in the present," he decided. He reread the last few pages. It was a pity to think that the past was going to be finally buried—his arrival in Paris, his first meetings with Dubreuilh, the trip to Djerba. " I've lived them ; that should be enough," he said to himself. But if you take that position then the present is also enough, life itself is enough. And it obviously wasn't, for he had to write to feel himself completely alive. Too bad then. In any case you can't salvage everything. The question was to know what to say about himself, about himself to-day. " How far have I come? What do I want?" It was funny—if you're so set on expressing yourself, it's because you feel you're unique. And he was not even able to say in what way he thought he was! " Who am I?" He did not ask himself that question in the past ; then it had always been the others who were defined, had limits. But not he. His books and life were still ahead of him. It enabled him to dismiss all adverse criticism, and from

the heights of his future works to look on everyone, even
Dubreuilh, with a little condescension. But now, he had to
admit to himself that he was a mature man: young people
treated him as an elder, adults as one of them, and some even
treated him with respect. Mature, bounded, finite, himself
and no one else, nothing but himself. But who was he? In a
way, his books would ultimately decide; but on the other
hand, he had to know the truth about himself in order to
write them. At first sight, the meaning of those months he had
just lived through was quite clear, but if you looked more
closely everything became hazy. Helping people to think
straight, to live better lives—was his heart really set on it, or
was it only a humanitarian daydream? Was he really interested in what happened to others, or only in soothing his own
conscience? And literature? What meaning did it now hold
for him? There's nothing more abstract than wanting to
write when you have nothing urgent to say. His pen hung
motionless above the paper and he thought irritably that
Paula was there behind him, watching him not write.

He turned around. "Are you going to see Grépin to-
morrow morning?" he asked.

Paula laughed. "God! When you get an idea in your
head!"

"Listen. That song fits you like a glove, you've told me you
like it, Bergère's music is delightful, and Sabriro will give you
an audition whenever you want. You could at least do a little
something about it. Instead of dozing there on that bed,
you'd be a lot better off doing something with your voice."

"I'm not dozing."

"Anyhow, now that I've made that appointment for you,
are you going to keep it?"

"I'd be very happy to have Grépin teach me to sing your
song," she replied.

"But you refuse to have an audition. Is that what you
mean?"

She smiled. "Something like that."

"You discourage me!"

"But you have to admit that I never encouraged you." She
smiled again. "Don't worry about me," she said tenderly.

He would have preferred worrying about her once and for
all and then never again feeling her there behind him like that,
spying on him. But perhaps she realised his motive. He had

spoken to Sabriro, had written two songs, had set up a whole repertoire, and had made an appointment with Grépin. He had done everything he could for her. She was willing enough to sing for him, indeed rather too often to suit his taste, but she remained stubbornly opposed to an audition. Cheerlessly, he went back to marshalling dead sentences.

For two hours he had been sticking doggedly to his task when suddenly he heard a brisk knocking at the door. He looked at his watch; it was ten minutes past midnight.

" Someone knocked."

Paula was dozing on the bed; she sat up. " Shall I open?"

Again there was a knocking and they heard a cheerful voice call out, " It's Dubreuilh. Am I disturbing you?"

Together they went downstairs and Paula opened the door. " Did something happen?"

" To whom?" Dubreuilh asked with a smile. " I saw the lights on and I thought you wouldn't mind if I came up. It's only a little after twelve. Were you going to bed?" He had already taken his customary place in the leather arm-chair.

" As a matter of fact, I was just in the mood to have a drink!" Henri said. " And I didn't feel like drinking alone. It must have been my bad angel who brought you over."

" Cognac?" Paula asked, opening a cabinet.

" With pleasure." Dubreuilh turned a beaming face towards Henri. " I have some news that ought to be of great interest to you. It's hot off the fire."

" What is it?"

" Because of the financial crisis that would probably have resulted, we more or less gave up the idea of making L'Espoir the organ of the S.R.L. Right?"

" Correct," Henri replied. He took the glass of cognac Paula handed him and, vaguely worried, drank a little.

" Well, I've just been with a fellow who's filthy with money and who's willing to back us if we need him. Did you ever hear of a certain Trarieux? A big shoe dealer who did a little fighting in the Resistance."

" Sounds vaguely familiar."

" He's up to his ears in millions and he has a limitless admiration for Samazelle, a happy combination that's already brought some very substantial help to the S.R.L. Samazelle took me over to his place to-night. He's ready to finance the

June meeting, and he'll supply all the necessary capital if L'Espoir becomes the movement's newspaper."

"Samazelle seems to have some pretty good connections," Henri said, emptying his glass. Dubreuilh's much too communicative cheerfulness irritated him a little.

"Samazelle is the 'dining-out' type," Dubreuilh said, laughing. "It's about the last thing in the world you or I could ever be forced into doing. I, personally, would rather beg in the streets. But he likes it, and, what's more important, he's liked. Well, so much the better; he's raking it in for us. From a financial standpoint, I honestly don't know where we'd be without him. He got to know Trarieux during the Occupation and he's been cultivating him ever since."

"Does he belong to the S.R.L., your millionaire shoemaker?"

"Why? Is that so surprising?"

Paula had sat down opposite Dubreuilh. She was smoking a cigarette and staring at him hostilely. She was about to open her mouth, but Henri anticipated the indignation in her voice and quickly said, "I can't say I'm very keen on your proposition."

Dubreuilh shrugged his shoulders. "Every paper, you know, will sooner or later be forced to accept private subsidies. The free press—that's another whopping lie!"

"L'Espoir is back on its feet now," Henri said. "If we stay what we are, we can keep on going for a long time."

"You can keep on going! And then what?" Dubreuilh said heatedly. "Yes, I understand—you created L'Espoir all by yourself and you want to stick it out on your own terms. I understand," he repeated. "But think of the rôle you could play! You've come to understand during the past month how much the S.R.L. needs a paper, haven't you?"

"Yes," Henri replied.

"And you agree as to the importance of what we're trying to accomplish. Well then?"

"If that fellow does finance L'Espoir, he'll want to stick his nose into it," Henri said.

"Completely out of the question!" Dubreuilh replied. "He will positively not intervene in the management of the paper. As a matter of fact, you'd be much more independent with a silent partner like him. After all, you are tied down to a certain extent by the fear of losing your readers."

"Your shoemaker seems to be a funny kind of philanthropist."

"If you met the man, you'd understand right off," Dubreuilh said.

"Nevertheless, I can't bring myself to believe he won't impose any conditions," Henri persisted.

"Absolutely none. I guarantee it. That's one thing you can be certain of."

"You're sure it's not just a lot of talk?"

"Listen, why don't you talk to him yourself?" Dubreuilh said. "Just pick up the phone and ring him. He's ready to sign to-morrow."

Dubreuilh had been speaking with such vivacity that Henri was forced to smile. "Slow down! First of all, I have to talk to Luc. And then, even if we decide to declare ourselves for the S.R.L., we might try to do it alone. I'd much prefer it that way."

"Personally, I'm convinced that *L'Espoir* won't lose its readers," Dubreuilh said. "I'm in complete agreement with giving it a try without Trarieux." He paused a moment. "But anyhow, I think it might be a good idea for you to have a talk with him."

"He won't tell me any more than he's told you," Henri said. "And as long as I can hold off by myself, I don't want him offering me any of his loot."

"As you like." Dubreuilh gave Henri a troubled look. "But please, try to decide soon. We've already lost so much time!"

"It's a serious thing, you know, that you're asking of me," Henri said. "I'm not the only one who's affected. Try to be a little patient on your part."

"I don't have much of a choice, do I?" Dubreuilh said with a sigh. He stood up and smiled broadly at Paula. "How about taking a little walk with me?"

"Where to?" Paula asked.

"Anywhere. It's a lovely night, a real summer night."

"No, I'm sleepy," Paula said, not very politely.

"So am I," Henri said.

"Too bad. I'll walk alone then," Dubreuilh said, going towards the door. "See you Saturday."

"Right."

Henri locked the door. When he turned around, Paula was standing in front of him, her face twisted with rage. "It's insane! He wants to steal your paper!"

"Listen, it has nothing to do with stealing," Henri said. He yawned exaggeratedly; it was in just such cases, when she agreed with him, that he was least able to tolerate talking to her. He, too, was upset. It was a strange sort of hocus-pocus —Dubreuilh had had only to ask for the paper to build up a sense of obligation in him. "He doesn't give a damn about my personal likes or dislikes; friendship counts for nothing once he's decided to use you."

"You should have sent him packing," Paula said. "He'll never take you seriously; you'll forever be the boy to whom he gave a start in literature, and who owes everything to him."

"After all, he's not really asking for anything extra-ordinary," Henri said. "I'm a member of the S.R.L. and I run L'Espoir; it's rather natural for the two things to merge."

"You won't be your own master any more; you'll be forced to take their orders." Paula's voice was trembling with indignation. "And then you'll be in politics right up to your neck; you won't have a minute to yourself. Even now you complain about not having enough time for your novel . . ."

"Don't get worked up; nothing's been decided yet," Henri said. "I very definitely did not say that I'd agree."

Henri's bitterness slowly dissipated as he listened to Paula's protests; their very vehemence made clear the frivolous motives which lay behind them. And they were the very same objections Henri himself had been turning over in his mind. "I'm rebelling because I'm afraid of being eaten up by politics, because I dread the thought of taking on new responsibilities, because I'd like some leisure, and especially because I want to stay master in my own house." All quite trifling reasons. On his way to the paper the next day, he hoped from the bottom of his heart that Luc would furnish better ones.

But Luc was overwhelmed by the recent turn of events. No question about it, Lachaume had rendered L'Espoir a dis-service; it was being whispered about that Henri was under Communist orders, which was all the more annoying since at that very moment he disapproved of many of their tactics; the way they were trying to identify the Resistance with the Party, their chauvinism, the demagogy of their election propaganda, their barefaced indulgences and arbitrary severities in regard to collaborators. But the rightist papers were eagerly exploiting the doubt and many of *L'Espoir's* readers were beginning to complain. Most of the men on the paper felt uneasy, and Lambert insisted on steps being taken to set things right.

So did Luc. " Label for label," he said after Henri had presented the situation, " it would be a lot better to represent the S.R.L. than to be taken for Communists."

That more or less expressed the general opinion.

" As for me, I don't believe in the S.R.L. and I don't believe in the Communist Party. It all amounts to the same thing," Vincent said. " It's up to you."

" They all agree," Henri concluded when he was alone again in his office. " They see no reason to refuse." His heart sank. So he would be forced to accept: the S.R.L. needed a newspaper and it stood for something he had to help. The world was wavering between war and peace, the future depended perhaps on an imponderable; it would be a crime not to try anything and everything to sway the balance in favour of peace. Henri looked at his desk, his chair, the walls; he listened to the purring of the presses; and suddenly it seemed to him as if he had just awakened from a long, futile dream. Up to now he had considered *L'Espoir* a sort of toy, a complete set of equipment for the little junior editor—life-size. A magnificent plaything! But it was in fact an instrument, a weapon; people had the right to hold him to account for the way he used it. He walked over to the window. Oh, he was exaggerating a little, of course; it hadn't been as futile as all that. The September euphoria had long since been dissipated. He had been quite emotional about this paper, but nevertheless he had always believed there was no one to account to but himself. He couldn't have been more wrong. " It's funny," he said to himself, " but whenever you do the decent thing, instead of it giving you certain rights it only creates more obligations." He had founded *L'Espoir*, and now that act was forcing him to throw himself body and soul into the political arena. Even now he could imagine Samazelle's intrusions, his

harangues, Dubreuilh's telephone calls, the conversations, the
conferences, the arguments, the deals. *I won't let myself be
eaten up,* he had promised himself. Well, the die was cast;
he was going to be eaten up. He left his office and went down
the stairs. Wrapped in fog and darkness, the city seemed to
him like a huge station. There was a time when he had liked
fogs, stations, but now he liked nothing; already he had let
himself be eaten up. Yes, that was why he found so little to
say when he tried to write about himself. *There are things
you value; tell us which.* Which? He loved neither Paula nor
Nadine, and travelling hardly tempted him; he never listened
to music any more, never took walks, never read for pleasure.
He no longer did anything at all for pleasure alone, no longer
stopped on street corners to look about idly, no longer took
time to savour an old memory. People to see, things to do;
he was living like an engineer in a mechanical world. No
wonder he had become as dry as a stone. He quickened his
pace. It terrified him, that dryness. At Christmas Eve he had
promised himself so firmly that he would find himself again.
And he had found nothing. In the bargain, he felt constantly
uneasy, constantly on the defensive, tense, irritable, irritated.
He knew only too well he was acquitting himself poorly of all
those drudgeries he inflicted upon himself; they brought him
nothing but remorse. " I don't know enough, don't see things
clearly, take sides too lightly; I haven't enough time, I'll never
have enough time." It was unbearable, that refrain. And now
it would grow even louder, he would never stop hearing it;
everything was going to be worse than before, infinitely
worse. Eaten up, devoured, picked clean to his very bones.
Writing would be out of the question, for writing is a way of
life and he was about to choose another; he would no longer
have anything to communicate to anyone. " That's not what
I want; I don't want it," he said to himself with revulsion.
No, his repugnance wasn't frivolous; on the contrary, with
only a little pathos, he could have told himself that the thing
was a matter of life or death, his life or his death as a writer.
He had to assert himself. " After all, the S.R.L. doesn't hold
the fate of humanity in its hands," he thought. " Nor do I
hold the fate of the S.R.L. in mine." People take themselves
too seriously, he had often said to himself. " When you get
right down to it, our acts don't count for much, this world

doesn't count for much—it's fibrous, porous, lacks body."
Passers-by were hurrying through the fog as if it were
important that they arrive a little sooner here or there. "In
the end, they'll all die, and so will I." How that thought eases
the strain of life! Nothing can be done against death; ergo,
nothing can really be done for anyone, nothing is owed to
anyone; it's useless to make a drudgery of existence. "Well,
then, why shouldn't I do only what I'm best capable of doing,
want most to do? Drop L'Espoir and the S.R.L., leave Paris,
settle down in a quiet corner of the Midi. And write, do
nothing but write." " Reap what you've sown," Lambert had
said. Try to be happy without waiting for everyone else in
the world to achieve happiness. Why not? Henri imagined a
solitary country home, pine trees, the smell of the scrub.
" But what will I write?" He continued walking, his head
empty. "The trap is well laid," he said to himself. " Just
when you think you're escaping, it slams down on you." To
recapture the past and preserve the present with words is all
very fine. But it can be done only if there is someone to
read them; there's no sense to it except if the past, if the
present, if life counts for something. If this world has no importance, if other men mean nothing, what point would there
be to writing? There would be nothing left to do but yawn in
boredom. Life can't be bought piecemeal; it has to be pur-
chased in bulk—all or nothing. Only there isn't time enough
for everything, that's the tragedy of it. Once more the refrain
began repeating itself insistently in Henri's head. He was
strongly attached to that paper, and his concerns about war,
peace, and justice weren't just idle nonsense; throwing all that
overboard was out of the question. And yet he was a writer,
he wanted to write. Up to now he had managed more or less
to reconcile everything, rather less than more. But if he gave
in to Dubreuilh, he'd never be able to extricate himself. What
then was he to do? Give in? Not give in? Get involved in
politics? Write?

He went home to bed.

Several days went by and Henri felt no less hesitant. " Yes
or no?" It ended by putting him in a bad humour, that obsession. He realised the extent of his temper when he looked
up at Lachaume's smiling face in the doorway. " Can you
give me five minutes?"

Lachaume often came to the paper to see Vincent, and

whenever he stopped off in Henri's office he was welcome. But this time, Henri said too sharply, "To-morrow, if you don't mind. I have to finish an article."

"But I'd like to talk to you to-day," Lachaume replied, unconcerned. He sat down firmly.

"About what?"

Lachaume looked at Henri seriously. "According to what Vincent says, it seems that L'Espoir might hook up with the S.R.L. Anything to it?"

"Vincent's just shooting his mouth off," Henri said. "The whole thing is still up in the air."

"Ah! That's what I wanted to hear!" Lachaume said.

"Why? What's it got to do with you?" Henri asked somewhat aggressively.

"It'd be a serious mistake," Lachaume replied.

"What's so serious about it?" Henri asked.

"I reckoned you didn't know," Lachaume answered. "That's why I wanted to warn you." His voice hardened. "In the Party, we believe the S.R.L. is becoming an anti-Communist movement."

Henri burst out laughing. "You're absolutely right! I'd really never have known!"

"It's nothing to laugh about!" Lachaume said.

"Then it must take a hell of a lot to make you laugh!" Henri said. He gave Lachaume an ironic look. "You throw bouquets at L'Espoir, in fact too many of them to suit me. But Dubreuilh, who says exactly what I do, is against you! What's going on?" he asked. "Lafaurie couldn't have been more friendly last week."

"A movement like the S.R.L. is very equivocal," Lachaume said in his sober voice. "It appeals to people on the left; there's no argument about that. But the moment it annexes a newspaper, the moment it organises a mass meeting, then the only conclusion to draw is that they mean to undermine us. In the beginning, the Communist Party wanted an alliance. But when they come out against us, we have no other choice but to fight back."

"What you mean to say is that if the S.R.L. continues to be a silent, humble little group, working meekly in your shadow, you'd tolerate it, even encourage it! But if we decide to exist in our own right, the sacred union is no longer in force. Is that what you have in mind?"

" I repeat: they're trying to split us up," Lachaume said. " And that being the case there can no longer be any sacred union."

" Yes, that's the way you people always reason!" Henri said. " Well, one bit of advice calls for another: don't start attacking the S.R.L. You'll never convince anyone that it's an anti-Communist movement, and you'll give justification to all those who believe the National Front is a hoax. It looks to me like it's true that you can't stand the existence of a leftist movement outside of your own!"

" There's no question for the moment of openly attacking the S.R.L.," Lachaume said. " We're just keeping an eye on it, that's all." With a deadly serious expression on his face, he gave Henri a penetrating look. " The day it has a newspaper to work with, the S.R.L. will become dangerous. Don't give them *L'Espoir*."

" Hold on! That sounds to me very much like blackmail," Henri said. " If it gives up the idea of having a newspaper, the S.R.L. can go on living modestly and peacefully, is that it?"

" Blackmail!" Lachaume said reprovingly. " If the S.R.L. stays in its place, we remain friends. If not, we don't. It's only logical."

Henri shrugged his shoulders. " When Scriassine told me that no one can work with the Communists, I didn't want to believe him. Well, he was right. Whoever works with you has to be at your beck and call, that's the whole story."

" You don't want to understand!" Lachaume said. " Why don't you stay independent? That was your strength," he added earnestly.

" If I go along with the S.R.L., I'll continue saying exactly the same things as before," Henri replied. " Things you approve of."

" But you'll be speaking in the name of a certain faction and therefore your words will take on another meaning."

" While up to now it was just splendid to let everyone believe I agreed with the Communist Party right down the line. That suited you pretty damned well, didn't it?"

" But is it true that you agree with us," Lachaume said ardently. " If you're tired of playing the lone wolf, why don't you join up with us? In any case, the S.R.L. has no future; it'll never win over the proletariat. In the Communist Party, if you spoke out, at least there'd be people who'd listen to you. You could really accomplish something."

" Yes, but something I wouldn't especially care for," Henri said.

Irritably, he thought, " It looks as if everyone in the world is taking a lien on me." Lachaume continued exhorting him. He should have realised that that kind of approach didn't make it likely that Henri would want to work more closely with them. Had he come as a friend to warn him, or simply to manœuvre him? Both motives no doubt were in operation; that was the nastiest part of it.

" We're wasting our time," Henri said brusquely, " and I have to finish my article."

Lachaume got up. " Just don't forget one thing: it's in Dubreuilh's interests to have L'Espoir, but not in yours."

" Don't worry, you can count on me to protect my own interests," Henri said.

They shook hands rather coldly.

Dubreuilh had been made aware of the Communist Party's sudden change of heart. Lafaurie had politely ordered him to give up the idea of a mass meeting. " They're afraid we might become too important," Dubreuilh said. " They're trying to intimidate us. But if we don't back down, they wouldn't dare attack us, not all out, in any case." He had firmly decided not to back down and Henri agreed wholeheartedly. But nevertheless, the issue had to be raised before the Committee, a matter of mere form, since the Committee always ended by siding with Dubreuilh. " What a waste of time!" Henri thought as he listened to the uproar of excited voices. Through the window, he looked at the clear blue sky. " I'd do a lot better for myself by taking a walk!" he thought. The first day of spring, the first peacetime spring, and he hadn't found a minute to take advantage of it! In the morning, there had been a conference with the American war correspondents, and afterwards an off-the-record talk with the North Africans. He had lunched on a sandwich while skimming through the daily papers, and now he was shut in this stuffy room. He looked at the others; not a single one who felt like even opening a window. Lenoir's voice was trembling with emotion and timidity; he was almost stuttering. " If the meeting is going to seem hostile to the Communist Party, I consider it a harmful thing."

" It would be harmful if we didn't denounce the Communist Party's tyranny," Savière said. " It's precisely because of that kind of cowardice that the left is slowly dying."

" I don't think I'm a coward," Lenoir said, " but I want to be able to sing with my comrades the night the bonfires are lit."

" Look here, basically we all agree ; it's only a question of tactics," Samazelle said.

Whenever Samazelle spoke up, everyone else grew silent ; there was no room for any other voice beside his. It was booming and mellifluous, and when he rolled it in his mouth it was as if he were savouring a rare red wine. He explained that in itself the meeting constituted a declaration of independence with regard to the Communist Party and that therefore it would be appropriate if the speeches to be given were neutral, even friendly. He made his point so cleverly that Savière thought he was suggesting a manœuvre destined to guarantee a rupture with the Communists, at the same time putting all the blame on them, while Lenoir understood him to be saying that the alliance would be maintained at all costs.

" But what good is all that cleverness?" Henri asked himself. " Masking our differences isn't going to help us surmount them." For the moment, Dubreuilh was easily able to impose his will. " But if the situation should become strained, if the Communists, for example, began attacking us, how would each man react?" The Communists seemed to fascinate Lenoir ; only his literary tastes and his friendship with Dubreuilh kept him from joining the Party. On the other hand, Savière, an old militant Socialist, was barely able to control his bitterness. As for Samazelle, Henri didn't quite know what went on in his mind and he vaguely distrusted him. He was the archetype of the polished politician ; his corpulence and the husky warmth of his voice made him seem solidly rooted in the earth ; he gave the impression of having a hearty liking for people and things, but in truth they served only to feed his impetuous vitality. And it was that vitality alone on which he became drunk. How he liked to speak! And to no matter whom! He was perfectly cast as a diner-out. When a man attaches more importance to the sound of his voice than to the meaning of his words, where is his sincerity? Brunot and Morin were sincere but hesitant, precisely the kind of intellectuals Lachaume had been talking about, intellectuals who want to feel that they're doing something useful without sacrificing their individualism. " Like myself," Henri thought. " Like Dubreuilh. As long as we can go along with the Communists without actually becoming Communists, well and good. But if they ever decided to excommunicate us, that would create a hell of a problem." Henri raised his eyes towards the blue sky. It was useless to try solving that problem now, for it couldn't even be correctly posed; if the attitude of the Communist Party changed, the whole perspective would change. " The one thing sure is that we mustn't let ourselves be intimidated." But everyone agreed to that and the whole debate was therefore rather futile. " While we're sitting in here talking a lot of nonsense, there are men out fishing," Henri thought. He didn't like fishing very much, but fishermen did. They were very lucky.

After the Committee finally decided unanimously in favour of the meeting, Samazelle came over to Henri. " The meeting must be a success!" he said. There was a vague tone of reproof in his voice.

" Yes," Henri replied.

" And to be successful, the pace of recruitment has to be stepped up considerably," Samazelle said.

" That is desirable."

" Do you realise that if we had a paper, we'd be assured of a much larger audience?"

" I know," Henri said.

Cheerlessly, he studied the solid face with its beaming smile. " If I go along, I'll be dealing with him at least as much as with Dubreuilh," he thought. Samazelle was indefatigable.

" It's becoming urgent now for us to know your answer," Samazelle said.

" I told Dubreuilh I'd need a few days to think it over."

" Yes, that was a few days ago," Samazelle shot back.

" I definitely do not like him," Henri said to himself. But reprovingly, he quickly added, " Now there's a perfect example of an individualist's reaction!" An ally didn't necessarily have to be a friend. " Besides, what really constitutes a friend?" he asked himself as he shook Dubreuilh's hand.

" Friends, but up to what point? And at what price? If I
refuse to give in, what will become of that friendship?"

" Don't forget, there's a stack of manuscripts waiting for
you at *Vigilance*," Dubreuilh said.

" I'm going there now," Henri said.

He would have willingly taken more interest in the magazine, for he enjoyed helping Dubreuilh gather articles and
make selections. But it was always the same refrain: he
needed time to go through the manuscripts, to write to the
authors, to talk things over with them. And that was out of
the question; he had to limit himself to skimming hastily
through anonymous writings. " I skimp everything," he
thought, sitting down behind the wheel of the little black
car. " I can't even take time out to do justice to a beautiful
day like this. In the end I'll just hurry through my whole
life."

" Did you come for your mail?" Nadine asked. With a
look of importance, she handed him a thick yellow envelope;
she took her secretarial job very seriously. " We just got some
stuff in from the clipping service. Would you like to take a
look at it?"

" Some other time," Henri replied. He looked pityingly at
the sheaves of paper piled high on the desk—black, red, and
green notebooks, packs of loosely tied sheets, ledgers. So
many manuscripts, and for their authors, each one important,
unique . . .

" Give me a list of the ones you're taking with you,"
Nadine said, busying herself with her index cards.

" I'll take this one," Henri replied, " and that one over
there. It seems pretty good," he added, pointing to a novel
the first page of which he had found interesting.

" Young Peulevey's book? He's nice, that little carrot-
top, but what can he write at his age? He's no more than
twenty-two." She placed an imperious hand on the note-book.
" Leave it here. I'll bring it to you this evening."

" I'm not at all sure that it's any good . . ."

" I'd like to look it over, anyhow," Nadine said. Her only
passion was that greedy curiosity of hers. " Will I see you
to-night?" she asked in a distrustful voice.

" All right. At ten o'clock in the café on the corner."

" Aren't you coming to Marconi's before then? We're
celebrating the fall of Berlin. Everyone's going to be there."

" I haven't got the time."

" It seems Marconi has all the latest records. I personally don't give a damn, but you, you claim to like jazz."

" I do, but I've got some things to take care of."

" You mean you haven't got a minute to spare between five o'clock and ten?"

" No. Tournelle finally gave me an appointment. I have to see him at seven."

Nadine shrugged her shoulders. " He'll laugh in your face!"

" I don't doubt it. But I want to be able to write to poor das Viernas that I actually spoke to him in person."

Nadine finished making up her list in silence. " Good! See you to-night," she said, raising her head.

Henri smiled at her. " See you to-night."

He would meet her at ten o'clock. At about eleven they would go to the little hotel across the street from the paper. It was she who had insisted upon sleeping with him again after their return to Paris. There was some consolation at least in thinking that that arid day would, in a few hours, fade into a warm, pink night. Henri climbed into the car and started off in the direction of the paper. The night was still far off, and the afternoon would drag cheerlessly to its end. Listening to new jazz recordings, drinking with friends, smiling at women—yes, certainly, he would have enjoyed all that. But time was short; even now at the paper some people were ticking off the minutes. He would have liked to pull the car up along a quay, lean against the railing, watch the dappled water; or ride off into the gentle countryside surrounding Paris. He would have liked a great many things. But no. This year again the old stones of Paris would become covered with green without him. " Never a breathing spell. Nothing exists but the future, a future which is always retreating. And that's what they call doing something!" Discussions, conferences—not a single one of those hours had been lived for itself. Now he would begin his editorial, see Tournelle, and there would be just time enough before ten to finish his article and rush it down to the composing room. He pulled up in front of the paper. Getting that car, at least, had been a stroke of luck; without it, he'd never have been able to get everything done. As he opened the door to get out, his eyes fell on the dashboard: 2,327 kilometres. Sur-

prised, he reread the figure. He was certain that the night
before the meter had registered only 2,102. Only four people
had a key to the garage: Lambert was in Germany, Luc had
spent the morning at the paper, and what earthly reason would
Vincent have had to drive 225 kilometres between midnight
and noon? He wasn't the kind to pick up some young thing
and take her out for a ride ; his taste ran exclusively to whore-
houses. Besides, where would he have got the petrol? And
then, he would have mentioned he was taking it. That was the
rule. Henri climbed the stairs and then stopped short in the
doorway of his office. This business about the car was beginning to intrigue him. He walked over to the editorial room
and put his hand on Vincent's shoulder.

" Look, there's something . . ."

Vincent turned and smiled. Henri hesitated. It was barely
a suspicion, but a little while ago, as he was reading the news
item at the bottom of the first page of *France-Soir,* he remembered a certain smile he had once noticed on Vincent's
face at the Bar Rouge. And now Vincent had that same
smile on his face. Henri thought again of the news item.
He left his question hanging and asked instead, " How
about having a drink with me?"

" You know me—I never say no," Vincent replied.

They went up to the bar and sat down at a table near a
door which opened on to the terrace. Henri ordered two
glasses of white wine. " There's something I wanted to ask
you," he resumed. " Was it you who took the car this morning?"

" The car? No."

" That's strange. Someone besides ourselves must have the
key then. I brought her back yesterday at midnight and since
then someone put 225 kilometres on her."

" You must have the numbers wrong," Vincent said.

" No, I'm sure I haven't. I noticed only last night that the
meter had just passed 2,100 kilometres." Henri paused a
moment and then continued, " Luc was here all morning. If
you didn't take the car out, I really wonder who it was. I've
got to know."

" Why's it so important to you?" Vincent asked. There was
something insistent in his voice, and Henri looked at him for
a moment in silence.

" I don't like mysteries," he replied.

" It's a pretty small mystery ! "

" You think so ? "

Again there was a brief silence and Henri asked, " Did you take it ? "

Vincent smiled. " Listen, I'm going to ask you a favour. Forget this business about the car ; forget the whole thing. The car didn't move since last night, that's all."

Henri emptied his glass. Two hundred and twenty-five kilometres, and Attichy is about one hundred kilometres from Paris. The news item in *France-Soir* reported that at dawn Dr. Baumal, suspected of having worked with the Gestapo and whose case had just been dismissed, had been found murdered in his house at Attichy. Henri studied Vincent again. The whole thing smelt of a cheap thriller. And Vincent, in the flesh was sitting there before him, smiling as large as life. Henri stood up. But at Attichy there was a very real corpse, and somewhere there were flesh-and-blood murderers.

" I think we can talk better out on the terrace," Henri said.

" Yes, it's a beautiful day," Vincent remarked, walking towards the railing beyond which could be seen an excellent view of the glistening roofs of Paris.

" Where were you last night?" Henri asked.

" Are you 'absolutely determined to find out?" Vincent said, smiling at some hidden thought.

" You were at Attichy," Henri said abruptly.

Vincent's smile vanished. He looked at his hands ; they remained steady. He quickly raised his eyes to Henri's. " What makes you say that?"

" It's only too clear," Henri replied.

As a matter of fact, he had tossed out words without really believing in them. But suddenly it was true. Vincent belonged to one of those gangs of murderers. He had been at Attichy last night.

" Is it as clear as all that?" Vincent asked, his voice sounding vexed. He was annoyed at having let himself be found out so easily, and he seemed perfectly indifferent to everything else.

Henri grabbed him by the shoulders. " You don't seem to realise what you've done. It's rotten, that kind of business, absolutely rotten."

" Dr. Baumal?" Vincent said calmly. " Isn't he the one they used to call over to the Rue de la Pompe to take care of the chaps who passed out? He'd bring them to, and the Nazis would start twisting their toes again. He did it for two years running."

Henri tightened his grip on Vincent's bony shoulders. " Yes, he was a lousy bastard. So what? What good do you think it does, having one less bastard on earth? Killing collaborators in '43, that was all right. But now there's no point to it. There's practically no risk involved, it's not action, it's not work, it's not even sport. It's just an unhealthy little game, and there are many better things to do."

" You can't deny that the way they're ' purging ' the collaborators is nothing but a dismal farce," Vincent said.

" And what you're doing is no less a dismal farce," Henri said. " You want me to tell you something?" he added sharply. " It's breaking your heart to think that all the adventure is over ; you're just trying to prolong it. But good God! It wasn't the adventure that counted ; it was the things we were defending."

" And we're still defending the same things," Vincent said in his unruffled voice. He spoke as if he were discussing a completely abstract problem in logic. " You know," he went on, " those little news items are useful for refreshing people's memories. And they need it damned badly. Just last week I ran into Lambert walking with his father. That's carrying things just a little too far, wouldn't you say?"

" I advised him to see him, if he felt like it," Henri said. " That's his business and his business only. Refreshing people's memories!" he went on with a shrug of his shoulders. " You'd have to be out of your mind to think that would change anything."

" Would you mind telling me who is changing anything?" Vincent asked ironically. " And if so, what?"

" You know why we're stalled?" Henri said angrily. " Because there aren't enough of us. It's your fault, and the fault of your pals and all the other idiots who are horsing around with murder and other crap instead of really working."

" I suppose you want me to join the S.R.L.?" Vincent said sarcastically.

" It would be a damned sight better idea," Henri said.

" Figure it out for yourself. What's the good of shooting up insignificant bastards no one gives a damn about anyhow? You can bet the rightists aren't going to be any the worse for it."

Vincent cut him off. " Lachaume says the S.R.L. serves the cause of reaction, and Dubreuilh tells us that the Communist Party is betraying the proletariat. Try to figure it out!" Deliberately he walked towards the french windows. " Forget the whole business. You have my promise I won't use the car any more," he added with a smile.

" I don't give a damn about the car," Henri said emphatically.

Vincent cut him short. " Don't worry about the rest."

They went through the bar together and Vincent asked, " Are you going over to Marconi's later?"

" No, I've got too much work to do."

" Too bad! If only once we could all enjoy the same thing together! We'll miss not having you with us!"

" And I'll miss not being there."

They went down the stairs in silence. Henri would have liked to add something, a clinching argument, but he found nothing to say. He felt very depressed. Vincent had a dozen corpses behind him; continuing to kill was his way of trying to forget them. And in between murders, he drank a great deal; to-night at Marconi's he was sure to get a good load on. Henri couldn't let him go on like that. But how was he to put a stop to it? " There's something rotten somewhere," Henri said to himself. " So many things to do! And yet so many people who don't know what to do with themselves! It should have worked out, but it hasn't. I'll send him off somewhere far away to do a long assignment," he decided. But that would be only a temporary solution. What he needed was something solid to offer Vincent. If the S.R.L. were coming along better, if it really represented a hope, Henri could have said to him, " We need you." But for the moment, they still had a good way to go.

When, two hours later, Henri drove over to the Quai d'Orsay, he was in a morose mood. He had only too well foreseen Tournelle's friendly greeting, his circumspect smile.

" Tell your friend das Viernas that his letter will be studied, but advise him to be patient," Tournelle said. " I'll see to it that your letter goes out in the pouch," he added. " Just leave

it with my secretary. But be very careful about what you say
in it, anyhow."

" Of course. They're already suspicious enough of the poor
old man!" Henri looked at Tournelle reproachfully.
" They're dreamers, they have no idea of what's going on in
the world. But nevertheless, they're completely right in wanting to kick Salazar out."

" Of course, they're right!" Tournelle said. There was a
trace of bitterness in his voice; Henri looked at him more
attentively.

" Well, then, don't you think we ought to try and help them
somehow or other?" he asked.

" How?"

" Frankly, I have no idea; that's your department."

Tournelle shrugged his shoulders. " You know the situation as well as I. How do you expect France to do anything
for Portugal, or for anyone else for that matter, when she
can't do anything for herself!"

Uneasily, Henri studied the angry face before him. Tournelle had been one of the first organisers of the Resistance;
he had never had any doubts about the ultimate victory. It
wasn't at all like him, this admission of defeat.

" We're not in such bad shape as all that," Henri said.

" You think so? Are you one of those people who feel
proud because France has been invited to San Francisco?
Well, don't deceive yourself. The simple truth is that we just
don't count any more."

" Granted, we don't carry much weight," Henri said. " But
at least we can speak out, defend our views, exert pressures . . ."

" How well I remember!" Tournelle said bitterly. " We
wanted to save the honour of France so that she could speak
to her allies with her head high. And there were people who
got themselves slaughtered for that! A lot of blood spilled
for nothing!"

" You're not going to tell me we shouldn't have resisted,"
Henri said.

" I don't know. All I can say is that it didn't do us a hell of
a lot of good!" Tournelle put his hand on Henri's shoulder.
" Don't repeat what I've said."

" Of course not!" Henri said.

A worldly smile reappeared on Tournelle's lips. "I'm
happy to have had the opportunity to see you again!"

"So am I," Henri said.

Walking rapidly, he went through the corridors and crossed
the courtyard. His heart was heavy. "Poor das Viernas!
Poor old men!" In his mind's eye, he saw their stiff collars,
their derbies, that righteous anger in their eyes. "France is
our only hope," they had said. But nowhere was there any
hope, no more in France than anywhere else. He crossed the
street and leaned against the railing of the quay. As seen
from Portugal, France still shone with the stubborn glitter
of a burnt-out star, and Henri had let himself be taken in by
this. Suddenly he realised that he was living in the moribund
capital of a very small country. The Seine was flowing in
its bed; the Madeleine, the Chambre des Deputés were in
their places, the Obelisk, too. One could easily have been
led to believe that the war had miraculously spared Paris.
"That's what we wanted to believe," Henri thought, turning
the car into the Boulevard St. Germain where the chestnut
trees were faithfully blossoming. They had all let themselves
be complacently fooled by those houses, those trees, those
benches which so perfectly aped the past. But actually the
once proud capital of the world had been utterly destroyed.
Henri was nothing but an insignificant citizen of a fifth-rate
power, and *L'Espoir* was a local sheet on the same level
as a village weekly. Mournfully, he climbed the stairs to his
office. *France can't do anything for herself.* Giving information to people who can do nothing, exciting their interest,
arousing their indignation—what good could it do? He had
written that series on Portugal with loving care, as if it could
stir up public opinion from pole to pole. And Washington
didn't give a damn, and the Quai d'Orsay was in no position
to help. He sat down at his desk and reread the beginning of
his article. What was the use? People would read it, nod
their heads, throw the paper into a waste-basket, and that was
it! What difference did it make if *L'Espoir* remained independent or not, if it had more or fewer readers, or even if it
went bankrupt? "It isn't even worth the trouble to be
stubborn over it!" Henri thought suddenly. Dubreuilh and
Samazelle believed they could make good use of the paper;
they believed, too, that France, if she didn't remain isolated,

still had an important rôle to play in the world. All hope was on their side; elsewhere, nothing but emptiness. "Well? Why not ring and tell them I accept?" Henri said to himself. For a long moment he looked at the telephone on his desk. But his hand remained frozen. He went back to his article.

"Hallo, Henri? It's Nadine." There was a frantic trembling in her voice. "Did you forget about me?"

He looked at his watch in surprise. "No, no. I was just coming down. It's not even a quarter past ten yet, is it?"

"Ten-seventeen."

"Well, I had a lot of work."

He hung up the telephone impatiently. She seemed to have a gift for that—always managing somehow to spoil their dates. During the long day, he had kept thinking of the moment when he would hold her smooth, fresh body in his arms; then, at last, he would have his share of springtime. And now, all at once, anger drowned his desire. "Another one who thinks she has a hold on me!" he said to himself as he went down the stairs. "As if Paula weren't enough . . ." He opened the door of the little café; Nadine was quietly reading, a glass of mineral water before her.

"What's the matter? Can't you wait twenty minutes?"

She raised her head. "I'm sorry, I didn't want to rush you. But I just can't help it. As soon as I start waiting, it seems I'll never again see the person I'm waiting for."

"People don't vanish just like that."

"You think so?"

He suddenly remembered she was only eighteen and had some very painful memories. Ashamed, he turned his head away.

"Did you order something?" he asked.

"Yes, they have steak to-night." With a conciliatory smile, she added, "You did well not coming over to Marconi's; it wasn't any fun."

"Did Vincent get drunk?"

"How did you know?"

"He always gets drunk. You ought to try converting him."

"Oh, Vincent! He can do anything he wants," Nadine said dreamily. "He's so different from the others—a sort . . . a sort of demigod."

She looked Henri in the eyes. "Well? Did you see Tournelle?"

"Yes. He says there's nothing he can do."

"I knew you were just breaking your neck for nothing," Nadine said.

"Don't you think I knew it too?" he replied.

"Then it really *wasn't* worth the trouble!" Nadine said, pouting again. She handed the black note-book to Henri. "I brought you the manuscript."

"What do you think of it?"

"He's got some very amusing things to say about Indo-China," Nadine replied in a noncommittal voice.

"Do you think we can put a few passages in the magazine?"

"Oh, definitely. I'd even put the whole thing in." She gave the manuscript a somewhat spiteful look. "You have to be completely without shame to dare talk about yourself the way he does. I'd never be able to."

Henri smiled at her. "You never feel like writing?"

"Never," Nadine said emphatically. "First of all, I don't see how anyone without genius can write."

"You know, sometimes I think that writing might help you," Henri said.

Nadine's face hardened. "Might help me? In what way?"

"To get along better in life."

"I get along quite well, thank you," she said, attacking her steak. "You're funny, you are," she added. "Worse than a dope addict."

"What makes you say that?"

"Dope addicts want to get everyone else to take dope; you want everyone to start writing."

Henri opened the manuscript and again, as he read, the typewritten sentences tinkled with a clear, sharp, happy sound, like a downpour of tiny pebbles.

"For a youngster of twenty-two, it's really good," he said.

"Yes, it is good," she agreed. "But," she added with a shrug of her shoulders, "how can you get excited about a guy you don't even know?"

"I'm not getting excited; I simply claim he has talent."

"So what? Aren't there enough talented writers in the

world? Would you mind explaining to me," she said with a
stubborn look, " why you—you and Father—feel such a need
to discover masterpieces in embryo?"

" If you write, it means you believe in literature," Henri
replied. "And it makes you happy to enrich it with a fine
book."

" You mean it reflects on your own activities and sort of
justifies them. Is that right?"

" Yes, in a way."

" That's what I thought," she said in a satisfied voice.
" When you get right down to it, the interest you take in
novices is simply a form of selfishness."

" Come now, that's rather cheap cynicism!"

" Don't people always do things out of selfishness?"

" Well, let's say that there are ways of being selfish that are
more or less helpful to others."

Above all, he did not want to argue with Nadine. He
watched her picking her teeth with a matchstick and the
sight set him on edge. She dropped the match to the floor.

" I expect you, too, think I was wrong to take that
secretarial job, don't you?"

" Why do you ask me that? You seem to be doing fine."

" I'm not talking about whether I'm good for the job, but
whether the job is good for me. Was I right or wrong to
take it?"

To tell the truth, he hadn't given the matter any thought.
Despite all her cynicism, Nadine would have been astonished
had she known just how indifferent he was to her problems.

" Of course, you could have gone on with your studies," he
said without enthusiasm.

" I wanted to be independent."

Working for her father's magazine was a strange kind of
independence. The truth was that although she worked hard
at scorning her parents, almost hating them in fact, she
couldn't have tolerated it if their life had not been her own.
She had to defy them at close range.

" You're the best judge," he said weakly.

" Then you think I was right?"

" What's right for you is right." He answered reluctantly,
for he knew that although Nadine loved to talk about herself
any judgment passed on her, even a favourable one, always

hurt her. As a matter of fact, there was nothing he felt like talking about just then ; all he wanted was to get in bed with her.

"You know what you'd do if you were nice?"

"What?"

"You'd go across the street with me."

Nadine's face darkened. "That's all you ever want to see me for," she said resentfully.

"I'm sorry, I didn't mean to insult you."

"I thought we'd have a little chat together," she said plaintively.

"Well, let's chat! Do you want a cognac?"

"You know I don't."

"Still as sober as a choir girl! No cigarettes either?"

"No."

He ordered a cognac and lit a cigarette. "What did you want to talk about?"

His voice was not very friendly, but Nadine didn't allow herself to be put out by it. "I feel like joining the Communist Party," she said.

"Join."

"But what do you think of the idea?"

"There's nothing for me to think about," he said sharply. "It's up to you to know what you want."

"But I'm not sure ; it's not so simple. That's why I wanted to talk to you about it."

"Discussions never convince anyone of anything."

"You discuss things with other people," Nadine said with a sudden bitterness in her voice. "But with me, you never want to. I suppose it's because I'm a woman, and women are only good for getting laid."

"I spend my days jabbering," he said. "If you only knew how fed up you can get . . ."

The fact was that with Lambert or Vincent he would not have tried to avoid the issue. Nadine needed help as much as they, but he had learned the hard way that coming to the aid of a woman always meant giving her a hold on him. They would somehow transform the least little token into an undying promise. He kept himself on the defensive.

"I'll tell you what I think: if you do join the Party you won't stay in it very long," he said with an effort.

"Well, let me tell you something: it isn't the scruples of

you intellectuals that are holding me back. One thing is sure," she said with feeling, " if I'd been a member of the Party, I wouldn't have felt so guilty when we saw those starving kids in Portugal."

Henri remained silent. Yes, getting rid of one's guilty feelings once and for all is certainly tempting. But to join the Party only for that is surely to miss the mark.

" What are you thinking about?" Nadine asked.

" I was thinking you ought to join if you really want to."

" But you, you'd rather stay in the S.R.L. than go over to the Communists, wouldn't you?"

" What reason would I have to change my mind?" Henri asked.

" Then you think that being a Communist is good for me but not for you?"

" There are a lot of Communist notions I can't accept; if you can, go right ahead."

" You see, you don't want to discuss it!" she said.

" But I am discussing it."

" Half-heartedly. You act as if you're bored to death with me!" she added reproachfully.

" I'm not bored with you, believe me. But I'm really beat to-night."

" You're always beat when you see me."

" Because I see you at night. You know it's the only free time I have."

" Listen," Nadine said after a brief silence, " I'm going to ask you something. But of course you'll refuse . . ."

" What?"

" Spend the week-end with me."

" But I can't," he replied. Again a feeling of rancour rose in his throat; she was refusing him the body he so much wanted and was demanding his time, his attention . . . " You know I can't."

" Because of Paula?"

" Exactly."

" How can a man allow himself to be a slave the rest of his life to a woman he no longer loves?"

" I never told you I didn't care for Paula any more."

" You pity her and you feel guilty. It's nauseating, all that sentimental crap. When you don't enjoy seeing people any more, you let them drop, that's all."

" If you look at it that way, you can never ask anything of anyone," he said, looking at her insolently. " And above all, you can't become indignant if someone says no to you."

" I wouldn't have been indignant if you'd told me frankly: ' I don't feel like spending the week-end with you,' instead of talking to me about your duty."

Henri laughed. " No," he thought, " this time I'm not going to let myself be taken in by that phony frankness business. She wants the truth? Well, she'll have it." Aloud, he said. " Well, let's suppose I did tell you that frankly?"

" You wouldn't have to say it twice."

She took her purse from the table and closed it smartly. " I'm not the clinging-vine type," she said. " I'm not a leech. And besides, I don't love you; you can set yourself at ease about that." She examined him for a moment in silence. " How can anyone love an intellectual! You have a set of scales where your heart should be and a little brain at the tip of your pecker. And fundamentally," she concluded, " you're all just a bunch of fascists."

" I don't follow you."

" You never treat people as equals; you deal with them according to the dictates of your little consciences. Your generosity is simply imperialism and your impartiality, conceit." She was speaking dreamily, without anger. She stood up and gave a thin, studied laugh. " Oh, don't put on that hurt expression. It bores you to go out with me, and to tell you the truth I don't get much of a kick out of it any more, either. There'll be no dramatics. We'll talk to each other when we run into each other. And without bitterness."

Nadine disappeared into the blackness of the street and Henri asked for the bill. He wasn't pleased with himself. " Why did I treat her like such a bastard?" She annoyed him, yes, but he still liked her a lot. " I'm much too irritable lately," he said to himself. " Everything gets on my nerves. Something's wrong somewhere." He emptied his glass of wine. After all, it wasn't surprising; he spent his days doing things he had no desire to do, lived his life half-heartedly from morning to night. " How did I ever come to this?" At first sight, the resolution he had made the day after the liberation—to rediscover his pre-war life and enrich it with a few new activities—didn't seem so very ambitious. He had believed he could manage L'Espoir and work for the S.R.L.

and still have time for writing and pleasure. He had been wrong. But why? It wasn't a question of time; if he had really wanted to, he would somehow have managed to take a walk that afternoon or to go to Marconi's. And even now, he still had time to work. He could ask the waiter to bring him some writing paper. But the very idea made him feel ill. " Funny kind of job!" Nadine had said. She was right. The Russians were sacking Berlin, the war was ending, or another one was beginning—how could one find pleasure in telling stories that never actually happened? He shrugged his shoulders. That was typical of the excuses you used when your work wasn't going well. Only a few years ago, the danger of war had hung menacingly over the world, the war itself had broken out, and still he had found pleasure in telling stories. Why not now? He left the café. He recalled another night, a night of fog and darkness when he had foreseen that politics would devour him. And now it had happened; he was devoured. But why hadn't he been able to defend himself better? What brought it on, that inner dryness, that paralysing dryness? Why was that youngster, whose manuscript he was holding in his hand, able to find things to say, and not he? When he had been twenty-two and had had things to say he had walked these very streets dreaming of his book—*the* book. He slackened his pace. They weren't the same streets. Then, they glittered with lights, they brightly streaked the capital of the world; to-day, the street lights shone far apart, and in their occasional light you noticed how narrow the streets were, how decrepit the houses. The City of Light had gone dark. If one day it should glitter again, the splendour of Paris would be that of other fallen world capitals— Venice, Prague, long-dead Bruges. Not the same streets, not the same world. Christmas Eve Henri had promised himself to put into words the sweetness of peace; but this peace was without sweetness. The streets were cheerless, Nadine's flesh grim; the springtime had nothing to offer him—the blue sky, the budding flowers obeying the season's routine, held no promise. *Tell about the flavour of my life.* But it no longer had any flavour because things no longer made sense. Yes, and that was why writing no longer made sense. Nadine was right about that, too. Those little lights along the Tagus—you can't enjoy describing them when you know they light a city dying of hunger. And starving people shouldn't serve as an excuse for writing. The past had been nothing but a mirage; the mirage vanished, what was left? Wretchedness, dangers, uncertain tasks, chaos. Henri had lost the world, had received nothing in return for it. He was nowhere, had nothing, *was* nothing; there was nothing he could speak about. "Then I just have to shut up," he thought. "If I really resign myself to the inevitable, maybe I'll stop tearing myself to pieces, maybe I'll be able to bear with a lighter heart the drudgeries I'm forced to do." He stopped in front of the Bar Rouge; through the window, he saw Julien sitting alone at the bar. He opened the door and heard his name whispered about the room. Only yesterday this would have excited him; but as he made his way through the crush of habitués, he grew steadily more angry with himself for having let himself be duped by a shabby mirage. Being a great writer in Guatemala or Honduras—what a laughable triumph! He had believed that he lived in a very special part of the world from which every word echoed across the entire planet. But he knew now that all his words died at his feet.

"Too late!" Julien said.

"Why too late?"

"The skull-busting. You missed it. Oh, it wasn't much," he added. "People don't even know how to bust skulls properly any more."

"What was it all about?"

"Some idiot called Pétain ' the Marshal,' " Julien said in an unsteady voice. He pulled a flat flask from his pocket. "Care for a real Scotch?"

"Pour it out."

"Mademoiselle, another glass and another bottle of soda, please," Julien said. He filled Henri's glass half full.

"Wonderful!" Henri said. He swallowed deeply. "Just what I needed! I had such a full day I don't know whether I'm coming or going. Did you ever notice how empty you feel after a full day?"

"Days are always full; not a single hour is ever missing. But with bottles . . . with bottles, unfortunately, it's not the same."

Julien pointed to the note-book which Henri had dropped on the bar. "What's that? Secret documents?"

"A novel by some young fellow."

"Well, tell your young fellow to use it for cutting out

paper dolls for his little sister. Let him become a librarian,
like me; it's a charming profession, and a whole lot healthier
than writing. Have you noticed? If you sold butter or can-
nons to the Krauts, they pardon you, kiss you on both cheeks,
decorate you. But if you wrote a word too much here or
there, then: Ready! Aim! Fire! You ought to write yourself a little article about that."

" I've been thinking about it."

" You think of everything, don't you?" Julien emptied the
flask of Scotch into the two glasses. " You can fill column
after column demanding the nationalisation of industry!
Work and justice! You think it'll be a riot?" He raised his
glass. " To the Berlin massacres!"

" The massacres?"

" What do you think they're doing in Berlin to-night, those
fine Cossacks? Killing and raping! What a bloody mess!
Well, that's victory, my friend. *Our* victory. Don't you feel
proud?"

" Now look, are you going to turn my stomach with
politics too?"

" Oh, no! Not me. The hell with politics, I say," Julien
answered.

" If you mean that this world isn't much fun," Henri said,
" I agree with you."

" So do I. Just take a look at this dive; they call it a bar.
Even the drunks talk about nothing but reviving France. And
the women! Not a single carefree woman in the whole district; nothing but a bunch of gloomy-faced breast-beaters."
Julien got off his stool. " How about going over to Montparnasse with me? At least you can find charming young girls
over there. Maybe they're not real, honest-to-God *nice* girls,
but they're obliging. And you won't find a breast-beater
among them."

Henri shook his head. " I'm going home to sleep."

" You're no fun, either," Julien said with disgust. " No, for
a post-war era, it isn't turning out very well!"

" It isn't turning out well!" Henri repeated to himself. With
his eyes, he followed Julien, who was walking with dignity
towards the door. Neither was he fun; in fact, he was turning
rather sour. But all in all, why should the post-war era be
fun? Yes, under the Occupation, there was a reason for
living. But that was ancient history now. The song of the

THE MANDARINS 215

to-morrows had been sung enough; to-morrow had become
to-day, and there was nothing to sing about. Paris had been
destroyed, really destroyed, and everyone had died in the war.
" So did I," Henri said to himself. " And what of it?" It's
no trouble being dead, if you give up pretending to be alive.
Writing finished, living finished. A single command: act, act
as a team, without worrying about yourself; sow, sow again,
and never reap. Act, unite, serve, obey Dubreuilh, smile at
Samazelle. He'd telephone and tell them, " The paper is
yours." Serve, unite, act. He ordered a double cognac.

CHAPTER FOUR

SURVIVING ONE'S own life, living on the other side of it like a spectator, is quite comfortable after all. You no longer expect anything, no longer fear anything, and every hour is like a memory. That's what I discovered during Nadine's absence. What a rest! The doors of the apartment no longer slammed, I could chat with Robert without frustrating anyone and stay awake late into the night without someone knocking at my door. I took advantage of it. I enjoyed recapturing the past in the depths of each instant. I needed only a brief moment of sleeplessness; a cluster of stars seen through the open window, and all the winters of my life, all the frozen fields, all the Christmases were brought to life again; the noise of clattering garbage bins made me relive every morning of Paris waking I had known since my childhood. There was still the same old silence in Robert's study as he wrote, his eyes red, deaf to the world, unaware of everything around him. And how familiar was the murmuring of those excited voices; They had new faces, were now called Lenoir, Samazelle; but the smell of dark tobacco, the violent disputes, the conciliatory laughs, how well I remember them! Evenings, I listened to Robert, looked about the room at our unaltering bric-a-brac, our books, our paintings, and I would say to myself that death was perhaps more merciful than I had suspected.

Only to continue believing that, I would have had to barricade myself in my tomb. For now, in the wet streets, we would pass men in striped pyjamas—the first deportees returning. On walls, in newspapers, pictures revealed to us that during all those years we hadn't formed the slightest idea of what the word " horror " really meant; once more dead men had come to increase the crowd of dead betrayed by our lives. And in my office I saw survivors appear, survivors who could not find rest in the past. " If I could only sleep a whole night without remembering," pleaded that tall girl whose cheeks were still fresh, but whose hair was completely white. Ordinarily, I knew how to protect myself. I gave only professional care to all those neurotics who had hidden their

216

aberrations during the war and who now released their complexes in a spirit of frantic vengeance. But before those returning ghosts I was ashamed, ashamed of not having suffered enough, of being undamaged and able to give counsel from the heights of my good health. How vain those questions I had been asking myself now seemed! Whatever the future of the world, I had to help these men and women to forget, to be cured. The only problem was that, although I worked far into the nights, my days were much too short.

And so much more so with Nadine back in Paris. She dragged in a large duffle bag filled with rust-coloured sausages, hams, sugar, coffee, chocolate; from her suitcase she brought forth cakes, sticky with sugar and eggs, stockings, shoes, scarfs, lengths of cloth, liqueurs. "You've got to admit I didn't do badly for myself!" she said proudly. She was wearing a Scotch-plaid skirt, a well-cut red blouse, a fluffy fur coat, and crêpe-soled shoes. "Get yourself a dress made quickly," she said. "My poor mother, you really are a mess!" She draped a piece of velvety cloth, rich with autumnal colours over my shoulders. For two whole days she vivaciously described Portugal to us. She was a poor teller of tales, and she used broad gestures to fill out sentences when the words wouldn't come. And there was a worried intensity in her voice, as if she had to dazzle us in order to enjoy remembering.

With an air of importance, she inspected the house. "The windows! The floors! How can you even think of doing everything yourself! No, now that more and more patients are coming back you've got to have someone to help out."

Robert also insisted on it, but I was a little repelled by the idea of being waited on. Nadine, however, said that those were petit-bourgeois scruples and the very next day she found me a neat, zealous, young charwoman named Marie. As things turned out, I almost sacked her the first week. Robert had gone out, abruptly, as he often did these days, and had left his papers scattered on his desk; hearing no noise in his study, I opened the door and saw Marie bending over a manuscript.

"What are you up to?"

"I'm putting things in order," Marie calmly replied. "While Monsieur isn't here . . ."

"I told you never to touch his papers. And you weren't putting things in order; you were reading!"

"I can't read Monsieur's writing," she said regretfully. She looked up at me and smiled, but the smile failed to brighten her expressionless little face. "It's funny to see Monsieur writing all day long. Does all that come out of his head? I just wanted to know what it looked like on paper; I didn't upset anything."

I wavered, but in the end I didn't have the heart. To spend one's days cleaning and making order—what a bore! Despite her sleepy look, she didn't seem stupid; I realised she was simply trying to find a few moments of distraction.

"All right," I said, "but don't do it again." I smiled and asked, "Do you like reading?"

"I never have time enough for it," Marie replied.

"Why? Do you have other work to do after leaving here?"

"There's six children at home and I'm the oldest."

"It's a shame she can't learn a real trade," I said to myself. I thought vaguely of speaking to her about it, but I hardly ever saw her and she was quite reserved.

"Lambert hasn't phoned," Nadine said to me a few days after her return. "And he knows perfectly well that Henri is back, and that I am, too."

"You told him twenty times before leaving that you'd be the one to get in touch with him. I suppose he's afraid of bothering you."

"Listen, if he wants to sulk, that's his business. But you do see now how easily he can get along without me."

I remained silent and she added aggressively, "I've been meaning to tell you: you were all wet about Henri. Fall in love with a chap like him? Not me! He's so cocksure of himself! And besides, he's boring," she concluded peevishly.

Certainly, she harboured no tender feelings for him. And yet the days she was to meet him, she applied her make-up with special care, and when she got home at night she would be more surly than usual. But to tell the truth, Nadine would use any pretext to get angry. One morning, she charged into Robert's study vengefully waving a newspaper.

"Look at that!"

On the front page of *Lendemain*, Scriassine was smiling at

Robert, who was staring straight ahead with an infuriated expression.

"Ah! They got me anyhow!" Robert said, grabbing the weekly. "It happened the other night at the Isba," he said to Nadine. "I told them to get the hell out, but they got me anyhow!"

"And they took you with that louse!" she said, her voice choking with anger. "They did it on purpose."

"Scriassine isn't a louse," Robert said.

"Everybody knows he's sold out to America. It's disgusting; what are you going to do about it?"

Robert shrugged his shoulders. "What do you want me to do?"

"Sue them. No one has the right to take your picture if you don't want them to."

Nadine's lips were trembling; she had always thought it loathsome that her father was a well-known person. Whenever a new professor would ask, "Are you Robert Dubreuilh's daughter?" she would freeze up in mute surliness. And yet she was proud of him; only she wished he could somehow be famous without it being known.

"A trial would make too much noise," Robert said. "No, against a thing like that we're totally unarmed." He threw the paper aside and turned towards me. "You said something very true the other day: that for us, nudity begins with the face."

I was always astonished by the preciseness with which he recalled words I had completely forgotten. Usually he gave them more meaning than I myself had intended; he was always generous to everyone.

"Nudity begins with the face, and obscenity with the word," he continued. "They decree that we are statues or ghosts, and then when they catch us existing in the flesh they accuse us of being impostors. That's why the slightest gesture so easily becomes scandalous. Laughing, talking, eating—just so many flagrant offences."

"Well, arrange things so that you won't be caught," Nadine said in an exasperated voice.

"Listen," I said, "it's not as tragic as all that."

"Oh, you! Of course! If they step on your toe, you pretend that they've stepped on a toe that just happens by chance to be yours."

As a matter of fact, I was none too happy myself about all the fuss they were making over Robert. Although he hadn't published anything since '39—except for articles in *L'Espoir* —they were making much more of him now than before the war. They pleaded with him to seek membership in the Académie and to ask for the Legion of Honour. Reporters followed him everywhere and a lot of lies were constantly being printed about him. " France likes to advertise its regional specialities—culture and *haute couture*," he would say to me. He, too, was annoyed by all that inane gossip surrounding him. But what could be done about it? I tried in vain to explain to Nadine that we were powerless; each time she read a bit of gossip about Robert or saw a picture of him in the papers, she would fly into a tantrum.

Once again doors began to slam, furniture to dance, books to fall noisily to the floor. And to make matters worse, the racket always began early in the morning; Nadine slept little. She believed sleeping was a waste of time, even though she did not know what to do with her time. Each occupation seemed meaningless to her when she considered all the others she was sacrificing for it; she couldn't make up her mind to stick to anything. One evening, when I saw her sitting before her typewriter, looking sullen, I asked, " Are you making any progress?"

" I'd do better to study my chemistry; I'm going to fail."

" Well, then, why don't you study your chemistry?"

" But a secretary has to know how to type." She shrugged her shoulders. " And it's so absurd to fill your head with formulas. After all, what have they got to do with real life?"

" Then drop chemistry if you're so fed up with it."

" You've told me a hundred times that one mustn't behave like a weather vane."

She was adept at turning against me all the advice with which I had wearied her childhood.

" There are times when it's stupid to be stubborn."

" Don't get excited! I'm not as stupid as you think; I'll pass that exam."

One afternoon she knocked at the door to my room. " Lambert's come to see us," she said.

" To see you," I said.

" He's leaving for Germany to-morrow and he'd like to

say good-bye to you." With a whining vivacity, she added,
" Please come ; it wouldn't be nice of you not to come."

I followed her into the living-room, but I knew that actually
Lambert liked me hardly at all. No doubt—and not without
reason —he held me responsible for all those things in Nadine
that pained him : her aggressiveness, her insincerity, her stubbornness. I thought, too, that he was only too inclined to
seek a mother in a woman older than he, and that he fought
that infantile temptation. His face, with its upturned nose
and soft cheeks, betrayed a heart and flesh haunted by dreams
of submission.

" You can't imagine what Lambert just told me," Nadine
said excitedly. " The Americans haven't repatriated one de-
portee in ten ; they're letting them rot where they are."

" The first few days, half of them died because they stuffed
them with sausages and tinned foods," Lambert said. " Now
they give them soup in the morning and coffee and a large
hunk of bread in the evening. And they're dropping like flies
from typhus."

" That should be known," I said. " We should protest."

" Perron's going to do it. But he wants unimpeachable
facts, and it's difficult to get them because they're not letting
the French Red Cross into the camps. That's why I'm going
back."

" Take me with you," Nadine said.

Lambert smiled. " There's nothing I'd like more."

" Did I say something funny?" Nadine asked angrily.

" You know very well it's impossible," Lambert replied.
" They're not letting anybody through but war correspondents."

" There are women war correspondents."

" But you're not one of them. And it's too late now ;
they're not accrediting any more. Anyhow, it's nothing to be
sorry about," he added. " It isn't the kind of job I'd suggest
for you."

He was speaking primarily for himself, but Nadine believed
she had detected a protective tone in his voice. " Why not? I
can do what you've done, can't I?"

" Do you want to see some pictures I brought back?"

" Yes, let's see them," she said eagerly.

He threw the pictures on the table. I'd have preferred not
looking at them, but I had no choice. The pictures of the

charnel houses were at least bearable—the number were too large for imagination to grasp, and then how can you feel sorry for piles of bones? But there is no escape for us when we're faced with the pictures of the living. All those eyes . . .

"I've seen worse," Nadine said.

Lambert took back the pictures without answering and said encouragingly, "You know, if you really feel like becoming a reporter, it wouldn't be very difficult. All you have to do is talk it over with Perron. Here in France there are a lot of things which could be investigated."

Nadine interrupted him. "What I want is to see the world as it is. Arranging words afterwards on paper wouldn't interest me."

"I'm sure you'd do all right," Lambert said warmly. "You've got a lot of guts, you know how to make people talk, you're clever, and you'd get through everywhere. As for putting it down on paper, that's something you learn pretty fast."

"No," she said stubbornly. "When you write you never tell the truth. Perron's series on Portugal—it's full of holes. And I'm sure yours is the same. I don't believe it; that's why I want to see things with my own eyes. But I wouldn't try to dress them up and then go and peddle them."

Lambert's face darkened. Quickly, I said, "For my part, I find Lambert's articles only too convincing. The Dachau hospital—you get the impression of having visited it yourself."

"Your impressions!" Nadine said impatiently. "What do they prove?" There was a brief silence and then she asked, "What the hell! Is Marie ever going to bring that tea or isn't she?" Authoritatively, she called out, "Marie!"

Marie appeared in the doorway in her blue uniform; Lambert stood up and smiled broadly. "Marie-Ange! What in the world are you doing here?"

She blushed fiercely and turned on her heel. I stopped her. "You might answer, you know."

Staring straight at Lambert, she said, "I'm the maid."

Lambert, too, was blushing, and Nadine looked at him suspiciously. "Marie-Ange? You know her? Marie-Ange who?"

There was an embarrassed silence and then she said brusquely, "Marie-Ange Bizet."

I felt a sudden flush of anger rise to my cheeks. "The reporter?"

She shrugged her shoulders. "Yes," she answered. "I'm leaving—I'm leaving immediately. You needn't bother to sack me."

"You came here to spy on us in our own home? I've never heard of such a dirty trick!"

"I didn't know you knew any reporters," she said, looking at Lambert.

"Why don't you slap her! What are you waiting for!" Nadine shouted. "She's listened to all our conversations, snooped everywhere, read our letters. She'll tell everything, to everyone . . ."

"Oh, you and your big mouth, you don't frighten me," Marie-Ange said.

I grabbed Nadine by the wrists just in time to keep her from striking Marie-Ange; she probably would have knocked her down. But she lacked the nerve to pull herself free from my restraint.

Marie-Ange walked to the door, and I followed her. In the hall she calmly asked me, "Don't you want me to finish doing the windows?"

"No. What I want to know is which paper sent you."

"None. I came on my own. I thought I'd be able to write a nice little article which would be easy to sell. You know, what they call a profile," she said in a professional voice.

"Yes . . . Well, I'm going to let all the papers know about this, and the one that buys your piece will pay dearly for it."

"Oh, I won't even try to sell it now; it's all spoiled." She removed the blue uniform and slipped on her coat. "That means my weeks of housework were all for nothing. And how I hate housework!" she added dejectedly.

I remained silent, but no doubt she felt my anger wavering, for she chanced a tiny smile. "You know, I never intended to write anything inconsiderate," she said in a little girl's voice. "I was only trying to get the atmosphere."

"Is that why you were going through our papers?"

"Oh, that! Believe me, I was reading them only for my own pleasure." In a sulky voice, she added, "Of course, it's easy for you to shout me down; I'm clearly in the wrong . . . But do you think it's simple to get a start? You, you're the wife of a famous man—it's all set up for you. But I have to make my own way. Listen," she said, "give me a chance. I'll bring you the article to-morrow and you can blue-pencil whatever you don't like."

"And then you'll go right ahead and sell it without cuts!"

"No, I swear I won't. If you want, I can give you a weapon to use against me—a complete confession, signed and sealed. You'll have me cold. Come on! Say yes. After all, I've washed stacks of dishes for you, and you've got to admit I had plenty of nerve."

"And you still have plenty."

I hesitated. If I had been told all this, I could imagine myself grabbing the shameless creature who had violated our privacy by the hair and throwing her down the stairs. But there she was, a swarthy, scrawny little girl, without beauty and with an overwhelming desire to get a start.

Finally, I said. "My husband never grants interviews. He won't permit it."

"Ask him. After all, the work's already done . . . I'll call you up to-morrow morning," she added quickly. "I hope you won't hold it against me, will you? I hate it when someone holds a grudge against me." She let out an embarrassed little laugh. "I can never hold a grudge against anyone."

"Neither can I," I said.

"That beats everything!" Nadine shouted, charging down the corridor with Lambert. "You'd let her publish her article! You stand there smiling at her! At that . . . at that informer!"

Marie-Ange opened the door and slammed it hard behind her.

"She promised to let me see the article first," I said.

"That informer!" Nadine repeated in a shrill voice. "She read my diary, she read Diego's letters, she . . ." Her voice broke; she was shaken by a blazing anger, like those of her childhood. "And instead of beating her, you're going to reward her!"

"I felt sorry for her."

"Sorry for her! You're always sorry for everyone! By what right?" She looked at me with a kind of hate. "Basically, it's nothing but contempt; you've never in your life had any real feeling for people."

"Calm down. It's not as serious as all that."

" Oh, I know; I'm wrong. Naturally! You never excuse me. And you're perfectly right! I don't want any of your pity!"

" She's not a bad sort, you know," Lambert said. " A little too ambitious, but nice."

" Well, why don't you go congratulate her, too. Go ahead, run after her."

Abruptly, Nadine ran to her room and loudly slammed the door.

" I'm terribly sorry," Lambert said.

" Oh, it's not your fault."

" Reporters these days have the morals of stool pigeons. I can understand Nadine getting angry ; in her place I'd see red, too."

He didn't have to defend her to me, but at least his intentions were good. " Yes, I understand too," I said.

" Well, I guess I'll be going," Lambert said.

" Have a nice trip," I said. " You ought to come see Nadine more often," I added. " She's very fond of you, you know."

He gave me an embarrassed smile. " You can hardly tell it by the way she acts!"

" She was very disappointed about not hearing from you sooner. That's why she wasn't very friendly."

" But she specifically told me not to ring her first."

" It would have made her happy if you'd have called her anyhow. She has to be very sure of a friendship to give herself wholeheartedly to it."

" She has no reason to doubt mine," Lambert said. Abruptly, he added, " I'm extremely fond of Nadine."

" Then make sure she realises it."

" I've been doing my best." He hesitated and then held out his hand to me. " In any case, I'll drop in as soon as I get back," he said.

I went back to my room without daring to knock at Nadine's door. How unfair she was! It's true that I willingly seek excuses for others and that indulgence does wither the heart, but if I'm demanding in regard to Nadine it's only because she isn't just another case stretched out on the couch. For her, I do feel something—that gnawing feeling, that worried sound in my breast.

She grumbled on principle when little Bizet's insignificant

article appeared. But her humour improved considerably
when the offices of *Vigilance* finally opened; given specific
duties, she showed herself to be an excellent secretary, and it
made her quite proud. The first issue of the magazine was a
great success; Robert and Henri were overjoyed and excitedly
began preparing the next one. From the day he convinced
Henri to unite the destiny of *L'Espoir* with that of the S.R.L.,
Robert overflowed with affection for him, and I, too, was
happy because Henri was in fact his only true friend. Julien,
Lenoir, the Pelletiers, the Canges—we'd spent some pleasant
moments with them, but it didn't go much further than that.
Among his old Socialist comrades, some had been collaborators and others had died in the concentration camps;
Charlier was taking a rest cure in Switzerland; and those who
remained faithful to the Party berated Robert, who in turn
berated them no less. He had disappointed Lafaurie by
founding the S.R.L., instead of rallying to Communism; their
relationship lacked warmth. Robert had lost practically all
contact with men of his own age. But he preferred it that
way: he held his whole generation responsible for that war
they hadn't known how to prevent, and he felt he had retained
only too many links with his past. He purposely wanted to
work with young men, for to-day politics and action had a
new face and new methods to which he felt he had to adapt
himself. He believed that even his ideas needed revising;
that's why he kept repeating so insistently that his major work
was still before him. In the essay he was now writing, he was
seeking to reach a synthesis of his old ideas and new perspective of the world. His goals, however, were the same as
always: above and beyond its immediate objectives, the task
of the S.R.L. was to maintain the hope of a revolution which
would fulfil its humanist intentions. But Robert was now
convinced that the revolution could not come about without
major sacrifices; the man of to-morrow would not be the one
Jaurès had so optimistically defined. What meaning, then,
what chance of remaining valid, did the old values have—
truth, freedom, individual morality, literature, thought? To
save them meant having to reshape them. And that's precisely
what Robert was attempting; it interested him profoundly
and I told myself with satisfaction that he'd once again found
a happy balance between writing and action. Of course, he

was very busy, but he enjoyed that. And my own life, too, had been full. Robert, Nadine, my patients, my book—there was no room in my days for a single regret, a single desire. The white-haired young woman was now sleeping without nightmares; she had joined the Communist Party, had taken lovers, too many lovers, and had begun drinking immoderately. True, it wasn't a miracle of adjustment, but at least she was able to sleep. And I was happy that afternoon, because little Ferdinand had drawn a house with windows and doors; for the first time, no iron fence. I had just finished calling his mother when the concierge brought the post. Robert and Nadine were both at the magazine—it was the day he received callers—and I was alone in the flat. I opened Romieux's letter and a sudden fear swept over me, as if I'd been projected into the stratosphere. A psychoanalytical congress was going to be held in New York in January, and I was invited. Arrangements could be made for lectures in New England, Chicago, and Canada. Shocked, I stood the letter on the mantelpiece and reread it. How I loved to travel! With the exception of a few people, there was nothing I loved more in the world. But it was one of the things I thought I was finished with forever. If I'd been offered a trip to Belgium or Italy, that would still have been within the realm of the possible. But New York! I was unable to take my eyes off that word which, no matter how often I saw it, always remained a fantasy-word to me. New York had always been for me a legendary city, and for a long time now I'd stopped believing in miracles: that scrap of paper wasn't enough to brush aside time, space, and common sense. I slipped the letter into my purse, left the house, and walked rapidly through the streets. Somebody important was making fun of me; someone was playing a trick on me and I needed Robert's help to straighten things out in my mind. I hurriedly climbed the stairway of the Mauvanes Publishing Company.

"You here?" Nadine said in a reproachful voice.

"As you see."

"Father is busy," she said importantly.

She was enthroned behind a desk in the middle of a large office which served as a waiting-room. A great many people were waiting—young and old, men and women—a real mob. Before the war Robert received quite a few visitors, but nothing to compare with this. What must have made him especially happy was that they were mostly young people. Many, no doubt, came out of curiosity, out of idleness, out of opportunism. But there were also many who had enjoyed Robert's books and who took an interest in his political activities. Good. So he was not a voice in the wilderness; his contemporaries still had eyes to read him, ears to hear him.

Nadine stood up. "Six o'clock! The office is closing!" she cried out in a cross voice. She followed the disappointed visitors to the door and turned the key in the lock.

"What a mob!" she said, laughing. "You'd think they were waiting for a free lunch." She opened the door to Robert's office. "All clear."

Robert smiled at me from the doorway. "Taking a holiday?"

"Yes, I felt like going for a little walk."

Nadine turned towards her father. "It's a scream to watch you functioning. You're like a priest in his confessional."

"I feel more like a fortune-teller reading palms."

Abruptly, as if someone had pressed a button, Nadine burst out laughing; her fits of gaiety were rare but strident. "Take a look at that!"

She pointed to a suitcase with well-worn corners; a label was pasted on the faded leather: "*My Life* by Joséphine Mièvre." "Talk about a manuscript!" she said between gasps of laughter. "It's her real name. And you can't imagine what she told me." In her eyes, glistening with pleasure, there was a triumphal light; laughter was her revenge. "She said to me, 'I, Mademoiselle, I am a living document!' Sixty years old. She lives in Aurillac. She starts at the very beginning and skips no details."

She kicked the suitcase and the top sprang open. Reams and reams of rose-coloured paper covered with green ink; not a single word scratched out. Robert picked up a page, skimmed it, and threw it back. "It isn't even funny."

"Maybe there are dirty passages," Nadine said hopefully, kneeling down in front of the suitcase. So much paper, so many hours! Tepid hours by a lamp at the fireside, surrounded by the smell of a provincial dining-room; hours so full and so empty, so deliciously justified, so stupidly lost.

" No, it isn't funny!" Nadine stood up impatiently; there was no longer any trace of gaiety on her face. " Well, shall we shove off?"

" Five more minutes," Robert replied.

" Hurry up; it stinks of literature in here."

" How does literature smell?"

" Like an old man who neglects himself."

It wasn't really an odour, but for three hours the air had been saturated with hope, fear, resentment, and through the silence one breathed in that vague sadness that follows a debilitating sickness. Nadine pulled a piece of garnet-coloured knitting from her drawer and began clicking the needles together rapidly. Ordinarily, she was quite wasteful of her time, but as soon as you asked her to be a little patient she hastened to prove that not a single one of her moments was to be wasted. My eyes lingered on her desk. There was something provocative about that black cover on which the words "Selected Poems: René Douce" were written in large red letters. I opened the note-book.

"Les prés sont vénéneux mais jolis en automne . . ."

I turned the page. "J'ai heurté, savez-vous, d'incroyable Florides . . ."

" Nadine!"

" What?"

" Someone who sends in selected poems by Apollinaire, Rimbaud, Baudelaire, and signs it all with his own name . . . He can't really believe they won't be recognised!"

" Oh, I know what that's all about," Nadine said indifferently. " The poor bastard gave Sézenac twenty thousand francs to write some poems for him. And you can imagine Sézenac wasting his time turning out original stuff for him!"

" But when he comes around, he'll have to be told the truth," I said.

" That doesn't matter. Sézenac's already pocketed the money and I'd be very surprised if his customer dared to protest. First of all, he has no recourse, and secondly, he'd be much too ashamed."

" Sézenac does things like that?" I asked in astonishment.

" How do you think he gets along?" Nadine said, throwing her knitting into the drawer. " Sometimes the things he cooks up are pretty funny."

" Paying someone twenty thousand francs to sign poems you haven't written—I find that pretty hard to believe," Robert said.

" Why? If you're determined to see your name in print . . ." Nadine said. Lowering her voice—in front of her father she watched her language—she muttered purely for my benefit, " You might just as well pay as break your ass doing the work."

When we reached the bottom of the stairs, she asked warily, " Are we going to have a drink at the café across the street, like last Thursday?"

" Of course," Robert said.

Nadine's face brightened and, after we were seated at one of the round marble tables, she said gaily, " You've got to admit I'm pretty good at protecting you!"

" Yes."

She gave her father a worried look. " Aren't you satisfied with me?"

" For myself. I'm delighted. It's you I'm worried about. This won't get you anywhere."

" No job does," Nadine said, stiffening suddenly.

" That depends. The other day you told me that Lambert suggested that you become a reporter. It seems to me that that kind of thing would be a lot more interesting."

" Oh, if I were a man, I wouldn't say no," Nadine replied. " But a woman reporter doesn't have a chance in a thousand of succeeding." With a gesture, she cut off our protestations. " Not what I call succeeding," she said loftily. " Women are always vegetating."

" Not always," I suggested.

" You think so?" she snickered. " Look at yourself, for example. All right, you get along, you have patients. But you'll never in all your life be a Freud."

She had never outgrown the childish habit of spitefully attacking me when her father was present.

" Between being Freud and doing nothing," I said, " there are a great many intermediate steps."

" I'm doing something; I'm a secretary."

" If you're satisfied with that," Robert said hastily, " that's the main thing, after all."

I was sorry he hadn't held his tongue to begin with; he had

needlessly spoiled Nadine's evening. I'd warned him often
about that, but he couldn't make up his mind to forget the
ambitions he had nourished for her.

"Anyhow," she said aggressively, "the fate of a single
individual is so unimportant to-day."

"*Your* fate is important to me," Robert said with a smile.

"But it depends on neither you nor me. That's why they
all make me laugh, those little idiots who want so desperately
to be someone." She cleared her throat and without looking
at us said, "The day I have the courage to take up something difficult, I'll go into politics."

"What are you waiting for? Why not start working for the
S.R.L. now?" Robert asked.

She drained her glass of mineral water. "No, I don't agree
with the S.R.L. And besides, you're against the Communists."

Robert shrugged his shoulders. "Do you think Lafaurie
would be so friendly if he believed I was working against
them?"

Nadine smiled thinly. "It seems that Lafaurie is going
to ask you not to hold your meeting," she said.

"Who told you that?" Robert asked.

"Lachaume, yesterday. They're not at all happy; they
think the S.R.L. is off on a wrong tack."

Robert shrugged his shoulders. "It may be that Lachaume
and his little band of leftists aren't happy, but they're wrong
to think that they are the Central Committee. It so happens,
I just saw Lafaurie last week."

"Lachaume saw him the day before yesterday," Nadine
said. "I assure you," she added, "it's serious. They held a
big council of war and decided that measures have to be
taken. Lafaurie is coming to talk to you."

Robert remained silent a moment. "If that's true, then
everything's hopeless!" he said.

"It is true," Nadine said. "They say that instead of working in harmony with them, your S.R.L. is preaching a policy
contrary to theirs, that your meeting is an open declaration of
war, that you are splitting the left, and that they're going to
be forced to start a campaign against you." Nadine's voice
sounded complacent; no doubt she had not weighed the
seriousness of what she was saying. When we're in real

trouble, it upsets her terribly, but our little setbacks merely divert her.

"Forced!" Robert said. "That's really something! And to say that I'm splitting the left! They haven't changed," he added angrily. "They'll never change! What they'd have liked is for the S.R.L. to obey them blindly. At the first sign of independence, they charge us with being hostile!"

"Obviously, if you don't agree with them, they consider you wrong," Nadine said in a reasonable voice. "And you do exactly the same thing."

"You can have different opinions and still maintain a unity of action," Robert said. "After all, that was the idea of the National Front."

"They consider you dangerous," Nadine said. "They say you preach a politics of doom, that you want to sabotage the reconstruction."

"Listen," Robert replied, "either take an interest in politics or don't take an interest in politics, but in any case don't be a parrot. If you used your own brains, you'd understand that it's their policies that are catastrophic."

"They can't act otherwise," Nadine said. "If they attempted to take power, America would intervene immediately."

"They have to gain time, granted. But they could certainly go about it differently," Robert said. He shrugged his shoulders. "I'm perfectly willing to admit that their position is difficult; they're more or less trapped. Ever since the death of the S.F.I.O., they've been forced to take a number of positions simultaneously: they're left of left and right of left in turn. But that's precisely why they ought to welcome the existence of another leftist party."

"Well," Nadine said, "they don't welcome it."

Abruptly she got up; she was satisfied with having created her little sensation and she wasn't at all anxious to let herself be dragged into a discussion in which she obviously would not have come out on top. "I'm going for a walk."

Robert and I left the café and walked home along the quays.

"I'm going to telephone Lafaurie now!" Robert said to me. "When you think how important it is for us to work together, side by side! And they know it! But they'll never

tolerate an independent leftist movement. The Socialists are
nothing any more; that kind of a National Front, of course,
they don't mind at all. But a vigorous young movement that
looks like it's getting off to a good start, that's something
else again . . ."

He continued talking angrily, and as I listened I thought,
" I don't want to leave him." In the old days, it never
bothered me to be away from him for a while: our love, like
our life, extended through eternity. But I now had come to
realise that we have only one life, a life already seriously
encroached upon, and threatened, by the future. Robert
wasn't invulnerable. And suddenly, he seemed even fragile.
He had committed a grave error in counting on the bene-
volence of the Communists; faced with their hostility, serious
problems would arise. " That's it; that's the impasse," I said
to myself. He could neither give up his programme nor maintain it against Communist opposition, and there were no
intermediate solutions. Maybe things would work out if the
Communists decided to tolerate the meeting. Robert's fate
wasn't in his own hands but in theirs. The thought horrified me. With a single word, they could destroy the beautiful
balance he had established. No, this wasn't the moment to
leave him.

When we entered the study, I said ironically, " Look at
what I got this afternoon!"

I handed Robert Romieux's letter and his face was suddenly transformed; I saw in it that joy that ought to have
been mine. " This is wonderful! Why didn't you tell me
before?"

" I'm not going to go away for three months," I said.

" Why not?" He looked at me in surprise. " It would be a
wonderful trip."

" I've got too much to do here," I murmured.

" What are you talking about? You've got plenty of time
between now and January to wrap things up. Nadine's big
enough now to get along without you—and so am I," he added
with a smile.

" America is very far away," I said.

" What's got into you!" he said, examining me critically.
" It'll do you a lot of good to get around a bit."

" We're going to take a bicycle trip this summer."

"That's not really getting around," Robert said. He smiled. "I'm sure of one thing. If someone came and told you that the whole thing had fallen through, you'd be damned disappointed."

"Possibly."

He was right; even now I was anxious to take the trip. And that was precisely one of the things that disturbed me. All those memories, all those desires that were awakening—what a nuisance! Why had they suddenly come to upset my quiet little moribund life? That evening, Robert and Henri vented their indignation on Lafaurie and encouraged each other to hold out. If the S.R.L. became a real force, the Communists would have to reckon with them and the union would be re-established. I listened and I was interested in what they were saying; and yet at the same time, a jumble of crazy pictures raced through my head. It wasn't any better the next day. Seated at my desk, I spent a solid hour asking myself, "Shall I accept? Or shall I refuse?" I ended by picking up the telephone and calling Paula; it was useless to pretend to work, and since I had promised Paula I would go to see her one day this seemed as good a time as any. Naturally, she was at home, alone; I started out on foot for her house. I'm really quite fond of Paula, but at the same time she frightens me a bit. Often, in the morning, I feel a suffocating shadow spread over me, the shadow of all the misfortunes that are awakening, and my first thought is of her. I open my eyes, and I'm awake; she opens hers, and immediately it's night within her. I say to myself: "If I were in her place, I'd never be able to stand that life." But I'm not in her place; she is, and for her it's certainly more bearable than it would be for me. Paula can stay shut up for days and weeks, doing nothing, seeing no one, without becoming bored. And she is still able not to admit to herself that Henri no longer loves her. But one of these days the truth will explode in her. And then what will happen? What advice could we give her then? Sing? But that would never be enough to console her.

I approached her house and felt a wrench at my heart. It was just like her to live in that village full of unfortunate people! I don't know where they had hidden themselves during the Occupation, but this springtime seemed to have brought them all back to life, with their goitres, their scars, their ragged clothes. Three of them were sitting next to a marble plaque covered with a wreath of faded flowers, their back against the iron fence surrounding the square. Their faces red with wine and anger, a man and a woman were fighting over a black oilcloth sack. They were hatefully hurling insults at each other, but their hands, clenched tightly on the shopping bag, hardly budged. The third was cheerfully watching them. I turned off into a little street. Faded wooden doors barricaded storerooms where ragpickers came each morning to unload their paper and scrap metal. Other doors with windows in them, opened on to waiting-rooms in which women were sitting with dogs on their knees. I had read in a prospectus that in these dispensaries " birds and little animals " were cared for or done away with without pain. I stopped in front of a sign, " Furnished Room To Let," and I rang. The same huge garbage can still stood at the bottom of the stairway, and no sooner did I begin walking up the stairs than a black dog began barking savagely. Paula, who had a taste for stage settings, achieved an easy theatrical effect whenever she opened the door of her apartment to a new visitor. I myself was always astonished by that sudden splendour—and by her exaggerated get-up. She preferred her own fancies to the conventional, and she always seemed to overdo things just a little. When she opened the door for me, she was wearing a long, full, mauve-coloured taffeta dressing-gown and sandal-like shoes with very high heels and lacing which criss-crossed her legs. Her collection of shoes would have made a fetishist turn green with envy.

" Come in and get warm," she said, leading me over to the fireplace in which heavy logs were crackling.

" It's not cold out."

She glanced at the tightly closed windows. " Yes, that's what they say." She sat down and leaned towards me with grave solicitude. " How are you?"

" All right. But I'm up to my ears in work. People don't have their daily ration of horror any more, so they're beginning to torture themselves again."

" And your book?"

" Progressing."

She questioned me out of politeness and I replied for the same reason ; I was well aware she had never been concerned with my work.

"Does it really interest you?" she asked.

"It fascinates me."

"You're very lucky!" Paula said.

"To do work that interests me?"

"To hold your fate in your own hands."

That was hardly the way I looked at it, but I hadn't come here to talk about myself. I said warmly, "Do you know what I've been thinking ever since I heard you sing again at the Christmas party? That you really ought to do something with your voice. It's all well and good to devote yourself to Henri, but after all, you count for something too . . ."

"Isn't that a coincidence! I just had a long discussion with Henri about that very same thing," she said indifferently. She paused and shook her head. "No, I shall never sing again in public."

"Why not? I'm sure you'd make a big hit."

"And what do you suppose that would mean to me?" she said with a smile. "My name on posters, my picture in the papers—really, it doesn't interest me. I could have had all that a long time ago, but I wanted no part of it. I'm afraid you misunderstood me," she added. "I'm not interested in personal glory. A great love, it seems to me, is so much more important than a career. The only thing I regret is that its success doesn't depend on me alone."

"But you don't have to choose between the two," I said. "You can continue to love Henri and sing."

She looked at me gravely. "A great love doesn't leave a woman free for anything else. I know the understanding that exists between you and Robert," she added. "But it isn't what I would call a great love."

I had no desire to discuss either her definitions or my life. "All the days you spend here, alone . . . you would have time to work."

"It isn't a question of time." She smiled at me reproachfully. "Why do you think I gave up singing ten years ago? Because I realised that Henri required all of me."

"You say he himself advised you to go back to work."

"But if I took him at his word he'd be shocked and dismayed!" she said cheerfully. "He'd never be able to tolerate a single one of my thoughts not belonging to him."

"What selfishness!"

"It isn't selfish to love." Gently, she smoothed her silken

skirt. " Oh, he asks nothing of me ; he's never asked anything
of me. But I know my sacrifice is necessary, not only for his
happiness, but for his work, his mission. And now more than
ever."

" Why is his success so important to you, and not yours?"

" Oh, I don't care in the least if he's famous or not," she
said vehemently. " Something entirely different is at stake."

" And what would that be?"

Abruptly, she stood up. " I made some mulled wine.
Would you care for some?"

" I'd love some."

I listened to her moving about in the kitchen, and I asked
myself uneasily, " What does she think—really think?" She
claimed to scorn glory, and yet it was precisely at the time
when Henri's name had begun to take on importance, when
they had honoured him as a hero of the Resistance and proclaimed him the hope of the new literature, that Paula had
once again wrapped herself in her mantle of love. I remembered how mournful and disillusioned she had been a
year earlier. How exactly did she feel about that love?
Why did she refuse to escape in work? How did she see the
world around her? I was shut in with her between those red
walls ; we were watching the fire, exchanging words, but I had
no idea of what was going on inside her head. I got up,
walked over to the window, and pulled the curtain aside.
Evening was falling, a man in a ragged coat was walking a
magnificent Great Dane at the end of a leash, and under the
mysterious inscription " Speciality: Rare and Saxon Birds " a
monkey chained to the bars of a window seemed also to be
perplexedly questioning the dusk. I let the curtain fall back
in place. What had I been hoping for? To see that familiar
setting for a fleeting moment through Paula's eyes? To know
from that setting the flavour of her days? No, the little
monkey will never see with the eyes of man. And I will never
slip into the skin of another.

Paula returned from the kitchen solemnly bearing a silver
tray on which two bowls were steaming, " You like it sweet,
don't you?"

I inhaled the red lava's burning aroma. " It smells deli-
cious."

Calm and collected, she slowly sipped the wine as if she were
taking a truth potion. " Poor Henri!" she murmured.

" Why poor?"

" He's going through a difficult crisis, and I'm afraid he'll suffer a great deal before he comes out of it."

" What crisis? He seems to be in fine shape and his recent articles are among the best he's ever written."

" Articles!" She looked at me with a kind of anger. " There was a time when he had nothing but contempt for journalism; he looked upon it merely as a way of earning his livelihood. He kept himself apart from politics, wanted to be an individual."

" But circumstances have changed, Paula."

" What do circumstances matter!" she said with feeling. " The important thing is that he mustn't change. During the war, he risked his life; that was noble. But to-day, the noble thing would be to turn his back on the world."

" What makes you say that?" I asked.

She shrugged her shoulders without answering. With a trace of annoyance, I added, " He surely must have explained to you why he's become involved in politics. As for me, I approve absolutely. Don't you think you ought to trust his judgment?"

" He's turned off on to a road that isn't his," she said categorically. " I know, and I can even prove it to you."

" That would surprise me," I said.

" The proof," she said emphatically, " is that he's become incapable of writing."

" Perhaps he's not writing at the moment," I said, " but that doesn't mean he'll never write again."

" I don't pretend to be infallible," Paula said. " But remember this: it was I who made Henri. I created him as he creates characters in his books, and I know him as he knows them. He's betraying his mission; it's up to me to lead him back to it. And there you have the reason why I can't start thinking about myself."

" You know, the only mission a person has is the one he assigns himself."

" Henri isn't just another writer."

" Of course," I said, " none of them are."

She shook her head. " If he were just a writer, I wouldn't be interested. There are so many writers! When I took him, at twenty-five, he thought only of literature. But I knew at once I could make him rise much higher than that. What I have taught him is that his life and his work should become a unit so completely realised, so pure, so absolute that it would serve as an example to all the world."

I thought anxiously that if she spoke that way to Henri he must be wearied beyond all measure.

" What you mean is that a man should be as careful with his life as he is with his books," I said. " But that doesn't prevent him from changing."

" On condition that the change is in harmony with himself. I've evolved a great deal myself, but I've always stayed on my own path."

" No one has a path laid out in advance," I said. " The world isn't the same any more, and no one can do anything about it. You have to try to adapt yourself to the way it is." I smiled at her. " For a few weeks, I too, was under the illusion that everything would once again be the same as before the war. But that was just plain nonsense."

Stubbornly, Paula stared at the fire. " Time itself is an illusion," she said. She turned abruptly towards me. " For example, think of Rimbaud. What do you see?"

" What do I see?"

" Yes, what image of him?"

" A picture of him as a young man."

" You see! There's a Rimbaud, a Baudelaire, a Stendhal. They were older, younger, but their whole lives are contained in a single picture. There's only one Henri, and I shall always be I. Time is powerless to change it; it's we who betray ourselves, not time."

" You're confusing things," I said. " When you're seventy you'll still be you, but you'll have a different relationship with people, with things." I paused briefly and added. " With your mirror."

" I've never looked at myself much in mirrors." She gave me a slightly suspicious look. " What are you trying to prove?"

I remained silent for a moment. Negating time—everyone no doubt is tempted at one time or another. I often was. I vaguely envied Paula her obstinate assurance.

" All I'm saying is that we live on earth and have to resign ourselves to it. You ought to let Henri do as he likes and pay a little attention to yourself."

" You speak as if Henri and I were two distinct beings,"

she replied dreamily. " Perhaps it's a kind of experience that's simply incommunicable."

I had lost all hope of convincing her. Besides, I no longer even knew of what. Nevertheless, I said, " But you are distinct, and the proof is that you criticise him."

" Yes, there's a superficial part of him against which I fight sometimes and which separates us," she replied. " But fundamentally, we're one single being. I used to feel it often ; in fact, I clearly remember my first awareness of it. I was almost terrified ; it's strange, you know, to lose yourself absolutely in another. But how rewarding it is when you find the other in yourself!" With an inspired look, she gazed at the ceiling. " You can be sure of one thing: my hour will come again. Henri will be returned to me as he truly is, as I will have returned him to himself."

There was an almost desperate violence in her voice, and I gave up discussing the matter with her any further. Spiritedly, I said, " Anyhow, it would do you good to see people, to get out a little. Wouldn't you like to come to Claudie's with me next Thursday?"

Paula's eyes came back to earth again ; she looked as if she had achieved some inner orgasm and that she now found herself released, lighter than air. She smiled at me. " Oh, no! No, thanks," she said. " Claudie came to see me last week and I think I've had enough of her to last me for months. Did you know that Scriassine was living with her? I wonder how he could ever have done that . . ."

" I suppose he was broke."

" Talk about a harem!" Paula said.

She let out a hearty laugh which made her look ten years younger ; that's how she always used to be with me. In Henri's presence, she would become stiff and unnatural, and nowadays she gave the impression that she always felt he was watching her. Perhaps if she had had the courage to live for herself she might have rediscovered her old cheerfulness. " I didn't know how to approach her ; I was clumsy," I said to myself reproachfully as I left the house. The existence she was leading wasn't normal, and at times she was quite clearly irrational. But with things as they are now, I would hardly have been capable of seriously attempting to set her straight. A normal existence—what could be more irrational? It's

fantastic the number of things you're forced not to think
about in order to go from one end of the day to the other
without jumping the track! And the number of memories
that have to be driven from your mind, the truths that have
to be evaded! "That's why I'm afraid to leave," I said to
myself. In Paris, near Robert, I manage without too much
difficulty to avoid the traps; I carefully mark them, and there
are alarm bells to warn me of dangers. But alone, under an
unknown sky, what would happen to me? What truths would
come suddenly to blind me? What chasms would open before
me? Oh, yes, chasms close, truths fade out—that's sure and
certain; I've seen it happen often enough before. We're like
those earthworms one vainly cuts in two, or those lobsters
whose legs grow back again. But the moment of false agony,
the moment you'd rather die than mend yourself once again—
when I think of it, I lose heart. I try to reason with myself:
"Why should anything happen to me? But why shouldn't
anything happen to me?" It's never safe to go off the beaten
path. It's true, I feel a little stifled here, but you get used to
being stifled. And a habit is never bad, despite what they
say.

"What's wrong with you?" Nadine asked me suspiciously
a few days later. She was in my room, lying on my couch,
wrapped in my dressing-gown. That's how I usually found
her when I came home; only the clothing, the furniture, the
lives of others had any value in her eyes.

"Why? Do I look as if something's wrong with me?" I
asked.

I hadn't spoken to her of Romieux's letter, but although she
had no real understanding of me, she always noticed my
slightest change of mood.

"You look as though you were walking in your sleep," she
said.

It was true that I usually questioned her in detail about her
days and that this evening I had taken off my coat and
combed my hair in silence.

"I spent the afternoon at St. Anne's. I expect I'm a little
tired," I explained. "And you? What did you do?"

"Are you really interested?" she asked grudgingly.

"Of course."

Nadine's face suddenly brightened; she gave up restraining

her pleasure any longer. " I've just met the man of my life!"
she said aggressively.

" The real one?" I asked with a smile.

" Yes, the real one," she replied seriously. " He's a friend of
Lachaume's, a really great man—not a scribbler like the
others. He's a militant, an honest-to-God militant. His name's
Joly."

She had broken with Henri a short time before; her reactions were so predictable that it astonished me how easily
she could be taken in by them. " Well, I suppose you'll be
joining the Party now, won't you?" I said.

" He was shocked when I told him I wasn't already a
member. He doesn't split hairs, you know, not him. He
ploughs right through everything. That's what I call a
man!"

" I've thought for a long time that you ought to have your
experiment with the Party, once and for all."

" Because, of course, for you it's just an experiment," she
said nastily. " I join, I leave. Youth must have its fling.
Is that it?"

" No, you misunderstand me. I didn't say anything like
that."

" Oh, I know what you're thinking. But Joly's power, you
understand, is that he believes in truths; he doesn't amuse
himself with experiments. He acts!"

For days on end I listened unflinchingly to the aggressive
eulogies she showered on Joly. On her desk, Das Kapital
lay open next to her chemistry book and her eyes wandered
sadly from one volume to the other. She soon began examining all my acts and words in the light of historical materialism. There were quite a few beggars in the streets at the
beginning of this cold springtime, and if I gave them a few
sous she would say sneeringly, " If you imagine that by giving
that poor outcast a handout you'll change the face of the
world . . ."

" Oh, I'm not aiming so high. If it makes him happy, it's
enough."

" And you ease your conscience. Everybody wins." She
always attributed shabby motives to me. " You think that
by refusing to go out in the world and by being rude to
people you're escaping your class. But you're just a shabbily
dressed bourgeoise, that's all."

I really didn't enjoy going to Claudie's. During the war, she had sent me quite a few packages from her Burgundy château, and now she imperiously summoned me to her Thursday gatherings. I couldn't, after all, refuse, but it was with great reluctance that I mounted my bicycle that snowy May evening. Winter had capriciously returned in the middle of spring: heavy flakes, warm to the eye, cold to the skin, were slowly drifting to earth from the white, silent sky, and I felt like riding straight ahead of me, far away, on one of those soft, fleece-covered roads. Social obligations seemed more dreadful to me now than they ever did before. Despite all Robert's efforts to hide, to run from reporters, decorations, academies, salons, first nights, they were nevertheless making him into a sort of public monument. And being his wife, even I was becoming public. I slowly climbed the stately stairway. I hate that moment when all faces turn towards me and when, with a single rapid glance, they identify and dismember me. Whenever that occurs I take stock of myself and I always wind up with a guilty conscience.

"What a miracle to see you again!" Laura Marva exclaimed. "You're so busy these days! We don't even dare invite you any more."

We had declined at least three of her invitations; among the people I recognised in that mob, there were very few to whom I felt obliged. They believed us to be haughty, misanthropic, or *poseurs*. The idea that we simply didn't enjoy going out in society I don't suppose ever dawned on those people who eagerly came here to bore themselves. Boredom was a scourge that had terrorised me ever since my childhood, and it was above all to escape it that I had wanted to grow up; I had in fact built my whole life around that avoidance. But perhaps those whose hands I was now shaking were so used to boredom that they didn't even feel it; perhaps they didn't even know that the very atmosphere could have a different tang.

"Couldn't Robert come with you?" Claudie asked. "Tell him I think his article in *Vigilance* is marvellous. I know it by heart, I recite it at table, in my bath, in bed. I sleep with it; it's my current lover."

"I'll tell him," I said.

She looked at me intensely and I felt ill at ease. Naturally, I don't like to hear people speak ill of Robert, but when they smother him with eulogies it embarrasses me; I feel an idiotic smile forming on my lips. If I say nothing, it seems to me an affectation; if I speak even a word, I feel garrulous.

"The publication of that magazine is an event of considerable importance," said the painter Perlène, who was in fact Claudie's current lover.

Guite Ventadour joined us. She had written several well-contrived novels and felt herself to be the most notable personality of that salon. Her dress, her manner indicated that she was conscious of no longer being young, but also that she remembered a little too well having been beautiful. She spoke somewhat breathlessly. "The extraordinary thing about Dubreuilh," she said, "is that with such a profound concern for pure art he can still take a passionate interest in the world of to-day. To love both words and men at the same time is very rare."

"Do you keep a diary of his life?" Claudie asked me. "What a document you could offer to the world!"

"I haven't the time," I replied. "And besides, I don't believe he'd like that."

"The thing that astonishes me," said Huguette Volange, "is that you can maintain a profession of your own while living with a man who has such an overpowering personality. As for me, I simply couldn't do it; my dear husband devours all my time. And besides, I think that's only natural."

I quickly rejected all the nasty answers that came to my lips and said as innocuously as possible, "It's simply a question of organisation."

"But I am well organised." She sounded annoyed. "No, it's rather a question of intellectual environment . . ."

They pierced me with their looks, demanded an accounting. It's always like that: they surround me and slyly question me, as if I were already a widow. But Robert is very much alive and I shan't help them to embalm him. They collect his autographs, vie for his manuscripts, set his complete works, decorated with inscriptions, between wooden shelves. I myself have only two or three of his books; no doubt I've purposely failed to demand the return of all those that were borrowed from me. And purposely, I've never sorted and filed his letters, many of which I know I've mislaid; they were intended only for me, are not a repository of information to be opened one day to those prying eyes. I'm not Robert's heir nor am I his witness: I'm his wife.

Guite must have detected my uneasiness. With the assurance of a sovereign who feels at home everywhere, she placed her small, soft hand on my wrist. " But nobody's offered you anything! Let me take you to the buffet." As she led me through the room, she gave me a conspiratorial smile. " I'd like so much to have a little chat with you one day; it's so rare to meet an intelligent woman." She made it seem as if she had just discovered the one person in the gathering who was capable of understanding her. " Do you know what would be nice?" she said. " If you and Dubreuilh could come over to my little place for dinner one evening."

That's one of the most painful moments of the entire ordeal: when, in an offhand or superior way, they suggest an appointment. When I answer with the ritualistic " Robert is so terribly busy these days " I feel their severe, accusing eyes on me. And I finish by admitting my guilt to myself: I'm his wife, yes, but first of all, by what right? And then that isn't any reason to monopolise him; a public monument, after all, belongs to everyone.

" Oh, I know what it is to be harried by one's work," Guite said. " I never go out either. It's quite by chance that you see me here!" Her laugh insinuated that I was pleasantly deluded, that in truth she wasn't there at all. " But this would be different—just a simple little dinner . . . And I'd invite only men," she added in a confidential tone. " I don't care for the company of women; I feel completely lost with them. Don't you?"

" No, I get along very well with women."

She gave me a look of dismayed reproof. " Curious, very curious . . . It must be I who's abnormal."

In her books she willingly proclaimed the inferiority of her sex. But she herself, she imagined, escaped it by the virility of her talent. And she believed she was even superior to men, since, gifted with the same qualities as they, she had in addition the singular and charming merit of being a woman. That trick irritated me. In a professional tone, I said, " You're not at all abnormal. Almost all women prefer men."

Her face froze solidly, and not too pointedly but deliberately she turned towards Huguette Volange. Poor Guite! She was torn between the desire to see justice rendered to her merits and to evade any reproach of narcissism. She therefore attempted to dictate to others what she wanted them to say about her. But if they didn't say it? Would she have to resign herself to being misunderstood? It was a painful dilemma.

Claudie noticed I was alone and, good hostess that she was, threw someone into my arms. " Anne, I don't believe you've ever met Lucie Belhomme. She used to be very friendly with Paula," she said, hurrying off to greet a late-comer.

" You know Paula?" I asked the tall dark woman who was wearing a black ottoman dress and diamonds.

She gave me a forced smile. " Yes, I used to know her very well," she said in an amused voice. "When I first opened Maison Amaryllis and she was opening at Valcourt's, I used to dress her gratis. For publicity reasons, you know. She was beautiful, but she didn't know how to wear clothes." Lucie Belhomme gave me one of her icy smiles. " I must say her taste wasn't very sound, and she refused to accept any advice. Poor Valcourt and I, how we suffered!"

" Paula has a style of her own," I said.

" But at that time she still hadn't found it ; she admired herself far too much to really know herself. And it hurt her in her work, too. She had a nice voice, but she didn't know what to do with it ; she was completely incapable of putting anything of herself into her singing. No, I'm afraid Paula would never have made the grade."

" I never heard her sing then, but I've been told she was quite successful. She was once booked for Rio, wasn't she?"

Lucie Belhomme laughed. " Yes, she had a brief success because she was so beautiful, but it wasn't long before she faded out. Singing is like anything else: it takes work, and work wasn't exactly what she craved. Brazil—I remember that story ; I was supposed to make her dresses for her. But it wasn't the tour that interested the fellow who made the arrangements, and she knew it very well. She wasn't as crazy as she wanted to make people believe. She pretended to think she was a diva, but at bottom all she wanted was to find some solid citizen to look after her, and when she found him she let everything else drop. And after all, you can't blame her ; she'd never have made a successful career of singing. How is she, by the way?" Lucie asked in a suddenly benevolent voice. "I was told her great man is giving her the gate. Is that true?"

"Absolutely not. They adore each other," I replied definitely.

"Oh . . . ? I'm glad to hear that," she said, completely unconvinced. "She waited long enough for him, poor kid."

I was disconcerted. Lucie Belhomme hated Paula; I wasn't going to accept that picture of her she had painted for me: an arrogant, lazy little whore who used her singing to find a protector. But it occurred to me that Paula had never actually told me anything about her first years in Paris, nor about her youth or her childhood. Why not?

"Do you mind if I say hallo to you? You don't hate me any more, do you?" Marie-Ange was smiling at me with an air of simulated confusion.

"You well deserve it!" I replied, smiling back at her. "You really took me in!"

"I was forced to," she said.

"Tell me, you don't really have six brothers and sisters, do you?"

"It's true I'm the oldest," she replied sincerely. "But all I have is one brother, and he's in Morocco." Her eyes greedily questioned me. "By the way, what was the great Ventadour telling you?"

"Not a thing."

"Oh, you can tell me," Marie-Ange said. "Anyone can tell me anything. It goes in here and comes out here," she said, pointing first to her ears and then to her mouth.

"That's what I'm afraid of. Tell me rather what you know about that one over there," I said, indicating Lucie with a slight nod.

"Oh, she's a terrific woman!" Marie-Ange replied.

"In what way?"

"At her age, she still has all the men she wants, and she manages to mix the useful ones and the pleasant ones. At the moment she has three, and they all want to marry her."

"And each believes he's the only one?"

"No. Each believes he's the only one to know there are two others."

"And yet she isn't exactly what you might call a Venus."

"It seems she was even uglier at twenty, but she managed to

fix herself up so that you could hardly tell. You find a few like that—ugly women who get places with their thighs," Marie-Ange said knowingly. " Only they really have to work at it. Lucie couldn't have been less than forty when she opened Maison Amaryllis with old man Brotteaux's money. She began raking it in heavily during the war, and now it's really skyrocketing. But in the beginning she had a hard time of it," Marie-Ange said sympathetically. " That's why she's so mean," she added.

" I see." I examined Marie-Ange. "What did you come looking for here? Scandalous little tidbits?"

" No, I came for pleasure. I adore going to cocktail parties. Don't you?"

" I really don't see what's so amusing about them. Explain it to me."

" Well, you see a lot of people you don't feel like seeing."

" That's crystal clear!"

" And then you've got to be seen around."

" Why?"

" If you want to be noticed."

" And you want to be noticed?"

" Oh, yes. What I like especially is having my picture taken." She bit her nails. " Is that normal? Do you think I ought to get myself psychoanalysed?"

" I understand. Things are really buzzing in that little head of yours."

" What? Complexes?"

" Something like that."

" But what will be left if they take them away from me?" she asked plaintively.

" Come over here," said Claudie. " Now that the bores have all left we can have a little fun."

There was always a moment at Claudie's when she announced that the bores had left, although the order of departure varied from one time to the next.

" I'm terribly sorry," I said, " but I'm afraid I have to leave with them."

" What! But you must stay for supper," Claudie insisted. " We're going to set up small tables; it'll be very nice. And I want you to meet some people who are coming later." She took me aside. " I've decided to take you under my wing," she said eagerly. " It's ridiculous to live like a savage ; no one knows you—I mean in the milieu where there's money to pick up. Let me launch you. I'll take you to the best dressmakers, I'll show you off, and in a year you'll have the plushiest practice in Paris."

" I've got more patients than I can handle even now."

" Half of whom pay poorly, and the other half not at all."

" That isn't the question."

" It is the question. With a patient who pays ten times as much, you can work ten times less. You'll have time to go out, to dress up."

" We'll talk about it again."

I was astonished at how little she understood me, but as a matter of fact I didn't understand her very well either. She believed that, for us, work was nothing but a means of achieving fortune and success, and I was vaguely convinced that all those snobs would have gladly traded their social position for intellectual talents and accomplishments. When I was a child, a teacher seemed to me a much greater person than a duchess or a millionaire, and through the years that hierarchy had not changed appreciably. Claudie, however, believed that the supreme reward for an Einstein would be to be received in her salon. We could hardly reach any real understanding.

" Sit down here. We're going to play ' Truth,' " Claudie said.

I detest that game ; I never tell anything but lies and it pains me to see the other players, anxious to exhibit their inner secrets and yet not reveal too much, questioning each other scrupulously and cunningly.

" What is your favourite flower?" Huguette asked Guite.

" The black iris," she answered amid a religious silence.

All of them had a favourite flower, a favourite season, their bedside book, their regular couturier.

Huguette looked at Claudie. " How many lovers have you had?"

" I've lost count. Twenty-five or twenty-six. Wait a second ; I'll take a look at the list in the bathroom." She returned and cried out triumphantly, " Twenty-seven!"

" What are you thinking of at this very moment?" Huguette asked me.

For me as well, the truth suddenly became irresistible. " That I'd like to be somewhere else." I stood up. " Seriously, I have some urgent work to do," I said to Claudie. " No, please don't get up."

I left the salon and Marie-Ange, who had been sitting list-lessly on a couch, followed behind me.

" It isn't really true, is it, that you have a crowded prac-tice?"

" I always have work to do."

" Can I invite you out to dinner?" she asked, giving me a pleading and promising look which she immediately sup-pressed.

" No, really, I haven't the time."

" Well, another time then. Couldn't we see each other occasionally?"

" I'm terribly busy!"

She held out the tips of her fingers to me unhappily. I mounted my bicycle and set off straight ahead. I would have enjoyed dining with her, but I knew only too well how it would have turned out: she feared men, played at being the little girl; she would have lost no time in offering me her heart and her frail little body. If I turned down her invitation, it wasn't that the situation frightened me, but rather that I fore-saw its inevitable outcome too clearly to be able to enjoy it. There was a great deal of truth in Nadine's reproach to me one day. " You never get involved in things," she had said. I looked at people through a doctor's eyes and it made it difficult for me to have any human contact with them. Anger, bitterness—I'm rarely capable of those emotions. And the nobler sentiments people show towards me touch me hardly at all; it's my job to evoke them. I have to submit patiently to the consequences of the transfers I generate, and I must cut them off at the proper moment. Even in my private life, I maintain that attitude: after cracking the subject's outer shell, I immediately diagnose his infantile troubles, see myself as I appear in his fantasies—mother, grandmother, sister, child, idol. I don't care much for the rites to which they abandon themselves before the idol they create, but there's nothing I can do but resign myself to it. And I suppose that if a normal individual ever became struck with the whim to attach himself to me, I'd unhesitatingly ask myself, " Whom does he see in me? What frustrated desires is he seeking to gratify?" And I'd be incapable of the least ardour.

I must have gone beyond the limits of Paris; I was riding alongside the Seine, on a narrow street bordered on the left by a railing and on the right by crooked little houses on which, at long intervals, ancient street lights cast a feeble glow. The cobblestone street was covered with slush, but a white coat of snow still lay on the sidewalk. I smiled at the sombre sky. In fleeing Claudie's salon, I had gained this hour for myself, owed it to no one; that no doubt was why the cold air seemed so cheerful. I remembered how I used to breathe in the pureness of the night, how it would go to my head, fill my whole being with joy, and I would say to myself that if such moments didn't exist living would hardly be worth the effort. Would they ever be reborn? I had been offered a chance to cross the ocean, to discover a continent, and all I could answer was, "I'm afraid." Of what was I afraid? I never used to be fainthearted. In the woods of Païolive or in the forest of Grésigne, I would place my knapsack under my head, roll myself in a blanket, and sleep alone under the stars as peacefully as if I were in my bed. It seemed perfectly natural to me to climb high dangerous mountains, slippery with patches of snow, without a guide, haphazardly. I scorned all suggestions of prudence, would sit alone in the dives of Le Havre and Marseilles, stroll alone through Algerian villages . . .

Abruptly, I swung my bicycle around towards Paris. It was useless pretending to ride towards the end of the earth; if I wanted to rediscover my old freedom, I would do far better to return to the house and this very evening say "Yes" to Romieux.

But I didn't answer him, and a few days later I was still anxiously seeking counsel, as if it were a question of an expedition to the bowels of the earth.

"If you were in my place, would you accept?"

"Of course," Henri said, astonished.

That was the night when huge, luminous Vs were dancing in the sky above Paris. They had brought champagne and records, and I had prepared a supper and had filled the house with flowers. Nadine remained in her room under the pretext of having urgent work to do, but in fact she was shunning a celebration which to her was an anniversary of death.

" A strange kind of celebration," Scriassine was saying.
" It's not an ending; it's a beginning—the beginning of the
real tragedy."

For him, the third world war was just starting. Cheerfully,
I said to him, " Now don't start playing Cassandra again to-
night. On Christmas Eve you were predicting all kinds of
horrible disasters. Remember? Well, I'd say you'd lost your
bet."

" First of all, we didn't bet," he said. " And then it hasn't
been a year yet."

" In any case, the French certainly aren't becoming fed up
with literature." I turned to Henri as my witness. " It's fabulous, isn't it, the quantity of manuscripts you're receiving at
Vigilance?"

" That only proves that France has chosen the destiny of
Alexandria," Scriassine said. " I'd prefer seeing *Vigilance* do
less well and not have an important paper like *L'Espoir*
threatened with bankruptcy."

" What are you talking about?" Henri said sharply.
" *L'Espoir* is doing fine."

" I was told you were going to be forced to seek private
subsidies."

" Who told you that?"

" I don't remember; it's a rumour going the rounds."

" Well, it's a false rumour," Henri said flatly. He seemed
strangely out of sorts, which was odd, for everyone else was
very gay, even Paula, even Scriassine whose chronic despair
failed for once to damp his spirits. Robert was telling stories
about another world—the twenties—and Lenoir and Julien
joined him in evoking that exotic age. Two American officers
no one knew were harmonising in a cowboy ballad, and a
W.A.C. was curled up on the couch, fast asleep. Despite all
the past dramas, the future tragedies, that night was a night
of celebration; I was sure of it, not because of the singing
and the fireworks, but because I felt like laughing and crying
all at once.

" Let's go see what's happening outside!" I said. " We'll
come back and have supper later."

Everyone agreed enthusiastically. Without too much
difficulty, we reached the underground entrance and boarded
a train which took us to the Place de la Concorde. But getting
out on to the square was another story; the stairway was

swamped by a sea of humanity. In order not to get separated, we locked arms, but just as I put my foot on the last step a violent surge ripped me away from Robert. I found myself alone with Henri, facing away from the Champs Elysées where we had originally planned to go. Instead, the stream carried us towards the Tuileries.

" Don't fight it," Henri said. " We'll all get together again over at your place in a little while. The only thing to do now is to follow the current."

Amid songs and laughter, we drifted to the Place de l'Opéra, brilliant with lights and red draperies. It was a little frightening, for if you tripped and fell you'd be trampled underfoot. But it was stirring, too ; nothing had really been settled, the past would not be reborn and the future was uncertain ; but the present was triumphant and you had only to let yourself be carried away by it, head empty, mouth dry, heart pounding.

" How about a drink?" Henri proposed.

" If it's possible."

Slowly and with much dodging, we managed to break out of the mob and found ourselves in the middle of a street which rose towards Montmartre. We went into a cabaret teeming with Americans in uniform who were singing at the top of their voices. Henri ordered a bottle of champagne. My throat was dry from thirst, fatigue, and emotion, and I emptied two glasses, one after the other.

" Well, it is a celebration, isn't it?" I said.

" Of course."

We exchanged a friendly look. It's rare for me to feel completely at ease with Henri ; there are too many people between us—Robert, Nadine, Paula. But that night he seemed very close to me, and the champagne gave me courage.

" You don't seem very happy this evening."

" Of course I am." He handed me a cigarette. The fact is that he definitely did not seem happy. " But I wonder who's spreading the rumour that *L'Espoir* is in trouble. It sounds to me as if that might very well be Samazelle's doing."

" You don't like him?" I said. " Neither do I. They're tiresome, those people who never forget the parts they're playing."

" But Dubreuilh is making a big fuss over him," Henri said.

"Robert? He finds him useful, but he doesn't care much for him."

"Is there a difference?" Henri asked.

His intonation seemed as strange to me as his question. "What do you mean?"

"Just now, Dubreuilh is so totally involved in what he's doing that his liking for people is measured solely by their usefulness, neither more nor less."

"But that isn't true at all," I protested indignantly.

He looked at me ironically. "I really wonder how friendly he'd still be to me if I hadn't put L'Espoir at the disposal of the S.R.L."

"Of course, he'd have been disappointed," I replied. "But he'd have been disappointed precisely for those reasons which finally made you accept."

"Yes, I suppose so. That kind of hypothesis is rather stupid, isn't it?" he said with too much vivacity.

I wondered if Robert had given him the impression of putting things on an all-or-nothing basis; he can be very rough when he wants, at any price, to achieve his ends. It would have pained me if he had wounded Henri. And he was alone enough as it was, was Robert; he shouldn't, above all, lose this friendship.

"The more Robert likes a person, the more he demands of him," I said. "I've noticed that with Nadine, for example. The moment he stopped expecting so much of her, he became a little indifferent."

"Ah! But to be demanding in the interest of someone else is quite different from being demanding in one's own interest. In the first case, yes, it's a proof of affection . . ."

"But with Robert, the two are inextricably mingled," I said.

Ordinarily, I disliked talking about Robert, but I wanted absolutely to dispel the bitterness I felt in Henri. "The joining of L'Espoir and the S.R.L. was a necessity in his eyes; therefore, the way Robert's mind works, you should have recognised that fact, too." I questioned Henri with my eyes. "You believe he was simply making use of you, but actually it shows he thinks highly of you."

"I know," Henri said with a smile. "He confidently believes that whatever is evident to him is evident to everyone else. You have to admit that that's a rather imperialistic form of esteem."

" After all, he wasn't so wrong, since you finally did agree," I said. " I really don't see what you can have against him."

" Did I say I had anything against him?"

" No, but that's the feeling I get."

Henri hesitated. " Oh, it's just a question of nuances," he said, shrugging his shoulders. " I'd have been very grateful to Dubreuilh if he would have just put himself in my place for a minute." He gave me a completely winning smile. " I'm sure you'd have done it."

" I'm not a woman of action," I said. " Yes," I added, " from time to time Robert purposely puts on blinkers. But that doesn't stop him, generally, from having a genuine concern for others, and disinterested feelings. You're unfair to him."

" Maybe," Henri said cheerfully. " You know, when you agree to do something against your will, you're bound to hold a small grudge against the person who pushed you into it. I admit it isn't very fair."

I looked at Henri almost remorsefully. " It weighs heavily on you, doesn't it, this new relationship between L'Espoir and the S.R.L.?"

" Oh, there's no longer any question about it now," he said. " I took the plunge."

" But you didn't want to take it, did you?"

He smiled, " No, not madly."

He had often stated that politics bored him to death, and now he was in it up to his neck. I sighed. " Anyhow, there's some truth in what Scriassine says: Never have politics been so all-devouring as to-day."

" That monster Dubreuilh isn't letting himself be devoured," Henri said with a trace of envy. " He's doing as much writing now as ever."

" As much . . ." I hesitated, but I felt a strong need to confide in Henri and continued: " He writes as much but less freely. That journal of his—you read a few passages from it —well, he's decided not to have it published; he claims they'd find too many weapons in it to use against him. It's sad, isn't it, to think that if you become a public figure you can no longer be completely sincere as a writer?"

Henri remained silent a second. "Yes, there's a certain freedom of expression which disappears, of course," he said. "Everything Dubreuilh publishes nowadays is read with an eye on its political implication, and he has to take that into account. But I don't really think that lessens his sincerity."

"The fact that those memoirs won't appear in print makes me very sad," I said.

"You're wrong," he said amiably. "The work of a man who confesses openly and completely, but without responsibility, would be neither more true nor more complete than that of a man who assumes full responsibility for everything he says."

"Do you think so?" I asked. "Have you had to face that question, too?"

"No," he replied. "Not in that way."

"But there *have* been questions?"

"It never stops raining questions, does it?" he said evasively.

But I insisted. "How's your light novel coming along?"

"That's just it; I'm not writing it any more."

"It turned sad? I warned you that would happen."

"I'm not writing," Henri said with an apologetic smile. "Not at all."

"Don't tell me that!"

"Articles, yes; they're finished then and there. But a real book . . . I can't any more."

He could no longer write; there was some truth then in Paula's ramblings. How had it happened to him, who loved writing so much?

"But why?" I asked.

"It's natural not to write, you know. It's the contrary that's abnormal."

"Not for you," I said. "You couldn't conceive of living without writing."

I looked at him uneasily. I had said to Paula, "People change"; but even though you know they change, you stubbornly look upon them as if they were, in many ways, immutable. Now here was another fixed star that had begun dancing in my sky.

"Do you think writing is futile nowadays?"

"Not at all," Henri replied. "If there are people for whom writing has meaning, so much the better for them. Personally, I don't feel like writing any more, that's all." He smiled. "I'm going to confess all to you; I don't have anything more to say; or rather, what I have to say seems too insignificant to me."

"It's just a passing mood," I said.

"I don't think so."

My heart was heavy; it must have been horribly sad for him to give up as he had. With both reproof and remorse, I said, "We see each other so often, and you never even spoke to us about it!"

"The opportunity never arose."

"Yes, it's true you've been talking nothing but politics with Robert." I had a sudden inspiration. "Do you know what would be a good idea? Robert and I are going on a bicycle trip this summer; come along with us for a couple of weeks."

"That could be nice," he said hesitantly.

"It would be." I hesitated in turn. "Only Paula doesn't ride a bicycle."

"Oh, in any case I'm not going to spend my whole holiday with her," he said quickly. "She's going to Tours to stay with her sister."

There was a brief silence. "Why," I asked abruptly, "doesn't Paula want to take up singing again?"

"If only you could tell me! I don't know what she has in her head these days," he said in a discouraged voice. He shrugged his shoulders. "Maybe she's afraid that if she makes a life of her own, I'll take advantage of it to do something about our relationship."

"And that's really what you're hoping for, isn't it?" I asked.

"Yes," he replied quickly. "After all," he added, "I haven't loved her for a long time. And besides, she's very well aware of it, even though she stubbornly insists that nothing's changed."

"I get the impression that she's living on two different planes at once," I said. "She's perfectly lucid, and at the same time she tells herself that you're madly in love with her and that she could have been the greatest singer of the century. I think that her lucidity will win in the end. But what's going to become of her then?"

" Ah! That I don't know!" Henri replied. " I don't want to be a bastard, but I'm not made to be a martyr, either. Sometimes the situation seems simple to me: when you're not in love any more, you're just not in love any more. But at other times, it seems unfair to have stopped loving her; after all, she's the same Paula."

" Loving, too, is unfair," I said.

"Granted. But what can I do about it?" he said.

He seemed truly tormented. Once more I thought to myself how fortunate I was to be a woman—because it's men with whom I have to deal, and that poses many fewer problems.

"Paula has to give a little, too," I said. " If she doesn't you're really trapped. You can't live with a bad conscience, but neither can you live with a lie."

" Well, maybe you have to learn to live a lie," he said with an obviously false nonchalance.

" No, I'm positive you don't!" I protested. " If you're not happy with your life, I don't see what else can justify it."

" Are you happy with yours?"

The question caught me off guard. I had spoken in the name of an old conviction, but how much did I myself still conform to it? I wasn't quite sure any more. Embarrassed, I said, " I'm not unhappy."

He studied me for a moment. " And is not being unhappy enough for you?"

" It's not so bad."

" You've changed," he said tenderly. " There was a time when you were satisfied with your lot in an almost defiant way."

" Why should I be the only one not to have changed?" I asked.

But he was no less insistent than I. " It sometimes seems to me your profession interests you less now than it used to."

" It still interests me," I replied. " But don't you think that in these times it's just a little futile to be treating states of mind?"

" Well, it's certainly important for those whom you cure," he said. " Just as important to-day as it ever was. What's the difference?"

I hesitated. " The thing is that I used to believe in happiness," I said. "I mean, I thought that people were meant to be happy. To cure a patient was to make a real person of him, a person capable of giving a meaning to his life." I shrugged my shoulders. "But you have to have a lot of faith in the future to believe that every life can have meaning."

Henri smiled; his eyes questioned me. "The future isn't as black as all that," he said.

"I don't know," I said. "Maybe I used to think of it as too rosy, and its greyness frightens me now." I smiled. "It's in that respect that I've changed most; I'm afraid of everything."

"That surprises me!" he said.

"I mean it. For example, several weeks have gone by since I was invited to attend a psychiatric congress in America in January. And I can't make up my mind to go."

"But why not?" he said, sounding shocked.

"I don't know. It tempts me, but at the same time I'm afraid. Wouldn't you be afraid? Would you go if you were in my place?"

"Of course!" he replied. "What in the world do you think might happen to you?"

"Nothing special." I hesitated. "It would be strange to see oneself and the people to whom one is attached from another world."

"It would be very interesting." He gave me an encouraging smile. "You're bound to make a few little discoveries, but I'd be very much surprised if they upset your whole life. The things that happen to us or the things we do, they're never really so important in the end."

I bowed my head. "It's true," I thought. "Things always turn out to be less important than I thought they'd be. I'll leave, I'll return; everything comes to an end and nothing ever happens." And my little tête-à-tête with Henri had already come to an end; it was time now to return to the house for supper. We could have prolonged the intimacy of that hour until dawn, perhaps even beyond the dawn, but for a thousand reasons it was better not to try. Was it better? In any case, we didn't try.

"I think we'll have to go back to the others now," I said.

"Yes," Henri agreed. "It's getting late."

We walked in silence to the underground and went to join the others.

Robert's talk with Lafaurie was courteously stormy; neither of them raised his voice, but each treated the other as if he were a war criminal. In a saddened voice, Lafaurie concluded, "We'll be forced to attack." That, however, didn't stop Robert from making active preparations for the June meeting. But one evening, after a long meeting with Samazelle and Henri, he asked me point-blank, "Am I right or wrong to go on with that meeting?"

I was stunned. "What makes you ask me that?"

He smiled. "To get an answer out of you!"

"You certainly know better than I do."

"You never can tell."

I continued examining him. "To give up the meeting would mean to give up the S.R.L., wouldn't it?"

"Naturally."

"After your dispute with Lafaurie, you explained to me in detail why it was out of the question to give in to him. Has something new come up?"

"No, nothing new has come up," Robert replied.

"Well? Why have you changed your mind, then? Have you stopped believing that it's possible to force the Communists' hand?"

"No. If we're successful, the chances are that they won't burn any bridges." Robert's voice remained doubtful; hesitantly, he continued, "It's just that I'm questioning myself about the whole thing."

"You mean the movement itself?"

"Yes. A socialist Europe—there are times when I wonder if it isn't just a utopian dream. But then every unrealised idea seems like a utopian dream. You'd never do anything if you thought that nothing was possible, except what already exists." He spoke as if he were defending himself against some invisible questioner, and I wondered where those doubts had suddenly come from. He sighed. "It isn't easy to distinguish between a real possibility and a dream."

"Wasn't it Lenin who used to say, 'Dreams are necessary'?"

"Yes, but only on the condition that you believe seriously in your dream. That's the whole question: Do I believe in it seriously enough?"

I looked at him in astonishment. "What do you mean?"

"Do you think my stubbornness might be due to pride, defiance, or a sense of self-satisfaction?"

"It's strange that you have doubts of that kind," I said. "You're not in the habit of suspecting your own motives."

"I'm even suspicious of my habits," Robert replied.

"Well, start suspecting that suspicion. Maybe you're tempted to give in out of fear of failure or because there might be a lot of complications.

"Maybe," Robert said.

"I suppose you're not very happy at the thought that the Communists will start a campaign against you?"

"No, I'm not happy about it," Robert replied. "You take so much trouble to make yourself understood! And then deliberately they will create worse misunderstandings. Yes," he added, "maybe it's the writer in me who faintheartedly counsels the political man to submit quietly."

"You see," I said. "If you begin examining your motives, you'll never finish with it As Scriassine would say, stay on objective ground."

"Unfortunately, even that ground shifts about quite a bit!" Robert replied. "Especially when you have only incomplete information. Yes, I believe in the possibility of a European left. But isn't it because I'm convinced it's needed?"

It upset me to hear Robert put the question that way. He had bitterly reproached himself for having too naïvely believed in the Communists' good will, but it shouldn't have made him doubt himself to that extent. It was the first time in my life I had ever seen him tempted by an easy way out.

"Since when have you been thinking about letting the S.R.L. drop?" I asked.

"Oh, I'm not thinking about it in a positive way," Robert replied. "I'm simply questioning myself."

"How long have you been questioning yourself like that?"

"About two or three days," Robert answered.

"And without any particular reason?"

He smiled. "Without any particular reason."

I studied him for a moment. "Don't you think it might simply be that you're tired?" I said. "You look tired."

"It's true," he said. "I am tired."

Suddenly, it was plain as day; he looked worn out. His

eyes were bloodshot, his skin grey, his face puffy. " After all, he isn't young any more," I thought anxiously. Oh, he still wasn't old, but nevertheless he couldn't allow himself his former excesses. The fact of the matter was, however, that he did work excessively, and indeed even more so than before, perhaps to prove to himself that he was still young. In addition to the S.R.L., *Vigilance*, and his book, there were the callers, the letters, the telephone calls. They all had urgent things to tell him: encouragements, criticisms, suggestions, problems. And if you didn't give them a hearing, didn't publish what they told you, you starved them, condemned them to misery, madness, death, suicide. Robert worked and listened far into the nights; he slept hardly at all.

" You're working much too hard!" I said. " If you go on like this, you'll kill yourself. One of these days you'll have a heart attack and I . . . I'll be in a pretty fix, won't I?"

" Just one more month to go, that's all," he said.

" And do you think a three or four week holiday will be enough to put you on your feet again?" I thought for a moment. " We ought to try finding a house in the suburbs," I said. " You'd go to Paris once or twice a week; and the rest of the time, no visits, no telephone calls—just peace and quiet."

" And will *you* find the house?" Robert asked mockingly.

Running from one agency to another, looking at houses— it did not appeal to me, and besides I had not the time to do it. But it was heartbreaking to see Robert driving himself. He had decided that the meeting would be held, but he continued to worry: the Communists would be intimidated only if the meeting were a huge success. But if it wasn't and they decided to burn the bridges, then what would happen to the S.R.L? For me, too, this was a desperately serious matter. I am even more concerned with the individual than is Robert, and with all the richness of the inner life—feelings, culture, happiness. I need to believe that in the classless society humanity will fulfil itself without giving up anything of itself.

Thank heavens, Nadine had stopped throwing at her father the reproaches of her Communist comrades. She no longer pounded us with diatribes against American imperialism, had definitely closed *Das Kapital*. I wasn't surprised when one evening she said abruptly to me, " When you come down to it, the Communists are no different from the bourgeoisie."

"What makes you say that?"

I was getting ready for bed, and she was sitting on the edge of my couch; it was often at that moment that she spoke to me of things that concerned her deeply.

"They're not revolutionaries. They're for order, work, the family, reason. Their justice is somewhere off in the future, and in the meantime they manage to live with injustice like all the others. And then their social system . . . Well, it'll just be another social system."

"Obviously."

"If you have to wait five hundred years to find out the world hasn't changed, I'm not interested."

"You don't imagine that the world can be remade in a single season, do you?"

"It's funny, you talk just like Joly. Mind you, I know what they're doing. But I can't see why I should join the C.P.; it's just a party like any other."

"Another venture gone wrong," I thought regretfully as I finished removing my make-up. And she needed one successful undertaking so badly!

"The best thing is to be completely independent, like Vincent," she said. "He's pure—a real angel."

An angel—the word she used to employ when speaking of Diego. She had probably rediscovered in Vincent that generosity and that extravagance which had once touched her heart. Only Diego put his madness into his writings, while there was reason to fear that Vincent let his take possession of his life. Was he sleeping with Nadine? I didn't suppose so, but they were seeing each other very often lately. I was in fact rather pleased about it, for although Nadine was restless she seemed quite gay.

It was without apprehension that I heard the doorbell ring at five o'clock one morning. Nadine hadn't come home yet and I imagined she had simply forgotten her key. But when I opened the door, I saw Vincent standing in front of me.

"Now, don't get upset!" he said.

Which of course, immediately upset me. "Something's happened to Nadine!" I said.

"No, no," he replied. "She's perfectly all right. Everything's going to be all right." He strode firmly towards the living-room. "Even Nadine's a woman!" he said disgustedly.

From a pocket of his jacket he pulled out a map which he spread on the table. " In a word, she's waiting for you at this crossroads," he said, pointing to the intersection of two small roads north-west of Chantilly. " You'll have to get yourself a car and go pick her up immediately ; I'm sure Perron will lend you the car. But don't explain anything to him ; just ask for the car and that's all. And above all, don't mention me."

He had spoken his piece in a single breath, in a calm, hard voice which failed to set my mind at ease. I was convinced that he was frightened. " What's she doing there? Did she have an accident?"

" I told you, no. Her feet hurt, that's all ; she doesn't know how to walk. But you'll get there in plenty of time to pick her up. You're sure you know where it is, now? I'll mark it with a cross to make certain. All you have to do is to blow the horn or call her ; she's in the little woods to the right of the road."

" What's this all about? What happened? I want to know," I insisted.

" Professional secret," Vincent replied. " You'd better ring Perron right away," he added.

I despised his sallow face, his bloodshot eyes, his finely chiselled profile. But it was an impotent fury. I dialled Henri's number and heard his surprised voice saying, " Hallo! Who's calling?"

" Anne Dubreuilh. Yes, it's I. I have a favour to ask you ; it's quite urgent. And please, don't ask me any questions. I need a car at once—with enough petrol for two hundred kilometres."

There was a very brief silence. " It's lucky we filled her up yesterday," he said in a very natural voice. " The car will be at your door in half an hour, the time to get it and bring it over."

" Take it to the Place St. André des Arts," I said. " Thank you."

" Perfect!" Vincent said with a broad smile. " I knew you could count on Perron. There's nothing at all to worry about," he added. " Nadine is in no danger—especially if you get there fast. Not a word to anyone, eh? She swore to me that we could depend on you."

" You can," I said, following him to the door. " But tell me what it's all about?"

"Believe me, it's nothing serious," he replied.

I felt like slamming the door violently behind him, but I closed it quietly so as not to awaken Robert. Happily, he must have been sleeping very soundly; I had heard him going to bed scarcely two hours before. I got dressed quickly. I remembered the two nights I had waited for Nadine while Robert was combing Paris for her. That horrible wait! This time it was even worse. I was sure they had done something very serious; Vincent was afraid. It must have been a burglary, or a hold-up, or God only knows what. And afterwards, Nadine couldn't make it by foot to the station, and I had to get there before the thing was discovered, before Nadine was discovered. Nadine who was waiting for me for hours, alone in the darkness, in the cold, in fear. It was a beautiful summer morning; the air smelled of tar and leaves. In a few hours, it would be very hot, but now, in the freshness and silence of the deserted quays, birds were singing. A cheerful, pleasant morning charged with anguish, like the morning of the flight from Paris.

Henri reached the square a few minutes after I did.

"Your carriage, Madame," he said cheerfully. He remained seated at the wheel. "Wouldn't you like me to go along with you?"

"No, thanks."

"Are you sure?"

"Yes."

"You haven't driven for a long time."

"I'm positive I'll know how."

He got out and I took his place behind the wheel. "Does it have something to do with Nadine?" he asked.

"Yes."

"Ah! They're using her to force our hand!" he said indignantly.

"Do you know what it's all about?"

"More or less."

"Tell me . . ."

He hesitated. "It's just supposition. Listen, I'll stay at home all morning; if there's any way I can be of help, just call me."

"Above all, I mustn't have an accident," I said to myself as I drove towards the Porte de la Chapelle. I forced myself to be careful and tried to reassure myself. Henri had seemed

to imply that Vincent was lying. Maybe there were many
people waiting for me ; maybe Nadine wasn't even with them.
How I wished that were true! I vastly preferred thinking of
myself as their prey than imagining Nadine numbed with
cold, fear, and resentment all through a long night.

The main road was deserted ; I took a smaller road to the
right, and then another. The crossroads, too, was deserted.
I sounded the horn several times and studied the map. I had
not mistaken the place, but supposing Vincent had made a
mistake? No, he had been very precise ; no possible error
there. I blew the horn again ; and then I turned off the motor,
got out of the car, went into the little woods on the right, and
called out, " Nadine!" At first I called softly, and then louder
and louder. Silence. Deathly silence—I finally understood
the meaning of those words. " Nadine!" No answer.
Exactly as if I had called out " Diego." She, too, had vanished into thin air ; she should have been there, precisely at
that place, and she wasn't. I turned in circles, crushed dead
twigs, fresh moss; I even stopped calling out her name.
" They've arrested her!" I thought with terror. I went back to
the car. Perhaps she'd grown tired of waiting—she wasn't
the patient sort—and had found the courage to walk to a
near-by station. I had to catch up with her, I had to ; they
would too easily notice her at this time of day on a deserted
platform. At Chantilly, she would have gone unnoticed ; but
Chantilly was quite far, and I would have met her on the
road. She must have chosen Clermont ; I stared at the map as
if it were possible to force an answer from it. There were
two roads to Clermont ; she had probably taken the shorter
one. I turned the key, tried the starter, and my heart began
beating desperately: the engine wouldn't start. Finally it
made up its mind, and the car began moving along the road
fitfully. My damp hands slipped on the wet steering wheel.
Around me, the stubborn silence continued, but daylight
was taking over; in the villages, doors would soon begin
opening. " They're going to arrest her." The silence, the
absence of people—this peacefulness was horrible. Nadine
wasn't on the road, nor in the streets of Clermont, nor in the
station. She didn't know the district, probably had no map. She
was wandering haphazardly around the countryside, and they
would find her first. I turned around, decided to go back to the
intersection by way of the other road. And then I would go up

and down each and every road until the petrol tank was empty.
And then? No questions now; just follow every road. This
one rose between green fields to a long flat stretch. And suddenly I saw Nadine coming towards me, a smile on her lips, as
if we had agreed on this rendezvous a long time ago. I slammed on the brakes and, unhurried, she walked over to the car.

In a completely natural voice, she asked, " Did you come to
get me?"

" No, I'm just taking a ride for the fun of it." I opened the
door. "Get in." She sat down beside me; her hair was
combed, her face powdered; she seemed rested. My foot
pressed the accelerator into the floorboard, and my hands
gripped the steering wheel too tightly.

With a half-mocking, half-indulgent smile, Nadine asked,
" Are you furious?"

Those two bitter tears which came to my eyes were indeed
tears of anger. The car skidded slightly; my hands, I suppose, were trembling. I slowed down, tried to relax my grip
and control my voice.

" Why didn't you stay in the woods?"

" I was getting bored." She took off her shoes and pushed
them under the seat. " I didn't think you'd come," she
added.

" Are you a complete idiot? Obviously I'd come."

" I wasn't sure. I wanted to take the train at Clermont; I'd
have got there sooner or later." Bending forward, she was
massaging her feet. " Oh, my poor feet!"

" What did you do?"

Nadine didn't answer.

" All right, keep your secrets," I said. " It will all be in the
papers to-night."

" In the papers!" Nadine straightened up, her face convulsed. " Do you think the concierge noticed that I didn't come
home last night?"

" She can't prove it, and if necessary I'll swear to the contrary. But I want to know what you did."

" Well, since you'll find out anyhow . . . There's a woman
in Azicourt," she began in a dejected voice. " She denounced
two Jewish kids who were living on a near-by farm. The kids
are dead. Everyone knows it's her fault, but with a lot of
wiggling and squirming she somehow managed to keep herself
out of trouble. Another rotten deal! Vincent and his pals

decided to punish her. I've known for a long time what
they've been up to and they knew I wanted to help them.
They needed a girl for this job and I went along. The woman
runs a tavern ; we waited until the last customers had left and,
just when she was closing up, I pleaded with her to let me in
for a minute to have a drink and rest. While she was serving
me, the others came in and jumped her ; they took her down
to the cellar."

Nadine stopped speaking, and I asked, " They didn't . . ."

" No," she replied quickly. " They shaved her head . . .I
didn't do my part too badly," she added in a suddenly proud
voice. " I closed the door and turned out the lights. Only the
time seemed to be passing slowly and I drank a brandy while
I was waiting for them to come up again. Naturally, I'm not
used to it and it hit me hard. We'd already walked God
knows how many kilometres coming from Clermont and they
wanted to leave from Chantilly. I just couldn't move. They
carried me over to the little woods and told me to wait for
you. After a little while, I began feeling better and . . ."

I interrupted her. " You're going to give me your word to
break with that gang or you're leaving Paris to-day."

" Anyhow, they wouldn't want anything more to do with
me," she said bitterly.

" That's not good enough for me ; I want your word or I
swear to you that to-morrow you'll be a long way away."

I hadn't spoken to her in that tone of voice for years. She
looked up at me with a submissive, imploring expression.

" Promise me something, too : don't tell Father anything."

I had almost never kept Nadine's stupidities from Robert,
but this time I felt that he really didn't need any new
worries. " A promise for a promise," I said.

" I'll promise anything you want," she replied sadly.

" Then I won't say anything." Anxiously, I asked, " Are
you sure you didn't leave any traces ? "

" Vincent said he checked everything. What would happen
if they arrested me ? " she asked fearfully.

" They won't arrest you. And you're only an accomplice.
And you're very young. But Vincent could be in real trouble,
and if he ends his life behind bars it would serve him right,"
I said furiously. " The whole thing is rotten. It's stupid and
rotten."

Nadine said nothing. After a brief silence, she asked, "Did Henri lend you the car without any questions?"

"I think he knows all about what's going on."

"Vincent talks too much," Nadine said. "With Henri or you it doesn't matter. But a chap like Sézenac could be dangerous."

"Don't tell me Sézenac was with you! That would be sheer madness!"

"No, he wasn't in on it. Vincent knows you have to be careful about a drug addict. Only they're great pals; they're always together."

"Someone has to talk to Vincent, convince him to give it up . . ."

"You'll never convince him," Nadine said. "Neither you nor I nor anyone else."

Nadine went to bed and I told Robert that I had gone out for a walk. He was so preoccupied these days that he suspected nothing. I called Henri and in a few vague sentences set his mind at ease. Taking an interest in my patients that day was quite a trial. I studied the evening papers; there was no mention of it. Nevertheless, I hardly slept at all that night. "Going to America is out of the question now," I said to myself. Nadine was in danger; she had promised me to break with that gang, but God only knows what else she would think up! And I thought sadly that even if I stayed near her I wouldn't be able to protect her. Being happy, feeling loved, was no doubt all she needed to make her stop destroying herself. But I could give her neither love nor happiness. How useless I was to her! The others, the strangers, I make them talk, untangle their complexes, rewind the strands of their memories, and when they leave I hand them neat little skeins which they stow away in their drawers. And sometimes it helps them. Nadine I can read without any effort, and yet I can do nothing for her. Long ago, I used to say to myself, "How can you breathe easily when you feel that the people you love are gambling with their eternal lives?" But the believer can pray, can try to make deals with God. For me, there no longer exists any communion of saints, and I say to myself, "This life is her only chance; there'll be no other truth but the one she'll have known, no other world but the one she'll have believed in."

The next morning, Nadine had deep circles under her eyes, and I continued eating my heart out. She spent the day with her nose in a chemistry book, and that evening, while I was removing my make-up, she said to me wearily, " This chemistry is a nightmare! I'm sure to fail."

" You've always passed your exams . . ."

" Not this time. Besides, pass or fail, it's all the same. I'll never make a career of chemistry." She reflected a moment. " I can't make a career of anything. I'm not an intellectual, and when it comes to action I just collapse. I'm worthless."

" You've been doing wonderfully at *Vigilance,* and you caught on right away."

" That's nothing to be proud of ; Father's perfectly right."

" When you find something that interests you, I'm sure you'll do well at it. And you'll find something."

She shook her head. " When you get down to it, I think I'm made to have a husband and children, like all other women. I'll scrub my pots and have a little brat every year."

" If you get married just for the sake of marrying, you won't be happy either."

" Oh, don't worry yourself about that! No man would be ass enough to marry me. They like to sleep with me, but after that it's ' Good night! ' I'm not the kind that grows on you."

I knew well the way she had of saying the most disagreeable things about herself in a perfectly offhand voice, as if with her nonchalance she could disarm and by-pass the bitter truth. Unfortunately, truth remained truth.

" You don't want to be," I said. " And if someone despite this is stubborn enough to like you, you refuse to believe it."

" If you're going to start telling me again that Lambert likes me . . ."

" For a whole year now, you're the only girl he's ever gone out with ; you told me that yourself."

" Naturally. He's a homosexual."

" You're crazy."

" He goes out only with boys. And it's obvious he's in love with Henri."

" You're forgetting Rosa."

" Oh, Rosa was so beautiful," Nadine said nostalgically. " Even a homo could fall in love with Rosa. You don't understand," she added impatiently. " Lambert is fond of me, yes, but in the same way he'd be fond of a man. Besides, that's all right with me. I have no desire to be a substitute." She sighed. " Men have all the luck! He's going to travel all over France and do a big series on the reconstruction of the devastated areas and all that. And he just bought himself a motor-cycle; you ought to see him! He's T. E. Lawrence chugging along on that hunk of scrap metal!" she said spitefully.

Her voice was so full of envy that it gave me an idea. I went over to *L'Espoir* the next afternoon and asked to see Lambert.

" You'd like to speak to me?" he asked courteously.

" Yes, if you have a minute."

" Would you like to go up to the bar?"

" Perfect."

No sooner had the bartender placed a glass of grapefruit juice before me than I attacked. " It seems you're going to make an extensive tour of France?"

" Yes, by motor-cycle. I'm leaving next week."

" Would it be possible to take Nadine with you?"

He looked at me reproachfully. " Does Nadine want to come along?"

" She's dying to go. But she'd never be the one to ask."

" Well, I haven't asked her because I'd have been very surprised if she accepted," he said stiffly. " She very rarely agrees to the things I suggest. And besides, I haven't seen much of her these days . . ."

" I know," I said. " She's been going around with Vincent and Sézenac; I don't think they're very good companions for her." I hesitated and then added very quickly, " They might even be dangerous companions; that's why I came to see you. If you care for her at all, you'll take her away from that gang."

Abruptly, Lambert's face was transformed; he suddenly seemed very young and totally defenceless. " You don't mean that Nadine is taking dope?"

That suspicion suited me perfectly. Reticently, I replied, " I don't know; I don't think so. But with Nadine, anything can happen. She's passing through a critical period just now. And frankly, I'm worried."

Lambert was silent for a moment; he seemed moved. " I'd be very happy if Nadine came with me," he said.

" Try it, then. And don't get discouraged. I imagine she'll
say no at first ; that's how she is. But be insistent ; you might
be saving her life."

Three days later, Nadine said to me casually, " Can you
imagine! Poor Lambert wants to take me with him!"

" On that trip through France? It would be pretty rugged,"
I said.

" Oh, I don't give a damn about that. But I can't leave the
magazine for two whole weeks."

" You're entitled to a holiday ; that's no problem. But if
you don't feel like it . . ."

" Oh, I'm sure it would be very interesting," Nadine said.
" But two weeks with Lambert, that's a high price to pay!"

I had above all to keep her from thinking I was pushing
her into taking that trip. " Is he really so boring?" I asked
naïvely.

" He's not boring at all," she said irritably. " Only he's so
careful, so formal ; everything shocks him. If I walk into a
café with a hole in my stocking, he gives me a dirty look. A
real gentleman, that one!" She paused and then said, " And
do you know he made up with his father? He's got absolutely
no backbone!"

" My God! How quick you are to condemn people!" I
said. " After all, what do you know about that story? What
do you know about Lambert's father or their relationship?"

I had spoken so heatedly that for a moment Nadine remained nonplussed. When I myself was really convinced of
something, I knew how to convince her. During her childhood, that was how I managed to exert my authority, but
after giving in to me she was usually so bitter that I re-
frained as much as possible from using that tactic. Now,
however, it exasperated me to see her so obstinately contrary.

Hesitantly, she said, " Lambert can't get along without his
dear little papa. It's infantilism, pure and simple. If you want
to know, that's just what annoys me about him: he'll never
be a man."

" He's twenty-five and he's had a strange adolescence. You
know very well yourself that it isn't easy to begin standing on
your own two feet."

" Oh, you can't make comparisons. I'm a woman."

" What of it? Being a man isn't any easier. They ask so
much of a man these days, and you not the least. They're still

wet behind the ears and they have to play at being heroes.
It's depressing. No, you have no right to be so hard on
Lambert. Say simply that you don't get along with him, that
you wouldn't enjoy the trip; that's something else."

" Oh, in a way, I always enjoy travelling."

Two days later, Nadine said to me half-furious, half-
flattered, " He's really something, that guy! Now he's trying
to blackmail me! He says that being a ' peace ' correspondent
gives him a pain and that if I don't go with him he'll give the
whole thing up."

" Well?"

" Well, what do you think?" she asked innocently.

I shrugged my shoulders. " Does he at least know how to
drive a motor-cycle? They're dangerous, those contraptions."

" They're not dangerous at all, and they're terrific!"
Nadine replied. " If I go," she added, " it'll be mostly because
of the motor-cycle."

Against all expectations, Nadine passed her chemistry
examinations. For the written part, it was rather close, but at
the oral test she easily bluffed her examiners with her glibness
and her composure. The three of us celebrated the triumph by
having a big champagne dinner in an open-air restaurant.
And then she left with Lambert. It was a stroke of luck, for
the S.R.L. meeting was to take place the following week; the
house was always full of people, and I was very happy to
have Robert to myself during those rare moments of freedom which were left to him. Henri helped him with a zeal
that touched me all the more since I knew how little enthusiasm he had for that kind of thing. Both of them agreed
that it looked as if the meeting would turn out to be a
success. " If they say it, it must be true," I thought as I went
down the Avenue Wagram. Nevertheless, I was worried;
Robert hadn't spoken in public for years. Would he still be
able to move people as he used to? I walked past the police
cars lined up along the kerb and continued on to the Place des
Ternes; I was early. Ten years before, on the evening of the
Salle Pleyel meeting, I was also alone and early; for a long
while I circled that square and then I went into the Lorraine
for a drink. This time, I didn't go into the café. The past was
past; I don't know why I suddenly missed it with such
anguish. Oh, simply because it was the past, no doubt. I retraced my steps to the theatre and went down the long sad

aisle. I remembered how uneasy I had felt when Robert mounted the rostrum; it had seemed as if they were stealing him from me. And this evening, too, the idea of seeing him on a stage, at a distance, frightened me. There still weren't very many people in the hall. "The public always comes at the last minute," one of the Canges said to me. I tried to speak to them calmly, but I anxiously kept one eye on the entrance. Finally, we were going to know whether or not people were going to follow Robert. Of course if they were behind him nothing was won yet, but on the other hand if the hall remained empty the defeat would be final.

It filled up. Every seat was taken when the speakers filed on to the stage to the audience's applause. It was disconcerting to see all those familiar faces transformed into public figures. Lenoir, by a sort of natural mimicry, blended in with the chairs and tables—a stick of dry wood. Samazelle, on the contrary, took up the whole platform; this was his natural habitat. When Henri began to speak, his voice changed the huge hall into a private room; he didn't see five thousand people before him, but rather five thousand times one person, and he spoke to them in an almost conversational voice. Little by little, I warmed up. Behind the words he spoke, the friendship he offered us was a certainty; listening to him, we felt sure that men were not condemned to hate each other, to fight each other. They applauded him for a long time. Méricaud gave a languid little speech, and then it was Robert's turn. What an ovation! As soon as he stood up, they began clapping their hands, stamping their feet, shouting. He waited patiently and I wondered if he was moved. I certainly was. Day after day I saw him bent over his desk, his eyes bloodshot, his back bent, alone and doubting himself. And it was this same man whom five thousand people were now acclaiming. What exactly did he stand for to them? He was both a great writer and a man who was part of the vigilance committees, the anti-fascist meetings; an intellectual dedicated to the revolution without repudiating himself as an intellectual. For the old, he stood for the pre-war era; for the young, the present and its promises. He effected the unity of the past and of the future. And no doubt he was a thousand other things to them besides; each loved him in his own way. They continued applauding and the noise grew within me, became immense. Fame, glory—ordinarily they leave me cold. This evening they seemed enviable. " Happy is he," I said to myself, " who can look the truth of his life full in the face and rejoice in it ; happy is he who can read it on friendly faces." At last they were silent. As soon as Robert opened his mouth, my hands became damp and my forehead was covered with beads of perspiration ; even though I knew that words came easily to him, I was frightened. Fortunately I was soon completely occupied with his speech. Robert spoke without affectation, with a logic so sharp that it seemed almost violent. He offered no programme, rather, he dictated tasks to us. And they were so urgent that you couldn't fail to carry them out: victory was assured by its very necessity. Around me, people were smiling, their eyes shone, each recognised his own assurance on the faces of his neighbours. No, that war will not have been in vain ; mankind now knows only too well the price of resignation and selfishness. They'll take their fate in their own hands, assure the triumph of peace, and they'll win freedom and happiness everywhere on earth. It was clear, it was certain, it was simple common sense: humanity cannot want anything but peace, freedom, and happiness, and what is there to prevent it from achieving what it wants? Humanity alone reigns on earth. Behind everything Robert said was that crystal-clear principle. It dazzled us. When he finished, we applauded for a long time, and it was the truth we were applauding. I wiped my hands with my handkerchief. Peace was assured, the future was guaranteed, the near and the distant were one, indivisible. I didn't listen to Salève ; he was as boring as Méricaud. But it didn't matter ; the game had been won, not just the meeting, but everything it stood for.

Samazelle spoke last. Immediately he began to scold, to thunder—a side-show barker. And I found myself back in my seat, amid a crowd as powerless as I, which was stupidly getting drunk on words. They were neither promises nor predictions—just words, nothing more. At the Salle Pleyel I had seen the same light on other attentive faces, and it hadn't prevented Warsaw, Buchenwald, Stalingrad, Oradour. Yes, we know the price of resignation and selfishness, but we've known it for a long time, and it's done us no good. No one has ever succeeded in ridding the world of evil, and it won't be got rid of soon, certainly not during our lifetime. And as for what will happen later, at the end of this long prehistory,

It must be admitted that we can't even begin to imagine it. No, the future isn't assured, neither the near nor the distant. I looked at Robert. Was it really his truth reflected in all those eyes? He was the scrutiny of other eyes, too—from America, from Russia, from the depths of the centuries. Whom do they see? Perhaps only an old dreamer, whose dream means little. And that might be the way he'll see himself to-morrow: he'll think that what he did served no purpose, or worse, that it served only to confuse people. If only I could reach a decision: Is there a basic truth? There is none. But—there will be one. Our life is there, heavy as a rock, and it has another side which we don't know. It's frightening. This time I was sure it was no early morning frenzy; I had had nothing to drink, it wasn't dark, and yet I was choked with fear.

" Are you satisfied?" I asked them, trying to sound nonchalant. Henri was satisfied. " It's a success," he said cheerfully. Samazelle said, " It's a triumph!" But Robert only grumbled, " Meetings don't prove very much." Ten years earlier, leaving the Salle Pleyel, he hadn't said anything like that; he was beaming then. And yet we had thought it more than likely that war would break out. Then what was the reason for that serenity? Ah, then we had time ahead of us! Beyond the impending war, Robert saw the stamping out of fascism, and he had already taken into account and resigned himself to the sacrifices it would entail. Now he feels his age; he needs certainties, and in the immediate future. The following days he remained sombre. He should have been happy when Charlier announced he was joining the S.R.L., but never had I seen him so downcast as after that interview. And I understood him. It wasn't so much because of Charlier's physical appearance—his hair hadn't grown back, his skin was red and lumpy, but at any rate since March he had gained twenty pounds and he was now wearing new teeth. Neither was it the stories he told; we had little left to learn about the horrors of the concentration camps. It was rather the way he told them that was unbearable. He, who had been the gentlest and the most stubborn of idealists, evoked the blows, the slaps, the tortures, the hunger, the colics, the brutalisation, the debasement with a laugh that wasn't even cynical. Infantile or senile? Angelic or idiotic? It was impossible to tell. And he laughed, too, at the idea that the

Socialists were waiting for him to rejoin their ranks. However, he retained his old loathing for the Communists. The S.R.L. won him over and he promised to bring to it the important faction that was regrouping behind him.

When he left us, Robert said to me, "You were surprised by my hesitations the other day. But the terrible thing about getting mixed up in political action nowadays is that you know only too well the price that has to be paid for making mistakes."

I knew he held himself and all the men of his age responsible for the war. And yet he was one of those who had fought most clearly and most fiercely against it; having failed he considered himself guilty. What surprised me, however, was that his meeting with Charlier could reawaken his remorse; usually he reacts to a whole picture, not to a detail.

"In any case, even if the S.R.L. is a mistake, I'm sure that no great disasters will result from it," I said.

"Little disasters count, too," Robert replied. He hesitated. "You have to be younger than I," he said, "to believe that the future will save everything. I feel that my responsibilities are more limited than before, but they are also heavier, clear."

"What do you mean by that?"

"Well, I'm beginning to think a little like you—that the death or unhappiness of an individual can't be ignored. Oh, I know I'm going against the stream," he added. "The young of to-day are much harder than we ever were; they're even downright cynical. And I'm becoming sentimental."

"Don't you think one might say rather that you're becoming more concrete than you used to be?"

"I'm not sure. What does concrete mean?" Robert said.

Yes, he was certainly more vulnerable than he had been before. Fortunately, the meeting bore fruit; each day new members were added to the rolls. And in the bargain, the Communists hadn't declared war on the S.R.L.; they merely spoke of it with a restrained ill will. There was hope that the movement would develop into something truly significant. The only dark cloud was that *L'Espoir* had nevertheless lost many of its readers and would soon be forced to call on Trarieux's money.

"Are you sure he'll come through?" I asked, examining myself disapprovingly in the mirror.

"Absolutely," Robert replied.

"Then why are you going to this dinner? Why are you dragging me along?"

"Well, it can't do any harm to keep him in a good mood," Robert said, sadly knotting his tie. "When you're about to unburden a man of eight million francs, you have to humour him a little."

"Eight million!"

"That's right!" Robert said. "They're as badly off as all that! It's Luc's fault, of course. What stubbornness! And there's no other way out; they'll be forced to take Trarieux's money. Samazelle made a little investigation of his own and he claims they can't hold out much longer."

"Well," I said, "then I'm resigned to it. *L'Espoir* is well worth a boring dinner."

We were all smiles as we entered the huge study. Samazelle, sporting a light grey flannel suit which emphasised his corpulence, was already there, together with his wife. Trarieux, too, was all smiles; he had no visible wife, but with him was a tall girl with lustreless hair who reminded me of my pious college classmates. In a dining-room with a black-and-white tiled floor, we were served a dinner chosen and prepared with meticulous care. With the coffee, Trarieux offered liqueurs but no cigars; Samazelle would certainly have appreciated a cigar; nevertheless he delighted openly in savouring an old cognac. It had been a long time since I last set foot in the home of a real bourgeois and the experience was comforting. Sometimes I think that all the intellectuals I know have something suspect about them, but whenever I meet a bourgeois my belief that they are no less suspect is promptly reaffirmed. Nadine and the life I permit her to lead are certainly strange, but that dried-up virgin who was pouring coffee with an oppressed air seemed much more dreadful. If I stretched her out on my couch, I'm sure she'd have a few things to tell me. And Trarieux! To me, his elaborate simplicity was extremely suspect. His ill-concealed vanity clashed violently with his too-enthusiastic admiration for Samazelle. For a short while they exchanged reminiscences about the Resistance; then they congratulated each other on the success of the meeting, and Samazelle declared, "The thing that augurs exceptionally well is that we're making progress in the provinces. A year from now we'll have two hundred thousand members, or we'll have lost the game."

"We won't lose it!" Trarieux said. He turned towards Robert, who until now had been quieter than he should have been. "Our movement had the great good fortune of being created precisely at the opportune moment. The proletariat is beginning to understand that the Communist Party is actually betraying its true interests. And a large number of clear-headed bourgeois realise, as I do, that they will have to accept the liquidation of their class."

"Which still won't give us two hundred thousand members one year from now. And the game won't be lost for all that," Robert said acidly. "There's no point in our lying to each other."

"My experience has taught me that if you're satisfied with a little, you won't get very much," Trarieux said. "There's no point, either, in limiting our ambitions!"

"What matters is that we don't limit our efforts," Robert said.

"Ah, permit me to say that we've a long way to go to fully exploit all our possibilities," Trarieux proclaimed authoritatively. "It's distressing that the organ of the S.R.L. is so terribly unequal to its task; L'Espoir's circulation is ridiculously low."

"But it's gone down because of its affiliation with the S.R.L.," I said.

Trarieux gave me an annoyed look, and I thought that if he had had a wife she wouldn't speak very often without being spoken to.

"No," he said almost rudely. "It's lack of vitality."

"The fact is that L'Espoir used to have a large audience," Robert said stiffly.

Softly, Samazelle said, "It took advantage of the surge of enthusiasm that followed the liberation."

"We have to look things in the face," Trarieux said. "We all admire Perron enough to have the right to talk about him in complete frankness. He's a marvellous writer, but he has no head for politics and he's not a businessman. And having Luc at his side doesn't help things much."

I knew that Robert more or less shared these opinions, but he shook his head. "In aligning himself with the S.R.L.,

Perron alienated both the right and the Communists. And his finances are too limited to fight an uphill battle."

" I'm absolutely convinced," Trarieux said, enunciating each syllable clearly, " that if a man like Samazelle were running *L'Espoir,* circulation would double in a very few weeks."

Robert's eyes lingered for an instant on Samazelle's face. Crisply, he said, " But he isn't."

Trarieux waited a moment, and then ventured, " Supposing I made Perron an offer to buy the paper for Samazelle, letting him pick his own price?"

Robert shrugged his shoulders. " Try it," he said.

" You don't think he'd accept?"

" Put yourself in his place."

" Very well, then. And if I asked to buy only Luc's share? Or, if necessary, a third of each of their shares?"

" It's their paper, you understand," Robert replied. " They created it, and they're determined to be their own masters."

" That's bad," Trarieux said.

" Perhaps. But no one can do anything about it."

Trarieux began pacing quietly before us. " I'm not the type who gives up easily," he said with a smile. " When someone tells me something is impossible, I immediately want to prove the opposite. Let me say this too—the interests of the S.R.L. seem much more important to me than any personal feelings, even the most honourable," he added gravely.

Samazelle looked disturbed. " If you're thinking about that plan you mentioned to me the other day," he said, " I've already told you that I can't go along with it."

" And I replied that I understood your scruples," Trarieux said, smiling briefly. He gave Robert a somewhat defiant look. " I buy up all of *L'Espoir's* debts and then let Perron make his choice: either he takes on Samazelle or I put him out of business."

" Perron would choose bankruptcy rather than give in to blackmail," Robert said scornfully.

" All right. He goes bankrupt and I start another paper with Samazelle at its head."

" No," Samazelle groaned.

" I hope you understand," said Robert, " that the S.R.L. would have absolutely nothing to do with such a paper. And such conduct on your part would lead to your immediate exclusion from the movement."

Trarieux studied Robert as if to gauge the strength of his opposition. He must have been quickly satisfied, for he hastened to beat a retreat. " I never actually thought of putting the plan into effect," he said cheerfully. " I merely thought of using it to force Perron's hand. But the success of that paper really ought to be a matter of grave concern to you," he added reproachfully. " Double the circulation and you double your troops!"

" I know," Robert replied. " But I repeat that in my opinion the only mistake Perron and Luc made was to insist stubbornly on working with far too little money. The day they have behind them the capital which you so generously put at their disposal, you'll see the difference."

" Certainly," Trarieux said with a smile. " Because when they accept the money they'll have to accept Samazelle along with it."

Robert's face hardened. " Excuse me," he said. " In April you told me you were ready to back *L'Espoir* without any conditions."

I studied Samazelle from the corner of my eye; he didn't seem at all embarrassed. His wife, however, looked tortured, but she always looked that way.

" I didn't say that," Trarieux replied. " I said that politically the policies of the paper would, of course, be decided by the leaders of the S.R.L., and that I wouldn't interfere. There was no question of anything else."

" Because there didn't seem to be anything else to be questioned," Robert said indignantly. " I promised Perron his complete independence, and it was on the strength of that promise that he took the enormous risk of affiliating *L'Espoir* with the S.R.L."

" You will admit that I don't have to consider myself bound by your promises," Trarieux said amiably. " Besides, I don't see why Perron should refuse. After all, Samazelle is his friend."

" That isn't the point. If he had any idea that we had plotted behind his back to force his hand, he'd become all the more stubborn. And I would understand it," Robert said vehemently.

He seemed extremely annoyed and so was I, especially since I knew Henri's feelings in regard to Samazelle.

" I can be stubborn, too," Trarieux replied.

" Samazelle's position would be pretty ticklish if he joined *L'Espoir* against Perron's will," Robert said.

" I agree completely!" Samazelle said. " Under different circumstances I'd feel that trying to breathe new life into a paper in trouble would be in my line. But I'd never let myself be forced on Perron against his will."

" You'll excuse me if I look on this deal as something that is in a sense my own personal problem," Trarieux said ironically. " I have no intention of making money out of it, but I absolutely refuse to squander millions for nothing. I want results. If Perron refuses to work with you, or you with him," he said to Samazelle, " I'll drop the whole thing. I never get involved in a venture if I feel it's bound to fail. That seems to me a sound point of view. In any case," he concluded dryly, "nothing can make me change my mind."

" It seems useless to me to argue about this until you've spoken to Perron," Samazelle said. " I'm convinced he'll be co-operative. After all, we're all interested in the same thing —the success of the movement."

" Yes, Perron will certainly understand the advisability of a few concessions, especially if you try to make him understand," Trarieux said to Robert.

Robert shrugged his shoulders. " Don't count on me," he replied.

The conversation dragged on for a little while longer. When we found ourselves at the foot of the stairway half an hour later, I said, " The whole thing stinks. Exactly what did Trarieux say to you in April?"

" We spoke only of the political aspects of the matter," Robert replied.

" And you promised Henri too much? You went too far?"

" Maybe," Robert replied. " If I'd been the least bit hesitant, I wouldn't have convinced him. Sometimes you're forced to go too far; otherwise you'd never accomplish anything!"

" Why didn't you put it squarely to Trarieux to-night?" I asked. " Either he keeps his promises without imposing conditions, or you break with him, you throw him out of the S.R.L."

" What then?" Robert said. " Suppose he chooses to break? The day Henri needs cash, what will he do?" We continued walking in silence, and then Robert said abruptly, " If Henri loses the paper because of me, I'll never forgive myself."

I thought of Henri's smile the night of the victory celebration. I had asked him, " You didn't want to get into the swim?" And he had answered, " Not madly." Subjecting *L'Espoir to* the domination of the S.R.L. had been painful to him ; he loved that paper, he loved his freedom, and he had no love at all for Samazelle. What was happening to him was downright shameful. But Robert looked so glum that I kept my thoughts to myself. I said only, " I can't understand why you put so much faith in Trarieux ; I don't take to him at all."

" I was wrong," Robert replied curtly. He thought for a moment. " I'm going to ask Mauvanes for the money."

" Mauvanes won't give it to you," I said.

" I'll ask others. There are plenty of people with money. I'm bound to dig up one who'll go along with us."

" It seems to me that to go along with you a man would have to be both a millionaire and a member of the S.R.L.," I said. " And that's a rather unusual combination."

" I'll keep looking," Robert said. " And at the same time I'll work on Trarieux through Samazelle. Samazelle can't let himself be foisted on somebody."

" It didn't seem to bother him too much," I said. I shrugged my shoulders. " Well, you can always try."

Robert saw Mauvanes the next day ; Mauvanes was interested, but naturally he didn't promise anything. Robert saw other people who weren't interested at all. As for me, I was worried ; the whole matter lay heavy on my heart. However, I didn't speak to Robert about it, because I try as much as possible not to be one of those women who doubles a man's worries by sharing them. But I thought of it constantly. " Robert shouldn't have done that," I would say to myself. And then I said, " He would not have done it before." An odd thought that! And what exactly did it prove? He said that his responsibilities seemed heavier and more limited than they used to be because he could no longer use the future as an alibi. Therefore, he was in more of a hurry to achieve his ends, which made him less scrupulous. I didn't like that idea. When one is as close to a person as I am to Robert, to judge him is to betray him.

Nadine and Lambert got back a few days later. For me, their return was a happy diversion; they were tanned, laughing, and as embarrassed as a young married couple.

"Nadine would make a first-class reporter," Lambert said. "When it comes to getting in anywhere and making anybody talk, she's terrific."

"Sometimes this business can be good fun," Nadine granted cockily.

But the thing in which she took the greatest pride was her discovery during the trip of the country house I had been futilely dreaming about for weeks. And only thirty kilometres from Paris! I was enchanted at first sight by the yellow façade with its blue shutters, the rank lawn, the small caretaker's cottage, the wild roses. Robert, too, was delighted by it, and we signed the lease at once. The interior was ramshackle, the paths full of nettles, but Nadine announced that she would take charge of putting everything in good shape. Suddenly, she lost interest in her secretarial job, left it for a while longer to her substitute, and together with Lambert set up quarters in the little cottage. They divided their time between planning their book, gardening, and painting walls. With his bronzed skin, his hands calloused from gripping the handlebars of his motorcycle, and his hair which Nadine systematically rumpled, Lambert looked a little less like a dandy. Nevertheless, he hardly gave the impression of being a manual labourer. But I had no other choice than to put my faith in them.

Nadine returned to Paris from time to time, but it wasn't until the eve of our departure for Auvergne that she permitted us to come to St. Martin. She rang us up and ceremoniously invited us to dinner.

"Tell Father we're going to have mayonnaise; it's Lambert's speciality."

But Robert declined the invitation. "Whenever Lambert sees me, he always feels he's got to attack me. Then I'm forced to answer him, which annoys everyone, and me most of all," he said regretfully.

As a matter of fact, Lambert always was aggressive in Robert's presence. It was quite rare to find people who didn't feel obliged to invent an attitude when they were with Robert. "When you come down to it, how alone he is!" I thought. It was never to him that they spoke, but to some distant, stiff, artificial person who had nothing in common with him but the name. He who so much used to enjoy being in the thick of the crowd was now unable to prevent his name from creating a barrier between himself and others; everyone constantly, mercilessly made him- remember it. And no one bothered about the man of flesh and blood Robert really was, with his laughter, his tenderness, his fits of anger, his insomnia. Just before leaving the house to take the bus, I asked him once more to come with me.

" It would be an unpleasant evening," he said. " Mind you, I don't dislike Lambert. But . . ."

" He's been very good for Nadine," I said. " This is the first time she's ever agreed to work with anybody."

Robert smiled. " And was she proud to see her name in print! That one who had nothing but scorn for literature!"

" So much the better!" I said. " It'll encourage her to continue. It's just the kind of work that suits her."

Robert put his hand on my shoulder. " Your mind's a little easier about your daughter's future now, isn't it?"

" Yes."

" Then why are you putting off writing to Romieux?" Robert asked sharply. " You haven't the slightest reason to hesitate any more."

" A lot of things can happen between now and January," I said quickly.

Romieux was clamouring loudly for an answer, but the thought of giving him a final yes or no panicked me.

" Listen," Robert said. " It's obvious that Nadine can get along perfectly well without you. Besides—and you yourself have said this often—nothing would do her more good than learning to do without us."

" That's true," I said without enthusiasm.

Robert looked perplexed. " You do want to take that trip, don't you?" he asked.

" Of course!" I replied, and immediately a feeling of panic overwhelmed me. " But I don't want to leave Paris. I don't want to leave you."

" How silly you are, my little silly," he said tenderly. " When you leave me, you always come back to find me exactly the same. And you've even admitted that you don't miss me when you're away," he added with a laugh.

" That was before," I said. " But now, with all the problems you've taken on yourself, I worry."

Robert studied me seriously. " You worry too much. Yesterday it was Nadine, to-day it's me. Don't you think it's becoming a mania?"

" Perhaps," I replied.

" No question about it," he said. " You're developing a little peacetime neurosis, like the others. You never used to be like that!"

Robert's smile was tender, but the idea that my absence might upset him seemed to him the invention of a sick mind. He could do perfectly well without me for three months, for at least three months. I could only share, not eliminate, that loneliness to which his name, his age, and people's attitudes condemned him. And if I didn't share it, it would weigh upon him neither more nor less heavily.

" Forget all those doubts!" Robert said. " Hurry up and write that letter, or that trip will slip right out from under your nose."

" I'll write to him as soon as I get back from St. Martin—if everything is really all right," I said.

" Even if everything isn't all right," Robert insisted.

" We'll see." I hesitated. " How are things going with Mauvanes?"

" I told you—he's taking a holiday and he'll give me a definite answer in October. But he practically promised me the money." Robert smiled. " He, too, wants to stay on the left."

" He really promised?"

" Yes. And when Mauvanes makes a promise he keeps it."

" That takes a weight off my heart," I said. Mauvanes was solid; I felt reassured. " You still don't intend to talk it over with Henri?" I asked.

" What for? What could he do? I got him into this mess; it's up to me to get him out of it." Robert shrugged his shoulders. " And then there's the chance he'll blow up and throw everything out of the window. No, I'll talk to him when I have the money."

" You're right," I said. I got up.

Robert got up, too, and smiled at me. " Stop worrying—and have a nice evening."

" I'll do my best."

Robert was, of course, right; that vague sense of worry I felt through my whole being dated from the liberation. Like so many others, I was having trouble readapting myself. The evening at St. Martin would teach me nothing new. It was neither because of Nadine nor because of Robert that I hesitated answering Romieux; my worry involved only me. All during the bus ride, I kept asking myself whether or not I would ever be able to shake it off. I pushed open the garden gate. A table was set under the linden tree and I could hear voices coming from inside the house; I went directly into the kitchen. Nadine was standing beside Lambert who, a napkin tied around his neck, was furiously beating a thin sauce.

" You've come at the height of tragedy!" she said to me cheerfully. " The mayonnaise is ruined!"

" Hallo," Lambert said sombrely. " Yes, it's ruined. And I never ruin it!"

" I tell you it can still be saved," Nadine said. " Keep going!"

" No, it's done for!"

" You're beating it too hard."

" I tell you it's done for," Lambert repeated angrily.

" Let me show you how to save a mayonnaise that hasn't come off," I said.

I poured the thin sauce down the drain and held out two new eggs to Lambert. " See what you can do with these."

Nadine smiled. " Sometimes you come up with a good idea," she said impartially. She took me by the arm. " How's Father?"

" Oh, he needs a good long holiday!"

" When you get back from your bicycle trip, the house will be ready and waiting," Nadine said. " Come and see what we've done with it already!"

Crowded with ladders and buckets of paint, the living-room to be still had the sad feeling of all unfinished construction. But the walls of my bedroom had been patched and were finished in a rough coat of dusty pink; Robert's room was done in pale ochre. They had done a good job.

" It's marvellous! Who did it? He or you?"

" Both of us. I give the orders, he carries them out. He's been working like a horse, and he's very obedient," she said, beaming.

I laughed. "You worked that out well!"

Nadine needed to give orders to be sure of herself; busy making herself obeyed, she stopped questioning herself. She thoroughly enjoyed playing the mistress of the house, and it had been a long time since I had seen her so cheerful. Between the salad bowls and platters of cold cuts, Lambert placed a large bowl of firm, smooth mayonnaise, and with Nadine not participating, we emptied a bottle of white wine. Enthusiastically, they told me of their plans: first Belgium, Holland, Denmark—all the occupied countries; and then the rest of Europe.

"And to think I'd made up my mind to drop newspaper work," Lambert said. "Without Nadine, I'd surely have given up. And let me tell you something: she's much better at it than I. Pretty soon she won't be wanting me to go along with her any more."

"That's why you don't want to let me drive your lousy motor-cycle," she sighed. "And it's so easy! I know it is!"

"Easy to break your neck, you little nut."

He smiled at her from the depths of his soul; in his eyes she was endowed with qualities which completely escaped me. I could never see her except from one point of view—as my daughter. For me, she had only two dimensions; she was flat. Lambert uncorked a second bottle of wine. He didn't know how to drink; his eyes were already glassy, his cheeks red, and beads of sweat were forming on his brow.

"Don't drink too much," Nadine said.

"Don't start playing mother," he said. "You know what happens when you start playing mother?"

Nadine's face hardened. "Don't talk nonsense," she said.

Lambert took off his jacket. "I'm not."

"You're going to catch cold."

"I never catch cold." He turned towards me and said, "Nadine doesn't want to believe it, but I'm pretty tough. I may not be a big bruiser, but there are some things I can take better than a professional athlete."

"We'll see about that when we cross the Sahara by motor-cycle!" Nadine said cheerfully.

"And we will cross it!" Lambert said. "You can go anywhere on a motor-cycle!" he looked at me and asked, "Don't you believe we can do it?"

" I have no idea," I replied.

" In any case, we're going to try," he said decisively. " You have to give everything a try! Just because a man's an intellectual, it doesn't mean he has to spend his life in slippers."

" Agreed," Nadine said, laughing. " We'll cross the Sahara, and the plateaus of Tibet, and we'll explore the jungles of the Amazon."

Lambert reached for the bottle; Nadine grabbed his wrist. " No, you've had too much already."

" Not at all." He got up and walked a few steps. " Am I staggering? A miracle of balance!"

" Let's see you juggle," Nadine said.

" One of my specialities," Lambert said to me. He took three oranges, threw them in the air, missed one, and fell full length on the lawn. Nadine let out one of her loud guffaws.

" Idiot!" she said tenderly. With a corner of her apron, she wiped Lambert's dripping brow; he happily abandoned himself to her care. " He really does have social talents," she said. " He knows such funny songs! Would you like to hear him sing one?"

" I'll sing *Heart of a Pig*," Lambert said decisively.

Nadine laughed so hard while he was singing that tears came to her eyes. As for me, I found in Lambert's gaiety an awkwardness that was almost pathetic; it almost seemed as if he were trying to slough off his skin by acting the part of a clumsy clown. But it stuck obstinately to his body. His grimaces, his comical voice, the sweat which streamed down his cheeks, the troubled fever in his eyes made me feel ill at ease. I was relieved when he finally threw himself down beside Nadine, who caressed his head with a happy, possessive look.

" You're a good little boy," she said. " Calm down now; rest."

She liked playing nurse, and he enjoyed being coaxed. And they had many things in common: their past, their youth, their rancour against words and ideas, their dreams of adventure, their vague ambitions. Perhaps they would be able to give each other confidence, contrive for themselves new undertakings, successes, happiness. One was nineteen, the other twenty-five; how young the future was! No, they weren't survivors. "And I?" I thought. "Am I really buried alive in the past? No!" I answered myself emphatically. "No!" Nadine and Robert could get along without me; they had only been excuses. I was simply a victim of my own cowardice, and suddenly it made me feel ashamed. An aircraft carrying me off, a giant city, and for three months no other task but to learn and to enjoy myself. So much freedom, so much that would be new to me! How I wanted it! It was no doubt foolhardy for me to go wandering in the world of the living, I who had built myself a sheltered little nest. Too bad! I'd have to chance it. I stopped trying to suppress the joy which was engulfing me. Yes, this very evening I'd answer yes. To survive is, after all, perpetually to begin to live again. I hoped I would still know how.

CHAPTER FIVE

HENRI TURNED over on his board; the wind was whistling through cracks in the stone walls and despite his blanket and sweaters he was too cold to fall asleep. But his head was hot and buzzing as if he had a touch of fever; and perhaps he did —a pleasant fever produced by the sun, fatigue, and too much red wine. Where exactly was he? In any case, somewhere where no one had any reason to be. But how restful it was! No regrets, no questions; those moments of insomnia were as serene as a dreamless sleep. He had given up a good many things: he no longer wrote, didn't enjoy each day; but what he had gained in exchange was tremendous—being at peace with his conscience. Far from the earth and its problems, far from the cold, from the wind, from his weary body, he was floating in a bath of innocence, and innocence can be every bit as exhilarating as voluptuousness. He raised his eyelids for a brief instant and, seeing the dark wooden table, the candle, and that man who was busily writing, he thought with satisfaction, " I must be in the Middle Ages!" And on that happy thought, the night closed in around him.

" Was I dreaming, or did I really see you writing last night?"

" I was getting a little work done," Dubreuilh replied.

" I thought you were Dr. Faustus."

Wrapped in blankets which were flapping in the wind, they were sitting in the doorway of the shelter. The sun had risen while they were still asleep and the sky was a pure, perfect blue. Below them a carpet of clouds stretched out into the distance. For brief instants, the wind tore the clouds apart, and through the gaps strips of farmland could be seen.

" He works every day," Anne said. " And the setting doesn't matter: it can be anywhere—in the stable, in the rain, on a public square. But he's got to have his four hours writing. After that, he'll do whatever you like."

" And what would you like to do now?" Dubreuilh asked.

" I think we might as well go down; we can do better than this for a view."

They wound their way down the mountain through the

heavy mist to the darkened village. Old women, sitting on their doorsteps, cushions bristling with pins in their laps, were already working their spindles. They drank a dark brew in the local bistro where they had left their bicycles and then set out again. The bicycles were old, war-wearied machines which looked as if they were about to fall apart; the paint was chipped, the mudguards were dented, and strange swellings bulged the tyres. Henri's was giving him so much trouble that he wondered anxiously if it would hold up until evening. He was relieved to see the Dubreuilhs stop alongside a stream which turned out to be the Loire; the water was too cold for swimming, but he doused himself from head to foot and when he got back on his bike he found that the wheels would still turn after all. Actually his body was the rustier of the two; putting it back in shape required real work. But after the initial stiffness had passed, Henri felt pleased that he had repaired such an excellent instrument; he had forgotten how efficient a human body can be. The chain and the wheels did their share, but actually the only source of power in that whole contraption was his muscles, his wind, and his heart. And together they ate up a respectable ration of kilometres, they valiantly climbed the hills.

"You seem to be doing all right now," Anne said. With her wind-blown hair, her tanned skin, her bare arms, she seemed much younger than she did in Paris. Dubreuilh, too, had tanned, grown thinner; with his shorts, his muscular legs, and the deep lines etched in his leathery face, he looked like one of Gandhi's disciples.

"Better than yesterday!" Henri said.

Dubreuilh slowed down and began riding alongside Henri. "You have to confess, though, that it was pretty bad yesterday," he said, cheerfully. "By the way, you haven't told us anything yet. What's been happening in Paris since we left?"

"Nothing special. It's been hot," Henri replied. "God, has it been hot!"

"And at the paper? You still haven't seen Trarieux?" The eager curiosity in Dubreuilh's voice sounded almost like anxiety.

"No, Luc's got an idea in his head that if we can hold out for another two or three months we'll pull out of it by ourselves."

" It's worth trying, only you mustn't go any deeper into debt."

" I know; we've stopped borrowing. Luc is counting on building up the advertising to pull us through."

" I must admit I didn't think circulation would drop as much as it did," Dubreuilh said.

" Well," Henri said with a smile, " if we end up by having to accept Trarieux's money. I won't let myself get sick over it. It's not too high a price to pay for the success of the S.R.L."

" The fact is that whatever success it's achieved up to now is due to you," Dubreuilh said. His voice was even more reserved than his words. He wasn't at all satisfied with the S.R.L., probably because he was too eager. After all, it is impossible to bring forth overnight a party as important as the old Socialist Party. Henri, on the other hand, had been happily surprised by the success of the meeting. But a meeting doesn't really prove very much. Nevertheless, he wouldn't soon forget those five thousand faces raised towards him. He smiled at Anne. " A bicycle has its points," he said. " In a way it's even better than a car."

They had slowed down, but the smell of the grass, the heather, the pine trees, the gentle coolness of the wind penetrated to their very bones. And the countryside was something much more than just a setting: they were conquering it bit by bit, by main force. In the weariness of the climbs, in the joy of the descents, they became part of it, lived it rather than looked at it as scenery. And the happy discovery Henri made on the very first day was that this life was enough to satisfy you completely. What silence inside his head! The mountains, the meadows, the forests, they all took charge of the business of living for him. " How wonderful it is!" he said to himself. " A peace that can't be mistaken for sleep!"

" You've chosen well," he said to Anne that evening. " It's beautiful country."

" It'll be nice to-morrow, too. Would you like to see the map?"

In the inn where they had just dined, they were drinking a murderously strong white liquor. Dubreuilh had already set up his paraphernalia at one end of an oilcloth-covered table.

" Yes," Henri said. His eyes obediently followed the pencil

point along red, yellow, and white lines. "How can you choose between those little roads?"

"That's the fun of it."

The fun of it, Henri thought the next day, was seeing how perfectly the future followed your plans: every turn, every upgrade and downgrade, every hamlet was in its foreseen place. What security! You felt as if your life was a cocoon spun from within your own body. And yet the metamorphosis of printed words and lines into real roads, real houses, gave you what no man-made creation can give: reality. That waterfall was forecast on the map by a little blue mark; it was for all that no less startling to come upon it, huge and foaming, at the end of a twisting gorge.

"How satisfying it is to look," Henri said.

"Yes, only there's no end to looking," Dubreuilh said regretfully. "Looking gives you both everything and nothing."

Dubreuilh didn't look at everything, but when he became fascinated with something then there really was no end to it. Henri and Anne had to climb down behind him, from rock to rock, to the foot of the watery cliff; barefooted, he went into the seething cauldron until the water reached the bottoms of his shorts. When he came back and sat down on the edge of the pool, he announced categorically, "That's the most beautiful waterfall we've ever seen."

"You always prefer what you're looking at," Anne said, laughing.

"It's all in black and white," Dubreuilh said. "That's what's so beautiful about it. I was looking for colours, but there's not a trace of colour. And for the first time I've seen with my own eyes that black and white are exactly the same. You ought to go into the water and walk as far as that big stone," he said to Henri. "That's where it hits you: the blackness of white, the whiteness of black. You actually see it!"

"I'll take your word for it," Henri said.

When you were with Dubreuilh, a stroll along the quays became as exciting as an expedition to the North Pole; Henri and Anne would often laugh together over this. The thing was that he didn't distinguish between seeing and discovering; no eye before his had ever seen a waterfall, no one knew what

water was, what black and white were. By himself, Henri
certainly would never have noticed all the details of that play
of mist and foam, the shape-shifting, the ghostly apparitions,
the tiny whirlpools which Dubreuilh scrutinised so closely, as
if he were trying to determine the destiny of each drop of
water. " You can get annoyed at him," Henri thought, looking
at Dubreuilh affectionately, " but you can't get along without him." When you were with him, everything seemed important, living became a great privilege—and you lived twice
as much. He transformed that leisurely trip across the French
countryside into a voyage of discovery.

" You'd really surprise your readers," Henri said, smiling at
Dubreuilh who, completely absorbed, was contemplating the
last rays of the sun.

" Why?" Dubreuilh asked in that shocked voice he always
affected whenever someone spoke to him about himself.

" You get the impression from your books that only people
interest you and that nature counts hardly at all."

" People live in nature, don't they?"

For Dubreuilh, a landscape, a stone, a colour, was a single
human truth ; things never moved him in memory or dream,
or by the feelings they might arouse in him, but only by the
meaning he detected in them. Of course, he stopped more
willingly to watch the peasants harvesting a crop than to look
at an empty meadow. And when he passed through a village
his curiosity became insatiable ; he wanted to know everything
—what the villagers ate, how they voted, the details of their
work, the shading of their thoughts. He would use any pretext to gain entrance to a farmhouse, from buying eggs to
asking for a drink of water. And whenever he could, he engaged his host in long conversations.

The evening of the fifth day out, Anne had a puncture half-
way down a hill. After walking for more than an hour, they
came to an isolated house inhabited by three toothless young
women ; each held a very dirty, rather chubby baby in her
arms. Dubreuilh set up shop in the middle of the dung-
splattered courtyard and began repairing the tube. While he
was glueing patches on it, he looked around greedily.

" Three women and no men . . . Peculiar, isn't it?"

" The men are in the fields," Anne said.

" At this hour?" He plunged the rust-coloured tube into

a tub and bubbles of air rose to the surface of the water.
" Another hole! Listen, do you think they might let us
sleep in the stable?"

" I'll ask them."

Anne disappeared inside the house and returned almost immediately. " They're a little upset at our wanting to sleep in
the hay, but they have nothing against it. Only they absolutely
insist that we drink something hot before turning in."

" I like the idea of sleeping here!" Henri said. " Because
when it comes to being out of touch with things, we really are
out of touch here!"

By the light of a smoky lamp, they drank barley coffee and
tried to carry on a conversation. The women were married
to three brothers who jointly owned that poor small farm ;
ten days before, their men had gone down to Basse-Ardèche
where they had hired themselves out to gather lavender, and
the women spent the long, silent days feeding the animals and
the children. They still knew how to manage a fleeting smile,
but they had almost forgotten how to speak. Here, chestnut
trees grew and the nights were chilly ; in Ardèche grew
bunches of lavender and it took much sweat to earn a few
francs. That was just about all they knew of the world. Yes,
they were out of touch with things, so far from everything
that when he stretched himself out in the hay, groggy from
all the smells and all the sun stored in that dried grass,
Henri dreamed that neither roads nor cities existed any
longer ; there was no return.

The next day, they followed a road which wound its way
among the chestnut groves and sank in sharp turns to the flatlands. Gaily they rode into the little town whose plane trees
indicated that they were nearing the heat and the bowling
greens of the Midi. Anne and Henri sat down at a table on
the deserted terrace of the town's largest café and ordered a
bite to eat while Dubreuilh went to buy the papers. They
watched him exchanging a few words with the vendor, and
then he slowly crossed the square, reading intently. He set the
papers down on the table and Henri saw the huge headline:
" U.S. Drops Atomic Bomb on Hiroshima." They read the
article in silence, and her voice unsteady, Anne said, " A
hundred thousand dead! Why?"

Japan, of course, would now capitulate ; it was the end of
the war. *Le Petit Cévenol* and *L'Echo de l'Ardèche* were ex-

ultant. But all three of them, sitting there, felt only one thing —horror.

"Couldn't they have threatened them first, frightened them?" Anne asked. "Couldn't they have demonstrated it in some deserted place? Did they really have to drop it?"

"Of course, they could have tried to bring pressure on the government before they did this," Dubreuilh said. He shrugged his shoulders. "On a German city, on white people, I wonder if they'd have dared! But yellow people! They hate yellow people."

"Nevertheless," Henri said, "it must upset them to vaporise a whole city."

"I think there's another reason for it," Dubreuilh said. "They're very pleased to be able to show the whole world just what they're capable of; that way they can carry out their policies as they will, and no one will dare to speak up."

"And they killed a hundred thousand people for that!" Anne exclaimed.

They sat stupefied before their coffees, their eyes frozen to the horrifying words, repeating one after the other and then all together the same useless phrases.

"My God! What if the Germans had succeeded in making that bomb! What a narrow escape!" Anne said.

"I'm not too happy to know that it's in American hands either," Dubreuilh said.

"They say here that the whole world can be blown up," Anne said.

"The way Larguet explained it to me," Henri said, "is that atomic energy—if some unfortunate accident should free it— wouldn't blow up the earth but would devour its atmosphere. The earth would become a sort of moon."

"That's hardly more cheering," Anne said.

But when they set out again on a sun-drenched road, the horrible words had become empty of meaning. No, it wasn't cheering. A city of four hundred thousand vaporised, Nature disintegrated—the words no longer awakened an echo in them. This day was in perfect order: the sky was blue, the leaves green, the thirsty sun a brilliant yellow, and the hours slipped by one by one from the freshness of dawn to the intense, quivering heat of noon. The earth was turning around the sun to which it had been assigned, indifferent to its cargo of destinationless passengers. How could one believe, under that infinitely tranquil sky, that those very passengers now had it within their power to transform the earth into a moon barren of life? Of course, after several days of wandering through nature, one came to realise that she, too, was a little mad; there was an exaggerated extravagance in the capricious majesty of the clouds, in the frozen actions and revolts of the mountains, in the scurrying of insects and the frantic pro-liferation of plant life. But it was a gentle, stereotyped mad-ness. How strange to think that when it passed through the human brain, this madness became organised into homicidal frenzy.

" And you still have the courage to write!" Henri said as he sat down at the edge of a river and saw Dubreuilh taking his papers out of his knapsack.

" He's a monster," Anne said. " He'd work in the ruins of Hiroshima."

" He is working in the ruins of Hiroshima."

" Why not?" Dubreuilh asked. " There have always been ruins somewhere."

He unscrewed his pen and for a long moment stared emptily into space; it wasn't, after all, so easy to write among those fresh, new ruins. Instead of bending over his paper, he said abruptly, " Ah, if only they didn't make it impossible for us to be Communists!"

" Who do you mean?" Anne asked.

" The Communists. Do you realise what a tremendous instrument of pressure that bomb is! I don't think the Yanks will drop one on Moscow to-morrow, but they can do it, and they won't let anybody forget that they can. They won't be able to control themselves. Now, if ever, is the moment to close our ranks, but instead we're simply repeating all the old pre-war mistakes."

" You say we," Henri said, " but it isn't we who started it."

" Oh, our conscience is clear. What of it?" Dubreuilh said. " That does us a lot of good, doesn't it? If the break occurs we'll be no less responsible for it than the Communists—in fact, even more so, since they're the stronger."

" I don't follow you,' Henri said.

" Agreed that they're obnoxious. But in what truly con-cerns us, that makes no difference at all. From the moment they make us their enemies, we'll be enemies, and it's useless to say; ' It's their fault.' Their fault or not, we'll be the enemies of the only large proletarian party in France. And that certainly is not what we want."

" What do you suggest then? That we give in to their blackmail?"

" I never thought that people who prefer to run away rather than yield were very clever," Dubreuilh said. " Blackmail or not, we've got to maintain the union."

" The only union they really look forward to is the dissolution of the S.R.L. and the adherence of all its members to the Communist Party."

" It might be that we'll even come to that."

" You would find it possible to join the C.P?" Henri asked with surprise. " But there are so many things that keep you apart from the Communists!"

" Oh, you learn to make the best of it," Dubreuilh said. " If I had to, I could keep my mouth shut."

He took his papers and began jotting down words. Henri pulled a couple of books from his saddlebag and spread them out on the grass; since he had stopped writing, he had read a great many books; books which had taken him virtually around the world. For the past few days he had been discovering India and China; there was nothing cheering about that, either. Many things became futile when one thought of those hundreds of thousands of hungry people. And perhaps his reservations in regard to the C.P. were also futile. What he held against them most of all was treating people as things; if you didn't believe in their right to freedom, in their judgment, in their good will, then individuals weren't worth bothering about. And if you do bother, you do it badly. But that particular grievance had no meaning except in France, in Europe, where people had attained a certain standard of living, a minimum of autonomy and sanity. When it came to huge masses brutalised by misery and superstition, what, after all, did " treating them as men " mean? They had to be fed, that's all. American domination meant the perpetual oppression and undernourishment of all the Oriental countries. Their only chance is the Soviet Union; the only chance to see humanity delivered from want, slavery, and stupidity is the Soviet Union. No effort, then, must be spared to help her. When millions of men are nothing but animals bewildered by need, humanism becomes laughable, and individualism a dirty lie. Judging, deciding, discussing freely—how can anyone

demand those superior rights for himself? Henri plucked a
blade of grass and thoughtfully chewed it. Since, in any case,
you can't live the way you'd really want to, why not renounce
doing so completely? To lose yourself in the bosom of a
large party, to blend your will with a huge collective will—
what peace, what power! You have only to open your mouth
and you speak in the name of the whole earth; the future
becomes your personal accomplishment. Considering all that,
it might well be worth it to submit to any number of unpleasant things. Henri tore off another blade of grass from the
ground. " Nevertheless, from day to day, I know I wouldn't
be able to take it easily," he said to himself. " It's impossible
to believe what you don't believe, want what you don't want;
to be a good militant, you need the faith of a fanatic. I don't
have it. And that isn't even the question," he thought, annoyed by his idealism. " What good would my joining the
Communist Party do? That's the only concrete question.
Obviously, it wouldn't provide a single grain of rice for a
single Hindu."

Dubreuilh had stopped questioning himself. He wrote, and
each day he continued writing. In that field, nothing could
silence him. One afternoon, while they were having lunch in
a village at the foot of Mt. Aigoual, a storm burst out so
violently that their bicycles were overturned; two saddlebags
were carried away, and Dubreuilh's manuscript drifted off on
a torrent of mud. When he fished it out, the words dripped
down in long black streaks on paper saturated with yellowish
water. Calmly, he dried the pages and recopied the more
damaged passages; he gave you the impression that, if
necessary, he would have started his whole book over again,
from beginning to end, with exactly the same equanimity.
Since he was able to find reasons doggedly to continue writing,
he was without doubt justified in doing so. And sometimes,
watching his hand slip along the paper, Henri felt a sort of
nostalgia in his own wrist.

" Can't we read a few pages of your manuscript? How far
have you got?" Henri asked one afternoon while they were
sitting in a shady café in Valence waiting for the heat to sub-
side.

" I'm writing a chapter on the idea of culture," Dubreuilh
said. " What's the meaning behind the fact that man can't
stop talking about himself? And what makes certain men

decide they can speak in the name of others? In other words, what is an intellectual? Doesn't that decision make him a species apart? And in what measure is humanity able to recognise itself in the picture it paints of itself?"

"And what's your conclusion?" Henri asked. "That literature still means something?"

"Of course."

"Writing to prove that you're justified in writing!" Henri said with a laugh. "That's wonderful!"

Dubreuilh looked at him curiously. "Look," he said. "You are going to start writing again one of these days?"

"Oh, not to-day, in any case," Henri replied.

"Well, what's the difference if it's to-day or to-morrow?"

"I'm pretty sure it won't be to-morrow either."

"But why not?" Dubreuilh asked.

"You're writing an essay; well and good. But you've got to admit that putting together a novel in these times is rather discouraging."

"No, I refuse to admit it! And I'll never understand why you gave up yours."

"Actually, it's your fault," Henri said, smiling.

"What do you mean, my fault?" Dubreuilh turned indignantly to Anne. "Did you hear him?"

"You preached action to me, and action made me fed up with literature." Henri signalled to the waiter who was standing against the cash register, half asleep. "I'd like another glass of beer. How about you?"

"No, I'm too warm," Anne replied .

Dubreuilh nodded his head in assent. "Explain yourself," he said, resuming the conversation.

"Why should people give a damn about what I think, what I feel?" Henri said. "My little personal stories don't interest anyone, and history, the big story, isn't in my opinion a fit subject for a novel."

"But we all have our little personal stories which don't interest anyone," Dubreuilh said. "That's why we're always discovering ourselves in our neighbour's. And if we know how to tell them well, in the end we wind up interesting everyone."

"That's what I thought when I started my book," Henri said. He drank a deep gulp of beer. He had little desire to explain himself. He looked at the two old men who were playing backgammon at the other end of the long red bench.

How peaceful it was in that café! Yet that was just another lie! He forced himself to answer Dubreuilh. " The trouble is the only personal things in an experience are the errors, the delusions. Once you've understood that, you no longer feel like telling about it."

" I don't quite see your point," Dubreuilh said.

Henri hesitated. " Suppose you see a string of lights at night along the bank of a river. It's a pretty sight. But when you know they light up cities where people are dying of hunger, they lose all their poetry, become nothing but a mirage. You'll tell me I can write about other things, about those people who are dying of hunger, for example. But I'd rather discuss those things at meetings or in articles."

" I wouldn't tell you that at all," Dubreuilh said spiritedly. " Those lights shine for everyone. Obviously, the basic need is to have food to eat, but what good is eating if you're denied all the little things that make life worth living? Why, for instance, are we taking this trip? It's because we believe that landscapes *aren't* mirages."

" All right," Henri said. " Let's admit that some day everything will make sense again. But just now, there are so many things which are so much more important."

" But it makes sense just now," Dubreuilh said. " Since it means something in our lives, it's going to mean something in our books." He said, beginning to sound annoyed, " To hear you talk, you'd think the left is dedicated to propagandist literature only, in which each and every word must enlighten the reader."

" You know that kind of literature doesn't appeal to me," Henri said.

" Yes, I know. But you're not trying to do anything else. And there's plenty to be done!" Dubreuilh looked at Henri pleadingly. " Of course, if you make a thing of beauty out of those lights and forget what lies behind them, you're an idiot. But that's just it: you've got to find a way to write about them which differs from the way the rightist aesthetes write; you've got to bring out at one and the same time the fact that they are pretty and that they shed light on misery. That's exactly the task that leftist literature should set itself," he said excitedly. " Making us see things in a new perspective by setting them in their true place. But let's not impoverish the world. **Personal experiences**—what you call mirages—do exist."

" Yes, they do **exist**," Henri said without conviction.

Perhaps Dubreuilh was right ; perhaps there was a way of retrieving everything, perhaps literature still had a meaning. But now, understanding the world seemed more urgent to Henri than recreating it in words. He preferred pulling from his saddlebag a bound and printed book rather than a sheet of blank paper.

" Do you know what's going to happen?" Dubreuilh continued vehemently. " Books written by the chaps on the right are going to wind up being better than ours, and the youth of the country will align itself with the Volanges."

" Oh, the Volanges will never capture the youth!" Henri said. " Young people don't like the defeated."

" It's we who may soon seem to be defeated," Dubreuilh said. He looked at Henri insistently. " I'm distressed that you're not writing any more."

" I may get back to it soon," Henri said.

It was too hot to argue. But he knew he wouldn't get back to it very soon. The advantage of not writing was that finally he had enough time to study and learn. In four months he had filled in a number of gaps, and when he returned to Paris in three days he would lay out a carefully planned course of studies ; in a year or two he hoped to have at least a basic knowledge of political culture.

" Provided Paula isn't back yet!" he said to himself the next morning while pedalling listlessly through a forest, whose thin shadows barely weakened the fury of the sky. He had let Dubreuilh and Anne ride on ahead of him and he was alone when he reached the clearing. Circles of sunlight quivered on the green grass, and he could not understand why he suddenly felt his heart grow heavy. It wasn't because of the burned-out hut which looked like so many other ruins, gently eaten away by indifference and time ; perhaps it was because of the silence—not a bird, not an insect, only the exaggerated sound of gravel crunching under the tyres. Anne and Dubreuilh had got off their bicycles and were looking at something. Henri joined them. They were looking at crosses, white crosses without names, without flowers. Vercors. That word, the colour of burnt gold, the colour of straw and ashes, coarse and dry as a wasteland but with a lingering mountain freshness, was no longer the name of a legend. Vercors. It was this mountainous country with its lacy forests and its moist, rust-coloured downs, where the hard sun lifted the crosses from the earth.

They rode off in silence. The road became so steep that they had to get off their bicycles and walk. The heat filtered through the pale shadows and Henri felt the sweat streaming down his face, watched it dripping from Anne's forehead and Dubreuilh's coppery cheeks. And in all their hearts there ran the same refrain: " A fresh green field where they could pitch their tents." It was one of those innocent, secret places of which one used to think, " Here at least war and hate will never manage to penetrate." But they knew now that there was no refuge anywhere. Seven crosses.

" There's the top!" Anne cried out.

Henri loved those moments when, after a long, blind ascent, he would look down upon a large patch of inhabited earth, with its fields, its hedgerows, its roads, its hamlets, dark slate and pink tile roofs glistening in a bath of sunlight. The first thing he saw upon reaching the top was a chain of mountains leaning against the sky. And then he saw the huge plateau roasting naked under the sun. As on all the other plateaus of France, there were farms, hamlets, villages ; but no tile, no slate, not a single roof. Only walls, walls of unequal height, capriciously hacked, sheltering nothing.

" It doesn't help to know," said Anne. " You only think you know."

They stood motionless for a moment and then cautiously began descending the rocky road upon which the sun was beating down in all its fury. For a whole week they had been talking of Hiroshima, repeating figures, exchanging sentences great with ghastly portents. Yet nothing stirred within them. And then, suddenly, a glance was enough. Horror was there, and their hearts shrank.

Dubreuilh abruptly slammed on his brakes. " What's going on?"

Through the haze trembling above the village there came a blare of bugles. Henri stopped and below him, along the main road, he saw a stream of military trucks, half-tracks, cars, pony traps.

" It must be the celebration," he said. " I wasn't paying

much attention, but I overheard some people at the hotel talking about a celebration somewhere."

" It looks like a parade," Dubreuilh said. " What shall we do?"

" Well, we can't go back again," Anne said. " Or stay here in the sun."

" No, I suppose not," Dubreuilh said in a dismayed voice.

They continued down the road. To the left of the burned-out village was a field of white crosses decorated with bouquets of red flowers. Senegalese soldiers in their brilliant fezzes were marching in parade step. Again the blare of bugles echoed above the silent graves.

" We're in luck," Henri said. " It looks as if it's just about over."

" Let's cut over to the right," Dubreuilh said.

The soldiers clambered aboard the trucks and the crowd dispersed. Old men and young, women and children, they were all dressed in black, sweltering in their heavy funeral clothes. In cars and buggies, on bicycles and motor-cycles and on foot, they had come from all the surrounding villages and hamlets. There were five thousand of them, perhaps ten thousand, vying with each other for the shade of dead trees and scorched walls. Squatting by the roadside, leaning against the cars and carriages, they unwrapped loaves of bread and bottles of red wine. Now that the dead had been fittingly gorged with speeches, flowers, and military music, the living could eat.

" I wonder where we'll be able to find a place to rest," Anne said.

After that morning's difficult stretch of road, they felt like lying down in the shade and drinking cold, fresh water. Sadly, they pushed their bicycles along the road teeming with widows and orphans. There was not even the faintest suggestion of a breeze, and the trucks going down into the valley were raising enormous clouds of white dust.

" Shade! Where can we find some shade?" Anne said.

" Those tables over there are in the shade," Dubreuilh said. He pointed to a group of long tables near a wooden shack, but every place seemed taken. Women were circulating with pans of mashed potatoes which they doled out with large ladles.

" Is it a banquet or a restaurant?" Anne asked.

" Let's go and ask. I could do with something other than hard-boiled eggs," Dubreuilh said.

It turned out to be a restaurant, and the customers closed ranks a little to make room on the benches for the new-comers. Henri sat down opposite Dubreuilh, next to a woman who was wearing a heavy crepe veil and whose eyes were bordered with red styes. A glob of potatoes dropped into his plate followed by a slice of rare meat which landed on top of the white paste. Baskets of bread and bottles of wine were passed from hand to hand. Everyone was eating in silence, and the stiff, unnatural gluttony of the diners reminded Henri of peasant funerals he had attended during his childhood. Only here they were in mourning by the hundreds—widows, orphans, and relatives, sharing each other's grief and sweat-ing profusely under the hot sun. An old man seated next to Henri passed him a bottle of red wine. " Pour her a drink," he said, pointing to the woman with the styes. " Her husband was one of the ones they hanged at St. Denis."

Across the table, a woman asked, " The one they hung by the feet?"

" No, not him. The one who was missing both eyes."

Henri poured the widow a glass of wine ; he lacked the courage to look at her, and suddenly he felt himself sweating under his light shirt. He turned towards the old man. " Was it parachute troops who burned Vassieux?"

" Yes, four hundred of them. As you can imagine, they didn't have much trouble. Vassieux had the most dead ; that's why they're entitled to the big cemetery."

" The big cemetery for all Vercors," the woman opposite him said proudly. " You're René's uncle, aren't you?" she said. " The lad they found in the grotto with Février's son?"

" Yes, I'm his uncle," the old man replied.

All around the table, tongues began loosening up, and as they drank the red wine they traded memories of scenes of horror. At St. Roch, the Germans had locked both men and women in the church, and then, after setting it afire, they allowed the women to come out. Two of them never came out.

" I'll be back in a minute," Anne said, rising suddenly. " I . . ."

She took a few steps and collapsed alongside the shack. Dubreuilh jumped up and Henri followed him. Her eyes were

closed, her skin white, her brow covered with sweat. " Sick,"
she mumbled, retching, her handkerchief to her mouth. After
a moment, she opened her eyes. " The wine . . . It'll pass."

" The wine, the sun, fatigue," Dubreuilh said, helping her
invent excuses. But he knew she was as strong as a horse.

" You ought to lie down in the shade and rest for a while,"
Henri said. " We'll look for a quiet place. Do you think you
can manage to ride for a few minutes?"

" Yes, of course. I'm all right now. Excuse me."

Fainting, weeping, vomiting—women have those expedi-
ences. But they, too, are useless ; in face of the dead, one is
without recourse. They mounted their bicycles. The air was
burning, as if for a second time the village were aflame ;
people were sprawled out at the foot of every haystack,
alongside every bush ; the men had removed their ceremonial
jackets and the women had rolled up their sleeves, unbuttoned
their blouses. Songs, laughter, little yelps and giggles drifted
through the air. What else were they to do, if not drink,
laugh, tickle each other? As long as they were alive, they had
to go on living.

They rode at least five kilometres before finding a narrow
patch of shade alongside the trunk of a half-dead tree. Anne
spread out her raincoat on the ground bristling with stubble
and rocks and curled up on it. From his saddlebag, Dubreuilh
took out his papers which had the smell of slime and looked
as if they were streaked with tears. Henri sat down and
leaned his head against the bark of the tree ; he could neither
sleep nor work. Suddenly, wanting to learn seemed idiotic
to him. France's political parties, the Don's economy, Iran-
ian oil, Russia's problems—all that had abruptly become part
of the past. The new era which was now opening had never
been foreseen in books. What, after all, was the good of a
solid political background when weighed against the brute
fact of atomic energy? The S.R.L., *L'Espoir*, action—what
a dismal joke! The so-called " men of good will " might just
as well quietly retire, for it was the scientists and technicians
who held the future in their hands, the men who were building
bombs, anti-bombs, super bombs. A jolly future! Henri
closed his eyes. From Vassieux to Hiroshima—they had gone
a long way in a single year. The next war would really be
something! And the next post-war period, that would be even
neater than this one! That is, if there is a next post-war

period—if the defeated don't take it into their heads to blow
up the world. And it could very well happen. Granted, it
wouldn't break into pieces; it would just continue turning on
its axis, frozen, barren. But that picture was hardly more
cheering. The thought of death had never bothered Henri, but
suddenly that lunar silence terrified him. Mankind would be
no more! In face of that deaf-and-dumb eternity, what
earthly sense was there in setting words on paper, holding
meetings? You had only to sit back and silently await the
universal cataclysm, or your own insignificant death. Nothing
meant anything.

He opened his eyes. The earth was hot, the sky glaring;
Anne was sleeping and Dubreuilh was writing a justification
for writing. Two peasants in mourning clothes, their shoes
white with dust and their arms laden with red roses, were
hurrying towards the village. Henri followed them with his
eyes. Did the women of St. Roch place flowers on their husband's ashes? Probably. Had they become respectable
widows? Or did people point accusing fingers at them in the
street? And deep inside themselves, how did they handle
things? Had they forgotten a little? Much? Not at all? A
year—how short it is; how long. Dead comrades had been
forgotten, and forgotten, too, was that future which the feverish days of August had promised. Fortunately it's unhealthy
to insist on living in the past, but you can't be very proud of
yourself when you realise you've more or less disowned it.
That's why they invented that dreadful compromise: com-
memoration. Yesterday blood, to-day red wine discreetly
salted with tears. Many people find release that way. But
there are others to whom it must seem horrible. Suppose one
of those women had loved her husband, really loved him.
What would all the speeches and fanfares in the world mean
to her? Henri stared at the reddish mountains. He saw
her standing in front of a mirror, adjusting her crepe veils;
a blare of bugles and she cries out, " I can't, I don't want to."
And they say to her, " You must." They put red roses in her
arms, plead with her in the name of the village, in the name
of France, in the name of the dead. Outside, the celebration
is beginning. She rips off her veil. And then? The picture
blurred. " Come now," Henri said to himself, " I made up
my mind to stop writing." But he remained motionless, his

eyes stared blankly off into space. It was absolutely necessary for him to decide what would become of that woman.

Henri got back to Paris before Paula. He rented a room across the street from *L'Espoir*, and, as things had slowed down considerably at the paper during the hot summer weather, he spent hours working at his desk. " It's fun writing a play!" he said to himself. That heavy afternoon red with wine, flowers, heat, and blood had become a play, his first play. Yes, there had always been ruins, there had always been reasons for not writing, but they didn't carry much weight once the urge to write seized you.

Without protesting, Paula accepted the idea that henceforth Henri would divide his nights between the red studio and the hotel, but the first time he stayed away from her all night he noticed such deep circles under her eyes the next day that he had to promise himself not to do it again. Nevertheless, from time to time he took refuge for a few hours in his room and it gave him the feeling of being a little freer. " You mustn't ask too much," he said to himself. " If you're modest enough in your demands, you can have a lot of little pleasures."

In the meantime, *L'Espoir's* financial situation remained precarious and Henri became seriously worried when he discovered one Thursday that the till was empty. But Luc only made fun of him, accused him of having the mental attitude of a small shopkeeper when it came to money matters. Perhaps he did. In any case, it was understood between them that the financial department was Luc's, and Henri gladly gave him carte blanche. And in fact Luc did find means to meet the payroll that Saturday. " An advance from a new advertiser," he explained. There were no further alarms. *L'Espoir's* circulation failed to pick up, but miraculously they were nevertheless able to hold out. On the other hand, although the S.R.L. hadn't become a large mass movement, it was steadily gaining ground in the provinces. And the thing that was especially gratifying was that the Communists had stopped attacking it ; the hope of a lasting union was reawakened. In November, the Committee unanimously decided to back Thorez against De Gaulle. " It makes life a lot easier when you feel you're working in harmony with your friends, your allies, yourself," Henri thought while chatting with Samazelle, who had come to bring him an article on the political crisis. The presses were purring, outside it was a beautiful autumn night, and from somewhere in the building he could hear Vincent singing in an off-key but happy voice. All things considered, even Samazelle had his good side. His book on the Maquis, from which *Vigilance* was publishing excerpts, appeared to be headed for a big success, and he was so naïvely happy over that future triumph that his heartiness seemed almost sincere.

" I'm going to ask you an indiscreet question," Samazelle said. He smiled broadly. " Someone once said that questions are never indiscreet, only the answers, and, of course, you don't have to answer me. But there's something that intrigues me," he continued. " With such limited circulation, how does *L'Espoir* manage to stay alive?"

" We've no secret funds," Henri replied cheerfully. " The explanation is that we're running a lot more advertising than we used to—classified ads, among others. It's a pretty big source of income."

" I believe I have a rather clear idea of what your advertising revenue is," Samazelle said. " And according to my figures, you ought to be deeply in the red."

" We've run up rather heavy debts."

" I know, but I know, too, that since July they haven't increased. That's what seems miraculous to me."

" You must have made a mistake in your figures," Henri said lightly.

" Yes, I suppose that's the answer," Samazelle said.

He didn't seem very convinced and Henri when he was alone again, became annoyed with himself: he should have been able to furnish Samazelle with precise figures. " Miraculous "—exactly the word that had come to his lips when Luc had drawn the payroll money from an empty till. *An advance from a new advertiser.* Henri had been foolish to have been satisfied with that explanation. What advertiser? How much of an advance? And had Luc told the truth? Again, Henri felt vaguely worried. Samazelle didn't have all the facts, but he did know how to figure. How exactly was Luc managing it? Who knows if he wasn't secretly borrowing money on a personal basis? He would never, of course, engage in anything dishonest, but nevertheless Henri felt he had to know where the money was coming from. When the building was empty, at about two in the morning, Henri went over to the editorial room. Luc was sitting at his desk, pouring over the books; no matter how late Henri left, Luc always remained after him, working on the books.

" Look; if you have a minute, let's have a look at the books together," Henri said. " After all, I think I ought to know a little about our finances."

" I'm up to my ears in work," Luc replied.

" I can wait," Henri said. " I will wait." He sat down on the edge of the table.

Luc was in his shirt sleeves; he was wearing braces, yellow braces. Henri stared at them for a long moment. Finally, Luc raised his head. " Why do you want to bother with these money problems?" he asked. " Just have confidence in me."

" Why do you ask me to have confidence in you when it's so easy to show me the books?" Henri asked.

" You wouldn't understand what it's all about anyhow. Accounting is a world of its own."

" You've explained to me before and I understood then. After all, it isn't witchcraft."

" We'll waste a hell of a lot of time."

" It won't be a waste of time. It bothers me not to know how you're managing. Come on now, show me the books. Why don't you want to?"

Luc shifted his legs under the table; his aching feet rested on a large leather cushion. " Not everything is entered in the books," he said irritably.

" That's precisely what I'm interested in," Henri said quickly, " the things that aren't entered." He smiled. " What are you hiding from me? Have you been borrowing again?"

" You said not to and I haven't," Luc grumbled.

" Well, what is it then? Are you blackmailing someone?" Henri asked in a voice which was only half jesting.

" Me turn L'Espoir into a blackmailing sheet? Me?" Luc shook his head. " You haven't been getting enough sleep."

" Listen," Henri said, " I don't like guessing games. But I don't want L'Espoir to live on makeshift expedients. Keep your secrets, but I'm going to ring Trarieux to-morrow morning."

" Now that's blackmail," Luc said.

" No, it's caution. I know the colour of Trarieux's money,

but the cash that fell into the till last Saturday—I have no idea where it came from."

Luc hesitated. " It was . . . it was a voluntary contribution."

Henri studied Luc apprehensively. A homely wife, three children, an expanding waistline, braces, the gout, a large sleepy face—the picture of a solid citizen. But in '41 he proved that an impetuous gust of wind could sometimes stir in that mass of flesh; in fact, it was thanks to it that *L'Espoir* was born. Had that wild wind started to blow again?

" Did you extort money from someone?"

" I'm afraid I wouldn't be capable of it," Luc said, sighing. " No, it was a gift, a plain gift."

" People don't give away that kind of money just like that. A gift from whom?"

" I promised to keep it secret," Luc replied.

" Whom did you promise?" Henri asked, smiling. " Come on, now you're pulling my leg. I don't believe that story of some generous mysterious contributor."

" I swear he exists," Luc said.

" It isn't Lambert by any chance?"

" Lambert! He doesn't give a damn about the paper. He never sets foot in here, except when he comes to see you. Lambert!"

" Well, who is it then? Spit it out," Henri said impatiently, " or I'll make that telephone call now."

" You won't say that I told you?" Luc asked hoarsely. " You promise?"

" I swear it on your own head."

" Well, it's Vincent."

Stupefied, Henri looked at Luc, who was looking at his feet. " Are you out of your mind? Don't you know how Vincent gets his money? How old are you?"

" Forty," Luc replied peevishly. " And I know Vincent's been getting gold from dentists who collaborated. And I don't see any harm in it. If you're afraid of getting involved, stop worrying; I've taken precautions."

" And what about Vincent? I suppose he's taken all sorts of precautions, too! One of these days he's going to get his fingers caught in a wringer, don't you know that? Do you have water on the brain, or something? The day that crackpot is hauled in, you'll feel mighty proud, won't you?"

" I never asked him for anything," Luc said. " If I'd turned down his money, he'd have given it to some dog and cat hospital."

" But don't you understand that by accepting it you encourage him to continue? How many times has he got us out of the hole?"

" Three times."

" And you were counting on things going on like that indefinitely? Why, you're as warped as he is."

Henri got up and walked over to the window. When he had learned in May that Nadine had joined Vincent's gang, he called him on the carpet and really let him have it. And then he sent him off to Africa for a month. When he returned, Vincent swore he had turned over a new leaf. A new leaf!

" I've got to find a way to frighten him," Henri said.

" You promised to keep it a secret," Luc said. " He made me swear you wouldn't get wind of it. Especially you."

" Naturally!" Henri came back to the table. " In any case, whether I talk to him about it or not, it's all the same."

" There's a bill coming due in ten days," Luc said. " We won't be able to meet it."

" I'm going to talk to Trarieux to-morrow," Henri said.

" If only we could hold out for another month or two . . . We're almost safe now."

" Almost isn't enough," Henri said. " What's the sense of being stubborn about it? Circulation isn't going up, and the longer we wait the more chance there is that Trarieux will change his mind." Henri put his hand on Luc's shoulder. " If we're as free as we were before, what difference can it make?"

" It just won't be the same," Luc said.

" It'll be exactly the same, except that money won't be a god-damned problem any more."

" But that was the most fun," Luc said with a sigh.

Henri, on the contrary, was rather relieved at the thought that the question of money was going to be settled once and for all. It was with a tranquil heart that he walked into Trarieux's office two days later, an office filled with books, pointing to an intellectual rather than a businessman. But Trarieux himself, thin, elegant, half bald, was the prototype of the rich industrialist.

" To think that all during the Occupation we worked so

near each other and yet never met!" he said, vigorously pumping Henri's hand. "You knew Verdelin well, didn't you?"

"Yes, I did. Were you in his group?"

"Yes. He was a remarkable man," Trarieux said in a discreetly funereal tone of voice. A proud smile rounded his face, producing a childlike effect. "It was through him that I met Samazelle." He indicated a chair to Henri and sat down himself. "In those days, it was human values that counted, not money."

"They already seem so far behind us," Henri said, for want of something to say.

"At any rate, it's some consolation to be able to spend money in defence of those values,"Trarieux said engagingly.

"Has Dubreuilh brought you up to date on the situation?" Henri asked.

"In a general way, yes."

Trarieux's face bore an imperiously questioning look; he knew all the facts, but he wanted time to study Henri. And the game had to be played his way. Henri began speaking without conviction; he, too, studied Trarieux who listened to him with a somewhat condescending affability. Certain of his privileges, and satisfied with having renounced them verbally, he felt superior both to those who had nothing and those who still hadn't resigned themselves to being dispossessed. According to Dubreuilh's description, Henri had pictured him somewhat differently; there was no trace of weakness or worry in his face—and no generosity either. If he belonged to the left, it could hardly have been for any other reason but opportunism.

"There I must disagree with you!" he said abruptly. "You say the drop in circulation was inevitable." He looked Henri in the eyes as if he were about to propound a dangerous truth. "I don't believe in inevitability; in fact, that's one of the reasons which prevent me from being a Marxist. My experience in life hasn't been the same as yours; I've always been a businessman, a man of action, and I've learned that the course of events can always be modified by the intervention of an opportune factor at the opportune moment."

"Do you mean to say that we might have been able to avoid that drop?" Henri asked rather stiffly.

Trarieux took his time in answering. "Well, in any case, I'm sure that as from to-day the circulation can be increased," he said. "I'm absolutely unconcerned about the money angle," he added with a sharp gesture, "but considering what *L'Espoir* represents, it seems of the utmost importance to me that it win back a large following."

Henri was amused to recognise Samazelle's vocabulary in Trarieux's words. "I want that as much as you do," he said. "But the thing that's holding us back is money. With enough capital, I'll guarantee to start investigations and have articles written which would win us a large public."

"Articles, investigations, yes, of course," Trarieux said in a far-off voice. "But that's not the main thing."

"What is the main thing?" Henri asked.

"I'm going to speak to you quite frankly," Trarieux said. "You're a very well-known person, indeed a very popular one. But allow me to say that your friend Luc is a nobody, a complete nonentity. And into the bargain, I've read articles of his which were, quite frankly, clumsy."

Henri cut him off sharply. "Luc is an excellent journalist, and the paper belongs to him as much as it does to me. If you've been thinking about getting rid of him, put it out of your mind."

"Don't you think it might be possible to convince him to withdraw of his own accord? By, let us say, buying him out at an interesting price and finding a good job for him?"

"Completely out of the question!" Henri replied. "He'd never agree, and besides I wouldn't ask him. *L'Espoir* is Luc and I; either you back both of us or you don't back us at all. There's no middle ground."

"Of course, for someone who's directly engaged in an enterprise, certain disassociations are more difficult than they would seem to an outside observer," Trarieux said lightly.

"I don't follow you."

"No law limits the board of a newspaper to two members," Trarieux replied. He smiled. "Considering the friendship between you, I'm sure there'd be no problem in making Samazelle the third."

Henri remained silent. So that was why Samazelle had been taking such an interest in *L'Espoir* these days! At last, he said frigidly, "I really don't see the need for it. Samazelle can write for us whenever he likes; that should be enough for him . . ."

"It isn't he, it's I who want that collaboration," Trarieux

said arrogantly. His voice hardened. " I believe that alongside your name, another, equally popular name is needed.
Samazelle's reputation is sky-rocketing ; to-morrow everyone
in France will be talking about him. Henri Perron and Jean-
Pierre Samazelle—now there's a masthead for you! And then
your paper needs a good strong dose of fresh dynamism ;
Samazelle is a human dynamo. Here's what I propose: I pay
off your debts and buy a half interest in L'Espoir, at a price
to be determined, and Luc, Samazelle, and you split the other
half among the three of you. Decisions would be made by
a majority vote."

" I admire Samazelle a great deal," Henri said. " But I'm
going to speak frankly, too. Samazelle is too strong a personality ; I could never feel at home where he feels at home. And
I'm determined to feel at home at the paper."

" That's a very personal objection," Trarieux said.

" Possibly, but after all we are talking about a paper which
does belong to me, personally."

" It's the organ of the S.R.L."

" One doesn't preclude the other."

" That's precisely the question," Trarieux said. " I am financing the organ of the S.R.L. and I intend to give it the
maximum chance of success," he added with a cutting gesture.
" L'Espoir is an extraordinary achievement ; believe me when
I tell you I truly appreciate its worth. But we're faced with
new difficulties now, and it's a question of succeeding on a
much vaster scale. The strength of a single man is no longer
enough."

" I repeat, I'm not alone," Henri said. " Together with Luc,
I feel perfectly capable of coping with any new situation."

Trarieux shook his head. " I've always taken a pride in
being able to judge a man's capabilities pretty exactly. You've
a hard, uphill battle to wage and you need someone like
Samazelle to help you."

" That isn't my opinion."

" But it's mine," Trarieux said in a suddenly discourteous
voice. " And no one can make me change it."

" Do you mean that if I turn down your proposition, you
won't finance L'Espoir?" Henri asked.

" You have no reason to turn it down," Trarieux replied, his
voice softening.

" You promised to help us with no conditions attached,"

Henri said. "And it was on the strength of that promise that I made *L'Espoir* the organ of the S.R.L."

"I'm not imposing any conditions; it's clearly understood that the political line of the paper will remain exactly as it is. I ask only that you take the necessary steps to assure an increase in circulation, an increase that you ought to want as much as I."

Henri got up. "I'm going to have this out with Samazelle!"

"Samazelle certainly won't join *L'Espoir* against your will," Trarieux said. "That's why it's preferable that this conversation remain between us. It doesn't matter whether the refusal comes from him or from you. I don't finance the paper unless he participates in its management."

"I'm going to talk it over with him, anyhow," Henri said, trying to control his voice. "Because I believed in your word, I jeopardised *L'Espoir's* security, brought it to the edge of bankruptcy. And you're taking advantage of the situation to blackmail me. I'd just as soon do without the help of a man capable of such dishonest behaviour!"

"You have no right to accuse me of blackmailing you!" Trarieux said, getting up. "All my dealings are conducted honestly and fairly, this one no less than any of the others. I never tried to conceal my belief that certain changes seemed to me indispensable for the good management of *L'Espoir*."

"That's not what Dubreuilh told me," Henri said.

"I'm not responsible for what Dubreuilh told you," Trarieux said, his voice rising. "I do know what I told him; if there was any misunderstanding, that's unfortunate, but I stated my views quite clearly."

"Did you tell him about your proposition?"

"Yes. In fact, we discussed it at great length."

The sincerity in his voice was so convincing that Henri was silent for a moment. "In any case, he probably didn't understand that it was a condition *sine qua non*," he finally said.

"I suppose he understood exactly what he wanted to understand," Trarieux replied with a trace of animosity. "Listen," he added in a conciliatory tone, "what makes my proposition so unacceptable to you? Yes, I know, you're annoyed because you believe yourself the victim of a dishonest manœuvre. But I'm sure a little chat with Dubreuilh will convince you of my good faith. And then you'll certainly understand what an

excellent opportunity my offer represents for you. Because—
and you can rest assured of this—no one else will risk backing
L'Espoir, with its six million in debts. You have to be devoted
to the S.R.L., as I am, to take that kind of gamble. Or else
you'll be asked to accept conditions quite different from mine
—political conditions."

"I don't think finding disinterested support is completely
hopeless," Henri said.

"But you've already found it!" Trarieux replied. He
smiled. "I consider this talk as simply an initial get-together.
As far as I'm concerned, negotiations remain open. Think it
over."

"Thanks for the advice!" Henri said.

He had answered irritably, but it wasn't Trarieux with whom
he was angry. Dubreuilh's optimism! His incurable optimism! But no, this time it wasn't just a question of optimism;
Dubreuilh was far from being so simple-minded. Suddenly,
the truth hit Henri with full force. "He made a fool of me!"
He sank down on one of the benches along Avenue Marceau.
In his head, in his body there was such a violent convulsion
that he thought for a moment he was going to faint. "He lied
to me, lied to me deliberately, because he wanted *L'Espoir*.
And I walked right into the trap." At midnight, he had
knocked at his door, he was smiling. Money without any
strings . . . come and take a walk . . . it's such a beautiful
night . . . And while he smiled, he was spreading his net.
Henri stood up and walked off rapidly; if he had slowed his
pace, he would have fallen over.

"What can he say? There isn't a thing he can say." He
crossed Paris almost without realising it and arrived at Dubreuilh's house. He stopped for a moment in front of the
door, waiting for the beating of his heart to calm down; he
wasn't quite sure his mouth could produce an articulate
sound.

"May I speak to Monsieur Dubreuilh?" Henri asked, and
was astonished at hearing his own voice, a normal voice.

"He's not in," Yvette replied. "No one's home."

"When will he be back?"

"I don't know."

"I'll wait," Henri said.

Yvette showed him into the study. Perhaps Dubreuilh
wouldn't be back before evening—and Henri had work to do.

But nothing existed for him any more, not *L'Espoir*, not the
S.R.L., not Trarieux, not Luc; nothing except Dubreuilh.
Not since that distant springtime when he had fallen in love
with Paula had he ever required anyone's presence as urgently
as now. He sat down in the arm-chair where he usually sat,
but to-day the furniture, the books set him on edge—all were
accomplices! On that little tea cart, Anne used to bring
ham and salads, and they would dine together gaily, among
friends. What a farce! Dubreuilh had allies, disciples, tools,
but no friends. What a good listener he was! How glibly he
spoke! And he was ready to step on your face at the first
opportunity. His warmth, his smile, that look of his which
never failed to win you merely reflected the intense interest he
had in everyone. "He knew how much that paper meant to
me! And he stole it from me!" It was he, perhaps, who had
suggested the substitution of Samazelle for Luc. "Go and see
Trarieux," he had advised, and in that way he was covered.
But he had given Trarieux instructions. "A plot, a trap!
And once caught in the trap, how to get out? Between Samazelle and bankruptcy, they're counting on me to choose
Samazelle. But they're in for a big surprise!" Henri tried to
find angry words in which to throw his decision in Dubreuilh's face. But his anger failed to stimulate him; on the
contrary, he felt worn out and even vaguely frightened,
vaguely humiliated, as if, after struggling for hours, he had
just been pulled from quicksand. He heard the outside door
open and then close again and he dug his nails into the arm
rests of the chair; he hoped desperately he could make
Dubreuilh feel the disgust he inspired in him.

"Have you been waiting long?" Dubreuilh asked, holding
out his hand. Mechanically, Henri shook it. The same hand,
the same face as yesterday; even when you knew, you
couldn't see through the mask.

"Not very long," he muttered. "I have to speak to you.
Urgently."

"What's wrong?" Dubreuilh asked in a voice which imitated solicitude to perfection.

"I was just over to see Trarieux."

Dubreuilh's face underwent a sudden transformation. "You
can't hold out any longer and Trarieux is making things
difficult, is that it?" Dubreuilh asked anxiously.

"That's just it! You told me he was ready to back

L'Espoir without conditions, and now he's insisting that I take on Samazelle." Henri looked Dubreuilh in the eyes. " It seems you know all about it."

" I've known about it since July," Dubreuilh said, " and I immediately went looking elsewhere for money. I thought for a while Mauvanes was going to come through ; he practically promised me. But I went over to see him this afternoon—he's just got back from a holiday—and it looks very much as though he were backing down." Dubreuilh looked at Henri anxiously. " Can you hold out for another month?"

Henri shook his head. " Impossible. Why didn't you let me know?" he asked angrily.

" I was counting on Mauvanes," Dubreuilh replied. He shrugged his shoulders. " I suppose I should have let you know. But you know how I hate to admit defeat. I was the one who got you into this mess and I swore to myself I'd get you out of it."

" You speak of July. But Trarieux maintains that he never at any time promised his unconditional support," Henri said.

" In April," Dubreuilh replied heatedly, " there was no question of anything but the political line of the paper, and he accepted it in full."

" But you promised me much more than that," Henri said. " Trarieux was supposed to keep his nose out of everything."

" Listen, as far as April goes, I have no reason to feel bad," Dubreuilh said. " I advised you then to go have a personal talk with Trarieux."

" You spoke with such assurance that it seemed superfluous for me to see Trarieux myself."

" I said what I believed, the way I believed it," Dubreuilh replied. " I could have been mistaken ; no one is infallible. But I certainly didn't force you to take my word for it."

" You aren't in the habit of being so badly mistaken," Henri said.

Suddenly, Dubreuilh smiled. " What are you getting at? That I intentionally lied to you?"

He himself had uttered the word ; all Henri had to do was answer " Yes." It was easy ; but no, it was impossible, not when faced with that smile, not in that study, not like that. " I think you took your wishes for truths without worrying in the least about my interests," Henri replied in a restrained voice. "Trarieux was paying, and in the end it didn't much matter to you what his conditions were."

"I may have taken my wishes for truths," Dubreuilh said, "but I swear to you that if I had suspected for even a second what Trarieux was cooking up I'd have dropped him and all his millions then and there."

There was a reassuring warmth in his voice, but Henri remained unconvinced.

"I'm going to have a talk with Trarieux this evening," Dubreuilh said, "and with Samazelle, too."

"That won't do any good," Henri said.

The conversation had started out all wrong! The transition from the words which you say to yourself to those you speak aloud isn't easy. A plot! Suddenly, it seemed absurd, seemed almost insane. Naturally, Dubreuilh had never rubbed his hands together and said to himself, "I'm brewing a plot." If Henri had dared throw that word in his face, Dubreuilh would only have smiled more broadly.

"Trarieux is a tough customer, but Samazelle can be got at," Dubreuilh said.

Henri shook his head. "You won't get to him. No, there's only one solution: I let L'Espoir drop."

Dubreuilh shrugged his shoulders. "You know damned well you could never do that."

"That's where you're in for a big surprise," Henri replied. "I'll do it."

"You'd sink the S.R.L? Do you know what you're saying? Can you imagine how the people opposing us would whoop it up! L'Espoir bankrupt, the S.R.L. broken up! That's a pretty picture!"

"I could turn over L'Espoir to Samazelle and buy myself a farm in the Ardèche. As for the S.R.L., it wouldn't be any the worse for it," Henri said bitterly.

Dubreuilh studied Henri, a look of distress on his face. "I can understand your being angry. I plead guilty. I was wrong in believing Trarieux so readily, and I should have spoken to you about the whole thing back in July. But I'm going to do everything in my power to right things." His voice took on an urgent tone. "I ask only one thing of you: Don't be pig-headed. We'll try to find a way out together."

Henri studied him silently. Admitting one's faults is a clever tactic; it's the best way of minimising them. But

Dubreuilh remained discreetly silent about the gravest fault
of all. Actually, he was guilty of a horrible abuse of confidence; in exchange for the sacrifices he demanded of your
friendship, he pretended to give you his, and he gave nothing
at all. Henri should have said to him, " You're playing me
and everyone else for suckers. For the love of the true and
the good, you'd sacrifice anyone; but the true is what you
think, and the good is what you want. You look on the whole
universe as your own work and there's no balance between
human beings and yourself. When you play at being
generous, that, too, is for your own glory." And he could
have told him a thousand other things besides. But then he
would have had to slam the door behind him, never to open
it again. " And that's just what I ought to do," Henri thought.
Whatever he might decide in connection with the paper, he
should break with Dubreuilh, then and there. He got up,
looked at the tea cart, the books, the picture of Anne, and he
faltered. For fifteen years that study had been the centre of
the world for him, his home. Here the truth appeared sure,
happiness important, and it seemed a great privilege just
being oneself. He couldn't imagine himself walking through
the streets with that door forever closed to him.

" It's useless; we're cornered," he said in a flat voice.
" I'm not being stubborn, but under those conditions running
L'Espoir wouldn't interest me any more. I'm sure my dropping out can be arranged so that it won't be harmful to either
the paper or the S.R.L."

" Listen, give me two days," Dubreuilh said. " If I don't
get anywhere in two days, then you can decide what you want
to do."

" All right. But the answer is quite obvious," Henri said.

When Henri found himself outside again, his head was
spinning. He took a few steps in the direction of the newspaper, but that was the last place in the world he wanted to
be. Facing Luc, Luc who would moan and wail or suggest
another raid on the dentists, was more than he could take.
And Paula, with her prophecies, her litanies, was also out
of the question. But he had to speak to someone. He felt
duped, as if he had just come from one of those gatherings
where a cunning magician pretends to reveal his tricks.
Dubreuilh was cheating, was about to be caught in the act.
And then, no! Hey presto! The marked card was neither in

his hands nor in his pockets. Exactly how much had he lied? And had he lied to himself too? At what point between cynicism and bad faith did his betrayal lie? Beyond any doubt it did exist, but it was impossible to put your finger right on it. "I let myself be manœuvred again!" The evidence once more seemed to be staring him in the face. It was a deliberate plot; Dubreuilh, chuckling while he did it, had pulled all the strings. Henri stopped in the middle of the bridge and leaned his hands against the railing. Was he building a fantasy? Or was he, on the contrary, foundering in imbecility when he doubted Dubreuilh's Machiavellism? In any case, if he remained alone, shifting from one view to the other, his head would shatter. He had to discuss the whole thing with someone. He thought of Lambert. "If I had taken his advice, I wouldn't be in the fix I'm in now," he said to himself. Lambert didn't like Dubreuilh, but he considered himself impartial and attempted to be so. He was the only one with whom Henri could imagine having a quiet conversation. He walked to the other side of the bridge and went into a telephone booth in one of the Biard cafés.

"Hallo! It's Perron. Can I come up to see you for a few minutes?"

"Of course. In fact, it's a damned good idea!" There was a note of surprise in Lambert's warm voice. "How are you?"

"All right. I'll be right up," Henri said.

The anxious warmth in that voice calmed him a little. Lambert's affection was somewhat awkward, but to him, at least, Henri wasn't just a pawn on a checker board. He hurried up the stairs; all day long he had been running up and down stairs, as if he were a candidate for the Académie.

"Come in," Lambert said happily. "Excuse the mess; I didn't have time to straighten the place up."

"Hey! You're really living!" Henri said.

A large bright room, a studied disorder, a gramophone, a record library, leather-bound books arranged according to their authors' names. Lambert was wearing a black sweat shirt and a yellow scarf. Henri felt a little out of his element in that setting.

"Cognac? Whisky? Soda? Fruit juice?" Lambert asked, opening a cabinet under the bookshelves.

"Whisky. Make it a double."

Lambert went to get some water in the pale green bathroom

and Henri caught a glimpse of a big terry-cloth robe, a whole assortment of brushes and soaps.

" How is it you're not over at the paper?" Lambert asked.

" I've got troubles."

" Troubles?"

It wasn't true that Lambert took no interest in the paper; rather, there was a hearty dislike between him and Luc, a dislike which was easily understandable when you saw them side by side. He listened to Henri's story with indignant attentiveness.

" Of course, it's a manœuvre!" he said. He thought for a moment. " Do you think Dubreuilh might be trying to work his way into the paper along with Samazelle? Or maybe in Samazelle's place?"

" No, I don't think so," Henri replied. " He's not interested in journalism, and in any case he controls L'Espoir through the S.R.L. But that doesn't change anything; whatever way you look at it, he laid a stinking trap for me." He gave Lambert a questioning look. " What would you do if you were in my place?"

" Chuck it all overboard if you will—just to louse them up," Lambert replied. " But what you must absolutely not do is to hand over the paper like a good little boy. That's exactly what they want."

" I don't want any scandal," Henri said, " but if it could be done quietly, I'd gladly let everything drop."

" That would be admitting defeat; they'd be only too happy."

" Well, you're the one who's been advising me to get out of politics; this looks like a good time to do it."

" L'Espoir is more than just a political thing," Lambert said. " You created it; it's your venture . . . No, stand up to them," he said heatedly. " If only I had real money! But I've got just enough not to know what to do with it."

" I'll never find enough—and they know it."

" Take Samazelle on and arrange with Luc to neutralise him."

" If he sides with Trarieux, they'll be as strong as we."

" Where did Samazelle ever get enough money to buy himself in?" Lambert asked.

" An advance on his book, or maybe Trarieux is helping him."

" Why does he insist on Samazelle?"

" How should I know? I can't even imagine what a chap like Trarieux is doing in the S.R.L."

" We have to find a way to block them," Lambert said. With a thoughtful air he began pacing the room. Suddenly, the bell rang twice, imperiously. Lambert blushed right down to the roots of his hair. " My father! I wasn't expecting him so early!"

" I'll get out," Henri said.

Lambert gave him an embarrassed, beseeching look. " Don't you want to say hallo to him?"

" Certainly, of course," Henri replied warmly.

Saying hallo to someone doesn't involve you in anything. And yet Henri was able to produce only a contrived smile when he saw that elderly man walking towards him, that man who had perhaps sent Rosa to her death and who had certainly done his best to serve the Germans. Under his greying hair, his sallow, puffy face was brightened by porcelain-blue eyes, a fresh, tender blue that was surprising in that worn-out face. Monsieur Lambert waited for Henri to offer him his hand, but it was he who spoke first.

" I've been very much interested in meeting you," he said. " Gerard has spoken so much about you!" A thin smile began to form on his lips; he suppressed it immediately. " How young you are!"

For him, Lambert was Gerard, was still hardly more than a child; it was at once natural and strange. They didn't resemble each other, but somehow you weren't surprised at their being father and son.

" Lambert's the young one," Henri said with spirit, " not I."

" You're young for a man who's so well known." Monsieur Lambert sat down. " You were talking . . . I don't want to disturb you," he said turning to his son. " I finished earlier than I expected. I didn't know where to go, so I came up."

" You did perfectly right! Would you like a drink? A fruit juice? Soda?" The confused eagerness with which Lambert reacted to his father only aggravated Henri's uneasiness.

" No, thank you. Those four stories are a little hard on my

old bones, but it's so restful here," he said, looking around him approvingly.

"Yes, Lambert is living in fine style," Henri said.

"It's a family tradition. I must say, though, that I appreciate his taste in clothes far less," Monsieur Lambert added. His voice was mild, but he looked distastefully at the black sweat shirt.

"Everyone to his own taste," Lambert mumbled without assurance.

There was a brief silence; Henri took advantage of it to get up and say, "I'm sorry, but I was just leaving when you rang. I've some urgent work to do."

"It's I who am sorry," Monsieur Lambert said. "I've read everything you've written most carefully, and there are certain things I'd have liked to discuss with you. But I don't suppose such a discussion would be of any interest except to me," he added, again curbing a smile. There was a weary charm in his flat voice, his restrained smiles, his gestures, a charm which he seemed unwilling to make use of. And that reserve made him seem both haughty and furtive at the same time.

"We'll surely have occasion to meet again more leisurely," Henri said.

"It isn't that sure," the old man replied.

In a few months, no doubt, he would be in prison, and he might not come out alive. In his day, he must have been quite a louse, that big-shot collaborator. But he had already crossed the line, he was now on the side of the condemned and no longer of the guilty. This time, Henri smiled effortlessly as he shook his hand.

"Can I see you to-morrow?" Lambert asked, accompanying Henri out into the hall. "I think I've got an idea."

"A good one?"

"You'll be the judge of that. But don't make any decisions before I've had a chance to speak to you. Will it be all right if I drop around about ten in the evening?"

"Fine. But not later than that; I've got an appointment with Scriassine."

"All right," Lambert said. "I promised the afternoon to Nadine, but you can count on me a little before ten."

In any event, Henri had no intention of making any decisions to-day; he no longer wanted to question himself about what he would do, and even less to discuss it. Nevertheless, he felt he had to get back to the paper. He told Luc coldly that his meeting with Trarieux had been postponed, and he threw himself into working on his correspondence. Neither would he tell Paula about it; as he turned the key in the lock, he hoped desperately that she was already asleep. But no matter at what hour he returned, he never found her sleeping; seated on the couch, freshly made-up and wearing her shimmering silk robe, she offered him her mouth which he brushed rapidly with his lips.

"Have a good day?" she asked.

"Very good. And you?"

She smiled without answering and asked instead, "What did Trarieux have to say?"

"He agrees to back us."

"It really doesn't bother you?" she asked, looking at him seriously.

"What?"

"Accepting his money."

"Not at all. That question was settled long ago," he replied sharply.

She hesitated and said nothing. She'd been hesitating for two days now. Henri knew what she was thinking, but he had no desire to help her get it off her chest. Her discretion irritated him. "She's decided not to rub me the wrong way, to handle me with care, to wait for the right moment," he thought peevishly. "Six months ago," he said to himself in an attempt to be fair, "she was cheerful and aggressive, and I held that against her too. What really annoys me, I suppose, is the way she always seems to be planning something." She knew she was in danger, and it was only natural for her to try to defend herself. But her wretched tricks only succeeded in making an enemy of her. He no longer spoke to her of singing; she had seen through his game and had deliberately turned down every appointment he had made for her. But in doing so, she had reasoned badly, for he held that stubbornness against her more than anything else, and now he had made up his mind to get rid of her without her co-operation.

"A letter from Poncelet," she said, handing him an envelope.

"I suppose he's turned it down, too," Henri said. He read the letter and passed it to Paula. "Naturally!"

It was the third time his manuscript had been rejected,

each time with profuse compliments: a very great work, but shocking, inopportune; impossible to take so great a risk; later, when feeling isn't running so high. Of course, the play displeased all those who wanted to forget the past, as well as those who were trying to adjust it to suit their wishes. And yet he had more affection for that play than for any of his books; he wanted very much to see it produced. You can't reread a novel; your eyes get trapped by the words. But that dialogue would one day be spoken by living voices, and he could hear it from afar with the satisfied detachment of a painter who looks at his canvas as at a partner.

" You've *got* to be produced," Paula said breathlessly.

" I ask for nothing more."

" I'm no more interested in success than you are," she continued, " but I feel you won't get back to your novel until you're delivered of that play."

" What a strange idea!" Henri said, surprised.

" Well, you haven't got back to it, have you?"

" No, but the play has nothing to do with it."

" Well then, why not?" she asked, studying Henri with a knowing look.

He smiled. " Let's say it's out of laziness."

" You've never known the meaning of laziness," she said gravely. She shook her head. " Obviously, it's a question of inner resistance."

" The novel got off to a bad start," Henri said. " I'd like to get back to it, but I know it's going to mean an enormous amount of work. So I've been putting it off, that's all."

She shook her head. " I've never seen you shy at an obstacle."

" Well, this jump I'm shying."

" Why haven't you ever shown me the manuscript?" Paula asked. " I might possibly have been able to give you some advice."

" I've told you a hundred times that my notes are completely shapeless."

" Yes, that's what you told me," she said with a meditative look.

" I did show you the play, didn't I?"

" Yes, you did. The first drafts were shapeless, too, and you showed them to me nevertheless."

He didn't answer. In his notes he had gone much too far

in speaking about himself—and about her; the novel he would one day attempt to form from them would be less indiscreet. Paula would just have to be a little patient.

He yawned. " I'm dead tired. By the way, I won't be home to-morrow; Scriassine won't let me get away before dawn and I might just as well go to the hotel."

" I don't understand the advantage of the hotel, at dawn or at dusk. But you may do what you will."

He stood up and she followed his example; it was a dangerous moment. Once in bed, he gave her a hasty kiss on the temple and turned towards the wall, pretending to fall asleep at once. But sometimes she would cling to him, begin trembling or mumbling words, and the only way to calm her was to sleep with her. He wasn't always able to, and never without difficulty. She couldn't possibly be unaware of it, and no doubt it was to compensate for his coldness that she spent herself in outbursts of passion so violent that they made him doubt the reality of her pleasure. Even more than her frenzied shamelessness, Henri hated her insincerity, and especially her humility. Fortunately, she remained still that night; she must have felt something was wrong. His cheek pressed again the freshness of the pillow, Henri lay there with his eyes open and, thinking over the events of that day, he no longer felt angry, but only sad. It wasn't he who was in the wrong; it was Dubreuilh. And that wrong he was unable to purge with either remorse or promises, lay more heavily on his heart than if he himself had committed it.

" Chuck it all overboard!" was Henri's first thought when he woke. He didn't telephone to Dubreuilh, and all through the day he kept repeating those words to himself, like a lulling refrain. Discuss, compromise, give in—when the paper had always been his uncontested property! No! The prospect weighed heavy on his heart. He much preferred retiring to the country, getting back to his novel, his true craft. He would sit by the fireside and read L'Espoir with an amused eye. The project seemed so attractive that at ten o'clock, when he saw the door of his office opening, he hoped the idea Lambert had come to give him was no good.

" It was really nice of you to stay a moment yesterday," Lambert said in a voice which seemed to apologise rather than thank. " You can't imagine how happy it made my father."

" I was interested in meeting him," Henri said. " He looks tired, but you get the feeling that at one time he must have had a great deal of charm, and there's still something left of it."

"Charm?" Lambert said in astonishment. "He was always authoritarian, authoritarian and scornful. And basically he still is."

" Oh, I can imagine he mustn't have been very easy to get along with."

" No, not easy at all," Lambert said. He made a gesture as if to chase away his memories. " Anything new with the paper?"

" Nothing."

"Then listen to what I have to suggest," Lambert said. Suddenly, he seemed embarrassed. " Of course, you might not be willing to go along with it . . ."

" Let's hear it first."

" You and Luc against Samazelle and Trarieux—you run the risk of being swallowed whole. But suppose I got into the act?"

" You?"

" I have enough money to buy as big an interest as Samazelle. If it's agreed that decisions are to be made by a majority of votes, we'll be three against two. We're in!"

" But you were undecided about staying in journalism."

" It's as good a profession as another. And then L'Espoir was my little adventure, too," Lambert said in a falsely ironical voice.

Henri smiled. " We don't always agree politically, you know."

" To hell with politics," Lambert said. " All I want is for you to keep your paper. In any case, you'll have my vote, and besides I haven't lost hope that you'll develop politically," he added cheerfully. " No, the only question is to find out if Trarieux will go along with it."

" He should be happy to know he's getting such a good reporter," Henri said. " It's a good thing you didn't get fed up with journalism," he added. " Your articles on Holland are damned good."

" Thanks to Nadine," Lambert said. " She got such fun out of it that it was fun for me, too." He looked at Henri anxiously. " Do you think Trarieux will agree?"

" I don't suppose they'd be too happy if I left ; so if I take Samazelle on, they've got to make some concessions."

" You don't seem very enthusiastic about the idea," Lambert said, looking rather disappointed.

" Oh, the whole damned thing gives me a pain! " Henri said. " I don't know what I want any more. Do you have your motor-cycle with you?" he asked, cutting the conversation short.

" Yes. Would you like me to drop you off somewhere?"

" Rue de Lille. Scriassine is living at Mother Belzunce's."

" Is he sleeping with her?"

" I don't know. Claudie's always putting up a lot of writers and artists ; it's hard to tell which ones are sleeping with her."

" Do you see Scriassine often?" Lambert asked as they went down the stairs.

" No," Henri replied. " He regally summons me from time to time. When I've turned him down for the tenth time, I end up by going over."

They mounted the motor-cycle and noisily rode along the quays of the Seine. Remorsefully, Henri looked at the back of Lambert's neck. It was decent of him to have made that offer. He had no real desire to buy into the paper. He was willing to do so for no other reason than to do Henri a favour. " And I didn't thank him gracefully," Henri said to himself. But in truth, he didn't feel at all grateful. " The best thing is to let it drop. I'd much rather let it drop," he repeated to himself. Keeping the paper, remaining in the S.R.L., meant continuing to work hand in hand with Dubreuilh, and you can't work hand in hand with someone when there's so much bitterness in your heart. He hadn't found the courage to make a clean break, but he certainly wouldn't play the game of friendship. " No, it's all over," he said to himself as the motor-cycle stopped in front of the Belzunce residence.

" Well, here you are," Lambert said in a disappointed voice.

Henri hesitated. He felt guilty about leaving Lambert so soon, after having so coldly greeted an offer in which he so obviously put his whole heart.

" Do you think you'd enjoy coming with me?" he asked.

Lambert's face lit up ; he loved to meet famous people. " I'd enjoy it very much, but don't you think it might be indiscreet?"

"Not at all. We'll wind up drinking vodka in some gypsy night club, and if he's in the mood Scriassine will invite the musicians to the table. No need for any inhibitions with him."

"I have a feeling he doesn't like me very much."

"But he does like the company of people he doesn't like. Come on," Henri said affectionately.

They circled the big mansion; all the windows were lit up and the sound of jazz music could be heard out in the street. Henri rang the bell at a small side door and Scriassine opened it. Lambert's presence didn't seem to surprise him in the least; he smiled warmly.

"Claudie's giving a cocktail party; it's horrible! The house is full of gigolos; I don't feel at home any more. Come inside for a moment and then we'll quietly get the hell out." His shirt collar was wide open and his eyes had a hazy glare. They went up a few steps; at the end of a corridor, a door opened on to a brightly lit room from which the sound of muffled voices was coming.

"You have guests?" Henri asked.

"It's a surprise," Scriassine replied with a satisfied look.

Somewhat apprehensively, Henri followed him, and when he saw them sitting there he involuntarily recoiled a step—Volange and Huguette. Cordially, Louis held out his hand. He had changed little: the lines in his forehead were a little deeper, his chin a little more assertive—a handsome, finely chiselled, well-preserved face. In a flash, Henri remembered that he had often promised himself, when reading the complacent articles Louis wrote in the Free Zone, to smash his fist into his jaw at the first opportunity. And he, too, held out his hand.

"I'm damned glad to see you again, old boy," Louis said. "I've never dared disturb you—I know you're busier than hell —but I've often felt like having a little chat with you."

"You haven't changed at all," Huguette said.

Neither had she changed. She was blonde, delicate, and as elegant as ever, and she still had the same perfumed smile. She would never change, but one day at the touch of a fingertip she would fall to dust.

"The fact is I hardly see anyone," Henri said. "I've been working like a horse."

"Yes, you must be leading a dull life," Louis said sympathetically. " But you've become a major name in the literary world. It doesn't surprise me either ; I was always convinced you'd end up on top. Do you know your book is selling for three thousand in the black market?"

" Just now, every book published is selling like hot cakes," Henri said.

" That's true. But you had wonderful reviews," Louis said encouragingly. He smiled. " I must say, though, you did hit on a golden subject ; you were really lucky. When you've a subject like that, the book writes itself."

Louis still had the same nonchalant smile, but there was an eagerness in his voice which contrasted sharply with his old cutting ways.

" And you, what have you been doing?" Henri asked.

He felt vaguely ashamed and couldn't decide whether it was for himself or for Louis.

" I'm hoping to be made literary critic of a weekly that's going to appear soon," Louis said, looking at his nails.

" Let's get the hell out of here," Scriassine said impatiently. " That music is intolerable. Let's go drink a little champagne at the Isba."

" I thought you were never going to set foot in that place again after what they did to your wallet," Henri said.

Scriassine smiled slyly. " It's their job to steal, the customer's to protect himself."

Henri hesitated. He was going to be rude, but why did they have to force his hand? He positively did not want to spend the evening with Louis. " I'm afraid I can't go with you," he said. " I dropped in for a moment because I told you I'd come, but I have to get back to the paper."

" I can't stand night clubs," Louis said. " Why don't we just stay here?"

" As you will," Scriassine said. He looked at Henri unhappily. " Anyhow, you do have time for a drink, don't you?"

" Of course," Henri replied.

Scriassine opened a cabinet and took out a bottle of whisky. " Not much left," he said.

" I don't drink and neither does Huguette," Louis said.

Claudie appeared in the doorway. " This is really charming! He drags himself half drunk to my party," she said, pointing to Scriassine, " insults my guests, and steals quietly away with all the interesting people! I'll never again have a Russian in my home."

"Stop shouting like that," Scriassine said, " or Cri-Cri will join us! Cri-Cri's the trumpet player," he added with a sigh.

Claudie closed the door. " I'm staying with you," she said firmly. " My daughter can be hostess for a while."

An embarrassing silence followed. Louis offered American cigarettes to everyone.

" And what are you doing these days?" he asked Henri with interest.

" I'm thinking about another novel," Henri replied.

" Anne told me you've written a very beautiful play," Claudie said.

" I wrote a play. Three producers have already turned it down," Henri said cheerfully.

" You must meet Lucie Belhomme," Claudie said.

" Lucie Belhomme? What's that?"

" You're extraordinary! Everyone knows you and you don't know anyone. She owns Maison Amaryllis, the big *maison de couture* everyone's talking about."

" I don't follow you."

" Lucie is the mistress of Richeterre, whose wife divorced him to marry Vernon, and Vernon is the producer who owns Studio 46."

" I still don't follow you."

Claudie laughed. " Vernon obeys his wife implicitly, so that she'll forgive him his male friends—because Vernon is as queer as they come. And Juliette's remained on the best of terms with her ex-husband, who obeys Lucie implicitly. You catch on?"

" It's crystal clear," Henri replied. " But what does Lucie expect to get out of it?"

" She has a ravishing daughter and she's trying to make an actress of her. You do have a part for a young woman in your play, don't you?"

" Yes, but . . ."

" You'll never get anywhere with ' buts.' As I say, the girl is ravishing. When you finally decide to come over, I'll introduce her to you. You've always passed up my Thursday gatherings, but I'm going to ask you a favour you can't possibly refuse me," Claudie said petulantly. " I've been sponsoring a home for the children of deportees, and it's expensive, too expensive for me alone. So I'm planning a series of lectures, the lecturers contributing their services free of charge. The snobs'll come pouring in by the bucketful; they'll be only too glad to pay a couple of thousand francs to see someone like you in the flesh, of that you can be sure. I'm putting you down for one of the first shows."

" I hate that kind of brawl," Henri said.

" For children of deportees, you can't refuse. Even Dubreuilh will accept."

" Can't your philanthropists contribute two thousand francs without annoying people?"

" They'd contribute once, but not ten times. Charity is all very nice, but people want to get something out of it. That's the principle of charity affairs." Claudine laughed. " Look at Scriassine! He's furious; he thinks I'm monopolising you."

" Excuse me," Scriassine said. " As a matter of fact, I did want to have a word with Perron."

" All right!" Claudine said. She sat down on the couch next to Huguette, and they began chatting quietly.

Scriassine turned to Henri. " You stated the other day that in affiliating itself with the S.R.L., L'Espoir didn't intend to stop telling the truth."

" That's right," Henri said.

" That's why I was so anxious to see you. If I brought you some devastating, indisputable facts about the Soviet régime, would you print them?"

" Oh, Le Figaro certainly would have published them already," Henri replied with a laugh.

" I have a friend who's just come from Berlin," Scriassine continued. " He gave me a precise account of the way the Russians squashed the German revolution in embryo. The story has to be released by a leftist paper. Are you prepared to do it?"

" What does your friend have to say?" Henri asked.

Scriassine looked from one face to the other. " Very roughly, here it is. There are certain suburbs of Berlin which remained fiercely Communist, even under Hitler," he said. " During the battle of Berlin, the workers of Köpenick and Wedding occupied the factories, raised the red flag, and organised committees. It could have turned out to be the beginning of a great popular revolution. The emancipation of

the workers by their own efforts was under way; the committees were prepared to furnish cadres for the new régime."
Scriassine paused. "But instead of that, what happens? The bureaucrats come trotting in from Moscow, wipe out the committees, liquidate the whole base of the revolution, and set up a state apparatus—a so-called 'occupation' government." Scriassine looked fixedly at Henri. "That doesn't mean anything to you? Contempt for man, bureaucratic tyranny! The case is open and shut!"

"You're not telling me anything new," Henri said. "Only you forgot to add that those bureaucrats were German Communists who had taken refuge in Russia and who had created the Committee for a Free Germany in Moscow a long time ago. It seems to me that they have more of a right to take over than those people who revolted during the fall of Berlin. Yes, I'm sure there were sincere Communists among the workers; but try to imagine who's what when sixty million Nazis plead in chorus that they were always against Hitler! I can understand the Russians being suspicious. But that hardly proves they're scornful of mankind in general."

"I was sure of it!" Scriassine said angrily. "Attacking America—for that you're always ready. But when it comes to opening your mouth against Russia, that's another story."

"It's obvious they were right to act as they did!" Henri said.

"I can't understand it!" Scriassine said. "Are you really blind? Or are you afraid? Dubreuilh's sold out, everyone knows that. But you!"

"Dubreuilh's sold out! You don't believe that yourself," Henri said.

"Oh, the C.P. doesn't buy you with money," Scriassine said. "Dubreuilh's getting old, he's famous, he's already got the bourgeois public. What he wants now are the masses."

"Go and tell the militants of S.R.L. that Dubreuilh's a Communist!" Henri said.

"The S.R.L.! What a dismal joke!" Scriassine said. Wearily he leaned his head against the back of his chair.

"Don't you find it distressing that one can no longer spend an evening among friends without arguing over politics?" Louis asked, smiling at Henri. "Taking part in politics is all right, but why discuss it interminably?"

He looked at Henri over Scriassine's head, trying to recapture the complicity of their youth. Henri, however, was all the more irritated to find that he agreed with Volange.

" I've been thinking the same thing," he said grudgingly.

" One ends by forgetting that other things exist on earth," Louis said. He looked at his nails demurely. " Things called beauty, poetry, truth—no one bothers about them any more."

" There are people around who still take an interest in those things," Henri said. He thought, " I ought to speak up, I ought to tell him I'll have nothing to do with him." But it isn't easy to insult your oldest friend without provocation. He set down his glass and was about to leave when Lambert began speaking.

" And who might they be?" he asked heatedly. " In any case, not the people who run *Vigilance*. For you to accept an article, it has to be stuffed with politics. If it's merely beautiful or poetic, you'd never publish it."

" As a matter of fact, that's precisely the fault I find in *Vigilance*," Louis said. " Of course, one can write very beautiful books based on political themes; your novel for one is an example," he added urbanely. " But I believe it to be immensely desirable to give pure literature its due."

" For me, the words ' pure literature ' have no meaning," Henri said. " And besides, they're dangerous words," he added sharply. " When you pretend to isolate literature from everything else, it's only too clear where it leads."

" That depends on the times," Louis said. " I was certainly wrong in '40 to think a person could divorce himself from politics. And you can rest assured that I understand now the full extent of my error," he added in a voice full of conviction. " But to-day, it seems to me that we once again have the privilege of writing as we will, for our own pleasure."

He gave Henri a courteous, questioning look, as if he were actually asking him for his permission. The feigned deference exasperated Henri all the more, but exploding would have served no purpose.

" Everyone's free to do as he pleases," he replied succinctly.

" Not as free as all that!" Lambert said. " You don't realise it, but it's hard to go against the current."

Louis shook his head sympathetically. " And it's all the more difficult when you consider that everything nowadays

is conspiring to convince the individual that he's nothing. If
ever he should find himself again, he'll discover a great many
things. But it's a vicious circle; he isn't given the opportunity."

"No, he isn't," Lambert said forcefully. He looked at
Henri excitedly. "Do you remember once at the Scribe? We
were discussing just that. I said that everyone should take an
interest in himself; I still believe it. If you think you're nothing, that you can do nothing, but you have rights to nothing, what can you expect to make of yourself? Take a look
at the people you know: Chancel got himself killed intentionally, Sézenac takes dope, Vincent drinks, Lachaume sold out
to the C.P. . . ."

"You're getting everything twisted!" Henri said. "I don't
see what pure literature could do for Vincent or Sézenac.
And as for your story about lost individuals finding themselves again," he said, turning to Louis, "that's a lot of nonsense, too. There are people who are nothing and others who
are something; it all depends on what you make of your life.
When you're young, you don't know what you're going to do
with it, and that's why you're confused and bewildered. But
as soon as you take an interest in something—in something
other than yourself—there are no more problems."

He had spoken in anger; it annoyed him to see Lambert
giving such importance to Louis' mouthings. He stood up.
"I must go."

Scriassine straightened up. "Have you really decided not
to pay any attention to my information?"

"You didn't give me any information," Henri said.

Scriassine poured himself a glass of whisky and swallowed
it in one gulp. As he reached for the bottle again, Claudie
jumped up and placed her hand on his arm.

"I think Papa Victor has had enough to drink!"

"Do you think I drink because I enjoy it?" Scriassine
shouted violently.

Henri smiled. "That might be a good reason."

"It's the only way I can forget!" Scriassine said, filling his
glass.

"Forget what?" Huguette asked with a frightened look.

"That in two years the Russians will occupy France, and
that you'll be welcoming them on your knees," Scriassine
replied.

" Two years! " Huguette exclaimed.

" Don't be silly," Henri said.

" You're handing over all of Europe to them ; every one of you is a party to it," Scriassine said. " And the real reason is that you're afraid! You're betraying your country because you're afraid."

" The real reason is that your hatred of Russia has gone to your head," Henri said. " You twist facts, spread all sorts of lies. It's a filthy business! By attacking Russia, you're attacking socialism in general."

" You know damned well that Russia and socialism have nothing to do with each other any more," Scriassine said, his voice thickening.

" Don't tell me that America is any closer to socialism! " Henri said.

Scriassine looked at Henri with eyes red with anger. " You call yourself my friend! And you defend a régime that's condemned me to death! The day they shoot me, you'll explain in *L'Espoir* that they had good reasons for doing it."

" My God! " Henri said. " The old veterans and their war stories weren't bad enough! Now we're going to start hearing about the executions of the future! "

Scriassine looked at Henri with hate-filled eyes. He took his half-filled glass and threw it with all his strength. Henri ducked and the glass shattered against the wall.

" You'd better go to bed," Henri said, walking towards the door. He gave a short wave of his hand. " So long."

" You mustn't hold it against him," Claudie said. " He's drunk."

" That's obvious."

Scriassine dropped back in his chair, his head in his hands.

" What a session! " Henri said as he stepped out into the courtyard with Lambert.

" Yes, I agree with Volange: political discussions ought to be prohibited."

" Scriassine doesn't discuss ; he prophesies."

" Well, in any case, that's the way it always goes," Lambert said. " You wind up throwing glasses at each other's heads and you don't even know what you're talking about. Neither of you knows what's happening inside East Germany. He's biased against Russia, and you're biased for it."

" I'm not biased. I don't doubt the fact that everything in

Russia isn't perfect. I'd be surprised if it was. But anyhow, they're the ones who are on the right road."

Lambert grimaced and remained silent.

" I wonder what Scriassine expected from the meeting," Henri said. " It must have been Louis who suggested it ; he's probably hoping I'll help him get cleared."

" Maybe he just wants to become friends again," Lambert said.

" Louis? What a joke! "

Lambert gave Henri a perplexed look. " Wasn't he your best friend? "

" A strange friendship!" Henri said. " When he came to high school in Tulle from Paris, he looked me over quite carefully and he found me to be less of a yokel than the others. But there never was any real friendship between us."

" I find him rather likeable," Lambert said.

" You find him likeable because politics bore you and because he was defending pure literature. But you understand why he does that, don't you?"

Lambert hesitated. " Whatever the reasons behind it, what he said is true. There are personal problems and it's not easy to solve them when everyone keeps repeating to you that you're wrong in posing them to yourself."

" I never took that position," Henri said. " Granted that they have to be posed. What I say is that they can't be isolated from other problems. In order to know who you are and what you want to do, you have to decide where you stand in the world."

Lambert mounted his motor-cycle and Henri got on behind him. " Only a year," he thought, " and here they are back again, as arrogant as the sinner convinced that he's worth ninety-nine of the righteous. Since they speak a different language than we do, Lambert and the others of his age are going to believe they've got something new to offer. They're going to be tempted. But we mustn't permit it," Henri said to himself. " We've got to stop them, no matter how."

When the motor-cycle stopped, he said warmly, " You know, I appreciate your offer enormously, and I'll be glad to accept your help. That was a wonderful idea you had! We'll remain masters in our own home!"

" You accept?" Lambert said happily.

" Of course. The whole business put me in a bad humour ; that's why I didn't jump for joy before. But really, you can't imagine how happy I am to be able to keep the paper ! "

" Do you think Trarieux will agree ? " Lambert asked.

" He'll have to," Henri replied. He shook Lambert's hand warmly. " Thanks ! See you to-morrow."

" No," he thought as he entered his room. " This isn't the moment to run out." His bitterness towards Dubreuilh wouldn't die quickly, but that didn't rule out working together towards a common goal ; personal feelings should certainly be secondary. What mattered was to prevent the return of the Volanges to win the game. He lit a cigarette. Being a member of *L'Espoir's* board would do Lambert a lot of good, and Henri would so arrange things that he would be brought closer and closer to the life of the paper. Lambert would evolve politically, would feel much less lost in the world, and once completely caught up in the paper he would stop wondering what to do with himself.

" It's true it isn't easy to be young in these times," Henri said to himself. He made up his mind to have a serious talk with Lambert one of these days. " And just what would I say to him ? " He began undressing. " If I were a Communist or a Christian, I'd be less at a loss. An ethical system based on universal values, yes, you can try to impose it on others. But the meaning one gives to one's own life is another story. I couldn't explain that in a few sentences ; Lambert would have to be made to see the world through my eyes." Henri sighed. And that's precisely where literature is useful—to show the world to others as you yourself see it. Only he had tried and he had failed. " Did I really try ? " he asked himself, lighting another cigarette and sitting down on the edge of the bed. He had wanted to write a book for his own pleasure, a book which would serve no purpose, was not needed, had no reason for being. No wonder he had become fed up with it so quickly. He promised himself he would be honest, but he had only been complacent. He had pretended to talk about himself without setting himself in either the past or the present. But the truth of one's life is outside one-self, in events, in other people, in things ; to talk about oneself, one must talk about everything else. He got up and drank a glass of water. At the time, it had suited him to believe that literature no longer had any meaning, but nevertheless it hadn't prevented him from writing a play that satisfied him. A play set in a definite place, at a definite time, a play that meant something. And that was precisely why he was satisfied with it. Then why not undertake a similar novel; why not tell a story of to-day in which the readers would find their own worries, their own problems? Neither demonstrate nor exhort, but bear witness. It took him a long time to fall asleep.

Dubreuilh hadn't succeeded in convincing either Trarieux or Samazelle. But no doubt they failed to understand how much insurance for Henri there was in Lambert's presence on the board of the paper, or else they were afraid of an explosion which might prove harmful to the S.R.L., or perhaps they didn't, after all, harbour any Machiavellian designs; for in any case they accepted Henri's proposition without raising any difficulties. At the paper, no one was very much alarmed about a change which seemed to be on a purely administrative level. Except for Vincent. One afternoon, when Luc and Henri were alone in the editorial room, he sauntered in and began his attack in a surly voice."

" I don't know what's going on any more."

" It's very simple!" Henri said.

" I don't know Trarieux, but a man who's got so much money must be dangerous. It might have been better not to take him in."

"We had to," Henri said.

" And why put Lambert on the board?" Vincent asked. " You're in for some bad surprises. When I think that he has made it up with his father, knowing what he knows!"

" There's no proof the old man informed on Rosa," Henri said. " Why don't you stop making snap judgments about people? I know Lambert, and I have complete confidence in him."

Vincent shrugged his shoulders. " The whole business depresses me!"

" You've got to admit we made a mess of things," Luc said with a sigh.

" Made a mess of what?" Henri asked.

" The whole thing," Luc replied. " There was some hope that things would change a bit, but once again it's only money that counts."

" Things couldn't change so fast," Henri said.

" Nothing ever changes!" Vincent said. Abruptly, he turned on his heels and walked out the door.

" He doesn't know I told you, does he?" Luc asked in a worried voice.

" No," Henri replied. " I didn't say anything to him and I don't intend saying anything to him. What good would it do?"

The day set for the signing of the contract, Paula had started a blazing fire in the fireplace—in spite of the mild November weather—and while she poked it idly she asked, " Have you positively made up your mind to sign?"

" Positively."

" Why?"

" I have no choice."

" There's always a choice," she said.

" Not in this case."

" There is." She drew herself up and turned towards Henri. " You could leave!"

There it was! Finally, she had let loose the words which she had been holding back so awkwardly for days. Motionless, her hands clutching the ends of her shawl, she seemed a martyr offering her body to the lions. Firmly, she continued, " I think it would be more dignified to leave."

" If you knew how little I cared about dignity."

" Five years ago, you wouldn't have hesitated," she said. " You'd have left immediately."

He shrugged his shoulders. " I've learned a few things in five years. Haven't you?"

" What did you learn?" she said in a theatrical voice. " To compromise? To come to terms?"

" I've explained to you why I accepted."

" Oh, there are always reasons; one doesn't compromise oneself without reasons. But that's just it; one must know how to reject reasons." Paula's face was drawn; in her eyes there was a beseeching, haggard look. " You used to know; you chose the most difficult roads—solitude and purity. Pisanello's little St. George, clad in white and gold: we used to say that was you . . ."

" You used to say . . ."

" Oh, don't start denying our past!" she cried out.

" I'm not denying anything," he replied peevishly.

" You're denying yourself; you're betraying your character.

And I know who's responsible," she added angrily. " One of these days I'm going to have it out with him."

" Dubreuilh? Please! Don't be absurd! You know me well enough to realise that no one can make me do what I don't want to do."

" Sometimes I feel as if I don't know you at all any more," she said, looking at Henri in despair. Bewildered, she added, " Is it really you?"

" It seems to be," he replied, shrugging his shoulders.

" But you aren't even sure yourself! I can see you as you were . . ."

He cut her off sharply. " Don't always be looking for me in the past. I'm as real to-day as I was yesterday."

" No, I know wherein our truth lies," she said excitedly. " And I'll defend it against everything."

" Look, can't we have an end to these arguments? I've changed: get that into your head. People do change, Paula. And ideas change, and so do feelings. Soooner or later, you've got to face it."

" Never," she said. Tears began welling in Paula's eyes. " Believe me when I tell you I suffer more than you in these arguments ; I wouldn't fight against you if I weren't forced to."

" No one's forcing you to."

" I have my mission, too," she said fiercely. " And I'll accomplish it. I won't permit you to be turned away from your true self."

He was helpless against those high-sounding words. Sullenly, he muttered, " You know what's going to happen? We'll end up by hating each other."

" You could hate me?" She buried her face in her hands ; after a moment, she raised it again. " If I must, I'll even tolerate your hate," she said. " Out of love for you."

He shrugged his shoulders without answering and walked towards his room. " I've got to end it. I must end it," he said to himself earnestly.

In November, the S.R.L. supported Thorez's demands, in exchange for which the Communists once more gave it the benefit of their good will. *L'Espoir* began to be read in the factories again. But the idyll didn't last long. The Communists sharply criticised an article in which Henri rebuked them for having voted in favour of the hundred and forty billion franc military budget, and one in which Samazelle made clear the differences between the Communists and the Socialists with respect to the policies of the Big Three. They renewed their efforts to kill the S.R.L., and they attacked it in every possible way. Samazelle wanted a clean break with them; according to him, the S.R.L. should become a political party and put up candidates at the June elections. His proposition was rejected, but the Committee did decide to take advantage of the elections to adopt a less passive policy regarding the C.P. They would start a campaign.

" We don't want to weaken the C.P., but we would like the Communists to change their line," Dubreuilh concluded. " Well, here's our opportunity to bring pressure to bear. What we say in the name of the S.R.L. bothers them barely at all. But they've got to take the voters' wishes into account. We'll urge people to vote for the parties of the left—but we'll urge them to set their own conditions. At the moment the proletariat has a good many grievances against the Communists; if we channel that discontent, if we translate it into precise demands, we stand a chance of bringing about a change of attitude among the Communist leaders."

Whenever Dubreuilh reached a decision, he gave the impression that the whole of his past life had been guided by it. Henri recognised this once again when, the session over, they went to have dinner in a little restaurant along the quays, as they did every Saturday. Dubreuilh outlined to Henri the article he was going to write that very night, and it seemed as if he had always planned to have it published on the exact date it would in fact be published. First of all, he would criticise the Communists for having supported the Anglo-Saxon loan; yes, it would hasten the return of prosperity, but the workers would not benefit from it.

" And do you really think this campaign will produce results?" Henri asked.

Dubreuilh shrugged his shoulders. " Well, we'll see. During the Resistance you maintained that people must act as if the efficacy of the action decided upon was guaranteed. It's a good principle, and I hold to it."

Henri examined Dubreuilh and thought, " That isn't the kind of answer he would have given last year." Dubreuilh was clearly worried these days.

" In other words, you're not really hoping for very much?"
he asked.

"Oh, hoping, not hoping—it's all so subjective," Dubreuilh replied. " If you guide yourself by your moods, there's
no end to it ; you become a Scriassine. When you must make
a decision, you shouldn't go looking inside yourself."

In his voice, in his smile, there was a kind of abandon which
once would have touched Henri. But ever since the
November crisis, he had lost all feelings of warmth for
Dubreuilh. " If he takes me into his confidence, it's only because Anne isn't here ; he has to have someone on whom to
try out his thoughts," he said to himself. But at the same time,
he blamed himself a little for his ill will.

Dubreuilh published a series of very strong articles in
L'Espoir, to which the Communist press retorted stingingly.
They compared the attitude of the S.R.L. to that of the
Trotskyites who had refused to participate in the Resistance
under the pretext that it served British imperialism. Nevertheless, that polemic, in which the C.P. and the S.R.L.
mutually accused each other of misunderstanding the true
interests of the working classes, was kept on a relatively
courteous tone. It was with complete amazement that Henri
one Thursday read an article in *L'Enclume* that viciously
attacked Dubreuilh. It was a criticism of an essay currently
appearing in *Vigilance*—the chapter from his book about
which he had spoken to Henri a few months before and
which touched upon political questions only very indirectly.
Using it as a point of departure, and without any apparent
reason, they drew up a staggering indictment against him :
he was a watchdog of capitalism, an enemy of the working
class.

" What's got into them? And how did Lachaume ever let
that article got through? It's disgusting of him," Henri said.

" Does that surprise you?" Lambert asked.

" Yes. And the tone of the article surprises me, too. After
all, there's a feeling of tolerance in the air these days."

" I'm not as surprised as you are," Samazelle said.
" Three months before the elections, they aren't going to drag
a paper like *L'Espoir* through the mud, a paper that's read by
thousands of workers—including Communists. As for the
S.R.L., that's basically the same thing, and it's in their interest

to handle it with care. But Dubreuilh—blackening him in the eyes of the young leftist intellectuals is all profit."

Samazelle's and Lambert's obvious satisfaction annoyed Henri. He felt himself stiffen a little when two days later Lambert announced cheerfully, almost teasingly, " I've been having a little fun writing a paper on the article in *L'Enclume*. Only I wonder if you'll print it?"

" Why?"

" Because I tell them both off, Lachaume and Dubreuilh. He damned well deserves what he's getting; it'll teach him not to play both sides. If he's an intellectual, then he shouldn't sacrifice intellectual virtues to politics; if he considers them a useless luxury, let him say so, and we'll knock on somebody else's door when it comes to thinking independently."

" As a matter of fact, I do doubt if I could print that in *L'Espoir*," Henri said. " Besides, you're unfair. Anyhow, let's take a look at it."

The article was skilfully written, incisive, and at times pertinent despite its maliciousness; it attacked the Communists intemperately and was extremely unkind to Dubreuilh.

" You have the gifts of a pamphleteer," Henri said. " Your paper is brilliant." He smiled. " Of course, it's unprintable."

" Isn't what I say true?" Lambert asked.

" It's true that Dubreuilh is a split personality. But I'm surprised to see you criticising him for that; I am like him, you know."

" I know, but it's only out of loyalty to him," Lambert replied, putting the article in his pocket. " Don't think I'm saying this because I'm so stuck on my article, but it's funny when you stop to think of it: if I wanted to have it published, I'd never be able to; I'm too anti-Communist for *L'Espoir* or *Vigilance*, and too far to the left for the people on the right."

" This is the first article of yours I've ever turned down," Henri said.

" Oh, ordinary reporting jobs, criticism—they're acceptable anywhere. But if I ever wanted to say what I think about something really important, all you'd offer me would be your regrets."

" Why don't you try it?" Henri said amiably.

Lambert smiled. " Fortunately, I have nothing important to say."

" Have you tried writing any new stories?" Henri asked.

" No."

" You got discouraged pretty fast."

" You know what discouraged me?" Lambert asked with a sudden aggressiveness. " Seeing Peulevey's thing in *Vigilance*. If that's the kind of literature you like, then I don't understand anything any more."

" Didn't you find it interesting?" Henri asked, surprised. " You really get the feel of Indo-China, the feel of what a colonist is, and at the same time the feel of a childhood."

" Why not say straight out that *Vigilance* publishes neither novels nor short stories, but only factual articles?" Lambert said. " All a man has to do is spend his childhood in the colonies and be against colonialism, and you'll declare he's full of talent."

" Peulevey has talent," Henri said. " The fact of the matter is that it's more interesting to tell about something than nothing," he added. " The big fault in your stories was that you chose to tell about nothing. If you'd write about your experiences, the way this fellow writes about his, you might turn out something really good."

Lambert shrugged his shoulders. " I once gave some thought to a story about my childhood, and then I let it drop. My personal experiences had no social significance ; they're purely subjective, and therefore, from your point of view, completely insignificant."

" Nothing is insignificant," Henri replied. " Your childhood has a meaning, too ; it's up to you to find it and make us feel it.'

" I know," Lambert said ironically. " With whatever you have at hand, you can produce a human document." He shook his head. " That's not what interests me. If I wrote, it would be to tell of things precisely because of their unimportance ; I would try to justify them only by the way I told them." He shrugged his shoulders. " Don't worry. I won't do it. I'd have a bad conscience. Only I don't like the same kind of literature you do, so I won't write anything at all ; that's the simplest thing."

" Listen, the next time we go out together, we'll talk this whole thing over seriously," Henri said. " If I'm responsible for discouraging you from writing, I'm really very sorry."

"Don't be sorry," Lambert said. "It's not worth it." He left the office without a smile; he almost slammed the door behind him. He was deeply hurt.

"He'll get over it," Henri said to himself. He had decided to stop taking things so much to heart; they always turn out less badly than you think they will. Samazelle wasn't as burdensome as Henri had feared—with the exception of Luc, he had won over the whole team by his friendliness—and Trarieux never set foot in the building. Circulation had gone up considerably and, to top it all, Henri felt as free as ever. But it was, above all, his new novel that made him feel optimistic; he had feared enormous difficulties—and the book was shaping up almost by itself. This time, Henri was practically certain he'd got off to a good start; he wrote happily. The only dark cloud was that Paula insisted on his working near her. And she wanted to see the rough drafts. He would refuse; she would become irritable. Again that morning, as they were finishing breakfast, she attacked.

"Your work going well?"

"So-so."

"When are you going to show me something?"

"I've told you twenty times already that it's still unreadable; it's shapeless."

"Exactly. You've been telling me that for so long, I thought it might have taken shape by now."

"I've begun all over again."

Paula leaned her elbows on the table and placed her chin in the hollow of her hands. "You don't have much confidence in me any more, do you?"

"Of course I do!"

"No, you no longer have any confidence in me. Ever since that bicycle trip . . ." she said meditatively.

Henri studied her for a moment in surprise. "What in the world could that trip have changed between us?"

"The fact is evident," she said.

"What fact?"

"Well, you don't believe what I tell you any more." She shrugged her shoulders and added quickly, "I can cite you twenty cases when you didn't believe me."

"For example?"

"For example, in September I told you you could sleep in

your hotel whenever you liked, and yet each time you do you ask my permission guiltily. You don't want to believe that I prefer your liberty to my happiness."

" Listen, Paula, the first time I slept at the hotel, your eyes were all swollen the next morning."

" I have a right to cry, haven't I?" she asked aggressively.

" But I don't want to make you cry."

" And do you think I don't cry when you refuse me your confidence, when I see that you lock up your manuscript—because you do lock it up . . ."

" That's really nothing to cry over," he said irritably.

" It's insulting," she said. She looked at Henri with a frightened, almost childlike expression. " I sometimes wonder if you aren't a sadist."

He poured himself a second cup of coffee without answering her, and she said angrily, " Are you afraid I'll look through your papers?"

" That's what I'd do if I were in your place," Henri replied with forced cheerfulness.

She stood up and pushed back her chair. " You admit it! You lock up your desk because of me. We've come to that!"

" So that you won't be led into temptation," he said, and this time the cheerfulness in his voice rang completely false.

" We've come to that!" she repeated. She looked Henri in the eyes. " If I swore to you I wouldn't touch those papers, would you believe me? Would you leave the drawer unlocked?"

" You've got that wretched manuscript so much on your mind that you yourself couldn't tell what you'd do. Of course, I believe in your sincerity, but I'll keep the drawer locked."

There was a brief silence and then Paula said slowly, " Never have you hurt me as much as you just have."

" If you can't stand the truth, don't force me to speak it," Henri said, pushing back his chair violently.

He went upstairs and sat down at his desk. She really deserved being shown the manuscript. That way he would be rid of her for good. Of course, he'd have to cut the manuscript a bit before publication—unless she should die before then. But in the meantime, when he reread it, he felt revenged. "In a way, literature is truer than life," he said to himself. "Dubreuilh played me for a sucker, Louis is a skunk, Paula poisons my life—and I go on smiling at them. On paper, you say exactly and completely what you feel." Once more, he read through the description of the break up. How easy it is to break things off on paper! You hate, you shout, you kill, you commit suicide; you carry things to the very end. And that's why it's false. "Yes, it's false," he said to himself, "but it's damned satisfying. In life you're constantly denying yourself, and others are always contradicting you. Paula exasperates me, and yet in a little while I'll take pity on her and she'll think that basically I still have some love for her. On paper, I make time stand still and I impose my convictions on the whole world; they become the only reality." He unscrewed the top of his pen. Paula would never read those pages, and yet he exulted in them as if he had forced her to recognise herself in the portrait he had drawn of her; a woman acting the part of a lover and loving only her histrionics and her dreams; pretending to be noble, generous, self-sacrificing, when in fact she is without pride and without courage, steeped in the egoism of her feigned passions. That was how he saw her, and on paper she matched that picture exactly.

In the days that followed, Henri did his best to avoid any further outbursts. But Paula had found a new reason for displaying her indignation: the lecture he had agreed to give at Claudie's. He tried at first to justify himself; even Dubreuilh had spoken at Claudie's . . . the purpose was to collect money for a children's home . . . It was impossible to refuse. . . . But since she wouldn't be appeased, he decided to hold his tongue. That tactic only succeeded in exasperating Paula all the more; she, too, grew silent, but she seemed to be turning over important decisions in her head. The day of the lecture, she looked at him so fiercely while he was knotting his tie in front of the mirror in their bedroom that he thought hopefully, "She's going to suggest that we break up."

"You're sure you don't want to go with me?" he asked in a friendly voice.

She let out such a guffaw that if he hadn't known her he would have thought her crazy. "What a joke! Go with you to that carnival?"

"As you like."

" I have better things to do," she said in a voice that invited a question.

He complied. " What do you have to do?" he asked.

" That's my business!" she replied haughtily.

This time he didn't insist, but as he was getting ready to leave she said aggressively, " I'm going over to *Vigilance* to see Dubreuilh."

Henri spun about; she had produced her effect. " Why do you want to see Dubreuilh?"

" I warned you I was going to have it out with him one of these days."

" For what reason?"

" I have many things to tell him, things that concern me, and that concern you."

" I beg you not to interfere in my relations with Dubreuilh," Henri said. " You've nothing at all to tell him, and you won't go to see him."

" Excuse me," she said, " but I've already waited only too long. That man is your evil genius and I alone can deliver you from him."

Henri felt the blood rush to his face. What was she going to tell Dubreuilh? In moments of anger or worry, Henri had expressed himself freely in front of Paula; he could not permit her to repeat some of the things he had said. But how to dissuade her? They were expecting him at Claudie's; he'd never be able to convince her in five brief minutes. He would have to tie her up, or lock her in.

" You're out of your mind," he stammered.

" You see," Paula said, " when one lives as solitary a life as I do, one has a great deal of time to think. I think about you and about everything that concerns you, and sometimes I see things. A few days ago I saw Dubreuilh with remarkable clarity, and I realised he'd do anything to destroy you completely."

" If you start having visions now!" he said. He tried to think of a way to intimidate her. He found only one: to threaten her with breaking up.

" It's not only my visions I rely on," Paula said in a deliberately mysterious voice.

" What else, then?"

" I made inquiries," she replied, looking at him teasingly.

He looked at her, perplexed. "Anne certainly didn't tell you Dubreuilh wants to destroy me."

"Who said anything about Anne?" she replied. "Anne! She's even blinder than you."

"Well, then, who is the super-clairvoyant you consulted?" he asked, feeling vaguely worried.

Paula's face became serious. "I spoke to Lambert."

"Lambert? Where did you see him?" Henri asked, his throat dry with anger.

"Here. Is that a crime?" Paula replied calmly. "I rang him up and asked him to come."

"When was that?"

"Yesterday. He doesn't like Dubreuilh either," she said with satisfaction.

"That's an abuse of confidence!" Henri said. To think that she had spoken to Lambert with her ridiculous vocabulary, her laughable vehemence! He felt like slapping her.

"You're always talking about purity and taste," he continued in a fury. "But a woman who shares a man's life, his thoughts, his secrets, and who gives them away behind his back, without letting him know, a woman who does a thing like that is behaving in a filthy manner! Do you hear?" he said, grabbing her by the wrist. "Filthy!"

She shook her head. "Your life is my life because I have sacrificed mine for yours; I have rights in it."

"I never asked you for any sacrifices," he said. "I tried to help you make a life of your own last year, but you didn't want to. That's your business. But you have no rights in me!"

"I didn't want to because of you," she said, "because you need me."

"Do you think I need these perpetual scenes? Well, you're badly mistaken! There are times when you make me feel like never setting foot here again. And I'm going to tell you something: if you go to see Dubreuilh, I'll never forgive you for it. You won't see me again."

"But I want to save you!" she said passionately. "Don't you understand that you're ruining yourself! You agree to all sorts of compromises, you give lectures in salons . . . And I know why you don't dare show me what you write any more: your failure is reflected in your work, and you feel it. You're ashamed. You're so ashamed that you lock your manuscript in a drawer. It must be really awful."

Henri looked at her with hate in his eyes. "If I show you the manuscript, will you give me your word you won't go to see Dubreuilh?"

Paula's face abruptly softened. "You'll show it to me?"

"Will you give me your word?"

She thought for a moment. "I give you my word I won't go to-day."

"That's good enough for me," Henri said. He opened the drawer, pulled out the thick, mottled note-book, and threw it on the bed.

"I can read it? Really?" Paula asked uncertainly. Her tragedienne's assurance had left her, and suddenly she seemed rather pitiful.

"You can."

"Oh, you can't imagine how pleased I am," she said. She smiled timidly. "This evening we'll discuss it together, like we used to."

He didn't answer. He looked at the note-book which Paula was caressing with the flat of her hand. Only paper and ink; it looked as inoffensive as the powders locked in the glass cabinet of his father's pharmacy. Actually, he was more despicable than a poisoner.

"Good-bye," she called out over the balustrade as he fled through the living-room.

"Good-bye."

He continued fleeing on the stairway, tried in vain to empty his head of all thoughts. That evening, when he saw Paula again, she would have read it. She would read every sentence, reread every word. It was murder. He stopped. Clutching the banister, he slowly climbed a few steps, and the dog, big, black, and barking, jumped at him. He hated that dog, that stairway, Paula's fanatical love, her silences, her outbursts, her unhappiness. He rushed down the stairs to the street.

It was a lovely winter day, a little hazy and with a faint pinkness permeating the air; through a bay window, Henri looked out upon a patch of silky sky. He brought his eyes back to his audience but found it more difficult to speak when he saw them. Little hats, jewels, furs; most of them were

women of the well-preserved variety who believe they know
how to display their remaining assets to the best advantage.
What earthly interest could they possibly have in the history of
French journalism? It was too warm; the air smelled of
perfume. Henri's eyes wandered from Marie-Ange's thin
smile to Vincent's laughing grimace. Somewhere between an
Argentine millionaire and a hunchbacked patron of the arts,
Lambert was seated, and Henri was afraid of seeing him face
to face again. He was ashamed. He lowered his eyes once
more and let the words flow from his mouth.

" Marvellous! "

Claudie had given the signal for applause; they clapped
their hands, let loose their voices, rushed towards the platform. Huguette Volange opened a little door behind Henri.
" Come this way. Claudie's going to get rid of all the old
bats; she's asked only a few of her intimate friends to stay,
and of course your friends too. You must be dying of thirst,"
she added, dragging Henri to the buffet where Julien, standing
alone opposite two servants, was finishing off a glass of champagne.

" I hope you'll forgive me, but I didn't hear a thing," he said
in a loud voice. " The only reason I came was to get drunk on
the house."

" You're forgiven. Lectures are as much of a bore to listen
to as they are to give," Henri said.

" I wasn't bored at all," Vincent said. " In fact, it was even
educational!" He laughed. " Nevertheless, I'm also going to
have a drink."

" Drink up!" Henri said.

A grey-haired woman wearing the Legion of Honour on her
breast rushed towards him; he quickly forced a gracious smile
to his face. "Thank you for your participation! It was
magnificent! Do you know you brought in more money than
anybody?"

" I'm delighted," Henri said. His eyes searched the room
for Lambert. What had Paula told him? Henri had never
spoken to Lambert about his private life. Of course, he must
have learned a few intimate things about him through Nadine.
But Henri didn't give a damn about that: the affair with
Nadine meant practically nothing to him. But Paula—that
was different.

He smiled at Lambert. " Would it be too much trouble to give me a lift on your motor-cycle when this carnival is over?"

" It'd be a pleasure!" Lambert replied in a completely natural voice.

" Thanks. It'll give us a chance to talk a bit."

Claudie charged headlong into the salon, directing herself unswervingly towards Henri. " Now you're going to be a perfect darling and sign your name in a few books. These ladies are ardent admirers of yours."

" With pleasure," Henri replied; and in a half-whisper added, " But I can't stay very long; I'm expected at the paper."

" You simply must stay to see the Belhommes; they're coming for the sole purpose of meeting you. They should be here any minute."

" In half an hour, I'm getting out," Henri said. He took the book a tall blonde was holding out to him. " Your name?" he asked.

" You don't know it yet," the blonde replied with a haughty little smile, " but you will know it one day. Colette Masson."

She thanked him with a second mysterious smile, and in another book he wrote another name. What a farce! He signed, smiled, smiled, signed. The little salon had filled up; they were legion, Claudie's intimate friends. They, too, smiled, shook Henri's hands; their eyes shone with a curiosity which bordered on the obscene, and they spoke words which they had spoken the last time to Duhamel, which they would indifferently repeat the next time to Mauriac or Aragon. From time to time, a zealous reader thought it necessary to proclaim her admiration: this one had been overwhelmed by the description of a sleepless night, that one by a sentence on cemeteries. They never failed to pick some insignificant passage, indifferently written. Reproachfully, Guite Ventadour asked Henri why he chose such sad gentlemen as heroes; and all the while she was smiling broadly at a lot of infinitely sadder people. " How hard they are on the characters in a novel!" Henri thought. " They don't allow them a single weakness. And how strangely all of them read! I suppose that instead of following the road laid out for them, most of them go wandering blindly through the pages from time to time, a word strikes a chord in them, awakening God only knows what memories or what longings. Or else they think they see a reflection of themselves in some image or other; they stop a moment, admire themselves, and gropingly set off again. It would be a lot better never to see your readers face to face," he thought.

He went over to Marie-Ange who had been observing him mockingly. "What are you snickering about?"

"I'm not snickering; I'm observing." Banteringly, she added, "You know, you're right to live a secluded life. You're not at all brilliant."

"What does one have to do to be brilliant?"

"Look at your friend Volange and take some lessons."

"I'm not gifted," Henri said.

Dazzling them failed to amuse him, and pretending to shock them was equally empty. Julien was holding forth while ostentatiously emptying glass after glass of champagne, and around him everyone laughed indulgently. "If I had a name like that," he was blaring, "I'd get rid of it damned fast. Belzunce, Polignac, La Rochefoucauld: they've been dragged through all the pages of French history; they're covered with dust." He could insult them, utter the worst improprieties, and they would never fail to be delighted. If a poet isn't sanctified with titles, prizes, decorations, then it's best he be a buffoon. Julien believed himself their master, and all he did was reinforce their belief in their own superiority. No, the only way was to keep your distance from people like that. The fashionable writers and the pseudo-intellectuals who eagerly flocked around Claudine, were, perhaps, even more depressing. They didn't enjoy writing, thinking didn't interest them, and all the boredom they inflicted on themselves was reflected in their faces. Their only concern was with the personalities they invented for themselves and the success of their careers, and they frequented one another only to envy each other at close range. A repulsive breed! Catching sight of Scriassine, Henri smiled warmly; he was a fanatic, a troublemaker, intolerable, but thoroughly alive, and when he made use of words it was because he felt something deeply, not because he wanted to trade them for money, compliments, honours. With him, vanity came only afterwards, and then it was nothing but a superficial whim.

"I hope you're not angry with me," Scriassine said.

"Of course not ; you were drinking. How's it going? You still hiding here?"

"Yes. I came down just to say hallo to you ; I was hoping that high society had already left. Is that what you spoke in front of and what Claudie wants me to speak in front of?"

"It isn't a bad audience," said Volange, who had non-chalantly come over to join them. He smiled a small haughty smile around the room, and his eyes came to rest on Lambert. "People who have a great deal of money affect futility, but in fact they often have a feeling for true values. Claudie's luxury, for example, is very intelligent."

"Luxury gives me a pain," Scriassine said.

Marie-Ange burst out laughing and Louis looked at her angrily.

"You mean false luxury," Huguette said indulgently.

"False, true—I don't like luxury."

"How can one not like luxury?" Huguette asked.

"I don't like people who like luxury," Scriassine said. "In Vienna," he added brusquely, "three of us lived to-gether in a miserable hole, and we had one overcoat between us. We were starving to death. Those were the happiest days of my life."

"Now there's evidence for you of a rather curious guilt complex," Volange said, sounding amused.

"I know my complexes and they've got nothing to do with it," Scriassine said curtly.

"Of course they have! Both of you are puritans, like all the others on the left," Volange said, turning to Henri. "Luxury shocks you because you can't bear to have a bad conscience. It's frightening, that austerity of yours. You reject luxury, and you'll end up by rejecting poetry and art."

Henri didn't answer. He attached no importance to Volange's words ; what interested him was to see how he had changed since their last meeting. There was no longer any trace of humility in his voice or in his smiles ; all his old arrogance had returned.

"Luxury and art aren't the same thing," Lambert said timidly.

"No," Louis answered, "but if everyone stopped having a bad conscience, if evil disappeared from the earth, art, too, would disappear. Art is an attempt at integrating evil. The organised progressives want to suppress evil, and in so doing they're condemning art to death." He sighed. " The world they promise us will be dismal indeed."

Henri shrugged his shoulders. " And you, the organised anti-progressives, you make me laugh! Now you prophesy that we'll never be able to suppress injustice ; now you proclaim that when we do, life will become duller than a pastoral. Your own arguments can be thrown right back at you!"

" That seems to me a very interesting idea, that evil is necessary to art," Lambert said, looking at Louis questioningly.

Claudie put her hand on Henri's arm. " There's Lucie Belhomme," she said, " that tall, very elegant brunette. Come over with me and I'll introduce you to her."

She indicated a tall, gaunt woman dressed all in black. Was she elegant? Henri had never really understood the meaning of that word ; for him, there were desirable women and others who weren't. This one wasn't.

" And this is Mademoiselle Josette Belhomme," Claudie said. The daughter was undoubtedly beautiful. But that fashionable figure wasn't right at all for the part of Jeanne. Furs, perfume, high heels, painted nails ; under the coils of her amber hair, she was just another luxurious doll among other dolls.

" I've read your play ; it's magnificent," Lucie Belhomme said in a positive voice. " And I'm sure it can make a lot of money ; I have a special feeling for things like that. I've spoken about it to Vernon, the producer of Studio 46, and he's very interested. He's a very good friend of mine."

" He doesn't find it too shocking?" Henri asked.

" Something shocking can make a play a hit, or it can make it a failure ; that depends on a great many things. I think I can convince Vernon to risk it." There was a brief silence and then, without any change of pace, almost insolently, she continued, " Vernon would be willing to give Josette her chance. She's played only small parts up to now— she's only twenty-one—but she's had experience, and she's remarkably good at getting the feel of character. I'd like you to hear her in the big scene in the second act."

" I'd be glad," Henri said.

Lucie turned to Claudie. " Do you have a quiet corner where Josette could run through the scene?"

" Oh, not now," Josette said.

Her eyes shifted from her mother to Henri in fright; she lacked the customary assurance of those luxurious mannequins she so much resembled. It seemed almost as if she were intimidated by her own beauty. And she was truly beautiful, with her large dark eyes, her slightly heavy mouth, and her clear, creamy skin under her tawny hair.

" It's a matter of ten minutes," Lucie said. .

" But I can't just like that," Josette said. " Not cold."

" There's no hurry," Henri said. " If Vernon really decides to take the play, we'll make an appointment."

Lucie smiled. " If it's agreed that Josette has the part, I can guarantee you he'll take the play."

Josette's tender white skin burst into flame, from her throat to the roots of her hair. Henri smiled at her gently. " Shall we set a date? Tuesday, at about four? Is that all right with you?"

She nodded her head in assent.

" Come over to my place," Lucie said. " You'll find it quite suitable for working."

" Does the part interest you?" he asked in a conversational voice.

" Of course."

" I must admit I didn't picture Jeanne as being so beautiful," he said cheerfully.

A polite smile wandered around her tragic mouth and failed to settle on it; she had been taught all the expressions required for success, but she executed them poorly. That rather broad face with its enormous eyes shattered every mask.

" An actress is never too beautiful," Lucie said, " When your leading lady comes on stage half undressed, what the public wants to see is this," she said, abruptly raising Josette's skirt and uncovering her long silky legs to mid-thigh.

" Mother!"

Josette's dismayed voice touched Henri. Was she really just a splendid doll, no different from all the others? " She certainly isn't going to set the world on fire," Henri said to himself. But he couldn't quite believe that there was nothing at all behind that pathetic face.

" Don't play the ingénue; it's not your type," Lucie Belhomme said sharply. "Aren't you going to write down the appointment?" she asked.

Obediently, Josette opened her purse and pulled out an appointment book. Henri caught a glimpse of a lace handkerchief and a little gold compact; there was a time when the inside of a woman's handbag seemed full of mystery to him. For a moment, he held her long, slender fingers—fingers which seemed to be carved from rock candy—in his hand.

"Till Tuesday, then."

"Till Tuesday."

"Do you like her?" Claudie asked with a wicked little smile after the two women had left. "If you want it, you know, it's there for the asking; she isn't very choosy, poor kid."

"Why 'poor?'"

"Lucie isn't easy to live with. You know, women who have a tough time of it before success hits them generally aren't softies."

At any other time, listening to Claudie's chitchat would have amused him, but Volange and Lambert were standing there together, chatting animatedly. Volange was holding forth, moving his hands in gracious gestures, and Lambert was nodding his head and smiling. Henri felt like breaking in; he was relieved when he saw Vincent detach himself from the buffet and turn towards them.

"I'd like to ask you a question, just one question," Vincent shouted loudly. "What's a man like you doing here?"

"As you can see," Louis replied calmly, "I'm chatting with Lambert. As for you, you're getting yourself drunk, which is equally obvious."

"Maybe no one told you," Vincent said, "but this meeting's for the benefit of the children of deportees. You are out of place here."

"Who knows his proper place in the world?" Louis said. "If you believe you know yours, it's no doubt because there's a special dispensation for drunkards."

"Oh, that Vincent!" Lambert said bitingly. "He's really something! He knows everything, judges everyone; he never makes a mistake, and he is always glad to give you a few free lessons."

Never had Vincent's face looked so pale; it seemed as if blood would begin dripping from his eyes at any moment.

"I know how to recognise a bastard," he muttered.

" I believe that young man needs medical attention," Louis said. " A boy of his age saturated with alcohol! It's a depressing spectacle."

Henri rushed over to join them. " You've suddenly become damned puritanical, haven't you?" he said. " You who so valiantly integrate evil. In his own way, Vincent's taking the part of the devil: he gets drunk. Do you know any good reason why he shouldn't?"

" A bastard, and the son of a bastard," Vincent mumbled with a cruel smile. " Naturally, they go well together."

" What did you say? Repeat that!" Lambert said.

Vincent's voice grew hard. " I said you have to be a real bastard to make up with the guy who put the finger on Rosa. Do you remember Rosa?"

" Come outside with me," Lambert said. " Let's settle this thing."

" Why not settle it here?" Vincent said.

Henri held Vincent back and Louis placed his hand on Lambert's shoulder. " Let it drop," Louis said.

" I'd like to knock his teeth down his throat."

" Some other time," Henri said. " You promised to give me a lift, and I'm in a hurry. And you, go home and sleep it off," he said amicably to Vincent, who was muttering unintelligible sounds.

Lambert let himself be led away, but while they were crossing the courtyard he said darkly, " You shouldn't have stopped me ; I'd have given him a good lesson. I know how to use my fists, you know."

" I believe you, but fist fights are stupid."

" I should have swung immediately instead of talking," Lambert said. " My reflexes don't work right. When I should swing, I talk."

" Vincent was drinking and, besides, you know he's a little cracked," Henri said. " Don't let what he said bother you."

" That's too simple," Lambert said angrily. " If he was really so crazy, you wouldn't be so close to him." He mounted his motor-cycle. " Where are you going?"

" Home. I'll go to the paper a little later," Henri replied.

A picture of Paula had just flashed through his mind: she was sitting in the middle of the living-room, motionless, staring blankly into space. She had read it. She had read the break-up scene sentence by sentence, word by word. She knew exactly what Henri thought of her. He had to see her, immediately. Lambert was speeding angrily along the quays ; as he stopped for the last red light, Henri asked, " Want to have a drink with me?"

He should see Paula at once, but at the thought of finding himself face to face with her again his heart sank.

" If you like," Lambert replied sulkily.

They went into the *café-tabac* at the corner of the quay and ordered two glasses of white wine at the counter.

" I hope you aren't going to hold it against me because I stopped you from slugging it out with Vincent," Henri said amiably.

" I don't see how you can stand that man," Lambert said heatedly. " His drunkenness, his filthy shirts, his filthy stories, and on top of it all his big show of being a desperado! I don't go for that. When he was in the Maquis he killed people ; so did a lot of others. But it's no reason to go through life with a chip on your shoulder. And Nadine calls him an angel, because he's half impotent! No, I don't see it," Lambert repeated. " If he's warped, let him go to a hospital and get himself a few good shock treatments. Maybe then he'll stop giving us a pain."

" You're being very unfair!" Henri said.

" If you ask me, you're the one who's biased."

" I like him," Henri said a bit sharply. " But it isn't Vincent I wanted to speak to you about," he added. " Paula told me a strange thing ; that she had you over yesterday and questioned you about Dubreuilh. I thought it was completely out of line ; it must have been rather embarrassing for you."

" Not at all," Lambert replied hastily. " I didn't quite understand what exactly she wanted from me, but she was very nice."

Henri studied Lambert's face ; he seemed completely sincere. Perhaps Paula had restrained herself in front of him. " Just now, she hates Dubreuilh," Henri said. " She's a woman who carries her feelings to extremes ; maybe you noticed it."

" Yes, but since I don't care much for Dubreuilh either, it didn't bother me," Lambert replied.

" Good! I was afraid the thing might have been unpleasant for you."

" Not in the least."

"Good!" Henri repeated. "See you later—and thanks for the lift."

Henri walked slowly down the street. There was no possible chance of another delay; in two minutes he would be facing Paula, feeling her eyes upon him, searching for words. "I'll deny everything. I'll tell her that Yvette has nothing in common with her, that I merely borrowed certain expressions and gestures from her, but that I twisted everything around." He stared up the stairs. "She'll never believe me!" he thought. "Maybe she won't even let me explain. Maybe . . ." He quickened his pace; his throat was tight and dry, and he ran up the last few steps. No barking, no bells ringing, no radio or gramophone music; not a sound. "A deathly silence," he said to himself. And horrified, he thought, "She's killed herself!" He stopped in front of the door; there was a murmur of voices coming from within.

"Come in."

Paula was alive, was smiling! The concierge, who was sitting on the edge of the couch, got up. "Here I've wasted your time with my stories," she said.

"Not at all," Paula said. "I found them very interesting."

"I'll speak to the landlord about it to-morrow," the concierge said. "You needn't worry about it."

"The ceiling's caving in," Paula explained cheerfully as the concierge closed the door behind her. "She's nice, that woman," she added. "She told me some surprising stories about the tramps in the neighbourhood; you could write a book about them."

"I suppose so," Henri replied. He looked at Paula with a mixture of disappointment and relief; she had spent the afternoon chatting with the concierge, hadn't had time to read the manuscript. He would have to go through the whole thing again, and he knew he wouldn't have the courage.

"Did she keep you from reading the novel?" he asked casually. He forced a smile to his face. "All that fuss over nothing!"

Paula looked at him, shocked. "Of course, I read it!"

"You did? What do you think of it?"

"It's masterly," she said simply.

He took the note-book and thumbed through the pages, trying to seem completely casual.

"What do you think of Charval? Does he appeal to you?"

"Not exactly, but he does have a true nobility," Paula replied. "I suppose that's what you were after, wasn't it?"

Henri nodded. "And do you like the Fourteenth of July scene?"

Paula reflected a moment. "It's not my favourite."

Henri opened the note-book at the fatal page. "And the break-up with Yvette, what did you think of it?"

"It's gripping."

"Really?"

She gave him a slightly suspicious look. "Why does that surprise you?" She uttered a little laugh. "Were you thinking of us when you wrote it?"

He threw the note-book on the table. "Don't be stupid!"

"It's going to be your finest book," Paula said authoritatively. Tenderly she ran her fingers through Henri's hair. "I really can't understand why you were so secretive about it."

"Neither can I," he said.

Henri felt almost overawed by the thickness of the silence; rugs, curtains, and draperies padded the large, richly furnished room. Through closed doors, not a whisper of a sound could be heard. Henri wondered if he wouldn't have to upset some of the furniture to awaken someone.

"Have I been keeping you waiting?"

"Not very long," he replied politely.

Josette remained standing in front of him, a frightened smile on her lips. She was wearing an amber-coloured dress, filmy and very indiscreet. "She isn't very choosy," Claudie had said. That smile, the silence, the fur-covered couches were an obvious invitation to all manner of boldness. Too obvious. If he had taken advantage of those abetments, Henri would have felt as if he were corrupting the morals of a minor under the watchful eye of a leering procuress. Somewhat stiffly, he said, "If it's all right with you, we'll start working immediately; I'm a bit pressed for time. Do you have a script?"

"I know the monologue by heart," Josette replied.

"Well, let's get started then."

He propped his copy on an end table and sat back comfortably in a big, deep arm-chair. The monologue was the most difficult scene in the whole play; Josette hadn't grasped it at all, and besides she was terrified. Henri felt embarrassed watching her frantically pouring out her heart in a desperate attempt to please him. No question about it: it made him feel like a wealthy pervert watching a very special performance in a particularly luxurious brothel.

"Let's do the third scene, second act," he said. " I'll cue you."

" It's hard to act and read at the same time," Josette said.

" Let's try it."

It was a love scene; Josette handled it a little better. She had excellent diction, and her face and her voice were truly exciting. " Who knows what a clever director might do with her?" Henri thought.

When she had finished the scene, Henri spoke to her cheerfully. " You haven't got it clear," he said. " But there's hope."

" Do you think so?"

" I'm sure of it. Sit down over here and I'll explain the character to you."

She sat down next to him. It had been a very long time since he had last found himself seated next to such a beautiful girl. As he spoke, he breathed in the sweet scent of her hair; her perfume smelled like perfume, like all perfumes, but on her it seemed an almost natural odour. And it gave Henri a terrible desire. Running his fingers through her hair, slipping his tongue inside the red mouth—it would be easy, too easy in fact. He could feel that Josette awaited his pleasure with truly discouraging resignation.

" Do you understand now?" he asked.

" Yes."

" All right then, go ahead; let's give it another try."

They began the scene again and she put so much feeling into every word that it was even worse than the first time.

" You're putting too much into it," he said. " Do it more simply."

" Oh, I'll never be able to do it right!" she said disconsolately.

" You will if you work at it."

Josette heaved a long sigh. " Poor kid! On top of it all, her mother's going to shout at her for not getting me to lay her," Henri thought, getting up. He felt a little sorry about his scruples. How desirable that mouth was! He recalled the rapture of sleeping with a really desirable woman.

" We'll make another appointment," he said.

" I'm wasting your time!"

" For me, it isn't wasted time," Henri replied. He smiled. " If you aren't afraid of wasting yours, perhaps we could go out together after the next session."

" We could."

" Do you like to dance?"

" Naturally."

" Good! I'll take you dancing then."

The following Saturday Henri met Josette at her apartment on Rue Gabrielle, in a living-room with pink-and-white satin covered furniture. Seeing her again gave him a little shock. Whenever you take your eyes away from true beauty, you immediately betray it. Josette's skin was paler, her hair darker than he remembered, and there was a sparkle in her eyes that made him think of a fresh mountain brook. While he distractedly read off her cues, Henri's eyes wandered over that young body moulded in black velvet, and he told himself that that figure, that voice were good enough to excuse a great deal of awkwardness. Besides, with good direction, he didn't see why Josette should be any more awkward than someone else. At times, she even struck a touching note. He made up his mind to give it a try.

" It'll be all right," he said warmly. " Of course, you've got a lot of hard work ahead of you, but it'll be all right."

" I want it to so very much!" she said.

" And now, let's go dancing," Henri said. " I was thinking we might go down to St. Germain des Prés. What do you say?"

" Whatever you like."

They went to a cellar club on Rue St. Benoît and sat down at a table beneath the portrait of a bearded lady. Josette was wearing a two-piece dress; removing a bolero, she uncovered round, mature shoulders which contrasted with her childlike face. " That's what I needed to have fun having fun," Henri said to himself happily. " A young, beautiful wench beside me!"

" Shall we dance?"

" Yes, let's."

Holding that warm, compliant body in his arms made him a little dizzy. How he used to love that kind of dizziness! He loved it again, now. And once again he loved jazz, smoke, young voices, the sight of others enjoying themselves. He was ready to love those breasts, that belly. Only, before making an attempt, he would have liked to feel that Josette liked him at least a little bit.

" Do you like this place?"

" Yes." She hesitated. " It's rather unusual, isn't it?"

" Yes, I suppose it is. What kind of places do you prefer?"

" Oh, it's very nice here," she replied hastily.

Whenever he tried to get her to talk, she looked frightened ; ner mother must have carefully taught her to keep quiet. They kept quiet until two in the morning, drinking champagne and dancing. Josette looked neither sad nor gay. At two o'clock, she asked to be taken home, and he couldn't tell whether it was out of boredom, fatigue, or discretion. He accompanied her to her apartment. In the car, she said with studied politeness, " I'd love to read one of your books."

" That's easy to arrange." He smiled at her. " Do you like to read?"

" When I have the time."

" But you don't often have the time?"

She sighed. " No, unfortunately."

Was she completely stupid? Or quite innocent? Or paralysed by timidity? It was difficult to decide. She was so beautiful that normally she ought to have been stupid, but at the same time her beauty gave her an air of mystery.

Lucie Belhomme decided that the contract should be signed at her home after a small, intimate dinner. Henri called up Josette and asked her to celebrate the good news with him. In a worldly voice, she thanked him for his book, which he had sent over to her with a nice inscription, and made an appointment to meet him that evening in a little Montmartre bar.

" Well, are you happy?" he asked, holding Josette's hand for a moment.

" With what?" Josette asked. She looked a little less youthful than usual, and not at all happy.

" The contract. We're going to sign ; it's all settled. Doesn't that make you happy?"

She lifted a glass of Vichy water to her lips. " It frightens me," she said in a low voice.

" Vernon isn't crazy, and neither am I. There's no need to be frightened, you'll be very good."

" But that wasn't the way you saw the part, was it?"

" I couldn't see her any other way now."

" Is that true?"

" Yes."

And it was true. She would play the part at best only fairly well, but he didn't want to imagine Jeanne as having any other eyes, any other voice than hers.

" You're so sweet!" Josette said.

She looked at him with true gratitude in her eyes, but whether she offered herself to him calculatingly or out of gratitude made no difference. That wasn't what Henri wanted. He didn't move. Between soft, languishing silences, they spoke of potential directors, of the cast, of the set. Josette remained troubled. He took her to her door and she held on to his hand.

" Well, till Monday," she said in a choked voice.

" You're not afraid any more?" he asked. " You're going to sleep now like a good little girl?"

" I'm still frightened," she said.

He smiled. " Aren't you going to ask me in for a night-cap?"

She looked at him happily. " I didn't dare!" she said.

She climbed the stairs quickly and, once inside the apartment, threw off her fur cape, revealing her bust sheathed in black silk. She gave Henri a tall glass in which the ice tinkled gaily.

" To your success!" he said.

Quickly she rapped her knuckles against the wooden table. " Don't say that! My God! It'd be so terrible if I turned out to be bad!"

" You'll be good!" he repeated.

She shrugged her shoulders. " I always mess everything up!"

He smiled. " That surprises me."

" But it's true." She hesitated. " I shouldn't tell you this, because you'll lose your confidence, too, but I went to see a fortune-teller this afternoon. She told me I had a grave disappointment in store for me."

" Fortune-tellers always exaggerate," Henri said firmly. " You haven't by any chance ordered a new dress, have you?"

" Yes, for Monday."

" Well, it won't look well on you. There's your disappointment!"

" Oh, but that would be awful!" Josette said. " What would I wear for the dinner?"

" A disappointment is always disappointing," he said, laughing. " But don't worry, you'll still be the most beautiful woman there," he added, " on Monday as always. And it's less disastrous than playing a part badly, isn't it?"

" You have such a nice way of arranging things!" Josette said. " It's a shame you can't take God's place."

She was very close to him. Was it only gratitude which swelled her mouth, veiled her eyes?

" But I wouldn't offer him mine," he said, taking her in his arms.

When Henri opened his eyes, he saw, in the half light of dawn, a pale-green tufted wall. The happiness of being alive on this morning made his heart jump with joy. It called for brisk, salty pleasures—cold water, a rough bath glove. He slipped out of bed without awakening Josette, and when he came out of the bathroom, washed, dressed, and starving, she was still asleep. He crossed the room on tiptoe and bent over her; she was lying there wrapped in her dampness, in her fragrance, with her bright locks flowing over her eyes, and he felt wonderfully happy to have that woman for himself, and to be a man. She half-opened an eye, just one, as if she were trying to retain her sleep in the other.

" You're up already?"

" I'm going to have a coffee in the bistro on the corner; I'll be back in a few minutes."

" No!" she said. " No! I'll make you some tea."

She rubbed her sleepy eyes and slid out from between the sheets, all warmth in her frothy nightgown. He took her in his arms.

" You look like a little faun."

" A fauness."

" A little faun."

She offered her mouth to him, as if enchanted. A Persian princess, a little Indian, a fox, a morning glory, a lovely wisteria—it always pleased them when you told them they looked like something, like something else. " My little faun," he repeated, kissing her gently. She put on a bathrobe and slippers, and he followed her into the kitchen. The sky was shining and the white tiles sparkled as Josette, with hesitant movements, busied herself making tea.

" Milk or lemon?"

" A little milk."

She set the tray down in the flesh-coloured boudoir, and he looked curiously at the ottomans and the little tables. Why did Josette, who dressed so well, whose voice and gestures were so harmonious, why did she choose to live in that hideous film set?

" Did you furnish this apartment yourself?"

" Mother and I."

She gave him a worried look and he said very quickly, " It's pretty."

When had she stopped living at her mother's? Why? For whom? Suddenly, he felt like asking her a great many questions. Behind her was a whole existence every day of which, every hour of which, had been lived separately. Yes, and every night! And he knew nothing at all about it. It wasn't the moment to cross-examine her, but he felt ill at ease among those tasteless decorations, those invisible memories.

" Do you know what we ought to do?" he said. " Take a walk together. It's such a beautiful morning."

" Take a walk? Where?"

" In the streets."

"' You mean on foot?"

" Yes. Walking on foot in the streets."

She looked baffled. " I'll have to get dressed then, won't I?"

He laughed. " It might be preferable. But you don't have to dress up as though you were going to a party, you know."

" What shall I put on?"

How does one dress to go walking on foot in the streets at nine in the morning? She opened closets, dresser drawers, hesitantly fingering scarfs and blouses. She slipped her legs into a pair of long silk stockings and Henri felt in his hands the memory of that silk filled with burning flesh.

" Is this all right?"

" You're ravishing."

She was wearing a dark little suit and a green scarf; she had put her hair up. She was ravishing.

" Don't you think this suit makes me look plump?"

" No."

She examined herself in the mirror with a worried look.

What did she see? Being a woman, being beautiful, how does
it feel from the inside? How does that silken caress along the
thighs feel, that glossy satin against the warmth of a belly?
" How does she think of our night?" he asked himself. " Has
her voice spoken other names in the night? Which? Pierre,
Victor, Jacques? And what does the name Henri mean to
her?"

" Did you read it?" he asked, pointing to his novel, which
was lying conspicuously on an end table.

" I looked through it." She hesitated. " It's silly, but I just
can't get myself to read."

" Does it bore you?"

" No, but as soon as I open a book, I start dreaming of
something else. I take off on a word."

" And where do you go? I mean, what do you dream
about?"

" Oh, it's all so vague. When you dream, it's always so
vague."

" Do you think about places, people?"

" Not about anything. I just dream."

He took her in his arms and asked with a smile, " Have
you been in love often?"

" Me?" She shrugged her shoulders. " With whom?"

" A lot of men must have been in love with you. You're
so beautiful."

" It's humiliating to be beautiful," she said, turning her head
away.

He let his arms drop to his sides. He had no idea why she
inspired so much compassion in him; she lived luxuriously, she
didn't work, had the hands of a lady. And yet, before her, he
melted with pity.

" It's funny being out in the streets so early," Josette said,
lifting a carefully made-up face to the sky.

" It's funny being here with you," he said, squeezing her
arm.

Joyously, he breathed in the clear, fresh air. Everything
seemed new that morning. The springtime was new; it was
barely beginning, but even now he could taste a warm complicity in the air. The Place des Abbesses smelled of cabbage
and fish; women in house-dresses, their hair frowsy with sleep
and tinged with strange colours produced by neither nature

nor art, were suspiciously examining the year's first crop of lettuce.

"Look at that old witch over there," he said, indicating an old woman dripping with make-up and jewels and wearing a filthy hat on top of her head.

"Oh, I know her," Josette said. She did not smile. "Maybe I'll be like her one day."

"I'd be very much surprised." They went down a few steps in silence ; Josette managed them unsteadily on her high heels. "How old are you?" he asked.

"Twenty-one."

"Your real age, I mean."

She hesitated. "I'm twenty-six. But don't tell Mother I told you," she added in terror.

"I've already forgotten," he replied. "But you look so young!"

She sighed. "Because I'm always watching myself ; it gets very tiring."

"Well then, stop tiring yourself!" he said tenderly, tightening his hold on her arm. "Have you always wanted to act?"

"I never wanted to be a model—and I don't like old men," she said between her teeth.

It was obviously her mother who had chosen her lovers for her ; perhaps it was true that she had never loved. Twenty-six years old, those eyes, that mouth, and never to have known love! Yes, she had a right to be pitied. "And I, what am I to her?" he asked himself. "What will I be?" In any case, her pleasure that night had been sincere, and so, too, was that trusting light in her eyes. They arrived on the Boulevard de Clichy where the sheds of a street fair were dozing quietly. Two children were happily riding a merry-go-round, but the little roller coaster was still fast asleep under a canvas cover.

"Do you know how to play Japanese billiards?"

"No."

She stood docilely beside him in front of one of the perforated boards. "Do you like street fairs?" he asked.

"I've never been to a street fair."

"You've never been on a roller coaster? Or through the tunnel of love?"

"No. When I was little we were too poor. Then Mother

put me in a boarding school, and when I got out I was already grown up."

"How old were you then?"

"Sixteen."

Diligently, she threw the wooden balls towards the round compartments. "It's hard."

"No, it isn't. Look! You almost won!" He took her arm. "One of these evenings, we'll take a ride together on the merry-go-round."

"You, you ride on merry-go-rounds?" she asked incredulously.

"Not when I'm alone, of course."

Again, she walked unsteadily down the steep hill.

"Are you tired?"

"My shoes hurt."

"Let's go in here," Henri said, opening the door of the nearest café, a tiny bistro with oilcloth-covered tables. "What would you like?"

"A Vichy."

"Why always Vichy?"

"Because of the liver," she explained sadly.

"A Vichy and a glass of red wine," Henri said to the waiter. He pointed to a sign hanging on the wall. "Look at that!"

In her deep, slow voice, Josette read, "Combat alcoholism by drinking wine." She burst out laughing. "It's funny! You certainly know funny places."

"I was never here before. But you know, you discover a lot of things when you wander around. Don't you ever wander around?"

"I haven't got the time."

"What do you do with your time?"

"There are always so many things: diction lessons, shopping, the hairdresser. You can't imagine how much time the hairdresser takes! And then there are teas, cocktail parties . . ."

"Do you enjoy all that?"

"Do you know any people who are enjoying themselves?"

"I know some who are happy with the lives they're living. Me, for example."

She said nothing and he gently put his arms around her. "What would you need to make you happy?"

"To be able to do without Mother and to be sure of never becoming poor again," she replied without hesitation.

"You'll get there one day. And then what will you do?"

"I'd be happy."

"But what will you do? Travel? Go out?"

She shrugged her shoulders. "I haven't thought about it."

She took a gold compact from her purse and did up her mouth. "I must go. I have a fitting at Mother's shop." She gave Henri a worried look. "Do you really think my dress won't look well on me?"

"Of course it will," he said with a laugh. "I'm sure the fortune-teller was all wrong; it happens sometimes, you know. Is it a pretty dress?"

"You'll see it Monday." Josette sighed. "I'm going to have to be seen around for publicity. That means I'll have to be well dressed."

"Isn't it a bother, having to be well dressed all the time?"

"If you only knew how tiring those fittings are! Afterwards, I have a headache all day long."

She rose and they went up the street to a hack stand. "I'll go along with you."

"Don't bother."

"For my own pleasure," he said tenderly.

"You're nice."

It went straight to his heart every time she said, "You're nice," in that voice of hers, with those eyes. In the taxi, he settled Josette's head on his shoulder and wondered, "What can I do for her?" Help her become an actress, yes, but she didn't especially like the theatre; it wouldn't fill that emptiness he felt in her. And what if she weren't a success? She wasn't at all satisfied with the obscure futility of her life, but what could he possibly interest her in? Try talking to her? unlocking her mind? He wasn't, after all, going to drag her through museums, take her to concerts, lend her books, explain the world to her. He gently kissed her hair. He would have had to be in love with her. With women it always came down to that; you had to love them with an exclusive love.

"See you this evening," she said.

"I'll be waiting for you in our little bar."

She gently squeezed his hand and he knew that they were both thinking, " Till to-night, in our bed." When she had disappeared inside the imposing building, he set off on foot towards the Seine. Eleven-thirty. " I'll get to Paula's early; it'll make her happy," he said to himself. That morning, he felt like making everyone happy. " And yet," he thought somewhat anxiously, " I've got to talk to her." After having held Josette in his arms, he could no longer stand the thought of spending his nights with Paula. " Maybe she won't even mind," he said to himself hopefully. " She knows very well I have no desire left for her." Paula had avoided recognising herself in the unhappy heroine of his novel ; and yet a change had come over her since reading it. She no longer made any scenes, hadn't protested when she saw Henri, little by little, transferring his papers and clothing to his hotel room. He had been sleeping there very often. Who knows if she might not accept a peaceful, friendly relationship? She might welcome it with relief. The spring sky was so gay that it seemed possible to live sincerely and without making anyone suffer. At the corner of the street, Henri stopped hesitantly in front of a flower cart ; he was tempted to bring Paula a big bunch of pale violets, as he so often used to. But he was afraid of her surprise. " A bottle of good wine ; that'll be less compromising," he decided as he went into the neighbourhood grocery. He was happy as he climbed the stairs. He was thirsty, hungry ; he could already feel the robust taste of the old Bordeaux in his mouth. He hugged the bottle to his heart as if it were filled with all the friendship he wanted to offer Paula.

Very quietly, without knocking, he put the key in the lock and opened the door, the way he used to years ago. She heard nothing. She was kneeling on the rug which was covered with old papers ; he immediately recognised his old letters. And she was holding a picture of him in her hands, looking at it with an expression he had never before seen in her face. She wasn't crying, and before those dry eyes he realised for the first time that in all tears there lingers a little hope. She was face to face with her fate, she expected nothing more of it, and still she was resigned to it. She was so alone before that lifeless image that Henri felt drained of his very being. He closed the door from outside and was unable to suppress an irritable feeling which paralysed his pity. When he knocked, he heard a shuffling of papers and the swishing of silk. "Come in," she finally called out in an unsteady voice.

"What in the world have you been doing?"

"I was rereading your old letters. I didn't expect you so early."

She had thrown the papers on an arm-chair and had hidden the picture. Her face was calm, but mournful; he should have remembered that she was never cheerful any more. Annoyed, he set down the bottle on the table.

"You'd do a lot better to stop wrapping yourself in the past and start living a little in the present," he said.

"Oh, the present, you know . . ." She looked blankly at the table. "I haven't set the table yet."

"Would you like me to take you to a restaurant?"

"No, no. It'll only take a minute."

She walked towards the kitchen and he started to reach for the letters. "Leave them alone!" she said violently.

She grabbed them and threw them into a cupboard. He shrugged his shoulders. In a way, she was right; all those old, stale words had become lies. Silently, he watched Paula busying herself at the table. It wouldn't be easy to speak to her of friendship.

They sat down opposite each other, facing an assortment of hors d'œuvres, and Henri uncorked the bottle.

"You like red Bordeaux, don't you?" he asked earnestly.

"Yes," she replied indifferently.

Of course. For her, it wasn't a celebration; pretending to celebrate his new love with Paula was the absolute pinnacle of blindness and egotism. But even as he reproached himself, Henri felt a furtive, barely detectable bitterness.

"Anyhow, you ought to go out a little," he said.

"Go out?" she asked, as if she were coming down from the clouds.

"Yes, stick your nose outside, see people."

"What for?"

"Why keep yourself shut up in this burrow all day? Is that getting you anywhere?"

"I liked my burrow," she replied with a sad smile. "I never get bored here."

"You can't go on like this all your life. You don't want to sing any more? All right; that's settled. But at least try to find something else to do."

" What, for example?"

" We'll look for something."

She shook her head. " I'm thirty-seven years old. I don't know any trade. I could become a ragpicker, but . . ."

" A trade can be learned; there's nothing to stop you from learning."

She gave Henri a troubled look. " You'd like me to earn my keep?"

" It isn't a question of money," he said quickly. " I just want you to take an interest in things, to keep yourself occupied."

" I'm interested in us," she said.

" That isn't enough."

" It's been enough for me for ten years."

He gathered all his courage. " Listen, Paula, you know very well things have changed between us; there's no sense in lying to each other. We once had a great and beautiful love, and now, let's face it, it's turning into friendship. That doesn't mean we'll see less of each other, not at all," he added earnestly. " But you've got to find an independent existence for yourself."

She riveted her eyes on him. " I'll never feel friendship for you." A little smile brushed her lips. " Nor you for me."

" You're wrong, Paula . . ."

She interrupted him. " Take to-day, for example. You couldn't wait until twelve-thirty; you got here twenty minutes early. And you knocked so feverishly! Do you call that friendship?"

" You're wrong."

His anger returned in face of her stubbornness, but he remembered that look of utter desolation he had glimpsed on her face and the hostile words withered in his throat. They finished the meal in silence; Paula's expression ruled out all small talk.

Getting up from the table, she asked in a casual voice, " Are you coming home this evening?"

" No."

" You don't come home very often any more," she said. She smiled sadly and added, " Is that part of your new friendship plan?"

He hesitated. " I suppose you can call it that."

She studied him intensely for a long moment and then said

slowly, " I told you I've now learned to love you with complete generosity, with an absolute respect for your freedom. That means I require no explanation of you: you can sleep with other women without telling me and not feel the least bit guilty. I'm becoming more and more indifferent to whatever is routine and commonplace in your life."

" But I've nothing to hide from you," he said uneasily.

" What I'm trying to tell you," she continued gravely, " is that you needn't have any scruples; no matter what you do, you can always come home to sleep without considering yourself unworthy of us. I'll be expecting you to-night."

" All right!" Henri thought. " She's asking for it!" Aloud, he said, " Listen, Paula, I'm going to speak to you very frankly. I don't think we should sleep together any more. You who are so attached to our past, you know what beautiful nights we once had; let's not spoil the memory of them. We just don't have enough desire for each other any more."

" You have no desire for me any more?" Paula asked incredulously.

" Not enough," he replied. " Nor you for me," he added. " And don't tell me you do; I have a memory too, you know."

" But you're wrong!" Paula said. " You're tragically wrong! It's all a horrible misunderstanding! I haven't changed at all!"

He knew she was lying, and no doubt to herself as much as to him. " In any case, I've changed," he said gently. " Maybe it's different with a woman, but it's impossible for a man to desire the same body indefinitely. You're as beautiful as ever, but you've become too familiar to me."

His eyes anxiously sought Paula's, and he tried to smile at her. She wasn't crying; she looked paralysed with horror. With a great effort, she managed to murmur, " You're not going to sleep here any more? Is that what you're trying to tell me?"

" Yes, but it really won't make that much difference . . ."

She cut him off with a gesture. She accepted only the lies she herself contrived; it was no less difficult to soften the truth for her than to force it upon her.

" Go away," she said without anger. " Go away," she repeated. " I've got to be alone."

" Let me explain . . ."

"Please!" she said. "Go away!"

He stood up. "As you like. But I'll be back to-morrow and we'll talk it over," he said.

She didn't answer. He closed the door behind him and stood on the landing for a moment, listening for the sound of a sob, a fall, a movement. But there was only silence. Going down the stairs, Henri thought of those dogs whose vocal cords are severed before they're subjected to the tortures of vivisection. Not a sign in the world of their suffering; it would be far less intolerable to hear them howling.

They didn't discuss it the next day, nor the following days; Paula pretended to have forgotten their conversation and Henri had no desire to bring it up again. "Sooner or later, I'll have to tell her about Josette. But not just now," he said to himself. He spent every night in the pale-green room, and they were very passionate nights; but when he got up the following morning, Josette never tried to keep him there. The day of the contract signing, they had agreed to stay together until late in the afternoon. It was she who left him at two o'clock to go to the hairdresser. Was it discretion? Indifference? It isn't easy to measure the feelings of a woman lavish with her body, but who has nothing else to offer. "And I? Am I going to become attached to her?" he wondered, absent-mindedly window shopping along the Faubourg St. Honoré. It was too early to go to the paper and he didn't know what to do with himself. He decided finally to drop in at the Bar Rouge. He always used to go there whenever he had a few moments to kill, but it had been months now since he last set foot in the place. Nothing had changed; Vincent, Lachaume, and Sézenac were sitting at their usual table. Sézenac still had the same sleepy look.

"It's a pleasure to see you!" Lachaume said, smiling broadly. "Have you deserted the neighbourhood?"

"More or less." Henri sat down and ordered coffee. "I've been wanting to see you, too, but not just for the pleasure of it," he said with a half smile. "It was rather to tell you that I think it was disgusting to have let that article on Dubreuilh go through last month."

Lachaume's face darkened. "Yes, Vincent told me you were against it. But what exactly were you opposed to? After all, a lot of the things Ficot said are true, aren't they?"

"No! That portrait as a whole is so completely false that

not a single detail is true. Dubreuilh an enemy of the working classes! Come now, don't you remember? Just one year ago, at this same table, you were telling me that we had to work together shoulder to shoulder, you, your pals, Dubreuilh, and I. And then you go and publish that filth!"

Lachaume looked at him reprovingly. " *L'Enclume's* never printed anything against you."

" It'll happen!" Henri said.

" You know damned well it won't."

" Why attack Dubreuilh in that way, and at this time?" Henri asked. " Your other publications have been more or less kind to him. And then all of a sudden, for no reason, in connection with a series of articles which weren't even political, you proceed to insult him viciously!"

Lachaume hesitated. " You're right," he said. " The moment was poorly chosen, and I realise Ficot went a little too far. But you've got to understand! The old chap's beginning to give us a pain with his lousy humanism. Politically, the S.R.L. doesn't bother us much. But as a theoretician, Dubreuilh has a glib tongue; there's a chance he might influence the young people. And what's he offering them? The reconciling of Marxism with the old bourgeois values! You've got to admit that that isn't what we need to-day! The thing to do with bourgeois values is to liquidate them."

" Dubreuilh is defending something quite different from bourgeois values," Henri said.

" That's what he claims. But that's precisely wherein the hoax lies."

Henri shrugged his shoulders. " I don't agree with you," he said. " But in any case, why didn't you say what you just told me instead of depicting Dubreuilh as a watchdog of the bourgeoisie?"

" If you want to make yourself understood, you've got to simplify," Lachaume replied.

" Come now! *L'Enclume* addresses itself to intellectuals, and they'd have understood perfectly," Henri said irritably.

" Look, I didn't write the article," Lachaume replied.

" But you accepted it."

Lachaume's voice took on an apologetic note. " Do you think I do what I want to? I just finished telling you that I thought the moment was poorly chosen and that in my opinion Ficot went too far. As for me, I believe we ought to discuss things with a fellow like Dubreuilh instead of insulting him. If we had our own magazine, my friends and I, that's what we'd have done."

"A magazine in which you could have spoken up freely," Henri said with a smile. "There's no chance of it any more?"

"No."

There was a brief silence; Henri studied Lachaume. "I know what discipline means. But, nevertheless, doesn't it bother you to stay on *L'Eclume* when you disagree with them?"

"I think it's better that I be there rather than someone else," Lachaume replied. "I'll stay on as long as they let me."

"You think they might not let you?"

"You know, the C.P. isn't the S.R.L.," Lachaume replied. "When you've got two opposing factions, the losers very easily become suspect."

There was so much bitterness in his voice that Henri said, "And you're the man who was urging me to join the C.P! It looks to me as if you might be quitting it soon yourself."

"I know some people who'd like nothing better! They're a nice basket of vipers, the intellectuals in the party!" Lachaume shook his head. "But I'll never quit. There are times when I've really felt like it," he added. "I'm not a saint. But you learn how to take it."

"I have a feeling I'd never be able to learn," Henri said.

"That's what you say now," Lachaume replied. "But if you were convinced that, in the main, it was the party that had the right idea, you wouldn't attach much importance to your little personal problems when you weighed them against the big things that are involved. You understand," he continued animatedly, "there's one thing I'm sure of: the Communists are the only ones who are doing useful work. So look down at me if you like, but I'd swallow anything rather than quit."

"Oh, I understand you," Henri said. To himself he thought, "Which one of us, after all, is being completely honest? I belong to the S.R.L. because I approve of its line, but I choose to ignore the fact that it will very likely never amount to anything. Lachaume's primary concern is with effectiveness, and so he accepts methods he disapproves of.

No one puts his whole being into each of his acts; the very nature of action prevents it."

He stood up. " I'm going over to the paper."

" So am I," Vincent said.

Sézenac started to rise. " I'll walk over with you."

" No, there's something I want to talk to Perron about," Vincent said nonchalantly.

When they got outside the bar, Henri asked, "What's Sézenac doing these days?"

" Not much. He says he's translating, but nobody knows what. He holes up with friends and eats whatever he can scrounge. Just now he's sleeping at my place."

" Be careful," Henri said.

" Of what?"

" Drug addicts are dangerous," Henri replied. " They'd squeal on their own mothers."

" I'm not crazy," Vincent said. " He's never known anything about anything. I rather like him," he added. " With Sézenac, there's no compromise—it's despair in its purest form."

They walked down the street in silence, and Henri asked, " Did you really have something to talk to me about?"

" Yes." Vincent sought Henri's eyes. " Is there any truth to the story that's going the rounds: that your play's going to open in October at Studio 46, and that the little Belhomme girl is going to star in it?"

" I'm signing to-night with Vernon. Why do you ask?"

" I suppose you didn't know that Mother Belhomme had her head shaven—and she had it coming to her. She's got a château in Normandy where she entertained lots of German officers. She used to sleep with them, and very likely the daughter did, too."

" Why do you come to me with such gossip?" Henri asked. " Since when are you acting the informer? And do you think I like to hear that sort of stuff?"

" It isn't gossip. There's a file on them, and I have friends who saw it—letters, snapshots. This guy collected the stuff thinking it might come in handy some day."

" Did you see it?"

" No."

" Of course not. In any case, I don't give a damn," Henri said indignantly. " It's none of my business."

" Stopping the bastards from taking over the country again, refusing to get involved with them—that's everybody's business."

" Go and recite your piece somewhere else."

" Listen," Vincent said, " don't get angry. I just wanted to warn you that Mother Belhomme is being watched; they've got their eye on her. It'd be stupid of you to get yourself involved in a mess because of that bitch."

" Don't worry about me," Henri said.

" All right," Vincent said. " I just wanted to warn you, that's all."

They walked the rest of the way in silence.

But a voice settled in Henri's breast and kept repeating, " The daughter did, too." And all through the afternoon, it kept repeating that refrain. Josette had practically admitted her mother had sold her, and more than once; and besides, all that Henri wanted of her was a few more nights, and perhaps another few. Still, throughout that interminable dinner, while he watched her smiling at Vernon with a sleepy acquiescence, he felt to the point of anguish the desire to be alone with her, and to question her.

" Well, are you happy now that it's signed?" Lucie asked.

Her gown and jewels clung so tightly to her skin that they almost seemed a part of her; she gave the impression that she was born in, slept in, and would die in a gown with an Amaryllis label. A golden lock rippled in her black hair, and Henri stared at it, fascinated. How would that face look beneath a shaven skull?

" I'm very happy," he replied.

" Dudule will tell you that when I take a thing in hand you can rest easy."

" Oh, she's an extraordinary woman," Dudule said calmly.

Claudie had told Henri that Dudule, Lucie's official lover, was a generous, honourable man. Actually, beneath his silvery hair, he had the sort of upright, relaxed face one encounters only among out-and-out rogues, those who are rich enough to buy their very consciences. Besides, perhaps he was honest, according to his own code.

" You'll tell Paula for me that it was horrid of her not to have come!" Lucie said.

" She was really much too tired," Henri said.

The women were all dressed in black, offset by sparkling

jewels; Josette, too, was in black, looking almost crushed
by the mass of her hair. He got up to leave and,
with a smile of studied politeness, she held out her hand to
him. During the whole evening, not the slightest glance or
movement had given the lie to her apparent indifference to
him. Did hypocrisy come so easy to her? At night, in her
nakedness, she was so simple, so frank, so innocent. In a
confused jumble of pity, tenderness and horror, Henri wondered if there were snapshots of her, too, in the file.

For the past several days, the taxis had been operating
freely again. There were three of them stationed at the Place
de la Muette and Henri took one to go up to Montmartre.
He had just ordered a whisky when Josette arrived. She dropped into a deep arm-chair beside him. " Vernon was wonderful," she said. " And he won't bother me! He's a homo,
you know. I'm really lucky!"

" What do you do when men start bothering you?"

" That depends. Sometimes it's very difficult."

" Did the Germans bother you much during the war?"
Henri asked, trying to make his voice sound natural.

" The Germans?" She blushed as once before he had seen
her blush, from the rise of her breasts to the roots of her hair.
" What makes you ask me that? What have they been telling
you?"

" That your mother entertained Germans in her château
in Normandy."

" The château was occupied; that wasn't our fault. Yes, I
know, the people in the village spread a lot of rumours because
they hate Mother. She had it coming to her, too; she really
isn't a very nice person. But she didn't do anything rotten;
she always kept the Germans at a distance."

Henri smiled. " And if things had been different you
wouldn't tell me, of course."

" Oh, why do you say that?" she asked. She looked at him
with a tragic pout and a mist veiled her eyes. The power he
held over that beautiful face frightened him a little.

" Your mother had her business to keep going and she isn't
exactly overburdened with scruples. In fact, she might even
have tried to make use of you."

" What are you getting at?" she asked, terrorised.

" Maybe you were a little careless, maybe you went out
with a few officers, for example."

"I was polite with them and nothing more. I spoke to them, and sometimes they took me home from the village in their cars." Josette shrugged her shoulders. "I really had nothing against them, you know. They were very correct and I was young; I didn't know what the war was all about. All I wanted was for it to be over. But," she added very quickly, "now I know how horrible they were, with those concentration camps and all."

"You don't know very much, but that doesn't matter," Henri said tenderly. In '43 she wasn't as young as all that; Nadine was only seventeen then. But you couldn't compare them: Josette had been raised badly, loved badly; no one had ever explained anything to her. She had smiled a little too amiably at the German officers when she passed them on the streets of the village, had got into their cars. And that was enough to shock the population—after the events. Was there more to it? Was she lying? She was at once so open and so hypocritical. How could he know? "And by what right?" he thought with sudden disgust. He was ashamed at having played the detective.

"Do you believe me?" she asked timidly.

"I believe you." He pulled her to him. "Let's not talk about all that any more," he said. "Let's not talk about anything. Let's go to your flat. Let's go there now."

Monsieur Lambert's trial took place in Lille at the end of May. His son's testimony probably helped, and in addition strong pressures must have been brought to bear. He was acquitted. "It'll make Lambert feel better," Henri thought when he heard the verdict. Four days later, Lambert was working at the paper when he received a call from Lille: his father, who was to arrive in Paris that evening on the express, had fallen from a door of the train; his condition was very serious. In fact, it was learned an hour later that he had been instantaneously killed. Lambert got on his motor-cycle without uttering a word, and when he returned to Paris after the funeral he shut himself up in his flat without giving any sign of life.

"I must go and see him," Henri said to himself after several days of silence. "I'll go this afternoon." He had tried in vain to call him up; Lambert must have disconnected the telephone. "A terrible blow," Henri repeated to himself while

looking doubtfully at the papers spread on his desk. He was
an old man and not very engaging, and Lambert had more
pity for him than affection ; nevertheless, Henri found himself unable to be casual about the matter. What a strange
prank of fate! That verdict. And then the accident. He tried
to concentrate on the typewritten pages.

"Noon already! Josette'll be here any minute and I won't
be through reading this report," he said to himself remorsefully. Karaganda, Tsarskoe, Uzbek—he couldn't bring those
barbaric names, those figures, to life. And yet it certainly
would have been desirable if he had familiarised himself with
the report before the afternoon meeting. The truth of the
matter was that he couldn't take any real interest in it, because
he didn't really believe it. What faith could be put in a document submitted by Scriassine? Did that mysterious Soviet
functionary, who had escaped from the Red hell for the express purpose of divulging that information, really exist?
Samazelle said it was true, claimed even to have identified the
man. Nevertheless, Henri remained sceptical. He turned a
page.

"Peekaboo!"

It was Josette, wrapped in a large white coat, her magnificent hair tumbling over her shoulders. Before she had a
chance to close the door, Henri was up and had her in his
arms. Usually, no sooner did he kiss her than he found himself transported into a miniature world, among gossamer play-
things. To-day, however, the metamorphosis was a little more
difficult to accomplish ; he was unable to shake off the anxiety
that had been troubling him all morning.

"So this is where you live!" she said gaily. "Now I know
why you never invited me here. It's horrible! But where do
you keep your books?"

"I don't have any. Once I've read a book, I lend it to
friends who never return it."

"I always thought writers lived between walls covered from
floor to ceiling with books." She looked at him suspiciously.
"Are you sure you're a real writer?"

He burst out laughing. "In any case, I write."

"Were you working? Am I too early?" she asked, sitting
down.

"Give me five more minutes and then I'll be all yours," he
said. "Would you like to look at the papers?"

She made a little grimace. " Anything sensational?"

" I thought you'd started reading political articles," he said reprovingly. " Is that all done with?"

" It's not my fault. I tried," Josette said, " but the sentences just sort of flit by under my eyes. I get the feeling that all that just doesn't concern me," she added with an unhappy look.

" Well, have fun with the story about the chap who hanged himself in Pontoise," he said.

Norilsk, Igarka, Absagachev. The names, the figures remained lifeless. For him as well, the sentences flitted by under his eyes; he, too, had the feeling that all that didn't concern him. It was all happening so far away, in a world so different, so difficult to judge.

" Do you have a cigarette?" Josette asked almost in a whisper.

" Yes."

" And matches?"

" Catch. Why are you whispering?"

" So as not to disturb you."

He stood up, laughing. " I'm finished. Where will I take you for lunch?"

" To the Iles Borromées," she replied firmly.

" That ultra-swank place that just opened? No, thanks; think of somewhere else."

" But . . . but I've already reserved a table," she said.

" It's easy to unreserve it," he said, reaching for the telephone. She stopped his hand.

" But they're expecting us."

" Who?"

She lowered her head, and he repeated, " Who's expecting us?"

" It's Mother's idea; she says I have to get started on a publicity build-up right away. The Iles is the place everyone's talking about now, so she asked some reporters to do a little picture-interview of us there. You know the kind: author-conferring-with-his-interpreter."

" No, my dear," Henri said. " Have yourself photographed as much as you like, but without me."

" Henri!" Josette's eyes were suddenly full of tears; she wept with such infantile ease that it overwhelmed him. " I had this dress made just for this luncheon. I was so pleased . . ."

"There are a lot of other nice restaurants, places where we'd be by ourselves."

"But they're expecting me!" she said in despair. She looked at him with her big, moist eyes. "After all, you could do something for me."

"But, my love, what do you do for me?"

"Me? I . . . I . . ."

"Yes, you . . ." he said gaily. "And I, too, I . . ."

She didn't laugh. "It isn't the same," she said gravely. "I'm a woman."

He laughed again and thought, "She's right, she's a thousand times right—it isn't really the same."

"Are you really so set on this luncheon?" he asked.

"You don't understand! It's necessary for my career. If you want to succeed, you've got to be seen and be talked about."

"Most of all, though, when you do something you've got to do it well. Act your part well and they'll talk about you."

"I want to give myself every possible chance," Josette said. Her face hardened. "Do you think it's fun having to beg from Mother? And when I walk into those salons, do you think it's fun when she says to me in front of everybody, 'Why are you wearing those horrid clogs?'"

"What's wrong with those shoes? They're very pretty."

"Oh, they're all right for lunching in the country, but much too sporty for the city."

"I've always found you very elegant."

"Because you don't know anything about it, my dear," she said sadly. She shrugged her shoulders. "You have no idea what it's like, the life of a woman who hasn't got there."

He placed his hand on her soft hands. "You'll get there," he said. "Let's go have our pictures taken at the Iles Borromées."

They went down the stairs, and she asked, "Do you have the car?"

"No, we'll take a cab."

"Haven't you noticed yet that I don't have any money? Don't you think you'd have the most beautiful shoes in all Paris if I did?"

"But why don't you have any money?" she asked after they had got into the cab. "You're much smarter than Mother, or Dudule. Don't you like money?"

" Everybody likes it, but to really have a lot of it you've got to like it more than anything else."

Josette thought for a moment. " It isn't that I like money more than everything else, but I like the things you can buy with it."

He put his arms around her shoulders. " Maybe my play will make us rich. Then we'll buy you all the things you'd like."

" And you'll take me to smart restaurants?"

" Occasionally," he said gaily.

But as he walked through the flowering garden, he felt ill at ease under the eyes of those too elaborately dressed women and those men with their smooth, polished faces. The rose bushes, the old linden tree, the cheerfulness of the pond, sparkling in the sun, all that vernal beauty left him cold. " What in the hell am I doing here, anyhow?" he asked himself.

" It's pretty, isn't it?" Josette said fervently. " I love the country," she added. A broad smile transfigured her usually resigned face, and Henri, too, smiled.

" Yes, very pretty. What would you like to eat?"

" I think I'll have grapefruit and something from the grill," Josette replied regretfully. " I've got to watch my weight."

She looked very young in her green linen dress which revealed her firm, satin-like arms ; fundamentally, under that mask of worldly sophistication, how very natural she was! It was no more than normal that she wanted to succeed, to be seen, to dress well, to have fun ; and she had the great merit of truthfully admitting her desires without worrying about whether they were noble or sordid. Even when she lied, she was more truthful than Paula, who never lied ; there was a strong touch of hypocrisy in that code of the sublime Paula had developed. Henri pictured the haughty mask she'd have put on in face of all that easy luxury, and Dubreuilh's astonished smile, Anne's shocked expression. When those pictures and that interview appeared in print, they would all shake their heads in dismay.

" It's true that we all have a little bit of the puritan in us," he thought. " Myself included. Because we hate it when our privileges are thrust in our faces." He wanted to avoid that luncheon so that he wouldn't have to admit to himself that he could afford it. " And yet when I'm at the Bar Rouge with the boys, I never count what I throw away in a single night."

He leaned towards Josette. " Are you happy?"

" Oh, you're so nice!" she said. " You're everything."

A man would have to be stupid to sacrifice a smile like that for the sake of childish taboos. Poor Josette! She didn't often have a chance to smile. " Women aren't cheerful by nature," he thought, studying her. His affair with Paula was ending shabbily and, as for Nadine, he had been unable to give her anything. But Josette . . . well, Josette would be different. She wanted to get somewhere; he would see to it that she did. He smiled at the two reporters who were heading towards them.

Two hours later, as he was stepping from a cab in front of Lambert's house, he saw Nadine coming out the main entrance. She smiled at him cordially; she believed she had played the better part in their affair and was always quite friendly towards him. " Well, well! You too! How they do flock around the dear little orphan!"

Henri looked at her, slightly shocked. " I don't think this thing's particularly funny," he said.

" Why should he give a damn about the fact that that old bastard is dead?" Nadine said. She shrugged her shoulders. " Oh, I know the part I should be playing—nurse and comforter, and all that. But I just can't. I was filthy with good resolutions to-day—and then Volange swaggers in. I got out fast."

" Volange is upstairs?"

" Naturally. Lambert's been seeing a lot of him lately," she replied. Henri couldn't make up his mind if he detected a false note in the offhand way she said it.

" I'm going up anyhow," Henri said.

" Have fun!"

He slowly climbed the stairs. Lambert had been seeing a lot of Volange; why hadn't he told him? " He's afraid it might annoy me," Henri thought. The fact was that it did annoy him. He rang the bell. Lambert smiled at him dispiritedly.

" Oh, it's you. Nice of you . . ." he said.

" What a happy coincidence," Louis said. " We haven't seen each other for months!"

"It has been months," Henri said. He turned towards Lambert. He was very much the orphan in his flannel suit with black crepe sewed to the lapels, a suit whose classic elegance Monsieur Lambert would certainly have approved of. "I don't suppose you feel very much like going out these days," he said, "but there's an important meeting this afternoon at Dubreuilh's. *L'Espoir* is involved and we'll have to make some decisions. I'd appreciate it if you would come along with me."

Actually, he did not need Lambert, but he wanted to tear him away from his brooding.

"I've got other things on my mind," Lambert replied. He threw himself into an arm-chair and said darkly, "Volange is sure that my father's death wasn't accidental. He was murdered."

Henri was startled. "Murdered?"

"Doors don't open all by themselves," Lambert said. "And I can't imagine him committing suicide just after he'd been acquitted."

"Don't you remember the Molinari 'accident,' between Lyon and Valence?" Louis asked. "And Péral? They also fell from trains a short time after their acquittal."

"Your father was old, tired," Henri said. "The strain of the trial might have gone to his head."

Lambert shook his head. "I'll find out who did it!" he said. "I'll find out!"

Henri suddenly clenched his hands; that's what had been bothering him all week, that suspicion. "No!" he pleaded silently. "Not Vincent! Not him or anyone else!" Molinari, Péral—he didn't give a damn about them. And maybe old Monsieur Lambert was as much of a bastard as they. But in his mind he saw too clearly that face which had bled on the gravel alongside the tracks, a yellow face brightened by eyes of an astonishing blue. It had to be an accident.

"There are gangs of killers roaming France; that is a known fact," Louis said, getting up. "How horrible it is, all those hates which refuse to die!" There was a brief silence, and then he said engagingly, "Come and have dinner with us one evening. We never see each other any more; it's too silly. There are so many things I want to talk to you about."

"As soon as I have a little time," Henri said vaguely.

When the door had closed behind him Henri asked. "Was it very hard to take, those three days in Lille?"

Lambert shrugged his shoulders. "It seems it isn't manly to be shaken up when your father's murdered," he replied in a voice heavy with bitterness. "That's too bad. I admit quite frankly that it hit me pretty hard!"

"I understand," Henri said. He smiled. "That's women's nonsense, all that stuff about manliness."

What exactly had been Lambert's feelings about his father? He would admit only to pity; he let you suspect bitterness; no doubt there were also added admiration, disgust, respect, and unrequited tenderness. In any case, that man had meant something to him.

As warmly as he could, Henri said, "Don't stay here in your corner like this, eating yourself up. Make an effort and come along with me. You'll find it interesting, and you'll be doing me a favour."

"Why?" Lambert asked. "You've got my vote."

"I'd like your opinion, too," Henri said. "Scriassine claims a high-ranking Soviet functionary, who recently escaped from Russia, has brought him some sensational information—devastating for the régime, of course. He suggested to Samazelle that L'Espoir, Vigilance, and the S.R.L. help make these facts known. But how valid are they? I've been studying them, but I have no way of evaluating them."

Lambert's face lit up. "Ah! that! That interests me!" he said. He got up abruptly. "That interests me a lot!"

When they walked into Dubreuilh's study, they found him alone with Samazelle.

"There's one thing you can be sure of," Samazelle was saying. "It would be a sensational scoop to be the first to publish these facts. The last Five-Year Plan started last March, and we still know practically nothing about it. The question of the labour camps, especially, is going to upset public opinion. Of course, the matter had already been raised even before the war—the group I belonged to was particularly concerned with it—but in those days we weren't able to create much of a stir. To-day everyone finds himself forced to take a stand in connection with the Russian problem, and here we are in a position to throw new light on it."

Dubreuilh's voice seemed small and timid after that powerful basso profundo. " A priori, evidence of this kind is doubly suspect," he said. " First, because the accuser managed for so long to put up with the régime he's denouncing ; secondly, because once he's made the break, you can hardly expect him to be moderate in his attacks."

" What exactly is known about him?" Henri asked.

" His name's George Peltov," Samazelle replied. " He was head of the Tebriuka Agricultural Institute. And a month ago he fled from the Russian Zone of Germany to the Western Zone. His identity has been established beyond any doubt."

" But not his character," Dubreuilh said.

Samazelle gestured impatiently. " In any case, you've studied the report Scriassine turned over to us. The Russians themselves admit the existence of the camps and of administrative internment."

" Granted," Dubreuilh replied. " But how many men in those camps? That's the whole question."

" When I was in Germany last year," Lambert said, " rumour had it that there had never been as many prisoners in Buchenwald as since the Russian liberation."

" Fifteen million seems to me a very conservative estimate," Samazelle said.

" Fifteen million ! " Lambert repeated.

A feeling of panic gripped Henri's throat. He had heard talk about those camps before, but only vaguely, and he had never given it a second thought. You hear so many things ! As for that report, he had thumbed through it without conviction ; he was suspicious of Scriassine, and on paper the figures had seemed to him as invented as the baroque-sounding names. But now it seemed that this Russian functionary actually existed, and that Dubreuilh was taking the matter seriously. Ignorance is quite comforting, but it doesn't give you a very clear factual picture. He had been at the Iles Borromées with Josette ; it was a beautiful day and his few little pangs of conscience were easily disposed of. And during that time, in every corner of the earth, men were being exploited, starved, murdered.

Scriassine entered the room hurriedly and everyone's eyes turned towards the stranger who was following him. His hair was silver and black ; his eyes, two hard, gleaming chunks of coal ; his face, stolid, unsmiling, unmoving like the face of a man blind from birth. Above the thin, sharp bridge of his

nose, his coal-black eyebrows joined together. He was tall
and impeccably dressed.

"This is my friend George," Scriassine said. "For the time
being we'll stick to that name." He looked around him. "Is
this place absolutely safe? No chance of our conversation
being overheard? Who lives upstairs?"

"A very inoffensive piano teacher," Dubreuilh replied.
"And the people below are on holiday."

It was the first time Henri didn't think of smiling at
Scriassine's weighty airs ; that tall, dark silhouette at his side
lent a disquieting solemnity to the scene. Everyone sat down,
and Scriassine said, "George can speak either Russian or
German. He has certain documents with him which he'll sum-
marise and comment upon. Of all the questions on which he's
in a position to throw a terrifying new light, the question of
the labour camps is the one of the greatest immediate importance. He'll begin with that."

"Let him speak in German ; I'll do the translating,"
Lambert said spiritedly.

"As you wish." Scriassine said a few words in Russian, and
George nodded his head without disturbing his mask ; he
seemed paralysed by a painful, indelible bitterness. Suddenly,
he began to speak. His eyes remained fixed, directed within
himself towards visions which were not of this world, but from
his lifeless mouth came a vivid, impassioned voice, now dry
and sharp, now full of emotion. Lambert's eyes were riveted
to his lips, as if he were trying to decipher the words of a deaf
mute.

"He says that we must understand, first of all, that the
existence of the labour camps isn't a casual phenomenon, and
that therefore we can't entertain any hope of their eventual
abolition," Lambert said. "The programme of the Soviet
State requires surpluses which can only be furnished by
excessively hard labour. But if the consumption of free
workers falls below a certain level, their productivity drops
accordingly. Therefore, the State resorted to the systematic
creation of a sub-proletariat receiving only absolutely minimal
sustenance in exchange for a maximum amount of labour.
Such a system is possible only when concentration camp
methods are brought into play."

A deathly silence had fallen over the room ; no one moved.
George began speaking again and Lambert turned the tragic

voice into understandable words. "Corrective labour has
existed ever since the beginning of the régime, but it was in
1934 that the NKVD was invested with the right to impose
sentences of internment in labour camps for periods not ex-
ceeding five years, on the basis of a simple administrative
order. For longer sentences, a preliminary trial is necessary.
The camps were partially emptied between '40 and '45 ; many
of the prisoners were incorporated into the army, others died
of famine. But for the past year, they've been filling up
again."

George now pointed to names and figures on the papers
spread out before him and Lambert recited them in French.
Karaganda, Tsarskoe, Uzbek. They were no longer merely
words ; they were stretches of the frozen Russian steppe,
swamps, miserable barracks where men and women worked
fourteen hours a day for a pound of bread. They died of the
cold, of scurvy, of dysentery, of exhaustion. As soon as they
became too weak to work, they were carted off to hospitals
where they were systematically starved to death. "But is it
true?" Henri asked himself in disgust. George was suspect,
Russia was so far away, and you hear so many things!

He looked at Dubreuilh, whose wooden face expressed
nothing.

Dubreuilh had chosen to doubt ; doubt is the first line of
defence, but you mustn't put your trust in that, either. Some
of the things you hear are true. In '38, Henri had doubted
that war would come to-morrow ; in '40, he had doubted the
gas chambers. Certainly, George was exaggerating, but it was
just as certain that he hadn't invented the whole thing. Henri
opened the thick report on his knees ; everything he had read
absently a few hours earlier suddenly took on a terrifying
meaning. There they were, translated into English, official
documents admitting the existence of the camps. And you
couldn't honestly challenge all that evidence, coming in part
from American observers, in part from deportees, delivered to
the Nazis and later found in prisons. It was impossible to
deny : in Russia, too, men were working other men to
death!

When George finished, there was a long silence.

"You have accepted—with the natural masochism of intellectuals—the idea of a dictatorship of the mind," Scriassine

said. " But these organised crimes against men, against all men, can you endorse that?"

" It seems to me there's no doubt about the answer," Samazelle replied.

" Excuse me, but for me there is a doubt," Dubreuilh said sharply. " I don't know why your friend escaped, nor why he collaborated for so long with the régime he's now denouncing before us ; I imagine his reasons are excellent. But I don't want to risk lending my hand to an anti-Soviet manœuvre. Besides, we're unable now to answer you in the name of the S.R.L. ; only half of the Committee is present."

" If we here agree, our decision will surely carry," Samazelle said.

" How can you hesitate?" Lambert's eyes blazed with indignation. " If only a fourth of what he says is true, it should be shouted immediately from every rooftop, through thousands of loud speakers. You have no idea what a concentration camp is like! Whether it be Russian or Nazi, it's all the same. We didn't fight the Nazis to encourage the Russians."

Dubreuilh shrugged his shoulders. " In any case, it isn't up to us to modify the Russian régime, but only to act, to-day, in France, on the idea we have of Russia."

" That's just why this thing is of direct concern to us," Lambert said.

" Granted. But it would be criminal of us to do anything without sufficient information," Dubreuilh replied.

" In other words, you doubt what George says?" Scriassine asked.

" I don't accept his word as gospel."

Scriassine slammed his hand down on the report lying on the desk. " And what about all this?"

Dubreuilh shook his head. " I don't believe a single fact has been genuinely established."

Scriassine began speaking volubly in Russian ; George answered him in an impassive voice.

" George says he'll undertake to furnish you with definite proof. Send someone to West Germany ; he has friends there who'll give you precise information on the camps in the Soviet Zone. And furthermore, documents transmitted by Russia after the Nazi-Soviet Pact were found in the archives of the Reich. They contain some very revealing figures."

" I'll go to Germany," Lambert said. " And right away."

Scriassine looked at him approvingly. " Look in and see me," he said. " It's a delicate mission requiring careful preparation." Scriassine turned towards Dubreuilh. " If we bring you the proof you demand, are you prepared to speak out?"

" Bring your proof and the Committee will decide," Dubreuilh replied impatiently. " At the moment all we have is gossip."

Scriassine and George stood up. " I ask all of you to keep the conversation we just had absolutely secret. George wanted to meet you personally, but you can imagine the danger he faces in a city like Paris."

Everyone nodded reassurance. George bowed stiffly and followed Scriassine without adding a word.

" I am sorry about this delay," Samazelle said. " There can be no possible doubt about the essential truth of the matter. We could proceed immediately to publish extracts from the law, and that alone would suffice to stir up public opinion."

" Stir up public opinion against Russia!" Dubreuilh said. " That's precisely what we ought to avoid, especially now!"

" But the right won't profit from such a campaign; the S.R.L. will. And it damned well needs it!" Samazelle said. " The situation has changed since the elections, and if we stubbornly continue playing both sides the S.R.L. is done for," he added vehemently. " The Communists' success is going to make a lot of hesitant people join the C.P., and a good many others, out of fear, are going to throw themselves into the arms of reaction. Nothing we can do about the former, but as for the others we can get them if we openly attack Stalinism and if we promise them the formation of a left independent of Moscow."

" A strange kind of left that would be," Dubreuilh said. " Gathering anti-Communists together on an anti-Communist platform!"

" Do you know what's going to happen?" Samazelle said in an irritated voice. " If we go on like this, in two months the S.R.L. will be nothing but a little group of intellectuals subjugated by the Communists, at once scorned and manœuvred by them."

" No one manœuvres us!" Dubreuilh said.

Henri heard those agitated voices as if they were coming to

him through a thick fog. For the moment, he didn't give a damn about the fate of the S.R.L. In what measure had George told the truth?—that was the only question. Unless the whole thing was nothing but a pack of lies, it would be impossible henceforth to think of the Soviet Union as he used to think of it. Everything had to be reconsidered. As for Dubreuilh, he wanted to reconsider nothing; he took refuge in scepticism. And Samazelle had eagerly been awaiting the opportunities to sound off against the Communists. Henri had no desire to break with the Communists, but neither did he want to lie to himself. He stood up. "The whole question boils down to knowing whether or not George was telling the truth. In the meantime we're speaking in a vacuum."

"That's exactly the way I feel," Dubreuilh said.

Lambert and Samazelle left with Henri. The door was hardly closed when Lambert grumbled, " It's true! Dubreuilh has sold out! He wants to bury the whole thing. But this time he isn't going to have his way."

"Unfortunately, the Committee always goes along with him," Samazelle said. " In fact, he *is* the S.R.L."

"But *L'Espoir* doesn't have to obey the S.R.L.!" Lambert said.

Samazelle smiled. " Ah! That's a serious question you've just raised!" In a dreamy voice, he added, " Of course, if we decided to speak out immediately, no one could stop us."

Henri looked at him with surprise. " Are you thinking of a break between *L'Espoir* and the S.R.L.? What's got into you?"

"At the rate things are going, in two months there'll no longer be an S.R.L.," Samazelle replied. " I'd like to see *L'Espoir* survive its death."

Samazelle walked off smiling his big, round smile and Henri leaned against the railing of the quay.

"I wonder what's hatching in that head of his!" he said.

" If he'd like to see *L'Espoir* become a free paper again, all I can say is that he's right," Lambert said. " In Russia, they've brought slavery back. Here, they commit murders! And they don't want us to protest!"

Henri looked at Lambert. " If Samazelle should propose a break, don't forget what you promised me: that you'd back me up, come what may."

"I won't forget it," Lambert replied. " Only I warn you:

if Dubreuilh insists on burying the thing, I'll leave the paper and sell my shares."

" Listen, nothing can be decided before the facts are established," Henri said.

" Who'll decide if they're established or not?" Lambert asked.

" The Committee."

" Dubrueilh, that is. But if he's prejudiced, he won't let himself be convinced!"

" There's prejudice also in letting yourself be convinced without proof," Henri said reproachfully.

" Don't tell me George invented all that! Don't tell me all those documents were forgeries!" Lambert said heatedly. He looked at Henri suspiciously. " You do agree that if it's the truth, it has to be told?"

" Yes," Henri replied.

" Well, all right then. I'm going to leave for Germany as soon as possible, and I promise you I won't waste my time there." He smiled. " Can I drop you off somewhere?"

" No, thanks. I feel like walking a bit," Henri replied.

He was going to Paula's for dinner and he was in no hurry to get there. He began walking slowly. Telling the truth—up to now it had never posed any serious problems. He had said yes to Lambert without hesitation; it was almost a natural reflex. But as a matter of fact, he knew neither what he should believe nor what he should do; he knew nothing at all. He was still dazed, as if he'd been hit a heavy blow on the head. Obviously, George hadn't invented everything. Maybe, even, it was true! There were camps in which fifteen million workers were being reduced to a sub-human state, but thanks to those camps Nazism had been defeated and a great country was being built, a country which held out the only hope for a thousand million sub-humans slowly dying of hunger in China and India, the only hope for millions of workers enslaved to inhuman conditions, our only hope. " Will it, too, fail us?" he wondered fearfully. He realised he had never seriously questioned it. He knew of the abuses, the imperfections of the Soviet Union; nevertheless, socialism, true socialism, the one in which justice and freedom belong to all men, would one day finish by triumphing in the Soviet Union, and through the Soviet Union. If, this evening, that certainty left him, then the whole future would sink into the shadows; nowhere else in the world could even a glimmer of hope be seen. " Is that why I'm taking refuge in doubt?" he asked himself. " Am I rejecting the evidence out of cowardice, because the air wouldn't be breathable if there were no longer a corner of the earth towards which mankind could turn with a little confidence? Or, on the other hand," he thought, " maybe I'm cheating by complacently accepting those horrifying pictures. Unable to rally to Communism, it would be a relief to hate it resolutely. If only you could be completely for, or completely against! But to be against, you've got to have other hopes to offer mankind. And it's only too evident that revolution will come about through the Soviet Union, or there'll be no revolution. And yet, if Russia has merely substituted one system of oppression for another, if she's re-established slavery, how can one have the least friendship for her? . . . Perhaps evil is everywhere," Henri said to himself. He remembered that night in a shelter in the Cévennes Mountains when he had voluptuously drowsed off in innocent delight. But if evil were everywhere, innocence didn't exist. Whatever he did, he'd be wrong: wrong if he printed a garbled truth; wrong if he hid the truth, even though it was garbled. He went down to the walk alongside the river. If evil is everywhere, there's no way out, neither for humanity nor for oneself. Would he have to come around to thinking that? He sat down and in a daze watched the water flowing by.

CHAPTER SIX

I WAS overflowing with joy and curiosity the evening we landed at La Guardia Airport; I spent the following week champing at the bit. Yes, I had a great deal to learn about the latest achievements of American psychoanalysis, and the sessions of the congress, as well as the conversations with my colleagues, were quite instructive. But I also wanted to see New York, and they prevented me from doing so with a distressing zeal. They imprisoned me in overheated hotels, air-conditioned restaurants, solemn offices, luxurious apartments, and it wasn't easy to escape them. When they took me back to my hotel after dinner, I would quickly cross the lobby and leave by another door; I would get up at dawn and stroll through the streets before the morning session. But I didn't get much out of those moments of stolen freedom; I soon realised that in America solitude doesn't pay. And when I left New York, I was apprehensive. Chicago, St. Louis, New Orleans, Philadelphia, again New York, Boston, Montreal—a wonderful tour, if only I had the means to take advantage of it. My colleagues had, of course, given me the addresses of people who would be delighted to show me their cities, but they consisted exclusively of doctors, professors, and writers, and I was dubious.

As for Chicago, the game was, in any case, lost in advance. I was to stay there only two days, and at the airport two dowagers were waiting for me. They took me to a luncheon where there were other dowagers and didn't let me out of their sight all day long. After my lecture, I ate lobster seated between two starched gentlemen, and boredom is so tiring that when I got back to the hotel I went directly to sleep.

It was anger that woke me the next morning. " It can't go on like this," I decided. I picked up the telephone. " I'm terribly sorry, please excuse me, but I've caught cold and I'm afraid I shall have to stay in bed to-day." And then I jumped joyously out of bed. But once in the street I lost some of the wind in my sails; it was extremely cold and between the streetcar tracks and the elevated I felt completely lost. It was useless walking about for hours; I would wind up nowhere. I opened my address book: Lewis Brogan, writer. Perhaps he would be better than nothing. Again I telephoned, told Brogan that I was a friend of the Bensons, who had probably written to let him know I was coming. All right, he would be in the lobby of my hotel at two in the afternoon. " I'll come by to pick you up," I said, and hung up. I hated my hotel with its smell of dollars and disinfectant, and it was a pleasure to take a cab to go some place definite, to see someone.

The cab crossed bridges and tracks, passed by warehouses, went down streets in which all the shops were Italian. It finally stopped at the corner of an alley that smelled of burned paper, damp earth, poverty; the driver pointed to a wooden porch projecting from a brick wall. " That's it." I walked alongside a fence. To my left, a saloon decorated with a red, unlit neon sign: " Schlitz "; to the right, on a large billboard, the ideal American family smilingly sniffing a bowl of hot cereal. A garbage pail was smoking at the foot of a wooden stairway. I climbed the stairs. On the porch, I found a windowed door on the inside of which hung a yellow shade; that was probably it. But suddenly I felt nervous. Wealth always has something public about it, but the life of the poor is an intimate thing; it somehow seemed indiscreet to knock at that windowpane. Hesitantly, I looked at the row of brick walls to which other stairways and other grey porches were monotonously tacked. Above the roof-tops, I saw an immense red-and-white cylinder: a gas tank; at my feet, in the centre of a naked square of earth, stood a black tree, and at its foot a little toy windmill with blue sails. In the distance, a train passed; the porch trembled. I knocked and there appeared at the door a rather tall, rather young man, his chest stiffened by a leather jacket. He looked at me in surprise.

" You found the house?"

" So it seems."

A black stove was crackling in the middle of a yellow kitchen; old newspapers were scattered about on the linoleum covering the floor, and I noticed there wasn't any refrigerator. With a vague gesture, Brogan pointed to the papers. " I was trying to clean up a bit."

" I hope I'm not disturbing you."

" No, not at all." He stood in front of me with an embarrassed look on his face. " Why didn't you want me to pick you up at your hotel?"

" It's a horrible place."

The trace of a smile finally appeared on Brogan's mouth. " It's the most beautiful hotel in Chicago."

" Exactly. Too many rugs, too many flowers, too many people, too much music, too much everything."

Brogan's smile crept up to his eyes. " Come on into the other room."

The first thing I saw was the Mexican blanket, and then Van Gogh's yellow chair, the books, the gramophone, the typewriter. It must have been good living in that room, a room which was neither the studio of an æsthete nor a specimen of the ideal American home. Enthusiastically, I said, " It's nice here."

" Do you think so?" Brogan's eyes questioned the walls. " It isn't very big." There was another silence, and then he said precipitately, " Don't you want to take off your coat? What would you say to a cup of coffee? I have a few French records. Would you like to hear them? Some Charles Trenet records?"

Perhaps it was because of the big, crackling stove, or the shadow of the black tree quivering on the shade golded by the cold February sun, that I thought at first, " How nice it would be to spend the day sitting on that Mexican blanket!" But the reason I had telephoned to Brogan was to inspect Chicago. Firmly, I said, " I'd like to see Chicago; I'm leaving to-morrow morning."

" Chicago's a big city."

" Show me a bit of it."

He touched his leather jacket and said in a worried voice, " Do I have to dress up?"

" Don't be silly! I hate stiff collars!"

Heatedly, he protested, " I never wore a stiff collar in my whole life."

For the first time, our smiles met, but he still didn't seem completely at ease.

" Would you like to see the slaughterhouses?"

" No. Let's just walk through the streets."

There were a great many streets and all of them looked alike; they were bordered by tired frame houses and scrubby little yards that tried to look like suburban gardens. We also went down straight bleak avenues; everywhere, it was cold. Brogan anxiously touched his ears. " They're stiff as a board; any minute now they're going to break in two."

I took pity on him. " Let's go into a bar and warm up."

We entered a bar. Brogan ordered ginger ale; I, bourbon. When we went out again, it was still just as cold. We entered another bar and began chatting. After the invasion, he had spent a few months in a prisoner-of-war camp in the Ardennes and he asked me a lot of questions about France, the war, the Occupation, Paris. I, in turn, questioned him. He seemed happy having someone listening to him but embarrassed talking about himself. He formed his sentences hesitantly and then threw them at me with such force that I felt as if I were receiving a present each time. He was born in South Chicago, the offspring of a Finnish grocer and a Hungarian Jewish mother. He was twenty when the great depression struck and for several years he lived the life of a hobo, crossing America hidden in freight cars, in turn peddler, dishwasher, waiter, masseur, ditch digger, bricklayer, salesman, and, when necessary, burglar. In some forgotten roadside lunchroom in Arizona where he earned a living washing glasses, he had written a short story which a leftist magazine accepted for publication. Then he wrote others. Ever since the success of his first novel, his publishers had been giving him an allowance which permitted him to live.

" I'd like to read that book," I said.

" The next one will be better."

" But that one is already written."

Brogan studied me, perplexed. " Do you really want to read it?"

" Yes, really."

He got up and walked over to the telephone at the other end of the room. A few minutes later he came back. " The book will be at your hotel before dinner."

" Oh! Thank you!" I said warmly.

The promptness of his gesture touched me; that's what I had immediately found so appealing about him—his spontaneity. Ready-made phrases and the ritual of etiquette were unknown to him; his thoughtfulness was pure improvisation, and it resembled the little inventions affection inspires. At first, I had found it amusing meeting in the flesh that classic American species: self-made leftist writer. Now, I began taking an interest in Brogan. Through his stories, you got the feeling that he claimed no rights on life and that nevertheless he had always had a passionate desire to live. I liked that mixture of modesty and eagerness.

" Whatever made you start writing?" I asked.

" I always liked printed paper. When I was a kid, I used to make up newspapers by pasting press clippings in note-books."

" There must have been other reasons."

He reflected. " I know a lot of different kinds of people ; what I want is to show each of them how the others really are. You hear so many lies!" He fell silent for a moment. " When I was twenty, I realised that everyone was lying to me, and it made me mad. I think that's why I started writing and why I'm still writing."

" And are you still angry?"

" More or less," he replied with a reserved little smile.

" Are you active in politics?" I asked.

" In a small way."

All in all, he was practically in the same position as Robert and Henri, but he reconciled himself to it with a calm bordering on the exotic. Writing, speaking on the radio and occasionally at meetings to denounce some abuse or other satisfied him fully. Yes, I had once been told that here intellectuals could live in security because they knew they were completely powerless.

" Do you have any friends who write?"

" Oh, no!" he replied decisively. He smiled. " I do have friends who started writing when they saw I was making money doing nothing but sitting in front of my typewriter. But they didn't become writers."

" Did they make any money?"

He burst out laughing. " One of them typed five hundred pages in a single month. He must have paid through the nose to have them printed and his wife made him stop. He went back to his old profession of pickpocket."

" Is that a good trade?" I asked.

" It depends. In Chicago, there's a lot of competition."

" Do you know many pickpockets?"

He gave me a somewhat mocking look. " Half a dozen."

" Any gangsters?"

Brogan's face became serious. " All gangsters are bastards."

He began explaining at length the rôle that gangsters had played as strike breakers during the past years. And then he told me a lot of stories about their relationship with the police, with politics, with business. He was speaking rapidly and I had a little trouble following him, but I found it as exciting as an Edward G. Robinson film. Abruptly, he stopped. " Are you hungry?" he asked.

" Yes, now that you've reminded me, I'm very hungry," I replied. " You do know a lot of stories," I added cheerfully.

" If I didn't know any, I'd make them up," he said. " For the pleasure of watching you listening to them."

It was after eight; time had passed quickly. Brogan took me to an Italian restaurant for dinner, and while eating pizza I wondered why I felt so comfortable with him. I knew almost nothing about him and yet he didn't seem at all a stranger to me. Perhaps it was because of his carefree poverty. Starch, elegance, and good manners create distances, but when Brogan opened his jacket revealing his worn sweater, when he closed it again, I felt the reassuring presence next to me of a body which could be warm or cold, a living body. He had shined his own shoes; one had only to look at them to become a part of his intimate life. When, on leaving the pizzeria, he took my arm to help me along the icy pavement, his warmth seemed to me immediately familiar.

" Let's go! I think I *will* show you a few bits of Chicago," he said.

We went to a burlesque show and watched women strip to music; we went to hear jazz in a little Negro dance hall; we had several drinks in a bar which looked like a flophouse. Brogan knew everyone; the pianist with the tattooed wrists at the burlesque house, the Negro trumpet player in the dance hall, the bums, the coloured people, and the old whores in the bar. He invited them to our table, made them talk, and looked happily at me because he saw I was enjoying myself. When we were out in the street again, I said animatedly, " Thank you for the best evening I've spent in America."

" There are a lot of other things I'd have liked to have shown you!" Brogan said.

The night was almost over, dawn would soon break, and Chicago would disappear for ever. But the steel framework of the elevated hid from us the leprous spot which began eating away at the sky. Brogan was holding my arm. Ahead of us, behind us, the black arches were repeated into infinity ; it was as if they formed a belt around the entire earth and we would be eternally walking beneath them.

" One day isn't enough," I said. " I'll have to come back."

" Come back," Brogan said, and quickly he added, " I don't want to think that I'm not going to see you again."

Silently, we walked to a hack stand. When he drew his face close to mine I couldn't keep myself from turning my head away, but I felt his breath against my mouth.

In the train a few hours later, while trying to read Brogan's novel, I chided myself severely. " It's ridiculous! At my age!" But like a virgin's my mouth still tingled. I had never kissed a man except those with whom I had slept ; and each time that shadow of a kiss flashed through my mind, it seemed as if I were going to rediscover burning remembrances of love in the deepest recesses of my memory. " I'll come back," I said to myself decisively. And then I thought, " What good would it do? We'd only have to leave each other again, and this time I wouldn't have the comfort of being able to say to myself, ' I'll come back.' No, it's better to stop right here."

I had no regrets about Chicago. I quickly realised that friendships without to-morrows, and the little anguishes of parting, were part of the pleasures of travelling. I resolutely avoided bores, saw only those who amused me. We spent afternoons taking long walks, nights drinking and talking, and then we would leave each other, never to meet again, and there were no regrets. How simple life was! No regrets, no obligations, my acts and gestures counted for nothing, no one asked my advice, and I knew no other rule but my whims. In New Orleans, after leaving a patio where I had got drunk on Daiquiris, I abruptly took a plane for Florida. At Lynch-burg, I hired a car and drove aimlessly for a whole week across Virginia's red earth. During my second stay in New York, I hardly closed my eyes ; I saw a great many people all at once and went everywhere. The Davieses asked me to go to Hartford with them and two hours later I was in their car and on my way. What a godsend it would be to live for a few days in an American country home. It was a very lovely frame house, all white and shiny, with little windows everywhere.

Myriam sculpted, the daughter took dance lessons, and the son wrote obscure poems. He was thirty, had the complexion of a child, large tragic eyes and a pert nose. The first evening while telling me of her heartbreaks, Nancy amused herself dressing me up in a long Mexican gown, and she let my hair down to my shoulders. " Why don't you always wear your hair like that?" Philip asked me. " One would think you purposely try to make yourself look older." He kept me up dancing late into the night. The following days, to please him, I continued disguising myself as a young woman. I was well aware of why he was paying me court: I came from Paris, and I was the same age as Myriam was during his adolescence. I was nevertheless quite touched. He arranged parties and invented cocktails for me, played me very pretty cowboy songs on his guitar, took me for walks through old, Puritan villages. The evening before I left we stayed in the living-room after the others, listening to records while drinking whisky, and in a disconsolate voice, he said to me, " What a pity I didn't know you better in New York. I would have loved going out with you in New York."

" Well, it might still be possible," I said. " I'll be back in New York in ten days. Do you think you might be there?"

" In any case, I can come down. Call me," he said, looking at me seriously.

We listened to a few more records, and then he accompanied me through the hall to the door of my room. I held out my hand, but in a low voice he asked, " Don't you want to kiss me?"

He took me in his arms ; for a moment, we remained motionless, cheek against cheek, paralysed by desire. And then we heard a light step and quickly drew apart. Myriam gave us a wry smile.

" Anne is leaving early ; don't keep her up too late," she said in her delicate voice.

" I was just going to bed," I said.

I didn't go to bed. I stood before my open window breathing in the odourless night air ; it was almost as if the moon froze the flowers' perfume. Myriam was asleep—or awake—in the next room and I knew Philip wouldn't come. At times I thought I heard the sound of steps, but it was only the wind walking through the trees.

Canada wasn't much fun. I was very happy when I landed

again in New York, and at once I thought, " I will telephone
to Philip." I was invited that same day to a cocktail party
where I would see most of my friends ; from my window, I
looked out upon a vast landscape of skyscrapers. But all that
was no longer enough for me. I went down to the bar of the
hotel ; in the blue-black light, a pianist was softly playing
languorous melodies, couples were whispering together, and
waiters were walking on tiptoe. I ordered a martini and lit a
cigarette ; my heart was palpitating. What I was about to do
wasn't very sensible: after a week with Philip, I surely
wouldn't be able to leave him without having serious regrets,
Well, too bad! First of all, I wanted him ; and as for the regrets, I'd have them anyhow. I already had them. The Queens-
boro Bridge, Central Park, Washington Square, the East River
—in a week, I would no longer see them either, and all in all
I'd rather miss a person than stones ; that would be far less
painful, it seemed to me. I took a sip of the martini. One
week—too short for new discoveries, too short for pleasures
without tomorrows. I no longer wanted to wander about in
New York as a tourist ; I had to live, really live, in that city.
That way, it would become a little mine and, in turn, I would
leave something of myself in it. I had to walk in the streets
holding the arm of a man who provisionally at least, would
be mine. I emptied my glass. Once during that trip a man had
held my arm. It was winter and I was finding it difficult to
walk on the icy pavement, but near him I felt warmth. " Come
back," he had said. " I don't want to think that I'm not
going to see you again." And I wouldn't go back ; I'd hold
another arm tightly against mine. For a moment I felt guilty
of treason. But there was no question about it: it was
Philip I had wanted all through a long night. I still wanted
him and he was awaiting my call. I got up, went into a telephone booth, and asked for Hartford.

" Mr. Philip Davies."

" Just a moment, I'll get him."

Suddenly, my heart began beating wildly. A moment
before, I was disposing of Philip as I pleased, was sum-
moning him to New York, was putting him in my bed. But
Philip existed in his own right, and now it was I who was
dependent upon him. I was alone, defenceless, in that narrow
cell.

" Hallo?"

"Philip? This is Anne."

"Anne! How nice it is to hear your voice!"

He spoke French with a slow perfection that suddenly seemed cruel.

"I'm calling from New York."

"I know. Dear Anne, Hartford's become so boring since you left us. Did you have a lovely trip?"

How close his voice is! It's brushing my face. But he, suddenly seems very distant; my hand is damp against the black bakelite of the receiver. Haphazardly, I throw out words. "I'd like to tell you about it. You asked me to give you a ring. Can you manage to get to New York before I leave?"

"When are you leaving?"

"Saturday."

"Oh!" he said. "Oh, so soon!" There was a brief silence. "I've got to go to Cape Cod to visit some friends this week. I promised I would."

"What a pity!"

"Yes, it is a pity! Can't you put off your departure?"

"No, I can't. Can't you put off your visit?"

"No, it's impossible," said his dismayed voice.

"Well, we'll see each other in Paris this summer," I said with polite cheerfulness. "Summer isn't far away."

"I'm so terribly sorry!"

"I'm sorry, too. Good-bye, Philip. See you this summer."

"Good-bye, dear Anne. Try to remember me a little."

I hung up the telephone, damp with sweat. My heart calmed down, and it left an emptiness under my ribs. I went to the Wilsons. There were many people there; they put a glass in my hand, smiled at me, called me by my name, clutched my arm, my shoulder, invited me left and right; I wrote down appointments in my note-book—and that emptiness in my breast was still there. I could take my body's disappointment, but that emptiness I found almost unbearable. They smiled at me and spoke to me. I spoke. I smiled. For a whole week more we would speak and smile, and then none of them would think of me again, nor I of them. This country was indeed real, I was indeed alive, and I would go away without leaving anything behind me, without taking anything with me. Between two smiles, I abruptly thought, "And suppose I went to Chicago?" I could call up Brogan this very evening and say to him, "I'm coming." If he no

longer felt like seeing me, well, he'd tell me. What difference
did it make? Two rebuffs wouldn't be worse than one. Between two other smiles, I looked inside myself and felt
ashamed: I couldn't have Philip, so I was going to throw
myself into Brogan's arms. What about those morals of a
bitch in heat? Actually, the idea of sleeping with Brogan
didn't mean much to me; I imagined him as being rather
awkward in bed. And I wasn't even sure I'd enjoy seeing him
again. I had spent only a single afternoon with him, and I
might be letting myself in for worse disappointments. No
doubt about it, the whole project was stupid. I felt like
moving about, like doing things, to mask my failure; that's
how you do really idiotic things. I decided to stay in New
York and continued noting down appointments—exhibitions,
concerts, dinners, parties. The week would pass quickly.
When I found myself out in the street again, it was midnight
on the big clock in Madison Square. Anyhow, it was too late
to call. No, it wasn't too late! It was only eleven in Chicago
and Brogan was reading in his room, or writing. I stopped
in front of the lighted window of a drugstore. *I don't want
to think that I'm not going to see you again.* I went in, got
change, and asked for Chicago.

"Lewis Brogan? This is Anne Dubreuilh."

There was no answer. "This is Anne Dubreuilh. Can you
hear me?"

"I hear you very well." Then, in a formless French, happily
stammering each syllable, he added, "*Bonjour, Anne. Comment ça va?*"

The voice wasn't as close as Philip's, but Brogan seemed less
distant.

"I can come and spend three or four days in Chicago this
week," I said. "What do you think?"

"The weather's wonderful in Chicago now."

"But if I come, it would be to see you. Do you have any
time?"

"I have all my time," he said, laughing. "My time is all
mine."

I hesitated a second; it was too easy. One said no and the
other yes, both with the same indifference. But it was too late
to retreat. "All right, then," I said. "I'll arrive to-morrow
morning on the first plane out of here. Reserve a room for me

in a hotel—and not the best one in Chicago. Where shall we meet?"

" I'll come get you at the airport."

" All right. See you to-morrow."

There was a brief silence, and then I recognised the voice which three months earlier had said to me, " Come back." It was saying, " Anne! I'll be so happy to see you again!"

" I'm happy, too. See you to-morrow."

" See you to-morrow."

It was his voice, it was really he just as I remembered him, and he hadn't forgotten me. Near him, I'd feel warmth again, like that winter. Suddenly, I was happy that Philip had answered no. It would all be so simple. We'd talk for a while in a softly lit bar and then he'd say, " Come and rest a bit at my place." We'd sit down next to each other on the Mexican blanket, I'd listen obediently to Charles Trenet, and Brogan would take me in his arms. Probably it wouldn't be a very exciting night, but I was sure that it would make him happy and that was enough for my own happiness. I went to sleep, deeply stirred by the thought that a man was waiting to hold me tightly pressed against his heart.

He wasn't waiting for me; there was no one in the waiting-room. " It's starting badly," I thought, sitting down in an arm-chair. I was completely helpless and told myself worriedly that I had not been very cautious. " Should I call Brogan, or should I not call him?" I had started by playing this game alone, and now I found myself involved in an escapade whose success no longer depended upon me only. All I could do was to watch the hands on the clock—and they did not move. This passiveness frightened me, and I tried to reassure myself. After all, if things went badly, I could always find an excuse for returning to New York to-morrow. In any event, a week from now the interlude would be ended. Securely back in my old life, I would smile indulgently at all my memories, the touching as well as the ridiculous. My anxiety subsided. Before opening my purse to find Brogan's telephone number in my address book, I had checked all the emergency exits, was guaranteed against all mishaps. When I raised my head again, he was standing in front of me; he was taking me all in, a gentle smile on his lips. I couldn't have been more stupefied if, at the other end of the world, I had met his ghost.

"*Alors? Comment ça va?*" he asked in his atrocious French.

I got up. He was thinner than I remembered him, his eyes were more alive. "*Ça va.*"

Still smiling, he drew his mouth to my lips. I was disconcerted by that public kiss which left a red smear on Brogan's chin. "Now you're all smeared," I said. I wiped off the lipstick with my handkerchief. "I got in at nine o'clock," I added.

"Oh!" he said reproachfully, and the reproach seemed directed at me. "They told me on the telephone that the first plane from New York was due at ten."

"They made a mistake."

"They never make mistakes."

"Anyhow, I'm here."

"Yes, you're here," he conceded. He sat down and I, too, sat down. Twenty minutes past nine. He had come twenty minutes late, forty minutes early. He was wearing a good-looking flannel suit and an immaculate shirt. I could imagine him standing before his mirror, eager to do me honour, unaccustomed to looking at himself, questioning his reflection with an eye now flattered, now perplexed, anxiously watching the clock. And I, treacherously, I was already waiting for him!

I smiled at him. "We aren't going to stay here all morning, are we?"

"No," he said. He thought for a moment. "Would you like to go to the zoo?"

"To the zoo?"

"It's near here."

"And what will we do there?"

"We'll look at the animals and they'll look at us."

"I didn't come here to exhibit myself to your animals." I got up. "Why don't we go to some quiet place, where I can have some coffee and a sandwich, and we'll look at each other?"

He, too, got up. "That's an idea!"

We were alone in the limousine which was taking us to the centre of the city. Brogan was holding my travelling bag on his knees; he kept silent, and again I had an anxious feeling. "Four days will be a long time with this stranger; how long! Four days will be short time to get to know him!"

"We should stop at the hotel first and leave my suitcase there," I said.

Brogan gave me an embarrassed smile.

"You did reserve a room for me?"

He continued smiling guiltily, but there was something challenging in his voice. "No!"

"You didn't! But I asked you on the telephone!"

"I didn't hear half of what you were saying," he replied, speaking rapidly. "Your English is even worse than it was last winter, and you speak like a machine gun. But it doesn't matter. We'll leave the bag in the checkroom." We got out of the car in front of the airline terminal. "Wait here for me," he said. He went through a revolving door and, suspiciously, I followed him with my eyes. That forgetfulness, was it negligence or a trick? It was probably as clear to him as it was to me that I'd spend that night in his bed, but I was overwhelmed with panic at the thought that, come evening, we might perhaps not really feel like it. I had sworn to myself that I would never again make the mistake of getting into bed with a man for whom I had no desire.

As soon as Brogan returned, I said nervously, "We've got to call up a hotel. I didn't sleep all night. I'd like to take a bath and a little nap."

"It's very hard to find a room in Chicago," he said.

"All the more reason to start looking right away."

He should have said, "Come and rest a bit at my place." But he said nothing. And the cafeteria he took me to didn't look at all like the warm, intimate bar I had imagined; it seemed more like a railroad-station restaurant. The bar we drifted into afterwards also looked like a waiting-room. Were we going to spend the whole day waiting? What were we waiting for?

"Whisky?"

"Gladly."

"Cigarette?"

"Thanks."

"I'll put a record on."

If only we could have chatted quietly, like the last time! But Brogan couldn't stay put; he went to get a bottle of Coca-Cola at the bar, put a nickel, then another in the juke box, bought cigarettes. When I finally got him to telephone, he stayed away so long that I thought he had disappeared for-

ever. I had, it would seem, been mightily mistaken in my
anticipations. It was almost as if he were purposely trying to
upset them; he barely resembled the man I remembered.
Spring had melted that stiff block into which winter had frozen
him. To be sure, he had become neither graceful nor supple,
but his bearing was almost elegant, his hair decidedly blond,
his eyes a well-defined grey-green. In that face which had
once seemed neutral to me I now saw a sensitive mouth,
slightly dilated nostrils, and a subtlety that I found disconcerting.

"I couldn't find anything," Brogan said when he sat down
next to me. "I ended up by calling the hotel association. I
have to call them back a little later."

"Thanks."

"What would you like to do now?"

"Suppose we just stayed here quietly?"

"Another whisky then?"

"All right."

"Cigarette?"

"Thanks."

"Would you like me to put on a record?"

"If you don't mind, no."

There was a silence; I attacked. "I saw your friends in
New York."

"I have no friends in New York."

"Of course you do. The Bensons, the ones who brought us
together."

"Oh, them! They're not friends."

"Well then, why were you willing to see me three months
ago?"

"Because you were French and I liked your name: Anne."
For a brief instant, he gave me a smile, but he withdrew it
immediately.

I tried again. "What have you been doing?"

"Every day I've got a day older."

"As a matter of fact, I think you look younger."

"That's because I'm wearing a summer jacket."

Again there was a long silence, and this time I gave up.
"All right. Let's go somewhere. But where?"

"Last winter you wanted to see a baseball game," he said
eagerly. "Well, there's a game going on to-day."

"All right, let's go."

It was nice of him to remember my old wishes, but he certainly might have realised that for the moment I wasn't the least bit interested in baseball. No matter. The best we could do was kill time while waiting. Waiting for what? Vacantly, I watched the strangely dressed players who were running about on the aggressively green grass, and anxiously I repeated to myself, " Kill time! When we don't have an hour to waste! Four days is so short a time ; we have to hurry. When are we finally going to meet?"

" Getting bored?" Lewis asked.

" I'm a little cold."

" Let's go somewhere else."

He took me to a bowling alley where we drank beer while watching the pins fall, and to a saloon where five mechanical pianos hammered out old dusty music one after the other, and to an aquarium where we looked at fish grimacing spitefully. We took streetcars, subways, other streetcars and other subways. I liked riding in the subways. Our foreheads pressed against the window of the first car, we were swallowed up in dizzying tunnels illuminated by pale blue bulbs. Brogan put his arm around me, and our silence was like the silence that unites confident lovers. But in the streets he kept his distance, and it made me sad to feel that we did not speak because we could find nothing to say to each other. Along about mid-afternoon I had to admit to myself that I had made an error in my calculations. In a week, to-morrow, this day would belong to the past and I'd have a chance to get over it. But first I had to live it hour by hour, and during all those hours a stranger was capriciously disposing of my fate. I was so tired and so disappointed that I wanted nothing more than to be alone.

" Please," I said, " call up once more. I really need a little sleep."

" I'll call up the hotel association again," Brogan said, opening the door of a drugstore. I remained standing, looking distractedly at the shiny covers of a row of paperbound books. He came out of the booth almost immediately, a satisfied smile on his face. " There's a room waiting for you two blocks from here."

" Ah! Thank you."

We walked in silence to the hotel. Why hadn't he lied? That surely was when he should have said, " Come and rest a bit at my place." Was he, too, unsure of his desires? I had counted on his warmth, on his initiative, to break the solitude of my body, but he left me its prisoner and I could do nothing for us.

Lewis went over to the desk. " I've just reserved a room." The clerk glanced at the register. " For two?" he asked.

" For one," I said. I wrote my name in the register. " My suitcase is at the airline terminal."

" I'll get it," Lewis said. " When do you want it?"

" Call me in two hours."

Had I dreamed it? Or had he exchanged a strange look with the clerk? Had he reserved the room for two people? But then he would have tried to find an excuse to go up with me. I could have given him twenty. His sorry tricks irritated me, and all the more so since I was only too willing to let myself be taken in by them. I ran my bath and submerged myself in the warm water, thinking how bad a start we had got off to. Was it my fault? Doubtless, there were women who would have been able to say from the beginning, " Let's go up to your place." Nadine would have said it. I lay down on the satin bedspread, closed my eyes. I was already dreading the moment when I would have to get up in that room where not even the familiarity of a toothbrush would greet me. So many different and yet indistinguishable rooms, so much opening and closing of suitcases, so many arrivals and departures, awakenings, delays, trips, flights. I was weary of existing through three months of days without to-morrows, weary of re-creating my life each morning, each evening, each hour. I wished passionately that some outer force would pin me to that bed forever. If only he would come up, knock at my door, come in! I listened for the sound of his step in the hallway with such impatience that it was like impassioned desire. Not a sound. I took refuge in sleep.

When I met Brogan in the lobby, I was calmed down. Soon, the outcome of this adventure would be decided, and in any case I would be asleep again in a few hours. We had dinner in a cozy little German restaurant, and I chatted jauntily. The bar to which we went afterward was bathed in a soft violet haze ; I felt at ease there. And Brogan was speaking to me in his old voice.

" The cab took you away," he was saying, " and I didn't

know anything about you. When I went home, I found the
New Yorker under my door, and there, right in the middle of
an article on a psychiatric congress, I find your name. As if
you had come back in the middle of the night to tell me who
you were."

" Didn't the Bensons tell you about me?"

" Oh, I never read their letters." He sounded amused as he
added, " In the article, they spoke of you as a brilliant
doctor."

" Did that surprise you?"

He smiled at me silently. When he smiled at me like that,
I seemed to feel his breath against my mouth.

" I thought they must have damned funny doctors in
France."

" When I got back to the hotel, I found your book there. I
tried to read it, but I was too tired. I read it the next day on
the train." I studied Lewis for a moment. " There's a lot of
you in Bertie, isn't there?"

" Oh, me, I'd never set fire to a farm," Brogan said ironically. " I'm much too afraid of fire and of the police." He got
up quickly. " Let's go roll the dice."

The sullen-eyed blonde seated behind the gaming table
handed us a dicebox. Brogan chose the six and bet a half
dollar. Dejectedly, I watched the little bone cubes roll across
the green felt. Why did he have to escape just when we were
beginning to find each other again? Did I also frighten him?
His face seemed to me at once very hard and very vulnerable ;
I was unable to read anything into it. " I won!" he said
happily, handing me the dicebox. I shook it violently. " I'm
playing our night," I decided in a flash. I chose the five. My
mouth was lined with parchment, my hands were damp. The
five came out seven times in the first thirteen throws, then
three more times. I had lost.

" It's a stupid game," I said, sitting down again.

" Do you like to gamble?"

" I hate to lose."

" I love poker and I always lose," Brogan said unhappily.
" It seems my face is too easy to read."

" I don't think it is," I said, looking at him defiantly. He
seemed embarrassed, but I didn't turn my eyes away. I had
played our night and I had lost it. Brogan refused to help me

and the dice had condemned me. I rebelled against that defeat with a violence that suddenly turned into courage.

" Ever since this morning," I said, " I've been asking myself if you were glad that I came. And I still don't know."

" Of course, I'm glad," he said, so earnestly that I was ashamed of the aggressive voice in which I had spoken.

" I hoped you were," I said, " because I'm happy to have found you again. This morning, I was afraid my memories had deceived me. But no, it's really you whom I remembered."

" I never doubted my memories," he said, and once again his voice was as warm as a breath.

I took his hand and spoke the words of all women trying to be tender. " I like your hands," I said.

" I like yours, too," he said. " Is that what you use to wring your poor defenceless patients' brains?"

" Let me work on yours. I think they need it."

" Oh, my brain's only half crippled."

Our hands remained entwined ; with a deep feeling of emotion, I looked at that fragile bridge thrown up between our lives, and my mouth dry, I asked myself, " Will I or won't I know those hands?"

The silence lasted a long time and then Brogan said, " Would you like to go back and hear Big Billy again?"

" I'd like it very much."

In the street, he took my arm ; I knew that at any moment he would draw me against him. The weight of that heavy day had slipped from my shoulders and I was finally walking towards peace, towards happiness. Abruptly, he dropped my arm ; a broad, unfamiliar smile lit up his face. " Teddy!"

The man and the two women stopped and smiled broadly back at him. A moment later I found myself sitting with them at a table in a dreary cafeteria ; they were all speaking very rapidly and I understood nothing of what they were saying. Brogan was laughing a great deal, his face was animated ; he seemed relieved to have escaped from our long tête-à-tête. It was only natural : these people were his friends ; they had a lot of things to talk about. What, after all, did he and I have in common? The women seated opposite him were young and pretty. Did they please him? I realised that there must certainly have been young, pretty women in his life ; but how could I experience so much anguish over that thought when we hadn't even exchanged a single real kiss? And I was suffering. Far off, very far off at the end of a tunnel, I saw one of the emergency exits that had made me feel so secure that morning. But I was much too tired to reach it, even on my knees. "What a to-do about not getting kissed!" I tried to tell myself. But cynicism didn't help. It was no longer important if I was being more or less ridiculous, worthy of my own approval or deserving of my own blame. I had no control over what was happening; bound hand and foot, I had put myself at the mercy of another. What foolishness! I no longer even knew what I had come looking for here; certainly I must have been out of my mind to imagine that a man who was nothing to me could do something for me. When we were out on the street again, and Brogan had taken my arm, I made up my mind to go right back to the hotel and go to sleep.

"I'm glad you had a chance to meet Teddy," he said, "He's the pickpocket-writer I told you about. Remember?"

"I remember. And the women, who are they?"

"I don't know them." Brogan had stopped at a corner. "If a streetcar doesn't come along, we'll take a cab."

"A cab," I thought. "It's our last chance. If the streetcar comes along, I'll give up; I'll go back to the hotel." For an infinite moment, I looked at the menacing glitter of the tracks. Brogan hailed a cab. "Get in," he said.

I didn't have time to say to myself, "Now or never." He was already pressing me to him, a furnace of flesh imprisoning my lips, a tongue was probing my mouth, and my body was rising from the dead. I staggered into the bar as Lazarus reborn must have staggered. The musicians were taking a break and Big Billy came over to our table and sat down. Brogan, his eyes beaming happily, joked with him; I wanted to share his happiness, but I was encumbered by my brand-new body: it was too large, too burning. The orchestra began playing again; vaguely, I watched the one-legged tap dancer with the shiny, plastered hair doing his number, and my hand trembled as I brought the jigger of whisky to my mouth. What would Brogan do? What would he say? For my part, I wouldn't be able to make a single move, to utter a single word. After what seemed to me a very long time, he asked in a lively voice, "Do you want to leave?"

"Yes."

" Do you want to go back to the hotel?"

In a whisper which lacerated my throat, I managed to stammer. " I don't want to leave you."

" Nor I you," he said with a smile.

In the cab, he took my mouth again, and then he asked, " Would you like to sleep at my place?"

" Of course," I said. Did he imagine I could throw away that body he had just given me? I leaned my head on his shoulder and he put his arm around me.

In the yellow kitchen, where the stove was no longer crackling, he held me fiercely against him. " Anne! Anne! It's like a dream! I've been so unhappy all day!"

" Unhappy? It's you who tortured me! You couldn't make up your mind to kiss me."

" I did kiss you and you wiped my chin with your handkerchief. I thought I was on the wrong track."

" You don't kiss in waiting-rooms! You should have brought me here."

" But you insisted on having a room at a hotel! I had everything all planned. I'd bought a big steak for dinner, and at ten o'clock I'd have said, ' It's too late to find a room.' "

" I knew that," I said. " But I'm cautious; supposing we hadn't rediscovered each other?"

" What do you mean, rediscover each other? I never lost you."

We were speaking mouth to mouth and I felt his breath on my lips. I murmured, " I was so afraid a streetcar would come."

He laughed boastfully. " I'd made up my mind to take a cab." He kissed my brow, my eyelids, my cheeks, and I felt the earth spin. " You're dead tired. You must go to bed," he said. Suddenly he looked dismayed. " Your suitcase!" he said.

" I don't need it."

He stayed in the kitchen while I undressed; I slipped in between the sheets, under the Mexican blanket. I could hear him walking about, puttering, opening and closing closets as if we were already an old married couple. After so many nights spent in hotel rooms, in guest rooms, it was comforting to feel at home again in that strange bed; the man whom I had chosen and who had chosen me was going to lie down at my side.

" Oh! You're already in bed!" Brogan said. His arms were laden with clean linens, and he looked at me questioningly. " I wanted to change the sheets."

" It's not necessary." He remained standing in the doorway, embarrassed by his ceremonious burden. " I'm very comfortable," I said, pulling the warm sheet up to my chin, that sheet in which he had slept the night before. He moved away, came back again.

" Anne!"

The way he said it moved me deeply. He threw himself on me and for the first time I spoke his name. " Lewis!"

" Anne! I'm so happy!"

Suddenly, he was no longer either awkward or modest. His desire transformed me. I who for so long a time had been without taste, without form, again possessed breasts, a belly, flesh; I was as nourishing as bread, as fragrant as earth. It was so miraculous that I didn't think of measuring my time or my pleasure; I know only that before we fell asleep I could hear the gentle chirpings of dawn.

The smell of coffee awakened me. I opened my eyes and smiled when I saw my blue woollen dress in the arms of a grey jacket on a chair next to the bed. The shadow of the black tree had grown leaves which were fluttering on the bright yellow blind. Lewis handed me a glass and in one gulp I drank the orange juice which had, that morning, a convalescent taste—as if voluptuousness were a sickness, or as if my whole life had been one long illness from which I was just beginning to recover.

It was a Sunday, and for the first time that year the sun was shining on Chicago. We sat on the grass by the side of the lake. There were children playing Indians among the bushes and many lovers holding hands; yachts were sliding by on the unruffled water; midget aeroplanes, red and yellow as shiny as toys, were circling above our heads. Lewis pulled a sheet of paper from his pocket. " Two months ago, I wrote a poem about you . . ."

" Let me see it."

I felt a little tug at my heart. Seated by the window, under the Van Gogh reproduction, he had written those lines for the chaste stranger who had refused him her lips. For two months he had thought of her tenderly, and I was no longer that woman. He must have noticed a shadow on my face, for he said anxiously, " I shouldn't have shown it to you."

" Of course you should have," I said. " I like it very much." I managed a smile. " But now those lips are yours."

" Now, at last," he said.

The warmth of his voice reassured me. That winter, my reserve had touched him, but obviously he was much happier now. There was no need to be upset; he was caressing my hair, speaking gentle, simple words, slipping an old copper ring on my finger. I looked at the ring, listened to those almost forgotten words being spoken in a strange foreign language; under my cheek, I heard the familiar beating of a strange heart. Nothing was asked of me; I had only to be exactly what I was and a man's desire transformed me into a miracle of perfection. It was so restful that if the sun had stopped in the middle of the sky, eternity would have slipped by without my noticing it.

But the sun sank closer to the earth, the grass felt chilly, the bushes grew silent, the yachts went to sleep. " You'll catch cold," Lewis said. " Let's walk a little."

It seemed strange to find myself back on my legs again, warmed by my own heat, and with a body which could move, which occupied space. All day long, it had been nothing but an absence, a negative; it was awaiting the night and Lewis's caresses.

" Where would you like to have dinner?" he asked. " We can go somewhere or eat at my place."

" Let's go somewhere."

That day had been so blue, so tender, that for the moment I felt that I had had enough of gentleness. Our past reached back only thirty-six hours, our horizon was reduced to a face, and our future was our bed. I found it a little stifling in that close atmosphere.

" Suppose we try that Negro club Big Billy mentioned yesterday?"

" It's pretty far," Lewis said.

" We'll get in a little walk that way."

I felt a need for distractions; those too-intense hours had tired me. In the streetcar, I dozed on Lewis's shoulder. I didn't try to figure out where I was in that city; it didn't

seem to me as if it had fixed arteries and precise means of
transportation like the others. It was necessary to conform
to certain rituals that Lewis knew, and then places would
surge up from nowhere. The Delisa Club surged up from
nowhere, crowned with a mauve halo. There was a full-length
mirror just inside the door and together we smiled at our re-
flections. The top of my head was on a level with his shoulder; we looked young and happy and I said gaily, " What a
handsome couple!" And then I felt a wrench in my heart.
No, we weren't a couple, we'd never be a couple. We could
have loved each other, I was sure of that. But at what point
in time, at what place in the world? Nowhere on earth, in
any case, and at no point in the future.

" We'd like to have dinner," Lewis said.

A very dark-complexioned *maître d'hôtel*, who looked like
a heavyweight boxer, led us to a booth near the stage. Baskets
filled with fried chicken were set before us. The musicians
hadn't arrived yet, but the place was full—a few whites and
many negroes, some of whom were wearing fezzes on their
heads.

" Why are they wearing fezzes?"

" It's one of those lodges," Lewis said. " We've got a lot of
them here. We've wandered into one of their conventions."

" But it's going to be terribly boring!"

" I'm afraid so."

His voice was sullen. No doubt he, too, was tired by our
long debauch of happiness; since the previous day, we had
been wearing ourselves out seeking each other, reaching each
other, embracing each other. Too little sleep, too much fever,
too much languor. While we were eating in silence, a tall
negro wearing a fez went up on to the stage and began orating
bombastically.

" What's he saying?"

" He's talking about the lodge."

" There will be a floor show, won't there?"

" Yes."

" When?"

" I don't know."

His answers came brusquely; our common lassitude failed
to draw us together, and suddenly I felt nothing but a watery
grey substance flowing in my veins. Perhaps it was an error to

have wanted to escape our cell. The air there was too heavy,
too rich, but outside the earth was void of people and it was
cold. The speaker cheerfully called out a name ; a red-fezzed
woman stood up and everyone applauded. Another face, and
then another rose above the crowd. Was every member of the
lodge going to be introduced one by one? I turned towards
Lewis. With glassy eyes, he was staring emptily before him ;
his jaw was hanging slack and he resembled the spiteful-look-
ing fish in the aquarium.

" If it's going to last very long, we'd do better to leave," I
said.

" We didn't come so far to leave so soon." His voice was
harsh ; in fact, I thought I discerned in it a trace of hostility
that fatigue alone did not suffice to explain. Perhaps he had
wanted to go back to the apartment when we left the lakeside ;
perhaps he was hurt because I had not wanted to go back to
our bed at once. The idea upset me. I tried to draw close to
him with words.

" Are you tired?"

" No."

" Bored?"

" I'm waiting."

" We aren't going to wait like this for two hours, are we?"

" Why not?"

His head was resting against the wooden partition, his expression was obscure and distant as the face of the moon ; he
looked ready to doze for two hours without saying a word.
I ordered a double whisky ; it failed to pick me up. On the
stage, old Negro women wearing red fezzes were bowing to
each other and bowing to the public amid such applause.

" Lewis, let's go back."

" No, it's ridiculous."

" Then speak to me."

" I have nothing to say."

" I can't bear staying here any longer."

" You wanted to come."

" That's no reason for staying."

He had already fallen back into his torpor. " I'm sleeping,"
I tried to tell myself. " It's a nightmare and I'll soon wake
up." But no, it was that too-blue afternoon which had been
a dream, and now we were awake. At the lakeside, Lewis had

spoken to me as if I were never going to leave him, and he had slipped a ring on my finger. And in three days I'd be gone forever—and he knew it. "He's holding that against me, and he's right," I thought. "If I couldn't stay, why did I come? He's holding it against me and his bitterness will separate us forever." It took so little to separate us forever; just a little while ago we were separated forever! Tears welled in my eyes.

"Are you angry?"

"No, not at all."

"What's wrong then?"

"Nothing."

In vain, I sought his eyes; I could have crushed my knuckles, fractured my skull against that blind wall,, and I wouldn't have shaken it. A group of young girls in graduation dresses lined up on the stage; a skinny little tan-skinned thing went up to the microphone and began singing affectedly.

"I'm leaving," I murmured desperately.

Lewis didn't budge and I wondered incredulously, "Is it possible that it's all over already? Have I lost him so soon?" I tried using a little common sense; I hadn't lost him for I had never had him, and I had no right to complain since I had only loaned myself to him. All right, I wouldn't complain, but nevertheless I was suffering: I touched my copper ring. There was only one way to stop suffering: renounce everything. I'd return his ring; to-morrow morning, I'd take the plane for New York, and that day would become nothing but a memory which time would eventually blot out. The ring slipped along my finger and once again I saw the blue sky, Lewis's smile; he was caressing my hair, calling me Anne.

I sank my head on his shoulder. "Lewis!"

He put his arm around me and tears streamed down my cheeks.

"Was I really that mean?"

"You frightened me," I said. "I was so afraid!"

"Afraid? Were you afraid of the Germans in Paris?"

"No."

"And I frightened you? I'm proud . . ."

"You ought to be ashamed." He lightly kissed my hair, his hand caressing my arm. "I wanted to give you back your ring," I murmured.

"Yes, I noticed," he said gravely. "I said to myself, 'I always spoil everything.' But I couldn't get myself to say a single word."

"Why? What happened?"

"Nothing happened."

I didn't insist, but I asked, "Would you like to leave now?"

"Yes."

In the cab, he said abruptly, "Don't you ever want to kill everybody, and yourself too?"

"No," I said. "And especially not when I'm with you."

He smiled and settled me on his shoulder. I had found his warmth again, his breath, but he remained silent and I thought, "I wasn't mistaken; there was a reason for that crisis. He thought our affair was absurd; he still thinks so."

When we went to bed he immediately turned off the lights; he took me in the darkness, in silence, without saying my name, without offering me his smile. And then, without a word, he turned away. "Yes," I said to myself in terror, "he's holding it against me; I'm going to lose him."

"Lewis," I pleaded, "tell me at least that you like me a little!"

"Like you? But I love you," he replied violently. He turned towards the wall and I wept for a long while, not knowing whether it was because he loved me or because I couldn't love him, or because one day he would stop loving me.

"I have to talk to him," I decided as soon as I opened my eyes the next morning. Now that the word "love" had been spoken I had to explain to Lewis why I refused to use it. But he drew me to him. "How rosy you are! How warm you are!" he murmured. And I lost heart. Nothing counted any longer except the happiness of being warm and rosy in his arms. We went on a tour of the city, walked arm in arm down streets bordered by ramshackle hovels in front of which shiny cars were parked. In one section, ditches ran along either side of the street and were spanned by stairways leading to houses built below street level; I felt as if I were walking on a dyke. Under the sidewalks of Michigan Avenue, I discovered a city without sun, a city in which neon signs burned all through the day. We went rowing on the river, drank martinis at the top of a tower which looked out on an endless lake and suburbs as vast as the lake itself. Lewis loved his city, and he told me all about it: the prairies, the Indians, the first log cabins, the narrow streets filled with grunting pigs, the great fire, the first skyscrapers. It was almost as if he had witnessed everything in person.

"Where would you like to have dinner?" he asked.

"Wherever you like."

"I was thinking we might eat at home. What do you say?"

"Yes," I replied, "let's eat at home." My heart skipped a beat; he had said "at home," as if we were husband and wife —and we had only two days left to live together. "I have to speak to him," I repeated to myself. I had to tell him that I might have been able to love him and that I couldn't. Would he understand? Or would he hate me?

We bought some ham, some salami, a bottle of Chianti, and a rum cake. The Schlitz sign was glowing red as we turned the corner. Among the garbage cans at the foot of the stairway, he held me tightly against him. "Anne! Do you know why I love you so much? It's because I make you happy." But as he drew my lips close to his mouth to drink in his breath, he suddenly let go of me. "There's someone on the porch," he said.

Rapidly, he climbed the steps ahead of me, and I heard him exclaim cheerfully, "Maria! What a pleasant surprise! Come on in."

He smiled at me. "Anne, Maria. Maria's an old friend of mine."

"I don't want to disturb you . . ." Maria said.

"You're not disturbing me."

She went in. She was young, but a little too heavy. She would have been pretty if she had worn a little make-up and done her hair more carefully. Her blue housedress left bare two white arms, one of which was covered with large bruises. She must have come on a neighbourly visit, without bothering to get dressed up. "An old friend." What exactly did that mean?

She sat down, and in a slightly rasping voice, said, "I had to talk to you, Lewis."

A bitter taste rose in my throat. "Lewis." She had pronounced that name as if it had been very familiar to her, and she looked at Lewis with lingering tenderness while he was uncorking the bottle of Chianti.

" Were you waiting long? " he asked.

" Two or three hours," she replied lightly. " The people downstairs were charming; they asked me in for coffee. You can't imagine how much they think of you." She tossed off a glass of Chianti in a single gulp. " I have some very important things to tell you." She eyed me from head to foot. " Personal things."

" You can talk in front of Anne," Lewis said, adding, " Anne is French; she's from Paris."

" Paris! " Maria said. She shrugged her shoulders. " Pour me a little more wine." Lewis filled her glass, which she emptied greedily. " You've got to help me," she said. " You're the only one . . ."

" I'll try."

" She hesitated, made up her mind. " Good. I'll tell you what happened."

I poured myself a little wine and wondered anxiously, " Is she going to stay here all night? " She got up and, leaning against the stove, she was blurting out a story that had to do with marriage, divorce, a thwarted vocation. " You suc-ceeded," she was saying aggressively. " But for a woman, it isn't so easy. I *have* to finish that book, and I can't write where I am." I barely listened to her. I was thinking angrily that Lewis should have found some way to get rid of her. He said he loved me, and he knew very well our hours were numbered. But——?

But politely he asked, " And your family? "

" Why do you ask me that? My family! " With a nervous gesture, Maria picked up the papers scattered on the table, crumpled them, and threw them violently towards the garbage pail. " I hate disorder! No," she continued, riveting her eyes on Lewis, " you're the only one I can count on."

He stood up, looking embarrassed. " Are you hungry? We were going to have dinner."

" Thanks," she replied. " I had some cheese sandwiches— American cheese," she emphasised in a vaguely aggressive voice.

" And where are you going to sleep to-night? " he asked.

She burst out laughing. " I'm not going to sleep; I drank ten cups of coffee."

" And where are you going to spend the night?"

" But you invited me here, didn't you?" She looked me up and down. " Of course, I can't agree to stay if you're going to have other women dragging around the house."

" Unfortunately, there *is* another woman," Lewis said.

" Throw her out!" Maria said.

" That isn't so easy," Lewis replied cheerfully.

At first I felt like laughing. It should have been apparent to me the moment she opened her mouth that Maria had escaped from an insane asylum. And then my blindness frightened me. How vulnerable I must have been to have seen a rival in that poor crazy girl! And in two days, I'd be leaving, abandoning Lewis to a hungry pack of women who would be free to love him. I couldn't stand that thought.

" I haven't seen him for ten years," Maria said to me peremptorily. " Let me have him to-night and you can have him for the rest of your life. That's fair enough, isn't it?"

When I didn't answer, she turned to Lewis. " If I leave here, I won't be back. If I leave, to-morrow I'll marry another."

" But this is Anne's home," Lewis said. " We're married."

Maria's face froze up. " Excuse me. I didn't know." She grabbed the Chianti and drank greedily from the bottle. " Give me a razor."

We exchanged an anxious look and then Lewis said, " I don't have one."

" Go on, now!" She got up and walked over to the sink. " This blade will do fine. Do you mind?" she asked me mockingly as she sat down. Her thighs spread wide apart, she began shaving her legs with frantic concentration. " That'll be better, much better!" She got up again, stood in front of the mirror, and shaved first one armpit and then the other. " That makes all the difference in the world," she declared. stretching herself in front of the mirror with a voluptuous smile. " Well, that's it! To-morrow, I'll marry that doctor. Why shouldn't I marry a nigger, since I work like a nigger?"

" Maria, it's late," Lewis said. " I'm going to find you a hotel room where you can lie down quietly."

"I don't want to lie down." She looked at him angrily. "Why did you insist on asking me in? I don't like it when people make fun of me." She raised her fist and brought it to within an inch of Lewis's face. "This is the dirtiest trick anyone's ever played on me in my whole life. When I think of all I've taken because of you!" she added, pointing to the bruises on her arm.

"Come, it's late," Lewis repeated calmly.

Maria's eyes fell on the sink. "All right, I'll go. But first heat up some water; I'm going to wash the dishes. I can't stand filth."

"There's some hot water on the stove," Lewis replied resignedly.

She grabbed the kettle and began washing the dishes in silent haste. When she finished, she wiped her hands on her housedress.

"All right, I'll leave you alone now with your wife."

"I'll go with you," Lewis said. Without looking at me, she walked towards the door: Lewis gave me a little signal, as if to say "I won't be long." I set the table and lit a cigarette. Now there was no chance of another reprieve. Lewis would return in a few moments; I would have to talk to him. But the words I had been turning over in my mind since early that morning no longer seemed to have any meaning. And yet it was all quite real: Robert, Nadine, my work, Paris. A single day wasn't enough to make it unreal.

Lewis reappeared in the kitchen and carefully locked the door. "I put her in a cab. She said to me, 'I guess the best thing, after all, would be to go back and sleep with the nuts.' It seems she escaped late this afternoon and came directly here."

"At first I didn't understand."

"Yes, I noticed. She's been in the asylum for four years. Last year she wrote to me and asked for a copy of my book; I sent her one with a little note. I scarcely knew her." He looked around him, smiling. "Since I've been living here, a lot of funny things have happened. It's this place. It attracts cats, lunatics, dope addicts . . ." He took me in his arms. "And the simple-minded."

He put some records on the gramophone, came back, and sat down at the table. There was still a little Chianti left, which I poured into our glasses. While we ate in silence, side by side, the gramophone played an Irish folk song. Under the Mexican blanket, the bed was awaiting us. It was like an ordinary, everyday evening which would be followed by a thousand other evenings, all alike. Lewis expressed my thought aloud. "You could almost believe I wasn't lying to Maria." Suddenly, he gave me a questioning look. "And who knows?"

I knew. I turned my head away; I could retreat no further. "Lewis," I murmured, "I haven't told you enough about myself. There are things I've got to explain to you . . ."

"Yes?" There was an apprehensive look in his eyes, and I thought, "It's all over!" One last time, I looked at the stove, the walls, the window, at that room in which I would soon be nothing but an intruder. And then, blindly, the words tumbling over one another, I began spouting sentences. In the mountains one day, I fell headlong down a ravine. I thought I was going to die and I felt nothing but indifference. Once more I recognised that feeling of resignation. Only I wished I could close my eyes!

"I didn't realise your marriage still meant so much to you," Lewis said.

"It does."

He remained silent for a long moment.

"Do you understand me?" I murmured.

He put his arm around my shoulders. "You're even more precious to me than before for having told me. You're more precious to me every day." I pressed my cheek against his and all the words I refused to say to him swelled in my heart.

"You ought to go to sleep," he said. "I'm going to pick things up a bit, and then I'll join you."

For a long while, I heard the sound of dishes rattling, and then I heard nothing; I slept. When I opened my eyes, he was sleeping beside me. Why hadn't he awakened me? What had he thought? What would he think to-morrow? What will he think when I'm gone? Quietly, I got out of bed, opened the kitchen door, and leaned against the railing of the porch. Beneath me, the black tree was shivering; between the earth and the sky, a huge crown of red bulbs was glowing in the night atop the gas tank. It was cold and I, too, began shivering.

No, I didn't want to leave. Not the day after to-morrow,

not so soon. I'd cable Paris; I could stay another ten days, two weeks . . . I could stay—and then what? Sooner or later, I'd have to leave. And the proof that I should leave immediately was that it was already costing me too much. It still wasn't much more than a shipboard affair; but if I stayed, it would become a true love, an impossible love, and that's when I'd suffer. I didn't want to suffer: I had seen Paula's suffering at too close range; I had stretched too many tortured woman, whom I was unable to cure, on my couch. " If I leave, I'll forget," I thought. " I'll be forced to forget. One forgets; it's simple mathematics. One forgets everything, forgets quickly; it's easy to forget four days." I tried to think of Lewis as of someone forgotten; he was walking through the house and he had forgotten me. Yes, he, too, would forget. To-day, it's *my* room, *my* porch, *my* bed; there's a heart overflowing with *me*—and I will never have existed. I closed the door, thinking with deep emotion, " It won't be my fault; I won't lose him through any fault of mine."

" You're not sleeping?" Lewis asked.

" No," I sat on the edge of the bed, close to his warmth. " Lewis, if I wanted to stay another week or two, would it be possible?"

" I thought they were expecting you in Paris," he replied.

" I can always cable Paris. Would you keep me here a little longer?"

" Keep you? I'd keep you all my life!" he replied.

He had hurled those words at me with such violence that I fell into his arms. I kissed his eyes, his lips; my mouth went down along his chest. His smell, his warmth made me dizzy as with drink and I felt my life leaving me, my old life with its worries, its weariness, its worn-out memories. Lewis held a totally new woman against him. I moaned, and not only with pleasure but with happiness. I used to value pleasure for what it was worth, but I never knew that making love could be so overwhelming. The past, the future, everything that was separating us died at the foot of our bed. Nothing separated us any longer. What a victory! Lewis, complete, was in my arms, and I in his. We wanted nothing else; we had everything, forever. Both together we said, " What happiness!" And when Lewis said, " I love you," I said it with him.

I spent two weeks in Chicago. For two weeks we lived without a future and without questioning ourselves; from our past, we drew stories and told them to each other. It was Lewis who did most of the talking; he spoke very rapidly, a little feverishly, as if he wanted to make up for a whole life of silence. I liked the way the words rushed after one another in his mouth; I liked what he said and his way of saying it. I was constantly discovering new reasons for loving him, perhaps because everything I discovered in him served as new pretexts for my love. The weather was lovely, and we spent a good deal of time walking through the city. When we were tired, we would come back to the room, usually at the hour when the shadow of the tree on the yellow blind was disappearing. Lewis would put a stack of records on the gramophone and slip into his white bathrobe; in my nightgown, I would lie quietly in his arms, waiting for desire to overtake us. I, who always question myself suspiciously about the feelings I inspire in others, never wondered who it was Lewis loved in me. I was certain it was myself. He knew neither my country, my language, my friends, nor my worries, only my voice, my eyes, my skin. But I had no other reality than that skin, that voice, those eyes.

Two days before I was due to leave, we had dinner in the old German restaurant, and then we went down to the lake shore. The water was black under the grey, milky sky; it was hot. A group of young boys and girls, half naked and dripping wet, were drying themselves around a camp fire. Farther off, fishermen were setting their lines; beside them, on the cement walk, were sleeping bags and thermos bottles. Little by little, the quay became deserted. We were silent. The lake heaved softly at our feet; it was as untamed as when the Indians camped on its marshy shores, as when the Indians didn't even exist. To the left, above our heads, we could hear the clamour of the city; car headlights swept the avenue with their beams, and tall, gleaming buildings rose up towards the sky. The earth seemed infinitely old, utterly young.

"What a lovely night!" I said.

"Yes, a lovely night," Lewis repeated. He pointed to a bench. "Would you like to sit down here for a while?"

"If you like."

"I love a woman who always answers, 'If you like!'" Lewis said gaily. He sat down beside me and put his arm around me. "It's funny that we get along so well," he said tenderly. "I've never been able to get along with anybody."

"I'm sure it must be their fault," I said.

"No, it's mine. I'm not easy to live with."

"I think you are."

"Poor little Gauloise! You're not very demanding."

I rested my head on Lewis's chest and listened to the beating of his heart. What more could I have asked for? Beating under my cheek was that stout, patient heart, and around me that pearl-grey night, a night made precisely for me. It was impossible to imagine that I might not have lived it. "And yet," I said to myself, "if Philip had come to New York, I wouldn't be here." I'd never loved Philip; of that I was sure. But I wouldn't have seen Lewis again; our love wouldn't have existed. The thought was as disconcerting as when you try to imagine that you might not have been born, or that you might have been someone else.

"When I think I might not have telephoned to you!" I murmured. "Or that you might not have answered!"

"Oh!" Lewis said. "I knew I had to meet you again."

There was such assurance in his voice that it took my breath away. I placed my lips where his heart was beating and promised myself, "He'll never regret this meeting." In two days, I was going to leave; once more the future existed. But we would wring happiness from it.

I raised my head. "Lewis, if you like, I'll come back for two or three months next spring."

"Whenever you come back, it will always be spring," Lewis said.

For a long while we remained clasped in each other's arms, watching the stars. One of them shot across the heavens and I said, "Make a wish!"

Lewis smiled. "I already did."

I felt a sudden tightness in my throat. I knew what he had wished and knew also that that wish wouldn't be granted. There, in Paris, my life was awaiting me, that life I'd been building for twenty years; putting it in question was inconceivable. I'd return next spring—but only to leave again.

I spent the following day shopping. I remembered Paris with its sad shop windows, its frowsy women, and I bought

things left and right for everyone I could think of. We
dined out, and when I climbed the wooden stairway holding
on to Lewis's arm I thought, "It's the last time!" The rubies
of the gas tank were glowing for the last time between the
earth and the sky. I went into the room. One would have
thought a cut-throat had just murdered a woman and ran-
sacked her closets. My two suitcases were open, and scattered over the bed, the chairs, the floor, were nylon lingerie,
stockings, cosmetics, dress material, shoes, scarfs. There was
a smell of love, of death, of disaster. In truth, it was a
funeral home, and all those objects were the relics of a dead
woman, the sacraments she would carry with her to the hereafter. I stood rooted to the spot. Lewis went over to the
dresser, opened a drawer, and took out a mauve carton. He
looked embarrassed as he held it out to me.

"I got this for you," he said.

Under the tissue paper was a large, white flower with an
overpowering fragrance. I took the flower, crushed it against
my mouth, and, sobbing, threw myself on the bed.

"You're not supposed to eat it," Lewis said. "Do they
eat flowers in France?"

Yes, someone had died; a happy woman, all rosiness and
warmth, who woke up smiling every morning. I bit into the
flower; I wanted to dissolve in its fragrance, to die completely and actually. But I fell asleep alive, and early in the
morning Lewis took me to the corner. We had decided to
part there. He hailed a cab, I got in, the door slammed, the
cab turned the corner—and Lewis had disappeared.

"Your husband?" the driver asked.

"No," I replied.

"He looked so sad."

"It wasn't my husband," I said.

He was sad. And so was I. But already it wasn't the same
sadness: we were each alone. Lewis returned to the empty
room alone. I climbed into the plane alone.

Eighteen hours: a short time in which to leap from one
world to another, from one body to another. I was still in
Chicago, crushing my burning face against a flower, when
Robert suddenly smiled at me. I, too, smiled, took his arm,
and began speaking. I had told him quite a bit in my
letters, and yet as soon as I opened my mouth I felt I was

unleashing a monstrous cataclysm. All those days I had just lived, those days so full of life, suddenly petrified; behind me there remained nothing but a frozen block of past, and Lewis's smile had taken on the rigidity of a false face cast in bronze. I was here, walking through the streets I had never left, clinging to Robert from whom I had never been separated, and unfolding a tale that had happened to no one. It was the end of May, the sky was very blue, lilies of the valley were being sold on every street corner, bunches of asparagus banded for half their length in paper were lying on the green canvas covering of pushcarts. Lilies of the valley, asparagus—on this continent they were great treasures. The women were wearing gaily coloured cotton skirts, but how dull their skin and hair seemed to me! The cars, scattered here and there along narrow streets, were old, puny, and dilapidated. And the displays on the faded velvet in the shop windows—how anæmic they looked! There could be no mistaking it: that austerity gave notice that I had once again set foot in reality. And even more irrefutable, I soon recognised that taste in my mouth, that taste of anxiety. Robert would speak only of me, evaded all my questions; obviously, things weren't going the way he wished. Poverty. Anxiety. No doubt about it: I was home.

We left for St. Martin the very next day; the weather was mild and we sat out in the garden. As soon as Robert began to speak, I saw I hadn't been mistaken; he was deeply troubled. The Communists had opened a campaign against him, that campaign he had feared a year earlier. Among other things, they had published an article in *L'Eclume* which had touched him to the quick. It hurt me as well. In it, Robert was depicted as an old idealist, incapable of adapting himself to the hard necessities of these times. For my part, I thought rather that he had made too many concessions to the Communists and had given up too many things of his past.

" It's sheer dishonesty," I said. " No one believes that of you, not even the person who wrote the article."

" I don't know," Robert said. He shrugged his shoulders. " Sometimes I think that I am, in fact, too old."

" You aren't old!" I protested. " You weren't when I left, and you promised me you wouldn't change."

He smiled. " Let's say I have a dated youth."

"You didn't answer them?"

"No. There'd be too many things to answer. And this isn't the moment to do it."

Since the fifth of May, large numbers of so-called sympathisers had taken advantage of the Communists' setback to turn their backs on them. The M.R.P. was winning, De Gaulle was beginning to move, the American party was watching for its chance. More than ever, the left had to stand together, and while awaiting the October referendum and the elections which were to follow the best thing the S.R.L. could do was lie dormant. But Robert hadn't reached that decision with a light heart. It was the Communists' fault if a re-grouping of the left couldn't be carried out without hurting them; he was bitter against them for their sectarianism. But if he refused to criticise them publicly, in private he didn't restrain himself. Several times during those two days he let loose violently against them. Obviously, being able to speak to me relieved him. And I said to myself that perhaps it wasn't precisely I whom he needed. But she— that woman whose place I occupied—was certainly useful to him. Yes, it was my place, without any doubt, my true place in the world.

But then, why wasn't I able to remain in peace in it? Why those tears? It was a very lovely springtime, I was in good health, I lacked for nothing. And yet while walking in the woods, I would stop from time to time and feel like crying, as if I had lost everything. Softly, I would call out, "Lewis!" What a silence! From dusk to dawn, from dawn to night, I had had his breath, his voice, his smile. And now: not a sign of them. Did he still exist? I listened: not a murmur. I looked: not a trace. I no longer understood myself. "I'm crying," I thought, "and yet I'm here. Don't I love Lewis enough? I'm here, and yet I'm crying. Don't I love Robert enough?" I admire people who can contain life in definite formulas. "Physical love is nothing," they say. "Or, "A love which isn't physical is nothing." But I was no less attached to Robert for having met Lewis; and Robert's presence, all-embracing as it was, couldn't make up for Lewis's absence.

Saturday afternoon, Nadine arrived at St. Martin with Lambert. She began questioning me at once, suspicion in her voice.

" You must have been having a good time to prolong your stay like that, you who never change your plans."

" As you see, sometimes I do change them."

" It's funny you spent so much time in Chicago. They say it's horrid."

" They're wrong."

She had gone on several assignments with Lambert during those three months, was living with him, spoke to him with a mocking but determined tenderness. Satisfied with her own life, she was scrutinising mine with uncertain spitefulness. I appeased her as best I could with accounts of my trip. Lambert appeared to me more relaxed and more cheerful than when I left. They spent the week-end in the little cottage. I had had a separate kitchen and a telephone extension installed there so that Nadine would be independent without feeling cut off from the house. She was so happy with her stay that Sunday evening she announced they would remain in St. Martin for their whole holiday.

" Are you sure Lambert likes this arrangement?" I asked. " He doesn't care much for your father, nor for me, either."

" First of all, he likes you both well enough," she replied sharply. " And if you're afraid of having us on your backs, stop worrying. We'll keep to ourselves."

" You know very well I'll be happy to have you here. I was only afraid that it might not be all you'd want in the way of privacy. I must warn you, among other things, that everything that's said in the garden can be heard in my room."

" What of it? Do you think I give a damn? I'm not the type to hide things; I don't surround myself with an air of mystery."

It was true that Nadine, so concerned about her independence, so unreceptive to all criticism, to all advice, willingly spread out her life in broad daylight. It was probably a means she chose to show herself superior to it.

" Mother seems to feel that it might annoy you to spend your holiday here. Will it?" she asked, getting on the motorcycle.

" Not at all, of course not," Lambert replied.

" You see!" she said to me triumphantly. " You're forever complicating everything. Besides, Lambert is always happy to do what I ask him to do. He's a good little boy," she said, ruffling his hair. She circled his waist with her arms and, as the motor-cycle sped off, fondly put her chin on his shoulder.

It was four days later that we learned from an item in *L'Espoir* that Lambert's father had been killed in a fall from a train. Nadine called us up and, in a sullen voice, told us that he had left for Lille and that she wouldn't come for the week-end. I didn't question her, but we were, nevertheless, very curious. Had the old man committed suicide? Had the trial affected his mind? Or had someone done him in? For several days, we speculated about it a great deal. And then we had other problems to worry about. Scriassine had arranged a meeting between Robert and a Soviet functionary who had just escaped through the Iron Curtain for the specific purpose of denouncing Stalin's misdeeds to the West. The day before the meeting, Scriassine came by, bringing along with him a sheaf of documents which he wanted personally to put into Robert's hands so that he could study them before the following day. We hardly ever saw him any more; every time we did there were arguments. But that morning he carefully avoided any thorny subjects and got out very quickly; we parted on good terms. Robert immediately began thumbing through the thick sheaf of papers; some of them were written in French, many in English, a few in German.

"Look them over with me," he said. I sat down beside him under the linden tree and we read together in silence. There was something of everything: reports, statements, statistics, extracts from the Soviet law, commentaries. I found it difficult to plough through that jumble, and yet there were certain texts that were very clear: testimony of men and women who had been imprisoned by the Russians in concentration camps tragically like the Nazi camps; descriptions of those camps by Americans who, as allies, had crossed great stretches of the Soviet Union. According to the conclusions set forth by Scriassine, fifteen to twenty million men were wallowing in the camps under horrible conditions, and that was one of the essential bases of the system we called "Russian Socialism."

I looked at Robert. "How much of all this is true?" I asked.

"Many things, certainly," he said curtly.

Until now, he hadn't attached much importance to the

meeting, and he had intended to go only so that he wouldn't be accused of trying to escape it. He was certain that the Russian's revelations would leave him cold, since he believed he had no illusions about the Soviet Union. Well, it would seem he had had illusions. And now suddenly he was disillusioned. In the thirties, he hadn't been fooled when his Communist friends boasted to him about the penitentiary system in the Soviet Union. Instead of imprisoning criminals, they would say, they were rehabilitating them by employing them at useful work ; the unions protected them and saw to it that they were paid union wages. Robert had explained to me that, in fact, the whole thing was simply a means of subduing rebellious peasants while at the same time procuring a labour force for practically nothing. Forced labour, there as everywhere, was penal servitude. But now that the peasants had been integrated into the régime, now that the war had been won, it would have seemed logical to imagine that things had changed. Yet, according to what we had just read, they had got worse. For a long while, we discussed every fact, every figure, every bit of testimony, every hypothesis ; even allowing the widest possible margin for exaggerations and lies, an absolutely staggering truth stood out. The camps had become an institution, leading to the systematic creation of a sub-proletariat. Crime wasn't punished by work. Rather workers were treated as criminals so that they could be exploited.

"Well, what are you going to do?" I asked after we had left the garden to have a bite in the kitchen.

"I don't know," Robert replied.

Obviously, Scriassine's idea was for Robert to help him divulge those facts, and it seemed to me that there could be no justification for suppressing them. Somewhat reproachfully, I said, "You don't know?"

"No."

"When it concerns only yourself, or even the S.R.L., I can understand your accepting a lot of things without flinching," I said. "But this is different. If we don't do everything in our power to blot out those camps, we're accomplices."

"I can't make up my mind just like that, between to-day and to-morrow," Robert said. "And first of all, I need additional information."

"And if it confirms what we've just learned," I said, "what will you do then?"

He didn't answer and I looked at him with alarm. Remaining silent would mean that he was willing to take anything from the Communists. It would mean the disavowal of everything he had undertaken since the liberation: the S.R.L., his articles, the book he was just finishing.

"You always wanted to be both an intellectual and a revolutionary," I said. "As an intellectual, you've taken on certain commitments—to tell the truth, among others."

"Give me time to think it over," he said a little impatiently.

We ate in silence. Usually, he likes to reason with himself in front of me; he had to be very upset to brood like that, without saying a single word. I, too, was upset. Labour camps or death camps. There were, of course, certain differences, but penal servitude is penal servitude. All those internees! I could see them with those same enormous foreheads, those same crazed eyes as the deportees. And it was in the Soviet Union that all that was happening.

"I don't feel like working. Let's go for a walk," Robert suggested.

We went through the village and climbed to the upland, which was covered with ripening wheat and apple trees in bloom. It was a little warm, but not too much so; in the sky, a few small clouds were rolling themselves into balls. We could see the village, its roofs the colour of good crusty bread, its walls sun-scorched, its bell tower toylike. The earth looked as if it were made expressly for men, and happiness seemed within the reach of every hand.

It was almost as if Robert had heard the whisper of my thoughts, for he said abruptly, "It's easy to forget how hard this world is."

Regretfully, I repeated, "Yes, it's easy."

I only wished that I, too, could have benefited from that uneasiness. Why had Scriassine come to upset us? But Robert wasn't thinking of the camps.

"You say that if I remain silent about the camps I'd be an accomplice," he said. "But in speaking out, I'd become an accomplice of the enemies of the Soviet Union, that is, of all those who want to keep the world as it is. It's true that those camps are a horrible thing. But you mustn't forget that horror is everywhere."

Suddenly, he began speaking volubly. He isn't the type for great historical frescoes, vast social panoramas and yet, that afternoon, as the words tumbled from his mouth, all the wretchedness of the world fell over that sun-drenched countryside: weariness, poverty, the despair of the French proletariat, the misery of Spain and Italy, the enslavement of the colonial peoples, the famines and plagues of China and India. All around us, men were dying by the millions without ever having lived; their agony blackened the sky, and I wondered how we still dared to breathe.

"So you see," Robert said, "my duties as an intellectual, my respect for the truth—that's all just so much idle chatter! The only question is to know whether, in denouncing the camps, you're working for mankind or against it."

"All right," I said. "But what reason have you for thinking that the Russian cause is to-day still identified with the cause of humanity? It seems to me that the existence of the camps makes it necessary to review the whole Soviet question."

"There are so many things that we should know!" Robert said. "Is it really a question of an institution that is indispensable to the régime? Or does it relate to certain policies that are subject to modification? Can we hope that they'll be quickly liquidated once Russia begins rebuilding? Before making any decision, I want to know all these things."

I didn't insist. What right, after all, did I have to protest? I'm much too incompetent. We went back to the house, and both of us spent the evening pretending to work. I had brought back with me from America quite a few documents, notes, and books on psychoanalysis, but I didn't touch them.

The next morning, Robert took the ten o'clock bus. Sitting in the garden, I watched for the mailman: no letter from Lewis. He had warned me it would be a week before he wrote, and letters from Chicago didn't come quickly. Certainly, he hadn't forgotten me, but he was infinitely distant. It was useless seeking help in that direction. Help against what? I went into the study and put a record on the gramophone. Something unbearable was happening to me: I was beginning to have doubts about Robert. "There was a time when he would have spoken out," I said to myself. There was a time when he was completely forthright, would let neither

Russia nor the Communist Party get away with anything. And one of the *raisons d'être* of the S.R.L. was to allow him to voice constructive criticism. Sullenly, he chose to remain silent. Why? Accusing him of being an idealist had wounded him deeply; he was trying to be a realist, to adapt himself to the hard necessities of these times. But it's only too easy to adapt oneself. I, too, adapt myself, and I'm not proud of it. Always pretending not to notice, always accepting—in the end, it adds up to betraying. I accept absence and I betray my love; I accept surviving the dead and I forget them, betray them. But at any rate, as long as it concerns only the dead and myself, there are no major victims. But betraying the living, that's serious!

"If I spoke out, I'd betray others," Robert would answer me. And in chorus, they would add, " You can't make an omelette without breaking eggs." But in the end, who's going to eat all those omelettes? The broken eggs will rot and fester in the earth. "It's already festering." Yes, that's true. Too many things are true; they make my head spin, all those truths fighting each other. I wonder how they keep from getting all mixed up. As for me, I don't know how to add four hundred million Chinese and fifteen million slave labourers. And besides, maybe what you have to do is subtract. In any case, all those calculations are false. One man plus one woman doesn't make two men; it will forever make one plus one. All right, I'm wrong in resorting to arithmetic; to make order out of chaos, you have to turn to dialectics. It's a matter of getting beyond the slave labourers to the Chinese people. Good. Let's get beyond. Everything passes; " all is vanity and vexation of spirit "; we'll be past all this some day. We'll have got beyond the camps, and we'll have got beyond my own existence. It's laughable, this little ephemeral life brooding over those camps which the future has already abolished! History takes care of itself and each one of us into the bargain. Let's just keep quiet, then, each in his own little hole.

Well, then, why don't they keep quiet? That's the question I asked Robert more than twenty years ago, when I was a student. He laughed at me, but I'm not sure to-day that he ever completely convinced me. They pretended to believe that humanity is a single, immortal person, that one day it will be rewarded for all its sacrifices, and that I, myself, will receive my due. But I don't accept that: death nibbles at everything. The sacrificed generations won't rise from their graves to take part in the final love feasts; what might console them is that the chosen ones will join them under the earth at the end of a very brief interval spent above it. Between happiness and unhappiness, there isn't perhaps as much difference as one might think.

I turned off the gramophone, lay down on the couch, and closed my eyes in relief. How even and mild the light of death is! Lewis, Robert, Nadine had become as light as shadows, no longer weighed on my heart. I could have borne the weight of fifteen million shadows, or four hundred million. Nevertheless, after a few moments, I went to get a detective story. You have to kill time. But time will kill me too—and there's the true, pre-established balance. When Robert came home that evening, it seemed to me as if I was seeing him from very far off, through binoculars: a disembodied image with emptiness all around it, like Diego at the window in Drancy, Diego, who even then was no longer of this world. He spoke, I listened, but nothing concerned me any more.

" Do you blame me for having asked for that delay?" Robert asked.

" I? Not at all."

" Well, what's wrong then? If you think those camps don't upset me, you're badly mistaken."

" It's the exact opposite," I replied. " I was thinking today that people are really wrong to torment themselves over anything and everything. Things are never as important as they seem; they change, they end, and above all, when all is said and done, everyone dies. That settles everything."

" That's just a way of escaping from problems," Robert said.

I cut him off. " Unless it's that problems are a way of escaping the truth. Of course," I added, " when you've decided that it's life that's real, the idea of death seems like escape. But conversely . . ."

Robert shook his head. " There's a difference. The fact of living proves you've chosen to believe in life; if one honestly believes that death alone is real, then one should kill oneself. Actually, though, even suicides don't think that."

"It may be that people go on living simply because they're scatterbrained and cowardly," I said. "It's easier that way. But that doesn't prove anything either."

"First of all, it's important that suicide be difficult," Robert said. "And then continuing to live isn't only continuing to breathe. No one ever succeeds in settling down in complete apathy. You like certain things, you hate others, you become indignant, you admire—all of which implies that you recognise the values of life." He smiled. "I'm not worried. We haven't done with discussing the camps and all the other things. Like myself, like everyone, you feel yourself powerless in face of certain overwhelming facts, so you take refuge in a generalised scepticism. You don't really mean it."

I didn't answer. To-morrow, of course, I'd begin discussing things again, a lot of things. Did that prove they would stop seeming insignificant to me? And if they did, maybe it would be because I'd be deceiving myself again.

Nadine and Lambert returned to St. Martin the following Saturday. It looked as if things weren't going well with them; Nadine didn't speak a single word during dinner. Lambert was to leave for Germany in two days to get information about the camps in the Russian Zone. By mutual agreement, he and Robert avoided touching on the heart of the problem, but they talked animatedly about the practical methods of conducting the investigation.

While we were having coffee, Nadine exploded. "This whole thing is completely idiotic! Of course those camps exist. They're beastly and they're necessary! But that's the system, and no one can do a thing about it!"

"You make up your mind easily, don't you?" Lambert said. He looked at her reproachfully. "You've really got a gift for shrugging off things that bother you."

"And you, your mind isn't made up, I suppose," Nadine said aggressively. "Come now! You're perfectly delighted to be able to think ill of the Soviet Union. And thanks to that, you've got yourself a nice little trip and you're going to make it like a great big important man. Quite a deal you're making for yourself!"

He shrugged his shoulders without answering, but they must have had quite a fight in the cottage during the night. Nadine spent the next day alone in the living-room with a book she didn't read. Speaking to her was useless; she answered me in monosyllables. Towards evening, Lambert called to her from the garden, and when she refused to budge he came inside.

"Nadine, it's time to leave."

"I'm not going," she said. "I don't have to be at *Vigilance* until to-morrow morning at ten."

"But I told you I had to go back to Paris to-night; I've got some people to see."

"Go see them. You don't need me for that."

"Nadine, don't be stupid!" he said impatiently. "I won't stay more than an hour with them. We said we'd go to the Chinese restaurant."

"I changed my mind. It happens to you, too," Nadine said. "I'm staying here."

"It's our last evening," Lambert said.

"You're the one responsible for that!" she said.

"All right, see you to-morrow," he said haughtily.

"I'm busy to-morrow. I'll see you when you get back."

"Oh! Good-bye forever, if that's what you want," he shouted furiously.

He closed the door behind him. Nadine looked at me and she, too, began shouting. "Above all, don't tell me I'm wrong; don't tell me anything! I know everything you could tell me, and I'm not interested."

"I didn't open my mouth."

"Let him take his trip! I don't give a damn!" she said. "But he should have consulted me before deciding. And I hate it when someone lies to me. That investigation isn't so damned urgent. He'd have done better to tell me straight out, 'I'd rather be alone.' Because that's what's really behind it; he wants to be able to cry peacefully over his dear little papa."

"That's only normal," I said.

"Normal? His father was an old bastard. First of all, he shouldn't have made up with him. And now he's going around crying like a baby. Yes, he cried real tears; I saw him!" she said triumphantly.

"What of it? That's nothing to be ashamed of."

"None of the other men I know would have cried. And then, to dress up the story, he claims the old man was done in on purpose. That's the best of all!"

"It isn't impossible," I said.

She turned a deep red. "Not Lambert's father! It's ridiculous!" she said.

Immediately after dinner, she wandered off into the countryside; we didn't see her again until breakfast. It was then, with a reproving, greedy look, that she handed me Lewis's first letter.

"There's a letter from America," she said. "From Chicago," she added, eyeing me insistently.

"Thank you."

"Aren't you going to open it?"

"It's nothing urgent."

I set the letter down next to me and tried to keep my hand from trembling as I drank my tea. I had as much trouble keeping the parts of my body together as when Lewis held me in his arms for the first time. Robert came to my help; he began asking Nadine questions about *Vigilance* until I could find a pretext to go up to my room. My fingers were so benumbed that I ripped the sheet of yellow paper in pulling it from the envelope, that sheet of paper from which Lewis's overwhelming presence would miraculously surge forth. The letter was typewritten, cheerful, pleasant, and empty, and for a long moment I stared in stupefaction at the signature which sealed it closed as implacably as a tombstone. I could have re-read that page a hundred times, could have twisted and turned it every way, and still I would not have been able to squeeze out a single new word, a single smile, a single kiss. And it would not help much to begin waiting again: at the end of my waiting, I would meet only another sheet of paper. Lewis had stayed in Chicago, he continued to live, he lived without me. I walked over to the window, looked at the summer sky, at the happy trees, and I realised that I was only beginning to suffer. The same silence: only there was no longer any hope in it; there would always be that same silence. When our bodies were no longer touching, when our eyes no longer looked at each other, what did we have in common? Our pasts had nothing in common, our futures receded from each other, we did not hear the same language spoken around us, and even the clocks laughed at us. Here the morning was gleaming brightly, and it was night in that room in Chicago.

We couldn't even meet in the sky. No, there was no path between us—except those sobs in my throat, those sobs I repressed.

It was a stroke of luck that Paula telephoned me that day and pleaded with me to come see her; perhaps in sharing her sadness I'd succeed in forgetting my own. Seated in the bus next to Nadine, who was mulling over some nasty deed, I asked myself, " Do people get used to it? Will I get used to it?" In the streets of Paris, I passed hundreds, thousands of men, who had, like Lewis, two arms and two legs, but never his face. It's fantastic how many men there are on the surface of the earth who aren't Lewis! It's fantastic the number of roads there are which don't lead into his arms, the words of love which aren't spoken to me! Everywhere promises of pleasure and happiness brushed against me, but never did that spring tenderness penetrate my skin. Slowly, I walked along the quays. Paula had made the immense effort of dragging herself over to the apartment a few days after my return and had cheerfully accepted her presents from America. But she had listened to my stories and answered my questions with a distant air. I had not yet been to see her, and it was with a sort of astonishment that I rediscovered the familiar street. It was the same as ever; nothing had changed during my absence, nothing had happened. The signs still read the same: " Speciality: Rare and Saxon Birds." And the little monkey chained to the bars of a window was still shelling peanuts. Sitting on a stairway, a tramp was smoking a cigar while keeping an eye on a bundle of rags. The downstairs door, when I opened it, slammed as always against a rubbish bin; every hole in the rug on the stairway was in its proper place; a telephone was ringing insistently. Paula was wrapped in a silk dressing-gown, a little rumpled.

" You're very sweet! I'm terribly sorry to bother you, but I'd never have had the courage to go into that lion's den alone."

" Are you sure I'm invited?"

" But it's because of you that the Belhomme called me three times; she begged me to bring you. She has Henri, she'd like to have Dubreuilh . . ."

She went up the stairs leading to her bedroom and I followed her.

"You can't imagine how pretty the house at St. Martin is," I said. "You must come out."

She sighed. "It's so far!" She opened the doors of her wardrobe. "What shall I wear? It's been such a long time since I've gone out."

"Your black dress."

"It's terribly old."

"The green one."

"I'm not so sure green looks well on me." She took out the black dress. "I don't want to look all moth-eaten. Lucie would be only too happy!"

"Why are you going there?" I asked. "You never go out."

"She hates me," Paula replied. "When I was younger and prettier than she I took quite a few of her lovers away from her. If I turn down all her invitations, she'll start thinking I've become an invalid. And she'll gloat!"

She had gone over to the mirror, and with her fingers she traced the curve of her thick eyebrows. "I should have plucked them. I really ought to follow the fashions; they're going to think I'm ridiculous!"

"Don't be afraid of them," I said. "You'll always be the most beautiful."

"Oh, not any more," she said. "No, not any more!"

She was looking at herself with an unfriendly eye, and suddenly, for the first time in a good many years, I, too, saw her with the eyes of a stranger. She looked tired, her cheeks had taken on a purplish tinge, and her chin was starting to sag; the two deep gashes at the sides of her mouth pointed up the strength of her features. There was a time when Paula's creamy skin, her velvety look, the black shock of her hair softened her beauty. Deprived of that banal charm, her face became strange; it was shaped too definitely to excuse the indecision of a curve, the faltering of a colour. Instead of artfully engraving itself, time had brutally marked that noble, baroque mask which still well-deserved admiration, but which would have been more in place in a museum than a salon.

Paula had slipped on her black dress and was brushing her long lashes.

"Shall I make my eyes longer? Yes or no?"

"I don't know."

I could easily see her defects, but I was incapable of suggesting a remedy. I wasn't even sure one existed.

"If only I've got a decent pair of stockings left!" She began feverishly rummaging in a drawer. "Do you think these two are the same colour?"

"No, this one is lighter than the other."

"How about this one?"

"It's got a ladder from top to bottom."

It took us a good ten minutes to pick out a pair of stockings that matched.

"You're sure now?" Paula asked anxiously. "They really match?"

Standing by the window, I drew the transparent silk over my outstretched fingers and consulted the light of day. "I don't see any difference."

"But they see everything, you know."

She laced her thick-soled sandals around her legs and asked, "Shall I wear my necklace?"

It was a heavy copper necklace, set with amber and bone, an exotic piece of jewellery, without monetary value, which would make diamond-bedecked women smile scornfully.

"No, don't wear it."

I hesitated. At any rate, with her curls, her timeless dress, her mask, her buskins, Paula was so different from her enemies that perhaps it might be better to underline her originality. "Wait. Yes, you'd better wear it. Oh, I don't know," I said impatiently. "After all, they aren't going to eat you up."

"Oh, yes," she said without a smile. "They'll eat me up."

We walked to a bus stop. In the street, Paula lost all her stately bearing; she hugged the walls furtively. "I hate to go out all dressed up in this neighbourhood," she said apologetically. "In the morning, I go around in any old thing. That's different. But at this time of day, in this outfit, I'm an outrage."

I tried to distract her. "How's Henri?"

She hesitated. "He's so complicated!"

Stupidly, I repeated, "Complicated?"

"Yes, it's strange. I'm only just now beginning to know him—after ten years." After a brief silence, she continued. "He did something very funny while you were away. He suddenly shoved a passage from his novel under my nose, a passage in which the hero tells a woman that she's making life miserable for him. And then he asked me, 'What do you think of it?' "

" What was he trying to make you answer?" I asked, trying to make my voice sound amused.

" I asked him if he had been thinking of me when he wrote it and he blushed with embarrassment. But for a moment, I did feel that he would have liked me to believe it."

" You astonish me," I said.

" Henri's really a case," she said pensively, adding, " He's been seeing a lot of the young Belhomme. That's another reason why I was determined to go to Lucie's—so that they won't think I attach any importance to that little passing fancy."

" Yes, I saw a picture of her . . ."

" Of her with Henri at the Iles Borromées!" She shrugged her shoulders. " It's sad. He isn't proud of it, you know. It's even strange: he suggested that we stop sleeping together, as if he no longer felt worthy of me," she concluded slowly.

I felt like saying to her, " Stop lying to yourself!" But what right did I have? And in a way, I even admired her obstinacy.

On the stairway, going up to Lucie Belhomme's apartment, she grabbed my wrist. " Tell me the truth. Do I look defeated?"

" You? You look like a princess."

But when the butler opened the door, I suddenly felt Paula's panic overtaking me. There was a clamour of voices, the air smelled of perfume and malice; I, too, was going to be happily torn to bits. That's never a pleasant thing to think about. Paula had regained her composure; she walked into the salon with queenly dignity. But I suddenly, was no longer quite sure both her stockings were the same shade.

Period furniture, vaguely Persian rugs, pictures with fine patinas, books bound in parchment, crystal, velvet, satin: one felt that Lucie was wavering between her bourgeois aspirations, her intellectual pretensions, and her own taste, which, despite its good reputation, was plainly vulgar.

" How happy I am to have you here!" She was dressed with a perfection that would have given the best-dressed women in the world an inferiority complex. It was only at second glance that one noticed the meanness of the mouth, the anxious malice in her look. There still doesn't exist the make-up artist who can change a look. While smiling, she appraised me in detail, and then she turned to Paula. "My little Paula! Twelve years since we've seen each other! I hardly recognised you!" For a moment, she held on to Paula's hand, examining it shamelessly, and then she took me by the arm. "Come and let me introduce you."

The women were much younger and prettier than in Claudie's salon, and no mental dramas disfigured their cleverly worked-over faces. There were quite a few models eager to become starlets, and starlets eager to ripen into stars. All of them were wearing black dresses and very high-heeled shoes, had hair of the very latest shade, long eyelashes, and a personality, different for each one of them, but all produced in the same workshop. If I had been a man, I would have found it impossible to choose between them. I would have done my shopping elsewhere. As a matter of fact, the handsome young men who came to kiss my hand seemed far more interested in each other. True, here and there there were a few adults with manly bearing, but they looked like salaried extras. Among them was Lucie's lover of record, whom everyone called Dudule. He was talking to a tall brunette with platinum blonde hair.

"It seems you've just returned from New York?" he said to me. "What a fantastic country, isn't it? It's like the gigantic dream of a spoiled child. Those enormous ice-cream cones they gorge themselves on! I see in that the symbol of all of America."

"I didn't like it there at all," said the bleached blonde. "Everything is too clean, too perfect. You end up by wanting to meet a man in a dubious shirt and with a two-days' growth of beard."

I didn't protest. I let them explain to me with well-worn slogans that country from which I had just returned. Overgrown children . . . A woman's paradise . . . Abominable lovers . . . A feverish and giddy life . . . Dudule boldly even used the word " phallus " in connection with the skyscrapers. Listening to them, I said to myself that people really had no right to endow intellectuals with sophisticated feelings. It was these men and women here—the worldly and pseudo-worldly—who went through life blinded by bad clichés, their hearts filled with banalities. Robert, Henri let themselves nonchalantly like what they liked, be bored with what bored them, and if a king were to go naked through the streets they wouldn't admire the fine embroidery of his cloak. They were well aware that they created the models that would be zealously copied by the snobs who affected elegant refinement, but their pride permitted them all manner of naïveté. On the other hand, neither Dudule nor Lucie nor the young, slender, glittering women who flocked around her ever allowed themselves a moment of sincerity. I felt a frightened pity for them. Their whole existences were made up of empty ambitions, burning jealousies, abstract victories and defeats. And yet, there were so many things on earth to love and hate solidly! Suddenly, I thought, " Robert is right. Indifference doesn't exist." Even here, where it was hardly worth the trouble, I plunged immediately into indignation or disgust, stated firmly that the world was filled with things to love and to hate, and knew clearly that nothing could drive that conviction from me. Yes, it was out of weariness, laziness, or shame of my ignorance that I had idiotically pretended the contrary.

" You've never met my daughter?" Lucie asked, aiming one of her thin smiles at Paula.

" No."

" You'll see her. She's very beautiful—exactly the same type of beauty you used to have." Lucie contrived and then erased a second smile. " You have many things in common."

I decided to be as rude as she. " Yes, they say your daughter doesn't look at all like you."

Lucie examined me with definite hostility. There was an almost worried curiosity in that inspection, as if she were wondering, " Is there another way than mine to be a woman and to profit from being a woman? Has something escaped me?" Her eyes shifted back to Paula. " One of these days, you really ought to come and see me at Amaryllis. I'd dress you up a bit. Being dressed well changes a woman so much."

" It would be a shame to change Paula," I said. " The world is swarming with fashionable women, but there's only one Paula."

Lucie seemed a bit disconcerted. " Anyhow, when you stop scorning fashion, you'll always be welcome at my shop.

And I know a beauty specialist who performs miracles," she added, pivoting on her high heels.

"You should have asked her why she doesn't make use of her services," I said to Paula.

"I've never known how to answer them," Paula said. Her cheeks were purplish, her nostrils pinched; that was her way of paling.

"Do you want to leave?"

"No, that would be a defeat."

Claudie rushed over to us, her eyes shining like those of a gossip in heat. "The little redhead who just came in is the young Belhomme," she said.

Paula turned her head; so did I. Josette wasn't little, and she was a redhead of the rarest kind—one of those who have the creamy skin of a blonde under their tawny hair. Her sad, voluptuous mouth, her enormous eyes, made her look as if she were startled by her own beauty. One could understand that a man would want to excite a face like that. I looked at Paula anxiously. She was holding a glass of champagne in her hand, and she stood motionless, staring, as if she were hearing voices—nasty voices.

My heart rebelled. What crime was she expiating? Why were they burning her alive when around us all those women were smiling? I was willing to recognise that she herself had forged her unhappiness: she never tried to understand Henri, she gorged herself on fantasies, she had chosen laziness together with enslavement. But after all, she had never harmed anyone; she didn't deserve to be punished so brutally. We always pay for our mistakes, only there are some doors on which creditors never bother to knock and others which they break down. It's unfair. Paula was among the unlucky, and I couldn't bear seeing those tears streaming from her eyes without her seeming to notice them. Sharply, I brought her out of her trance. "Let's get out of here," I said, taking her by the arm.

"Yes."

When, after hastily saying our good-byes, we found ourselves in the street again, Paula looked at me gravely. "Why didn't you ever warn me?" she asked.

"Warn you? About what?"

"That I was on the wrong track."

" But I don't think that."

" It's strange that you didn't."

" Do you mean that you've lived too secluded a life?"

She shrugged her shoulders. " I haven't had my final say. I know I'm a little idiotic, but when I understand, I understand."

When she got off the bus, she nevertheless forced herself to smile. " Thanks for going with me. You did me a real favour. I won't forget it."

Nadine remained in Paris all week. When she reappeared at St. Martin, I asked her if she had heard anything from Lambert. He had written her, she said; he was returning in a week. " And are the sparks going to fly!" she added in a jubilant voice. " I saw Joly and we slept together again. Just picture Lambert's face when I tell him that!"

" Nadine! Don't tell him!"

She gave me a puzzled look. " You've told me a thousand times that decent people don't lie to each other. Truth above all!"

" No. What I said was that you have to try to build relationships in which it would be inconceivable to lie. But you haven't reached that stage with Lambert, not at all. And besides," I added, " it isn't out of love of the truth that you want to tell him about something that happened in your life. You brought it about deliberately in order to hurt him when you tell him about it."

Nadine grinned doubtfully. " Oh, you! When you go into your witch-doctor act!"

" Am I wrong?"

" Naturally, I wanted to punish him; he asked for it."

" You yourself admit that he always does everything you want; you could be a good sport about the one time he didn't give in."

" He does what I want because he enjoys playing the little boy. It's all an act. But the truth is that anything at all counts more than I: Henri, the paper, his father, an investigation . . ."

" You're blind. Lambert is completely devoted to you."

" That's what you say! But he's never said anything like that to me on his own."

" You mustn't have given him very much encouragement."

"Naturally, I didn't go begging him for declarations of love."

I looked at her, puzzled. "You do sometimes talk to each other about your feelings, don't you?"

"You don't talk about things like that," she replied, looking shocked. "What kind of an idea is that?"

"Talking helps one to understand."

"But I understand everything perfectly."

"Then you ought to understand that Lambert would never tolerate your being unfaithful to him. You're going to make him suffer terribly, and you'll spoil the whole affair beyond recall."

"It's really hilarious that it's you who's advising me to lie!" She sneered, but she seemed rather relieved. "All right, I won't tell him."

Lambert arrived two days later. He spoke little about his trip; he was planning to leave again in September to gather more precise information. Nadine appeared to have made up with him. Side by side, they took long sun baths in the garden, went walking together, read, talked, made plans. Lambert let himself be cuddled by Nadine and gave in graciously to her whims. But from time to time, he would feel a need to prove his independence, would get on his motor-cycle and zoom along the roads at a speed which visibly frightened even himself. Nadine always hated the self-sufficiency of others, but this time envy was added to her jealousy. In face of Lambert's resistance and my formal opposition, she had given up her ambition to drive the motor-cycle, but she tried, at any rate, to adopt it. She had painted the fenders a bright red and had attached mascots to the handlebars; however, despite her efforts, the motor-cycle remained in her eyes the symbol of all the masculine pleasures of which she wasn't the source and in which, to make matters worse, she was unable to share. That was the most frequent pretext for her quarrels with Lambert, but they, at least, didn't amount to anything more than little tiffs without bitterness.

One evening, while I was in my room preparing for bed, they came out and sat down in the garden.

"In short," Lambert said, "you feel I wouldn't be capable of managing a paper by myself?"

"I didn't say that. I said that if Volange uses you as a straw man, you won't be managing anything at all."

"And that he has enough confidence in me to offer me a position like that without his having any ulterior motives, that seems incredible to you!"

"You're naïve! Volange is still too hot to dare use his own name, and he's counting on manœuvring you from behind the scenes."

"Oh, you, you think you're pretty smart because you play the cynic. But malice can also be blinding. Volange is a somebody."

"Yes," she said calmly, "he's a bastard."

"All right, so he made a mistake. But I prefer people who have their errors behind them to those who have them ahead of them," Lambert said viciously.

"You mean Henri? I never made a hero out of him, but he's a decent enough chap."

"He was, but now he's letting himself be swallowed up by politics and by the figure he cuts in public."

"He's gained by it, if anything," Nadine said impartially. "That play he just wrote is the best thing he's ever done."

"Oh, no!" Lambert said. "I think it's foul. And it's a bad thing to do: the dead are dead; let them lie in peace. There's no reason to go stirring up hate between Frenchmen."

"On the contrary!" Nadine said. "People damned well need to have their memories refreshed."

"Dwelling on the past doesn't get you anywhere," Lambert said.

"Well, I don't approve of people forgetting it," Nadine said, adding sharply, "and I can't understand forgiving."

"And who are you and what did you do to be so stern?" Lambert asked.

"I'd have done at least as much as you if I were a man," Nadine replied.

"Even if I'd done ten times more, I wouldn't permit myself to condemn people without appeal," he said.

"That'll do!" she said. "We'll never agree about that. Let's go to bed."

There was a silence, and then Lambert said emphatically, "I'm certain that Volange will do great things."

"I doubt it," Nadine said. "In any case, I don't see how

that concerns you. There's nothing great about managing some vague sheet which won't even be really yours."

"Do you think I'll ever do anything great?" he asked, in a slightly bantering voice.

"Oh, I don't know," she replied. "And I really don't give a damn. Why is it so absolutely necessary to become important?"

"All that you expect of me is that I be a good little boy submissive to your every wish and whim—is that it?"

"But I expect nothing; I take you as you are."

Her tone was affectionate, but it clearly indicated that she was resisting saying the words Lambert wanted to hear. He persisted, his voice a little crotchety. "And what am I? What abilities do you see in me?"

"You know how to make mayonnaise," she replied cheerfully. "And you drive a motor-cycle."

"And something else I won't mention," he said with a little snicker.

"I hate it when you're vulgar," she said. She yawned loudly. "I'm going to sleep."

The gravel crunched under their feet and then I could hear nothing more in the garden but the insistent concert of the crickets. I listened to them for a long time. The night was beautiful; not a star was missing from the heavens, nothing was missing anywhere. And yet there was an emptiness inside me which seemed inexhaustible. Lewis had written me two other letters; he spoke to me much better now than he did in the first letter. But the more I felt him alive and real, the more his sadness overwhelmed me. I, too, was sad, and that drew us no closer together. I murmured, "Why are you so far away?" Echoing my words, he answered, "Why are you so far away?" and his voice was heavy with reproach. Because we're separated, everything separates us, even our efforts to join each other.

They, however, could have turned their love into happiness; their bungling annoyed me. The next day, they decided to spend the afternoon and evening in Paris. A little before one, Lambert came out of the cottage, wearing an elegant flannel suit and a well-chosen tie. Nadine was lying on the grass, clad in a flowered skirt full of spots, a cotton blouse and heavy sandals. A little peeved, he called out to her, "Hurry up and get ready! We're going to miss the bus."

"I told you I wanted to take the motor-cycle," Nadine said. "It's a lot more fun."

"But we'll be filthy by the time we get there. And you look ridiculous on a motor-cycle when you're even a little dressed up."

"I have no intention of getting dressed up," she replied firmly.

"You're not going to Paris in that get-up?" he asked. She didn't answer and, turning to me as a witness he said sadly, "What a shame! She could be so attractive if only she didn't insist on dressing like an anarchist." He examined her with a critical eye. "All the more so, since sloppiness doesn't become you at all."

Nadine believed herself ugly, and it was out of spite, more than anything, that she disdained looking feminine. You would hardly suspect from her surly carelessness how sensitive she was to any remarks concerning her physical appearance. Her face suddenly hardened. "If you want a woman who primps herself from morning to night, you'd better go to another counter."

"It wouldn't take long to slip on a clean dress," Lambert said. "I can't take you out anywhere if you stay like that, looking like a savage."

"But I don't have to be taken out. Do you think I feel like parading myself, hanging on your arm in places where there are maîtres d'hôtel and women dressed in their skin? To hell with that! If you're so set on playing Don Juan, hire yourself a model to go out with you."

"I don't see what's so revolting about going to dance in a decent night club where we could hear some good jazz." He turned to me. "You can understand that, can't you?" he asked.

"I don't believe Nadine cares much for dancing," I replied cautiously.

"She could be a good dancer if she wanted!"

"Exactly. I don't want to be a good dancer," she said. "I get no fun out of acting the monkey in the middle of a dance floor."

"You could get as much fun out of it as anyone else," Lambert said, reddening slightly. "And you could get fun out of dressing up, out of going out, if only you were sincere. People say, 'I don't get any fun out of it,' but they're lying.

All of us are hypocrites, overrun with inhibitions. I often wonder why. Why should it be a crime to like good-looking furniture, fine clothing, luxury, amusement? Fundamentally, everyone really likes these things."

"I swear to you I don't give a damn about them," Nadine said.

"That's what you say! It's funny," he continued with a vehemence that disconcerted me, "people always have to be affected, always have to be denying themselves. We're not supposed to laugh or cry when we feel like it, or do what we want to do, or think what we think."

"But who tells you not to?" I asked.

"I don't know, and that's the worst thing of all. Everyone's deceiving everyone else, and no one knows why. They say they're sacrificing themselves to purity. But where is there any purity? Let someone show it to me! And it's in the name of purity that we reject everything, do nothing, get nowhere."

"And just where do you want to get?" Nadine asked sarcastically.

"You can sneer, but that, too, is hypocrisy. You're a lot more impressed by success than you let on. You did go on that trip with none other than Perron, didn't you? And you'd speak to me in another tone of voice if I were a somebody. Everybody admires success, and everybody likes money."

"Speak for yourself," Nadine said.

"And why shouldn't people like money?" Lambert continued. "As long as the world's the way it is, you might just as well be among those who have it. Come now! You were mighty proud to have a fur coat last year, and you're dying to travel all over. You'd be delighted to wake up a millionaire, only you'd never admit it. You're afraid of being yourself!"

"I know who I am and it suits me perfectly," she said in a biting voice. "You're the one who's afraid of being what you are: a little bourgeois intellectual. You know damned well you aren't made for great adventure. So you're gambling on social success, money, and all the rest. You'll become a social climber and a filthy snob, that's all."

"There are times when all you deserve is a good slap in the face," Lambert said, turning on his heels.

"Why don't you try it! Believe me, there'd be some fun!"

I followed Lambert with my eyes, wondering what the reason was for his outburst. What was he reluctantly stifling inside himself? A taste for ease? An unconfessed ambition? Did he want, for example, to accept Volange's proposition without daring to risk the disapproval of his friends? Perhaps he had persuaded himself that the taboos he felt surrounded by were preventing him from becoming a somebody? Or did he want to be told that it was perfectly all right for him to be a nobody?

"I wonder what was going on in his head?" I asked.

"Oh, he builds himself little dreams," Nadine replied scornfully. "Only when he wants to bring me into them—excuse me, please!"

"I must say you don't encourage him much."

"No. In fact, it's even funny, because when I feel he wants me to say one thing, I immediately say the opposite. Can you understand that?"

"A little."

I could understand that very well; with Nadine, especially, I knew that sort of resistance.

"He always wants to get someone's permission. Why can't he just take it?"

"Nevertheless, you could be a little more conciliatory," I said. "You never make any concessions; you ought to give in to him when occasionally he asks something of you."

"Oh, he asks for more than you think," she said. Wearily, she shrugged her shoulders. "First of all, he asks me to sleep with him every night. I'm fed up with it."

"You can always refuse."

"You can't imagine what a fuss he makes when I refuse! And into the bargain," she added irritably, "if I didn't take precautions he'd knock me up every time." She was looking at me out of the corner of her eye. She was well aware of the fact that I hated to discuss such intimate details.

I shrugged my shoulders. "I can't imagine why you insist on making love if it's such a drudgery for you."

"How do you expect me to have affairs with men if I don't go to bed with them? Women bore me; I don't enjoy myself except with men. But if I want to go out with them, I have to sleep with them; I have no choice. Only there are some who do it more or less often, who are more or less fast. With Lambert, it's all the time and there's no end to it."

One of the paradoxical things about Nadine was that although she had slept in any number of beds, although she would use fantastic obscenities without blinking, she was extremely sensitive regarding her sexual life. Whenever, as he did only too often, Lambert permitted himself an allusion to their intimacies, she would bristle.

"There's one thing you don't seem to realise," I said. "Lambert loves you."

She shrugged her shoulders. "You've never wanted to understand," she said in a reasoning voice. "Lambert loved one woman in his life—Rosa. Afterwards, he wanted to console himself and settled on the first girl who came along—me. But at first he didn't even want to sleep with me. It was only when he found out that Henri was laying me that he started getting ideas. But I've never been his type. He thinks it's more manly having a woman of his own than chasing after tail. And it's easier, too. But I really don't mean anything to him."

She had a talent for jumbling the true and the false with such skill that I was overwhelmed by the effort I'd have to make to contradict her. Weakly, I said, "You've got everything all twisted."

"No, I know what I'm saying," she replied.

In the end, she put on a clean dress and they went to Paris. But they returned more sullen than ever, and soon a new scene broke out. I was working in the garden that morning; the sky, heavy with storm clouds, was weighing on my shoulders and pinning me to the earth. Near me, Lambert was reading and Nadine was knitting. "Fundamentally," she had said to me the day before, "holidays are an awful bore. Every day you have to invent ways of spending your time." She was obviously fed up. For a moment, her eyes remained riveted to the back of Lambert's neck, as if she were trying to make him turn his head by the sheer power of her look.

"Haven't you finished the Spengler yet?" she asked.

"No."

"Let me have it when you're finished."

"Yes."

Nadine couldn't see a book in someone else's hands without asking for it. She would take it to her room, and there it would futilely enlarge the pile of works that filled her future. Actually, she read very slowly, with a kind of hostility, and would grow tired after a few pages.

"It seems that it's nothing but a lot of crap!" she said, sneering.

This time, Lambert raised his head. "Who told you that? Your little Communist pals?"

"Everyone knows Spengler's an ass," she said with assurance. She stretched herself out on the ground and grumbled, "You'd do better taking me for a ride on the motor-cycle."

"I don't feel the least bit like it," Lambert said flatly.

"We could have lunch in Mesnils and then take a walk in the woods."

"And get drenched by the storm. Look at that sky."

"There won't be any storm. Why don't you just say it bores you to go riding with me?"

"It would bore me to go for a ride," he said impatiently. "I just told you that."

She got up. "Well, it bores me to spend the day in this cabbage patch. I'm taking the motor-cycle and going for a ride without you. Give me the ignition key."

"You're crazy. You don't know how to drive it."

"I've already driven it. It's not very difficult. The proof of that is that you can do it."

"And the very first turn, you'll break your neck. Nothing doing. I won't give you the key."

"You don't give a damn if I break my neck! You're afraid I might damage your little plaything, that's all. You're a selfish louse! I want that key!"

Lambert didn't even answer. For a moment, Nadine remained motionless, an empty look in her eyes. Then she rose and picked up the large basket that served her as a purse. "I'm bored silly here," she said to me. "I'm going to spend the day in Paris."

"Have a nice time."

She had chosen her revenge skilfully. Knowing Nadine would be in Paris with friends he hated would certainly make Lambert suffer. As she left the garden, he followed her with his eyes, and then he turned to me.

"I can't understand why our arguments become so bitter so quickly," he said disconsolately. "Do you understand it?"

It was the first time he had ever tried to strike up an intimate conversation with me. I hesitated. But since he was

willing to listen to me the best thing, no doubt, was to try
to speak to him.

"It's mostly Nadine's fault," I said. "A trifle can upset
her, and then she becomes unfair and aggressive. But you
must understand that the reason she becomes so easily hurt
is that she's very vulnerable."

"Well, she could try understanding that others are vulnerable, too," he said bitterly. "Sometimes, she's really unbe-
lievably insensitive."

He looked quite defenceless and very young, with his fresh
complexion, his slightly upturned nose, his eager mouth—a
sensual, perplexed face, torn between too-gentle dreams and
too-arduous tasks. I made up my mind. "To understand
Nadine, you have to go back to her childhood."

As well as I could, I told Lambert everything I had rehashed a thousand times within myself. He looked moved;
he listened to me in silence. But when I spoke Diego's name,
he interrupted me eagerly.

"Is it true he was fabulously intelligent?"

"Yes, he was."

"Were his poems good? Did he really have talent?"

"I believe so."

"And he was only seventeen! Did Nadine admire him?"

"Nadine never admires. No, what made her so attached
to Diego was that he belonged to her unreservedly."

"But so do I. I love her," he said sadly.

"She isn't sure of it," I said. "She's always afraid you're
comparing her to someone else."

"I'm much more devoted to Nadine than I ever was to
Rosa," he murmured.

That surprised me. In spite of everything, it seemed I had
become wedded to Nadine's opinions. "Have you told her
that?"

"It isn't something you can say."

"But it's something she needs to hear."

He shrugged his shoulders. "She knows very well that for
more than a year I've been living only for her."

"She's convinced that that's nothing more than a form of
friendship. And—how shall I explain it to you?—it's as a
woman that she mistrusts herself. She needs to be loved as a
woman."

Lambert hesitated. "But on that score, too, she's difficult. Maybe I shouldn't tell you this, but I just don't understand it; I'm completely at a loss. If a single evening goes by without anything happening between us, she feels insulted. But practically every amorous advance shocks her, so naturally she remains cold, and she hates me for it."

I remembered Nadine's surly confidences. "Are you sure it's she who doesn't want to let a single night go by . . .?"

"Absolutely sure," he replied sullenly.

This contradiction didn't surprise me very much; I had come across any number of similar cases. It always indicated that neither of the lovers was satisfied with the other.

"Nadine feels mutilated when she accepts her femininity and also when she rejects it," I said. "That's what makes the relationship so difficult for you. But if you have enough patience, I'm sure things will work out."

"Oh, I've got all the patience you could want! If only I were sure she didn't hate me!"

"What an idea! She's fiercely devoted to you."

"Often, I think she's scornful of me because I am, as she says, nothing but a little intellectual. An intellectual who hasn't even any creative gifts," he added bitterly. "And who can't make up his mind to use his own wings."

"Nadine could never be interested in anyone but an intellectual," I said. "She loves to argue, to explain herself; she has to put her life into words. No, believe me, the only thing she really has against you is not loving her enough."

"I'll convince her," he said, his face brightening. "If I could only believe she loved me a little, nothing else would matter."

"She loves you a lot. I wouldn't tell you that if I weren't certain of it."

He went back to his book and I to my work. The sky was becoming darker hour by hour; it was completely black when, after lunch, I went up to my room to try to write to Lewis. He had learned to speak to me; it was easier for him than for me. Those people, those things he described had existed for me; through the yellow pages, I could once more see the typewriter, the Mexican blanket, the window opening on the trees, shiny cars rolling along the broken-up street. But this village, my work, Nadine, Lambert were nothing to him. And how to tell about Robert? How to keep quiet about him? The words Lewis whispered to me between the lines of his letters were easy to say: "I'm waiting for you . . . Come back . . . I'm yours . . ." But how to say: "I'm far away . . . I won't come back for a long time . . . I belong to another life?" And if I wanted him to read, "I love you!" how was I to say it? He was calling me, and I, I was unable to call him; I had nothing to give him when I refused him my presence. I re-read my letter and was ashamed. How empty it was, and yet my heart was so heavy! And what shabby promises: I'll come back—but not soon, and then only to leave again. My hand froze as it touched the envelope which, in a few days, his hands would touch, real hands, which I had really felt on my skin. Yes, he really existed! Sometimes, he seemed to me a creation of my heart, and I dealt with him too freely. I would sit him down by the window, brighten his face, awaken his smile, and he had no way of defending himself. That man who overcame me, who overwhelmed me, would I ever find him again in flesh and blood? I left my letter on the desk and leaned against the window sill. Dusk was falling and the storm had broken; in the clouds, armies of horsemen were galloping, lance in hand, and the wind was raging madly in the trees. I went down to the living-room, started a blazing fire in the fireplace, and called up Lambert to invite him to come have dinner with us. When Nadine wasn't there to start an argument, Robert and he tacitly avoided all thorny questions. After the meal, Robert went back to his study, and while Lambert was helping me clear the table Nadine appeared, her hair wringing wet.

He smiled at her pleasantly. "You look like a water nymph. Do you want something to eat?"

"No, I had dinner with Vincent and Sézenac," she replied. She took a napkin from the table and rubbed her hair. "We spoke about the Russian camps. Vincent thinks as I do. He says it's disgusting, but if they start a campaign against it the bourgeois would be only too happy."

"You can't get very far with that kind of reasoning," Lambert said. He shrugged his shoulders irritably. "He'll try to persuade Perron not to speak out."

"Of course," Nadine said.

"I hope he'll be wasting his time," Lambert said. "I've

warned Perron that if he hushes up the matter I'll leave
L'Espoir."

"Now there's an argument that carries weight!" Nadine
said sarcastically.

"Oh, don't go putting on your superior airs now!" Lambert said cheerfully. "Fundamentally, you don't think as
badly of me as you'd like me to believe."

"But perhaps not as much of you as you believe," she
said without any trace of affability.

"That isn't very nice of you!" Lambert said.

"And you? Was it nice of you to let me go to Paris
alone?"

"But you didn't seem to want me to come!" Lambert
said.

"I didn't say I wanted you to come. I said you might have
offered to go with me."

I walked to the door and left the room. I could hear
Lambert saying, "Come on, let's not argue!"

"I'm not arguing!" Nadine said.

I assumed they were going to argue all evening.

I went down to the garden early the next morning. Under
the blue sky, softened by the rains of the previous night, the
countryside was a shambles; dead branches were scattered
over the lawn, the road was full of potholes. I wiped off the
wet table, and as I was setting my papers on it I heard the
roar of the motor-cycle. Nadine, her hair flowing in the
wind, her skirt tucked up high around her bare thighs, was
speeding along the pitted road. Lambert came out of the
cottage and ran over to the fence shouting, "Nadine!" Then
he came towards me, looking frenzied.

"She doesn't know how to drive it!" he said in a frantic
voice. "And with that storm there are broken branches and
fallen trees across the road. She's going to have an accident!"

"Nadine is careful in her own way," I said to reassure
him. But I, too, was worried. She valued her skin, yes, but
she wasn't very skilful.

"She took the ignition key while I was sleeping. She's so
stubborn!" He looked at me reproachfully. "You say she
loves me. But she certainly has a funny way of loving. All I
asked for last night was to make peace. You saw how I was
trying. It didn't do much good."

"It isn't easy to learn to get along," I said. "Just have a little patience."

"With her, you need a lot!"

He went off and I thought sadly, "What a mess!" Nadine was speeding along roads, her hands clenching the handlebars, crying to the wind, "Lambert doesn't love me. No one ever loved me except Diego, and he's dead." And meanwhile, Lambert was pacing in his room, his heart full of doubts. It's difficult to become a man at a time when that word is so heavily weighted with meaning: too many of his dead, tortured, decorated, famous seniors offer themselves as examples to a boy of twenty-five who's still dreaming of a mother's tenderness and a father's protection. I thought of those primitive peoples who teach their five-year-old boys to stick poisoned thorns into the flesh of living animals. With us as well, a male, to win to the dignity of adulthood, must know how to kill, must make others suffer, must suffer himself. Girls are weighed down with restrictions, boys with demands—two equally harmful disciplines. If they had really wanted to help each other, perhaps Nadine and Lambert would have succeeded together in accepting their age, their sex, their real place on earth. Would they ever decide to want to help each other?

Lambert had lunch with us. He was wavering between fear and anger.

"This thing's no longer a joke!" he said agitatedly. "No one has the right to frighten people out of their wits like this. It's pure malice; it's blackmail! She deserves a good slap in the face."

"She doesn't realise you're so worried," I said. "And actually, there's no reason to be. She's probably fast asleep in a meadow or having a sun bath."

"If she isn't lying in a ditch somewhere with her head split open," he said. "She's insane! She's a madwoman!"

He seemed truly anguished. I could understand him. I was far less unworried than I pretended to be. "If something happened, we'd have got a call by now," Robert was saying to me. But perhaps the motor-cycle was skidding at that very moment, and Nadine was smashing into a tree. Robert tried to distract me, but by evening he no longer hid his worry. He was considering calling the local police when, at last, we heard the roar of the motor-cycle. Lambert reached the road ahead of me. The machine was covered with mud; so was Nadine. She dismounted, laughing, and I saw Lambert give her two hard slaps.

"Mother!" Nadine had thrown herself at him, was slapping him in turn. She was shouting, "Mother!" in a high-pitched voice. He grabbed her by the wrists. When I finally reached them, he was so pale that I thought he would faint. Nadine's nose was bleeding, but I knew she could make her nose bleed at will—it was a trick she had learned during her childhood when she would fight with her playmates around the fountains of the Jardin du Luxembourg.

"Aren't you ashamed of yourselves," I said, placing myself between them as I would have separated two children.

"He struck me!" Nadine shouted in a hysterical voice.

I put my arm around her shoulders; I dabbed her nose gently. "Calm yourself," I said.

"He struck me because I took his lousy motor-cycle. I'll smash it to pieces!"

"Calm yourself," I repeated.

"I'll smash it!"

"Listen," I said, "Lambert was very wrong to slap you. But it's only natural that he was beside himself. We have all been terribly worried. We thought you'd had an accident."

"He wouldn't have given a damn! All he was thinking about was his motor-cycle. He was afraid I'd damage it."

"I'm sorry, Nadine," Lambert said unhappily. "I shouldn't have done it. But I was terribly upset. You could have killed yourself."

"Hypocrite! You don't give a damn! I know it. I could drop dead and you wouldn't bat an eyelash. You buried another one easily enough."

"Nadine!" He had turned from white to red; there was no longer anything childlike in his face.

"Buried, forgotten! It didn't take long," she shouted.

"How dare you! You! You who betrayed Diego with the whole American army!"

"Shut up."

"You betrayed him."

Tears of anger were streaming down Nadine's cheeks. "Maybe I betrayed him dead. But you, you let your father denounce Rosa when she was alive."

He was silent for a moment, and then he said, "I never want to see you again. Never."

He got on his motor-cycle, and I could find no words with which to stop him. Nadine was sobbing.

"Come and rest," I said. "Come."

She pushed me away, she threw herself on the grass, she cried out, "A man whose father denounced Jews! And I slept with him! And he slapped me! It serves me right! It serves me right!"

She wept. And there was nothing to be done but to let her weep.

CHAPTER SEVEN

PAULA SPENT the summer at Claudie de Belzunce's and Josette went to tan herself at Cannes with her mother. Henri set out for Italy in a little used car. He loved that country so much that he succeeded in forgetting *L'Espoir,* the S.R.L., all his problems. When he returned to Paris, he found in his mail a report that Lambert had sent from Germany and a sheaf of documents gathered together by Scriassine. He spent the night studying them. In the morning, Italy was very far away. It was possible to have doubts about the documents found in the archives of the Reich, documents that pointed to nine million eight hundred thousand prisoners; it was possible to hold suspect the statements of the Polish internees who were liberated in '41. But to reject systematically all the testimony of men and women who survived the camps you would have to decide once and for all to blindfold your eyes and plug your ears. And then, in addition to the articles on law, with which Henri was already familiar, there was that report published in Moscow in 1935 which enumerated the tremendous works carried out by the Ogpu camps; there was the Five Year Plan of 1941 which allocated fourteen per cent of all construction work to the NKVD. The Kolyma gold mines, the coal mines of Norilsk and Vorkuta, the Starobelsk iron fields, the Komi fisheries—how exactly did people live in those places? How many slave labourers were there altogether? On that point, there was a considerable difference of opinion. But what was certain was that the camps existed on a large scale and in an institutionalised manner. " It has to be brought out in the open," Henri concluded. " If not, I'll be an accessory to the crime, an accessory and guilty of abusing my readers' confidence." He threw himself on his bed without undressing, thinking, " This is going to be great! " He was going to quarrel with the Communists, and *L'Espoir's* position would be a difficult one. He sighed. It made him happy to see workers buying *L'Espoir* at the corner stand every morning. They would stop buying it. And yet how could he remain silent? He could plead that he didn't know enough about it to speak out: it was the régime taken as a whole which gave those camps their true significance, and how poorly informed one was! But on the other hand, he didn't know enough about it to keep quiet. Ignorance is no alibi: he had long ago accepted that fact. When in doubt, and since he had promised his readers the truth, he had to tell them what he knew. There would have had to be definite reasons to make him decide to hide it from them. His reluctance to tangle with the Communists was no such definite reason; it concerned only himself.

Happily circumstances gave him a short respite. Neither Dubreuilh nor Lambert nor Scriassine was in Paris, and Samazelle made only vague allusions to the affair. Henri forced himself to think about it as little as possible; besides, there were quite a few other things he had to think about, unimportant but urgent things. The rehearsals of his play were stormy. Salève was extravagantly Slavic; the frequency of his outbursts made them no less dreadful and they reduced Josette to tears. Vernon began to be afraid of a scandal and suggested completely unacceptable cuts and changes. He had assigned the costumes to Maison Amaryllis, and Lucie Belhomme refused to understand that Josette was supposed to be coming out of a burning church and not a dressmaker's shop. Henri was obliged to spend hours at the theatre.

"I really should call Paula," he said to himself one morning. While she was away, she had sent him only a few mysterious postcards, and since her return to Paris a few days earlier she had given him no sign of life. But, of course, she was anxiously waiting for the telephone to ring; her discretion was simply a manœuvre, and it would have been cruel of him to take advantage of it. However, when he called her up, she set an appointment in such a calm voice that he had a glimmer of hope as he climbed the stairs: maybe she had broken with him for good. She was smiling when she opened the door; dumbfounded, he asked himself, "What's happened to her?" Her hair was put up, revealing the thick nape of her neck; her eyebrows were plucked; she was wearing a suit which was too tight for her. She looked almost vulgar.

Still smiling, she said, "Why are you looking at me like that?"

He, too, forced himself to smile. " You're dressed rather
strangèly . . ."

" Do I surprise you?" She took a long cigarette holder
from her purse and stuck it in her mouth. " I'm hoping to
surprise you a great deal." She looked at him, her eyes
shining with mischief. " And first of all, I will tell you a bit
of news: I'm writing."

" You're writing?" he said. " And what are you writing?"

" You'll find out one day," she replied.

She was chewing on her cigarette holder with a mysterious
air ; Henri walked over to the window. Paula had often put
on tragic acts for him. but this kind of comedy was unworthy of her. If he hadn't feared complications, he would
have ripped that cigarette holder from her mouth, would
have shaken her, messed up her hair.

He turned around. " Did you have a nice holiday?"

" Very nice. And you? What have you been doing with
yourself?" she asked almost indulgently.

" Oh, I've been spending my days at the theatre. At the
moment we're marking time. Salève's a good director, but it
doesn't take much to get him excited."

" Will the youngster do?" Paula asked.

" I think she'll be excellent."

Paula took a puff of her cigarette, inhaled, choked,
coughed. " Is your affair with her still on?"

" Yes."

She studied him almost solicitously. " That's strange,"
she said.

" Why?" he asked. He hesitated. " It isn't just a passing
whim. I'm in love with her," he said decisively.

Paula smiled. " Do you really believe that?"

" I'm positive of it. I love Josette," he said firmly.

" Why do you tell me that, in that tone of voice?" she
asked, looking surprised.

" What tone of voice?"

" A strange tone."

He gestured impatiently. " Tell me about your holiday
instead. You wrote so little . . ."

" I was very busy."

" Was it a nice place?"

" I liked it," Paula replied.

It was tiring asking questions that she only answered with

short sentences heavy with mysterious innuendo. Henri became so fed up with it that he left after ten minutes. She didn't try to hold him back nor did she ask to see him again.

Lambert got back from Germany a week before the opening. He had changed. Since his father's death, he had become sullen and withdrawn. He immediately began speaking volubly about his investigation and the testimony he had gathered. He looked at Henri suspiciously.

"Are you convinced now or not?" he asked.

"Yes, on the essentials."

"That's something, at least!" Lambert said. "And Dubreuilh? What's he got to say about it?"

"I haven't seen him since I got back. He doesn't budge from St. Martin and I haven't had time to go there."

"But it's important to start taking action," Lambert said. He frowned. "I hope he'll have enough good faith to admit that this time the facts have been established."

"No doubt," Henri replied.

Again Lambert examined Henri distrustfully. "Personally, are you still in favour of speaking out?"

"Personally, yes."

"And if the old man is against it?"

"We'll put it before the Committee."

Lambert's face darkened, and Henri added, "Listen, give me another week. At the moment, I don't know whether I'm coming or going, but I'll go speak to him right after the opening and we'll settle the question once and for all. I'm going over to the theatre," he added in a friendly voice. "Would you like to come along?"

"I read your play. I don't like it," Lambert replied.

"That's your privilege," Henri said cheerfully. "But I thought you might like to watch a rehearsal."

"I've got work to do. I have to get my notes in order," Lambert said. There was an embarrassed silence, and then Lambert seemed to have made up his mind. "I saw Volange in August," he said in a noncommittal voice. "He's starting a big literary weekly, and he offered me the job of editor in chief."

"I've heard about that project," Henri said. "*Les Beaux Jours*, isn't it? I suppose he doesn't dare run it himself, openly."

"Are you trying to say he intends to use me? As a matter

of fact, he wanted us to run the paper together. That doesn't make his offer any less interesting."

"In any event, you can't work for both *L'Espoir* and a rightist sheet at the same time," Henri said sharply.

"It's going to be a purely literary weekly."

"That's what they always say. But people who claim they're apolitical invariably turn out to be reactionaries." Henri shrugged his shoulders. "Anyhow, how can you hope to reconcile our ideas and Volange's?"

"I don't feel so far from him. I've often told you I shared his contempt for politics."

"You don't seem to understand that with Volange that contempt is also a political attitude, the only one possible for him at the moment."

Henri stopped talking; Lambert had begun to look stubborn. Volange, no doubt, had known how to flatter him, and then he was holding out to him the opportunity of mixing good and evil in such a way as to absolve his father of guilt and also to justify his own burdensome wealth. "I'll have to work things out so I can see him often and talk to him," Henri said to himself. But for the moment, he didn't have the time. "We'll talk about all that again," he said, shaking Lambert's hand.

It hurt him a little to hear Lambert speak so sharply about his play. Doubtless because of his father, it had embarrassed Lambert to have the past stirred up. But why that note of hostility? "It's a pity!" Henri said to himself. He would really have liked to have an outsider witness one of the last rehearsals and tell him what he thought. He was completely at a loss. Salève and Josette didn't stop wailing, Lucie Belhomme steadfastly refused to tear Josette's dress, Vernon was stubbornly insisting on giving a party after the opening. Henri could protest and rail all he wanted: no one listened to a word he said. And he had a feeling they were racing towards disaster. "After all, whether a play's a hit or a failure isn't that important," he tried to tell himself. Except that there was Josette; and if he personally could take a failure, she needed a hit. He decided to telephone the Dubreuilhs, who had just returned to Paris. Could they come to the theatre to-morrow? They were running through the whole play and he was anxious to have their opinion.

"To-morrow's fine," Anne said. "We'd be tremendously

interested. And it would make Robert take a little rest; he's working like a madman."

Henri was a little afraid that Dubreuilh would lose no time in bringing up the matter of the camps. But perhaps he, too, was in no hurry to make a decision; he didn't once mention it. Henri was feeling very nervous when the rehearsal began. Already it bothered him when he saw somebody reading one of his novels; sitting beside the Dubreuilhs while they were listening to his script seemed somehow to have something obscene about it. Anne seemed moved and Dubreuilh interested. But in what didn't he take an interest? Henri didn't dare question him. The last line fell in a glacial silence. And then Dubreuilh turned to Henri.

"You can be very happy about it!" he said warmly. "It plays even better than it reads. And I told you when I read it that it's the best thing you've ever done."

"There's no doubt about it!" Anne said enthusiastically.

They continued to pour out glowing eulogies; they said the very words Henri wanted to hear. It was certainly pleasant, but it was also a little frightening. During those three weeks he had done his best to give the play every possible chance, but he hadn't wanted to question himself on its worth, on its success. He had forbidden himself both hope and fear, but now he felt his caution melting. The best thing he had ever done. Was that good? Would the public find it good?

The evening of the opening, his heart was beating too rapidly. Hidden behind a prop, he listened to the confused uproar coming from the invisible audience. Vanities, mirages —for years he had been guarding himself against counterfeits. But he had never forgotten the dreams of his youth. Glory: he had believed in it, had promised himself that one day he would hold it against him, embrace it as one embraces one's love. Glory is difficult to grasp; it has no face. "But at least," he thought, "it can reveal itself as a noise." He had heard it once. He had mounted the platform, had come down again, his arms laden with books, and his name sounded above the din of the applause. Perhaps he would once again know that childhood glorification. One can't always be modest, one can't always be proud and ignore all this evidence. If you spend the best of your days trying to communicate with others, it's because others count, and from time to time you need to know that you've succeeded in counting for them. You need festive moments in which the present gathers up in itself all of the past, and all of the triumphs of the future . . .

Henri's musings were sharply interrupted by the three taps signalling the start of the play. The curtain rose on a dark cave in which people were sitting, silent, their eyes blank. There was so little connection between that calm scene and the menagerie noises that had filled the last half hour that one wondered from where they had come. They didn't seem completely real. The truth was that scorched village, the sun, the shouting, the German voices, the fear. Someone in the theatre coughed, and Henri knew that they, too, were real—the Dubreuilhs, Paula, Lucie Belhomme, Lambert, the Volanges, and so many others he knew, so many others he didn't know. What exactly were they doing here? He remembered an afternoon red with sun, with wine and with bloody memories. He had wanted to tear it whole from that hot August, to tear it from time. He had dwelt on it in dreams, and a story had grown, as well as ideas which became words. He had wanted the words, the ideas, the story to become a living thing. That mute assemblage, was it there to give them life? There was a burst of machine-gun fire, and Josette crossed the deserted square in her too-beautiful, unmistakably Amaryllis dress. She collapsed downstage as shouts and raucous orders came from the wings. From the auditorium, too, came shouting; a woman wearing a hat of yellow bird-of-paradise feathers noisily left her seat, crying, "Enough of these horrors!" Amid booing and applause, Josette gave Henri a hunted look, and he smiled back at her calmly. She began speaking again. He was smiling, but what he wanted was to jump up on the stage or whisper new words to Josette, persuasive, over-powering words. He had only to stretch his hand to touch her arm, but the footlights excluded him from that world in which the play continued to unfold itself inexorably. It was then that Henri knew why they had been summoned: to deliver the verdict. It wasn't a glorification; it was a trial. He recognised those sentences he had chosen so hopefully in the indulgent silence of his room; to-night they had a criminal flavour. Guilty, guilty, guilty. He felt as alone as the accused man in a courtroom silently listening to his lawyer. He was pleading guilty and all he asked for was the jury's mercy. Again, someone shouted, "It's shameful!" and he was powerless to say a word in his own defence. When the curtain fell on the first act to applause mingled with a few boos, he noticed that his hands were damp. He left his vantage point in the wings and shut himself up in Vernon's office. In a few minutes, the door opened.

"They told me you didn't want to see anyone," Paula said. "But I don't suppose I'm someone." There was a studied ease in her voice; she was wearing a black dress and to-night again her quiet elegance made her seem eccentric. "You must be delighted!" she added. "It's a lovely scandal."

"Yes," he said. "That's the impression I got."

"You know, the woman who protested is a Swiss who spent the whole war in Geneva. There was also a nice little scuffle in the rear of the orchestra. And Huguette Volange pretended to faint."

Henri smiled. "Huguette fainted?"

"Very elegantly. But he's the one you ought to see. Poor Louis! He smells a success and he's livid."

"A mighty strange success!" Henri said. "Wait and see: in the second act everyone who applauded is going to start booing."

"So much the better!" Paula said haughtily, adding, "The Dubreuilhs are delighted."

Naturally, all his friends were pleased with that joyous commotion. To intellectuals, a scandal always seems favourable when it's someone else who creates it. Those hates and angers which Henri had unleashed were directed at him alone. Men had been burned alive in a church, and Josette had betrayed the husband she truly loved. The emotions, the bitterness of the audience made those cardboard crimes real. And he was the criminal! Once again, leaning against a prop in the shadows, he studied his judges and, stupefied, he thought, "That's what I've done! I did it!" A year had passed; the August sun was still beating down on the skeleton village, but crosses had sprung up above the graves. They were watering them with speeches, the air was filled with patriotic music, and widows draped in black were parading with flowers in their arms. Again a hostile buzzing spread through the night.

"I'm ridiculing the merchants of death, and they're going

to accuse me of flouting the corpses." he thought. His hands were dry now, but in his throat he felt a sulphurous vapour. "Am I so vulnerable?" he wondered with revulsion. The others, when you shook their hands in the wings, seemed always to have a detached, nonchalant air. Did they, too, secretly have these childish fears? How was he to compare himself with them? On everything else, they explain themselves complacently; they do not hesitate to communicate to the world at large a detailed catalogue of their vices and the exact dimensions of their tools. But no writer has ever been presumptuous enough or humble enough to lay out in broad daylight his ambitions and his disappointments. "Our sincerity would be as shocking as that of a child," Henri said to himself. "We lie as they do, and like them each of us is secretly afraid of being a monster." The curtain fell for the second time, and Henri assumed a detached, nonchalant air while shaking hands with the curious. It was like the receiving line after a church ceremony—but had it been a wedding or a funeral?

"It's a triumph!" Lucie Belhomme cried out, rushing towards him as he entered the huge restaurant in which a perfumed crowd was jabbering away. She placed her gloved hand on Henri's arm; on her head a big, black, sad-looking bird was poised. "You've got to admit that Josette really looked stunning when she came on in that red dress."

"To-morrow night I'm going to take that dress, drag it through the mud, and give it a few good rips here and there."

"You've no right to do that. It's an Amaryllis original!" Lucie said sharply. "Besides, everyone thought it was very beautiful."

"It's Josette they thought was beautiful!" Henri said. He smiled at Josette, who smiled dolefully back at him. At the same moment, they were blinded by a magnesium flash. He made a move, but Lucie's hand clutched his arm.

"Be nice. Josette needs the publicity."

There was another flash, and then another. Paula observed the scene with the air of an outraged vestal. "Why can't she stop making a fuss over everything?" he thought irritably. He didn't know whether he had won or lost his case; you need the heart of a child to recognise the sober but assumed glory of the awarding of honours. But suddenly, he felt like being gay. Something had just happened to him, one of the things he had dreamed about confusedly fifteen years earlier when he saw the flamboyant posters on the cylindrical billboards of Paris: his first play had been produced and people had found it good. He smiled across the room at the Dubreuilhs and took a few steps in their direction when Louis stopped him. He was holding a martini in his hand; his eyes were a little bleary.

"Well, it looks as if you've got what they call a big Parisian hit on your hands!"

"How's Huguette?" Henri asked. "I heard she wasn't feeling well."

"Oh, that's because you put your audience's nerves to a pretty severe test!" Louis replied. "I'm not one of those who becomes indignant, you understand. Why should one refuse a priori to employ melodramatic tricks, or even, as your detractors say, Grand Guignol devices? But Huguette is a sensitive type; she just couldn't take it. She left after the first act."

"I'm terribly sorry!" Henri said. "You shouldn't have felt obliged to stay."

"I was obliged to come and congratulate you," Louis said with an open smile. "After all, I'm your oldest friend." He looked around him. "I'm certainly the only one here who knew that little high-school boy in Tulle who worked so hard. If anyone deserves success, it's you."

Henri repressed a number of answers. No, he couldn't exchange insults with Louis; it was unpleasant enough imagining what was going on at that moment in his envious head. It would be better not to stir up any new eddies in it.

He cut the conversation short. "Thanks for coming. And my apologies to Huguette," he said, leaving Louis with a brief smile.

Yes, Louis was the only one who shared with him those memories of his childhood and his youth, memories which had finally blossomed that night. Suddenly, Henri felt revolted by them. He had no luck with his past. It often seemed to him that all the years gone by remained at his call, intact, like a book you've just closed and which you can reopen at will. He had promised himself that before his life was over he would sum it up. But for one reason or another, his attempts always miscarried. At any rate, it was hardly the moment to try piecing his whole existence together; there were too many hands to shake; and under the assault of ambiguous compliments, he was losing his footing.

"Well, you made it!" Dubreuilh said. "Half the people are furious, the other half enchanted. But they all predict three hundred performances."

"Josette was good, wasn't she?" Henri said.

"Yes, and she's so lovely," Anne replied a little hastily. Caustically, she added, "But the mother! What a filthy bitch! I overheard her snickering with Vernon a little while ago . . . Really, she has no shame at all."

"What was she saying?"

"I'll tell you later," Anne replied. She looked around her. "She certainly has horrid friends!"

"They're not her friends, nor anyone else's," Dubreuilh said. "They're the high-fashion Parisians. There's nothing worse." He smiled at Henri apologetically. "I'm going to beat it."

"I'll stay a while," Anne said. "To see Paula."

Dubreuilh shook Henri's hand. "Will you drop over to the house to-morrow or the next day?"

"Yes, we have to make a decision," Henri replied. "It's becoming urgent."

"Give me a ring," Dubreuilh said.

He walked rapidly to the door; he was happy to leave and didn't try to hide it. And it was apparent, too, that Anne was staying only out of politeness; she felt ill at ease. What exactly had Lucie said? "That's why Lachaume and Vincent didn't come to the party," Henri thought. "They're all blaming me for association with these people." He stole a glance at Paula, who was frozen into a reproachful statue, and while continuing to greet the elegant guests whom Vernon was introducing to him he wondered, "Is it I who's at fault? Or have things changed?" There was a time when you knew your friends and your enemies, when you liked people at the peril of your life or hated them unto death. Now, however, reservations and grudges found their way into every friendship; hate had been dissipated. No one was willing any more to give his life or to kill.

"It's quite an interesting play," Lenoir said stiffly. "A complex play." He hesitated. "I only regret that you didn't wait a little while to have it put on."

" Wait for what? The referendum?" Julien said.

" Exactly. This isn't the moment to underline the weaknesses the parties of the left may have."

" Bilge! Fortunately Perron finally made up his mind to kick over the traces. Conformism doesn't become him, not even when it's dyed in red." Julien turned to Henri and chuckled. " The Commies are going to give you such a working-over that you won't feel like singing in their choir any more."

" I don't believe Perron is capable of harbouring resentment," Lenoir said with troubled ardour. " God knows I myself have suffered rebuffs at the hands of the C.P.! But I shan't let myself become discouraged. They can insult me, slander me, but they'll never make me sink into anti-Communism."

" In other words, kick me in the face and I turn the other cheek," Julien said with a guffaw.

Lenoir turned very red. " Anarchism is also a type of conformism," he said. " You'll be writing for *Figaro* one of these days."

He turned and walked quietly away. Julien put his hand on Henri's shoulder. " You know, your play isn't bad, but it would have been a lot better if you'd made it a farce." He looked over the assemblage and gestured vaguely. " A satire on all these lovely people—you'd really have something!"

" You write it!" Henri said irritably. He smiled at Josette, who was displaying her golden-brown shoulders to a circle of admirers. He started to walk towards her when he caught Marie-Ange's trapped look; Louis had pinned her against the buffet and was speaking to her nose to nose while drinking a martini. Men usually reacted to Louis' intellectual seduction, but he had never been successful with women. There was a greedy eagerness in the smile he offered Marie-Ange; you felt as if he were ready to withdraw it the moment it had achieved its purpose. He seemed to be saying, " I want you; but hurry up and give in, because I have no time to waste." A few steps from them, Lambert stood, gloomily pensive. Henri stopped beside him.

" What a brawl!" he said, smiling at him. He did not find in his eyes the understanding he had hoped to find.

" Yes, a real brawl!" Lambert said. " Half the people here want nothing better than to kill the other half. And that's only natural, since you've chosen to straddle the fence."

"You call this straddling? I've made everybody unhappy."

"'Everybody' takes in too much territory," Lambert said. "That comes out to 'nobody.' A scandal of this kind is simply for publicity."

"I know you didn't like the play, but that's no reason to be nasty about it," Henri said in a conciliatory voice.

"But it's important!" Lambert said.

"Why? Even supposing the play's a failure, there's nothing so important about that."

"The important thing is that you've stooped to this kind of success!" Lambert said, his voice restrained. "The subject you chose, the tricks you use—it's catering to the public's basest instincts. We have a right to expect something else of you."

"You people make me laugh!" Henri said. "You're all asking me to do things: to join the C.P., to fight it, to be less serious, to be more so, to give up politics, to consecrate myself to it body and soul. And all of you are disappointed, all of you shake your heads reproachfully."

"Would you like us to forbid ourselves to judge you?"

"I'd like to be judged on the basis of what I do, and not on what I don't do," Henri replied. "It's funny: when you're starting out, you're welcomed with open arms, readers are grateful for the positive things you bring them. But later, all you have are debts, and no credit."

"Don't worry," Lambert said, "the reviews will be excellent." He did not sound very friendly.

Henri shrugged his shoulders and walked over to Louis, who was declaiming loudly to Marie-Ange and Anne. He couldn't handle liquor, and he looked completely drunk. It was the price he had to pay for his sobriety.

"Look at that thing," he was saying, pointing to Marie-Ange. "It sleeps with everybody, it paints its face, it shows its legs, it pads its breasts. And then all of a sudden it starts playing the Blessed Virgin."

"Nevertheless, I do have the right to sleep with whom I please," Marie-Ange said querulously.

"The right? What right? Who gave it any rights?" Louis shouted. "It thinks nothing, it feels nothing, it barely breathes, and it demands its rights! There's democracy for you! It's a lot of . . ."

"And where do you get the right to give everyone a pain in the neck?" Anne said. "Look at that man who thinks he's Neitzsche just because he's calling a woman names!"

"Oh, a woman! Naturally, you've got to prostrate yourself before a *woman*!" Louis said. "Talk about goddesses! They think they're goddesses, but that doesn't stop them from behaving like everyone else."

"You've had too much to drink; you're acting like a boor. I think you'd better go home and sleep it off," Henri said.

"Naturally, you defend them! Women are a part of your humanism," Louis said in a voice which was growing thick. "You throw them on their backs but you respect them! What a joke. They don't mind spreading their thighs, but they want to be respected. That's the way it is, huh?"

"And being a foul-mouthed bore, is that part of your mysticism?" Henri said. "If you don't shut up at once, I'll throw you out of here."

"You're taking advantage of me because I've been drinking," Louis said. He walked away angrily.

"Is he often like that?" Marie-Ange asked.

"All the time. Only he rarely drops his mask," Anne replied. "To-night, he's insanely jealous."

"Would you like a drink to calm your nerves?" Henri asked.

"I'd love one. I didn't dare drink with him around."

Henri handed Marie-Ange a glass, and then he caught sight of Josette standing in front of Paula, who was talking volubly to her. Her eyes were pleading for help; he went over and stood between the two women.

"You look terribly serious, you two. What are you talking about?"

"We were having a woman-to-woman talk," Paula replied, looking rather tense.

"She says she doesn't hate me. I never thought she hated me," Josette whined.

"Come now, Paula! Don't get emotional," Henri said.

"I'm not being emotional. I wanted to define my position clearly," Paula said haughtily. "I detest ambiguity."

"There's no ambiguity."

"So much the better," she said. And she walked nonchalantly to the door.

" She frightens me," Josette said. " I was looking at you so that you'd come and get me out of it. But you were much too busy flirting with that swarthy little girl."

" I was flirting with Marie-Ange? Me? But my darling, just look at her and then look at yourself."

" Men have such strange tastes." Josette's voice was trembling. " That fat old woman who was telling me you're hers for ever, and you standing there giggling with a bow-legged girl!"

" Josette, my little faun! You know perfectly well I love only you."

" What do I know?" she said. " Does one ever know? After me there'll be another. Maybe she's here now," she said, looking around her.

" It seems to me it's I who have a right to complain," he said cheerfully. " They were really paying court to you to-night."

She shivered. " Do you think I like that?"

" Don't be sad. Believe me, you gave a beautiful per-formance."

" I didn't do too badly—for a pretty girl. Sometimes I wish I were ugly," she said sorrowfully.

He smiled. " May the heavens not hear your plea."

" Oh, don't worry. They never hear anything up there."

" You really surprised them," he said, pointing to the crowd.

" Oh, no, you're wrong there! Nothing ever surprises them; they're much too mean."

" Come on, let's go home. You've got to get some rest," he said.

" You want to leave already?"

" Don't you?"

" Oh, yes! Very much. I'm tired. Just give me five minutes."

Henri followed her with his eyes as she was saying her good-byes, and he thought, " Yes, it's true: nothing surprises them. You can neither move them nor make them indignant; what goes on in their heads has no more weight than their words." As long as they were lost in the remoteness of the future, or the darkness of the theatre, you could easily delude yourself about them. But as soon as you saw them face to face, it was clear there was nothing to hope for and nothing to fear from them. Yes, that was the most disappointing thing of all: not that the verdict was uncertain, but that it was given by those people. In the end, nothing that had happened that night had any importance; the dreams of his youth had been meaningless. Henri tried to tell himself, "This isn't the real public." Yes, from time to time, there would be a few men, a few women in the theatre to whom it would be worth-while speaking. But they would always be isolated cases. He would never face friendly audiences who held the same truths as his in their hearts. They didn't exist, at any rate not in this society.

"Don't be sad," he said, sitting down next to Josette in her little car.

Without answering, she leaned her head against the back of the seat and closed her eyes with a sigh of exhaustion. Was it true that the public had received her rather coldly? In any case, that was what she believed. And he had wanted so much for her to feel triumphant, at least for one night! He was driving in silence along a narrow street when he passed a woman walking rapidly. Henri recognised Anne and slowed down.

"Want to get in? I'll drop you."

"Thanks, but I feel like walking," she replied.

She gave him a friendly little wave and he pressed down on the accelerator. He had seen tears in her eyes. "Why? For nothing, probably. And for everything," he thought. He, too, was tired of that evening, of others, of himself. "This is not what I wanted!" he said to himself with a sudden feeling of despair, not knowing if he was thinking of Anne's tears, or of Lambert's mournful face, of Josette's disappointment, of his friends, of his enemies, of those who were absent, of that evening, of the past two years, or of his whole life.

"Meat for the beasts!" Henri said to himself. When you throw a novel into the critics' den, they bite into it one after the other. But with a play, you get hit in the face all at once with that mud in which both flowers and spit are mixed. Vernon was delighted—even the bad reviews would help the play along. But Henri looked at the clippings spread out on his desk with a disgust bordering on shame. He remembered something Josette had once said and he thought, "Fame, too, is humiliating." To exhibit oneself is always to yield, to stoop. Anyone who pleased had the right to give him a kick or bestow a smile on him. He had learned to defend himself, had his own little tricks. He could clearly conjure up his detractors' faces: the ambitious, the bitter, the failures, the imbeciles. And those who congratulated him were worth neither more nor less than the others. Only their sympathy could pass for discernment, and through the subterfuge they regained enough worth so that one could give their praise a certain measure of value. "How difficult good faith is!" Henri said to himself. The truth of the matter was that neither the insults nor the compliments proved anything; the thing about them that hurt was that they imprisoned Henri within himself, inexorably. If his play had been a complete failure, he could have looked upon it as a minor accident and consoled himself with promises. But in it he rediscovered himself and he knew clearly what his limitations were. *The best thing you've ever done.* Those words of Dubreuilh's still plagued him. He didn't find it pleasing to hear it said that his first book was still the best of all; but neither was it comforting to think that that play of uncertain merit outclassed the rest of his works. He had told Nadine one day that he avoided comparing himself with others; but there are moments when you're forced to do so, when the others force you to it. And then you begin asking yourself unnecessary questions: "Who am I actually? What am I worth?" It's agonising, it's useless. And yet, perhaps, it's cowardly never to ask oneself such questions. Henri was relieved to hear footsteps in the hall.

"Can we come in?" Samazelle asked. Luc, Lambert, and Scriassine followed him.

"I've been waiting for you."

Except for Luc who drowsily dragged his big, gouty feet, they all looked as if they had come to demand an accounting. They sat down around the desk.

"I must admit I don't really understand the point of this meeting," Henri said. "I'm going to see Dubreuilh in a little while."

"Precisely. A decision has to be made before you meet him," Samazelle said. "When I spoke to him, he couldn't have been more reticent. I'm convinced he's going to ask for further delays. But Peltov and Scriassine insist on prompt action, and I'm in complete agreement. I'd like it to be established that, in the event of Dubreuilh's opposition, the paper will disengage itself from the S.R.L. and without it proceed to publish these documents."

"We'll bring the question before the whole Committee whether Dubreuilh says yes or no," Henri replied sharply. "And we'll abide by its decision."

"The Committee will follow Dubreuilh."

"Then I'll follow him, too. Besides, I don't see why we're wasting time discussing the matter before knowing his answer."

"Because his answer is only too predictable," Samazelle replied. "He'll use the referendum and the elections as pretexts to get out of it."

"I'll try to convince him. But I won't break with the S.R.L.," Henri said.

"Does the S.R.L. still exist? It's been fast asleep for three months now," Samazelle said.

"For the past three months, the S.R.L. has done nothing to check the Communist offensive," Scriassine said. "For the past three months, Dubreuilh has no longer been attacked by the Commy press. And there's an excellent reason for it, a reason which throws a completely new light on the situation." He paused dramatically. "Dubreuilh has been enrolled in the C.P. since the end of June."

"Come now!" Henri said.

"I have proof," Scriassine said.

"What proof?"

"Both his card and his file were seen." Scriassine smiled with satisfaction. "Since '44, a lot of people have joined the Party who actually are no more Stalinists than you or I. They've just been looking for a way to play safe. I know more than one of them, and, in private, there's nothing they like better than to talk. I've been suspicious of Dubreuilh for a long time; I asked questions and I got answers."

"Your stool pigeons were either lying or mistaken," Henri said. "If Dubreuilh had wanted to join the C.P., he'd have begun by quitting the S.R.L. and explaining why."

"He's always been careful to make sure that the S.R.L. doesn't become a political party," Samazelle said. "In principle, a Communist can belong to the movement. And conversely a member of the movement can believe that he has the right to join the C.P."

"But he'd have let us know," Henri said. "The C.P. isn't a secret society."

"You don't know them!" Scriassine said. "It's in the C.P.'s interest to have certain of its members pose as independents. The proof is that if I hadn't opened your eyes you'd have fallen into the trap."

"I don't believe you," Henri said.

"I can get you to meet one of my informants," Scriassine said, reaching for the telephone.

"I'll put the question to Dubreuilh and to him alone," Henri said.

"And you believe that he'll answer you honestly? Either you're naïve or you have your own reasons for evading the truth," Scriassine said.

"I feel that this new fact radically changes our relationship with the S.R.L.," Samazelle said.

"It isn't a fact," Henri retorted.

"Why should Dubreuilh lend himself to that kind of manœuvre?" Luc asked.

"Because the C.P. told him to and because he's ambitious," Scriassine replied.

"Perhaps he's got the senile idea that the happiness of humanity is in Stalin's hands," Samazelle said.

"He's an old fox who imagines the Communists have won and that it's better to get on their side," Scriassine said. "And in a way he's right: you've got to have a taste for martyrdom to maintain a critical attitude and yet not do anything to stop them from coming to power. When they get there, you'll find out the price you'll have to pay for that absurd approach."

"Those personal considerations don't touch me," Henri said.

"And the labour camps, do they or don't they touch you?" Lambert asked.

"Have I refused to speak out about them? I said I'd do it in accord with Dubreuilh, that's all. And that's my last word on the matter. This discussion is completely beside the point. In two or three days, the Committee will have been consulted and we'll let you know its answer," Henri said, turning to Scriassine.

"L'Espoir's board might have a different answer," Samazelle said, getting up.

" That remains to be seen."

They walked to the door, but Lambert remained standing in front of Henri's desk.

" You should have agreed to see Scriassine's informer," he said. " Dubreuilh is your friend, but he's also the leader of the movement you belong to. Under the plea of trusting in him, you're betraying the trust that others have placed in you."

" But this whole thing is just a lot of nonsense!" Henri said.

Actually, he wasn't as sure of it as all that. If Dubreuilh had finally decided to join the C.P., he wouldn't have consulted Henri. He always went his own way without consulting anyone, without taking heed of anyone; Henri had no illusions on that score. Pinned down, perhaps he would hesitate to lie; but until now, no one had asked him any questions, and his conscience, without a doubt, adapted itself to mental reservations.

" You're going to let yourself be taken in by his sophisms," Lambert said unhappily. " As for me, I feel that not to reveal the truth completely and immediately in a case like this would be a crime. I warned you in June: if you don't publish those documents, I'll sell you my holdings and you can dispose of them as you like. When I bought into the paper, it was in the hope that you'd soon stop all collaboration with the C.P. If it continues, I have no choice but to leave."

" I have never collaborated with the C.P."

" I call it collaboration. If it concerned Spain, or Greece, or Palestine, or Indo-China, you'd have refused from the very first day to remain silent about it. Come now, face the facts! They tear a man from his family, from his life, without even the pretence of a trial. They throw him in a prison camp, make him work to the limits of his strength, barely feed him. And if he should get sick they starve him to death. Can you permit that? Every one of them, the workers, the managers—they all know it can happen to them from one minute to the next. They live with that terror constantly hanging over their heads! Can you permit that?" Lambert repeated.

" No, of course not!" Henri replied.

"Then hurry up and protest. During the Occupation, you weren't gentle with people who didn't protest!"

"I'll protest," Henri replied impatiently. "That's settled."

"You said you'd follow Dubreuilh," Lambert said. "And Dubreuilh will oppose this campaign."

"You're wrong," Henri said. "He won't oppose it."

"Suppose I'm not wrong?"

"Listen, first I've got to talk to him; then we'll see," Henri replied.

"Yes, we'll see!" Lambert said, walking to the door.

Henri listened to the sound of his step fading away in the hall. He felt as if it were his own youth that had just appealed to him; he wouldn't have considered remaining silent for one second if he had seen, through the eyes of a young man of twenty, those millions of slaves imprisoned behind barbed wire. And Lambert had seen through him: he was hesitating. Why? He didn't want the Communists to see him as an enemy, and, more important, he would have liked to hide from himself the fact that in Russia, too, something was rotten. But all that was nothing but cowardice. He got up and walked down the stairs. "A Communist would have the right to choose silence," he thought. "His positions have been stated, and even when he lies, he's not, in a way, deceiving anyone. But I, who profess to independence, if I use my credit to stifle the truth, I'm a swindler. I'm not a Communist precisely because I want to be free to say what the Communists don't want to say and can't say. It's often a thankless rôle, but one whose usefulness they themselves fundamentally recognise. Certainly Lachaume, for example, would be grateful to me for speaking out—he and all those who want to see the camps abolished, but who aren't permitted to protest openly against them. And who knows? Perhaps they'll attempt something officially; perhaps pressures applied by the various Communist parties themselves will make the Soviet Union modify its penitentiary system. Oppressing men in secret and oppressing them in front of the whole world isn't the same thing. To keep my mouth shut would be defeatism; it would be both refusing to look things in the face and denying that they can be changed; it would be condemning the Soviet Union irrevocably under the guise of not judging her. If there's really no chance for

her to become what she should be, then there's no longer
any hope left on earth ; what we do, what we say, no longer
has any meaning. Yes," Henri repeated to himself, climbing
the stairway to Dubreuilh's apartment, "either speaking out
means something, or nothing means anything. We've got to
speak out. And unless Dubreuilh has actually joined the
Party, he must agree." Henri rang the bell. "But if Dubreuilh has joined, would he tell me?"

"How are you?" Dubreuilh said. "How's the play
going? All in all, the reviews were very good, weren't they?"

Henri had the feeling that that cordial voice rang false—
perhaps because inside himself something was ringing false.

"Yes, they're all right," he replied. He shrugged his
shoulders. "Let me tell you, I've had a bellyfull of that play.
All I ask is to be able to think of something else."

"I know how you feel," Dubreuilh said. "There's something disheartening about success." He smiled. "People are
never happy: failures aren't very pleasant, either."

They sat down in the study, and Dubreuilh continued,
"Well, it so happens that we do have something else to talk
about."

"Yes, and I'm anxious to know what you think," Henri
said. "As for me, I'm convinced now that, substantially,
Peltov told the truth."

"Substantially, yes," Dubreuilh said. "The camps do exist.
They're not death camps like the Nazis', but nevertheless they
are prison camps. And the police do have the right to send
people to them for five years, without a trial. That said, I'd
very much like to know how many internees there are, how
many of them political prisoners, and how many are sentenced for life. Peltov's figures are completely arbitrary."

Henri nodded his head in agreement. "In my opinion, we
shouldn't publish his report," he said. "We'll decide together which facts seem definite to us, and we'll draw our
own conclusions. We'll speak in our own name, stating our
own point of view clearly."

Dubreuilh looked up at Henri. "My own opinion is to
publish nothing at all. And I'll tell you why . . ."

Henri felt his heart skip a beat. "So it was the others
who saw things clearly," he said to himself. He interrupted
Dubreuilh. "You want to bury this?"

"You know damned well it won't stay buried. The rightist

press will eat it up. Let them have the pleasure; it isn't up
to us to put the Soviet Union on trial." He cut off Henri
with a gesture. " Even though we took every imaginable precaution, what people would see in our articles would be an
indictment of the Soviet régime. And that's one thing I
don't want at any price."

Henri remained silent. Dubreuilh had spoken decisively.
He had taken his position and he wouldn't budge from it.
Further discussion would serve absolutely no purpose. He
had made his decision by himself, and he would force it on
the Committee. Henri would have no choice but to submit
to it meekly.

" There's a question I've got to ask you," he said.

" Go ahead."

" Certain people claim you've recently joined the Communist Party."

" Really?" Dubreuilh said. " Who?"

" The rumour's making the rounds."

Dubreuilh shrugged his shoulders. " And you took it
seriously?'

" It's been two months since we've talked to each other,"
Henri replied, " and I don't suppose you'd have sent me an
announcement."

" Of course I would have sent out announcements!" Dubreuilh retorted vehemently. " It's absurd. How could I have
joined without advising the S.R.L. and without having
publicly explained my reasons?"

" You might have wanted to defer your explanation for a
few weeks," Henri replied, quickly adding, " I must say it
would have surprised me, but anyhow I did want to ask you
about it."

" All those rumours!" Dubreuilh said. " People say anything that pops into their heads."

He looked sincere, but it was the way he would have looked
if he had lied. As a matter of fact, Henri couldn't quite see
why he would have done it, and yet Scriassine seemed so
absolutely certain of what he was saying. " I should have
seen that informer," Henri said to himself. Confidence can't
be feigned: either you have it, or you don't. Since he no
longer had any confidence in Dubreuilh, his refusal had been
a falsely noble gesture.

Noncommittally, he resumed, " At the paper, everyone's in

agreement on breaking the story. Lambert has made up his mind to quit *L'Espoir* if we don't speak out."

"That wouldn't be a great loss," Dubreuilh said.

"It would make for a very delicate situation, especially since Samazelle and Trarieux are ready to break with the S.R.L."

Dubreuilh thought a moment. "Well," he said, "if Lambert leaves I'll buy up his share."

"You?"

"I'm not interested in journalism. But it's the best way to defend ourselves. You'll surely be able to convince Lambert to sell me his share. As for the money, I'll manage somehow."

Henri was taken aback. He didn't like that idea, he didn't like it at all. Suddenly, in a flash of light, the whole thing came clear. It was a rigged deal! Dubreuilh had spent the summer with Lambert and he knew the latter was getting ready to resign. Everything became perfectly clear. The Communists had assigned Dubreuilh to put the brakes on a campaign that would prove embarrassing to them, and to annex *L'Espoir* for them by worming his way into the management of the paper. The only way he had any chance of succeeding was by carefully concealing his affiliation with the Party.

"There's only one thing wrong with that," Henri said sharply. "And that is that I want to speak out, too."

"You're wrong!" Dubreuilh said. "Get this clear: if the referendum and the elections don't turn out to be a triumph for the left, we'll be running the risk of having a dictatorship. This isn't the moment to lend ourselves to anti-Communist propaganda."

Henri examined Dubreuilh. The question wasn't so much knowing the value of his arguments; it was whether or not he was speaking in good faith.

"And after the elections," he asked, "would you agree to speak out?"

"By then you can be sure the matter will already have been given plenty of space," Dubreuilh replied.

"Yes, Peltov will have taken his information to *Figaro*," Henri said. "Which means it's not really the outcome of the elections that's in question, but only our own attitude. And from that point of view, I don't see what advantage we would have in letting the right get the jump on us. In any event, we'd be forced to clarify our position. And how would we look then? We'd be trying to temper the anti-Communist attacks without frankly siding with the Soviet Union. We'd look like a bunch of crooks."

Dubreuilh interrupted Henri. " I know perfectly well what we'd say. My conviction is that these camps aren't essential to the régime, as Peltov maintains. They're tied in with certain policies which can be deplored without questioning the whole régime. We'd dissociate the two things: we'd condemn corrective labour, but we'd defend the Soviet Union."

" All right," Henri said. " But it's as plain as day that our words would carry much more weight if we were the first to denounce the camps. Then no one could believe we were following a line. We'd get the credit and we'd be cutting the ground right out from under the anti-Communists' feet. They're the ones who would look like partisans when they started following suit."

" Oh, that wouldn't change anything; people would believe them anyhow," Dubreuilh said. " And our intervention would give them a strong arguing point: even the sympathisers were so shocked that they turned against the Soviet Union. That's what they'd say! And that would upset people who otherwise wouldn't have believed a word of it."

Henri shook his head. " This matter has to be taken in hand by the left. The Communists are used to the slanders of the right; they leave them cold. But if the whole left, throughout all of Europe, rises up against the camps, there's a good chance it might upset them. Situations change when a secret becomes a disgrace. Russia might end up by changing its penitentiary system."

" You know that's a dream! " Dubreuilh said scornfully.

" Listen," Henri said angrily. " You've always maintained that we could exert certain pressures on the Communists; in fact, that's the whole idea of our movement. Here, if ever, is the time to try. Even if we have only a slim chance of succeeding, we've got to risk it."

Dubreuilh shrugged his shoulders. " If we're the ones who open the campaign, we'll deprive ourselves of any chance of working together with the Communists. They'd put us down as anti-Communists, and that wouldn't be wrong. Don't you see," Dubreuilh continued, "the part we're trying to play is that of an opposition minority, outside the Party, but allied with it. If we appeal to the majority to combat the Communists on any question whatsoever, then it becomes something more than just opposition. We'd be declaring war on them, changing sides. They'd have the right to accuse us of being traitors."

Henri studied Dubreuilh; he wouldn't have spoken differently if he had been an undercover Communist. His resistance only confirmed Henri's feeling that he was right in wanting to break the story. If the Communists wanted the left to remain neutral, it proved that the left did have a certain power over them and that, therefore, his intervention stood a chance of being effective. "In short," he said to Dubreuilh, "in order to be able to influence the Communists at some later date, you refuse to use the weapons we now have at hand. Opposition isn't permitted us except in so far as it has no effectiveness. Well I don't like that," he added decisively. "The thought that the Communists are going to spit all over us isn't any more pleasant to me than it is to you. But I've thought it all over very carefully; we have no choice." He cut Dubreuilh off with a gesture; he wasn't going to let him speak before he had had his say. "Being a non-Communist either means something or it means nothing. If it means nothing, let's become Communists or go and pick daisies. But if it does have a meaning, that implies certain duties—among others, to be able, if necessary, to tangle with the Communists. To humour them at any price without joining them outright is to choose the easiest kind of moral comfort. It's plain cowardice."

Dubreuilh was tapping impatiently on his desk blotter. "Those are moral considerations; they don't touch me," he said. "I'm interested in the results of my actions, not in what they make me appear to be."

"It isn't a question of appearance . . ."

"But it is," Dubreuilh said brusquely. "The heart of the matter is that it bothers you to appear as if you're letting yourself be intimidated by the Communists."

Henri stiffened. "It would bother me very much to let ourselves be intimidated by them. It would go against everything we've attempted for the past two years."

Dubreuilh continued tapping his desk blotter, and Henri

added sharply, "You're putting the discussion on a rather strange level. I could just as well ask you why you're so afraid of displeasing the Communists."

"I don't give a damn about pleasing or displeasing them," Dubreuilh said. "I don't want to start an anti-Soviet campaign, especially now. I think it would be criminal."

"And I think it would be criminal not to do everything in my power against the camps," Henri said. He looked at Dubreuilh. "I could understand your attitude much better if you were enrolled in the Party; I'd expect a Communist to deny that the camps existed, or to defend them."

"I told you I wasn't enrolled," Dubreuilh said in an irritated voice. "Isn't that enough for you?" He got up and took a few steps across the room.

"No," Henri thought, "that definitely is not enough for me. There's nothing to prevent Dubreuilh from lying to me cynically; he's already done it. And moral considerations don't touch him. But this time, I'm not going to let myself be had," he said to himself bitterly.

Dubreuilh continued pacing the room in silence. Had he felt Henri's distrust? Or was it merely his opposition that irritated him? He seemed to be having difficulty controlling himself. "Well, we've only to call the Committee together," he said. "Its decision will settle the matter."

"You know perfectly well they'll go along with you!" Henri said.

"If your reasons are good, they will convince them," Dubreuilh replied.

"Come now! Charlier and Mericad always vote with you and Lenoir is on his knees to the Communists. Their opinion doesn't interest me," Henri said.

"What are you getting at? That you'd act against the Committee's decision?" Dubreuilh asked.

"If necessary, yes."

"Are you trying to blackmail me?" Dubreuilh asked in a tense voice. "Either we give you free rein or L'Espoir breaks with the S.R.L., is that it?"

"I'm not trying to blackmail you. I've made up my mind to speak and I'll speak, that's all."

"Do you realise what this break means?" Dubreuilh said, his face as tense as his voice. "It's the end of the S.R.L., and L'Espoir goes over into the anti-Communist camp."

"The S.R.L. is a cipher now," Henri said. "And *L'Espoir* will never become anti-Communist; you can count on me for that."

For a moment they eyed each other in silence.

"I'll call the Committee together at once," Dubreuilh said finally. "And if it agrees with me, we'll publicly disavow you."

"It'll agree with you," Henri said. He walked to the door. "Disavow me; I'll answer you."

"Think it over again," Dubreuilh said. "What you're going to do is known as a betrayal."

"It's all thought over," Henri said.

He crossed the hall and closed the door behind him, that door he would never again open.

Scriassine and Samazelle were anxiously waiting for him at the paper. They took no pains to conceal their satisfaction. However, they were a little let down when Henri announced that he himself intended to prepare the articles on the camps, alone and with a completely free hand. They could take it or leave it. Scriassine tried to argue, but Samazelle quickly persuaded him to agree. Henri immediately set to work. He sketched the Soviet Union's penitentiary system in broad outline, emphasising its shocking character and quoting documents to back him up. But he took great care to point out that, on the one hand, the faults of the Soviet Union in no way excused those of capitalism, and, on the other, that the existence of the camps damned a certain policy but not the whole régime. To a country in the throes of the severest economic difficulties, they no doubt represented a facile solution. One had the right to hope for their elimination. Everyone for whom the Soviet Union embodies a hope, and the Communists themselves, had to do everything they could to secure the abolition of the camps. The very fact that their existence had been divulged had already changed the situation. That was why he had chosen to speak out against them. To have remained silent would have been defeatism and cowardice.

The article appeared the next morning. Lambert declared himself very dissatisfied with it, and Henri had a feeling that it was being vigorously argued about in the editorial room. That evening, a messenger brought Dubreuilh's letter. The Committee of the S.R.L. had expelled Perron and Samazelle; the movement no longer had any connection with *L'Espoir*. It deplored the exploitation, to the profit of anti-Communist propaganda, of facts which could be judged only within the total framework of the Stalinist régime. Whatever their exact import, the C.P. was to-day the only hope of the French proletariat, and if one sought to discredit it, it was because one chose to serve the cause of reaction. Henri immediately wrote an answer. He accused the S.R.L. of yielding to Communist terrorism and of betraying its original programme.

"How did we ever come to this?" Henri asked himself in a kind of stupor when he picked up a copy of *L'Espoir* the next day. He was unable to take his eyes from that front page. He had been of one opinion, Dubreuilh of another; there had been a slight raising of voices, a few impatient gestures, all in private. And suddenly, spread out in black and white for all the world to see were those two columns filled with insults.

"The telephone hasn't stopped ringing," his secretary said to him when he arrived at the paper around five o'clock. "There was a Monsieur Lenoir who said he'd be here at six."

"Let him come in when he arrives."

"And wait till you see the mail! I haven't even finished sorting it for you yet."

"Well, it looks as if this thing's got people excited," Henri said to himself, sitting down at his desk. The first article had appeared only the day before, and already a lot of readers were congratulating him, insulting him, voicing surprise. There was a telegram from Volange: "I clasp your hand, old friend." Julien, too, congratulated him in a lofty style which he found completely surprising. The trouble was that everyone seemed to think *L'Espoir* was going to become a second *Figaro*. He'd have to straighten them out. Henri raised his head. The door to his office had just opened, and Paula was standing before him. She was wearing an old fur coat and he saw from her face that it was one of her bad days.

"What brings you here? What's up?" Henri asked.

"That's what I came to ask you," Paula said. She threw a copy of *L'Espoir* on the desk. "What's up?"

"It's all explained in the paper," Henri replied. "Dubreuilh didn't want me to publish those articles on the Soviet camps; I did anyhow, and we broke." Impatiently, he added, "I'd have told you all about it to-morrow at lunch. What made you come here to-day?"

"Am I bothering you?"

"I'm glad to see you, but I'm expecting Lenoir any minute now. And I have a lot of work to do. I'll give you all the details to-morrow; after all, it isn't as urgent as all that."

"Yes, it is urgent. I've got to understand," she said. "Why this break?"

"I just told you." He forced a smile to his face. "You ought to be happy; you've been hoping for it for a long time."

Paula looked at him anxiously. "But why now? You don't break up a friendship of twenty-five years' standing because of a disagreement on a miserable political question."

"Well, that's what happened. The fact is that that miserable question is very important."

Paula's face hardened. "You're not telling me the truth."

"Believe me, I am."

"You haven't been telling me anything for a long time," she said. "I believe I've found out why. That's the reason I came to see you; you've got to have confidence in me again."

"You know I've always had confidence in you. But let's talk about it to-morrow," he said. "I haven't the time now."

Paula didn't budge. "I displeased you the other night when I was explaining my position to Josette. I apologise," she said.

"It's I who should apologise. I was in a bad mood."

"Above all, don't apologise!" She looked up at him, her face trembling with humility. "The night of the opening and in the days that followed, I came to understand a great many things. There's no standard by which you can be measured against other people, against me. To want you as I had dreamed of you and not as you are was to prefer myself to you. It was pure presumptuousness. But that's over. There's only you; I'm nothing. I accept being nothing, and I'll accept anything from you."

"Listen, stop getting excited," he said, embarrassed. "I said we'd talk about it to-morrow."

"You don't believe I'm sincere?" Paula said. "It's my fault; I had too much pride. The road to self-abnegation isn't easy, you know. But I swear to you now: I'll ask nothing more for myself. You alone exist, and you can demand anything of me."

"My God!" Henri thought. "If only she'll leave before Lenoir gets here!" Aloud, he said, "I believe you. But all I ask of you for the moment is to be patient until to-morrow and let me get back to my work."

"You're laughing at me!" Paula said violently. Her face softened. "I repeat that I'm totally yours. What can I do to convince you? Would you like me to cut off an ear?"

"And what would I do with it?" Henri asked, trying to make a joke of it.

"It would be a token." Tears welled in Paula's eyes. "It's intolerable to me that you doubt my love."

The door half opened. "Monsieur Lenoir. Shall I show him in?"

"Ask him to wait a few minutes." Henri smiled at Paula. "I don't doubt your love. But as you see, I have an appointment. You'll have to leave."

"You really aren't going to put Lenoir before me!" Paula said. "What is he to you? And I who love you so!" Now she was weeping large tears. "If I went out in society, if I tried to write, it was only out of my love for you."

"Yes. I know."

"Perhaps someone told you I had become vain, that nothing mattered to me except my work. The person who told you that was lying. To-morrow, I'll throw all my manuscripts in the fire before your very eyes."

"That would be stupid."

"I'll do it," she said. In a sudden burst, she added, "In fact, I'll do it as soon as I get home."

"Please! Don't be foolish. Where will that get you?"

Paula's face fell again. "Does that mean that nothing can convince you of my love?"

"But I am convinced," he replied. "I'm profoundly convinced."

"Oh, God! I'm boring you," she said, bursting into tears. "What shall I do? These misunderstandings must be straightened out!"

"There's no misunderstanding."

"There! I'm still boring you," she said desperately. "I'm still boring you and you won't want to see me any more!"

"No," he thought, "not any more." Aloud, he said, "Of course I will."

"You'll end up by hating me and you'll be right. To think that I'm quarrelling with you! *I* quarrelling with *you*!"

"But you aren't quarrelling with me."

"You see perfectly well I am," she said, the tears streaming down her cheeks.

"Calm yourself, Paula," he said as tenderly as he could. He felt like beating her—and he began smoothing her hair. "Calm yourself."

He continued caressing her for several moments, and then she finally decided to raise her head.

"All right, I'll leave," she said. She gave him an anguished look. "Will you come for lunch to-morrow? Promise?"

"I swear."

"Stop seeing her altogether, that's the only solution," he said to himself after she closed the door behind her. "But how will I get her to accept the money if I stop seeing her? Scrupulous women don't accept a man's help unless they can inflict their presence upon him. I'll work it out somehow. But I don't want to see her any more."

"Excuse me for keeping you waiting," he said to Lenoir. Lenoir made a little gesture with his hand. "It's of no importance." He coughed, he was already red; he had, of course, prepared every word of his diatribe in advance, but Henri's presence made his sentences fall apart. "I suppose you realise the object of my visit."

"Yes, you stand with Dubreuilh and my attitude shocks you. I gave my reasons; I'm sorry they didn't convince you."

"You didn't want to conceal the truth from your readers. But with what truth are you dealing?" Lenoir said. He had found one of the key words of his discourse; everything else would easily follow from it. Ambiguous truth, partial truth: Henri knew the tune only too well. He awakened when Lenoir finished his generalisations. "Police restraints play the same rôle in the Soviet Union as economic pressure in capitalist countries. I can see only advantages in the fact that it plays it in a more systematic manner. A régime in which the workers aren't threatened by layoffs or the managers by bankruptcy is forced to invent new types of penalties."

" But not necessarily these," Henri said. " And you aren't going to compare the lot of an unemployed man with that of a forced labourer."

" At least their daily needs are assured. I'm convinced their lot is less awful than anti-Communist propaganda would have it. And we tend to forget that a Soviet man's way of thinking is different from ours; he finds it natural, for example, to be relocated according to the needs of production."

" Whatever his way of thinking, no man finds it natural to be exploited, undernourished, deprived of all his rights, imprisoned, brutalised by work, condemned to die of cold, scurvy, or exhaustion," Henri said. He thought, " Politics are really incredible!" Lenoir literally couldn't have stood seeing a fly suffer, and yet he gladly accepted the horrors of the camps.

" No one wants evil for the sake of evil," Lenoir said. " And the Soviet Union less than any other government. If they take those measures, it's because they're necessary." Lenoir became even redder. " How dare you condemn the institutions of a country whose needs, whose difficulties, you know nothing about? It's an intolerable presumption."

" I spoke about its needs and its difficulties," Henri replied. " And you know very well I didn't condemn the Soviet régime in its totality. But to accept it blindly, in its totality, is cowardice. You can justify anything you want by invoking that idea of necessity. But it's a two-edged sword. When Peltov says the camps are necessary, it's to prove that socialism is a Utopian dream."

" They can be necessary to-day without being so permanently," Lenoir said. " You forget that conditions in the Soviet Union are war conditions; the capitalist powers are only waiting for the right moment to pounce on her."

" Even so, that still doesn't prove the camps are necessary," Henri said. " No one wants evil for the sake of evil, and yet it happens often enough that evil is committed uselessly. You won't deny that in the Soviet Union, as everywhere, there were mistakes made—famines, rebellions, massacres which could have been avoided. Well, I think the camps, too, are a mistake. You know," he added, " even Dubreuilh shares that opinion."

Lenoir shook his head. " Necessity or mistake, whichever the case, you've committed a wrong," he said. " Attacking the Soviet Union won't change what goes on in the Soviet Union, and it serves the capitalist powers. You've chosen to work for America and for war."

" Not at all!" Henri protested. " You can criticise Communism without its being any the worse for it. After all, it's sturdier than that!"

" You've just proved again that one can't want to be extra-Communist without in fact becoming anti-Communist," Lenoir said. " There's no middle road. The S.R.L. was condemned from its very inception to become allied with reaction or to perish."

" If that's the way you think, the only thing for you to do is join the C.P."

" Yes, that's the only thing for me to do. And it's what I'm going to do," Lenoir said. " I just wanted to make things clear: from now on, you'll have to consider me an adversary."

" I'm sorry," Henri said.

Embarrassed, they looked at each other for a moment, and then Lenoir said, " Well, good-bye."

" Good-bye," Henri said.

Yes, that was one of the possible retorts—denying the facts and the figures, denying one's own intelligence and reason itself by a blind act of faith: everything Stalin does is right. " Lenoir isn't a Communist; that's why he's being excessively zealous," Henri said to himself. What he would have found interesting would have been to speak to Lachaume or any other intelligent and not-too-sectarian Communist.

" Have you seen Lachaume lately?" he asked Vincent.

" Yes."

Vincent had been deeply stirred by the business of the camps. In the beginning, he thought they should not be mentioned, and then he went over to Henri's side.

" What does he think of my articles?" Henri asked.

" He's very much opposed to what you're doing," Vincent replied. " He says you're acting like an anti-Communist."

"Oh!" Henri said. "And the camps? Don't they bother him? What does he think of the camps?"

Vincent smiled. "That they don't exist, that they're an excellent institution, that they'll disappear all by themselves."

"I see," Henri said.

Definitely, people don't enjoy asking themselves questions. One way or another, they all manage to defend their systems. The Communist journals went as far as to sing the praises of an institution they baptised "Rehabilitation and Corrective Labour Camps." And all the anti-Stalinists saw in that affair was a pretext to rekindle well-established indignations.

"More congratulations!" Samazelle said, throwing the telegrams on Henri's desk. "It looks as though we've stirred up public opinion," he added happily. "By the way, Scriassine is waiting outside. Peltov and two other fellows are with him."

"His project doesn't interest me," Henri said.

"Nevertheless, they really ought to be given a hearing," Samazelle said. He pointed to some papers he had placed in front of Henri. "And I'd like very much for you to take a look at these remarkable articles Volange just sent us."

"Volange will never write for L'Espoir," Henri said.

"Too bad!" Samazelle said.

The door opened, and Scriassine came in, smiling seductively. "You have five minutes, don't you? Our friends are getting impatient. I brought along Peltov and Bennet, an American journalist who spent fifteen years in Moscow as a correspondent. And Moltberg. Moltberg was still a militant Communist in Vienna at the time I left the Party. Can I have them come in?"

"Yes, have them come in."

They entered the office and their faces were heavy with reproach, either because Henri had kept them waiting or because the world wasn't giving them their due. Henri motioned them to sit down and, addressing himself to Scriassine, he said, "I'm afraid this meeting is going to be completely futile. I made it very clear in our conversations together and in my articles that I haven't become anti-Communist. You should take your project to the Gaullists, not me."

"Don't talk to me about De Gaulle," Scriassine said. "When he was in power, his first act was to fly to Moscow. That's a thing that shouldn't be forgotten."

"No doubt you haven't had time to look carefully into our programme," Moltberg said reprovingly. "We're men of the left; the right is backed by big business and there's no question of our allying ourselves with it. What we want to do is unite the living forces of democracy against Russian totalitarianism." With a courteous gesture, he pushed aside Henri's objections. "You say that you haven't become anti-Communist, that you've revealed certain abuses and want to go no further. But actually, you can't stop half-way; against a totalitarian country, our involvement must also be total."

Scriassine quickly jumped in. "Don't tell me you're so distant from us. After all, the S.R.L. was created to prevent Europe from falling into the hands of Stalin. And we, too, want an autonomous Europe. Only we realise it can't be achieved without America's help."

"A mere nothing!" Henri said. He shrugged his shoulders. "A Europe colonised by America is precisely what the S.R.L. wanted to avoid. In fact it was our first objective, since we never thought Stalin had any intention of annexing Europe."

"I can't understand this prejudice against America," Bennet said in a melancholy voice. "You've got to be a Communist to see in her only the citadel of capitalism. For it's also a country of workers, the country of progress, of prosperity, of the future."

"It's the country that everywhere and always systematically takes the side of the privileged. In China, in Greece, in Turkey, in Korea, what are they defending? It isn't the people, is it? It's capital, it's the big land holdings. When I think that they're supporting Franco and Salazar . . ."

Henri had learned that very morning that his old Portuguese friends had finally fomented a rebellion. It ended up with nine hundred arrests.

"You're speaking of the policies of the State Department," Bennet said. "You forget there's also an American people. I assure you that you can put your trust in the leftist trade unions and that whole segment of the nation which sincerely believes in liberty and democracy."

"The unions have never opposed the government's policy," Henri said.

"You've got to look things squarely in the face," Scriassine said. "Europe can't defend itself against the Soviet Union except with America's help. If you forbid the European left to accept it, a deplorable confusion will be established between the interests of the right and those of democracy."

"If the left engages in rightist policies, it's no longer a left," Henri replied.

"In short, then," Bennet said in a menacing voice, "given a choice between America and the Soviet Union, you'd choose the Soviet Union?"

"Yes," Henri replied, "and I've never made a secret of it."

"How can you compare the abuses of American capitalism and the horror of police oppression?" Bennet said. His voice swelled, he began prophesying, and Moltberg chimed in with him while Scriassine and Peltov talked volubly in Russian. None of those men bore any resemblance to one another, but all of them had that same look, a look lost in an awful, vengeful dream from which they refused to awaken. All of them were determined to be deaf and blind to the world, gripped by the horrors of the past. Sharp, grave, solemn, or vulgar, they all spoke in prophetic voices. Of all the evidence they brought to bear against the Soviet Union, that, perhaps, was the most disturbing—that angry, distrustful, ever-hunted air which the Stalinist experience had etched on their faces. There was no stopping them when they began throwing their memories in your face, not because they had any hope of thus forcing a decision from you—they were too intelligent for that—but rather it was a verbal purging necessary to their inner hygiene. Bennet suddenly fell silent, as if exhausted.

"I don't know what we're doing here!" he said abruptly.

"I warned you we'd be wasting our time," Henri said.

They got up. Moltberg looked Henri in the eyes for a long moment. "Perhaps we'll meet again sooner than you think," he said almost tenderly.

After they left the office, Samazelle snorted, "It's difficult having a discussion with those fanatics. The funny part about it is that they all hate each other. Every one of them considers that the one who remained a Stalinist a little longer

than he did is a traitor. And the fact is they're all suspect.
Bennet stayed in Moscow for fifteen years as a correspondent; but if the régime filled him with as much indignation as
he claims to-day, what a coward he was! They're marked
men," he concluded with a satisfied look.

"At any rate, they have enough integrity to refuse to compromise themselves with Gaullism," Henri said.

"They lack political sense," Samazelle said.

Samazelle had failed on the left; nothing, therefore, seemed
more natural to him than to rally to the right, since he was
interested only in the number of his listeners and not in the
meaning of his speeches. He had suggested the publication
of Volange's articles, had spoken with measured sympathy
of the Gaullist programme. Henri pretended not to understand his insinuations. But it was a futile ruse; Samazelle
didn't hesitate long before attacking openly.

"There's a great game to be played by whoever sincerely
wants to form an independent left," he said. "Scriassine is
right in thinking that Europe couldn't exist without the help
of the United States. Our rôle should be the coalescence, to
the profit of an authentic socialism, of all the forces opposed
to the Sovietisation of the Occident. We should accept American aid in so far as it comes from the American people,
should accept an alliance with the Gaullists in so far as
they can be oriented towards a leftist policy. That's the
programme I'd propose for us," he concluded, staring at
Henri with a stern and domineering look.

"Well, don't count on me to carry it out," Henri said.
"I'll continue fighting American politics with everything at
my command. And you know perfectly well that Gaullism is
reaction."

"I'm afraid you aren't very well aware of what the situation is," Samazelle said. "Even though you took every
possible precaution, here we are classified as anti-Communists. That cuts down our readers by half. The paper's only
chance is to win over new ones. And to do that we can't stop
half-way; we've got to move ahead in the direction we've just
taken."

"That is, become in effect an anti-Communist sheet!"
Henri said. "Out of the question. If we have to go bankrupt, we'll go bankrupt, but we'll maintain our line to the
very end."

Samazelle didn't answer. Trarieux, of course, was of the same opinion, but he knew that Lambert and Luc would always stand behind Henri. There was nothing he could do against that coalition.

"Have you seen *L'Enclume*?" he asked happily two days later. He threw the weekly on Henri's desk. "Read it."

"What's so special about *L'Enclume* this week?" Henri asked nonchalantly.

"An article about you by Lachaume," Samazelle replied. "Read it," he repeated.

"I'll take a look at it later," Henri said.

The moment Samazelle left the office, he opened the paper. "The Masks Removed" was the title of the article. As Henri read it, he felt his throat contracting with anger. By means of garbled excerpts and distorted summaries, Lachaume explained that all Henri's work betrayed a fascist tendency and implied a reactionary ideology. His play, particularly, was an insult to the Resistance. He had a fundamental scorn for other men; the vile articles he had just published in *L'Espoir* proved it blatantly. It would have been more honest of him to declare himself openly anti-Communist than to affirm his sympathy for the Soviet Union at the very moment he was opening that slanderous campaign against her. The coarseness of that ruse clearly showed in what wretched esteem he held his fellow beings. The words "traitor" and "sold out" weren't written in black and white, but they were easily read between the lines. And it was Lachaume who had written that! Lachaume: Henri saw him again, at the time he was hiding in Paula's apartment, happily waxing the floors. He saw him at the Gare de Lyon wrapped in an overcoat which was too long and embarrassed by his emotion when the good-byes were being said. The Christmas sparklers were crackling, and seated at a table in the Bar Rouge he was saying, "We've got to work side by side." A little later, with a confused look, "We've never attacked you." Henri tried to think, "It isn't his fault. The guilty one is the Party; yes, the Party picked him out purposely to do the job." And then, a red anger suffused his face. It was he who had made up each sentence, one by one. You never confine yourself to obeying; you recreate. And he had less excuse than his accomplices, for he knew perfectly well he was lying. "He knows I'm no fascist and that I'll never become one."

He got up. Answering that article was out of the question; Lachaume already knew everything Henri could possibly say. When words no longer had any meaning, the only thing left to do is use your fists. He got into his car. At that time of day, Lachaume should be at the Bar Rouge. Henri set out for the Bar Rouge. He found Vincent drinking with some friends. No Lachaume.

"Lachaume isn't here?"

"No."

"Then he's probably at *L'Enclume*," Henri said.

"I don't know," Vincent replied. He got up and followed Henri to the door. "Got your car with you? I'm going over to the paper."

"I'm not," Henri said. "I'm heading for *L'Enclume*."

Vincent went outside with him. "Let it drop," he said.

"Did you read Lachaume's article?" Henri asked.

"Yes. He showed it to me before it was printed, and I argued with him. It's a filthy piece of work. But where will it get you to create a scandal?"

"I don't often feel like fighting," Henri said, "but this time it's a positive need. If it creates a scandal, so much the better."

"You're wrong," Vincent said. "They'll use it as an excuse to write another article—and in that one, they'll go even further."

"Further? But they accused me of being a fascist," Henri said. "They can't go any further than that. And anyhow, I don't give a damn." He opened the door of the car. Vincent grabbed his arm.

"You know, once they've made up their minds to get a chap they don't stop at anything," Vincent said. "There's a weak point in your life; they'll go after you through that."

Henri looked at Vincent. "A weak point? You mean Josette and that dirt they made up about her?"

"Yes. Maybe you don't realise it, but everyone knows about it."

"They wouldn't dare. Not that!" Henri said.

"Wouldn't they?" He hesitated. "I gave Lachaume so much hell when he showed me his article that he cut out ten lines. But the next time, you can be sure he'll leave them in."

Henri remained silent. Poor Josette! So vulnerable! It
sent a shiver up his spine to picture her reading those ten
lines Lachaume had cut out. He sat down behind the wheel.
" Get in ; you've won. Let's get back to the paper."

He started the car and added, " Thanks!"

" I'd never have believed it of Lachaume," Vincent said.

" Of Lachaume or anyone else," Henri said. " Attacking
a man's private life, and in that way, is just too damned
filthy."

" It's filthy all right," Vincent said. He hesitated. " But
there's one thing you've got to understand: you don't have
any more private life."

" What do you mean?" Henri said. " Of course I have a
private life, and it's nobody's business but my own."

" You're a public figure ; everything you do falls into the
public domain. Isn't all this proof enough? You've got to be
invulnerable, all along the line."

" There's no possible defence against slander," Henri said.
For a moment, they drove along in silence. " When I think
they picked out Lachaume to do the job!" Henri said. " Lachaume and none other! That's really twisting the knife."
He added, " How they must hate me!"

" You don't think they love you, do you?" Vincent said.

They drew up in front of the paper, and Henri got out of
the car. " I have to go and get something. I'll be up in five
minutes," he said. There was nothing he had to get, but he
wanted to be alone for a few minutes. He began walking
straight ahead of him. " You don't think they love you, do
you?" No, he didn't, but he hadn't gauged the extent of
their hostility. Worn-out catchwords had drifted between his
heart and his lips: loyal adversaries . . . fight honourably
. . . they were two-year-old words, centuries-old words, words
no one any longer understood. He knew the Communists
would attack him officially, but he told himself that many
of them would secretly keep their esteem for him and that
he would even cause them to think things over. " But the
truth is they hate me!" he said to himself. He continued
walking aimlessly. Under the smoky golden colours of
autumn, Paris was beautiful and melancholy, like long-dead
Bruges. And hate was at his heels. It was a new experience
for him, a rather horrible one. " Love is never completely
directed at you," Henri thought. " Friendship is as precari-

ous as life. But hate never misses its mark, and it's as
certain as death." Henceforth, wherever he went, whatever
he did, that certainty would accompany him everywhere.
"I'm hated!"

When Henri returned to the office, he found Scriassine
waiting there for him. "He's read *L'Enclume*; he thinks
iron should be struck while it's hot!" Henri said to himself.

"You want to talk to me?" he asked. With feigned solicitude, he added, "Something wrong with you? You aren't
looking well."

"I have a horrible headache—not enough sleep and too
much vodka. Nothing serious," Scriassine replied. He
straightened up in his chair, his face under control. "I came
to ask you if you've changed your mind since the other
day?"

"No," Henri replied. "And I won't change it."

"Doesn't it make you think a bit, the way the Communists
are treating you?"

Henri laughed. "Oh, I think. I think a lot. In fact, that's
all I do!"

Scriassine heaved a deep sigh. "I was hoping you'd end up
by seeing things our way."

"Come on, don't be unhappy. You don't really need me,"
Henri said.

"You can't count on anyone," Scriassine said. "The left
has lost its warmth. The right hasn't learned anything." In a
doleful voice, he added, "There are times when I feel like
retiring to the country."

"Why don't you?"

"I don't feel I have the right," Scriassine replied. With
a harassed air, he passed his hand across his brow. "What
a head!"

"Would you like a couple of aspirins?"

"No, no. I've got to meet some people in a little while—
old friends. It's never very pleasant, so I'd rather not be too
clear in the head."

There was a silence. "Are you going to answer Lachaume?" Scriassine asked.

"Certainly not."

"Too bad. When you want to, you know how to stand up
for yourself. Your answer to Dubreuilh was well put."

"Yes, but was it right?" Henri asked. He looked at

Scriassine questioningly. "I wonder if your informant can really be trusted."

"What informant?" Scriassine asked, running a shaking hand over his face.

"The one who claims to have seen Dubreuilh's card and his file."

"Oh!" Scriassine said. A little smile crossed his face. "He never existed."

"Impossible! You made that all up?"

"In my eyes, Dubreuilh's a Communist, enrolled or not. But I had no way of making you share my conviction, so I cheated a little."

"And suppose I had agreed to meet your man?"

"The most elementary psychology guaranteed me you'd refuse."

Henri looked at Scriassine in dismay. He couldn't even bring himself to hold a grudge against him for a lie admitted so naturally! Scriassine gave him a confused smile. "Are you angry?"

"It's beyond me how anyone could do a thing like that!" Henri replied.

"As a matter of fact, I did you a favour," Scriassine said.

"You'll permit me not to thank you," Henri said.

Scriassine smiled without answering. He got up. "I have to leave for my appointment."

For a long moment, Henri remained motionless, his eyes blank. If Scriassine hadn't made up that story, what would have happened? Perhaps things would have turned out the same way; perhaps not. In any case, he hated to think that he had played with marked cards; it gave him a consuming desire to replay the hand. "Maybe I ought to try talking it over with Nadine," he said to himself abruptly. Vincent saw her occasionally; he decided to ask him the date of their next meeting.

The following Thursday, when he went into the café in which Nadine was waiting, Henri felt vaguely moved. And yet he had never attached much importance to Nadine's judgment. He stood in front of her table. "Hallo."

She raised her eyes. "Hallo," she said indifferently. She didn't even seem surprised.

"Vincent asked me to tell you he'd be a little late. May I sit down?"

She nodded her head without replying.

"I'm really glad to have a chance to talk to you," Henri said with a smile. "We had our own personal relationship, the two of us, so what I'd like to know is whether you consider my break with your father as a break with you as well."

"Oh, as far as a personal relationship goes, we'd see each other when we happened to meet," Nadine said coldly. "You don't come over to *Vigilance* any more, we never see each other—there's no problem."

"Excuse me, but there is one for me," Henri said. "If we aren't angry with each other, there's nothing to stop us from having a drink together from time to time."

"There's nothing to force us to, either," Nadine said.

"From what I can see, we are angry with each other," Henri said. She didn't answer, and he added, "But you do see Vincent and he's on the same side I am."

"Vincent didn't write the letter you wrote," Nadine replied.

Henri quickly retorted, "You've got to admit your father's wasn't friendly, either!"

"That's no reason. And yours was just plain rotten."

"All right," Henri said. "It was because I was angry." He looked Nadine in the eyes. "Someone swore to me, with proof to back him up, that your father was enrolled in the Communist Party. It made me furious to think that he hid it from me. Try putting yourself in my place."

"You didn't have to believe that rot," Nadine replied.

When she was wearing that stubborn look, there was no hope of convincing her of anything. And besides, Henri couldn't have justified himself without accusing Dubreuilh. He let it drop.

"Is the letter the only thing you've got against me?" he asked. "Or did your Communist pals convince you that I'm a social traitor?"

"I don't have any Communist pals," Nadine replied. She looked at Henri icily. "Social traitor or not, you're no longer what you once were."

"That's completely idiotic," Henri said irritably. "I'm exactly the same as ever."

"No."

" In what way have I changed? Since when? What have you got against me? Explain yourself."

" First of all, you're hanging around with that filthy crowd," Nadine said. Suddenly, her voice rose. " I thought that you, at least, wanted people to remember. You say some very fine things in your play—that we mustn't forget. and all that. And actually you're just like the others!"

" So Vincent's been telling you things!" Henri said.

" Not Vincent. Sézenac." Sparks were flying from Nadine's eyes. " How can you even touch that woman's hand? I'd sooner be skinned alive."

" I'll repeat to you what I told Vincent the other day: my private life is nobody's business but my own. And furthermore, I've known Josette for a year now. It isn't I who changed; it's you."

" I haven't changed. It's just that last year I didn't know what I know now. And then, I used to have confidence in you!" she added provocatively.

" And why did you stop?" Henri asked angrily.

Nadine lowered her head stubbornly.

" You were against me in the matter of the camps? That's your right. But to conclude from that I'm a bastard is a damned big jump. No doubt that's your father's opinion," he added irritably. " But you were never in the habit of taking everything he said as the gospel."

" Speaking out about the camps doesn't make you a bastard. In itself, I think it's even defensible," Nadine said soberly. " The question is to know why you did it."

" I explained why, didn't I?"

" You gave a few public reasons," Nadine replied. " But your own reasons, no one knows about them." Again, she stared icily at Henri. " The whole right is covering you with flowers; it's embarrassing. You'll say there's nothing you can do about it; nevertheless, it's still embarrassing."

" Listen, Nadine, you don't seriously think that that campaign was a manœuvre to draw myself closer to the right?"

" At any rate, the right is drawing itself closer to you."

" It's idiotic!" Henri said. " If I wanted to pass over to the right, I'd have done it by now! But you can plainly see that *L'Espoir's* line hasn't changed. And believe me, it hasn't been easy! Did Vincent tell you what happened?"

"Vincent is blind when it comes to his friends. Naturally, he defends you. That proves the purity of his heart and nothing else."

"And you, when you accuse me of being a bastard, what proof have you got?" Henri asked.

"None. And besides, I'm not accusing you of anything; I'm suspicious, that's all." She smiled without warmth. "I was born suspicious."

Henri got up. "All right. Suspect all you want to. As for me, when I feel a little friendship for someone, I try rather to believe in him. But you're right, that isn't the way you are. I was wrong to come here. I'm sorry."

"Suspicion—there's nothing worse," he said to himself on his way back to his room. "I'd rather they dragged me through the mud, the way Lachaume did. At least you know where you stand." He pictured them sitting in the study having coffee: Dubreuilh, Nadine, Anne. They weren't saying, "He's a bastard." No, they were too high-principled for that. They suspected. What can you say to someone who suspects? A criminal can at least look for excuses. But a suspect . . . a suspect is totally disarmed. "Yes, that's what they've made of me," he angrily repeated to himself the following days. "A suspect. And into the bargain, they all blame me for having a private life!" But he was neither a statesman nor a zealot; he was determined to have a life of his own, a private life. On the other hand, he was fed up with politics. There's no end to it; every sacrifice creates new duties. First, it was the paper, and now they wanted to deprive him of all his pleasures, all his desires. In the name of what? In any case, he wasn't doing any of the things he wanted to do; in fact, he was doing the exact opposite. That being the case, why should he restrain himself? He made up his mind to stop restraining himself and to act as he damned well pleased. At the stage he was at, it really didn't matter.

Nevertheless, the evening he found himself seated between Lucie Belhomme and Claudie de Belzunce in front of a bottle of too-sweet champagne, Henri suddenly thought in astonishment, "What am I doing here?" He liked neither the champagne, nor the crystal chandeliers, the mirrors, the velvet covering of the chairs, nor those women who so abundantly displayed their tired skin. He liked neither Lucie, nor

Dudule, nor Claudie, nor Vernon, nor the ageing young actor who was said to be his lover.

"Then she went into the bedroom," Claudie was saying. "She saw him there, spread out on the bed, all naked." The three men burst out laughing and Lucie, somewhat sharply, said, "Very funny!" She found it flattering to associate with a wellborn woman, but the coarse tone Claudie deliberately adopted whenever she went out with her inferiors never failed to irritate her. Lulu's efforts to display a distinction equal to her elegance were truly pathetic. She turned to Henri.

"Ruéri would be good in the husband's part," she whispered, indicating the handsome fellow who was sipping Vernon's sherry cobbler through a straw.

"What husband?"

"Josette's."

"But you never see him. He dies at the beginning of the play."

"I know. But for the film, your story is much too sad. Brieux suggests that you let the husband escape. He'd join the Maquis and at the end he'd pardon Josette."

Henri shrugged his shoulders. "Brieux will film the play I wrote or nothing at all."

"You aren't going to spit on two million just because they want you to bring a dead man back to life!"

"He pretends to scorn money," Claudie said. "But what with the price of butter nowadays, it certainly comes in handy. Even when the Fritzes were here, it cost less."

"Don't talk like that in front of a resistentialist," Lucie said.

This time they all laughed together, and Henri smiled with them. If they could have heard them, seen him, they would all have blamed him together—Lambert as well as Vincent, Volange as much as Lachaume, and Paula, Anne, Dubreuilh and Samazelle, and even Luc, and that whole anonymous throng of those who were expecting something of him. That was precisely why he was there, with those people—because he shouldn't have been. He was wrong, radically wrong, without reservations, without excuses. What a relief! Sooner or later, you get fed up with constantly asking yourself, "Am I right or wrong?" That one evening at least, he knew the answer, "I'm wrong, completely wrong." He had made a clean break with Dubreuilh, the S.R.L. had disavowed him, and most of his old comrades felt a shiver of shame when they thought of him. At *L'Enclume*, Lachaume and his friends—and how many others throughout Paris, throughout France— were calling him a traitor. In the wings of Studio 46, machine guns were rattling, the Germans were burning a French village, and anger and horror were reawakening in sluggish hearts. Everywhere, hate was flaring. Yes, that was his reward: hate. And there was no way of overcoming it. Drink. He understood Scriassine ; he refilled his glass again.

"That was a courageous thing you did," Lucie said.

"What?"

"Denouncing all those horrors."

"If that takes courage, then there are thousands of heroes in France," Henri said. "When you attack the Soviet Union nowadays, you don't run any risk of being shot."

She examined Henri, looking slightly perplexed. "Yes, but you more or less established a position for yourself on the left. That affair must have compromised it."

"But think of the positions I can now find on the right!"

"Right, left, those are outmoded notions," Dudule said. "What people have to be made to understand is that the collaboration of capital and labour is necessary for the country's recovery. You did a useful piece of work in disposing of one of the myths opposed to their reconciliation."

"Don't congratulate me too soon!" Henri said.

That was the worst solitude of all : being approved of by these people. Eleven-thirty, the night's most fearful hour. The theatre was emptying, all those minds he had held captive for three hours were being unleashed together, and as one they would turn against him. What a massacre!

"Old man Dubreuilh must be foaming at the mouth," Claudie said with a satisfied look.

"Tell me, who's his wife sleeping with?" Lucie asked. "Because, after all, he's practically an old man."

"I don't know," Henri replied.

"She did me the honour of coming over once," Lucie said. "What a prig! How I hate these women who dress like poor relations to show they have a social conscience."

Anne was a prig ; Dudule, who had seen the world, declaimed that Portugal was a paradise ; and they all thought that wealth was a kind of merit and that they merited their wealth. But since he had taken his place beside them of his own free will, Henri could do nothing but remain silent.

" 'Evening," Josette said, placing her little sequined purse on the table. She was wearing her green dress with the generous decolletage. Henri couldn't understand why, since men's desire offended her, she offered herself so generously to their stares. He disliked the idea of that tender flesh being as public as a name. She sat down beside him at the end of the table, and he asked, " Did it go well? No booing?"

" Oh, for you, it's a triumph," she replied.

On the whole, the critics hadn't treated her too badly—a debut, like so many others. With those looks and a little patience, she had every chance of making an honourable career for herself. And yet, she was disappointed. Her face suddenly came alive. "Did you see? At that table back there . . . Felicia Lopez. She's really beautiful!"

" What she has are very beautiful jewels," Lucie corrected.

" She's beautiful!"

" My dear," Lucie said, giving her a tight-lipped smile, " never say in front of a man that another woman is beautiful. Because he might possibly imagine that you're less so. And you can rest assured that no other woman would ever be silly enough to return the compliment."

" Josette can allow herself to be frank," Henri said. " She has nothing to worry about."

" With you, maybe," Lucie said in a slightly contemptuous voice. " But there are others who wouldn't enjoy having that mournful face in front of them. Give her a drink. A pretty woman ought to be gay."

" I don't want to drink," Josette said. Her voice cracked. " I've got a pimple in the corner of my mouth; I'm sure it's from my liver. I'll have a Vichy."

" What a generation!" Lucie said, shrugging her shoulders.

" The good thing about drinking," Henri said, " is that you end up by getting drunk."

" You aren't drunk, are you?" Josette asked anxiously.

" Oh, getting drunk on champagne is a herculean task," he replied, reaching for the bottle.

She stopped his arm. " Good. Because I've got something to tell you." She hesitated. " But promise me first you won't get angry."

He laughed. " I really can't promise without knowing what
it's all about."

She looked at him impatiently. "Then you don't love me
any more."

" Go ahead."

" Well, I was interviewed by *L'Eve Moderne* the other
night . . ."

" And what did you tell them?"

" I said we were engaged. Oh, it wasn't at all to force you
to marry me," she added quickly. " We'll announce our
break-up whenever you like. But we're seen together all the
time, and being engaged . . . well, it makes it look better,
you understand."

From her glittering purse, she pulled out a magazine page
and unfolded it with a satisfied air. " For once, they wrote
something nice."

" Let's see," Henri said. He murmured, " I look pretty
good!"

Josette was sitting next to Henri behind two champagne
glasses ; she was wearing a very low-cut dress, and they were
both laughing. " Exactly the way we are now," he thought,
annoyed. " And from this it's only a short step to imagining
that I spend my nights swilling champagne, that I've sold
out to America. They won't waste much time taking that
step." And yet, he had no real liking for all that inane
glitter. He frequented the fashionable places to make Josette
happy, but for him it didn't count ; those moments remained
marginal to his real life. He continued staring at the picture.
" But the fact of the matter is that it's I, and that I'm here."

" Are you angry?" Josette asked. " You promised not to
get angry."

" No, I'm not the least bit angry," he replied. And then
he thought decisively, " Let them all go to hell!" He owed
no one anything, and yet he was blaming himself for everything. Was that what real freedom meant?

" Let's dance," he said.

When they got out on the dance floor, crowded with men
in dinner jackets and women in low-cut gowns, Josette asked,
" Does it really bother you when I look sad?"

" What bothers me is your *being* sad."

She shrugged her shoulders. " It isn't your fault."

" Nevertheless, it bothers me. There's no reason for your

being sad, you know. Your reviews were excellent, there's no
doubt in my mind that you'll get other parts . . ."

"Yes. It's stupid. It's because I'm stupid. I thought that
the day after the opening everything would suddenly be
changed; for example, that Mother wouldn't dare speak to
me any more the way she does. And I thought that, inside,
I'd feel all different."

"After you've done a lot of acting, when you're sure of
your talent, then everything will seem different to you."

"No. What I imagined . . ." She hesitated. "Well, it was
like magic." She was touching when she tried to dress up her
uncertain thoughts in words. "When someone falls in love
with you, really in love, it's just like magic. Everything
changes. I thought it would be like that after the opening."

"You told me once that no one had ever been in love
with you."

She blushed. "Oh, just once. It happened once, when I
was very young. I'd just got out of boarding school. I don't
even remember it any more."

"But it seems you do remember it," Henri said tenderly.
"Who was he?"

"A young man. But he left. He left for America. I've
forgotten him. It's an old story."

"And we two?" Henri asked. "Isn't there just a little bit
of magic in it?"

She looked at him, vaguely reproachful. "Oh, you're nice;
you tell me nice things. But it isn't love unto death."

"Neither was it with the young man," Henri said, "since
he left." There was a note of annoyance in his voice.

"Oh, don't keep harping on that story," Josette said in an
irritated voice which was new to Henri. "He left because
there was nothing else he could do."

"But he didn't die of it, did he?"

"What do you know about it?" she said.

"Excuse me, my dear," he said, surprised by her violence.
"Is he dead?"

"He's dead. He died in America. Are you happy now?"

"I didn't know. Don't get angry," Henri murmured,
leading her back to the table. Was she capable then, after
ten years, of still having such poignant memories? Unhappily, he asked himself, "Is she capable of loving more
than she loves me? Well, so much the better if she doesn't

love me. That way I have no responsibilities; I'm not at
fault." He drank several glasses of champagne, one after
the other. Suddenly, all the objects around him began
chattering. Those messages which they emitted with disconcerting speed, and which he alone could understand, were
fascinating. Unfortunately, he immediately forgot them.
That wooden stick laid negligently across one of the glasses
—he no longer remembered its significance. And the chandelier, that enormous crystal chandelier, what did it represent? The bird poised on Lucie's head was a tombstone;
dead, stuffed, it was its own funeral monument—like Louis.
And why hadn't Louis disguised himself as a bird? The truth
was that they were all disguised animals. From time to time
a little electric shock would occur in their brains, and then
words would begin pouring from their mouths.

"Look," he said to Josette. "They've all been turned into
men—the chimpanzee, the poodle, the ostrich, the seal, the
giraffe. And they're all speaking, they're speaking but no
one understands what the others are saying. You see? You
don't understand me. The two of us, too, we don't belong
to the same species."

"No, I don't understand," Josette said.

"Well, it doesn't matter," he said indulgently. "It doesn't
matter in the least." He got up. "Let's dance."

"What's wrong with you? You're stepping on my gown.
Have you had too much to drink?"

"Never too much," he replied. "Don't you really want to
drink? It makes you feel so good. It makes you feel you
can do anything you want to—beat up Dudule or kiss your
mother . . ."

"Now really, you're not going to kiss Mother? What's got
into you? I've never seen you like this."

"You'll see me," he said. A lot of memories were dancing
capriciously in his head, and he suddenly remembered something Lambert had said. "You see," he said solemnly, "I'm
integrating evil!"

"What in the world are you talking about? Let's sit
down."

"No, let's dance."

They danced, sat down, danced again. Little by little,
Josette cheered up. "Look at that tall fellow who just came

in. It's Claude Sylvère!" she said in a dazzled voice. "This night club is really fine. We'll come back again."

"Yes, it's fine," Henri said.

He looked around him in surprise. What in hell was he doing there? The objects had suddenly grown silent; he was sleepy and there was a lump in his stomach. That must be what they call debauchery. At least you escaped. With a little luck and a lot of whisky, you could escape for at least one night, as Scriassine, who knew about such things, would say. And it worked with champagne, too. You forgot your wrongs and your rights, forgot hate, forgot everything.

"It's fine," Henri repeated. "And besides, as they say, we're not having fun just to have fun, are we? We'll come back, my dear. We'll come back."

CHAPTER EIGHT

LIVING A love while refusing it is a very strange business. Lewis's letters broke my heart. "Will I go on loving you more and more each day?" he wrote. And another time, "You played a funny trick on me. I can't casually bring women home with me any more. And I no longer have anything to offer those to whom I might have given a little corner of my heart." How I wanted to throw myself into his arms when I read those words! Since it was forbidden me, I should have told him, "Forget me." But I didn't want to say it. I wanted him to love me, wanted him to suffer all the pain I was causing him. I suffered his sadness in remorse. But I suffered, too, on my own account: how slowly time passed, how quickly it passed! Lewis remained as far from me as ever, but each day brought me closer to old age. Our love was ageing; it would die one day without ever having lived. The thought was intolerable. I was happy to leave St. Martin and return to Paris, where once again I found my patients, my friends, noise, pursuits that kept me from thinking of myself.

I had seen hardly anything of Paula since the month of June. Claudie had taken her under her wing and had invited her to spend the summer in her Burgundy château. To my great surprise, Paula had accepted. When, upon my return to Paris, I telephoned her, I was put off by the distant, cheerful politeness of her voice.

"Of course . . . I'd be delighted to see you. Are you free to-morrow to go to the opening of Marcadier's exhibition?"

"I'd rather see you more quietly. Don't you have another free moment?"

"I'm so busy these days . . . Wait! Can you come to-morrow after lunch?"

"That suits me perfectly. See you then."

For the first time in years, Paula was in street clothes when she opened the door to me. She was wearing a grey worsted suit of the very latest style and a black blouse; her hair was swept upwards and a row of bangs covered her forehead;

she had plucked her eyebrows; her face had thickened, and her cheeks were slightly blotched.

"How are you?" she said affectionately. "Did you have a nice holiday?"

"Excellent. And you? Did you have a good time?"

"It was delightful," she replied in a voice that seemed to me charged with undertones. She scrutinised me with a look at once embarrassed and provocative. "Don't you find me changed?"

"You seem to be in excellent shape," I replied. "And that's a very lovely tailored suit you have on."

"Claudie gave it to me. It's from Balmain."

There was nothing you could say against the refined cut of that suit, nor against those elegant pumps. Perhaps it was only that I wasn't accustomed to her new style, but Paula seemed more bizarre to me than in the old-fashioned outfits she used to create for herself. She sat down, crossed her legs, lit a cigarette. "You know," she said with a little laugh, "I'm a new woman."

I didn't know quite what to say and asked inanely, "Claudie's influence?"

"Claudie was only an excuse. Although, mind you, she's a very remarkable person," Paula said. She mused for a moment. "People are much more interesting than I used to think. As soon as you stop keeping them at a distance, they ask for nothing more than to be nice." She examined me critically. "You ought to go out more often."

"Maybe," I said irresolutely. "Who was down there?"

"Oh, everybody!" she replied in a radiant voice.

"Are you going to start a salon, too?"

She laughed. "You think I wouldn't be capable of it?"

"On the contrary."

She raised her eyebrows. "On the contrary?" There was a brief silence, and then she said curtly, "In any case, I have something else on my mind just now."

"What?"

"I'm writing."

"Good!" I said, loading my voice with enthusiasm.

"I never could imagine myself a writer," she said with a smile. "But at the château they all told me it was a crime to let so much talent go to waste."

"And what are you writing?" I asked.

"You can call it what you like—short stories or poems. I can't be classified."

"Did you show your work to Henri?"

"Of course not. I told him I was writing, but I've shown him nothing." She shrugged her shoulders. "I'm sure he'd be upset. He's never tried to create new forms. Besides, for the experiment I'm trying I've got to try alone." She looked me in the face and said solemnly, "I've discovered solitude."

"You're not in love with Henri any more?"

"I am, but I love him as a free woman." She threw her cigarette in the empty fireplace. "His reaction was curious."

"He realised that you had changed?"

"Naturally. He isn't stupid."

"No, he isn't."

I did feel stupid. I looked at Paula questioningly.

"First of all, when he returned, I didn't get in touch with him," she said in a satisfied voice. "I waited for him to call —which he did almost immediately." She communed with herself for a second. "I was wearing my beautiful suit, and I opened the door for him very calmly. Immediately his face changed; I could feel he was quite agitated. He pressed his forehead against the window pane, turning his back to me to hide his face while I talked to him calmly about us, about myself. And then he looked at me very strangely. And I knew he had come to the decision to put me to the test."

"Why should you be put to the test?"

"For a moment he was on the verge of suggesting that we live together again. And then he took hold of himself. He wants to be sure of me. And he has the right to doubt. I haven't been easy to get along with these past two years."

"And then?"

"He explained to me very seriously that he's in love with the little Josette." She burst out laughing. "Can you imagine that?"

I hesitated. "He's been having an affair with her, hasn't he?"

"Of course. But he didn't have to come and tell me he loved her. If he really loved her, he certainly wouldn't have told me. He was watching my reaction, you see. But I had won in advance, since all I need is myself."

"I see," I said, gathering all my courage into a broad, trusting smile.

"The funniest thing about it," she said cheerfully, "is that at the same time he was flirting outrageously. He doesn't want me to be a burden on him, but if I stopped loving him I believe he'd be capable of killing me. For instance, he spoke to me about the Musée Grévin."

"In connection with what?"

"Just like that, out of a blue sky. It seems some member of the Académie is going to have his statue in the museum. You can imagine how little Henri cares about that! Actually, it was an allusion to that famous afternoon when he fell in love with me. He wants me to remember it."

"It's rather involved," I said.

"Not at all," she said. "It's naïve. Besides, there's only one very simple thing to be done. The opening's in four days: I'll have a talk with Josette."

"What are you going to tell her?" I asked with a feeling of anxiety.

"Oh, everything and nothing. I want to win her over," Paula said, laughing lightly. She got up. "You really don't feel like going to the exhibition?"

"I'm afraid I haven't the time."

She stuck a black beret on her head and slipped on a pair of gloves. "Honestly, how do you think I look?"

It was no longer from inside myself, but from her face, that I took my answer. "You are perfect!" I replied with conviction.

"We'll see each other Thursday, at the opening," she said. "Are you coming to the party?"

"Of course."

I went downstairs with her. Her way of walking had changed, too. She went straight ahead with assurance, but it was the assurance of a sleepwalker.

Three days before the opening, Robert and I went to a rehearsal of The Survivors. Both of us were gripped by it. I like all of Henri's books; they move me deeply and personally. But I felt that never before had he done anything as good as that play. It was something new for him, that verbal violence, that lyricism both comic and gloomy at the same time. And then, this time there was no separation of plot and ideas. You had to pay attention to the tale and the meaning of the play came clear to you. And as that remarkable meaning was welded to a strange and convincing story, it had the richness of reality. "That's real theatre!" Robert said. I hoped that all those who went to see it would react the same way we did. Only this drama, woven from both farce and tragedy, had the flavour of raw meat, which ran the risk of shocking them. When the curtain went up, the night of the opening, I felt extremely worried. Little Josette was plainly lacking in ability, but she held up well when people began making a row. After the first act, the applause was enormous. And it was even greater at the end. It was a real triumph. Really, in the life of a writer who isn't too unlucky, there are moments of great joy. It must be very moving to find out that, in a flash of applause, that you've achieved your goal.

When I entered the restaurant, I felt a great surge of feeling for Henri. True simplicity is so rare! All around him, everything rang false—the smiles, the voices, the words—while he was being himself, exactly the same as always. He looked happy, he was a little embarrassed, and I wanted to tell him all kinds of nice things. But I shouldn't have waited; after five minutes, my throat was tied in knots. It must be said that I had bad luck; I ran into Lucie Belhomme at the moment she was saying to Volange, indicating two young Jewish actresses, "It wasn't crematories the Germans had; it was incubators!" I knew the joke, but never had I heard it used so pointedly. I was horrified not only by Lucie Belhomme but by myself. And I held it against Henri, too. In his play he said some very fine things about forgetfulness, but he, too, was rather forgetful. Vincent claimed that Mother Belhomme had had her head shaven and that she well deserved it. And Volange, what was he doing there? I no longer felt like congratulating Henri, and I believe he felt my constraint. I stayed a short while because of Paula, but I felt so ill at ease that I drank immoderately. It hardly helped. I recalled the words Lambert had spoken to Nadine and I wondered, "What right have I to insist upon remembering? I did less than the others, suffered less. If they've forgotten, if one has to forget, then I, too, have only to forget." But I chided myself in vain; I felt like insulting someone, or weeping. Making up, pardoning—what hypocritical words! You forget, that's all. And forgetting the dead isn't enough. Now we're forgetting the murders, forgetting the murderers. All right, I have no right to remember.

But if tears come to my eyes, that's something that concerns only me.

Paula had spoken at length with Josette that night; I did not know what she had told her. During the following weeks, I felt she was avoiding me. She went out, wrote; she was busy and important. I didn't worry about her very much; I was too busy myself, with too many things. Returning to the house one afternoon, I found Robert livid with anger. It was the first time in my life I had ever seen him beside himself. He had just broken with Henri. He told me what had happened in a few crisp sentences and then, sharply, he said, " Don't try to excuse him. He's inexcusable."

I didn't try immediately; I was speechless. Fifteen years of friendship wiped out in a single hour! Henri would never sit in that arm-chair again, we would no longer hear his cheerful voice. How alone Robert would be! And Henri! What a void in his life! No, it just couldn't be final. I found my voice again.

" It's absurd," I said. " Both of you lost your heads. In a case like this, you could consider Henri politically wrong without withdrawing your friendship. I'm certain he's acting in good faith. It isn't easy to have a clear picture of this thing. I must say that if I had to make the decision on my own responsibility, I'd be damned embarrassed."

" You seem to believe I kicked Henri out," Robert said. " I wanted nothing more than to settle things in a friendly way. He's the one who walked out and slammed the door."

" Are you sure you didn't put him in a position where he would have to yield or break off?" I asked. " When you asked him to make L'Espoir the organ of the S.R.L., he was convinced that if he refused he'd have lost your friendship. This time, since he didn't want to yield, he probably preferred bringing it to an end immediately."

" You didn't witness the scene," Robert said. " He flaunted his ill will from the moment he came into the room. I don't say that a conciliation would have been easy, but at least an outright break could have been avoided. Instead of that, he rejected all my arguments, refused to discuss the matter with the Committee, went as far as to insinuate that I was secretly enrolled in the Communist Party. Do you want me to tell you something? He wanted this break."

" What an idea!" I said.

Henri certainly had nursed real resentments against Robert, but he'd had them for a long time. Why should he want to break now?

Robert stared off into space, his face hard. "I embarrass him, you understand."

"No, I don't understand," I replied.

"He's going downhill fast," Robert said. "You've seen the kind of people he goes around with? We're his bad conscience; all he wants is to be rid of it."

"You're being unfair!" I said. "I, too, was disgusted the other night, but you yourself explained to me that having a play produced nowadays necessarily entails certain compromises. And with Henri, it doesn't involve very much. He hardly ever sees those people. Yes, he's sleeping with Josette, but you certainly can be sure that it's not she who's influencing him."

"Granted that, in itself, that party was of no importance," Robert said. "But it's a sign. Henri is the kind who pampers himself, and he wants to be able to pamper himself in peace and quiet, without having to account to anyone."

"He pampers himself?" I said. "He spends his time doing things that bore him. You've often admitted yourself that he's damned self-sacrificing."

"Yes, when he feels inclined. But the fact is that politics do bore him. He isn't seriously interested in anything but himself." Robert cut me off with an impatient gesture. "That's what I hold against him most: all he's thought of in this whole business is what people would say about him."

"Don't tell me the existence of the camps leaves him cold," I said.

"It doesn't leave me cold, either. That's not the question," Robert replied. He shrugged his shoulders. "Henri doesn't want people to accuse him of letting himself be intimidated by the Communists; he prefers actually to go over into the anti-Communist camp. Under those circumstances, it suits him better to have broken with me. He can freely cut the fine figure of a big-hearted intellectual, whom the whole right will applaud."

"Henri isn't interested in pleasing the right," I said.

"He wants to please himself, and that will inevitably lead him to the right. Because on the left fine figures don't find many admirers." Robert reached for the telephone. "I'm going to call a meeting of the Committee for to-morrow morning."

All evening Robert worked on the letter he intended to submit to the Committee, an angry look on his face. My heart was heavy the morning I unfolded *L'Espoir* and saw the two letters in which he and Henri exchanged insulting repudiations. Nadine, too, was dismayed. She still felt a great deal of friendship for Henri, but, on the other hand, she couldn't stand seeing her father attacked publicly.

" It's Lambert who pushed Henri into it," she said to me furiously.

I really would have liked to have understood what had gone on in Henri's head. Robert's interpretations were too full of ill will. The thing that made him most indignant was that Henri hadn't had any confidence in him. But after all, I told myself, he had given him a few reasons to be mistrustful. And if he answered that by saying that, since that time, Henri could well have wiped the slate clean? That was all very fine, but you can't forget the past at will! And I know from experience that you can easily be unjust to people whom you aren't in the habit of judging. I myself have occasionally had doubts about Robert, doubts based on the fact that in small things he has aged a bit. I realise now that if he decided to remain silent about the camps, it was for solid reasons, but I *had* believed it was out of weakness. So I can understand Henri. He, too, admired Robert, blindly; although he knew his imperialistic ways, he always followed him, in everything, even when it forced him into doing things that went against the grain. The Trarieux affair must have left its mark on him precisely because of that. And since Robert had been capable of deceiving him once, Henri believed that he had become capable of anything.

At any rate, it was useless to keep on analysing the matter; the clock could not be turned back. The question now was knowing what would become of the S.R.L. Divided, disorganised, without a newspaper, it was condemned to wither away rapidly. With Lenoir as an intermediary, Lafaurie suggested its fusion with the para-Communist groups. Robert replied that he wanted to wait until after the elections before deciding anything. But I knew he wouldn't go along with them. The discovery of the camps had not left him cold, but he didn't have the least desire to make common

cause with the Communists. The individual members of the
S.R.L. were free to join the C.P., but the movement as such
would simply cease to exist.

Lenoir was the first to join. He expressed satisfaction that
the downfall of the S.R.L. had opened his eyes. Many others
followed his example. It was amazing the number of people
whose eyes opened in November, after the Communists'
success. Little Marie-Ange came one day to ask Robert for
an interview. It was for *L'Enclume*.

"But since when are *you* a Communist?" I asked.

"Since I realised you've got to take sides," she replied,
looking me over with an air of weary superiority.

Robert refused to be interviewed by her. He was annoyed
by all those conversions going on around him. And despite
his bitterness against Henri, Lachaume's article sickened him.
When Lenoir returned to the charge, he listened to him
impatiently.

"It's the finest answer the Communists could give to that
filthy campaign—their success in the elections," Lenoir said
enthusiastically. "Perron and his clique weren't able to
change a single vote." He looked at Robert engagingly.
"Just now, the S.R.L. would follow you to a man if you
spoke up for the fusion we were talking about the other
day."

"The S.R.L. is dead," Robert replied. "And I'm through
with politics."

"Come now," Lenoir said. He smiled. "The members of
the S.R.L. are still alive. All that's needed to rally them is a
single word from you."

"I have no intention of speaking it," Robert said. "Even
before the affair of the camps, I didn't see eye to eye with
the Communists. I'm certainly not going to throw myself
into their arms now."

"The camps? But you refused to take part in that hoax,"
Lenoir said.

"I refused to speak out about the camps, but not to believe in their existence," Robert replied. "A priori, you've
always got to believe the worst; that's true realism."

Lenoir frowned. "Granted, you've got to be able to
anticipate the worst—and then go on," he said. "So tax the
Communists with what you will, that shouldn't stop you from
going along with them."

"No," Robert repeated. "Politics and I—that's all over. I'm crawling back into my hole."

I knew very well that the S.R.L. no longer existed and that Robert had no new plans. Nevertheless, it disturbed me a little to hear him declare that he was crawling back into his hole for good. As soon as Lenoir left, I asked, "Are you really through with politics?"

Robert smiled. "I have the impression that it's politics that is through with me. What can I do?"

"I'm sure that if you looked you'd find out," I said.

"No," he said. "There's one thing I'm beginning to be convinced of: a minority no longer has any chance to-day." He shrugged his shoulders. "I don't want to work with the Communists or against them. What's left?"

"Well, devote yourself to literature," I said cheerfully.

"Yes," Robert said without enthusiasm.

"You can always write articles for *Vigilance*."

"Yes, I will, when the opportunity presents itself. But what one writes decidedly doesn't carry much weight. It's true what Lenoir was saying about Henri's articles having no influence on the elections."

"Lenoir seems to believe Henri's broken up by it," I said. "But that's very unfair. According to what you yourself told me, he wasn't hoping to cause a Communist setback."

"I don't know what he was hoping for," Robert said grumpily. "I'm not even sure he himself knew."

"In any case," I said quickly, "you've got to admit that *L'Espoir* hasn't gone in for anti-Communism."

"Up to now, no," Robert said. "But let's see what happens next."

It irritated me to think that Robert and Henri had broken over a matter that turned out to be a complete fizzle. There was no question of a reconciliation, but, noticeably, Robert felt very much alone. It wasn't a happy winter. The letters I received from Lewis were cheerful, but they failed to comfort me. It was snowing in Chicago, people were skating on the lake, Lewis spent days on end without leaving his room. He told himself stories, told himself that in May we'd go down the Mississippi by boat, that we'd sleep together in a cabin, lulled by the sound of the water. He seemed to believe it. No doubt, from Chicago the Mississippi didn't seem so far. But I knew that for me that cold, grey day which commenced with every awakening would endlessly repeat itself. "We'll never be together again," I thought. "It will never be spring."

It was one of those evenings without future that I heard Paula's voice on the telephone. Her voice was urgent.

"Anne! Is that you? Come over right away. I've got to speak to you. It's important."

"I'm terribly sorry," I said, "but I'm having guests for dinner. I'll come over to-morrow morning."

"You don't understand. Something terrible has happened and you're the only one who can help me."

"Can't you come over here for a moment?"

There was a silence. "Who are you having for dinner?"

"The Pelletiers and the Canges."

"Henri won't be there?"

"No."

"Are you sure?"

"Of course, I'm sure."

"All right, I'll come. But for God's sake, don't tell them anything."

A half-hour later, she rang the bell, and I led her into my bedroom. Her hair was hidden under a dark kerchief, and the powder she had spread over her face failed to camouflage her swollen nose. Her breath had a strong odour of mint and cheap wine. Paula had been so beautiful that it never occurred to me she could one day cease completely to be so—there was something in her face that would resist everything. And suddenly, you could see: like everyone else's, it was made of spongy flesh—more than eighty per cent water. She pulled off her kerchief and sank down on the couch.

"Look what I just got."

It was a letter from Henri, a few lines of neat handwriting on a small sheet of white paper. "Paula, we're only hurting each other. It's better that we stop seeing each other completely. Try not to think of me any more. I hope one day we'll be able to become friends. Henri."

"Can you make anything out of it?" she asked.

"He was afraid to speak to you," I replied. "He preferred sending you a letter."

"But what does it *mean*?"

"It seems clear to me."

" You're lucky."

She looked at me questioningly, and finally I muttered, " It's a letter breaking things off."

" Breaking things off? Did you ever see a letter that broke things off written like this?"

" There's nothing extraordinary about it."

She shrugged her shoulders. " Please! And besides, what's there to break between us? Since he accepts the idea of friendship and I want nothing more."

" Are you sure you didn't tell him you love him?"

" I'll love him beyond the grave. Why should that interfere with our friendship? And besides, he demands that love," she said violently, in a voice that suddenly reminded me of Nadine's. " That letter is revoltingly hypocritical! Just reread it once. ' Try not to think of me any more.' Why doesn't he simply say ' don't think of me any more '? He's giving himself away. He wants me to torture myself trying, but not to succeed. And at the same time, instead of tritely calling me ' Dear Paula,' he writes ' Paula.' " Her voice wavered in pronouncing her name.

" He was afraid ' Dear ' might seem hypocritical to you."

" Not at all. You know perfectly well that in love, during the most passionate moments, you say only the name. He wanted to make me hear his bedroom voice, you understand."

" But why?" I asked.

" That's just what I came here to ask you," she replied, looking at me accusingly. She turned her eyes away. " ' We're only hurting each other.' That's the last straw! He claims I'm tormenting him!"

" I imagine he's suffering from making you suffer."

" And he thought this letter was going to make me happy? Come, come! He isn't so stupid."

There was a silence, and then I asked, "What's your impression?"

" It's not clear to me," she replied. " Not clear at all. I never imagined he could be so sadistic." With a look of exhaustion, she passed her hands over her cheeks. " I felt as if I had almost won. He became confiding and friendly again. More than once, I felt he was about to tell me the test was over. And then, the other day, I must have made a wrong move."

" What happened?"

" The papers had announced his engagement to Josette. Naturally, I didn't believe it for a minute. After all, how could he marry Josette, since I'm his wife? I realised immediately it was part of the test. He came and admitted to me it was all a lie."

" Yes?"

" That's what I said, didn't I! Are you starting to mistrust me, too?"

" I simply said ' yes.' It wasn't a question."

" What you said was ' yes?' Oh, let it go . . . He came over. I tried explaining to him that he could put an end to the comedy, that nothing that could happen to him in this world from now on could possibly touch me, that I loved him with complete abnegation. I don't know whether I was clumsy about it or whether he's crazy, but he misunderstood every word I spoke. It was horrible."

There was a long silence, and then I asked cautiously, " But what do you really think he wants of you?"

She examined me suspiciously. " Listen," she said, " what kind of a game are you playing?"

" I'm not playing any game."

" You're asking stupid questions."

After another silence, she resumed, " You know perfectly well what he wants. He wants me to give him everything and ask for nothing. It's simple. What I don't know is whether he wrote that letter because he believes I still require his love, or because he's afraid I'll deny him mine. The first case would be a continuation of the comedy. The second . . ."

" The second?"

" Would be pure vengefulness," she said darkly. Again her eyes fell upon me, hesitant, mistrustful, and yet insistent. " You've got to help me."

" How?"

" You've got to speak to Henri and convince him."

" But Paula, you know very well Robert and I have just broken with Henri."

" I know," she replied vaguely. " But you see him anyhow."

" Of course not."

She hesitated. " All right, let's say you don't. At any rate, you *could* go to see him. He wouldn't throw you down the stairs."

"He'd believe it was you who sent me, and my words would carry no weight."

"Are you or aren't you my friend?"

"Of course I am!"

She looked defeated. And then, suddenly, her face slackened and she melted into tears. "I'm beginning to doubt everything," she said.

"Paula, I'm your friend," I said.

"Then go and speak to him," she said. "Tell him I can't take any more, that I've had enough. Maybe I've been wrong at times, but he's been torturing me too long. Tell him to stop!"

"Supposing I do it," I said. "Will you believe me when I tell you what Henri's said?"

She got up, wiped her eyes, arranged her kerchief. "I'll believe you if you tell me the truth," she replied, walking to the door.

I knew that speaking to Henri would be completely useless; as for Paula, all friendly conversation would henceforth be futile. The only thing to do would have been to lay her down on my couch and start treating her. Fortunately we are not allowed to treat someone we know intimately; I would have felt as if I were abusing a confidence. I was relieved, in a cowardly way, when she refused to answer the telephone and when she replied to my two letters with a laconic, "Excuse me. I need to be alone. I'll get in touch with you when I want to see you."

The winter continued to drag on. Nadine had become very unstable since her break with Lambert; except for Vincent, she stopped seeing anyone. She gave up journalism, confined herself to her work at *Vigilance*. Robert read enormously, often took me to the cinema, and spent hours listening to music. He began buying records like mad. Whenever he becomes involved that way in a new preoccupation, it means his work isn't going well.

One morning, while we were having breakfast and thumbing through the newspapers, I ran across an article by Lenoir. It was the first time he had written for a Communist paper, and he laid it on with a vengeance. Mercilessly, he took all his old friends and executed them methodically. Robert was the least abused; but on the other hand, he let loose full blast at Henri.

"Look at this," I said.

Robert read it and threw the paper aside. "You've got to give Henri a lot of credit for not becoming anti-Communist."

"I told you he'd hold up under it!"

"They must really be wrangling on the paper," Robert said. "You get the definite feeling from Samazelle's articles that he'd like nothing more than to slip over to the right. Trarieux, too, of course. And Lambert is more than doubtful."

"Oh, Henri isn't having an easy time of it!" I said. I smiled. "When you come down to it, he's more or less in the same position as you: both of you are at odds with the whole world."

"It must bother him more than me," Robert said. His voice sounded almost benevolent; I had the impression that his bitterness against Henri was beginning to dissipate itself.

"I'll never understand why he broke with you that way," I said. "I'm sure he's sorry about it now."

"I've thought about it often," Robert said. "At first, I reproached him for worrying too much about himself in that business. But now I'm beginning to think he wasn't so wrong. In effect, we had to decide what can and what should be the rôle of an intellectual to-day. To remain silent was to choose a very pessimistic solution. At his age, it's only natural that he demurred."

"The paradox is that Henri was far less anxious than you to play a political rôle," I said.

"Maybe he understood that there were other questions involved," Robert replied.

"For example?"

Robert hesitated. "Do you want to know what I really think?"

"Naturally."

"An intellectual no longer has any rôle to play."

"What do you mean? He can still write, can't he?"

"Oh, you can amuse yourself stringing words together like you string pearls—being very careful not to say anything. But even that's dangerous."

"But look here," I said, "in your book you defend literature."

"I hope that what I said will one day come true again," Robert replied. "For the moment, I really believe the best thing we can do is to make people forget us."

"You're not going to stop writing?" I asked.

"Yes. When I finish this book, I will not write again."

"But why?"

"Why do I write?" Robert said. "Because man doesn't live by bread alone and because I believe in the need for that added element. I write in order to capture all the things action ignores—the truths of the moment, the individual, the immediate. Up to now, I thought that that task went hand in hand with the revolution. But no; it hinders it. At the moment all literature that aspires to give man something besides bread is exploited to prove that he can very well do without bread."

"You've always avoided that misunderstanding," I said.

"But things have changed," Robert said. "You see, to-day the revolution is in the hands of the Communists and of them alone. There is no longer any place for the values we used to defend. Maybe one day we'll find them again; let us hope so. But if we stubbornly insist on maintaining them now, we serve the cause of the counter-revolution."

"No, I don't want to believe that," I said. "The taste for truth, respect for the individual—things like that certainly aren't noxious."

"When I refused to speak out against the labour camps, it was because the truth seemed noxious to me," Robert said.

"That was a special case."

"A special case identical with hundreds of others. No," he said, "either you speak the truth or you don't. If you can't make up your mind to speak it always, the best thing is to remain silent and not interfere."

For a moment, I studied Robert. "Do you know what I think? You still believe it was right to keep silent about the Russian camps, but inwardly you're paying heavily for it. And when it comes to sacrifices, you're the same as I am: we don't like them; they make us feel guilty. It's to punish yourself that you're giving up writing."

Robert smiled. "Let's say, rather, that in sacrificing certain things—essentially, what you would call my duties as an intellectual—I became aware of how vain they were. Do you remember the Christmas Eve party in '44?" he asked. "Somebody said that there might come a day when literature would lose its rights. Well, it's come! And it isn't through any lack of readers. But the books I could offer them would be either harmful or meaningless."

I hesitated. "There's something that doesn't ring true in what you're saying."

"What?"

"If the old values really seemed so futile to you, you'd go along with the Communists."

Robert nodded. "You're right: something doesn't ring true. And I'll tell you what it is: I'm too old."

"What's your age got to do with it?"

"I realise only too well that many of the things I once set store by are no longer important; I'm being led to want a future very different from the one I used to imagine. Only I can't change myself, and therefore I see no place for myself in that future."

"In other words, you're hoping for the triumph of Communism, knowing that you'd never be able to live in a Communist world. Is that it?"

"Yes, that's about it. I'll talk to you of it again," he added. "Now I'm going to write about it. It will be the ending of my book."

"And when the book is finished, what are you going to do then?" I asked.

"I'll do the same as everybody else. There are two and a half billion men who don't write."

I didn't want to worry too much about it. Robert still had the S.R.L.'s failure to get out of his system. He was going through a crisis; he would soon be back on his feet. But I must admit I didn't like that idea: do the same thing as everyone else. Eating to live, living to eat—that had been the nightmare of my adolescence. If it meant going back to that, it would be just as well to turn on the gas at once. But I suppose everyone thinks of things like that: let's turn on the gas at once. And you don't turn it on.

I felt rather depressed during the days that followed and didn't feel like seeing anyone. I was very much surprised when one morning a messenger put an enormous bunch of red roses in my arms. Pinned to the tissue paper was a short note from Paula. "Light! the misunderstanding has been dispelled! I am happy and I send you roses. See you this afternoon, at my place."

I said to Robert, "It's not getting any better."

"There was no misunderstanding?"

"None."

He repeated what he had already told me several times: "You ought to take her to see Mardrus."

"It won't be easy to talk her into it."

I wasn't her doctor, but neither was I her friend as I climbed the stairway to her apartment, my mouth filled with lies and a professional look lurking in the depths of my eyes. The smile I contrived as I knocked at her door seemed to me a betrayal, and I was all the more ashamed when Paula greeted me with an unaccustomed gesture: she kissed me. She was wearing one of her long, ageless gowns; she had stuck a red rose in her loose-hanging hair, another over her heart. The flat was full of flowers.

"How nice you are to come!" Paula said. "You're always so nice. I really don't deserve it; I was horrid with you. I'd completely lost control of myself," she added apologetically.

"It's I who should be thanking you; those were glorious roses you sent me."

"Oh, it's a great day!" Paula said. "I wanted so much to have you join in the celebration." She smiled happily at me. "I'm expecting Henri any minute. It's starting all over again."

It was starting all over again? I doubted it very much. Rather, I imagined that Henri had decided to pay her this visit out of pity. In any case, I did not want to see him. I took a step towards the door. "I told you we'd broken with Henri. He'd be furious if he found me here. I'll come back to-morrow."

"Please! Don't go!" she said.

There was such a look of panic in her eyes that I threw my purse and gloves on the couch. Too bad, I told myself, I'd have to stay. With long silken strides, Paula walked to the kitchen and returned carrying a tray on which there were two glasses and a bottle of champagne. "We'll drink to the future."

The cork popped, and after filling the glasses we clinked them together.

"What's happened?" I asked.

"I must really be stupid," Paula said cheerfully. "I've had all the clues in my hand for God knows how long. And it was only last night that the pieces of the puzzle finally fell into place. I wasn't sleeping, but my eyes were closed, and then suddenly I saw it, just as clearly as on the post card: the large pool at Claudie's château. At dawn, I sent Henri a special delivery letter."

I looked at her anxiously. Yes, I had done well to stay; it wasn't getting any better, it wasn't getting anywhere at all.

"You don't understand? It's as silly as a musical-comedy plot!" Paula said. "Henri is jealous." She laughed with genuine heartiness. "It seems inconceivable, doesn't it?"

"Yes, rather."

"Well, it's the truth. He's been having fun torturing me sadistically, and now I know why." She rearranged the rose in her hair. "When he suddenly told me that we shouldn't sleep together any more, I thought it was for reasons of moral delicacy. I was completely wrong. The fact is that he imagined I had become cold and it wounded his ego horribly. I didn't protest with enough conviction, and that irritated him even more. And then on top of it, I began going out, dressing up, and that, too, annoyed him. I said good-bye to him cheerfully, much too cheerfully for his taste. And while I was in Burgundy, I committed one monumental mistake after another. I swear to you that I didn't do it on purpose."

At that moment, there was a quiet knock at the door. Paula gave me such a startled look that I got up. It was a woman holding a basket in her hand.

"Excuse me, I'm sorry," she said. "I can't find the concierge. It's about having a cat altered."

"The clinic is on the ground floor," I said. "The door on the left."

I closed the door, and my laughter froze inside me when I saw Paula's bewildered look.

"What does that mean?" she asked.

"That the concierge wasn't in," I said cheerfully. "It can happen."

"But why did she knock here?"

"Just by chance. After all, she had to knock somewhere."

"By chance?" Paula said.

I smiled engagingly. "You were talking to me about your holiday. What did you do to hurt Henri?"

"Oh, yes." There was no longer any animation in her voice. "Well, I sent him the first post card. I told him what I had been doing and I wrote that unfortunate sentence: 'I've been taking long walks about the countryside; they say it looks like me.' Obviously, he immediately got the idea I had a lover."

"I don't see . . ."

"'They,'" she said impatiently. "The 'they' was suspect. When 'they' compare a woman to a landscape, it generally means the 'they' is her lover. And on top of that, I sent him a second card when he was in Venice; it had a picture of the Belzunce grounds with the pool in the centre."

"So?"

"You yourself told me that fountains, basins, pools were psycho-analytical symbols. Henri thought I was throwing the fact that I had taken a lover in his face! He must have known that Louis Volange was there. Didn't you notice, at the party after the opening, the withering look he gave me when I was talking to Volange? It's as simple as two and two. From there on it all fits together perfectly."

"Is that what you told him in your special delivery letter?"

"Yes. Now he knows everything."

"Did he answer you?"

"Why should he? He'll come; he knows I'm waiting for him."

I remained silent. Deep within herself, Paula knew he wouldn't come; that was why she had pleaded with me to stay. At some point, she would have to admit to herself that he hadn't come, and then she would break down. My only hope was that Henri had understood she was going mad and that he would come to see her out of pity. In the meantime, I could find nothing to say. She stared at the door with a persistence I found intolerable; the fragrance of the roses seemed to me a mortuary fragrance.

"Are you still writing?" I asked.

"Yes."

"You promised to show me something," I said, struck by a sudden inspiration. "And you never have, you know."

"Are you really interested?"

"Of course."

She walked over to her desk and took out a sheaf of blue paper covered with round handwriting. She put it on my knees. She had always made mistakes in spelling, but never in such great number. I read over one of the sheets; it gave me something to do, but Paula continued staring at the door.

"I can't read your writing very well," I said. "Would you mind very much reading it aloud?"

"As you like," Paula replied.

I lit a cigarette. At least, while she was reading, I knew what sounds were forming in her throat. Although I hadn't been expecting much, I was nevertheless surprised: it was devastating. In the middle of a sentence, the downstairs bell rang. Paula got up. "You see!" she said triumphantly. She pressed the button that controlled the opening of the door. With an ecstatic look on her face, she remained standing.

"Special delivery."

"Thank you."

The man closed the door and she handed me the blue envelope. "Open it. Read it to me."

She sat down on the couch; her cheeks and lips had become violet.

"Paula: There never was any misunderstanding. We'll be friends when you've accepted the fact that our love is dead. In the meantime, don't write to me any more. Until then."

She threw herself full length on the couch with such violence that the petals of one of the roses on the mantel dropped off. "I don't understand," she moaned. "I don't understand anything any more." She was sobbing, her face hidden the cushions, and I began saying meaningless words to her, for no other reason than to hear the purr of my voice. "You'll get well, you've got to get well. Love isn't everything . . ." And I knew very well that in her place I would never want to get well and bury my love with my own hands.

I had just returned from St. Martin where I had spent the week-end, when I got her special delivery letter. "The dinner will take place to-morrow night at eight." I picked up the telephone. Paula's voice seemed icy.

"Oh, it's you. Why are you calling?"

THE MANDARINS 547

"I just wanted to tell you it's all right for to-morrow night."

"Naturally, it's all right," she said, and hung up.

Although I was anticipating a difficult evening, I was, nevertheless, shocked when Paula opened the door; never had I seen her face without make-up. She was wearing an old skirt and an old grey sweater; her hair was drawn back in a severe bun. On the table, to which she had added extensions and which stretched from one wall of the room to the other, she had set twelve plates and as many glasses. Simpering, she held out her hand and greeted me with, "Did you come to offer me your condolences or your congratulations?"

"In connection with what?"

"My breaking off with my lover."

I didn't answer, and looking over my shoulder at the empty corridor, she asked, "Where are they?"

"Who?"

"The others."

"Which others?"

"Oh! I thought there were many more of you," she said uncertainly, closing the door. She looked at the table. "What would you like to eat?"

"Anything at all. Whatever you have."

"The thing is I have nothing," she said. "Except maybe some noodles?"

"I'm not really hungry," I said hastily.

"I can let you have some noodles without ruining anyone," she said ominously.

"No, really. I often skip dinner."

I sat down, unable to take my eyes from that banquet table. Paula, too, had sat down; she was studying me in silence. In her eyes, I had previously seen reproach, suspicion, impatience; but to-day, there was no mistaking it: black, cold and hard, it was hate.

I forced myself to speak. "Who were you expecting?" I asked.

"All of you!" She shrugged her shoulders. "I must have forgotten to send the invitations."

"All? Who do you mean?" I asked.

"You know perfectly well," she replied. "You, Henri, Volange, Claudie, Lucie, Robert, Nadine—the whole conspiracy."

"Conspiracy?"

"Don't play the innocent," she said in a hard voice. "All of you have formed a conspiracy. The question I wanted to ask you to-night is this: Towards what end have you been acting? If it's for my good, I'll thank you and I'll leave for Africa to take care of lepers. If not, the only thing left for me is to take revenge." She stared at me. "Since I'll have to take my revenge first on those who were dearest to me, I've got to be absolutely sure before I decide." There was such a dark passion in her voice that I stole a look at the purse she had placed in her lap; she was pulling the zipper nervously back and forth. Suddenly, everything had become possible. That red living-room—what a beautiful setting for a murder! I decided to counter attack.

"Listen, Paula, you seem extremely tired these days. You give a dinner and you forget to invite people, you forget to prepare the meal. And now you're building up a persecution mania. You've got to see a doctor at once. I'll make an appointment for you with Mardrus."

For a moment, she seemed to have lost her assurance. "I do have headaches," she said. "But that's secondary. First, I've got to discover the meaning of things." She reflected. "I know I have an artistic temperament. But a fact is a fact."

"What are the facts?"

"Why did Claudie mail her last letter to me from the post office near the zoo? Why was there a monkey—a little ape—making faces at me from the house across the street? Why, when I said I wouldn't be capable of holding a salon, did you answer: 'On the contrary'? You accuse me of having aped Henri in trying to write, of having aped Claudie, her way of dressing, her society life. You reproach me, all of you, for accepting Henri's money and for looking down my nose at the poor. You're all in league to convince me of how low I am." Again, she looked at me menacingly. "Is it to save me, or to destroy me?"

"What you call facts, are incidental events which mean nothing," I said.

"Come, come. Clouds don't form a definite pattern like that! Don't deny it," she added impatiently. "Answer me frankly, or we'll never get anywhere."

"No one ever thought of destroying you," I said. "Listen, Paula, why would I wish you any harm? We're friends."

" That's what I used to tell myself," Paula said. " Whenever I would see you again, I'd stop believing in my suspicions. It was like some sort of magic charm . . ." She got up abruptly, and her voice changed. " I'm being a terrible hostess," she said. " There must be some port left somewhere." She went to look for the port, came back with it, filled two glasses, and simulated a smile. " How's Nadine? "

" So-so. Ever since her break with Lambert, she's been rather depressed."

" Who's she sleeping with? "

" Just now, I really don't believe she's sleeping with anyone."

" Nadine? You must admit that's strange," Paula said.

" Not as strange as all that."

" Does she go out with Henri often? "

" I told you we'd broken with Henri," I said.

" Oh, yes. I was forgetting about that story about a breakup! " Paula said with a snicker. The snicker halted abruptly. " I'm no fool, you know."

" Look, you read Henri's and Robert's letters in *L'Espoir.*"

" I read them in the copy of *L'Espoir* I had in my hands."

I examined her for a moment. " Do you mean to say that copy was made up purposely for you? "

" Obviously! " Paula replied. She shrugged her shoulders. " For Henri, it was mere child's play."

I remained silent; it would have been senseless to argue the point. Again, she attacked. " Then according to you, Nadine doesn't see Henri any more? "

" No."

" She never loved him, did she? "

" Never."

" Why did she go to Portugal with him? "

" You know very well why. She thought it would be fun having an affair with him, and, primarily, she wanted to travel."

I felt as if I were undergoing a police interrogation; at any moment I would be pounced upon and given the third degree.

" And you let her go with him, just like that," Paula said.

" Since Diego's death, I've always left her free to do as she wanted."

" You're a strange woman," Paula said. " They talk too

much about me, and not enough about you." She refilled my glass. " Finish up the bottle."

" Thank you."

I didn't see what she was getting at, but I felt more and more uneasy. What exactly did she have against me?

" You haven't been sleeping with Robert for quite a long time, have you?" she asked.

" A very long time."

" And you never had any lovers?"

" Occasionally . . . A few unimportant affairs."

" A few unimportant affairs," Paula repeated slowly. " And are you having one now, an unimportant affair?"

I didn't quite know why I felt I had to answer her, as if I were hoping the truth would somehow be able to neutralise her madness. "I'm having a very important affair, in America," I said. " With a writer. His name is Lewis Brogan . . ."

I was ready to tell her everything, but she cut me off. " Oh, America! That's far away," she said. " I mean, in France."

" I love this American," I said. " I'm going back in May to see him. Having another affair would be completely unthinkable."

" And what does Henri have to say about it?" Paula asked.

" What's Henri got to do with this?"

Paula got up. " Come! Let's put an end to this game," she said. " You know very well that I know you're sleeping with Henri. I want you to tell me when it began."

" Look," I said, " Nadine's the one who slept with Henri. Not me."

" You threw her into Henri's arms to hold him for yourself. I've realised that for a long time now," Paula said. " You're very clever, but nevertheless you've made mistakes."

Paula had taken her purse with her when she got up, and she was still playing with the zipper. I couldn't take my eyes off her hands. I, too, got up.

" If that's what you think, I'd better leave," I said.

" I guessed the truth that night in May of '45 when you pretended you'd got lost in the crowd," Paula said. " And then I said to myself I must be raving. What an idiot I was!"

"You *were* raving," I said. "You're raving now."

Paula leaned against the door. "Let's get it over with," she said. "Did you stage that act to get rid of me, or in my best interests?"

"Go and see a doctor," I said. "Mardrus or someone else —any doctor. But go and see one and tell him everything. He'll tell you you're raving mad."

"You refuse to help me?" Paula said. "Oh, I expected it. Well, it doesn't matter. I'll end up by seeing it through without your help."

"I can't help you; you refuse to believe me."

For a moment that seemed interminable, she looked deeply into my eyes. "You want to go? They're waiting for you?"

"No one's waiting for me. But there's no use in my staying."

She stepped away from the door. "Get out! You can tell them everything; I have nothing to hide."

"Believe me, Paula," I said, holding out my hand to her, "you're sick. You've got to get yourself treated."

She took my hand. "Thank you for coming. Good-bye."

"Good-bye," I said.

I went down the stairs as fast as I could.

The next day, while we were having coffee after lunch, the bell rang. It was Claudie.

"Excuse me. I know it isn't very polite to drop in on you like this without any warning." Her voice was troubled and heavy with importance. "I've come to see you about Paula. I have a feeling that something's wrong."

"What happened?"

"She was supposed to have lunch at the house. At half-past one, she still hadn't come. I called her up and she answered me with a big guffaw. I told her we were going to start lunch and she shouted, 'Start lunch! Go ahead and start lunch!' And all the time she was laughing like a madwoman!"

Claudie's big eyes sparkled with gleeful solicitude. I got up. "We must go and see her," I said.

"That's what I thought. But I didn't dare go alone," Claudie said.

"Well, let's go together," I said.

A few minutes later, we stepped out of Claudie's car in

front of Paula's house. To-day the familiar sign, "Furnished Rooms To Let," seemed pregnant with sinister meaning. I rang the bell. The door didn't open. I rang again, this time insistently. There was a clicking of heels in the hall and then Paula appeared. Her hair was hidden beneath a violet shawl: she began to laugh. "Only two of you?" She held the door open only a crack and examined us with mean-looking eyes.

"I don't need you any more, thank you."

She slammed the door shut violently, and I heard her shouting loudly as she moved away, "What a farce!"

We stood motionless on the pavement.

"I think we ought to get in touch with the family," Claudie said. Her eyes no longer sparkled. "In cases like this, it's the best thing to do."

"Yes, she has a sister." I hesitated. "Nevertheless, I'm going to try to talk to her."

This time, I pressed the first button and the door opened automatically. The concierge stopped me on the way in. She was a frail, discreet little woman who had been cleaning Paula's flat for many years.

"Are you going to see Mademoiselle Mareuil?"

"Yes, she doesn't seem to be very well."

"That's why I stopped you. I've been worrying about her," the concierge said. "She hasn't eaten a thing for at least five days, and the people under her told me she paces the room all night long. When I clean up for her, she's all the time mumbling things aloud. That I'm accustomed to, but lately, she's been acting peculiar."

"I'm going to try to take her away for a rest."

I went up the stairs, Claudie following behind me. It was dark on the top landing; in the darkness, something was shining—a large white sheet of paper tacked to the door. Written on it, in printed letters, was "The Society Ape." I knocked, in vain.

"How awful!" Claudie said. "Maybe she's killed her-self!"

I looked through the keyhole. Paula was kneeling in front of the fireplace; bundles of paper were scattered all around her and she was throwing them into the fire. I knocked again, loudly.

"Open up, or I'll have the door broken in!"

She got up, opened the door, and put her hand behind her back.

"What do you want from me?"

She knelt in front of the fire again. Tears were streaming down her cheeks and her nose was dripping. She was throwing her manuscripts and her letters into the flames. I placed my hand on her shoulder, and she shook it off in horror.

"Leave me alone!"

"Paula, you're going to go with me to see a doctor now. You are losing your mind."

"Get out! I know that you hate me. And I hate you, too. Get out!" She stood up and began shouting, "Both of you get out!" In another moment, she would have begun shrieking. I walked to the door and left with Claudie.

Claudie sent a telegram to Paula's sister; I called up Mardrus to ask his advice and sent a note to Henri. That evening, during dinner, the bell rang; we were so on edge that all of us started. Nadine jumped up and raced to the door. It was only a young boy who handed me a scrap of paper. "It's from Mademoiselle Mareuil. I'm the concierge's nephew," he said. I read it aloud. "I don't hate you, I'm waiting for you. Come immediately."

"You're not going to go?" Nadine said.

"Of course I'll go."

"It won't do a bit of good."

"You never can tell."

"But she's dangerous," Nadine said. "All right," she added. "If you go I'm going with you."

"I'm the one who'll go with you," Robert said. "Nadine's right: you oughtn't to go there alone."

I protested weakly, "Paula will think it strange."

"A lot of things seem strange to her these days."

As a matter of fact, when I found myself again in front of that demented house, when once more I climbed the stairway with its threadbare carpet, I was very happy to have Robert with me. The sheet of paper was no longer on the door. Paula didn't offer us her hand, but her face was calm. She made a ceremonious gesture.

"Won't you be good enough to come in."

I stifled an exclamation. All the mirrors were shattered and slivers of glass were scattered over the carpet; an acrid smell of burnt cloth filled the room. "I'm glad you came,"

Paula said solemnly. "I wanted to thank you." She motioned us to sit down. "I wanted to thank all of you—because I understand now."

Her voice seemed sincere, but the smile she gave us twisted her lips as if she were no longer capable of controlling them.

"There's no need to thank me," I said. "I haven't done anything."

"Don't lie," she said. "You've been acting for my good, I admit it. But you mustn't lie to me any more." She scrutinised me. "It was for my good, wasn't it?"

"Yes," I replied.

"Yes, I know. I deserved that test, and you were right to inflict it on me. I owe you my thanks for making me look myself in the face. But now I need your advice; should I take a dose of prussic acid or try to redeem myself?"

"Not the prussic acid," Robert said.

"All right. But then how shall I live?"

"First of all, you're going to take a sedative and get some sleep," I replied. "You can't stand up any more."

"I don't want to think about myself any more," she said violently. "I've had enough of thinking about myself. Don't give me bad advice."

She let herself fall into a chair. It was only a question of waiting; any minute now she would collapse completely, and then I would give her a sedative and put her to bed. I looked around me. Did she really have prussic acid in her possession? At the beginning of the war, I recalled, she had shown me a little brownish phial, explaining that she had got hold of some poison "in case." Perhaps the phial was in her purse. I didn't dare touch the purse. My eyes returned to Paula. Her lower jaw hung slack, all her features had sagged. I had seen a good many faces in that state, but Paula wasn't a patient; she was Paula, and it hurt me deeply to see her like that.

She made an effort. "I want to go to work," she said. "I want to pay Henri back. And I don't want the tramps to insult me any more."

"We'll find work for you," Robert said.

"I was thinking of becoming a charwoman," she said. "But that would be unfair competition. Is there any kind of work where you're not competing with someone?"

"We'll find something," Robert replied.

Paula passed her hand across her brow. "Everything is so difficult! A little while ago, I started burning my dresses. But I have no right to." She looked at me. "If I sell them to the rag-pickers, do you think they'll stop hating me?"

"They don't hate you."

Abruptly she stood up, walked over to the fireplace, and gathered up an armful of clothing. The shimmering silk dresses, the grey worsted suit were nothing now but crumpled rags.

"I'm going to give them away now," she said. "Let's go down together."

"It's rather late," Robert said.

"The Café des Cloches stays open very late."

She threw a coat over her shoulders. How was I to stop her from going down? Robert and I exchanged a look; doubtless, she caught it. "Yes, it's an act," she said wearily, "Now, I'm beginning to ape myself." She took off her coat, threw it on a chair. "That's an act, too. I saw myself throwing off my coat." She dug her fists in her eyes. "I'm always seeing myself!"

I went to get a glass of water and dissolved a powder in it. "Drink this," I said. "And go to bed."

Paula looked at me uncertainly, and then she threw herself into my arms. "I'm sick! I'm so sick!"

"Yes, but you're going to take care of yourself and you'll get well," I said.

"Take care of me, you've got to take care of me!"

She was trembling, tears were streaming down her cheeks; she was so feverish and damp that I felt as if she were going to melt away completely at any moment, leaving behind only a puddle of pitch, black as her eyes.

"To-morrow I'll take you to a hospital," I said. "In the meantime, drink this."

She took the glass. "Will it make me sleep?"

"I'm sure it will."

She emptied the glass in a single swallow.

"Now, go upstairs and get into bed."

"I'm going," she said obediently.

I went up with her and while she was in the bathroom I opened the zipper of her purse. In the bottom was a little brownish phial which I slipped into my pocket.

The next morning, Paula went quietly to the hospital with

me, and Mardrus promised me she'd be cured—a matter of a few weeks or a few months. She'd be cured, but once in the street again I asked myself anxiously, "What exactly are they going to cure her of? And afterwards, who will she be?" Oh, after all, it wasn't difficult to foresee. She'd be like myself, like millions of others: a woman waiting to die, no longer knowing why she's living.

And then at last it was May. There, in Chicago, I would once more rediscover myself in the body of a woman in love, a woman loved. I found it hard to believe. And sitting in the plane, I still couldn't believe it. It was an old, battered crate which had come from Athens and which was flying very low; it was full of Greek shopkeepers who were going to seek their fortunes in America. As for myself, I didn't know what I was going there to seek; there was no living image in my heart, no desire in my body. It wasn't that gloved traveller whom Lewis was expecting: I was expected by no one. "I knew it: I'll never see him again," I thought when the plane turned back over the ocean. One of the engines had failed, and we were returning to Shannon. I spent two days overlooking a fjord, in an imitation village with toy-like houses. In the evening, I drank Irish whisky; during the day, I took walks through the green and grey country-side, a countryside as melancholy as you could wish. When we landed in the Azores, a tyre burst, and for twenty-four hours they parked us in a waiting-room with cretonne cur-tains. After Gander, the plane was caught in a storm and, to get out of it, the pilot turned towards Nova Scotia. I had the feeling that the rest of my life would be spent revolving around the earth, eating cold chicken. We flew over a dark gulf swept by the beam from a lighthouse. Again, the plane set down; another landing strip, another waiting-room. Yes, I was condemned to wander endlessly from landing strip to landing strip with my head full of noise and a blue overnight bag at my feet.

And then, suddenly, I saw him: Lewis. We had agreed that he would wait for me at his flat, but he was there, in the crowd watching at the door to the customs area. Strangely enough, he was wearing a stiff collar and gold-rimmed glasses, but the strangest part of it was that I had seen him and had felt nothing. That whole year of waiting, all the regrets, the remorse, that long voyage—and perhaps I was about to find out I no longer loved him. And he? Did he still love *me*? I wanted to run over to him, but the customs men seemed in no particular hurry. The suitcases of the Greek shopkeepers were filled with lace goods, and they appraised them one by one, joking and laughing. When they finally let me go, Lewis was no longer there. I got into a cab and wanted to give the address to the driver, but I couldn't remember the number. My ears were buzzing and that noise in my head wouldn't let up. Finally, I thought of it: 1211. The cab started off; down one avenue, up another, neon signs, other neon signs. I had never learned to find my way around in that city, but nevertheless, it seemed to me the ride shouldn't have taken that long. Perhaps the driver was going to take me to some deserted dead-end street and choke me to death. In the mood I was in, that seemed to me much more credible than seeing Lewis again.

The driver turned around. " There is no 1211."

" There is. I know the house well."

" Maybe they changed the numbers," the driver said. " We'll turn around and go back up the street."

He began driving slowly along the street, close to the pavement. I seemed to recognise certain corners, vacant lots, tracks. But tracks and vacant lots all look alike. A dock, a viaduct seemed familiar; it was as if the things were still there but had changed place. " What lunacy!" I thought. You leave, you say, " I'll come back," because it's too hard to leave for good. But you're lying to yourself: you don't come back. A year passes, things happen, nothing is the same. To-day, Lewis was wearing a stiff collar, I had seen him without my heart beating any faster, and his house had vanished into thin air. I shook myself. " All I have to do is ring him up," I said to myself. " But what's the number?" I had forgotten it. Suddenly, I saw the red sign, " Schlitz," and the inane faces laughing on the billboard.

" Stop! Stop!" I shouted. " Here it is!"

" This is 1112," the driver said.

" Yes, 1112. That's it!"

I jumped out of the cab and, in the lighted frame of a window, I saw a bending silhouette. It was watching, watching me; it hurried down. It was he. He was wearing neither a stiff collar nor glasses, but there was a baseball cap on his head, and his arms smothered me. "Anne!"

"Lewis!"

"At last! It's been such a long wait! It's been so long!"

"Yes, it was long; it was so terribly long!"

I know he didn't carry me and I don't remember using my rubbery legs to climb the stairs. And yet, there we were, embracing each other in the middle of the yellow kitchen. The stove, the linoleum, the Mexican blanket—everything was there, in its place.

I stammered, "What are you doing with that cap on?"

"I don't know. It was lying around." He pulled off the cap and threw it on the table.

"I saw your double at the airport. He wears glasses and stiff collars. He frightened me. I thought it was you and I didn't feel anything."

"I had a fright, too. About an hour ago, two men passed by outside carrying a woman. She had either fainted or she was dead, and I thought it was you."

"But now," I said, "it's really you, it's really I."

Lewis hugged me very tightly and then loosened his hold. "Are you tired? Thirsty? Hungry?"

"No."

Again, I clung to him; my lips were so heavy, so numb, that they would no longer form words. I pressed them against his mouth; he carried me over to the bed. "Anne! I waited for you every night!"

I closed my eyes. A man's body was once more weighing on me, heavy with all its confidence and all its desire. It was Lewis. No, he hadn't changed, nor had I, nor had our love. I had left, but I had come back; I had found my place again and I was released from myself.

We spent the following day packing suitcases and making love—a long day that lasted until the next morning. In the train, we slept cheek to cheek. I still wasn't fully awake when, tied to a dock on the Ohio, I saw the side-wheeler Lewis had spoken about in his letters. I had thought so much about it without believing in it that, even now, I could hardly believe my eyes. And yet, it was indeed real: I boarded it. Stirred with emotion, I inspected our cabin. In

Chicago, I lived in Lewis's apartment; this was our cabin, it belonged to us both. That made us truly a couple. Now I knew: it was possible to come back, and I would come back every year. Every year, our love would pass through a night longer than the polar night; and then, one day, happiness would rise like the sun, and for three or four months it would not sink again. From the depths of the night, we would await that day, await it together. Absence would no longer separate us; we were united forever.

" We're leaving. Come quickly! " Lewis said. He ran up the stairs and I followed him. He leaned over the rail, his head turning in every direction.

" See how pretty it is—the sky and the earth blending in the water."

The lights of Cincinnati were glittering under a vast star-speckled sky, and we were gliding over flaming ripples. We sat down and for a long while watched the neon signs fade away and then disappear. Lewis was holding me against him.

" To think I never believed in all that," he said.

" All what? "

" Loving and being loved."

" What did you believe in? "

" Having a roof over my head, eating regularly, bringing home a girl now and then—security. I didn't think you had any right to ask for more. I thought that everyone was alone, always. And here you are! "

Above our heads, a loud-speaker was blaring out numbers: the passengers were playing bingo. They were all so old that I felt as if my age was reduced by half. I was twenty. I was living my first love, and this was my first trip. Lewis kissed my hair, my eyes, my mouth.

" Let's go down. Would you like to? "

" You know I never say no."

" But I like so much to hear you say yes. You say it so nicely! "

" Yes," I said. " Yes."

What a pleasure to have only to say yes! With my frayed life, my skin no longer brand-new, I was creating happiness for the man I loved. What happiness!

It took us six days to go down the Ohio and the Mississippi. At each stop we fled the other passengers and walked headlong through the hot, dark cities. The rest of the time, stretched out on the deck in the sun, we would talk, read, and smoke without doing anything. Each day the same view of water and grass, the same sound of engine and water. But we liked it that way—a single morning being reborn from morning to morning, a single evening from evening to evening.

Yes, that's what happiness is: everything seemed good to us. And we were glad, too, when we left the boat. Both of us had been to New Orleans before, but for Lewis and for me it wasn't the same city. He showed me the crowded neighbourhoods where fifteen years earlier he used to hawk bars of soap, the docks where he would feed himself on stolen bananas, the narrow streets of the red-light district he walked through, his heart beating, his pockets empty. At times, he seemed almost to miss those days of misery, of anger, of the violence of his unsatisfied desires. But when I took him walking in the French Quarter, when he strutted as a tourist through its bars and its patios, he seemed delighted, as if he were playing a good trick on destiny.

He had never been in an aeroplane; during the whole flight, his nose was glued to the window, and he laughed at the clouds. I, too, was delighted. What a change! When the fixed stars begin waltzing in the heavens, when the earth takes on a new skin, it's almost as if you were changing skins yourself. For me, Yucatan was nothing but a word without reality, printed in little letters in an atlas. I had no ties to it, not even a desire or a mental image, and all of a sudden I was discovering it with my own eyes. The plane began its descent, rushed towards the ground, and, spread out beneath us from one end of the sky to the other, I saw a land of verdigris velvet on which the shadows of the clouds formed black lakes. We drove along a bumpy road between fields of blue century plants above which the vigorous red of a flat-topped tropical tree exploded from time to time. We went down a street bordered by little adobe houses with thatched roofs. The sun was huge and hot. We left our suitcases in the lobby of the hotel, a sort of luxuriant, stagnant greenhouse in which, perched on one leg, pink flamingoes were sleeping. And then we set out again. In the white squares, sitting in the shade of glazed trees, men dressed in white were dreaming under their straw hats. I recognised the sky, the silence of Toledo and Avila ; finding Spain again on this side of the ocean bewildered me even more than saying to myself, " I'm in Yucatan."

" Let's take one of those little hacks," Lewis said.

On one side of the square was a line of black, stiff-backed hacks. Lewis awakened one of the drivers, and we sat down on the narrow seat. Lewis began to laugh. " And now, where to? Got any idea?"

" Tell him to just drive us around and then take us to the post office. I'm expecting some letters."

Lewis had learned a few words of Spanish in southern California. He made a little speech to the driver, and the horse began walking, slowly. We went along avenues at once sumptuous and seedy. The rain, poverty had gnawed away at the mansions built in a harsh Castilian style ; the statues were rotting behind the rusty iron gates of the gardens ; luxuriant flowers, red, violet, and blue, were wilting at the foot of half-bare trees ; lined up along the tops of walls, large, black birds were watching. Everywhere there was a smell of death. I was happy when we reached the edge of the Indian market place ; under the sun-beaten canvas roofing, the teeming crowd was very much alive.

" I'll be back in a minute," I said to Lewis.

He sat down on the stairway and I went into the post office. There was a letter from Robert ; I opened it immediately. He was reading the final proofs of his book ; he was writing a political article for *Vigilance*. Good. I had been right in not worrying too much about him. Despite all his mistrust of politics and writing, he wasn't ready to give them up. He said it was grey in Paris. I put the letter in my purse and went out. How far away Paris was! How blue the sky here! I took Lewis's arm. " Everything's fine."

We made our way through the crowd, in the shade of the canvas roofing. They were selling fruits, fish, sandals, cotton wear ; the women were wearing long, embroidered skirts. I liked their glistening braids and their placid faces. The Indian children laughed a great deal, showing their teeth. We sat down in a café which smelled of the sea, and they served us a dark, foamy beer on our barrel-top table. There were only men there, all young ; they were chattering and laughing.

"They look happy, those Indians," I said.

Lewis shrugged his shoulders. "That's easy to say. On a sunny day, when you take a walk through Little Italy in Chicago, the people look happy, too."

"That's true," I said. "You have to look more closely."

"I was thinking about that while I was waiting for you," Lewis said. "For us, everything's a holiday because travelling is a holiday. But I'm sure they aren't celebrating a holiday." He spat out an olive pip. "When you travel around like this, as a tourist, you don't know what's going on."

I smiled at Lewis. "Let's buy a little house here. We'll sleep in hammocks, I'll make you tortillas, and we'll learn to speak Indian."

"I'd like that," Lewis said.

"Ah!" I sighed. "If only people could have several lives."

Lewis looked at me. "You're not doing so badly," he said with a little smile.

"What do you mean?"

"It seems to me you manage to have two lives."

The blood rushed to my cheeks. Lewis's voice wasn't hostile, but neither was it very affectionate. Was it because of that letter from Paris? Abruptly, I realised I wasn't alone in thinking about our problems; in his own way, he, too, was thinking about them. I said to myself, "I came back, I'll always come back." But perhaps he was saying to himself, "She'll always leave again." What could I answer him? I was at a loss.

Anguished, I said, "Lewis, we'll never be enemies, will we?"

"Enemies? How could anyone ever be your enemy?"

He looked frankly bewildered; those words I had spoken so thoughtlessly had, of course, been silly. He was smiling at me; I smiled at him. But suddenly I was afraid; would I be punished some day for having dared to love without giving my whole life?

We dined at the hotel between two pink flamingos. The tourist agency at Mérida had assigned us a little Mexican to whom Lewis was listening impatiently. I wasn't listening at all. I was still wondering what was going on in his head. We never spoke of the future, Lewis never asked me any questions; perhaps I should have asked him questions. But after all, the year before, I had told him everything I had to say. There was nothing new to add. And besides, words are dangerous; you run the risk of getting things all mixed up. Now, our love had to be lived; later, when it was well established, it would be time enough to talk about it.

"Madame cannot go to Chichen Itza in a bus," the little Mexican said. He gave me a big smile. "You would have the car at your disposal all day to visit the ruins. And the driver would act as your guide."

"We hate guides and we like to walk," Lewis said.

"The Hotel Maya has a special rate for customers of the agency."

"We'll stay at the Victoria," I said.

"It is impossible. The Victoria is an inn for natives," said the native.

In face of our silence, he bowed with a sad little smile. "You will have a very trying day!"

Actually the bus that took us to Chichen Itza the next evening was quite comfortable, and when we walked past the garden of the Hotel Maya and heard the babble of American voices we felt proud of our stubbornness. "Listen to them!" Lewis said to me. "I didn't come all the way down to Mexico to see Americans!"

He was holding a little travelling bag in his hand and we groped our way along the muddy road; heavy drops of water were dripping from the trees which hid the sky from us. It was pitch-black and the oppressive smell of mould, rotting leaves, and dying flowers made me dizzy. In the darkness, invisible cats with glittering eyes were jumping up and down. I pointed to those bodiless pupils. "What's that?"

"Fireflies. We have them in Illinois, too. Put five of them in a lantern and you can see clearly enough to read."

"That would be a help just now!" I said. "I can't see a thing. Are you sure there's another hotel?"

"Absolutely."

As for me, I began to have my doubts. Not a house, not a human sound. Finally, we heard voices speaking Spanish; a wall became faintly visible. Not a light. Lewis pushed open a gate, but we didn't dare go in. Pigs were grunting, chickens cackling, and somewhere there was a chorus of toads.

"It's a robber's den," I murmured.

Lewis shouted, "Is this a hotel?"

There was a stir, a candle flickered; and then the lights went on. We were in the courtyard of an inn, a man was smiling politely at us. He said something in Spanish. "He apologises. A fuse blew out," Lewis said. "He has rooms."

The room faced a courtyard on one side, the jungle on the other; it was bare, but the sheets were spotless under white mosquito netting. For dinner, they served us tortillas which stuck to our teeth, violet-coloured beans, and a bony chicken with a sauce which set my throat on fire. The dining-room was decorated with carnival bric-a-brac and coloured lithographs. On a calendar, half-naked Indians dressed up in feathers were playing basketball in an ancient stadium. Sitting on a bench in the courtyard, amid the pigs and chickens, a Mexican was strumming a guitar.

"How far away Chicago seems!" I said. "And Paris! How far away everything seems!"

"Yes, now we're beginning to travel," Lewis said in an excited voice.

I squeezed his hand. At that moment, I was sure of what was in his head: the sound of the guitar, the chorus of toads, and me. I heard the toads and the guitar, and I was completely his. For him, for me, for us, nothing existed but us.

All night long, the concert of the toads penetrated into our room; in the morning, we awakened to the chatter of thousands of birds. We were alone when we entered the enclosure where the ancient city stood. Lewis ran off towards the temples, and I followed him slowly. I was even more taken aback than I had been when I arrived in Yucatan. Until now, antiquity for me was tied up with the Mediterranean. On the Acropolis, in the Forum, I had contemplated my own past without surprise; but nothing connected Chichen Itza with my life. A week earlier, I didn't even know the name of that immense geometrical Mecca with its blood-soaked stones. And there it was, huge, mute, crushing the earth under the weight of its mathematically exact architecture and its fanatical sculpture. Temples, altars, the stadium pictured on the calendar, a market place with a thousand columns, other symmetrical temples with crazy bas-reliefs. I looked around for Lewis and found him at the very top of the tallest pyramid. He was waving his hand; he looked tiny. The stairway was steep, and I climbed it without watching my feet, my eyes riveted on Lewis.

"Where are we?" I asked.

"That's what I'm wondering."

Beyond the walls of the enclosure, the jungle stretched out as far as the eye could reach; here and there, one of the red tropical trees burst through the vast expanse of green. Not a field.

"But where in the world do they grow their corn?" I asked.

"Didn't they teach you anything in school?" Lewis said smugly. "When they're ready to begin sowing, they burn out a patch of the jungle. After the harvest, the trees grow back again. You can't see the scars."

"How do you happen to know that?"

"Oh, I've always known it."

I began to laugh. "You're lying! You read it in a book, probably last night while I was sleeping. Otherwise, you'd have told me yesterday in the bus."

He looked crestfallen. "It's funny," he said. "Even in little things, you always manage to find me out. Yes, I found a book last night at the hotel and I wanted to dazzle you."

"Dazzle me. What else did you learn?"

"The corn grows by itself. The peasants don't have to work more than a few weeks a year. That's how they had the time to build so many temples." With a sudden violence, he added, "Can you imagine the lives they must have led! Eating tortillas and heaving stones. And under the sun! Eating and sweating, sweating and eating, day after day! The people they used as human sacrifices, that was far from being the worst part of it—there were only a handful of them. But think of those millions of miserable creatures turned into beasts of burden by the warriors and the priests. And why? Out of stupid vanity!"

He looked angrily at those pyramids which had once shot up towards the sun and which now seemed to us to be crushing the earth. I didn't share his anger, perhaps because I had never had to sweat in order to eat and because all that misery was too ancient. But neither could I lose myself without mental reservations in the contemplation of that dead beauty, as I would have ten years earlier. It had left nothing behind it, that civilisation which had sacrificed so many human lives to its games of building blocks. Even more than its cruelty, its sterility offended me. Only a handful of archæologists and æsthetes still took an interest in those monuments which the tourists photographed so casually.

"What about going down now?" I said.

"How?"

Looking down, it seemed as if all four walls rising to the platform were perfectly vertical. One of them was streaked with shadows and shafts of light on which it was unthinkable to set foot. Lewis began to laugh. "Didn't I ever tell you I get terribly dizzy whenever I'm six feet above the ground? I climbed up here without noticing it, but I'll never be able to get down."

"But you've got to!"

Lewis retreated to the centre of the platform. "Impossible." He smiled again. "Ten years ago, in Los Angeles, I was starving to death. Then I found a job—plastering the top of a factory smoke-stack. They hoisted me up in a basket; I stayed in that thing for three hours without daring to budge. Finally, they let me down and I went off with my pockets empty. And I hadn't eaten a thing in two days. That's just to show you!"

"It's strange you get dizzy," I said. "You've gone through so much, seen so many things. I'd have thought you were tougher." I walked over to the stairway. "There's a whole American family getting ready to come up. Let's go down."

"Aren't you afraid?"

"Yes, I'm afraid."

"All right, let me go first then," Lewis said.

Hand in hand, we walked sideways down the stairs. We were drenched in sweat when we reached the bottom. A guide was explaining the mysteries of the Mayan soul to a group of tourists.

"What a funny thing travelling is!" I murmured.

"Yes, it really is," Lewis said. He hurried me along. "Let's go back and have a drink."

It was a very hot afternoon; we spent it dozing in hammocks in front of the door to our room. And then suddenly, with the compelling force of a tropism, curiosity made me turn my head towards the forest.

"I want to take a walk in those woods," I said.

"Why not?" Lewis replied.

We made our way into the deep, damp silence of the jungle. Not a tourist anywhere. Troops of red ants bearing sharp blades of grass on their shoulders were marching towards invisible citadels. We also came upon swarms of butterflies which flew off, pink, blue, green, and yellow, at the sound of our steps. Water trapped by the lianas stirred and fell on us in large drops. From time to time, at the end of a path, a mysterious mound loomed up: the ruins of a temple or a palace wrapped in its own rocky matrix. Some had been half exhumed but were now smothered by grass.

"You get the feeling no one has ever been here," I said.

"Yes," Lewis replied indifferently.

"Look down there . . . at the end of the path. It's a great temple."

"Yes," Lewis said again.

It was a very large temple. Golden lizards were warming themselves among the stones. Except for a grinning dragon, the sculptured figures were all in ruins. I pointed out the dragon to Lewis; his face remained expressionless.

"Do you see that dragon?" I asked.

"I see it," Lewis answered.

Suddenly he kicked the dragon in the face.

"What are you doing?"

"I kicked it," Lewis replied.

"Why?"

"I didn't like the way it was looking at me."

Lewis sat down on a rock, and I asked, "Don't you want to look around the temple?"

"You go ahead. I'll wait for you."

I wandered through the temple, but my heart wasn't in it. I saw only stones piled one on top of the other and having no meaning at all. When I got back, Lewis hadn't budged and his face was so empty that it seemed as if he had taken leave of his very self.

"Have you seen enough?" he asked.

"Do you want to start back?"

"If you've seen enough."

"Yes, quite enough," I said. "Let's start back."

It was beginning to get dark. We could see the first fire-flies. Anxiously, I said to myself that, after all, I didn't know Lewis very well. He was so spontaneous, so outspoken, that he seemed uncomplicated to me. But who is? When he kicked that statue, he wasn't pleasant to look at. And what did his dizzy spells indicate? We walked along in silence. What was he thinking of?

"What are you thinking of?" I asked.

"I'm thinking of the flat in Chicago. I left the light on. People who pass by in the street are going to think someone is home. And there's no one there."

There was a sadness in his voice.

"Are you sorry you're here?" I asked.

Lewis gave a little laugh. "Am I here? It's funny. You're like a child; everything seems real to you. But for me, all this is like a dream, a dream dreamed by someone else."

"But just the same you really are here," I said. "And so am I."

Lewis didn't answer. We came out of the jungle. It was completely dark; in the heavens, the old constellations were scattered chaotically among clusters of brand-new stars. When he saw the lights of the inn, Lewis smiled. "Finally! I felt lost."

"Lost?"

"All those ruins are so old! They're too old."

"I like the feeling of being lost," I said.

"Not me. I was lost too long; I thought I'd never find myself again. I wouldn't go through that again for anything in the world."

There was a tone of defiance in his voice, and I felt vaguely menaced. "Sometimes, you've got to get lost," I said. "If you never take any chances, you'll never have anything."

"I'd rather not have anything than take that chance," Lewis said decisively.

I understood him. He had had so much trouble winning a little security that he was determined, above everything else, to protect it. And yet how rash it was of him to have loved me! Was he going to regret it?

"That kick you gave the dragon, was it because you felt lost?" I asked.

"No, I didn't like that beast."

"You really looked nasty."

"It's because I am nasty," Lewis said.

"Not with me."

He smiled. "With you, it's hard. I tried it once, last year, and right away you started to cry."

We went into our room, and I asked, "Lewis, you don't hold anything against me, do you?"

"Such as what?"

"I don't know. Everything, nothing. Having two lives."

"If you had only one, you wouldn't be here," Lewis said.

I gave him a worried look. "Do you hold that against me?"

"No," Lewis replied, "I don't hold it against you." He pulled me to him. "I want you."

He pushed aside the mosquito netting and threw me on the bed. When we were naked, our bodies pressed together, he said happily, "These are our most beautiful journeys!"

His face had brightened; he no longer felt lost. And I was no longer worried. The peace, the joy we found in each other's arms would overcome everything.

Travelling, running around the world to see with your own eyes what no longer exists, what doesn't concern you, is indeed a dubious pastime. Lewis and I both agreed about that, but, nevertheless, it didn't stop us from enjoying ourselves enormously. It was a Sunday when we visited Uxmal, and the Indians were unpacking picnic baskets in the shade of the temples. Gripping a chain handrail, we climbed up a long flight of dilapidated stairs behind a group of women in long skirts. Two days later, we flew over forests saturated with rain. The plane climbed high into the sky and it didn't come down: it was the ground that rose up to meet us. Spread out amid its greenery, it presented us with a blue lake and a flat city with blocks as regular as graph paper— Guatemala City; the dry poverty of its streets lined with long, low houses, the teeming market place, the barefoot peasants clad in princely rags bearing baskets of flowers and fruits on their heads. In Antigua, in the garden of the hotel, avalanches of red, violet, and blue flowers tumbled along the trunks of trees and smothered the walls. It was raining furiously—a dense, warm rain—and a parrot on a chain ran up and down its perch, laughing. On the shores of Lake Atitlán, we slept in a bungalow covered with huge bunches of carnations. A boat took us to Santiago, where women with red bands around their foreheads were cradling infants shrouded from head to shoulders in cylindrical hoods. We got out of a bus one Thursday in the middle of the market place of Chichicastenango. The square was covered with tents and stands; women wearing embroidered bodices and colourful skirts were selling grain, meal, bread, shrivelled fruit, scrawny fowl, pottery, purses, belts, sandals, and miles of fabric in colours of stained glass and ceramics, so beautiful that Lewis himself fingered them delightedly.

" Buy this red material?" he said. " Or maybe the green, with all the little birds?"

"Wait!" I said. "We must look at everything."

The most wonderful of all these wonders were the very old capes some of the peasants were wearing. I showed Lewis one of those capes with its antique embroidery in which a vivid blue blended tenderly with dull reds and golds.

" There's what I'd like to buy, if it were for sale."

Lewis examined the old Indian with the long braids. " Maybe she'll sell it."

" I'd never dare ask her. And besides, in what language?"

We continued wandering through the market place. Women were kneading tortilla dough in the palms of their hands, pots filled with a yellow stew were simmering over fires, families were eating. The square was flanked by two white churches to which access was gained by flights of stairs. On the steps, men dressed like operetta toreadors were swinging incense burners. Through a thick cloud of smoke which made me recall my pious childhood, we climbed the stairway leading to the larger of the two churches.

" Do you think we can go in?" I asked.

"What can they do to us?" Lewis said.

We went in, and a heavy odour of incense gripped me by the throat. No pews, no chairs, not a place to sit down. The flagstone floor was a flower bed of flickering pink-flamed candles; the Indians were mumbling prayers while passing ears of corn from hand to hand. On the altar lay a mummy covered with brocade and flowers; opposite the altar, weighed down by fabrics and jewels, was a large, gory Christ with a tortured face.

" If only we could understand what they're saying!" Lewis said.

He was looking at an old man with rough, calloused feet who was bestowing blessings on kneeling women. I pulled him by the arm. "Let's get out of here. I'm getting a head-ache from all that incense."

When we were outside again, Lewis said to me, "I don't think those Indians are very happy. Their clothes are gay—but they are not."

We bought belts, sandals, fabrics. The old woman with the wonderful cape was still there, but I didn't dare approach her. In the café-grocery on the square, a few Indians were sitting around a table and drinking; their wives were seated at their feet. We ordered tequila, which was brought to us with salt and little green lemons. Two young Indians were half-staggering, half-dancing together; they looked so incapable of enjoying themselves that it touched my heart. Outside, the merchants were beginning to fold their stands; with their pottery, they erected intricate edifices which they set on their backs. Their foreheads straining against a band of leather that helped them support their loads, they went off at a dog-trot.

"Will you look at that!" Lewis said. "They think they're beasts of burden."

"I suppose they're too poor to have donkeys."

"I suppose so," he said. "But they look so well adapted to their misery; that's what's so irritating about them. Shall we go back to the hotel?" he added.

"Let's."

We returned to the hotel, but he left me at the door. "I forgot to buy cigarettes. I'll be straight back."

A fire was blazing in the fireplace; that sunny little city was perched higher above earth than the highest village in France, and the nights could be quite cool. I lay down in front of the flames and sniffed the good odour of resin. I liked that room, with its pink plaster walls and all its rugs. I thought of Lewis; I was happy to be alone for a few minutes because it gave me a chance to think about him. The picturesque obviously didn't impress Lewis. No matter what you showed him—temples, scenery, market-places—he immediately saw through them, and saw men. And he had his own ideas about what a man should be: above all, some-one who doesn't resign himself to things, someone with desires and who fights to satisfy them. For himself, he was satisfied with little, but he had violently refused to be

cheated out of everything. In his novels, there was a strange
mixture of tenderness and cruelty, because he despised the
too-complacent victims almost as much as their oppressors.
He reserved his sympathy for people who at least made an
attempt to escape—in literature, art, dope, at worst in
crime, preferably in happiness. And the only ones he really
admired were the great revolutionaries. He had no more of
a head for politics than I, but in a very sentimental way he
liked Stalin, Mao Tse-tung, Tito. The American Communists seemed to him simple-minded and soft, but I imagine he
would have been a Communist in France—at least he would
have tried. I turned my head towards the door. What was
keeping him so long? I was beginning to get impatient when
he finally returned, a package under his arm.

"What have you been doing?" I asked.

"I was on a special mission."

"Who sent you?"

"Myself."

"And did you carry it out?"

"Of course."

He threw me the package; I ripped off the paper. And the
vivid blue filled my eyes. It was the wonderful cape.

"It's pretty filthy!" Lewis said.

With my finger, I fondly traced the capricious and yet
deliberate design of the embroidery. "It's magnificent. How
did you get it?"

"I took the desk clerk with me and he did all the negotiating. The old girl wouldn't hear of selling her old rag,
but when we offered her a new cape in exchange she gave in.
She even looked at me as if I were an idiot. Only afterwards
I had to buy the desk clerk a drink, and he wouldn't let me
get away. He wants to go to New York and make his
fortune."

I threw my arms around Lewis's neck. "Why are you so
nice to me?"

"I've told you before that I'm not nice. I'm very selfish.
The thing is, you've become a little piece of me." He hugged
me tightly. "You are so sweet to love."

Ah, how useful our bodies were during those moments
when we were choked with tenderness! I pressed myself
against Lewis. How could his flesh be so familiar and yet

so overpowering? Suddenly, his warmth burnt from my skin to my very bones. We sank down on the rug in front of the crackling flames.

"Anne! You know how much I love you, don't you? Even though I don't say it often, you do know, don't you?"

"I know. And you do, too, don't you?"

"Yes, I do."

We threw off our clothes, letting them lie where they fell.

"Why do I want you so much?"

He took me on the rug, he took me again in the bed, and for a long while I lay beside him, my head in the hollow of his shoulder.

"How I love being against you!"

"How I love having you against me."

After a while, Lewis raised himself on an elbow. "My throat's parched. How about you?"

"I'd love a drink."

He picked up the telephone and ordered two whiskies. I slipped on my dressing-gown and he his old, white bathrobe.

"You ought to get rid of that monstrosity," I said.

He drew the terry-cloth robe tightly around him. "Never! It'll have to give me up first."

He wasn't at all stingy, but he hated to throw things away, especially his old clothes. They brought us the whiskies, and we sat down beside the fire. Outside, it was beginning to rain; it rained every night.

"I feel wonderful," I said.

"So do I," Lewis said. He put his arm around my shoulders. "Anne," he said, "stay with me."

My breath caught in my throat. "Lewis! You know how much I want to! I want to so very much! But I can't."

"Why not?"

"I told you why last year."

I emptied my glass in a single gulp, and all the old fears overwhelmed me—those of the Club Delisa, of Mérida, of Chichen Itza, and still others which I had very quickly smothered. That was the foreboding I had: one day he would say to me, "Stay," and I would have to answer no. And then what would happen? If I lost Lewis the year before, I would still have been able to console myself. Now, I might just as well be buried alive as be deprived of him.

"You are married," he said. "But you can get a divorce.

We can live together without being married." He bent over me. "You're the only woman in my life."

Tears welled in my eyes. "I love you," I said. "You know how much I love you. But at my age, you can't throw your whole life overboard; it's too late. We met each other too late."

"Not as far as I'm concerned," he said.

"You think so?" I said. "If I asked you to come and live in Paris for the rest of your life, would you come?"

"I don't speak French," Lewis replied quickly.

I smiled. "You can learn. Life isn't any more expensive in Paris than in Chicago, and a typewriter is easy to move. Would you come?"

Lewis's face darkened. "I couldn't write in Paris."

"I suppose not," I said. I shrugged my shoulders. "You see, in a foreign country you wouldn't be able to write and your life would no longer have any meaning. I'm not a writer, but there are things that mean as much to me as your books do to you."

Lewis remained silent for a moment. "And yet you do love me, don't you?" he asked.

"Yes," I replied. "I'll love you till the day I die." I took his hands in mine. "Lewis, I can come back every year. If we're sure of seeing each other every year, there won't be any separation, only waits. And when you love strongly enough, you can wait in happiness."

"If you love me the way I love you, why waste three-fourths of our lives waiting?" Lewis said.

I hesitated. "Because love isn't everything," I said. "You ought to understand me; it isn't everything for you, either."

My voice was trembling, and my eyes were pleading with Lewis to understand, to go on loving me with that love which wasn't everything, but without which I would be nothing.

"No, love isn't everything," Lewis said.

He looked at me with a hesitant air, and I said fervently, "I don't love you any less because other things mean something to me. You mustn't hold that against me. You mustn't love me any less for it."

Lewis touched my hair. "I guess if love were everything for you, I wouldn't love you as much. You wouldn't be you any more."

My eyes filled with tears. If he accepted me just as I was, with my past, my life, with everything that separated him from me, our happiness was saved.

I threw myself into his arms. "Lewis! It would have been so awful if you hadn't understood! But you do understand. Oh, I can't tell you how happy I am!"

"Why are you crying?" Lewis asked.

"I was so afraid. If I had lost you, I couldn't go on living."

He crushed a tear on my face. "Don't cry. When you cry, I'm the one who's afraid."

"I'm crying now because I'm happy," I said. "Because we'll be happy. When we're together, we'll store up happiness for the whole year. Won't we, Lewis?"

"Yes, my little Gauloise," he said tenderly. He kissed my wet cheek. "It's funny, but sometimes you seem like a very wise woman, and sometimes you're just like a little child."

"I suppose I'm really a stupid woman," I said. "But if you love me, I don't care."

"I love you, my stupid little Gauloise," Lewis said.

The following morning, riding in the bus that was taking us to Quezaltenango, my heart was full to overflowing. I no longer feared the future, or Lewis, or words; I feared nothing. For the first time, I dared to make plans aloud: next year, Lewis would rent a house on Lake Michigan and we would spend the summer there; the year after, he would come to Paris and I would show him France and Italy . . . I held his hand tightly in mine and he smilingly approved of my plans. We passed through dense forests; the rain that was falling was so warm and fragrant that I lowered the window in order to feel it against my face. Shepherds watched us pass, standing motionless in their straw capes; they looked as if they were carrying huts on their backs.

"Is it really true we're twelve thousand feet up?" Lewis asked.

"It would seem so."

He shook his head. "I don't believe it. I'd be dizzy."

From far away, those plateaus as high as glaciers and covered with luxuriant trees had always seemed to me an impossible wonder. But now I actually saw them, and they became as natural as a French meadow. In fact, with its slumbering volcanos, its lakes, its pastures, its superstitious peasants, highland Guatemala was very much like Auvergne. But I was beginning to grow tired of it and I was happy when, two days later, we descended to the coast. And what a descent it was! At dawn, we shivered with cold on the twisting road which wound through green grazing lands. And then the deciduous plants disappeared in a surge of dark vegetation with hard, glazed leaves. At the foot of a mountain pasturage covered with hoar-frost there appeared a bare Andalusian village brightened by hibiscus and bougain-villaea. A few turns of the wheel and we dropped down several more levels of the spiralling road. The sky was blazing as we passed through banana plantations dotted with huts among which bare-breasted Indians were wander-ing. The station at Mazatenango was a fairground; women were sitting on the tracks amid their flaring skirts, their bundles, their fowl. A bell sounded in the distance, the employees began shouting, and a little train appeared, pre-ceded by an ancient clamour of clanking metal and hissing steam.

It took us ten hours to cover the seventy-five miles separat-ing us from Guatemala City. The next day, flying above dark mountains and a sparkling coast line, a plane carried us to Mexico City in five hours.

" At last, a real city! A city where things happen!" Lewis said in the cab. " I like cities," he added.

" So do I."

We had made reservations at a hotel, and our mail was waiting for us there. I read my letters in the room, seated beside Lewis. Now I could think of my Paris life without feeling as if I were robbing him of something; now I could share everything with him, even those things which separ-ated us. Robert seemed in good spirits; he said that Nadine was sad but peaceful, and that Paula was almost well again. Everything was fine.

I smiled at Lewis. " Who wrote to you?"

" My publishers."

"What do they have to say?"

" They want some facts about my life—for the launching of the book. They're planning a big publicity campaign."

Lewis's voice was sullen. I looked at him questioningly.

"That means you're going to make a lot of money, doesn't it?"

"Let's hope so!" Lewis replied. He slipped the letter in his pocket. "I have to answer them right away."

"Why right away?" I asked. "Let's see Mexico City first."

Lewis began to laugh. "Such a stubborn little head! And eyes that never get tired of looking!"

He was laughing, but something in his voice bothered me. "If you don't feel like going out, we'll stay in," I said.

"You'd be much too unhappy!" Lewis said.

We went down the Alameda. On the pavement, women were weaving huge funeral wreaths, and others were street-walking. The word "Alcazar" was glowing joyously on the façade of a funeral parlour. We went down a wide crowded avenue and then several disreputable little streets. I liked Mexico City at first sight. But Lewis was preoccupied. It didn't surprise me. Sometimes, he'll decide a thing in a flash, but often he can hesitate for hours before he packs a suit-case or writes a letter. I let him meditate in silence through-out the whole dinner. As soon as we got back to the room, he sat himself down in front of a sheet of white paper. His mouth half open, his eyes glassy, he looked like a fish. I fell asleep before he had set down a single word.

"Did you finish your letter?" I asked the next morning.

"Yes."

"Why did you have so much trouble writing it?"

"I didn't have any trouble." He began to laugh. "Oh, stop looking at me as if I were one of your patients. Come and take a walk with me."

We did a lot of walking that week. We climbed to the tops of tall pyramids and sailed in flower-filled boats; we strolled along Jalisco Avenue, wandered through its shabby market places, went into its dance halls, its vaudeville theatres; we roamed around the city's outskirts and drank tequila in infamous bars. We were planning on staying a little longer in Mexico City, spending a month visiting the rest of the country, and then returning to Chicago for a few days.

But one afternoon, when we returned to our room for a siesta, Lewis said to me abruptly, "I have to be in New York on Thursday."

I looked at him in surprise. "In New York? Why?"

"My publishers want me there."

"Did you get another letter from them?"

"Yes. They want me to come up for two weeks."

"But you don't have to accept," I said.

"That's just it: I do have to," Lewis replied. "Maybe it isn't the same way in France," he added, "but here a book is a business, and if you want it to make money for you you've got to spend time on it. I'll have to see people, go to parties, give interviews. It won't be much fun, but that's the way it is."

"Didn't you tell them you wouldn't be free until July? Can't they put the whole thing off until July?"

"July is a bad month; they'd have to wait until October, and that's too late." Impatiently, Lewis added, "I've been living off my publishers for four years now. If they want to get back what they laid out, I'm not the one who's going to throw a monkey wrench in the machinery. And I need money, too, if I want to go on writing whatever I feel like writing."

"I understand," I said.

I understood, and yet I felt a strange emptiness in the pit of my stomach.

Lewis began to laugh. "Poor little Gauloise! How pitiful she looks when she doesn't get her way!"

I blushed. It was quite true that Lewis's only concern was to make me happy. I shouldn't have felt browbeaten when, for once, he thought about his own interests. He thought I was selfish; that's why his voice was a little aggressive.

"It's your fault," I said. "You've been spoiling me too much." I smiled. "It's going to be nice seeing New York together. Only the thought of changing all our plans gave me a shock, and you told me about it without giving me any warning."

"How should I have told you about it?"

"I'm not blaming you," I said cheerfully. I looked at Lewis questioningly. "Had they already asked you in the first letter?"

"Yes," Lewis replied.

"Why didn't you tell me?"

"I knew it wouldn't make you happy," Lewis replied.

His downcast look softened me. I understood now why he

had taken such pains with his answer: he was trying to
rescue our trip to Mexico, and he was counting so strongly
on succeeding that it had seemed useless to him to worry
me. But he had failed. And having failed, he was trying
now to smile in the face of bad luck, and my reluctance
irritated him a little. He prefers being irritated to being sad;
I can understand that.

"You could have spoken to me about it, you know; I'm
not as delicate as all that," I said. I smiled at him tenderly.
"You see, you do spoil me too much."

"Maybe," Lewis said.

Again, I felt vaguely worried. "We're going to change all
that," I said. "When we get to New York, I'll be the one
to do your bidding."

Lewis looked at me, laughing. "You really mean that?"

"Yes, I really mean it. Turn and turn about."

"Why wait till we get to New York? Let's start right
now." He grabbed me by the shoulders. "Come and do
my bidding," he said a little defiantly.

It was the first time, in giving my mouth, that I thought,
"No." But I wasn't accustomed to saying no; I couldn't.
And besides, it was already too late for me to retreat without creating an issue. Of course, I had on two or three
occasions said yes without really wanting to, but my heart
was always willing. To-day, however, it was different. There
was an aggressiveness in Lewis's voice that made me freeze
up. His gestures, his words had never before shocked me
because they were as spontaneous as his desire, as his pleasure, as his love. But to-day I felt uneasy participating in
the familiar gymnastics which seemed to me grotesque,
frivolous, incongruous. And I noticed that Lewis failed to
say "I love you." When was the last time he had said it?

He didn't say it the following days. He spoke only of
New York. In '43 when he sailed for Europe, he had spent
a day there, and now he had a burning desire to go back.
He hoped to get in touch with some old Chicago friends, he
hoped many things. In Lewis's eyes, the future and the past
have much more value than the present. I was with him,
New York was far away; it was New York, with which he
was obsessed. It didn't upset me too much, but, nevertheless,
his cheerfulness did sadden me. Didn't he have any regrets

at all about giving up our trip together? I had too many fresh memories to fear that he had already grown tired of me, but perhaps he was getting a little too used to me.

New York was broiling. No more torrential nocturnal rains. The sky blazed all day long. Lewis left the hotel early, and I continued to doze under the purring fan. I read, took showers, wrote a few letters. At six o'clock, I was dressed and waiting for Lewis. He got back at seven-thirty, full of excitement.

"I found Felton!" he said.

He had told me a great deal about this Felton who played the drums by night, drove a cab by day, and took dope day and night. His wife walked the streets and took dope as well. They had left Chicago for urgent reasons of health. Lewis didn't know their exact address. As soon as he had finished with his agent and publisher, he set out to look for him and after a thousand frustrations he finally reached Felton by phone.

"He's waiting for us," Lewis said. "He's going to show us New York."

I would have preferred spending the evening alone with Lewis, but I said readily, "I'm sure I'll enjoy meeting him."

"And he'll take us to a lot of places we'd never have discovered without him. Places I'll bet your psychiatrist friends didn't show you!" Lewis added gaily.

Outside, it was very hot and humid. It was even hotter in Felton's top-floor room. He was a tall fellow with a sallow face and he laughed heartily as he shook Lewis's hand. As it turned out, he didn't show us very much of New York. His wife came in with a couple of young men and a supply of cartons of beer cans. They emptied can after can while talking about a lot of people of whom I knew nothing, people who had just gone to jail, who were coming out, who were looking for a proposition, who had found one. They spoke, too, of dope peddling and the price of cops in New York. Lewis was enjoying himself hugely. We went to eat pork chops in a Third Avenue bar. They continued talking for a long while. I was quite frankly bored and I felt rather depressed.

I remained so the following days. On one point I hadn't been mistaken: once in New York, Lewis became somewhat disenchanted. He didn't care at all for the kind of life they were inflicting upon him—the social events, the publicity. Joylessly, he went to the luncheons, the parties, the cocktail parties, and he would come back from them in bad humour. As for me, I didn't know what to do with myself. Lewis halfheartedly suggested that I accompany him, but I was in no mood this year to make casual friendships, nor even to see my old friends again. I went walking in the streets, alone and aimlessly; it was too hot, the tar melted under my feet, I immediately began sweating, and Lewis's absence left a painful void in me. The worst part about it was that when we were together it wasn't much gayer. It bored Lewis to tell about boring gatherings, and I had nothing to tell about. We therefore spent our time going to cinemas, to a prize fight, to a baseball game, and often Felton came along with us.

"You don't care much for Felton, do you?" Lewis asked me one day.

"It's just that I have nothing to say to him nor he to me," I replied. I looked at Lewis curiously. "Why are all your best friends pickpockets, or drug addicts, or pimps?"

Lewis shrugged his shoulders. "I find them more interesting than other people."

"But you, haven't you ever been tempted to take dope?"

"Oh, no!" he replied quickly. "You know how I am: I love everything that's dangerous—but from a distance."

He was joking, but he was speaking the truth. Whatever was immoderate, unreasonable, or dangerous fascinated him, but he had made up his mind to live moderately, reasonably, and without taking risks. It was that contradiction which so often made him restless and hesitant, and, sadly, I wondered whether it didn't figure in his attitude towards me. Lewis had fallen in love with me spontaneously, rashly; was he now blaming himself for it? At any rate, I could no longer hide it from myself: he had changed in the past few weeks.

That evening, he seemed in very high spirits when he came back to the room. He had spent the afternoon recording an interview for the radio, and I was expecting the worst. But he kissed me happily.

"Hurry up and get dressed!" he said. "I'm having dinner with Jack Murray, and you're coming along with me. He's dying to meet you, and I'm anxious for you to meet him."

I didn't hide my disappointment. "This evening? Lewis,

aren't we ever going to spend an evening alone again, just you and I?"

"We'll leave him early!" Lewis replied. He emptied his pockets on to the dresser and took his new suit out of the cupboard. "I don't often like a writer," he said. "If I tell you that you'll like Murray, you can believe me."

"I believe you," I said.

I sat down in front of the vanity and applied my make-up.

"We'll have dinner outdoors, in Central Park," Lewis said. "It seems the place is pretty and the food very good. What do you say?"

I smiled. "I say it's perfect, if we can really get away early, you and I."

Lewis looked at me hesitantly. "I really hope you'll like Murray."

"Why?"

"Because we've made plans!" Lewis replied cheerfully. "But you've got to like him, or else it won't work out."

I looked at Lewis questioningly.

"He owns a house in a little town near Boston," Lewis said. "He's invited us to stay as long as we want to. It would be a hell of a lot better than going to Chicago; it must be even hotter in Chicago than it is here."

Again, I felt a vast emptiness in the pit of my stomach. "Does he stay in that house, or doesn't he?"

"He lives there with his wife and two kids. But don't worry," Lewis added in a slightly mocking voice, "we'll have a room of our own."

"But Lewis, I don't feel like spending this last month with other people," I said. "I'd rather be too hot in Chicago and be alone with you."

"I don't see why we have to be alone night and day just because we love each other!" Lewis said brusquely.

Before I could answer, he had gone into the bathroom and had closed the door.

"What does it mean?" I asked myself in anguish. "Is he really bored with me?" I put on a lace blouse, a rustling skirt I had bought in Mexico, and a pair of golden sandals. And then I stood motionless in the middle of the room, completely at a loss. "Is he bored? Or what?" I touched the keys he had thrown on the dresser, the billfold, the packet of Camels. How could I understand so little about Lewis when

I loved him so much! Among the scattered papers, I noticed a letter on his publisher's letterhead. I unfolded it. "Dear Lewis Brogan, Since you prefer coming to New York right away, we'll make all the necessary arrangements accordingly. When you get in on Thursday . . ." I read the rest of the letter through a fog; the rest of the letter did not interest me. ". . . you prefer coming to New York right away, you prefer, you . . ." The night Paula gave her banquet, I had felt the floor swaying under my feet. Now it was worse. Lewis wasn't crazy; it had to be me! I fell into a chair. He had written his letter only a week after that night in Chichicastenango, that night when he said, "I love you, stupid little Gauloise." I remembered everything: the flames, the rugs, his old bathrobe, the rain beating against the windows. And he had said, "I love you." That was a week before we arrived in Mexico, and during that week nothing had happened. Why then? Why had he decided to cut short our trip together? Why had he lied to me? Why?

"Oh, come now, stop making such a face!" Lewis said when he came out of the bathroom.

He thought I was sulking because of Murray's invitation; I didn't disabuse him. I was incapable of uttering a single word. During the whole cab ride we didn't unclench our teeth.

It was cool in the Central Park restaurant. Or, at least, the grass and trees, the damask tablecloths, the buckets filled with ice, the bare shoulders of the women made it seem cool. I drank two martinis in quick succession and, thanks to that, I was able to articulate a few sentences politely when Murray arrived. At the time when I used to enjoy casual friendships, I would certainly have been happy to meet him. Everything about him was round, his head, his face, his body; perhaps that was what made you feel like clinging to him as to a buoy. And how pleasant his voice was! Listening to it, I realised how cold Lewis's had become. He spoke to me about Robert's books, and Henri's; he seemed to know about everything. It was easy talking to him. The refrain continued hammering insistently in my head: ". . . you prefer coming to New York, you prefer New York." But it was a nightmare that went on without me while I ate a shrimp cocktail and drank white wine. Murray asked me what the French thought of the Marshall Plan and he began discussing the Soviet Union's probable reaction with Lewis. He seemed to have a better understanding of politics than Lewis; on the whole, his mind was better organised and he had a wider range of knowledge. Lewis was more than happy to discover his own opinions confirmed by a man who was so well able to defend them. Yes, in many ways Murray had much more to give him than I. I could understand Lewis wanting to make a friend of him; I could even understand his wanting to spend that month at his home. But still, it didn't explain the lie in Mexico; it didn't explain the main point.

"Can I drop you off somewhere?" Murray asked, heading towards the parking lot.

"No thanks," I replied quickly. "I feel like walking."

"If you like walking, then you must come to Rockport," Murray said with a broad smile. "It's beautiful country to walk in. I'm sure you'll like the place. And I'd be delighted to have both of you there as my guests."

"It would be nice!" I said warmly.

"You can come whenever you like after next Monday," Murray said. "You don't even have to bother to let us know beforehand."

He got into his car, and we set out on foot through the park.

"I think Murray wanted to spend the evening with us," Lewis said, a little reproachfully.

"Maybe he did," I said. "But not I."

"But you seemed to be getting along so well together," Lewis said.

"I think he's very nice," I said. "But there's something I want to talk to you about."

Lewis's face darkened. "It can't be that important!"

"It is." I pointed to a flat rock in the middle of the grass. "Let's sit down."

Grey squirrels were hopping about on the ground; in the distance, the tall buildings were glowing. In a matter-of-fact voice, I said, "A little while ago, while you were taking your shower, you left some letters lying on the dresser." I sought Lewis's eyes. "Your publishers didn't insist on your being in New York now. You were the one who suggested it. Why did you tell me the opposite?"

"Ah! So you read my mail behind my back!" Lewis said, irritated.

" Why not? You lie to me."

" I lie to you and you go through my papers. We're even," Lewis said angrily.

Suddenly, all my strength left me and I looked at him, stupefied. This was he, this was I. How did we ever come to this?

" Lewis, I don't understand anything any more. You love me. I love you. What's happening to us?" I asked in bewilderment.

" Nothing at all," Lewis replied.

" I don't understand!" I repeated. " Tell me. We were so happy in Mexico. What made you decide to come to New York? You knew we'd see hardly anything of each other here."

" Indians and ruins, ruins and Indians! I was getting fed up with it," Lewis said. He shrugged his shoulders. " I felt like a change of scenery. Nothing tragic about that, is there?"

It was no answer, but for the time being I decided to be satisfied with it. " Why didn't you tell me you had enough of Mexico? Why the manœuvring?" I asked.

" You wouldn't have let me come here; you'd have forced me to stay there," Lewis replied.

I was as shaken as if he had slapped me. What resentment there was in his voice!

" Do you really believe what you're saying?"

" Yes," Lewis replied.

" But look here, Lewis, when did I ever prevent you from doing what you want? Yes, you were always trying to please me, but you seemed to get pleasure out of it, too. I never had the feeling I was tyrannising you."

I reviewed our past in my mind. Everything had been love, understanding, and the happiness of giving each other happiness. It was awful to think that behind Lewis's considerateness hidden resentments smouldered.

" You're so stubborn you don't even realise it," Lewis said. " You arrange things in your head and then you won't budge an inch. Everyone's got to do exactly as you please."

" But when did I ever act like that? Cite me an instance," I said.

Lewis hesitated. " I'd like to spend this month at the Murrays' and you refuse."

I interrupted him. " You know you're being unfair. When was I like that before Mexico?"

" If I hadn't done something to force you, I know damned well we'd have stayed in Mexico," Lewis said. " According to your plans, we were supposed to spend another month there, and you'd have proved to me that we had to do it."

" First of all they were our plans," I said. I thought for a moment. " I suppose I would have put up an argument. But since you wanted so much to come to New York, I would certainly have yielded in the end."

" That's easy to say," Lewis retorted. He stopped me with a gesture. " In any case, it would have taken a hell of a lot of work to convince you. To save time, I told a little lie. That isn't so serious, is it?"

" I think it's serious," I replied. " I always thought you never lied to me."

Lewis gave me a slightly embarrassed smile. " As a matter of fact, it was the first time. But you're wrong to get yourself all worked up over it. Whether you lie or whether you don't, the truth is never said."

I studied him for a moment. I was perplexed. Obviously there were strange things going on in his head, and something was disturbing him deeply. But what exactly? I shook my head. " I don't believe that," I said. " People can talk to each other, can get to know one another. All that's needed is a little good will."

" Yes, I know that's what you believe," Lewis said. " But that's the worst lie of all: pretending that people tell each other the truth." He got up. " Well, on that point at least I've spoken and I have nothing to add to it. Do you think we can leave here now?"

" Yes," I said.

We crossed the park in silence. His explanation had explained nothing at all to me. One thing only was clear— Lewis's hostility. But where did it come from? He was much too antagonistic to tell me; it would do no good to question him.

" Where are we going?" Lewis asked.

" Wherever you want."

" I don't have any ideas."

" Neither do I."

" You seemed to have made plans for this evening," Lewis said.

" Nothing special," I replied. " I thought we might go to a quiet little bar and just talk."

" You can't make conversation like that, to order," he said crossly.

" Let's go to Café Society and listen to some jazz," I said.

" Haven't you heard enough jazz in your life?"

A flush of anger rose to my face. " Good. Let's go back to the hotel and go to sleep," I said.

" I'm not sleepy," Lewis replied innocently.

He was teasing me, but it was not in fun. " He's doing it on purpose to spoil this evening. He's doing it on purpose to spoil everything!" I thought bitterly.

" Then let's go to Café Society," I said sharply, " since I feel like going and you don't feel like doing anything."

We took a cab. I recalled what Lewis had said to me the year before: that he was constitutionally unable to get along with anyone. It was true then! He was on good terms with Teddy, Felton, Murray, because he saw them only rarely. But he would never be able to stand living together with someone for very long. He had loved me impetuously, and even now that love seemed to him a restraint. Again, a feeling of anger gripped my throat; in a way, it was comforting. " He should have foreseen what was happening to him," I thought. " He shouldn't have let me get involved body and soul in this affair. And he has no right to act the way he's acting. If I'm a burden to him, let him say so. I can go back to Paris; I'm ready to go back now."

The orchestra was playing a Duke Ellington piece. We ordered two highballs. Lewis looked at me somewhat anxiously.

" Are you unhappy?"

" No," I replied, "not unhappy. I'm angry."

" Angry? You certainly have a calm way of being angry."

" Don't let it fool you."

" What are you thinking about?"

" I'm thinking that, if this affair is a burden to you, all you have to do is say so. I can take a plane for Paris to-morrow."

Lewis smiled briefly. " What you're suggesting is pretty serious."

" You act as if it were unbearable that for once we're out by ourselves," I said. " I think that's the key to the way you're behaving: you're bored with me. So I might as well go."

Lewis shook his head. " I'm not bored with you," he said seriously.

My anger left me as quickly as it had come, and again I felt weak. " What is it then?" I asked. " There's something. What is it?"

There was a silence, and then Lewis replied, " Let's say that from time to time you irritate me just a tiny little bit."

" That's rather obvious," I said. " But I'd like to know why."

" You once explained to me that love isn't everything for you," Lewis said in a sudden burst of volubility. " All right. But then why do you insist on its being everything for me? If I feel like coming to New York, like seeing some friends, it makes you angry. You aren't satisfied unless you are all that matters, unless nothing else exists for me but you, unless I devote my whole life to you while you sacrifice nothing of yours. It isn't fair!"

I remained silent. There was a good deal of distortion in his reproaches, and a good deal of incoherence as well. But that wasn't the question. For the first time that evening I saw a ray of light; it wasn't at all reassuring.

" You're wrong," I murmured. " I insist on nothing."

" Oh, yes! You come and go whenever the spirit moves you. But while you're here I've got to make you completely happy."

" You're the one who's unfair," I said. My voice choked up in my throat. Suddenly I saw it all clearly: Lewis was holding it against me that I refused to stay with him permanently. The trip to New York, the plans made with Murray, were nothing but reprisals!

" You're harbouring a grudge against me," I said. " Why? You know very well I'm not to blame."

" I have no grudge against you. I think only that you shouldn't ask for more than you give."

" You *are* holding a grudge against me!" I repeated. I looked at Lewis in despair. " And yet, when we talked things over that night in Chichicastenango, we agreed, you understood me. What's happened since then?"

" Nothing," Lewis replied.

" Well, then? You said you wouldn't love me so much if I were different. You said we'd be happy . . ."

Lewis shrugged. " I said the things you wanted me to say."

Again I felt as if I had been slapped full in the face. " What do you mean by that?" I stammered.

" I wanted to tell you a lot of other things, but you began weeping with joy. And that kept me quiet."

Yes, I remembered. The flames were crackling, and my eyes were full of tears. It's true that I had hastened to weep with joy on Lewis's shoulder ; it's true that I had forced his hand.

" I was so afraid," I said. " I was so afraid to lose your love."

" I know. You looked terrified. And that, too, kept me from talking," Lewis said. Bitterly, he added, " How relieved you were when you knew I'd do everything you wanted! Nothing else mattered to you."

I bit my lip ; this time, at any cost, I had to keep myself from crying. And yet, what was happening to me, was horrible. The flames, the rugs, the rain against the windows, Lewis in his white bathrobe—all those memories were false. I saw myself crying on his shoulder ; we were united forever. But I was united alone. He was right: I should have tried to find out what was going on inside his head instead of contenting myself with words I forced out of him. I had been cowardly, selfish and cowardly. And I was being well punished for it. I gathered together all my courage ; now, I could no longer escape.

" What would you have said if I hadn't cried?" I asked.

" I would have said you can't love someone who isn't all yours the same way as someone who is."

I steeled myself and tried to fight back. " You said just the opposite: you said that if I were different you wouldn't love me so much."

" There's no contradiction there," Lewis said. " Or if there is, it's because feelings can be contradictory."

It was useless discussing the matter any further ; logic played no part here. At first, probably, Lewis's feelings had been confused, and to gain time he had spoken appeasing words to me. Or perhaps it was afterwards that he began bearing me a grudge. It mattered little. To-day he no longer loved me the same way as before; how could I resign myself to that? Despair was suffocating me. To keep myself from thinking, I continued talking.

"You no longer love me the way you used to?"

Lewis hesitated. "I think that love is less important than I once believed."

"I see," I said. "Since I must leave, it doesn't make much difference if I'm here or if I'm not."

"Something like that," Lewis replied. He looked at me, and suddenly his voice changed. "And yet, how I awaited you!" he said with deep feeling. "All year long, I thought of nothing else. How I wanted you!"

"Yes," I said sadly. "And now . . ."

Lewis put his arm around my shoulders. "Now I still want you."

"Oh, in that way," I said.

"Not only in that way." His hand tightened on my arm. "I'd marry you this very moment."

I lowered my head. I recalled the shooting star above the lake. He had made a wish, and that wish hadn't been fulfilled. And I, who had promised myself never to disappoint him, had disappointed him irremediably. I alone was guilty. Never again would I be able to hold anything against him.

We stopped speaking. We listened to a little jazz and then we returned to the hotel. I couldn't sleep. I asked myself sadly if I would be able to save our love; it could still triumph over absence, waiting, everything, but on the condition that both of us wanted it. Would Lewis want it? "For the moment he's wavering," I said to myself. "He's determined to protect himself from regrets, suffering, melancholy, but he who loathes getting rid of an old bathrobe won't be able to throw off our past so easily. He's more generous than proud." I went on, trying to encourage myself, "More eager than careful; he wants things to happen to him." Only, I knew too the value he attached to his security, his independence, and how bent he was upon living moderately and reasonably. It can seem unreasonable to love across an ocean. Yes, that's what seemed to me the thing most to be feared about Lewis—that mania for carefulness which overtakes him from time to time. That's what I had to fight against. I had to prove to Lewis that he had more to gain than to lose in this affair. While having breakfast, I attacked.

"Lewis, I was thinking about us all night."

"You'd have done better to get some sleep."

His voice was friendly; he looked relaxed. No doubt, it had relieved him to say what was on his mind.

"You told me yesterday that I annoy you because I ask for more than I give," I said. "Yes, that's wrong; I won't do it any more. I'll take what you give me and I'll never demand anything."

Lewis wanted to interrupt me, but I continued speaking. First of all, we would go to Murray's; that was settled. And then, I didn't want him to feel constrained by that faithfulness which until now he had imposed upon himself; in my absence, he should feel as free as if I had never existed. And if he were ever to love another woman, so much the worse for me; I wouldn't protest. Since our affair failed to bring him everything he hoped it would, at least it wouldn't deprive him of anything.

"So now, stop imagining I laid a trap for you," I said. "Stop spoiling things simply for the sake of spoiling them."

Lewis had listened to me attentively. He shook his head. "It isn't as simple as that."

"I know," I said. "As soon as you love someone, you're no longer free. But anyhow, loving a woman who believes she has claims on you isn't at all the same as loving one who doesn't."

"Oh, a woman can believe she has all the claims in the world on me, but as long as I don't recognise them it's all the same to me," Lewis said. "Let's not talk about all that," he added. "You only get things all messed up when you talk about them."

"They also get messed up when you're silent about them," I said. I leaned towards him. "There's one thing I want to ask you: are you sorry you met me?"

"No," he replied. "I'll never be sorry about that."

His tone of voice gave me courage. "Lewis, we'll see each other again, won't we?"

He smiled. "Surest thing in the world," he said.

Hope returned to my heart. I knew my speech had only half convinced him, and, in fact, it was indeed wrong to speak to him of freedom while at the same time asking him not to drive me from his heart. "But if only he's not deter-

mined to harbour resentment," I said to myself, "I'll prove
to him our love can be happy." Doubtless, I had already
struck a responsive chord in him, or perhaps his grievances
had vanished the moment he had put them into words. He
took me to Coney Island that afternoon and was just as
cheerful, as tender, as on our happiest days together. Suddenly, he had a thousand things to tell me: about the literary
life in New York, about people, about books. He talked and
talked as if we had just that moment met again. And if only
he had said, "I love you," I would have been able to
believe that everything that night was exactly the same as it
used to be.

"Are you sure you don't mind going to Murray's?" he
asked in a slightly hesitant voice the following Monday.

"Not at all. I look forward to it."

"Good. Let's leave this evening, then."

I looked at him in surprise. "I thought you still had a
lot of things to do here?"

Lewis began to laugh. "I guess I just won't do them."

The next morning, we were drinking coffee with the
Murrays in a room with large bay windows. The house was
a little outside the town, perched on a rocky ledge; the blue
of the sky and the sound of the ocean drifted in through the
open windows. Lewis was talking his head off while stuffing
himself with buttered toast. To look at his happy face, you
would have believed he had finally realised his most cherished
dream. It had to be admitted that everything was perfect:
the place, the weather, the breakfast, our hosts' smiles. And
yet I felt ill at ease. Despite her graciousness, Ellen intimidated me; her discreet elegance, the charm of her home,
her two glowingly healthy children testified to the fact that
she was an accomplished young matron, and women who
plan all the details of their existence so successfully always
frightened me a little. And here I was, about to be caught in
the close-knit web of that life to which I didn't belong. I
had the feeling both of being bound hand and foot and of
drifting along with the current.

Dick, their little boy, was eight. He immediately took a
great liking to Lewis and led us down a steep path to a little
cove at the foot of the rocks. Lewis spent the morning
playing ball with him in the water and on the beach. I swam
and read; I wasn't bored, but nevertheless I continued asking

myself, "What am I doing here?" In the afternoon, Murray took us for a drive along the coast; Ellen didn't come. When we returned to the house, Lewis and I remained alone in the living-room for a while, drinking highballs. I suddenly realised we would often be left alone together: Murray intended to spend his days in front of his typewriter, and Ellen obviously didn't have a minute to herself. I took a sip of the highball; I was beginning to feel good.

"How lovely it is here!" I said. "And how nice Murray is! I'm really happy."

"Yes, it's nice here," Lewis said.

The radio was playing an old tune, and for a moment we listened to it in silence. The ice tinkled in our glasses, we could hear the children's laughter, a good smell of baking mingled with the smell of the sea.

"This is how people ought to live!" Lewis said. "A house of your own, a woman you love neither too much nor too little, children . . ."

"You think that's how Murray feels about Ellen?" I asked curiously. "Neither too much nor too little?"

"It's obvious," Lewis replied.

"And Ellen? How does she love him?"

Lewis smiled. "Too much and too little, I suppose, like all women."

"He's got it in for me again," I thought a little sadly. No doubt it was because of that little dream of family happiness which had just passed through his head.

"Do you think you'd be happy like that?" I asked.

"At least I'd never be unhappy."

"That isn't so certain. Not being happy makes a lot of people unhappy. I think you're that kind."

Lewis smiled. "Maybe," he said. He reflected a moment. "At any rate, I envy Murray for having children. You get tired of always living by yourself, for yourself. After a while, it begins to seem very empty. I'd like to have children."

"Well, one day you'll get married and you will have children," I said.

Lewis looked at me hesitantly. ". It won't happen to-morrow or the day after to-morrow," he said. "But later, in a few years, why not?"

I smiled at him. "Yes," I said, "why not? In a few years . . ."

That was all I wanted—a few years. I was too old for pledges of eternal love; I lived too far away. I asked only that our love live long enough so that it would die out gently, leaving untarnished memories in our hearts and a friendship that would never end.

The dinner was so ample and Murray so cordial that I finally began to feel at ease. I was in an affable mood when, during coffee, people began to arrive. It was the beginning of the season and there were still only a few holidaymakers in Rockport; they all knew one another and were eager to see new faces. We were the centre of attention. Lewis soon withdrew from the conversation; he helped Ellen make sandwiches and shake cocktails. As for me, I did my best to answer all the questions they heaped on me. Murray began a discussion on the relationship between psychoanalysis and Marxism, a subject I knew more about than the others, and since he urged me on I did a lot of talking. Later, when we were alone together in our room, Lewis examined me with an intrigued air.

" I'm going to wind up believing there's a brain inside that little skull," he said to me.

" It was a good imitation, wasn't it?" I said.

" No, you really have a brain," Lewis replied. He continued studying me, and there was a slight look of reproach in his eyes. " It's funny, but I never think of you as a brainy woman. To me, you're something entirely different!"

" With you, I feel entirely different!" I said, slipping into his arms.

How tightly he hugged me! Ah, suddenly there were no more questions. He was there, that was enough. His legs were entangled in mine, his breath, his smell, his eager hands on my body. He was saying, " Anne!" the way he used to, and once again his smile gave me his heart along with his flesh.

When we awakened, the sky and the sea were glistening. We borrowed the Murrays' bicycles and went into town. We walked along the wharf, spent a while watching the boats, the fishermen, the nets, the fish. I breathed in the fresh salty smell of the ocean, the sun was caressing my body, and Lewis, smiling, was holding my arm.

" What a magnificent morning!" I said ardently.

"Poor little Gauloise!" Lewis said tenderly. "How little she requires to feel that she's in paradise!"

"The sky, the sea, the man I love—after all, that isn't so little."

He squeezed my arm. "You aren't very demanding."

"I'm satisfied with what I have," I said.

"You're right," Lewis said. "You've got to be satisfied with what you have."

The sky became still bluer, the sun warmer, and inside me I heard a great, joyous carillon. "I've won!" I said to myself. I was right in agreeing to come here. Lewis felt free, he knew now that my love deprived him of nothing. On the beach he spent part of the afternoon playing with Dick again and I admired his patience. I hadn't seen him so relaxed for a long time. After dinner, Murray took us to visit friends, and this time Lewis didn't try to remain on the side lines; he bubbled over with exuberance. Really, he would never stop surprising me; I didn't believe he could be brilliant at a social gathering. He was. In telling about our trip, he made such skilful cuts and added such convincing fictions that his Guatemala was more real than Guatemala itself. Everyone wanted to go. When he imitated the little Indians trotting along under their burdens, one of the women exclaimed, "You'd make a wonderful actor!" And another, "He really knows how to tell a story!"

Lewis stopped short. "What patience you have!" he said, smiling. "Personally, I can't stand listening to travelogues," he added.

"Oh, please go on," said a blonde.

"No, I've finished my number," he replied, walking over to the buffet. He finished off a large Manhattan while beautiful golden-shouldered young women and less beautiful matrons, their eyes heavy with soulfulness, crowded around him. It annoyed me a little to find out that he was attractive to women. I believed he had subtly seduced me precisely through his lack of seductiveness. And all of a sudden I discovered he was indeed seductive. But in any event, what he was to me he was to no one else. "For me alone, he's unique," I thought with a kind of pride.

I also drank, danced, chatted with a guitarist who had just been cashiered from radio for holding advanced ideas, and then with musicians, painters, intellectuals, writers. Rockport, during the summer, is an annex of Greenwich Village; it's full of artists.

Suddenly, I realised Lewis had disappeared. I asked Murray, "What happened to Lewis?"

"I have no idea," Murray replied in his placid voice.

I felt a prick of anguish in my heart. Had he gone for a stroll in the garden with one of his beautiful admirers? If that were the case, he wouldn't be very happy to see me appear. Well, too bad! I glanced into the foyer, the kitchen, and then I went outside. The only sound was the insistent chirping of the crickets. I took a few steps and saw the glow of a cigarette. Lewis was sitting on a lawn chair, alone.

"What are you doing out here?" I asked.

"Resting."

I smiled. "I thought those bitches were going to eat you up alive."

"You know what we ought to do with them?" Lewis said vindictively. "We ought to load them in a boat, throw them all into the ocean, and bring back a cargo of little Indian women in their place. Do you remember the little Indians in Chichicastenango, sitting modestly on the ground at their husbands' feet? How quiet they were, and their faces were so placid!"

"I remember."

"They still have their pretty faces and their black braids," Lewis said. "And we'll never see them again." He sighed. "How far away it all is!"

There was the same nostalgia in his voice as when, in the jungle at Chichen Itza, he spoke to me of the apartment in Chicago. "If I become a memory in his heart, he'll think of me, too, with that same tenderness," I thought. But I didn't want to become a memory."

"Perhaps one day we'll go back again to see the little Indians."

"I doubt it very much," Lewis said. He got up. "Come, let's take a walk. The night smells so good."

"We'd better go back inside, Lewis. They're going to start missing us."

"What of it? I have nothing to say to them, nor they to me."

"But they're friends of the Murrays. It wouldn't be nice to disappear just like that."

Lewis sighed. "How I'd like a little Indian wife who'd follow me wherever I go without protesting!"

We went back inside. Lewis had lost all his cheerfulness. He drank a great deal and replied with grunts to the questions they asked him. He sat down beside me and listened to the conversation disapprovingly. I said to Murray that a good many writers in France were wondering what point there was in writing in this day and age. Thereupon everyone began discussing the subject animatedly. Lewis's face grew darker and darker. He hated theories, systems, generalisations. I knew why: for him, an idea wasn't merely a collection of words; it was a living thing. Those he accepted stirred in him, upset everything. He was forced to exert a great effort to restore a semblance of order in his mind; that frightened him a little. In that domain as well, he had a yearning for security, detested feeling lost. Often, he withdrew completely. It was obvious that he was withdrawing now. And then, suddenly, he exploded.

"Why does one write? For whom does one write? If you begin asking that, you stop writing! You write, that's all. And people read you. You write for the people who read you. It's writers nobody reads who ask themselves questions like that!"

That cast a chill over the room. And it was all the more penetrating because, as a matter of fact, there were several writers present whom no one read and whom no one would ever read. Happily, Murray managed to smooth things over. Lewis withdrew into his shell again. Fifteen minutes later, we took our leave.

All the next day, Lewis was sullen. When Dick came down to the beach, pistols in hand and shouting, he looked at him darkly. Boiling mad, he reluctantly gave him a boxing lesson and took him swimming. That evening, while I chatted with Ellen and Murray, he buried himself in the newspapers. I knew Murray wouldn't take offence so easily, but I was worried about Ellen. "He had too much to drink last night; to-morrow he'll be in a better mood," I said to myself hopefully as I fell asleep.

I was wrong. The next morning, Lewis didn't give me a

single smile. Ellen was touched because he took the vacuum cleaner from her and cleaned the house from cellar to attic. But that sudden passion for housework was suspect. Lewis was trying to compose himself; what was he fleeing from? During lunch he was relatively amiable, but as soon as we were alone together on the beach he said furiously, "If that lousy brat comes around and starts bothering me again, I'll break his neck."

"It's your own fault, you know," I said in annoyance. "You shouldn't have been so nice to him the first day."

"I always let myself be had the first day," Lewis said in a voice full of rancour.

"Yes, but there are other people in the world," I said warmly. "You've got to realise that."

There was a sound of rolling pebbles above our heads; Dick was coming down the path. He was wearing a pair of black-and-white checkered trousers, an immaculate shirt, and a cowboy belt. He ran over to Lewis.

"Why did you come to the beach? I was waiting for you up at the house. Yesterday you said we'd go for a bike ride after lunch."

"I don't feel like going riding," Lewis replied.

Dick looked at him reproachfully. "You said yesterday we'd go to-morrow. Well, to-morrow's to-day."

"If it's to-day, then it isn't to-morrow," Lewis said. "What have they been teaching you at school? To-morrow's to-morrow."

Dick's mouth dropped open; he looked wretched. "Aw, come on! Let's go!" he said, grabbing Lewis by the arm.

Lewis pulled his arm away sharply. He had just about the same expression on his face as the day he kicked the stone dragon. I put my hand on Dick's shoulder.

"What would you say if I went bicycle-riding with you instead? We'll go into town, we'll look at the boats and we'll eat lots of ice-cream."

Dick considered my suggestion without enthusiasm. "He promised to come," he said, pointing to Lewis.

"He's tired."

Dick turned to Lewis. "Are you staying here? Are you going for a swim?"

"I don't know," Lewis replied.

"I'll stay with you. We can box," Dick said, "and then we can go swimming."

Once again, he raised a trusting face to Lewis.

"No!" Lewis said.

I put my hand on Dick's shoulder. "Come," I said. "He's got things to think about, we'd better leave him alone. Anyhow, I've got to go to Rockport and I'd be lonely all by myself. How about keeping me company? You can tell me all the things you did last winter. And I'll buy you comic books; I'll buy you anything you want!" I said with the strength of desperation.

Dick turned his back to Lewis and began walking up the path. I was furious with Lewis. You don't act that way with a child! And into the bargain, I had no desire to be saddled with Dick. Fortunately, by profession I know how to set a child at ease; he soon relaxed. We had a bicycle race, and I let myself be beaten in a close finish; I stuffed him with strawberry ice-cream; we went aboard a fishing boat. In the end, I did so much and did it so well that he didn't want to leave me until dinner time.

"Well," I said to Lewis as I came into our room, "you can thank me for taking that boy off your hands. You were nasty to him," I added.

"He's the one who should thank you," Lewis said. "Another minute and I'd have broken every bone in his body."

He was lying on the bed in a T-shirt and his old cotton pants, smoking a cigarette while gazing at the ceiling. I thought bitterly that he really should have thanked me. I took off my beach dress and began doing my hair.

"It's time to get dressed," I said.

"I am dressed," Lewis replied. "Can't you see I have clothes on my body? Do I look naked?"

"You don't intend to go down like that, do you?"

"I damned well do! I don't see why people have to change their clothes just because the sun happens to be setting."

"Murray and Ellen change, and you're their guest," I said. "And besides, they're having people for dinner."

"Again!" Lewis said. "I didn't come here to live the same kind of stupid life as in New York."

"And neither did you come here to be unpleasant to everyone," I said. "Last night, Ellen was already beginning to look at you in a funny way." I stopped abruptly. "Oh, why should I give a damn, after all!" I said. "Do whatever you like!"

Lewis ended up by getting dressed, muttering to himself. "It was he who insisted on coming here, and now he's purposely trying to make it unbearable," I said to myself angrily. I was doing my best to be agreeable, and he was spoiling everything. I made up my mind that I wouldn't bother with him that evening; it was too tiring trying to keep up with his constantly shifting moods.

I did what I had promised myself I would do: I talked with everyone and ignored Lewis. On the whole, I found Murray's friends rather congenial; I spent an enjoyable evening. Around midnight, most of the guests left; Ellen went to bed and so did Lewis. I remained downstairs with Murray, the guitarist, and two other men, and we continued talking until three in the morning. When I went up to our room, Lewis turned on the light. He sat up in his bed.

"Well? Did you finally finish making noises with your mouth? I never thought any woman could make so much noise all by herself."

"I enjoy talking to Murray," I said, starting to undress.

"Yes, and that's just what I have against you!" Lewis said, his voice rising. "Theories, always theories! You don't make good books with theories! There are people who explain how to write books and others who write them: they're never the same."

"Murray doesn't pretend to be a novelist. He's a critic, an excellent critic; you yourself acknowledge it."

"He's a big blabbermouth! And all of you sit there, listening to him with intelligent smiles on your faces! It makes me feel like knocking your heads against a wall to put some good common sense in them!"

I slipped into my bed. "Good-night," I said.

He turned out the light without answering.

My eyes remained open. I wasn't even angry any more; I just didn't understand anything! Lewis was bored with those gatherings. All right. But after all, they did leave us peacefully alone all day long, and there was really nothing pedantic about Murray. Until now, Lewis, too, had enjoyed his conversation. Why that sudden hostility? Without any doubt it was I whom Lewis was aiming at when he chose to

spoil his stay; his grudges had endured. But then he should
have kept his bad humour for me alone; he must have been
angry with himself to take it out like that on everyone. Perhaps he was reproaching himself for those moments when
he had seemed to be giving me all his tenderness. The
thought was so unbearable that I wanted to call out to him,
to speak to him. But my voice shattered against my teeth.
I listened to his even breathing; he was sleeping, and I
didn't have the heart to awaken him. It's touching to see a
man asleep; so innocent a sight. Everything becomes possible, everything can begin, or begin all over again. He would
open his eyes, he would say, " I love you, my little Gauloise."
But no, he wouldn't say it; that innocence was nothing but a
mirage. To-morrow would be exactly like to-day. " Is there
no way out?" I asked myself in desperation. I suddenly had
a spasm of revolt. "What does he want? What will he do?
What is he thinking?" There I was, torturing myself with
questions, while he was sleeping peacefully, far from his
thoughts. It was too unfair! I tried to empty my mind;
but no, I couldn't fall asleep. Quietly, I got out of bed. Dick
had kept me from going swimming that afternoon and, suddenly, I had a desire to feel the coolness of water on my body.
I put on my bathing suit and my beach dress, took Lewis's
old bathrobe, and went barefoot through the sleeping house.
How immense the night was! I slipped on my sandals, ran
all the way to the beach, and lay down on the sand. It was
very mild out; I closed my eyes under the stars, and the purr
of the water put me to sleep. When I woke up, a huge red
globe was emerging from the sea. It was the fourth day of
Creation and the sun had just been born; the suffering of man
and beast had not yet come to pass. I plunged into the
ocean and floated on my back; my body lost all its weight,
and my eyes were full of sky.

" Anne!"

I turned towards the shore—an inhabited land, a man
calling out. It was Lewis in pyjama bottoms, his chest bare.
I felt the weight of my body again and began swimming
towards him. "Here I am!"

He walked out to meet me; the water was up to his knees
when he took me in his arms.

" Anne!" he repeated. " Anne!"

"You're going to get all wet! Let me dry myself off," I said, edging towards the beach.

He didn't loosen his hold. "Anne, how frightened I was!"

"I frightened you? It was my turn, after all!"

"I opened my eyes: the bed was empty. I waited, and you didn't come back. I went downstairs; you were nowhere in the house. Then I came here and at first I didn't see you."

"You didn't really think I had drowned myself?" I said.

"I don't know what I thought. It was like a nightmare!" Lewis said.

I picked up the white robe. "Rub me. And dry yourself."

He obeyed, and I slipped on my dress; he wrapped himself in his bathrobe. "Sit down beside me," he said.

I sat down again and he took me in his arms. "You're here! I didn't lose you."

"You'll never lose me through any fault of mine," I said impulsively.

For a long moment, he smoothed my hair in silence. And then, abruptly, he said, "Anne, let's go back to Chicago."

A sun rose in my heart, more brilliant than the one climbing in the sky.

"I'd like nothing better!"

"Let's go back," he repeated. "I want so much to be alone with you! The very night we arrived here, I realised what a stupid thing I'd done!"

"Lewis, there's nothing in the world I'd like more than to be alone with you," I said. I smiled at him. "Is that what put you in such bad humour? You were sorry you came here?"

Lewis nodded. "I felt as if I were caught in a trap; I couldn't see any way out. It was terrible!"

"And now you see a way?" I asked.

Lewis looked at me as if inspired. "They're still sleeping. Let's pack our bags and just take off."

I smiled. "Why not try explaining things to Murray?" I said. "I'm sure he'll understand."

"And if he doesn't understand, that's just too bad!" Lewis said.

I gave him a somewhat worried look. "Lewis, are you absolutely sure you want to go back? It isn't just a whim, is it? You're sure you won't regret it?"

Lewis smiled. "I know very well when I'm indulging myself in a whim," he replied. "I swear on your head that this is no whim."

Again I sought his eyes. "And when we return home, do you think we'll return to all the rest? Will it be just like last year? Or almost?"

"Just like last year," Lewis replied in a serious voice. He took my head in his hands and looked at me for a long while. "I tried to love you less. I couldn't."

"Don't try any more," I said.

"No, I won't try any more."

I'm not quite sure what Lewis told him, but Murray was all smiles when he accompanied us to the airport the next evening. Lewis hadn't lied: in Chicago, everything was given back to me. At the corner, before parting, he held me tightly in his arms, saying, "I've never loved you as much as now."

CHAPTER NINE

HENRI'S SECRETARY opened the door. "A special delivery."

"Thanks," ie said, quickly taking the blue paper. "Paula has killed herself," he thought. Despite Mardrus's assurances that she was harbouring no suicidal thoughts and that she was almost well again, there was something ominous these days in the ringing of the telephone, and especially in special deliveries. He was relieved when he saw Lucie Belhomme's signature. "It is extremely important that I see you. Call in at my house to-morrow morning." He was puzzled as he reread the peremptory message. Never before had Lucie taken that tone with him. Josette was in wonderful shape; she was delighted with her part in the film, *La Belle Suzon,* and was going dancing that night at the Lace Ball in a magnificent Amaryllis creation. Henri really couldn't understand why Lucie wanted to see him. He stuffed the special delivery in his pocket. There was certainly another bit of trouble in prospect, but what difference did one more or one less make? He thought of Paula again, and he reached for the phone. But then he let his hand drop. "Mademoiselle Mareuil is resting comfortably." Neither the answer nor the nurse's cold competent voice ever varied. They had forbidden him to see Paula; they were all agreed that it was he who had driven her insane. Well, so much the better; they spared him the lash of self-accusation. Paula had inflicted the rôle of hangman on him for so long that his feelings of remorse had frozen inside him; he no longer felt them. Besides, ever since he had come to understand that no matter what you do you're always wrong—especially when you believe you've been right—he had felt strangely carefree. He swallowed his daily ration of insults like warm milk.

"I'm the first one here?" Luc asked.

"As you see."

Luc dropped into a chair. He purposely came in shirt sleeves and slippers because he knew Trarieux detested such informality.

"Tell me, what do we do if Lambert runs out on us?" he asked.

" He won't run out on us," Henri replied quickly.

" He's one hundred per cent for Volange," Luc said. " I'm convinced that's why Samazelle suggested his articles—to goad Lambert into putting us in the minority."

" Lambert promised me his vote," Henri said.

Luc sighed. " I wonder what that little twerp's up to. In his place, I'd have left a long time ago."

" I suppose he'll go one of these days," Henri said. " But he won't play their game. I've lived up to my commitments ; he'll live up to his."

Henri had made a point of defending Lambert against Luc and Luc against Lambert under all circumstances. But actually the situation was equivocal ; Lambert wasn't going to continue voting against his convictions indefinitely.

" Quiet! The enemy approaches!" Luc said.

Trarieux entered first, followed by Samazelle and a sullen-faced Lambert. No one was smiling, except Luc ; he alone enjoyed that war of attrition, in which no one as yet was worn out.

" Before discussing the question which brings us together to-day, I would like to make an appeal to everyone's good will," Trarieux said, staring intently at Henri. " All of us have an affection for L'Espoir," he continued warmly, " and yet, because of our lack of agreement, we're leading the paper to bankruptcy. One day Samazelle says white, the next day Perron says black. The reader becomes confused and buys another paper. It is of the greatest urgency that we establish a common platform which will transcend our differences of opinion."

Henri shook his head. " For the hundredth time, I repeat that I will make no concessions. I suggest instead that you make up your minds to stop opposing me. I will continue to hold L'Espoir to the line it has always followed."

" A line which the failure of the S.R.L. has doomed and which has become anachronistic," Samazelle said. " Remaining neutral in regard to the Communists is out of the question nowadays ; you've got to be emphatically for or against." He tried to force one of his jovial laughs. " Considering the way they've been treating you, I'm surprised that you stubbornly continue to try to get along with them."

" I'm surprised that men who call themselves leftists can

support the party of the capitalists, the militarists, and the Church," Henri said.

"Let's get a few things straight," Samazelle said. "All my life I've fought against militarism, against the Church, and against capitalism. But you've got to recognise the fact that De Gaulle is something quite different from a militarist, that the aid of the Church is necessary to-day to defend the values we cherish, and that Gaullism can very well be an anti-capitalist movement if men of the left assume positions of command in it."

"I suppose listening to things like that is better than being deaf," Henri said. "But not much!"

"Nevertheless, I believe it would be in your own interest to find a common ground with us," Trarieux said. "Because it might happen, you know, that you'll find yourself in the minority."

"I'd be very much surprised," Henri said, smiling at Lambert. Lambert didn't smile back ; apparently, his loyalty was weighing heavily upon him and he intended to show it.

"In any case, if that happened, I'd resign," Henri said. "But I won't accept any compromises." Impatiently, he added, "It's useless spending the whole day discussing the matter. We have a decision to make. Let's make it. For my part, I categorically refuse to publish Volange's articles."

"So do I," Luc said.

Everybody looked at Lambert who, without raising his eyes, said, "Their publication doesn't seem opportune to me."

"But you thought they were excellent!" Samazelle exploded. "You're letting yourself be intimidated!"

"I've just said their publication doesn't seem opportune to me. That's clear, isn't it?" Lambert said haughtily.

"You were hoping to split us up? Well, you missed the mark," Luc said jeeringly.

Trarieux stood up abruptly and gave Henri a withering look. "One of these days, L'Espoir is going to go bankrupt. That'll be your reward for your stubbornness!"

He walked to the door ; Samazelle and Luc left behind him.

"Can I talk to you for a moment?" Lambert asked in a mournful voice.

"I was just going to ask you the same question," Henri

replied. He could feel a false smile on his lips. It had been months, in fact a whole year, since he had last had a really friendly conversation with Lambert. It wasn't because he hadn't tried, but Lambert had been sulking and Henri no longer knew how to speak to him.

"I know what you're going to tell me," he said. "You feel your position has become untenable. Is that it?"

"Not any longer," Lambert replied. He looked at Henri reproachfully. "You have a right not to like De Gaulle, but at least you could maintain a benevolent neutrality towards him. In those articles you turned down, Volange lucidly dissociates the concepts of Gaullism from those of reaction."

"Dissociating concepts is a children's game!" Henri said. "Well, then," he added, "you want to sell your holding?"

"Yes."

"And you'll work at *Beaux Jours* with Volange?"

"Exactly."

"Too bad," Henri said. He shrugged his shoulders. "You see, I was right. Volange was preaching abstention, but he was waiting for his moment. He didn't lose much time taking the plunge into politics."

"It's your own fault," Lambert replied sharply. "You've mixed politics into everything! If you want to keep the world from being completely eaten up by politics, you have to play politics."

"In any event you won't stop anything!" Henri said. "But it's useless discussing it; we don't speak the same language any more," he added. "Sell your interest. Only, that poses a problem. If we divide it up among the four of us, we go back to the situation you helped me avoid. You, Luc, and myself will have to get together and agree upon someone who's in a position to buy you out."

"Pick whoever you like; I don't care," Lambert said. "Only, try to make it fast. I don't want to have to repeat what I did to-day."

"I'll start looking, but give me a little time," Henri said. "We can't replace you just like that."

He had spoken those last words as an afterthought, but Lambert seemed touched. Innocent phrases would often wound him, and sometimes he attributed warmth to words spoken casually.

" Since we don't speak the same language any more, the first one who comes along will do better than I," he said sullenly.

" You know very well that in addition to the man's ideas, there's the man himself," Henri said.

" I know, and that's what makes things complicated," Lambert replied. " You and your ideas make two." He got up. " Are you coming to the Lenoir festival with me?"

" We might do better going to a film," Henri replied.

" Oh, no! This is one thing I don't want to miss."

" All right, pick me up at eight-thirty."

The Communist papers had announced the reading of a master-piece in four acts and six scenes in which Lenoir " reconciles the demands of pure poetry with the concern for delivering a broadly human message to mankind." Julien intended to sabotage the meeting in the name of the old para-human group. In the articles written by Lenoir since his conversion, there was such a servile fanaticism, and he had put his friends and his own past on trial with such malignant zeal, that Henri was looking forward without displeasure to seeing him put in his place. And then, it was as good a way as any of killing the evening; since Paula's illness, he couldn't stand being alone. And into the bargain, there was Lucie Belhomme's note, which intrigued him unpleasantly.

The auditorium was overflowing. The whole Communist intelligentsia was gathered together—all the old guard and many new recruits. A year earlier, many of those neophytes were indignantly denouncing the errors and faults of the Communists. And then suddenly, in November, they understood—they understood that it could help to belong to the Party. Henri went down the centre aisle in search of a seat and, as he passed, faces filled with hateful disdain. In that respect, Samazelle was right: they weren't the least bit appreciative of his honesty. All the year long, he had laboured mightily defending L'Espoir against the pressures of the Gaullists, had firmly taken his stand against the war in Indo-China, against the arrest of the Madagascan deputies, against the Marshall Plan. All in all, he had taken exactly the same position as theirs, but that didn't stop them from calling him a liar and a traitor. He went as far as the front rows. Scriassine looked up at him and smiled, but the

young people grouped around Julien eyed Henri with
hostility. He retraced his steps and sat down on a stairway in
the back of the auditorium.

"I must be something like Cyrano de Bergerac," he said.
"All I have is enemies."

"It's your own fault," Lambert said.

"It costs too much to make friends."

At one time, he had enjoyed the pleasures of comradeship,
teamwork. But that was in another age, in another world.
To-day, as things were, he was just as well off being severely
alone; that way, he had nothing to lose. Nothing much to
gain either, but on this earth who ever gains anything?

"Take a look at the little Bizet," Lambert said. "It didn't
take her long to pick up the approved style."

"Yes, a splendid example of the female militant," Henri
said gaily.

Four months earlier, he had turned down an article of hers
on the German problem and she had whined, "I suppose the
only way to succeed in journalism is to sell yourself to
Figaro or *L'Humanité.*" Before leaving, she had added,
"Anyhow, I really can't take this article over to *L'Enclume.*"
And then a week later, she telephoned, "Well, I brought the
article over to *L'Enclume* anyhow." And now she was writing regularly for the weekly, and with deep feeling Lachaume
would cite "our dear Marie-Ange Bizet." Flat shoes, badly
made-up, she was coming back up the centre aisle shaking
people's hands, and looking important. She passed in front
of Henri; he got up and grabbed her by the arm.

"Hallo!"

"Hallo," she said without smiling, trying to break away.

"You're in quite a hurry. Did the Party forbid you to
speak to me?"

"I don't believe we have much to say to each other,"
Marie-Ange replied. Her childish voice had become acid.

"Let me congratulate you anyhow. You're doing all right
for yourself."

"I feel I'm doing useful work."

"Bravo! You already have all the Communist virtues!"

"I hope I've lost a few bourgeois failings."

She sailed off, and at that moment there was a burst of
applause: Lenoir was climbing to the stage. He sat down at
a table and spread out his papers before him while a well-

disciplined clique counterfeited enthusiasm. Then he began reading a kind of manifesto. He read in a choppy voice, leaping desperately at each word, as if he had seen dizzying crevasses opening between the syllables. Quite obviously, he was frightening himself. And yet, he spouted nothing but the most tried and tested clichés about the poetry of the real world and the social mission of the poet. When he stopped, there was another salvo of applause. The enemy camp held its fire.

"Can you imagine the depths to which they've fallen to applaud that!" Lambert said.

Henri didn't answer. Of course, all you had to do to make the scorn of these dishonest intellectuals seem meaningless was to look at them. It was out of opportunism, or fear, or for moral comfort that they had become converts; and there was no limit to their servility. But you had to be equally dishonest to be satisfied with that too-easy victory. It wasn't these people whom Henri had in mind when he would say to himself, his heart heavy, "They despise me." No, he was thinking rather of the thousands of men who used to read *L'Espoir*, who read it no longer, and for whom Henri's name had become synonymous with traitor. *They* were sincere, and the stupidity of that evening would in no way diminish their sincerity—nor their hate.

His voice now calm, Lenoir began attacking a scene written in Alexandrine metre. A young man was bemoaning his melancholy state: he wanted to leave his home town. Parents, teachers, friends, each urged resignation, but he swept aside all bourgeois temptations while a chorus commented on his departure in sibylline stanzas. A few obscure images and a few flowery words underlined the solid banality of the declamation.

Suddenly, a voice burst out, "Faker!"

Julien stood up and shouted, "They promised us poetry! Where's the poetry?"

"And the realism?" another voice cried out. "Where's the realism?"

"The masterpiece! We want the masterpiece!"

"How about the reconciliation?"

They began shouting "Reconciliation!" in chorus, stamping their feet in rhythm. At the same time, there were cries of "Throw them out! . . . Call the police! . . . Trouble-

makers! ... Tell us about the camps! ... Long live peace!
... Shoot the fascists! ... Don't insult the Resistance! ...
Long live Thorez! ... Long live De Gaulle! ... Long live
freedom!"

Lenoir looked defiantly at his executioners. You felt he
was going to fall to his knees, baring his breast, or else that
he was about to begin dancing a jig. Without any apparent
reason, the noise abated, and he resumed his reading. Now
the hero was wandering across the earth, searching for an
impossible escape. A light and provocative harmonica melody
floated across the auditorium; a little later there came the
honking of a horn. Julien punctuated each Alexandrine
with a guffaw which made Lenoir's mouth quiver spasmodically. The laughter spread from seat to seat; everywhere
people were laughing, and Henri, too, joined in. After all,
that's what he had come for. Someone shouted "Bastard!"
at him, and he laughed all the harder. Applause broke out
amid the laughter and the boos. Again, voices cried out,
"Send them to Siberia! ... Go back to Moscow! ... Long
live Stalin! ... Informer! ... Traitor! ..." Someone even
shouted, "*Vive la France!*"

"I was hoping it would be more fun," Lambert said as
they stepped out into the street.

"As a matter of fact, it wasn't any fun at all," Henri
said. Hearing Scriassine's breathless voice behind him, he
turned around.

"I saw you inside, and then you disappeared. I've been
looking all over for you."

"You were looking for me?" Henri asked. He felt a
sudden tightening of his throat. What did Scriassine want of
him? All evening long, he had felt it—something terrible
was going to happen.

"Yes, let's go and have a drink at the New Bar," Scriassine replied. "We've got to drink a toast to this little affair,
You know the New Bar?"

"I do," Lambert replied.

"Good. I'll see you there in a few minutes," Scriassine
said, suddenly vanishing in the crowd.

"What's this New Bar?" Henri asked.

"That's right, it's been months since you've set foot in the
old neighbourhood," Lambert said, getting into Henri's car.
"Ever since the Commies took over the Bar Rouge, the old

non-Commie crowd has been going to a new place next door."

" On to the New Bar," Henri said.

He started the motor, and a few moments later they turned into the familiar little street.

" Is this it?"

" This is it."

Henri slammed on the brakes; he recognised the scarlet glow coming from the Bar Rouge. He opened the door of the New Bar. " This tearoom is pretty ugly," he said.

" Yes, but you've got a better clientèle here than next door," Lambert said.

" Oh, I have my doubts about that," Henri said. He shrugged his shoulders. " Fortunately, keeping bad company doesn't frighten me."

They sat down at a table. A lot of young people, a lot of noise, a lot of smoke. Henri knew none of those faces; when he took Josette out, they went to a completely different kind of place. And besides, he didn't go out very often.

" Scotch?" Lambert asked.

" Yes."

Lambert ordered two Scotch-and-sodas in the elegantly blasé voice he had borrowed from Volange. They waited for their drinks in silence. It was truly sad: Henri could no longer find anything to say to Lambert. Nevertheless, he made an effort.

" It seems Dubreuilh's book just came out."

" The one they printed excerpts from in *Vigilance*?"

" Yes."

" I'm anxious to read it."

" So am I," Henri said.

Dubreuilh always used to give him the galley proofs to read; this book Henri would buy in a bookshop. And he would discuss it with whom he wished, but not with Dubreuilh, the only person with whom he would have liked to discuss it.

" I dug up that article of mine on Dubreuilh—the one you turned down," Lambert said. " Remember it? It wasn't so bad, you know."

" I never said it was bad," Henri said.

He recalled that conversation; it was the first time he had felt a kind of hostility in Lambert.

" I'm going to work it up into a detailed study of Dubreuilh," Lambert said. He hesitated almost imperceptibly. " Volange has asked me to do it for *Les Beaux Jours*."

Henri smiled. "Try not to be too unfair."

" I'll be completely objective," Lambert said. " They're also going to publish a story of mine," he added.

" Oh! You've written some new stories?"

" I've written two. Volange likes them very much."

" I'd love to see them," Henri said.

" You wouldn't like them," Lambert said.

Julien appeared in the doorway and walked over to their table. He had slipped his arm under Scriassine's; their common hatred took the place of friendship for the moment.

" To work, comrades!" he said in a loud voice. " The moment has finally come to reconcile man and whisky."

He was wearing a white carnation in his lapel and his eyes had regained a little of their old brightness, perhaps because he hadn't had anything to drink as yet.

" A bottle of champagne!" Scriassine called out.

" Champagne! Here?" Henri said, shocked.

" Let's go somewhere else!" Scriassine said.

" No, no, I'll go along with the champagne, but no gipsies, please!" Julien said, sitting down hurriedly. He smiled. " Lovely party, wasn't it? Highly cultural party! I'm only sorry no blood was spilled."

" A lovely party, yes, but there have to be sequels," Scriassine said. He looked at Julien and Henri urgently. " I got an idea during that session: we ought to organise a group to squelch all traitorous intellectuals in every way and at every opportunity."

" And how about a group to squelch all groups?" Julien asked.

" Hey, now! Aren't you becoming just a bit fascist?" Henri said to Scriassine.

" Damn it! There you have it!" Scriassine said. " There's why all our victories are without to-morrows."

" To hell with to-morrows!" Julien said.

Scriassine's face had clouded. " After all, we've got to do something."

" Why?" Henri asked.

" I'm going to write a paper on Lenoir," Scriassine said. " He's a remarkable case of political neurosis."

"Oh, come on! I know a few who would be more than a match for him," Henri said.

"We're all neurotics," Julien said. "But nevertheless, none of us writes in Alexandrines."

"That's right!" Henri said. He began to laugh. "I was just thinking how you'd have looked if Lenoir's piece had turned out to be good."

"And suppose Thorez had come to dance the French cancan? How would you have looked?" Julien said.

"After all, Lenoir did write some good poems," Henri said.

Lambert shrugged his shoulders irritably. "Before giving up his freedom."

"The freedom of a writer—it would be interesting to know what that means," Henri said.

"It means nothing," Scriassine said. "It means nothing to be a writer any more."

"Precisely," Julien said. "So much so that it even makes me feel like going back to writing."

"You really ought to," Lambert said with a sudden animation. "It's so rare these days to find a writer who doesn't believe he has to have a mission."

"That was for my benefit," Henri thought. But he said nothing.

Julien laughed. "That's how it goes," he said. "I'm immediately given a mission: to prove that a writer doesn't have to have a mission!"

"No, no!" Lambert protested.

Julien put a finger to his lips. "Silence alone is certain."

"Good God!" Scriassine exclaimed abruptly. "We have just witnessed a tragic spectacle; we saw a man who was once our friend reduced to abjection by the Communist Party. And you sit here and talk about literature! Haven't you got any hearts?"

"You take the world too seriously," Julien said.

"Yes? Well, if there weren't any men like me to take the world seriously, the Stalinists would be in power, and I don't know where you'd be, my friend."

"Six feet under, resting peacefully," Julien replied.

Henri laughed. "You think the Communists want your hide?"

"Even my hide doesn't like them," Julien replied. "I'm very sensitive." He turned to Scriassine. "I ask nothing of

anybody. I'll continue to enjoy living as long as I get any
fun out of living. And when that's no longer possible, I'll put
an end to things."

"You'd liquidate yourself if the Communists were in
power?" Henri asked jocularly.

"Yes, and I'd strongly advise you to do the same," Julien
replied.

"That's really something!" Henri said. He looked at
Julien, stupefied. "You think you're sitting around talking
to your friends, and then, suddenly, you realise one of them
thinks he's Napoleon!"

"Tell me this: what would you do in case of a Gaullist
dictatorship?"

"I don't like speeches or military music, but with a little
cotton wool in my ears I'd get along."

"I see. Well, I'm going to tell you something: you'd end
up by removing the cotton wool and applauding the
speeches."

"No one can accuse me of having any love for De Gaulle,"
Scriassine said. "You know that. But you can't compare
what a Gaullist France would be like with a Stalinised
France."

"Oh, you too!" Henri said, shrugging his shoulders.
"Soon you'll be shouting: 'Long live De Gaulle.'"

"It isn't my fault if the anti-Communist forces grouped
themselves around him," Scriassine said. "When I wanted
to form a left against the Communists, you refused."

"As long as you're an anti-Communist, why not be a
militarist?" Henri said. "Talk about a left!" he added
irritably. "You used to say there are the American people,
there are unions. And in your articles, you defend Marshall
and Company."

"It is a fact that to-day the world is divided into two
camps. You have to choose either America or Russia."

"And you choose America!" Henri said.

"There aren't any concentration camps in America,"
Scriassine replied.

"Those camps again! You make me feel sorry I ever
spoke about them," Henri said.

"Don't say that! It was the finest thing you ever did,"
Lambert said. His voice was a little thick; he was on his
second drink and he didn't handle liquor very well.

Henri shrugged his shoulders. "What good did it do? The right used the camps to discredit the Communists, as if it was completely justified in doing so. As soon as you talk about exploitation, unemployment, famine, they answer you with 'and how about the slave labour camps?' If they didn't exist, they would have invented them."

"But the fact is they do exist," Scriassine said. "Disturbing, isn't it!"

"I feel sorry for people who aren't disturbed by it," Henri replied.

Lambert suddenly stood up. "Excuse me, but I have an appointment."

"I'll go with you," Henri said, getting up. "I'm going home to get some sleep."

"Sleep! This early! On a night like this!" Julien said.

"Yes, it's a great night!" Henri said. "But I'm tired." He gave a little wave of his hand and walked to the door.

"Where's your appointment?" he asked Lambert.

"I don't have an appointment. I was just fed up. They get on my nerves," Lambert said. Bitterly, he added, "When will we be able to spend an evening without talking politics?"

"We weren't talking; we were shooting lines."

"Shooting lines about politics."

"I did suggest going to a film."

"Politics or films!" Lambert said. "Is there really nothing else in the world?"

"I imagine there is," Henri replied.

"What?"

"I wish I knew!"

Lambert kicked the pavement angrily. In a somewhat dictatorial voice, he asked, "Aren't you going to have a drink with me?"

"Let's go."

They sat down in an outdoor café. It was a beautiful night; people seated at the little tables were laughing. What were they talking about? Tiny cars zigzagged along the street; young people passed by, arm in arm; under the sidewalks, in smoky cellar clubs, couples were dancing and the echo of first-rate jazz drifted up into the street. Of course, there were many other things in this world besides politics and films—for other people.

"Two double Scotches," Lambert ordered.

"Double! You're hitting it hard!" Henri said. "Are you taking to drink, too?"

"Why the ' too '?"

"Julien drinks, Scriassine drinks . . ."

"Volange doesn't and Vincent does," Lambert said.

Henri smiled. "It was just idle talk ; you're the one who sees political undertones in everything."

"Nadine didn't want me to drink either," Lambert said, his face already displaying a foggy stubbornness. "She didn't think I could take it ; she didn't think I could do anything. Just like you. It's exasperating, but people don't seem to trust me," he concluded gloomily.

"I've always trusted you," Henri said.

"No. For a while, you were indulgent, that was all. Nothing more." Lambert drank half his glass of Scotch and continued angrily, "In your gang, if you aren't a genius, you've got to be a monster. Vincent is no problem: he's a monster. But me, I'm neither a writer nor a man of action nor a great hell-raiser—just a good, solid son of a well-to-do family. And I don't even know how to get drunk properly."

Henri shrugged his shoulders. "No one asks you to be either a genius or a monster."

"You ask nothing of me because all you feel for me is contempt," Lambert said.

"You're completely out of your mind!" Henri said. "I'm sorry you have the opinion you have, but I have no contempt for you."

"You think I'm a bourgeois," Lambert said.

"And I? I'm not a bourgeois?"

"Oh, but you, you're you!" Lambert said rancorously. "You say you feel superior to no one, but in reality you're contemptuous of everyone—Lenoir, Scriassine, Julien, Samazelle, Volange, and all the others, and me as well. Obviously," he added in a voice at once admiring and grudging, "because you have such high principles! You're disinterested, honest, loyal, courageous, true to yourself. Not a flaw! Ah, it must be great to feel above reproach!"

Henri smiled. "I can assure you that isn't my case."

"Come on! You're flawless and you know it," Lambert said in a disheartened voice. "As for me, I know damn' well I'm not flawless," he added angrily, "but I don't give a damn. I am what I am."

" Who's blaming you?" Henri said. He studied Lambert a
little remorsefully. He had blamed him for taking the easy
way out, but Lambert had excuses enough: a difficult childhood, Rosa dead when he was only twenty. And Nadine
hadn't helped matters much. What he was asking for was,
after all quite modest: that he be permitted to live a little
for himself. " And I've offered him hardly anything but
tasks," Henri thought. That's why Lambert was going over
to Volange's side. But perhaps it wasn't too late to offer him
something else.

" I have a feeling you're holding a lot of grievances against
me," he said affectionately. " You'd do well to get them off
your chest once and for all and we'll try to iron things out."

" I don't have any grievances ; it's just that you're always
blaming me. You spend half your time blaming me," Lambert said dolefully.

" You're completely mistaken. When I happen to differ
with you about something, that doesn't mean I blame you.
First of all, we aren't the same age. What matters to me
doesn't necessarily matter to you. For example, I've had my
youth ; I can well understand your wanting to enjoy yours a
little."

" You understand that?" Lambert asked.

" Of course."

" Oh, even if you don't, I don't give a damn," Lambert
said.

His voice wavered ; he had drunk too much to be able to
hold to talk sensibly. And besides, there was no hurry.

Henri smiled at him. " Listen, it's late and we're both of us
a little beat. Let's go out together some evening and try to
have a real talk. It's been a long time since we've done that."

" A real talk? Do you think that's possible?" Lambert
asked.

"It is, if you want to have one," Henri replied. He got up.
" Can I drop you somewhere?"

" No, thanks, I'm going to stick around and see if anybody
turns up," Lambert replied vaguely.

" Well, see you soon," Henri said.

Lambert held out his hand. " See you soon."

Henri returned to his hotel. There was a package in his
mailbox—Dubreuilh's book. While he climbed the stairs, he
tore off the wrapping and opened the volume to the flyleaf.

Naturally, it was blank. What had he imagined? It was Mauvanes who had sent him the book, as he had sent him a lot of others.

" Why?" he asked himself. " Why did we break off?" He had often asked himself that question. Dubreuilh's articles in *Vigilance* struck exactly the same note as Henri's editorials. Actually, nothing separated them. And they had broken off. It was one of those facts which could be denied, but nothing could explain it. The Communists hated Henri, Lambert was leaving *L'Espoir*, Paula was insane, the world was rushing towards another war. The break with Dubreuilh made neither more nor less sense.

Henri sat down at his desk and began cutting the pages of the book. He had already read large portions of it. He turned immediately to the final chapter, a long one which must have been written in January, after the dissolution of the S.R.L. He found it a little disconcerting. The thing that was so admirable about Dubreuilh was that he never hesitated to re-examine his ideas, and each time he did he would start again from scratch. But this time, the reorientation was radical. " To-day a French intellectual can do nothing," he declared. That was only too obviously true: the S.R.L. had failed; Dubreuilh's articles in *Vigilance* caused a stir but had no influence on anybody; he was accused of being now a crypto-Communist, now a tool of Wall Street; he had nothing but enemies. It couldn't have been any picnic for him. Henri was roughly in the same position, and neither was it a picnic for him. But it wasn't the same. Henri lived from day to day, adapted himself; Dubreuilh, with his fanatical side, was surely unable to adapt himself. Besides, he went quite a bit further than Henri: he doomed literature itself. Henri continued reading. Dubreuilh went even further: he doomed his own existence. To the old humanist philosophy which had long been his, he opposed a new humanism, more realistic, more pessimistic, in which force figured large and the concepts of justice, freedom, truth hardly at all. Victoriously, he demonstrated that that was the only ethics adequate to the present state of relations among mankind. But to adopt it, one had to throw so many things overboard that he, personally, was incapable of doing so. It was indeed strange seeing Dubreuilh preaching a truth he was unable to make his own. It meant that he considered himself as dead. "It's my fault," Henri thought. "If I hadn't been so obstinate, the S.R.L. would have continued in existence, and Dubreuilh wouldn't believe himself defeated for good." Ineffectual, isolated, doubting that his work had any meaning, cut off from the future, challenging his past—it wrung Henri's heart to think of it. Abruptly, he said to himself, "I'll write to him!" Perhaps Dubreuilh wouldn't answer, or would answer angrily. What difference did it make? Pride? Henri no longer knew what it meant. "To-morrow I'll write to him," he decided, getting into bed. "To-morrow I'll have a real talk with Lambert," he said to himself, turning out the light. "To-morrow. Why does old lady Belhomme want to see me to-morrow morning?" he wondered.

The chambermaid stepped aside and Henri went into the living-room. Bearskin rugs, thick carpets, low couches, the same collusive silence as when he had met a tacitly offered Josette here. Surely Lucie couldn't have summoned him to offer him her middle-aged charms! "What does she want with me?" he asked himself, trying to think of possible answers.

"Thanks for coming," Lucie said. She was wearing a severe housedress; her hair was carefully arranged, but she had not pencilled her eyebrows, and that nakedness above her eyes made her look strangely old. She motioned him to sit down.

"I have a favour to ask of you. It isn't so much for myself; it's for Josette. Are you fond of her, or not?"

"You know very well I am," Henri replied. Lucie's voice was so normal that he felt vaguely relieved. "She wants me to marry Josette," he thought, "or join her in some deal or other." But that lace handkerchief she was holding in her right hand, why was she squeezing it so hard?

"I don't know how far you'd go to help her," Lucie said.

"Tell me what it's all about."

Lucie hesitated; she was wringing her crumpled handkerchief in her hands. "I'll tell you. I have no choice." She smiled a thin smile at him. "I'm sure you've heard that during the war we were not exactly members of the Resistance."

"So I heard."

" No one will ever know what I went through to get control of the Maison Amaryllis and to turn it into a big establishment," Lucie said. " Besides, that doesn't concern anyone, and I have no illusions about softening you up with the story of my life. Only, you've got to understand that after all those years of struggling, I would have slit my throat rather than see it go to pieces. And the only way I could save it was by using the Germans. I used them, and I won't pretend to you that I'm sorry I did. But obviously, you get nothing for nothing. I entertained them in my house in Lyon, gave parties . . . in short, I did what I had to. It caused me a little trouble after the liberation. But that was a long time ago now ; it's been forgotten."

Lucie looked around her, and then her eyes met Henri's. Calmly, he murmured, " Go on." It seemed to him that this scene had already taken place. When? In his dreams, perhaps. Ever since he received that note he had known what Lucie was going to tell him ; he had been expecting this moment for a year.

" There's a man named Mercier who used to take care of my business for me. He'd often come to Lyon. He filched some photographs, some letters, picked up bits of gossip. If he squeals, Josette and I are certain to be officially denounced."

" So that story about the file is true," Henri said. He felt nothing but a great weariness.

" Oh, you knew about it?" Lucie asked in surprise. Her face relaxed a little.

" Did you use Josette, too?" Henri asked.

" Use Josette! Josette never did me a bit of good," Lucie said bitterly. " She compromised herself in a completely useless way: she fell in love with a captain, a handsome, sentimental boy without any influence whatsoever. He sent her a lot of impassioned letters before getting himself killed on the Eastern Front, and of course she had to leave them lying around all over the place. And then there were some snapshots of the two of them together. Lovely documents, I assure you. It didn't take Mercier long to realise their value."

Henri got up suddenly and walked over to the window. Lucie was watching him, but he didn't give a damn. He recalled Josette's languid face that morning, the first morning, and her so-truthful voice which was lying: " Me? In

love? With whom?" Yes, she had loved, and it was someone else she had loved, a handsome German. He turned to
Lucie and, with considerable effort, asked, " He's blackmailing you?"

Lucie laughed. " You really don't imagine I'm coming to
you for money? I've been forking out for three years now,
and I was willing to go on forking out. I went so far as to
offer him practically everything I own in return for the file.
But he's clever; he looks ahead." She looked Henri in the
eyes and said challengingly, " He was an informer for the
Gestapo and he's just been arrested. He got word to me that
if I don't get him out of it he'll drag us under with him."

Henri was silent. The bitches who slept with the Germans
had, until now, belonged to a different world, a world for
which there could be only one possible feeling: hate. But
Lucie was talking, he was listening; that contemptible world
was his world; there was only one world. Josette had
slipped into his arms from those of the German captain.

" You realise what this affair could do to Josette?" Lucie
said. " Being the person she is, she'd never stand up under
it. She'd turn on the gas."

" What do you want me to do about it? What do you
expect of me?" he asked irritably. " There isn't a lawyer
alive who can do anything for a Gestapo informer. The only
advice I can give you is to take off for Switzerland as fast as
you can."

Lucie shrugged her shoulders. " Switzerland! I still say
that Josette would kill herself. She's been so happy these
days, the poor darling," Lucie said with a sudden tenderness.
" Everyone says she's a sensation on the screen. Sit down,"
she added impatiently, " and listen to me."

" I'm listening," Henri said, sitting down.

" As far as a lawyer goes, I've already got myself one:
Truffaut. Know him? He's a very devoted friend, and
besides he owes me a few favours," Lucie said with a mysterious smile. She looked Henri squarely in the eyes. " We've
studied the whole matter together, from every conceivable
angle. He says the only solution is for Mercier to claim he
was a double agent. But of course, it won't hold water unless
some prominent member of the Resistance backs him up."

" I'm beginning to understand!" Henri said.

" It's quite easy to understand," Lucie said coldly.

Henri laughed mirthlessly. "You think it's simple, do you? Unfortunately, all my comrades in the Resistance know that Mercier never worked with me."

Lucie bit her lip; suddenly, all her swagger was gone, and he was afraid that she might burst into tears. That would have been a sickening spectacle. He studied her crestfallen face with malicious pleasure, and words rushed through his head like the wind: "In love with a German captain ... She really took me ... Idiot! What an idiot!" He had felt so certain of her pleasure, of her tenderness. Idiot! She had never for a moment considered him as anything but a tool. Lucie was a smart woman; she looked ahead; if she had taken Henri's interest in hand, if she had thrown Josette into his arms, it was not to promote the career of a daughter about whom she didn't give a damn; it was to gain a useful ally. And Josette had played her game. She had told Henri she had never loved in order to excuse the reticence in her heart, but all the love of which that futile heart was capable had been given to a German captain, a young, handsome, German captain. He felt like reviling her, beating her, and he was being asked to save her!

"The group was secret, wasn't it?" Lucie asked.

"Yes, but among ourselves we knew who was with us."

"Won't the judge take your word? And would your friends contradict you, if they're brought to confront you?"

"I don't know and I don't want to run the risk of finding out," Henri replied irritably. "You don't seem to understand that giving false testimony is a serious thing. You want to hold on to your business; well, there are certain little things I also want to hold on to."

Lucie had regained her composure. In a matter-of-fact voice, she said, "The principal charge against Mercier is that he denounced two girls; it happened on the Pont de l'Alma the twenty-third of February, 1944." She looked at Henri questioningly. "In the Resistance, they went under the names of Lisa and Yvonne; they spent a year in Dachau. Does that bring anything back to you?"

"No."

"Too bad. If you had known them, it might have helped us. Anyhow, they know you, of course. If you state that Mercier was somewhere else that day, with you, won't that take the wind out of their sails? And if you declare that you secretly used Mercier as a double agent, would anyone dare contradict you?"

Henri reflected. Yes, it had a lot of merit; a bluff might work. In '44, Luc was in Bordeaux, and Chancel, Varieux, Galtier were all dead now. As for Lambert, Sézenac, and Dubreuilh, if they had any doubts they would keep them to themselves. But he wasn't going to give false testimony for a little tart whose body happened to please him. She certainly had kept her secret damned well, the poor sweet innocent thing!

"Better be on your way to Switzerland fast," he said. "You'll find a lot of your kind there. In Switzerland, or in Brazil, or in Argentina—it's a big world. It's a fallacy to think that you can live only in Paris."

"You know how Josette is, don't you? She was just beginning to have a taste for life again. She'll never be able to take it," Lucie said.

Henri felt a sudden twinge in his heart. "I've got to see her," he said to himself. "Now."

He stood up abruptly. "I'll think it over."

"Here's Truffaut's address," Lucie said, pulling a slip of paper from her pocket. "If you decide to help us, get in touch with him."

"And suppose I do help?" Henri said. "How can you be sure he'll surrender the file?"

"What could he do with it? First of all, he has no interest in making you angry. And secondly, the day the file is brought out in the open your testimony becomes suspect. No, if you get him out of it, his hands are tied."

"I'll ring you to-night," Henri said.

Lucie got up and, for a moment, stood facing him hesitantly. Again he was afraid she might burst into tears or throw herself at his feet. But she only let out a sigh and walked with him to the door.

He ran down the stairs, got into his car, and drove over to Rue Gabriel. In his pocket, he still had the key Josette had given him that beautiful night a year earlier. He opened the door to the apartment and went into her bedroom without knocking.

"Who's there?" Josette said. She opened her eyes and smiled sleepily. "It's you? What time is it? How sweet of you to come to give me a kiss!"

He didn't kiss her. He drew the curtains and sat down on an ottoman. Between those quilted walls, among those knick-knacks, those cushions, that satin, it was difficult to believe in scandal, prison, despair. A face was smiling, a very rosy face framed in a shock of tawny hair.

"I've got to talk to you," he said.

Josette pushed herself up a litle on her pillows. "About what?"

"Why didn't you tell me the truth? Your mother's just finished telling me everything. And this time, I want the truth," he said in a furious voice. "Did she throw you into my arms because she thought I'd be able to do the two of you a favour some day?"

"What's happening?" Josette asked, looking at Henri in terror.

"Answer me! Did you sleep with me to obey your mother?"

"Mother told me to drop you a long time ago," Josette replied. "What she'd like is to see me set up with some rich old man. What's happening?" she repeated in a pleading voice.

"The file," he said. "You have heard about that file, haven't you? The man who has it has been arrested and he's threatening to spill the whole story."

Josette buried her face in the pillows. "Will there never be an end to it!" she said in despair.

"Do you remember that first morning, here in this very room—you told me you'd never been in love. Later, you spoke to me vaguely about some young man who died in America. Well, your young man turned out to be a German captain! What a fool you made out of me!"

"Why do you talk to me like that?" Josette whined. "What did I ever do to you? When I was in Lyon, I didn't know you."

"But when I questioned you, you did know me. And you lied to me with such innocence!"

"What good would it have done to tell you the truth? Besides, Mother forbade me to. And after all, you were a stranger."

"And for a whole year I remained a stranger to you?"

"What reason was there to talk about all that?" She began weeping softly in her hands. "Mother says if I'm

denounced I'll go to prison. I don't want to go to prison!
I'd rather kill myself."

"How long did your affair with that captain last?"

"A year."

"Was he the one who set you up in this flat?"

"Yes. Everything I have, he gave me."

"And you loved him?"

"He loved me, he loved me like no other man will ever
love me. Yes, I loved him," she said, sobbing. "That's no
reason to throw me in jail."

Henri got up, took a few steps among the furniture chosen
by the handsome captain. Actually, he had always known
that Josette was capable of giving herself to Germans. "I
didn't know what the war was all about," she had once
admitted. He had supposed that she had smiled at them,
had even flirted vaguely with them, and he excused her for
it. A sincere love should have seemed to him even more
excusable. But the fact was that he couldn't bear imagining
a grey-green uniform draped over that chair and the man it
belonged to lying in bed with her, body to body, mouth to
mouth.

"And do you know what your mother wants me to do?
Give false testimony to save your skins. False testimony—I
suppose that doesn't mean anything to you," he added.

"I won't go to jail! I'd kill myself first," Josette repeated between sobs. "Besides, I don't care any more. I
don't care if I die."

"It's not a question of your going to jail," Henri said
more gently. No point in pretending to play the judge. He
was, quite simply, jealous. In all justice, he really couldn't
hold it against Josette that she had loved the first man who
fell in love with her. And what right did he have to blame
her for her silence? He had no right whatsoever.

"At worst, you'll have to leave France," he continued.
"But France isn't the only place people can live, you know."

Josette continued sobbing. Of course, it was nonsense,
what he had just said. Shame, flight, exile—Josette would
never be able to take it. Even now, she wasn't so very fond
of life. He looked around him, and a feeling of anguish rose
in his throat. Life seemed frivolous indeed in that Hollywood
film set, but if one day Josette turned on the gas it would be
between those quilted walls, lying between those pink sheets

that she would meet death. And she would be buried in that
frothy nightgown. No, the frivolousness of that room was
nothing but an optical illusion: Josette's tears were real
tears, a real skeleton was hidden under her fragrant skin. He
sat down on the edge of the bed.

"Don't cry," he said. "I'll get you out of it."

She brushed aside the locks of hair flowing over her wet
face. "You will? But you look so angry!"

"No, no, I'm not angry," he said. "I promise you I'll get
you out of it," he repeated vigorously.

"Oh, please! Save me! I beg you!" Josette said, throwing herself into his arms.

"Don't be frightened. Nothing bad will happen to you,"
he said gently.

"You're so nice!" Josette said, clinging to him and offering him her mouth. He turned his face away. "I disgust
you?" she murmured in a voice so humble that Henri felt
suddenly ashamed, ashamed of being on the side of right.
He was a man facing a woman, a man with money, a name,
culture, and, above all, principles! A little tarnished lately,
those principles, but they still gave the illusion of being
there. At times, he himself was taken in.

He kissed the mouth stained with salty tears. "No, I
disgust myself," he said.

"You?"

She looked at him with eyes that understood nothing, and
he kissed her again, feeling pity well up in him. What
principles had they given her? What weapons? What
hopes? There had been the slaps from her mother, the vul-
garities of men, the humiliating beauty, and now there had
been planted in her heart a remorse which bewildered her.

"I should have been nice instead of barking at you," he
said.

She looked at him anxiously. "You really don't hold it
against me?"

"I don't hold it against you. And I'll get you out of it."

"How will you do it?"

"I'll do what I have to do."

She let out a sigh and put her head on Henri's shoulder.
He fondled her hair. False testimony: the thought horrified
him. But what of it? In perjuring himself, he would do no
one any harm. Of course, he would save Mercier's head

and that was regrettable, but there were so many others who deserved to be dead and who were walking around hale and hearty! If he refused, Josette would be quite capable of doing away with herself, or, in any event, her life would be ruined. No, he couldn't hold back: on the one side, there was Josette, on the other, qualms of conscience. He twisted a lock of her hair around his finger. At any rate, there was damned little to be gained from having a clear conscience. The thought wasn't new to him: you were just as well off being frankly in the wrong. Now he was being offered a fine opportunity to say to hell with morality; he wasn't going to let it go by.

He withdrew his hand and ran it over his face. Playing the part of the devil didn't suit him. He would give that false testimony because he couldn't do otherwise, that's all. "How did I ever come to this?" It seemed to him at the same time both completely logical and absolutely impossible. Never had he felt sadder.

Henri didn't write to Dubreuilh, nor did he have a heart-to-heart talk with Lambert. Friends meant accountings to give; to do what he was going to do, he had to be alone. Now that his decision was made, he forbade himself remorse. Neither was he afraid. Of course, he was taking a big chance; exposure was always possible, and what a lovely scandal there would be if he were ever convicted of giving false testimony! Mixed with the Gaullist or Communist sauces, it would make quite a spicy stew. But he had no illusions about his importance to the world, and as for his personal future, he didn't give a damn. He and Truffaut fabricated a likely career for Mercier, and he felt no more than slightly squeamish the day he walked into the office of the examining magistrate. It was an office like thousands of others, but it seemed to him less real than a theatrical set. The magistrate, the clerk were merely actors in an abstract drama; they were playing their parts, Henri would play his. The truthful word meant nothing here.

"Of course, a double agent is required to give certain token information to the enemy," he explained calmly. "You know that as well as I. Mercier couldn't possibly have helped us without compromising himself. But we always decided together on the information he would furnish the

Germans; there was never the slightest leak concerning the true activities of the group. And if I'm here to-day, if so many of my comrades escaped death, if *L'Espoir* was able to continue its clandestine existence, it's thanks to him."

He spoke with a warmth that he felt was convincing, and Mercier's smile corroborated his words. He was a passably handsome young man, thirtyish, modest-looking, with a rather likeable face. "And yet," Henri thought, "it might have been he who informed on Borel or Fauchois. He informed on others—without hate, without love, for money. They were killed, they killed themselves, and he goes on living, honoured, well-off, happy." But between those four walls, he felt so far away from the world in which men live and die that it didn't seem to matter much.

"It's always a delicate matter determining the exact point at which a double agent becomes a traitor," the magistrate said. "What you do not know is that, unfortunately, Mercier crossed that boundary."

He gestured to the bailiff, and Henri stiffened. He knew that Yvonne and Lisa had spent twelve months in Dachau, but he had never seen them. Now, he saw them. Yvonne was the dark one and she seemed healthy again; Lisa had chestnut-brown hair and she was still pale and thin, as if she had just returned from the dead. Vengeance wouldn't have given her back her colour, but they were both very real, and it was going to be difficult to lie to their faces.

It was Yvonne who repeated their deposition, and her eyes never left Mercier's face. "On the twenty-third of February, 1944, at two o'clock in the afternoon, I had an appointment to meet Lisa Pelloux, here present, on the Pont de l'Alma. The moment I greeted her three men came up to us, two Germans and this man here who pointed us out to them. He was wearing a brown overcoat, no hat, and he was clean-shaven, as he is to-day."

"There is an error in identification," Henri said firmly. "At two o'clock on the twenty-third of February, Mercier was in La Souterraine with me; we had arrived there together the day before. Friends of ours were to give us the location of certain ammunition dumps which the Americans bombed three days later, and we spent the entire day with them."

"Nevertheless, he's definitely the one," Yvonne said.

She looked at Lisa, who said, " Yes, he is definitely the one!"

"Couldn't you be mistaken about the date?" the magistrate asked.

Henri shook his head. "The bombing took place on the twenty-sixth; the information was transmitted the twenty-fourth, and I spent the twenty-second and twenty-third there. You don't forget dates like that."

"And you're positive you were arrested on the twenty-third?" the magistrate asked, turning to the young women.

"Yes, the twenty-third of February," Lisa replied. Both of them seemed dumbfounded.

"You saw the man who denounced you for only a brief moment, and at a time when you were very much upset," Henri said. "I worked with Mercier for two years; it is impossible for me to confuse him with someone else. Everything I know about him tells me he would never have informed on a member of the Resistance. That's only an opinion, but what I swear to under oath is that on February twenty-third, 1944, he was in La Souterraine with me."

Henri looked intently at Yvonne and Lisa; the two women looked at each other in distress. They were no less sure of Mercier's identity than of Henri's loyalty, and there was a look of panic in their eyes.

"Then it must have been his twin brother," Yvonne said.

"He has no brothers," the magistrate said.

"It was someone who looks enough like him to be his brother."

"A lot of people look like each other at a distance of two years," Henri said.

There was a silence, and then the magistrate asked, "Do you still adhere to your testimony?"

"No," Yvonne replied.

"No," said Lisa.

Unwilling to doubt Henri, they consented to doubt their own most positive recollections. But along with the past, the present—and even reality itself—was reeling around them. Henri was horrified by that bewildered perplexity in the depths of their eyes.

"Would you mind reading this over and signing it?" the magistrate said.

Henri read through the typewritten page. Translated into

that impersonal style, his deposition seemed to lose all significance, and signing it didn't upset him. But with his eyes, he hesitantly followed the young women as they left the room; he felt like running after them, but he had nothing to say to them.

It was a day just like any other day, and no one could read on his face the fact that he had just perjured himself. Back at the paper, Lambert passed him in the hall without smiling, but that was for an entirely different reason: he was hurt because Henri still hadn't set a date for that "real conversation." "I'll invite him out for dinner to-morrow." Yes, friendship was once again permissible; the precautions, the scruples were of the past. The thing had gone so smoothly that it was almost possible to imagine that nothing at all had happened. "Well, let's imagine it," Henri said to himself, sitting down at his desk. He went through his correspondence. A letter from Mardrus: Paula was cured, but it would be desirable if Henri didn't attempt to see her again. Perfect. Pierre Leverrier wrote that he was interested in buying Lambert's interest. Good. He was honest and austere; he wouldn't restore L'Espoir's lost youth, but you could work with him. Ah! They had brought him additional information on the Madagascan affair. Henri read the typed pages. One hundred thousand Madagascans massacred as against one hundred and fifty Europeans; terror reigned on the island; all the deputies had been arrested even though they had disavowed the rebellion; they were being subjected to tortures worthy of the Gestapo; an attempt had been made on their lawyer's life with a hand grenade; the trial was fixed in advance—and there was not a single newspaper to denounce the scandal. He took out his pen. Someone had to be sent there: Vincent would like nothing better. In the meantime, he would take special pains with his editorial. He had just written the first few lines when his secretary opened the door.

"There's someone to see you," she said. It was Truffaut. Henri felt a twinge in his heart. Lucie Belhomme, Mercier, Truffaut—something had happened. He had accomplices.

"Show him in."

The lawyer was holding a thick leather brief case in his hand. "I won't disturb you for long," he said, adding in a pleased voice, "Your deposition was admirable; a dismissal of the case is sure. I'm extremely happy about it. Prison would not have helped that young man to make up for the mistakes he might have made. You gave him a chance of becoming a new man."

"And of committing new atrocities!" Henri said. "But that isn't the question. All I hope is that we hear no more of him."

"I've advised him to leave for Indo-China," Truffaut said.

"Excellent idea!" Henri said. "If he kills as many Indo-Chinese as he did Frenchmen, he'll become a famous hero. In the meantime, did he give back the file?"

"Precisely my reason for coming here," Truffaut replied. He took a thick package wrapped in brown paper from his brief case. "I wanted to give it to you personally."

Henri took the package. "Why to me?" he asked hesitantly. "It should be turned over to Madame Belhomme."

"You can do whatever you like with it. My client's wish is that it be turned over to you," Truffaut said noncommittally.

Henri tossed the package into a drawer. In some mysterious way, the lawyer was indebted to Lucie; that didn't mean he had a soft spot for her in his heart. Perhaps he was treating himself to some kind of revenge.

"Are you sure everything is in there?"

"Positive," Truffaut replied. "The young man understands perfectly well that making you angry could prove very costly to him. No, I'm convinced we'll hear nothing further from him."

"Thank you for your trouble," Henri said.

The lawyer didn't get up. "You do not think we need worry about a contradiction of your testimony?" he asked.

"I don't think so," Henri replied. "Besides, the matter received no publicity."

"Happily, no. It was quickly stopped."

There was a silence which Henri made no attempt to break. Finally, Truffaut decided to take his leave. "Well, I'll let you get back to your work. I do hope I'll have the pleasure of seeing you again one of these days at Madame Belhomme's." He stood up. "If you ever have the slightest trouble, don't fail to let me know."

"Thank you," Henri said curtly.

As soon as the lawyer left, Henri opened the drawer; his

hand froze on the brown paper. He shouldn't touch it; he should take the package to his room and burn it without a single glance inside. But he was already breaking the strings, spreading out the documents on his desk. Letters in German, in French, statements, depositions, snapshots. In low décolleté and dripping with jewellery, Lucie among a group of Germans in uniform; Josette laughing exuberantly, seated between two officers behind a champagne bucket; and then there was Josette standing in the middle of a lawn with the handsome captain's arm around her waist, and she was smiling at him with that look of happy confidence which had so often overwhelmed Henri—in a light-coloured dress, her hair falling free over her shoulders, she seemed even younger than she was now. And so much gayer! And how she was laughing! Putting the photographs back on the desk, Henri noticed that his fingers had left damp marks on their shiny surfaces. He had always known that Josette had been laughing while thousands of Lisas and Yvonnes were suffering agonies in concentration camps. But all that had been an old story, well hidden behind the convenient curtain that veils the past, absence, and nothingness. But now he could see that the past had once been the present, that it was still part of the present.

"My dearest beloved." The captain wrote in a painstakingly correct French, sprinkled with little phrases in German, little impassioned phrases. He seemed to have been very stupid, very much in love, and very sad. She had loved him, he had died; she must have wept a great deal. But first, she had laughed. How she had laughed!

Henri rewrapped the package, put it into a drawer, and locked it up. "I'll burn it to-morrow." At the moment, he had to finish his article. He picked up his pen. He was going to speak of justice and truth, protest against murders, tortures. "I've got to do it," he said to himself emphatically. If he gave up doing what he had to, he became doubly guilty. Whatever opinion he might have of himself, there were those men there whom he had to try to save.

He worked until eleven at night without taking any time for dinner; he wasn't hungry. As on every other evening, he went to pick up Josette at the theatre, and he waited for her in his car. She was wearing a diaphanous mist-hued cloak; she was heavily made up, and she was very beautiful.

She sat down beside him and carefully arranged the cloud that enveloped her.

"Mother says that everything went well. Is that true?" she asked.

"Yes," he said. "You needn't worry any more. All the papers have been burned."

"Honestly?"

"Honestly."

"And they won't suspect you of lying?"

"I don't think so."

"I was so afraid all day!" Josette said. "I'm all worn out. Will you take me straight home?"

"All right."

They drove in silence towards Rue Gabriel. Josette put her hand on his sleeve. "Did you burn the papers yourself?"

"Yes."

"Did you look at them?"

"Yes."

"What was in them, anyhow? Certainly no nasty pictures of me," she said in a worried voice. "No one ever took nasty pictures of me."

"I don't know what you call nasty pictures," he said with a half smile. "You were with the German captain and you were very pretty."

She didn't answer. Sitting there beside him was the same Josette he had always known, but beyond her he once more saw the beautiful, too-cheerful girl who was laughing in a picture, indifferent to all misery. From now on, she would always be between them.

He stopped the car and followed Josette to the street door. "I'm not coming up," he said. "I'm tired too, and I have a lot of things to do."

Her eyes were large and frightened. "You're not coming up?"

"No."

"Are you angry?" she said. "The other day you said you weren't, but now you are, aren't you?"

"No, I'm not angry. That boy loved you and you loved him; you were free to do as you pleased." He shrugged his shoulders. "Maybe it's jealousy. I just don't feel like coming up to-night."

" As you like," Josette said.

She smiled at him sadly and unlocked the door. When she disappeared, he stood there for a long moment looking at the little lighted window above the door. Yes, perhaps it was merely jealousy; it would have been unbearable to take her in his arms to-night. " I'm not being fair," he said to himself. But fairness had no part in this; you don't sleep with a woman out of fairness. He drove away.

When Henri invited him to dinner the next day, Lambert was still sullen. " I'm sorry, but I'm busy to-night," he said.

" How about to-morrow?"

" To-morrow, too. As a matter of fact, I'm tied up all this week."

" Well, we'll make it for next week then," Henri said.

It would have been impossible to explain to Lambert why he hadn't asked him out sooner. Nevertheless, a few days later, Henri decided to give it another try: Lambert would certainly be touched by his insistence. He was on his way up to his office, turning over a persuasive little speech in his mind, when he bumped into Sézenac on the stairway.

" Well, well! Where have you been keeping yourself?" he asked amiably. " What are you doing these days?"

" Nothing special," Sézenac replied.

He had put on weight, and he was considerably less good-looking than he used to be.

" How about coming back up for a minute? It's been ages since I last saw you," Henri said.

" Not to-day," Sézenac replied.

He turned away abruptly and went down the stairs. Henri climbed the last few steps. Lambert was leaning against the wall in the hall. He seemed to be waiting for him.

" I just bumped into Sézenac," Henri said. " Did you see him?"

" Yes."

" You see him occasionally, don't you? What's he doing?" Henri asked, opening the door to his office.

" I believe he's a police informer," Lambert replied in a strange voice.

Henri looked at him in surprise; there were beads of sweat on his forehead.

" What gives you that idea?"

"Some things he told me."

"A drug addict who needs money—obviously that's the kind of man they can make an informer of," Henri said. Curious, he asked, "What did he tell you?"

"He offered me a strange kind of deal," Lambert replied. "He promised to tell me who the sons-of-bitches were who killed my father in exchange for certain information."

"What information?"

Lambert looked Henri in the eyes. "Information on you." Henri felt the pit of his stomach contract.

"In what way would I be of any interest to the police?" he asked in a surprised voice.

"You're of interest to Sézenac." Lambert's eyes didn't leave Henri's. "It seems you testified the other day in favour of a certain Mercier, a fellow who did some black-marketing around Lyon and who was chummy with the Belhommes. You claimed he worked in our group in '43 and '44 and that he went with you to La Souterraine on February twenty-third in '44."

"That's right," Henri said. "What of it?"

"You never met Mercier before this past month," Lambert said in a triumphant voice. "Sézenac knows that, and so do I. I followed you around like a shadow that year; there wasn't any Mercier about. Your trip to La Souterraine took place on February twenty-ninth; there was some talk about my going with you, and the date stuck in my mind. Chancel was the one you took."

"You're completely out of your mind!" Henri said. He felt as indignant as if Lambert had suspected him unjustly. "I made two trips to La Souterraine, the first with Mercier which no one knew about but myself." In an irritated voice, he added, "You don't even deserve an answer—because what you're doing is accusing me of false testimony, nothing less!"

"On the twenty-third, you were in Paris," Lambert said. "I've got it all written down in my note-books. I'll check it again, but I know you made only one trip. We talked enough about it! No, don't tell me any stories. The truth is that Mercier has got something or other on the Belhommes, and to save those two collabos you whitewashed a Gestapo informer!"

"I'd knock anyone else's teeth down his throat," Henri

said. "Get out of this office immediately! And don't ever set foot in here again!"

"Wait," Lambert said. "I've one more thing to say to you. I didn't spill anything to Sézenac. And yet I swear to you that I wanted him to talk. I didn't spill anything to him," he repeated. "So now, I feel we're even. I'm taking back my freedom."

"You've been waiting for an excuse for a long time," Henri said. "You ended up by having to invent one. I congratulate you!"

"I didn't invent anything," Lambert said. "Good God!" he added. "What a fool I've been! I always thought you were so honest, so unbiased . . . It frightened me! I thought I had to be loyal to you. Talk about loyalty! You're always passing judgment on everyone, but scruples don't hold you back any more than the next person."

He walked to the door with so much dignity that Henri almost felt like smiling. His anger had subsided, and he was left with only a vague feeling of anguish. Should he try to explain the whole story to him? No, Lambert was too unstable, too easily swayed. To-day, he had refused to give Sézenac any information, but to-morrow an admission could become a dangerous weapon in his hands, in Volange's hands. He had to deny everything; the danger was great enough as it was. "Sézenac is looking for evidence against me; he knows it would bring a good price," Henri thought. Dubreuilh had never heard of Mercier; he might remember that on February 23, 1944, Henri had been in Paris. If Sézenac should take him by surprise, he would have no reason to doctor the truth. "I've got to warn him." But Henri was loath to ask him to become an accomplice before he had even tried to make up with him. Besides, he couldn't imagine himself confessing the truth to him. It was strange; he was saying to himself, "If I had to do it over again, I'd do it again." And yet, he couldn't stand the thought of someone else knowing what he had done: he would have been ashamed of it then. He would feel justified only as long as he wasn't found out. And how long would that be? "I'm in danger," he said to himself. Someone else was, too: Vincent. Even if it wasn't his gang who had executed the old man, Sézenac certainly must have had a lot of other things on him. He had to warn him. And he had to go immediately to see Luc, who was home nursing an attack of the gout, and draft a letter of resignation with him. Luc had long been expecting a crisis; he probably wouldn't take it too hard. Henri got up. "I won't sit down at this desk again," he thought. "It's all over; *L'Espoir* isn't mine any more!" He was sorry about having to give up the campaign he had just started on the Madagascan situation; of course, the others would quickly bury it. But apart from that, he was far less moved than he would have thought possible. Going down the stairs, he said to himself vaguely, "It's the price you have to pay." The price for what? Sleeping with Josette? Wanting to save her? Trying to hold on to a private life when political action requires a man's whole being? Insisting on engaging in politics when he didn't give himself to it without reservations? He didn't know. And even if he had known, it wouldn't have changed anything.

The night the presses were printing his letter of resignation, Henri instructed the desk clerk in his hotel: "Tomorrow I'm not in to anyone. No visitors, no phone calls." Cheerlessly, he opened the door to his room. He hadn't slept with Josette again; she didn't seem to be too upset about it, and that was good. Nevertheless that didn't keep that bed in which Henri slept alone from seeming as austere to him as a hospital cot. It's wonderful to blend one's sleep with the sleep of another body, a warm and trusting body. You wake up feeling nourished. Now when he woke up, he felt empty. He had trouble falling asleep. He was worn out in advance by all the comments his resignation was going to stir up.

He got up late and had just finished dressing when a messenger brought him a special delivery. His heart leaped when he recognised Dubreuilh's handwriting. "I just read your farewell letter to *L'Espoir*. It's really absurd that our attitude accentuates only our differences when so many things draw us together. As for me, I'm still your friend." There was a postscript. "I'd like to speak to you as soon as possible regarding someone who seems to wish you ill." Henri stared at those blue-black lines for a long time. He had thought of writing to him—and it was Dubreuilh who had written. You could impute his generosity to pride, but that was because pride with him was a generous virtue. " I'll go see him straight away," Henri said to himself and he felt as if an army of red ants had been let loose inside his breast. What had Sézenac said? If he had raised suspicions in Dubreuilh, how would he be able to lie with enough conviction to still them? Since Dubreuilh was offering him his friendship, it was, no doubt, still not too late for lying. But how abominable it would be to reply to such an offer with an abuse of confidence! And yet, what else was there to do? Even Dubreuilh would be shocked by an admission, and then Henri would feel at fault. He got into his car. Now, for the first time, harbouring a secret weighed heavily upon him. It requires you either to deceive someone else or betray yourself ; friendship becomes almost impossible. He hesitated for a long time in front of Dubreuilh's door before he could make up his mind to ring.

Dubreuilh opened the door, smiling.

" I'm so glad to see you! " he said in a natural, business-like voice, as if they had important things to discuss after a brief absence.

" I'm the one who's glad," Henri said. " When I got your note, it made me feel wonderful." They went into the study, and he added, " I've often thought about writing to you."

Dubreuilh interrupted him. " What happened? " he asked. " Did Lambert run out on you? "

The same old curiosity was shining in his eyes, those eager, crafty eyes which hadn't changed.

" Samazelle and Trarieux have been wanting to go over to the Gaullists for months," Henri replied. " Lambert ended up by going along with them."

" The little bastard! " Dubreuilh said.

" He has his reasons," Henri said, embarrassed. He sat down in his old chair and lit a cigarette, the way he used to. He had to keep Lambert's real reasons to himself. Dubreuilh hadn't changed, nor had the study, nor the ritual, but he was no longer the same. There was a time when they could have skinned him, dissected him, without uncovering any surprises. But now he was hiding a shameful tumour inside his body. Quickly, he said, " We had an argument and I pushed him too far."

" It was bound to end up like that," Dubreuilh said. He laughed. " Well, it looks as if the circle is closed. The

S.R.L. is dead and they've stolen your paper from you. We're right back to nothing again."

"And it's my fault," Henri said.

"It's no one's fault," Dubreuilh said sharply. He opened a cabinet. "I have some very good armagnac. Would you like some?"

"With pleasure."

Dubreuilh filled two little glasses and handed one to Henri. They smiled at each other.

"Is Anne still in America?" Henri asked.

"She'll be back in two weeks. How happy she's going to be!" Dubreuilh added cheerfully. "She thought it was so silly, our not seeing each other."

"It *was* very silly," Henri said.

He wanted to make a clean breast of things; he felt that the break would never be really healed unless they discussed it freely. And he was quite ready to admit that he had been wrong. But once more, Dubreuilh changed the subject.

"I hear that Paula is cured. Is she really?"

"It seems so. She doesn't want to see me any more, and I'd just as soon have it that way. She's going to move in with Claudie de Belzunce."

"All in all, then, you're as free as the air now!" Dubreuilh said. "What are you planning to do?"

"I'm going to finish my novel. After that, I don't know. Everything's happened so fast, I'm still dizzy."

"Doesn't it make you happy to think you're finally going to have some time to yourself?"

Henri shrugged his shoulders. "Not especially. Oh, no doubt it'll come, but for the moment what I feel most is remorse."

"But what in the world for?" Dubreuilh said.

"No matter what you say to the contrary, I'm the one who's responsible for everything that happened," Henri said. "If I hadn't been so stubborn, you would have bought Lambert's interest, *L'Espoir* would now belong to us, and the S.R.L. would have held out."

"The S.R.L. was lost in any event," Dubreuilh said. "*L'Espoir*, yes, we might have saved it. And then what? Oppose both blocs? Remain independent? That's what I'm trying to do in *Vigilance*, but I really don't see what good it's doing."

Henri looked at Dubreuilh with astonishment. Was he hastening to absolve Henri out of kindness? Or did he want to avoid having his own conduct questioned?

" You think that even in October the S.R.L. didn't have a chance?" Henri asked.

" I think it never had a chance," Dubreuilh said sharply.

No, he wouldn't be speaking like that out of tactfulness; he was convinced, and Henri felt baffled. He would have liked to tell himself that he bore no responsibility for the S.R.L.'s failure, and yet Dubreuilh's admission made him feel ill at ease. In his book, Dubreuilh pointed out the impotence of French intellectuals, but Henri hadn't imagined that he gave retrospective significance to his conclusions.

" When did you first start thinking that?" he asked.

" A long time ago." Dubreuilh shrugged his shoulders. " The game was between Russia and the United States from the start. We were completely out of it."

" Nevertheless, what you used to say still doesn't seem so false to me," Henri said. " That is, that Europe—and France in Europe—had a definite part to play."

" It was false; we were trapped. After all," Dubreuilh added in an impatient voice, " let's face it. What weight did we carry? None at all."

He was very definitely still the same. He would impetuously force you to follow him and then, suddenly, would leave you standing there and set out in a new direction. Henri had often said to himself, " There's nothing one can do." But it disturbed him to hear Dubreuilh express the same thought with so much authority.

" We were always aware that we were only a minority," Henri said, " but you maintained that a minority could do effective work."

" In certain cases, but not in that one," Dubreuilh replied. He began speaking very rapidly. Obviously many things had been weighing heavily on him for a long time. " For the Resistance, fine! A handful of men was enough; all we wanted, after all, was to stir up trouble. Stirring up trouble, sabotage, resisting—that's the job of a minority. But when you set out to build, that's an entirely different story. We thought all we had to do was take advantage of the running start we had got while actually there was a radical difference between the Occupation period and the one that followed the liberation. It was up to us to see that there was no collaboration; what came afterwards was no longer our concern."

"Nevertheless, it did concern us a little," Henri said. He could see clearly why Dubreuilh was claiming the opposite: the old man didn't want to think he had had possibilities of action and hadn't exploited them properly. He preferred to accuse himself of a mistake in judgment rather than admit to a defeat. But Henri remained convinced that in '45 the future was still open; it wasn't just for the fun of it that he had involved himself in politics; he had felt, with evidence to support him, that what was going on around him did in fact concern him. "We failed to achieve our goal," he said. "That doesn't prove we were wrong to try."

"Oh, we never did anyone any harm," Dubreuilh said. "And you're better off going in for politics than getting drunk; it's rather less harmful to the health. But nevertheles, we were on the wrong track. When you reread what we wrote in '44 and '45, it makes you feel like laughing. Try it and you'll see!"

"I suppose we were too optimistic," Henri said. "That's understandable."

"I'll grant us all the extenuating circumstances you want," Dubreuilh said. "The success of the Resistance, the joy of the liberation—to a very great extent, they excuse us. Righteousness was triumphing. The future was promised to men of good will. With our old bedrock of idealism, all we wanted to do was to believe that." He shrugged his shoulders. "We were children."

Henri was silent. He was attached to that past. He was attached to it precisely as one is attached to childhood memories. Yes, they were like one's childhood, those days when you could distinguish unhesitatingly between friends and enemies, good and evil, those days when life was as simple as a painting book. His very unwillingness to reject it all proved that Dubreuilh was right.

"According to you, then, what should we have done?" he asked. "Join the Communist Party?" he added with a smile.

"No," Dubreuilh replied. "As you were saying to me one day, you can't keep yourself from thinking what you think; it's impossible to escape yourself. We would have been very bad Communists." Brusquely, he added, "Besides, what have they accomplished? Nothing at all. They, too, were trapped."

"What then?"

"Nothing. There was nothing we could do."

Henri refilled his glass. Perhaps Dubreuilh was right; but if that was the case, then it was all one big joke. Henri recalled that spring day when he was nostalgically watching the fisherman. He had said to Nadine, "I don't have the time." He never had any time; there were too many things to do. And actually he had had nothing to do.

"Too bad we didn't realise it sooner. We would have avoided a lot of trouble."

"We couldn't have realised it sooner!" Dubreuilh said. "Admitting that you belong to a fifth-rate nation and to an outmoded era isn't something you can do overnight." He shook his head. "It takes a lot of practice to resign yourself to impotence."

Henri looked at Dubreuilh admiringly. Hey presto! Now you see it, now you don't! There had never been any defeat, only a mistake. And the mistake itself was justified, therefore obliterated. The past was as clean as a cuttlebone, and Dubreuilh a spotless victim of historical necessity. Yes? Well, Henri didn't find that at all satisfying! He didn't like to think that he had been taken in by that affair from beginning to end. He had had great struggles of conscience, he had had doubts and enthusiasms, and, according to Dubreuilh, the cards had always been stacked. He often asked himself who he was, and this was the answer he now got: he was a French intellectual made drunk by the victory of '44 and brought back by events to the clear awareness of his own uselessness.

"You've become damned fatalistic!" he said.

"No, I don't say that action in general is impossible. It is just now, for us."

"I read your book," Henri said. "All in all, you think it's possible to do something only by going along unconditionally with the Communists."

"Yes. It isn't that their position is striking, but the fact is that, besides them, there's nothing."

"And yet you're not going along with them."

"I can't remake myself," Dubreuilh said. "Their revolution is too unlike the one I used to hope for. I was wrong;

unfortunately, you can't suddenly become someone else simply by realising your errors. You're young; you still might be capable of making the leap. Not I."

"Oh, as for me, I stopped wanting to get mixed up in things a long time ago," Henri said. "I'd like to retire to the country, or even get the hell out of France entirely—and write." He smiled. "According to you, we aren't even entitled to write any more."

Dubreuilh returned his smile. "Maybe I exaggerated a little. After all, literature isn't as dangerous as all that."

"But you feel it no longer has any meaning."

"You think it has?" Dubreuilh asked.

"Yes, since I'm still writing."

"That's no reason."

Henri looked at Dubreuilh suspiciously. "Are *you* still writing, or have you stopped?"

"Obsessions have never been cured by proving they're senseless," Dubreuilh replied. "Otherwise, the lunatic asylums would be empty."

"Ah, good!" Henri said. "You haven't even been able to convince yourself. That's a little better!"

"I may succeed one day," Dubreuilh said impishly. He changed the subject deliberately. "Listen, I wanted to warn you. I had a strange visitor yesterday. Young Sézenac. I don't know what you ever did to him, but he certainly does not wish you well."

"I fired him from *L'Espoir*. But that was a long time ago," Henri said.

"He began by asking me a lot of questions without head or tail," Dubreuilh said. "If I knew a certain Mercier, if you were in Paris I don't remember what day in '44. First of all, I don't remember anything, and secondly, what business was it of his? I told him off rather sharply, and then he began making up a completely incredible story."

"About me?"

"Yes. He's a pathological liar, that young fellow; he could be dangerous. He told me that you gave false testimony to whitewash a Gestapo informer, that you were being black-mailed through the young Belhomme. He's got to be stopped from spreading such stories."

Henri was relieved to realise from Dubreuilh's tone that he hadn't for one moment believed that Sézenac was telling the truth. All he had to do was smilingly to toss off a non-chalant sentence and the incident would be closed. He was unable to find that sentence.

Dubreuilh looked at him inquisitively. "Did you know he hated you that much?"

"He doesn't really hate me," Henri replied. Abruptly he added, "the fact is, his story is true."

"Oh? It's true?" said Dubreuilh.

"Yes," Henri replied. Suddenly he was humiliated by the thought of lying. After all, since he was able to adjust himself to the truth, the others didn't have to be so damned fastidious; what was good enough for him was good enough for them as well. He continued, a bit defiantly, "I gave false testimony to save Josette, who had slept with a German. You often used to reproach me for my uncompromising morality; I'm making progress, you see," he added.

"Then that Mercier fellow was really an informer?" Dubreuilh asked.

"Yes. He thoroughly deserved to be shot," Henri replied. He looked Dubreuilh in the face. "You think I did something abominable? I didn't want Josette's life to be completely ruined. If she had turned on the gas, I would never have been able to forgive myself. While one Mercier more or less on earth doesn't make me lose any sleep."

Dubreuilh hesitated. "All the same, one less is better than one more," he said.

"Yes, of course," Henri said. "But I'm certain Josette would have done away with herself. Could I let her die?" he asked vehemently.

"No," Dubreuilh said. He seemed perplexed. "You must have had a difficult moment!"

"I made up my mind almost immediately," Henri said. He shrugged his shoulders. "I don't say I'm proud of what I did."

"Do you know what it proves, this story?" Dubreuilh said with sudden animation. "That personal morality just doesn't exist. Another one of those things we used to believe in and which have no meaning."

"You think so?" Henri said. He very definitely didn't care for the kind of consolation Dubreuilh was dispensing to-day. "True, I found myself trapped," he went on. "At that particular moment, I no longer had any choice. But nothing would have happened if I hadn't had that affair with Josette. I suppose that's where the fault lies."

" Oh, you can't deny yourself everything," Dubreuilh said with a kind of impatience. " Asceticism is all right if it's spontaneous, but for that you've got to have positive satisfactions elsewhere. And in the world of to-day, there aren't many. Let me tell you something. If you hadn't slept with Josette, you would have had regrets about it, regrets which would have led you to some other foolishness."

" That's quite possible," Henri said.

" You can't draw a straight line in a curved space," Dubreuilh said. " You can't lead a proper life in a society which isn't proper. Whichever way you turn, you're always caught. Still another illusion that has to be got rid of," he concluded. " No personal salvation possible."

Henri looked at Dubreuilh uncertainly. " Then what's left to us?"

" Not very much, I'm afraid," Dubreuilh replied.

There was a silence. Henri didn't feel satisfied with that generalised indulgence. " What I'd like to know is what you would have done in my place," he said.

" I can't tell you, because I wasn't in your place," Dubreuilh replied. " You'd have to tell me everything in detail," he added.

" I'll tell you everything," Henri said.

CHAPTER TEN

THE PLANE flew nonstop from Gander to Paris and arrived two hours early. I left my baggage at the Gare des Invalides and took a bus. It was a grey, lonely morning; the city was still asleep, and my unannounced arrival, when they believed me still far off in the clouds, bordered upon indiscretion. A man was sweeping the pavement in front of the still tightly closed street door, and the garbage cans hadn't yet been emptied. I was arriving before the scene was set and the actors made up. Of course, you aren't an intruder when you return to your own life, and yet, as I opened and closed the door to the flat, softly in order not to awaken Nadine, my furtive movements gave me a vague feeling of being at once at fault and in danger. No sound from Robert's study. I turned the porcelain door knob and, almost immediately, he lifted his head, and smiled, pushed back his chair, and put his arm around me.

" Poor little creature! Coming home all alone like this! I was going to meet you."

" The plane was two hours early," I said, kissing his bristly, unshaven cheeks. He was wearing a bathrobe; his eyes were swollen from sleeplessness. " You've been working all night, haven't you? That's not good."

" I wanted to finish something before you got back. Did you have a good trip? You aren't tired?"

" I slept the whole time. And you? When no one's here to watch over you, you just don't know how to take care of yourself."

We had talked to each other gaily, but when Robert went into the bathroom I once more experienced that silence which had choked me up when, on opening the door, I had seen him writing, head lowered, far away from me. How full that study was—that room in which there was no place for me! The air was saturated with smoke and work; an all-embracing mind summoned together here at will the past, the future, the whole world. Everything was here, nothing was missing. On top of a bookcase, a picture of me was smiling, an old photograph which would never grow

older. That was in its place. But to make room for me in
his overcrowded days Robert had had to work all night.
And there was something he hadn't finished because I had
returned too soon. I got up. I know that on home-coming
days, on the days when you leave, you make discoveries that
are no truer than everyday truths. But even though you
know, even though you have spotted all the traps, you nevertheless fall stupidly into them. And recognising that fact
didn't help me to get out of them. I couldn't get out of
them. How empty my room was! And while I wandered
uncertainly between the window and the couch, it remained
just as empty. There was a pile of mail on my desk ; people
were asking me when I would reopen my office ; Paula had
got out of the hospital and invited me to pay her a visit. I
noticed that her handwriting was less childish than before
and that she no longer misspelled words. A note from
Mardrus assured me she was cured. I went to give Nadine a
kiss, and she greeted me with forbearance ; she had a thousand things to tell me and I promised her my evening. Robert,
Nadine, friends, work—and yet I stood motionless in the
hall, asking myself in bewilderment, "What am I doing
here?"

"Were you waiting for me?" Robert asked. "I'm ready."

I was glad to leave that flat, to walk through streets that
were neither teeming nor empty—the quays, Avenue des
Gobelins, Place d'Italie. We walked for a long time,
stopping here and there in an out-door café, and we had lunch
in the restaurant in the Parc Montsouris.

Robert sensed that I didn't feel much like talking, and he
had a lot of things to tell me. He told them to me. He was
much more cheerful than before my departure ; it wasn't
that the international situation seemed more hopeful to him,
but he had recaptured a taste for his life. He was very
happy about his reconciliation with Henri, and his book had
created such a stir that, against all logic, he had started
another one. Political action remained impossible, but he
very definitely hadn't given up thinking ; in fact, he felt that
he was only just beginning now to see things a little clearly.
I listened to him. And he was so forcefully alive that he
imposed on me the past of which he was speaking. It was
my past ; I had no other, nor any other future than the one
he proclaimed. Soon, I would see Henri again and I, too,

would be very happy; soon I, too, would read those letters Robert had received about his book, and they would amuse me or move me as they had him. And soon I would be as delighted as he was to leave for Italy.

"Are you sure you don't mind making another trip after so much travelling?" he asked.

"Not at all. I have absolutely no desire to stay in Paris."

I looked out at the lawns, the lakes, the swans. One day, soon no doubt, I would once again like Paris, would have my troubles, pleasures, preferences; my life would emerge from the fog, my real life, my Old-World life, and I would be taken up with it completely. Suddenly, I began to speak, for I had to confirm the reality of that other world as well, that world from which I was separated by an ocean, by a single night. I talked about my last week there. But it was even worse than remaining silent; as in the previous years, I felt guilty, horribly guilty. Robert understood everything—only too well. There, Lewis was awakening in a room destroyed by my absence; he was silent, he no longer had anyone. He was alone, and in his bed, in his arms, my place was empty. Nothing would ever make up for the desolation of that morning; the pain I was inflicting on him couldn't be expiated.

When we returned home that evening, Nadine told me, "Paula rang up to find out if you'd got back."

"That's the third time she's called," Robert said. "You ought to go see her."

"I'll go to-morrow. Mardrus claims she's cured," I added, "but do you know how she is really? Has Henri seen her again?"

"No," Nadine replied.

"Mardrus wouldn't have let her out if she weren't really cured," Robert said.

"There are cures and cures," I said.

Before going to bed, I had a long talk with Nadine. She was going out with Henri again and she was very pleased about it. She bombarded me with questions. The next day, I telephoned Paula to let her know I was coming; her voice was crisp and calm. It was about ten o'clock at night when I turned into that street which had seemed so tragic to me the past winter, and I was upset by its reassuring look. The windows were open to the mildness of the evening, people

were calling to each other from house to house, a little girl
was skipping with a rope. Under the sign "Furnished Rooms
To Let" I rang Paula's bell, and the door opened, normally.
Too normally. Of what use were all those frenzies, those
distortions, if everything had returned to its place, if reason
and routine had triumphed? Of what use was my impassioned remorse if it was ordained that I would one day awake
in indifference? I was almost hoping to see a hostile and
haggard Paula appear in the doorway of her apartment.

But I was greeted by a plump, smiling woman wearing an
elegant black dress. She returned my kiss neither warmly nor
coldly; the room was in perfect order, the mirrors had been
replaced, and for the first time in years the windows were
wide open.

"How are you? Did you have a nice trip? Your blouse
is lovely, did you buy it there?"

"Yes, in Mexico. You'd like that country." I put a
package in her arms. "Here! I brought you back some
material."

"How nice of you!" She broke the string and opened
the package. "What marvellous colours!"

While she was unpacking the embroidered fabrics, I went
over to the window. As always, one saw Notre Dame and its
gardens, the stubborn weight of stones visible through a silk-
like curtain of yellowing skeletal leaves. Along the river, the
bookstalls were padlocked, Arab music was drifting up from
the café across the street, a dog was barking and Paula was
cured. It was an evening out of the distant past; I had
never met Lewis and I couldn't miss him.

"You must tell me about the places you visited," Paula
said. "You must tell me everything else. But let's not stay
here. I'll take you to a very amusing club—L'Ange Noir. It
just opened and you see everybody there."

"Who's everybody?" I asked, a little apprehensively.

"Oh, everybody," Paula repeated. "It isn't far; we'll walk
there."

"All right."

"You see," Paula said as we were going down the stairs,
"six months ago, I would have asked myself immediately,
'What made her say: Who's everybody?' And I would
have found a lot of answers."

I smiled, with a big effort. "Are you sorry things have changed?"

"That would be saying a little too much. But you can't imagine how rich the world was in those days. The least little thing had a thousand facets. I would have questioned myself about the red in your skirt; that tramp over there I would have taken for a dozen people all at once." There was a sort of nostalgia in her voice.

"And now the world seems rather flat to you?"

"Oh, not at all!" she replied firmly. "I'm glad to have that experience behind me, that's all. But I can assure you that my life isn't going to be flat; I'm crawling with plans."

"Tell me about them."

"First of all, I'm going to get out of that flat; I'm tired of it. Claudie's suggested that I move in with her, and I've accepted. And I've decided to become famous," she said. "I want to go out, travel, meet people; I want love and glory. I want to live." She declaimed those last words in a solemn voice, as if she were taking a vow.

"Are you thinking of singing or writing?" I asked.

"Writing. But not the kind of nonsense I once showed you. A real book, in which I'll tell about myself. I've already given it a lot of thought; there won't be anything amusing about it, but I believe it'll create quite a sensation."

"Yes," I said, "you have a wealth of things to say. You should say them."

I had spoken warmly, but I was sceptical. Paula was cured—there was no doubt about that—but her voice, her gestures, her expressions, made me feel as uncomfortable as did those false young faces that had been fashioned by the surgeon's knife out of old flesh. She would probably play the part of a normal woman until the day she died, and it was a performance that made it difficult for her to be sincere.

"This is it," Paula said.

We went down into a cellar as hot and as damp as the jungles of Chichen Itza. It was full of noise, of smoke, and of boys and girls in dungarees who weren't our age. Paula chose a table near the orchestra, a table in full view of everybody, and authoritatively ordered two double Scotches. She didn't seem to sense that we were completely out of place there.

"I don't want to begin singing again," she said. "Not that I have an inferiority complex—physically, if I don't hold quite the same trumps as I used to, I know I have others—only in a singing career you've got to depend on too many people." She looked at me cheerfully. "On that point, you were right: depending upon others is disgraceful. What I want is to do something vigorous."

I nodded my head. In my opinion, she no longer had any of the qualities necessary to captivate an audience; she was better off attempting almost anything else.

"Are you planning on fictionalising your story or telling it as it is?" I asked.

"At the moment, I'm looking for a form," she replied. "A new form—something Henri, as a matter of fact, never succeeded in inventing. His novels are all tediously classical." She emptied her glass in a single gulp. "It wasn't easy, what I went through, but if you only knew how happy I am to have finally found myself!"

I wished I could have said something affectionate to her: that I was glad to see her happy; that . . . But the words froze on my lips.

It was that wilful voice and that rigid face which chilled me; Paula seemed to me more a stranger now than when she was mad. Uneasily, I said, "You must have gone through some pretty bad moments."

"Yes, indeed!" she said. She looked around her wonderingly. "There were days when everything seemed so funny to me I almost died laughing! And other days were pure horror; they had to put me in a strait jacket."

"Did they give you any shock treatments?"

"Yes. I was in such a strange state of mind that at the time I wasn't even afraid. But the other night, I dreamt someone had fired a pistol into my temple and I felt an intolerable pain. Mardrus told me it was probably an unconscious memory."

"Mardrus is good, isn't he?" I said uncertainly.

"Mardrus? He's wonderful!" Paula said fervently. "It's extraordinary with what certainty he found the key to the whole story! I must say, though, that I didn't offer much resistance," she added.

"Is the analysis over?"

"Not completely, but the main part is done."

I didn't dare question her, but she needed no prompting.
"I never told you about my brother, did I?" she asked.

"Never. I didn't know you had a brother."

"He died when he was fifteen months old; I was four. It's easy to understand why my love for Henri immediately took on a pathological character."

"Henri was also two or three years younger than you," I said.

"Exactly. When my brother died, my childish jealousy gave rise to a feeling of guilt, which explains my masochism in connection with Henri. I made myself a slave to that man; I agreed to give up all personal success for him; I chose obscurity, dependence. Why? To redeem myself; so that through him my dead brother would eventually consent to absolve me." She began to laugh. "To think that I made a hero of that man! A saint! Sometimes it makes me burst out laughing just to think of it!"

"Have you seen him again?" I asked.

"Oh, no! And I won't see him again," she said spiritedly. "He took unfair advantage of the situation."

I kept silent. I was quite familiar with the kind of explanations Mardrus had used; on occasion, I myself made use of similar ones, and I valued them for what they were worth. Yes, to release Paula it was necessary to reach back into the past in order to destroy her love. But I thought of those microbes which can't be exterminated except by destroying the organism they are devouring; Henri was dead for Paula, but she, too, was dead. I didn't know that fat woman with the sweaty face and the bovine eyes who was swilling Scotch beside me.

She stared at me. "And you?" she asked.

"Me?"

"What did you do in America?"

I hesitated. "I don't know if you remember," I said, "but I told you I had an affair there last year."

"I remember. With an American writer. Did you see him again?"

"I spent all three months with him."

"Do you love him?"

"Yes."

"What are you going to do?"

"Go back and see him next summer."

" And then what?"

I shrugged my shoulders. What right did she have to ask me those questions, the answer to which I was hoping so desperately to ignore? She leaned her chin on her fist and looked at me even more insistently.

" Why don't you rebuild your life with him?"

" I have no desire to rebuild my life," I replied.

" And yet you love him, don't you?"

" Yes, but my life is here."

" Only because you think it is," Paula said. " There's nothing to stop you from starting a new one somewhere else."

" You know very well what Robert means to me," I said somewhat ungraciously.

" I know you imagine you can't do without him," Paula said. " But what I don't know is where that hold he has on you comes from. And neither do you know." She continued to scrutinise me. " Have you ever thought of getting yourself analysed again?"

" No."

" Are you afraid?"

I shrugged my shoulders. " Not at all. But what for?"

Of course, I might have learned a lot of little things about myself from an analysis, but I couldn't see where that would have helped me. And if it had begun to go any further than that, I would have rebelled; my feelings aren't illnesses.

" You have a lot of complexes," Paula said meditatively.

" Maybe, but as long as they don't bother me . . ."

" You'd never admit they bother you. That's precisely a part of your complexes. Your dependence upon Robert certainly stems from a complex. I'm sure an analysis would free you."

I laughed. " But why do you want me to leave Robert?"

The waiter placed two more Scotches in front of us ; Paula gulped half of hers down immediately.

" There's nothing more injurious than living in the shadow of someone else's glory," she said. " One wastes away. You, too, have got to find yourself. Drink up," she said abruptly, pointing to my glass.

" Don't you think we're drinking too much?" I asked.

" Why too much?" she said.

Why, indeed? I, too, enjoy the turbulence that alcohol

unleashes in my blood. A body fits so snugly, it's so tight, that at times you feel like splitting the seams. They never split, but there are moments when you feel almost as if you were about to jump out of your skin. I drank along with Paula.

"No man deserves the adoration they demand of us," she said firmly. "Not one! You're being taken in, too. Give Robert some paper and the time to write, and he'll have everything he wants."

She was speaking very loudly to make herself heard above the blare of the orchestra, and it seemed to me that surprised faces were turning in our direction. Fortunately, almost everyone was dancing, lost in a frozen frenzy.

Irritably, I murmured, "It isn't because I feel it's my duty that I'm staying with Robert."

"If it's only habit, then that isn't any better," she said. "We're far too young for resignation!" Her voice grew excited, and her eyes clouded over. "I'm going to get my revenge. You can't imagine how happy I feel!"

Tears streaked down her perspiring face; she ignored them. Perhaps she had shed so many that her skin had become insensitive to them. I felt like weeping with her over that love which for ten years had been the meaning and the pride of her life and which had now become a shameful sore. I took a sip of the Scotch and squeezed the glass in my hand, as if it were a talisman. "I'd rather die of suffering," I said to myself, "than ever sneeringly scatter the ashes of my past to the winds."

I slammed my glass down on the saucer. "I, too, will end up that way!" I thought. "You sneer, more or less, but you always end up like that; the whole past can never be presented intact. I want to remain faithful to Robert; so one day my memories will betray Lewis. Absence will kill me in his heart, and I will bury him in the depths of my memory." Paula was still speaking, and I was no longer listening to her at all. "Why should it be Lewis whom I have doomed?" "No," I had said to him, and at the time no other answer seemed possible to me. But why? "Give Robert some paper, some time, and he'll have everything he wants," Paula had said. I saw the study again, that study which was so full without me. There were times, like last year, when I wanted to feel important, but even then I knew that in all things that counted for Robert I was of no help whatsoever to him. Faced with his real problems, he was always alone. Over there there was a man who was hungry for me; I had my place in his arms, my place which remained empty. Why? I was very strongly attached to Robert, I would have given my life for him, but he never asked me for it; in fact, he had never really asked me for anything; the joy his presence brought me involved only myself. Staying with him or leaving him—my decision involved only myself. I emptied my glass. Settle down in Chicago? come to Paris from time to time?—it wasn't, after all, so very impossible. Robert would look up at me and smile each time I arrived, as if we had never been separated; he would barely notice that I no longer breathed the same air he did. What taste would my life have without him? That was difficult to imagine. But I knew only too well the taste of my days to come should I spend them here: a taste of remorse and irrationality, an utterly intolerable taste.

I got home very late. I had drunk a great deal. I slept badly. While we were having breakfast, Robert examined me sternly.

" You look terrible."

" I didn't sleep well. And I had too much to drink."

He came behind my chair and put his hands on my shoulders. " Are you sorry to be back?'

" I don't know," I answered. " There are moments when it seems absurd for me not to be there, where someone needs me—a real need, like no one before has ever had for me. And I'm not there."

" Do you think you could live in America, so far from everything? Do you think you'd be happy?"

" If you didn't exist, I would try it," I replied. " I know I'd try it."

Robert removed his hands from my shoulders, took a few steps, and looked at me perplexedly. " You'd have no profession, no friends; you'd be surrounded by people who share none of your interests, who don't even speak the same language as you; you'd be cut off from your whole past and everything that counts for you . . . I don't believe you'd hold out very long."

" Maybe not," I said.

Yes, my life with Lewis would have been quite cramped.

A foreigner, an outsider, I would have been able neither to make a life for myself nor to blend into the life of that huge country which would never be mine. I would have been only a woman in love clinging to the man she loved. I didn't feel myself capable of living solely for love. But how weary I was of taking up each morning the empty, ponderous weight of yet another day in which I was needed by no one! Robert hadn't answered me by saying that he needed me. Never had he said that to me. Only, previously the question never arose; my life was neither necessary nor gratuitous; it was simply my life. But now, Lewis had questioned me: "Why not stay with me, always? Why not?" And I, who had promised never to disappoint him, had answered, "No." That no had to be justified—and I could find no justification. His voice pursued me: "Why not? Why not?" Suddenly, I thought, "But nothing is irreparable!" Lewis was still alive, and so was I; we could always speak across the ocean. He had promised to write me first, in a week. If he still called to me in his letter, if his expressions of regret had the sound of a call. I would find the strength to give up my old security; I would answer, "Yes, I'll come, I'll come to stay with you as long as you want to keep me."

Robert and I laid out our trip. I figured carefully and sent Lewis a cable telling him to address his letter "General Delivery, Amalfi, Italy." For twelve days my destiny would be hanging in suspense; in twelve days I might decide to take a mad chance on an unknown future, or else I would settle down again in absence, in waiting. For the moment, I was neither here nor there, neither myself nor another, nothing but a machine for killing time, time which usually dies so quickly, but whose agonies now seemed endless. We took a plane, buses, boats; once again I saw Naples, Capri, Pompeii; we discovered Herculaneum, Ischia. I followed Robert; he interested me in the things that interested him; I remembered his memories. But as soon as he left me alone, I was completely lethargic. I made hardly any attempt to read, or even to look at whatever happened to be surrounding me. At times, I would relive, with schizophrenic precision, my arrival in Chicago, that night in Chichicastenango, our farewell. Mostly, I slept; never have I slept so much.

Robert liked Ischia; we prolonged our stay there and arrived in Amalfi three days later than planned. "At least I

don't have to worry," I said to myself, stepping out of the
bus. " The letter is here." I left Robert and our suitcases in
the middle of the square and walked towards the post office,
trying to keep myself from running. Like all post offices,
this one smelled of dust, glue, and boredom; it was neither
dark nor light, the employees hardly stirred in their cages.
It was really one of those places where the same gestures
are repeated all day long, the same days all year long, without anything ever happening; it seemed preposterous that
my heart could beat so violently while I stood in line at one
of the windows. A young woman tore open an envelope, and
a broad smile lit up her face. It gave me courage. With an
engaging air, I showed the clerk my passport; he disdained
the pigeonholes lined up behind him, took a bundle of letters
from a closet, thumbed through them, and handed me an
envelope. A letter from Nadine.

" There's another one," I said.

" Nothing more."

Nadine's letter proved that the mails were functioning, that
letters arrived when they were sent.

" I know that there's another one," I insisted.

With a pleasant Italian smile, he placed the bundle in
front of me. " Look for yourself."

Denal, Dolincourt, Dellert, Despeux. I went through the
D's a second time and then inspected the bundle from A to
Z. All those letters! Some were weeks old and no one came
to claim them. Why couldn't a deal be made? An exchange?

" What about the pigeonholes?" I asked in desperation.
" Are you sure there's nothing for me under D?"

" All letters for foreigners are in this bundle."

" Take a look, anyhow."

He looked and shook his head. " No, nothing."

I left the post office, stood on the pavement, my arms hung
limp at my sides. What dreadful legerdemain! I was no
longer sure of the ground under my feet, nor of the calendar,
nor even of my own name. Lewis had written and letters
were arriving; therefore, his letter had to be here. It was not
here. It was too soon to cable, " No letter. Worried "; too
soon to burst into tears; it was, after all, merely a normal
delay; I wasn't permitted the refuge of unbounded despair;
I had figured wrong, that's all, and one rarely dies from a

mistake in calculation. And yet, while I dined with Robert on a flowery terrace overhanging the sea, I was certainly not alive. He spoke to me of Nadine who was going out assiduously with Henri; I answered; we drank our wine, on the label a moustachioed gentleman smiled at us; the lights of the fishing boats shimmered on the sea; all around us hung a powerful fragrance of romantic plants; nothing was missing, anywhere, except black marks on a yellow sheet of paper, and they would have been the symbol of an absence; the absence of an absence, which is really nothing, which devours everything.

The letter was there the following day. Lewis wrote from New York. His publishers had given a big party in honour of his book, he was seeing a lot of people, he was enjoying himself very much. Oh, he hadn't forgot me; he was cheerful, he was tender. But it was impossible to decipher the slightest call between his lines. I sat down in an outdoor café facing the post office, by the edge of the sea. Little girls in blue jumpers and round hats were playing on the beach, and I watched them for a long while, my heart empty. For the past two weeks, I had been treating Lewis as a puppet; his face hesitated between reproach and love; he held me against him; he said, " I never loved you as much as now "; he said, "Come back." And he was in New York, with an unknown face, with smiles that weren't directed at me, as real as that man walking by. He didn't ask me to come back. Was he still hoping for my return? That doubt alone was enough to strip me of the strength to want to. I would wait, like the previous year; only, I no longer knew why I had condemned myself to the horrors of waiting.

There were others letters, in Palermo, in Syracuse. Lewis sent me one each week, as before; and, as before, they all ended with that word "Love," which means everything and signifies nothing. Was it still a word of endearment, or the most banal of formulas? Lewis's tenderness had always been so discreet that I didn't know how much I could attribute to his discretion. When I used to read the sentences he created for me, I would rediscover his arms, his mouth. Was it his fault or mine if they no longer aroused me? The Sicilian sun burned my skin, but inside me it was always cold. I would sit out on my balcony or lie down on the sand; I would look at the flaming sky, the sea, and I would shiver,

On certain days, I hated the sea; it was monotonous and infinite, like absence; its waters were so blue that they somehow seemed syrupy. I would close my eyes or I would run away.

When I found myself back in Paris, in my house, with things to do, I thought, "I've got to pull myself together." Pull oneself together the way one salvages a sauce that has turned—it can be done, it's feasible. You step back and, with the knowing eye of a connoisseur, you look at your worries, your troubles. I would sit down beside Robert and we would talk; or I would drink Scotch with Paula and pour out my heart to her. Besides, I was quite capable of studying my lesson, all by myself. Lewis was merely an episode in my existence, an episode to which circumstances had made me attach an exaggerated value. After years of abstinence, I had been hoping for a new love, and I had very deliberately brought this one about. I had magnified it out of all proportion because I knew my life as a woman was drawing to a close. But actually, I could get along very well without it. If Lewis should give me up, I could easily return to my old austerity; or I could seek other lovers—and they all say that when one looks, one finds. My mistake was to take my body so seriously; I needed an analysis that would teach me to be more easy going. Ah, it's difficult to suffer without giving way! Once or twice, I tried to tell myself, "One day this affair will end and I'll be left with a beautiful memory; I might just as well make up my mind to it straight away. "But I rebelled. What a ridiculous farce! To maintain that I alone hold our affair in my hands is to substitute a puppet for Lewis, to transform myself into a ghost and our past into anæmic memories. Our love isn't a story I can pull out of the context of my life in order to tell it to myself. It exists outside of myself; Lewis and I bear it together. Closing one's eyes isn't enough to do away with the sun; disavowing that love is only blinding myself. No, I rejected cautious thinking, and false solitude, and sordid consolations. And I realised immediately that that rejection was still another sham; the truth is I was in no way master of my heart. I was powerless against that anguish which gripped me each time I opened one of Lewis's letters, and my sensible speeches would never fill the emptiness inside of me. I was without recourse.

What a long wait! Eleven months, nine months, and there was still just as much earth and water and uncertainty between us. Autumn replaced summer and, one day in October, Nadine came to me and said, "I have news for you."

There was a disturbing mixture of defiance and confusion in her eyes.

"What is it?"

"I'm pregnant."

"Are you sure?"

"Absolutely. I saw a doctor."

I studied her for a moment. She knew how to protect herself, and there was a sly glimmer in her eyes.

"Did you do it on purpose?" I asked.

"And what if I did?" she said. "Is it a crime to want a baby?"

"Is it Henri's?"

"I suppose so, since he's the one I've been sleeping with," she replied, snickering.

"Does he agree?"

"He doesn't know about it yet."

I persisted. "But did he want a child?"

She hesitated. "I didn't ask him."

There was a silence, and then I asked, "Well, what do you intend to do?"

"What do you expect me to do with a child? Make patties out of it?"

"I mean, do you intend to marry Henri?"

"That's up to him."

"You do know what you want, don't you?"

"What I want is to have a baby. As for the rest, I'm not asking anything of anyone."

Never had Nadine breathed a word to me of that maternal desire. Was it ill will that prompted me to think that she had primarily hoped through that manœuvre to force Henri into marrying her?

"Someone will have to be asked for something," I said. "For a while at least, either your father or Henri will have to support the child."

She began laughing with an air of amused condescension. "Go ahead, give me some advice. I can see you're just dying to."

" You'll hold it against me for a long time."

" Let's hear it, anyhow."

" Don't suggest to Henri that he marries you without being sure he really wants to. I mean, wants to selfishly, for himself, and not just for you and the baby. Otherwise, it would be a disastrous marriage."

" I won't suggest anything at all to him," she said in her sharpest voice. " But who told you he doesn't want to? Naturally, if you ask a man whether he wants a baby, he becomes frightened. But once the baby's there, he's delighted with it. If you ask me, I think it would do Henri a lot of good to be married, to have a home. His kind of artistic bohemianism is out of date." She stopped, out of breath.

" You asked me for advice and I gave you some," I said. " If you sincerely believe that marriage won't be a burden either to Henri or to you, get married."

I had my doubts about whether Nadine could find happiness in a domesticated, married life; it was difficult for me to see her completely absorbed in devoting herself to a husband and a child. And if Henri married her only through a sense of duty, wouldn't he always bear her a grudge for it? I didn't dare question him; it was he who broached the subject first. One evening, instead of going as usual directly to Robert's study, he knocked on the door to my room.

" I'm not disturbing you, am I?"

" Not at all."

He sat down on the couch. " Is this where you do your operating?" he asked with a smile.

" Yes. Would you like to try it?"

" Who knows?" he said. " As a matter of fact, maybe I do need an explanation of why I feel so desperately normal. Suspicious, isn't it?"

" There's nothing more suspicious!" I replied with so much spirit that he looked at me in surprise.

" Then I really must get myself treated," he said cheerfully. " But that isn't what I wanted to talk to you about," he added. He smiled. " I've come, as it were, to ask you for your daughter's hand."

I returned his smile. " Will you make her a good husband?"

" I'll try hard. Do you have any doubts about me?"

I hesitated and then replied frankly, " If you get married only to do right by Nadine, yes, I'd be a little doubtful."

" I understand what you mean," he said. " But you needn't worry. The affair with Paula taught me a lesson. No. First of all, I'm fond of Nadine ; and secondly—this may surprise you—I believe I'm cut out to be a father."

" You do surprise me," I said.

" Nevertheless, it's true. I was surprised by it myself, but when Nadine told me she was pregnant I was really moved. I don't know how to explain it to you. You put so much into writing books that everyone criticises, or plays that shock people. And then, just by giving in to my body, I created a living thing. Not a character on paper, but a real flesh-and-blood child. And so easily . . ."

" I hope I'll hurry up and discover that I'm cut out to be a grandmother," I said. " I imagine you'll get married as soon as possible. But where are you going to live? You'll need an apartment."

" We don't want to stay in Paris," Henri replied. " I'd even like to get out of France entirely for a while. It seems there are places in Italy where you can rent houses for next to nothing."

" And in the meanwhile?"

" You know, we really haven't had too much time to work out our plans."

" You're always welcome to stay with us at St. Martin," I said. " The house is quite big enough."

The idea didn't displease Nadine. She didn't want to live in the cottage, because, I suppose, she still had bad memories of it ; instead, she fixed up two large rooms on the second floor. She gave up her secretarial job and began perusing child-care books and knitting baby clothes the dazzling colours of which happily violated all traditions ; she was having a wonderful time. It was, it seemed, a time of plenty. Henri was congratulating himself on having escaped the torments of political life, and Robert didn't appear to be missing them too much. Paula, too, was delighted with her new life. She was living at the Belzunce town house, where she performed mysterious secretarial functions ; Claudie lent her dresses and took her everywhere. She spoke to me eagerly of her doings, of her lovers, and she wanted to drag me along in the wake of her glory.

"At least get an evening gown for yourself," she said to me. "Don't you feel like dressing up, being seen?"

"Seen by whom?"

"In any case, you do need an afternoon dress. What did you do with that marvellous Indian cloth?"

"I don't know. It must be among my other things."

"We've got to find it."

She began looking in my closet for that princely rag, which at the other end of the world, the other end of time, had protected the shoulders of an old Indian woman.

"Here it is! We can have it made into a really wonderful blouse!"

In a kind of stupor, I touched the cloth with its colours of stained glass and mosaic. One day, in a distant city which smelled of burning incense, a man who loved me had placed it in my arms. How could it have possibly materialised here, to-day? From that old dream to my real life, there was no road. Yet the cape was here. And suddenly, I no longer knew where I, myself, really was: here, a prey to delirious memories? or elsewhere, dreaming I was here, but just about to awake in Lewis's arms, close by an Indian market place?

"Let me take it with me," Paula said. "Claudie will have it done over by a dressmaker, and I'll see to it that it's returned to you before Thursday. You *will* come Thursday, won't you? Promise?"

"I'd much rather not."

"I promised Claudie I'd bring you. I'd like so much to pay her back a little for everything she's doing for me." Paula's voice was as pathetic as when she had pleaded with me to speak to Henri.

"I'll drop in for a moment," I said.

To dress up her Thursday gatherings, Claudie had thought up the idea of financing a literary prize to be awarded by an all-woman jury, over which, of course, she would preside. She had hastened to announce that great event to the world, and although the project was still rather vague she had summoned Paris's smart set as well as a number of reporters to gather at her house the coming Thursday. She would have got along quite well without me, but an imperious note from Paula accompanied the package I received Wednesday evening, a package in which lay, metamorphosed, the old cape. Now, it was cut to my size, was irreproachably in style. And yet, there lingered in it a smell of the lost past, and when I slipped it on I could feel something akin to hope coursing through my veins. With my skin I was touching the proof that there *was* a road between vanished happiness and my present torpor; therefore, there *could* be a return. Freshened by a new coat of make-up, my reflection in the mirror was satisfying. "No, six months from now, I shan't have aged much; I'll see Lewis again and he'll still love me." And when I entered Claudie's salon, I wasn't far from thinking, "After all, I'm still young!"

"I was so afraid you wouldn't come!" Paula said, leading me to a corner of the foyer. "I've got to speak to you," she added, looking worried and important. "I'd like you to do one more thing for me."

"What is it?"

"Claudie has her heart set on your being a member of our jury."

"But I'm not qualified. And I haven't the time."

"You won't have anything to do."

"Then why does she have her heart set on me?" I asked, laughing.

"Well, because of your name," Paula replied.

"Robert's name," I said. "Mine isn't worth very much."

"It's the same name," Paula said hastily. She pushed me into a small deserted sitting-room. "I'm afraid I didn't explain this project too well to you. It isn't just a parlour game, you know."

I sat down, resigned. Since she had been cured, Paula would ramble on endlessly about all manner of inanities. It was distressing to see her take as deep an interest in this idiotic idea as she once did in Henri's destiny. She praised the virtues of the number seven at great length; there *had* to be seven members on this jury. I managed a sudden burst of energy. "No, Paula," I said, "it isn't for me. No."

"Listen," she said with a worried look, "at least tell Claudie you'll think it over."

"If you like, but it's all thought over."

She got up, and her voice became casual as she asked, "Is it true what they're saying—that Henri's going to marry Nadine?"

"It's true."

She began to laugh. "That's really funny!" Her voice

became serious again. " I mean, as far as Henri is concerned it's funny. But I feel sorry for Nadine. You ought to intervene."

" She does what she wants, you know."

" For once, use your authority," Paula said. " He'll destroy her, the way he wanted to destroy me. Of course, for Nadine, Henri is a substitute for Robert," she added dreamily.

" It's quite possible."

" Anyhow, I wash my hands of it," Paula said. She walked to the door. " I shouldn't monopolise you! Come quickly!" she said with a sudden restlessness.

The drawing-room was teeming with people; a small orchestra was spiritlessly playing jazz tunes, a few couples were dancing. Most of the guests were busy drinking and eating. Claudie was dancing with a young poet who was wearing a pair of lavender coloured velvet trousers, a white sweat shirt, and a gold ring in one ear; he was a bit startling, to say the least. There were many young people there—candidates for the new literary prize, no doubt—and all of them affected the manner of embassy attachés. I was glad to see a familiar face—Julien's. He, too, was correctly dressed, and he didn't seem drunk. I smiled at him, and he bowed to me.

" May I invite you to dance?"

" Oh, no!" I said.

" And why not?"

" I'm too old."

" No more so than others," he said, glancing at Claudie.

" No, but almost as old," I said, laughing.

He, too, laughed, but Paula said seriously, " Anne is overflowing with complexes!" She looked at Julien coquettishly. " But I'm not."

" How fortunate you are!" Julien said, moving away.

" Too old!" Paula said to me, sounding annoyed. " What an idea! I've never felt younger."

" One feels the way one feels," I said.

That little spark of youth which had dazzled me for a moment fizzled out all too quickly. Glass mirrors are too indulgent; the faces of these women of my own age, that flabby skin, those blurred features, those drooping mouths, those bodies so obviously bulging under their corsets—these were the true mirrors. "They're old, worn-out hags," I thought, "and I'm the same age as they."

The music stopped, and Claudie pounced on me. "It was nice of you to come. It seems you're very interested in our project. I'd be so happy for you to join us in it."

"I'd love to," I said, "only I have so much work these days."

"So it seems. You're becoming Paris's most fashionable psychoanalyst. Let me introduce you to a few of my protégés."

I was glad, but a little put out, that she wasn't more insistent. Her heart apparently wasn't as set as all that on my participation; Paula had been imagining things. I shook a great many hands—young people, and others less young. They brought me champagne, petits fours; they were eager to please; some of them had a way with compliments; all of them, between smiles, confided some little dream to me— an interview with Robert, an article by him for a new quarterly which was about to appear, an introduction to Mauvanes, a friendly review in *Vigilance,* or even of seeing their name in print. A few, more ingenuous or more cynical, asked me for advice: what must one do to win a prize, and, in a general way, to succeed? It was their belief that I must know all sorts of tricks! I had my doubts about their futures; you can't tell at first sight whether someone has or hasn't any talent, but you can tell quickly enough whether he has real reasons for wanting to be a writer. All these salon-haunters wrote only because it's difficult to do otherwise when you're bent on leading a literary life. But none of them really enjoyed the tête-à-tête with blank paper; they wanted success in its most abstract form, and, after all, that isn't the best way of achieving it. I found them as disagreeable as their ambition. One of them practically said to me, "I'm prepared to pay." There were many whom Claudie made pay—in kind. She was beaming as she talked to the reporters, surrounded by an admiring circle of fresh young bodies. Paula failed to take advantage of the windfall; she had set her sights on Julien. Seated beside him, her legs crossed high—legs which were still very beautiful—she had concentrated her whole soul into her eyes, and she was talking a blue streak. It would have been difficult for a novice, stunned by so many words, to turn her down; but

Julien knew all the answers. I listened to the urgent voice of a tall old man whose high forehead made him look like the traditional picture of a genius, and I made a vow to myself. If ever I lost Lewis, when I had lost Lewis, I would immediately and forever stop believing myself still a woman. I did not ever want to be like them.

" You see, Madame Dubreuilh," the old fellow was saying, " it isn't a question of personal ambition with me, but the things I have to say must be heard. No one else dares to say them ; it takes an old fool like myself to take the chance. And there's only one man courageous enough to back me up ; your husband."

" I'm sure he'd be very interested," I said.

" But his interest has to be *active*," he said vehemently. " They all tell me it's remarkable, it's fascinating! But when it comes to publishing it, they get frightened. If Robert Dubreuilh understands the importance of this work, to which I have—and I can say it without exaggerating—consecrated many years of my life, he owes it to himself to lend it his support. A preface by him would suffice."

" I'll speak to him about it," I said.

He was getting on my nerves, that old man, but I felt sorry for him. When you succeed, you have a lot of problems, but you have them too when you don't succeed. It must be dismal to speak and speak without ever awakening an echo. He had previously published two or three obscure books ; this one represented his last chance, and I was afraid it wasn't any better than the others. I was suspicious of every person in that room.

I edged my way through the mob and touched Paula's arm. " I think I've done my duty. I'm leaving. Ring me up."

" Do you have a second?" She grabbed my arm with the air of a conspirator. " I must ask your advice in connection with my book ; it's been bothering me for days. Do you think it would be a good idea to have the first chapter published in *Vigilance*?"

" That depends," I replied. " On the chapter and on the book as a whole."

" Without any doubt, the book is made to be read in a single, overpowering sitting," Paula said. " The reader ought to be hit in the stomach and not be given a chance to recover. But on the other hand, publication in *Vigilance* is a guarantee of its serious intent. I don't want to be taken for a society woman who writes for housewives . . ."

"Send me the manuscript," I said. "Robert will give you his opinion."

"I'll have a copy brought over to you to-morrow morning," she said. She left me standing there and ran over to Julien. "Are you going already?"

"I'm terribly sorry, but I've got to leave."

"You won't forget to ring me, will you?"

"I never forget anything."

Julien went down the stairs with me and said to me, in his precise voice, "A truly charming woman, Paula Mareuil! Only she's too fond of peckers. Not that of itself a pecker isn't a bad thing. But collectors bore me."

"It seems to me you're somewhat of a collector yourself," I said.

"No! What defines the collector is the catalogue; I've never kept a catalogue."

I was in a bad mood when I left Julien; it pained me to hear Paula spoken of in that way. But while changing from my going-out finery to a dressing-gown, I asked myself, "After all, why should it? She doesn't give a damn about what people think of her, and she's probably right." I wanted to be different from those overripe ogresses, but actually I had other tricks which were no better than theirs. I hasten to tell myself, "I'm finished, I'm old." In that way, I cancel out those thirty or forty years when I will live, old and finished, grieving over a lost past; I'll be deprived of nothing since I've already renounced everything. There's more caution than pride in my sternness, and fundamentally it covers up a huge lie: by rejecting the compromises of old age, I deny its very existence. Under my wilting skin, I affirm the survival of a young woman with her demands still intact, a rebel against all concessions, and disdainful of those sad forty-year-old hags. But she doesn't exist any more, that young woman; she'll never be born again, even under Lewis's kisses.

The next day, I read Paula's manuscript—ten pages as empty, as flat as a story in *Confidences*. But there was no point in getting upset about it; actually she wasn't as determined as all that to be a writer; a failure certainly wouldn't be tragic. She had insured herself once and for all against tragedy; she was reconciled to everything and anything. But I couldn't resign myself to her resignation. In fact, it saddened me to such an extent that I became more and more disgusted with my profesion; often I felt like saying to my patients, "Don't try to be cured; you'll heal as much as you need to by yourself." I had many patients, and that winter, as a matter of fact, I met with success in several difficult cases. But my heart wasn't in it. I really no longer understood why it is proper for people to sleep at night, make love with ease, be capable of acting, choosing, forgetting, living. Setting free all those neurotics imprisoned in their narrow misfortunes—when the world, after all, was so vast— used to seem terribly important to me. Now, however, when I tried to rid them of their obsessions, I was merely obeying a set of old slogans. Now I myself was becoming like them! The world was still as vast as ever, and I was no longer able to take an interest in it.

"It's shameful!" I said to myself that evening. They were having a discussion in Robert's study; they were talking about the Marshall Plan, the future of Europe, the future of the whole world; they were saying that the chances of war were increasing, and Nadine, listening to them, appeared frightened. War concerns all of us, and I didn't take those troubled voices lightly. And yet, I was thinking only of that letter, of a single line in that letter: "Across an ocean, the tenderest arms are cold indeed." Why, in confessing to me a few unimportant affairs, had Lewis written those hostile words? I hadn't asked him to be faithful to me; with all that water, all that foam, between us, it would have been stupid. Obviously, he resented my absence. Would he ever forgive me for it? Would I see his real smile again one day? Around me, they were pondering the fate menacing millions of men; it was my fate as well, and all I could worry about was a smile, a smile which wouldn't stop atomic bombs which could do nothing against anything—nor for anyone. It hid everything from me. "It's shameful," I repeated to myself. Truly, I couldn't understand myself. After all, being loved isn't an end in itself, a *raison d'être*; it changes nothing, it leads nowhere. Even I, it could lead me nowhere. I'm here, Robert is talking to Henri; how could what Lewis thinks there possibly affect me? I'd have to be out of my mind to make my fate dependent upon one heart, one heart among millions of others. I was trying to listen, but in vain ; I was saying to myself, "My arms are cold. After all," I thought, "just a single spasm of my heart, which, too, is only one heart among millions of others, and this vast world will cease to concern me, forever. The measure of my life might just as well be a single smile as the entire universe ; choosing one or the other is also arbitrary." Besides, the choice was not mine.

I answered Lewis and must have found the right words, for his next letter was relaxed and confiding. From then on, it was in a tone of friendly complicity that he kept me up to date on his life. He had sold his book to Hollywood, he had money, he was renting a house on Lake Michigan. He seemed happy. It was springtime. Nadine and Henri were married ; they, too, seemed happy. Why not I? I gathered up all my courage and wrote, "I'd love to see the house on the lake." He could ignore that sentence or else tell me, "You'll see the house next year," or perhaps, "I don't think you'll ever see it." When I held the envelope in my hands, the envelope that contained his answer, I became as rigid as if I were facing a firing squad. "I mustn't fool myself," I thought. "If he says nothing, it means he doesn't want to see me again." I unfolded the sheet of yellow paper and the words leaped immediately to my eyes: "Come at the end of July ; the house will be ready by then." I collapsed on the couch ; I had been reprieved at the very last second. I had been so terribly afraid that at first I felt no joy. And then, plainly, I felt Lewis's hands against my skin and I gasped, "Lewis!" Sitting beside him last year in the hotel room in New York, I had asked, "Will we ever see each other again?" And now he replied, "Come." Between the question and the answer, nothing had happened ; that phantom year had been obliterated, and I once more found my living body. What a miracle! I pampered it as if it were a prodigal child ; I, who usually worry so little about my body, wanted it polished, varnished, elegantly decked out, and for a whole month I lavished attentions on it. I had beach dresses made and shorts and halters ; in the flowered cotton clothes, I was already beside the blue lake, I could already feel his kisses. In the shop windows that year, they were showing long, silky, absurd petticoats ; I bought several. And I allowed Paula to give me a bottle of Paris's most expensive perfume. This time, I trusted travel agencies, passports, visas, airways. When I boarded the plane, it seemed as safe to me as a commuters' train.

Robert made arrangements to have dollars available for me in New York. I went to the same hotel where I had stayed on my first trip, and they gave me, within a few stories, the same room. In the hallway, with its slightly stuffy smell and its dim red light, I found again the same silence I had met two years before when curiosity was my only passion. For a few hours, I again felt carefree. Paris no longer existed, Chicago was not yet; I walked through the streets of New York and I thought of nothing. The next morning, I busied myself peacefully in various banks and offices. And then I went back to my room to get my suitcase. I looked in the mirror at the woman Lewis would take in his arms that evening. He would let down that hair, and, with his lips on mine, I would rip off that now well-tailored blouse which once had covered the shoulders of an old Indian woman. I pinned a rose to it, a rose which would soon be crushed, and I dabbed the perfume Paula had given me on the nape of my neck. I felt vaguely as if I were preparing a victim for a sacrifice, a victim who wasn't I. I examined her one last time; it seemed to me she could be loved—if I were loved.

The plane landed in Chicago four hours later. I took a cab and this time I found the house without any trouble. Everything was as it should be. The red Schlitz sign was glowing in front of the big bill-board; Lewis was sitting at a table on the porch, reading. He waved to me, smiling, ran down the stairs, took me in his arms, and spoke the anticipated words: "You're back! You're back at last!" Perhaps the scene was unfolding with a fidelity which was too precise, for it didn't seem completely real; it was like a slightly blurred copy of our first day together the previous year. Or perhaps it was simply that I was disturbed by the bareness of the room: there was not a picture, not a book in it.

"How empty it is!" I said.

"I've sent everything to Parker."

"Is the house ready? How does it look?"

"You'll see," he said. "You'll soon see." He cradled me

against him. "What a strange smell!" he said with a surprised little smile. "Is it the rose?"

"No, that's me."

"But you never smelled like that before."

Suddenly, I felt ashamed of Paris's most expensive perfume, of the stylish cut of my blouse, of my silk petticoats. What good were all those artifices? He hadn't needed them to desire me. I sought his mouth. It wasn't that I was that eager to make love, but I wanted to be certain he still desired me. His hands crumpled the silk of my petticoat, the rose fell to the floor, my blouse followed it, and I stopped asking myself questions.

I slept for a long time; it was past noon when I awakened. While I had breakfast, Lewis began telling me about the neighbours we would have in Parker, and, among others, about Dorothy, an old friend who had been divorced after an unhappy marriage and who, with her two children, was now living with her sister and brother-in-law two or three miles from our house. I wasn't very interested in Dorothy and perhaps he felt it, for he asked me abruptly, "Would you mind if I turned on a baseball game?"

"Not at all. I'll read the papers."

"I saved all the New Yorkers for you," Lewis said eagerly, "and I've marked the interesting articles."

He set a pile of magazines on the night table and turned on the radio. We stretched out on the bed, and I began thumbing through the New Yorkers. But I was ill at ease. It often happened, in those other years, that we would read or listen to the radio side by side, without speaking. But to-day, I had just arrived; I found it strange that Lewis could think only of baseball when I was lying there beside him. The year before, we had spent the whole first day making love. I turned the page, but I was unable to concentrate on reading. This time, before entering into me, Lewis had turned out the light; he hadn't given me his smile, hadn't spoken my name. Why? I had fallen asleep without asking myself any questions, but to dismiss a question isn't to answer it. "Maybe he hasn't quite found me again," I thought. "Finding someone after a whole year isn't easy. I must be patient. He'll find me again." I began an article and stopped, my throat tight. I didn't give a damn about Faulkner's

latest book, about anything else. I should have been in
Lewis's arms, and I wasn't. Why? That baseball game
seemed endless. Hours passed and Lewis was still listening.
If, at least, I could have slept—but I was gorged with sleep.
Finally, I made up my mind.

"You know something, Lewis? I'm hungry," I said
cheerfully. "Aren't you?"

"Just ten more minutes," he replied. "I bet three bottles
of Scotch on the Giants. Three bottles of Scotch is pretty
important, don't you think?"

"Very important."

I recognised Lewis's old smile, and that jesting, affectionate voice of his. Any other day, all that would have been
very normal. After all, perhaps it was normal for to-day, as
well, to be like any other day. But all the same, those last
ten minutes seemed horribly long to me.

"I won!" Lewis said happily. He got up and turned off
the radio. "Poor little starveling! We're going to feed
you!"

I, too, got up and combed my hair. "Where are you taking
me?"

"How about the old German restaurant?"

"That's a good idea!"

I liked that restaurant; I had pleasant memories of it.
We chatted cheerfully while eating sausages and red cabbage. Lewis told me about his Hollywood experience. Next,
he took me to the saloon with all the tramps and then to the
little Negro dance hall where Big Billy used to play. He was
laughing, I was laughing; the past was coming to life again
And then, suddenly, I thought, "No, it's just a good imitation!" What made me think that? What was wrong?
Nothing, nothing at all. It must have been I, imagining
things; the plane trip and the emotional impact of my
arrival had exhausted me. Quite obviously, I must be light-
headed. A year earlier, Lewis had said to me, "I'll stop
trying not to love you . . . I've never loved you as much
as now." He had said it to me: that was yesterday, and I
was still I, he was still he. In the cab which was taking us
back to our bed, I settled myself in his arms. It was indeed
he; I recognised the rough warmth of his shoulder. But I
didn't find his mouth again; he didn't kiss me. And above
my head, I heard a yawn.

I didn't move. But I felt myself sinking into the depths of the night. " This is the way it must feel when you're mad," I thought. Two blinding lights pierced through the darkness, two truths equally true, and which couldn't both be true together: Lewis loves me; and when he's holding me in his arms, he yawns. I climbed the stairs. I got undressed. I had to ask Lewis one question, one very simple question. Even now, it was tearing at my throat; but anything was better than that confused horror. I got into bed. He lay down beside me and wrapped himself in the sheets.

" Good-night."

He had already turned his back to me. I gripped his shoulder, clung close to him.

" Lewis, what's wrong?"

" Not a thing. I'm tired."

" I mean all day, what was wrong? Didn't you find me again?"

" I found you again," he replied.

" Then you don't love me any more, is that it?"

There was a silence, a decisive silence. It left me numb. All evening long, I had been afraid, but I hadn't seriously believed my fear was justified. And then, suddenly, there was no longer any possible doubt.

" You don't love me any more?" I asked again.

" I'm still very fond of you! I have a great deal of affection for you," Lewis replied dreamily. " But it isn't love any more."

There it was; he had said it. I had heard those words with my own ears, and nothing could obliterate them, ever. I was silent. I no longer knew what to do with myself. I was still exactly the same; and the past, the future, the present, everything was reeling. It seemed to me that even my own voice itself no longer belonged to me.

" I knew it!" I said. " I knew that I'd lose you. I've known it from the very first day. That's why I cried at the Club Delisa—because I knew. And now it's happened. How did it happen?"

" It's rather that *nothing* happened," Lewis said. " I waited for you this year without impatience. Yes, a woman is nice to have around; you talk, you sleep together, and then she leaves. It's nothing to lose your head about. But I kept telling myself that maybe when I saw you again something would happen."

"I understand," I said feebly. "And nothing happened . . ."

" No."

Bewildered, I thought, " It's because of that strange smell, those silks. I just have to begin all over again; I'll wear the suit I wore last year . . ." But obviously, my petticoats had nothing to do with it. I heard my voice from a long way off. " Well," I was saying, " what are we going to do?"

" Why, I hope we're going to spend a pleasant summer together!" Lewis replied. " Didn't we have a nice day?"

" It was a hellish day!"

" Really?" He looked distressed. " I thought you didn't notice anything."

" I noticed everything."

My voice gave out; I could no longer speak, and besides what good would it have done? The year before, when Lewis had tried to stop loving me, I had felt, in spite of his rancour and his bad moods, that he was having difficulty in succeeding; I had always continued to hope. But this year, he wasn't forcing himself; he no longer loved me; it was plain as day. Why? How? Since when? It mattered little; all questions were futile. Understanding is important when you still have hope, and I was certain I had nothing to hope for.

" Well, good-night," I murmured.

For an instant, he held me against him. " I wouldn't want you to be unhappy," he said. He smoothed my hair. " It isn't worth it."

" Don't worry about me," I said. " I'm going to sleep."

" Sleep," he said. " Sleep well."

I closed my eyes; yes, I would surely sleep. I felt even more exhausted than after a fever-ridden night. " Well, that's it," I thought coldly. " Nothing has happened, and that's normal. The abnormal thing was that one day something _had_ happened. What? Why?" Actually, I had never understood that love is always undeserved. Lewis had loved me without any valid reason; it hadn't surprised me. Now, he no longer loved me; neither was that surprising, it was even very natural. Suddenly, the words exploded in my head: " He doesn't love me any more." It was I he didn't love; I wanted to howl until I died. I began to weep. Each morning he used to ask, " Why are you laughing? What makes you so rosy and warm?" I would no longer laugh. " Anne!" he used to say. Never again would he say it in that way. Never again would I see that loving, delighted look on his face. "Everything has to be paid back," I thought through my sobs. "Everything that was given me, without my asking for it, has to be paid for with its weight in tears." A siren wailed in the distance, train whistles pierced the night air. I wept. Shuddering violently, my body emptied itself of its warmth ; I became cold and limp, like an old corpse. If only I could have done away with myself entirely! At least, while I wept, I had no future, I had nothing left in my head. It seemed to me I could have gone on sobbing until the end of time without ever tiring.

It was the night that tired first ; the kitchen shade grew yellower, and a leafy shadow imprinted itself upon it firmly. Soon, I would have to stand up, speak words, face a man who had slept without tears. If at least I could have held it against him, it would have drawn us together. But no, he was simply a man to whom nothing had happened. I got up. In the kitchen, the morning was silent and familiar, like so many other mornings. I poured myself a drink of Scotch and swallowed a benzedrine with it.

" Did you sleep?" Lewis asked.

" Not much."

" That was pretty silly of you!"

He began busying himself in the kitchen. His back was turned to me, and that made it easier for me to speak. "There's one thing I don't understand," I said. " Why did you let me come? You should have warned me."

" But I wanted to see you," Lewis replied warmly. He turned around and smiled at me innocently. " I'm glad you're here ; I'm glad we're going to spend the summer together."

" You're forgetting one thing," I said. " The fact that I love you. It isn't much fun living with someone you love, but who doesn't love you."

" You won't always love me," Lewis said lightly.

" Maybe not. But now I love you."

He smiled. " You've got too much good sense for it to last very long. Seriously," he added, " to really love someone, you've got to get all worked up. When two are playing the game, it can be worth it; but if you're playing alone, it becomes silly."

I looked at him, puzzled. Was he really callous, or was he just pretending to be? Perhaps he was speaking sincerely; perhaps love had lost all importance in his eyes since he stopped loving me. In any case, deliberate or thoughtless, his egotism proved to me that I now meant almost nothing to him. I lay down on the bed. I had a headache. Lewis began putting books in wooden crates, and suddenly I realised that I hadn't touched bottom. I was lying on the Mexican blanket, I was looking at the yellow shade, the walls; I was no longer loved, but I still felt at home. And perhaps it all belonged to someone else. Perhaps Lewis was in love with another woman. There had been other women in his life the past year; he had written me about them, and none of them had seemed worth worrying about. But perhaps he had met one whom he hadn't written me about on purpose.

I called to him. "Lewis!"

He raised his head. "Yes?"

"I have to ask you a question: Is there another woman?"

"Great God, no!" he exclaimed. "I will never be in love again!"

I sighed. The worst had been spared me. That face I would never see again, that voice I would never hear again, at least they didn't exist for anyone else.

"Why do you say that?" I asked. "You can never tell."

Lewis shook his head. "I think I'm not made for love," he replied in a slightly hesitant voice. "Before you, no woman had ever meant anything to me. I met you at a time when my life seemed very empty. That's why I rushed so headlong into that love. And then it ended up by ending." He studied me silently. "And yet," he added, "if ever there was someone who was made for me, it was you. After you, there can be no one else."

"I see."

Lewis's friendly voice made my despair complete. If he had been aggressive, unfair, I would no doubt have tried to defend myself. But no, he seemed almost as distressed as I was by what was happening to us. My head was hurting me more and more, and I gave up questioning him any further. It was useless asking the only conclusive question: "Lewis, if I had stayed, would you have gone on loving me?" For I hadn't stayed.

Lewis went to buy me some sedatives; I took two of them and I slept. I awakened with a start. "It ended up by ending!" I said to myself immediately. I sat down by the window; behind me, Lewis was packing dishes. It was already very hot; children were playing ball among the weeds of a vacant lot, a little girl was wobbling on a red tricycle, and I was biting my lips to keep myself from bursting into tears. With my eyes, I followed a long, luxurious car as it drove slowly down the street, close to the pavement. I turned my head away: the same view, the same room, the same black shadow embossed on the yellow shade; Lewis was wearing a pair of his old patched pants, he was whistling softly. The past was showing open defiance; I couldn't stand it any more.

"I'm going out for a while," I said, getting up.

I took a cab to the Loop and walked around for a long time; walking keeps one almost as busy as crying does. The streets seemed hostile to me. I had liked that city. I had liked that country. But things had changed in two years, and Lewis's love no longer protected me. Now, America meant atomic bomb, threat of war, nascent fascism. Most of the people I passed were enemies; I was alone, scorned, lost. "What am I doing here?" I asked myself. Towards the end of the afternoon, I found myself walking past the Schlitz sign; in an alley, smoke was rising from ash cans, giving off a good autumnal smell. I climbed the wooden stairs and stood looking at the red-and-white checkerboard that camouflaged the gas tank; a train passed in the distance and the porch shook. It was exactly like this the first day, the other days. "I'd do better going back to Paris," I said to myself. I could see the corner where my departure was already awaiting me. The cab that would take me away was cruising somewhere in the city; Lewis would hail it with a familiar gesture, and then the door would slam shut. It had slammed shut before—once, twice, three times, and this time it would be forever. What was the use of going through three months of agony? "As long as I see Lewis, as long as he smiles at me, I'll never have the strength to kill the love within me. But from a distance, everyone is capable of killing." I gripped the railing. "I don't want to kill it."

No, I didn't want Lewis to be as dead for me one day as Diego.

"I hope you'll like the house," Lewis said to me the next morning.

"Oh, I'm sure I will," I said.

He was filling a box with the remaining canned goods, the last few books. I was glad to leave Chicago. At least, in Parker things wouldn't insist upon parodying the past. There would be a garden, and we would have separate beds; it would be far less stifling. I began packing my suitcase. I buried the Indian blouse at the very bottom. Never again would I wear it; it seemed to me as if there were something malignant in its embroidery. Reluctantly, I touched all those skirts, those blouses, those beach clothes I had so carefully chosen. I closed the suitcase, and poured myself a stiff drink of Scotch.

"You shouldn't drink so much," Lewis said.

"Why not?"

I took a benzedrine; I needed help to go through those days in which I had to remind myself hourly that he no longer loved me. And to-day, friends were coming to pick us up in a car; I wouldn't have a minute to go cry quietly in some corner.

"Anne, this is Evelyn and Ned."

I shook hands. I smiled. The car went through the city and then through parks and suburbs. Evelyn spoke to me: I answered. We crossed an immense flatland bristling with smokestacks, housing developments, well-kept woods, and stopped at the end of a road which was obstructed by giant weeds. A gravel path led to a white house; in front, a lawn fell in a gentle slope towards a pond. I looked wide-eyed at the glistening dunes, the floating water lilies, the curtain of leafy trees. For two months, I was going to live here, as if I were in my own home. And then I would leave, never to return.

"Well?" Lewis said.

"It's magnificent!"

At the far end of the lawn, several people were sitting around a brick barbecue pit from which smoke was rising. They welcomed us gaily. I shook hands: Dorothy, her sister Virginia, her brother-in-law Willie who worked in one of the nearby factories, and Bert, a heavy-set fellow who taught in a Chicago elementary school. Hamburgers were sizzling on the black grill in the pit; there was a good smell of fried onions and burning wood. Someone handed me a glass of whisky and I gulped it down. I needed it badly.

"Isn't the house a jewel?" Dorothy said. "The lake is just beyond the dunes. There's a little boat to cross the pond; you're at the beach in five minutes."

She was a swarthy woman with a hard, tired face, an aggressive voice. She had once loved Lewis; perhaps she still did. And yet, there was a sincere warmth in her eyes.

"It'll be wonderful in the evenings," she said, "cooking your dinner out here in the open. The woods are full of dead branches; all you have to do is pick them up."

"I'll buy you a little hatchet," Lewis said gaily, "and when you don't behave yourself, you'll have to chop wood as punishment." He grabbed me by the arm. "Come and see the house."

Once again I saw on his face the happy fire of impatience; he used to look at me that way, with that smile glowing with pride.

"The rest of the furniture is coming to-morrow. We'll put the beds in here; that room in the back will be the library."

One would have really thought we were a pair of lovers preparing our nest. And when we returned to the garden, I was conscious of the avid curiosity in everyone's face. "Are you keeping the place in Chicago?" Virginia asked.

"Yes, we're keeping it."

They looked at us as if we were one, and I was saying "Lewis and I," I was saying "we." We would stay here all the summer; no, we didn't have a car; we're hoping you'll come to see us often. Lewis too was saying "we." He was speaking animatedly. We had not spoken to each other very much since my arrival, and it was the first time I had seen him cheerful. Now, he needed others to be cheerful. It was much cooler than in Chicago, and the smell of grass made me dizzy. I wanted to throw off that weight that was crushing my heart and be cheerful myself.

"Anne, would you like to go out in the boat?" Lewis asked me.

"Oh! I'd love to," I said.

Fireflies were flickering in the dusk as we walked down the

little stairway. I sat down in the boat, and Lewis shoved us free of the bank ; gelatinous weeds wrapped themselves around the oars. On the pond, on the dunes, it was a true country night; but above the bridge, the sky was red and violet, a sophisticated, big-city sky, scorched by the fires of the blast furnaces.

" It's as lovely as the skies above the Mississippi," I said.

" Yes. And in a few days, we'll have a full moon."

A campfire was crackling alongside the dunes. Here and there a window shone through the trees ; one of them was ours. Like all windows shining at night in the distance, they promised happiness.

" Dorothy is nice," I said.

" Yes," Lewis said. " Poor Dorothy. She works in a drugstore in Parker and her ex-husband pays her a little alimony. Two children, her whole life here, and not even a home of her own. It's hard."

We were speaking intimately of others, the black water isolated us from the world, Lewis's voice was affectionate, his smile the smile of an accomplice. I asked myself suddenly, " Is everything really all over?" I had given in immediately to despair, out of pride, so as not to be like all those women who lie to themselves, and out of caution, so as to spare myself the anguish of doubt, of waiting, of disappointment. Perhaps I had been too hasty. Lewis's nonchalance, his excessive frankness weren't natural ; in reality, he's neither thoughtless nor brutal, wouldn't crudely parade his indifference if it weren't the result of a considered decision. He had decided to stop loving me. All right. But making a decision and holding to it are two different things.

" We have to christen our little boat," Lewis said. " What would you say to calling it ' Anne '?"

" I'd be very proud!"

He was looking at me now the way he used to, and it was he who had suggested that lovers' outing. Perhaps he was beginning to tire of his false caution ; perhaps he was hesitating to banish me from his heart. We returned to the garden, and our guests soon left. We lay down side by side on the narrow bed, temporarily set up in the library. Lewis turned out the light.

" Do you think you'll like it here?" he asked.

" I'm sure I will."

I pressed my cheek to his bare shoulder; he was gently stroking my arm, and I held myself tight against him. It was his hand on my arm, it was his warmth, his smell, and I no longer had either pride or caution. I found his mouth again, and as my hand crept over his warm belly my body burned with desire. He, too, desired me, and between us desire had always been love. Something was beginning again that night. I was sure of it. It all happened so fast that I remained dumbfounded.

I spoke first. "Good-night," I said.

"Good-night," said Lewis, turning towards the wall.

A desperate anger gripped my throat. "He has no right to do this," I murmured. Not for an instant had he given me his presence; he had treated me as a pleasure machine. Even if he didn't love me any more, he shouldn't have done that. I got out of bed; I hated his warmth. I went into the living-room, sat down, and cried myself out. I simply couldn't understand it. How could our bodies, those bodies which had loved each other so well, how could they have become such total strangers? He said, "I'm so happy, I'm so proud." He said, "Anne!" He gave me his heart. With his hands, his lips, with his whole body. That was yesterday. All those nights the memories of which were still burning inside me—under the Mexican blanket, in our berth rocked by the Mississippi, in the shadow of mosquito netting, in front of a fire which smelled of resin—all those nights. Would they never come to life again?

When I went back to bed, exhausted, Lewis raised himself on his elbow. Irritably, he asked, "Is that your programme for the summer? Spending a pleasant day and then crying all night?"

"Oh, don't try to sound so superior!" I said hotly. "I was crying because I was angry. Sleeping together cold like that, it's . . . it's horrible! You shouldn't have . . ."

"I can't give you warmth I no longer feel," Lewis said.

"Then you shouldn't have slept with me."

"You wanted it so much," he said calmly. "I didn't want to refuse."

"It would have been better to refuse. I think we should decide never to sleep together again."

"It would certainly be better if it's going to make you cry all night. Now try to get some sleep."

There was no hostility in his voice, only indifference. His calmness upset me. I lay on my back, staring blankly at the ceiling; in the distance, the lake was pounding the shore with the throb of an engine. Was Lewis speaking the truth? Was I the guilty one? Yes, without any doubt, I was guilty —not so much for having begged his caresses but rather for having deluded myself with false hopes. Certainly, Lewis's conscience wasn't perfectly clear, which accounted for his temperamental behaviour. But for a man such as he, there's very little distance between a refusal to love and an absence of love. He had deliberately decided to stop loving me. The result was that he no longer loved me. The past was unmistakably dead—a death without a corpse, like Diego's. That's what made it so difficult to believe. It would really have helped if I'd had a tombstone to weep over.

"This stay's off to a pretty bad start," Lewis said to me the next morning, looking worried.

"Not at all," I said. "Nothing very serious has happened. Give me a chance to get used to it, and everything's going to be fine."

"I want that so much," Lewis said. "I feel we could have a good time together. When you aren't crying, I get along so well with you."

His eyes were questioning me. There was a good deal of insincerity in his optimism, and he gave scant consideration to my feelings in the matter. And yet, his anxiety was sincere; causing me pain truly upset him.

"I'm sure we'll have a lovely summer together," I said.

It looked like a lovely summer. Each morning we could row across the weedy pond and climb over the dunes which always burned my feet. To the right, the deserted beach stretched out into infinity; to the left, it died at the foot of flame-spouting blast furnaces. We swam; we tanned ourselves in the sun while watching a flock of white birds, perched on stilt-like legs, pecking at the sand. And then we would return to the house, loaded down like Indians with sticks of dead wood. I spent hours reading on the lawn in the company of grey squirrels, blue jays, butterflies and large brown birds with red breasts. In the distance, I would hear the clacking of Lewis's typewriter. Evenings, we would light a fire in the barbecue pit, and I would melt a cake of ice in which a disjointed chicken was mummified; or Lewis would saw off a petrified steak from a side of beef and would roast ears of corn wrapped in damp leaves in the hot ashes. Side by side, we would listen to records or watch an old film or a fight on television. Our happiness was so well counterfeited that it often seemed to me it would become real from one moment to the next.

That bait caught Dorothy; it fascinated her. She would often ride over in the evening on her red bicycle, sniff the smell of the hamburgers, breathe in the smoke of the burning twigs. "What a magnificent night! Do you see the fireflies? Do you see the stars? And the campfires on the dunes?" Avidly, she would describe to me that life which would never be hers and which wasn't really mine. She overwhelmed me with compliments, advice, and devotion. It was she who had furnished the house; it was she who went shopping for us, and, in addition, she did us a thousand superfluous favours. She always arrived bearing some miraculous message; a recipe, a new kind of soap, a leaflet extolling the virtues of the latest model washing machine, a review of a sensational new book. She could dream for weeks about the advantages of an improved refrigerator capable of keeping a barrel of cream fresh for six months. She had no roof of her own and yet she subscribed to an expensive architectural magazine in which she would delightedly contemplate the fabulous residences of multimillionaires. I listened patiently to her incoherent plans, her shrieks of enthusiasm, all the frantic chatter of a woman who has nothing left to hope for. Lewis often became annoyed with her. "I'd never have been able to live with that woman!" he said to me. No, he would never have been able to marry Dorothy, and I hadn't been able to marry him, and he no longer loved me. That garden, that house promised a happiness that wasn't for any of us.

Naturally, it was Dorothy who dragged us one Sunday to the fair in Parker; she adored mass expeditions. Bert came to pick us up in his car, and Dorothy took Virginia, Willie, and Evelyn in her old car. Lewis felt he couldn't refuse, but he was not very enthusiastic about it. As for me, I was dismayed by the prospect of that afternoon of merriment, to be followed by a supper at Virginia's. I was always afraid, when exposed too long to the searching looks of others, of not being able to play out to the very end my rôle of a happy woman.

" My God, what a mob! What dust!" Lewis complained upon entering the amusement park.

" Oh, don't start grumbling," Dorothy said. She turned to me. " When he decides to be sullen, he'd like to turn off the sun!"

Her face was glowing with a slightly mad hope as she rushed over to a stand and began throwing darts at toy balloons. From stand to stand, she seemed to be anticipating some extraordinary revelation. As for me, I concentrated on smiling. With all the curiosity I could muster, I watched the trained monkeys, the naked dancers, the seal man, the half-woman. I much preferred the games that demanded my complete physical attention; ardently, I knocked over bowling pins and tin cans, steered midget automobiles on moving floors, steered planes through painted skies.

Lewis watched me sardonically. " It's incredible how seriously you can take things!" he said. " It's almost as if you were playing for your life!"

Should I have read hidden meanings into his smile? Was he thinking I had brought to love the same futile seriousness, the same false ardour? Dorothy retorted spiritedly, " It's a lot better than putting on big, blasé airs all the time." She took my arm firmly. As we passed in front of a photographer's stand, she smoothed my silk dress with her rough hand. " Anne, have your picture taken with Lewis! Your dress is so pretty, and that hair-do suits you so well."

" Yes, do!" Virginia said. " We'd so much like a picture of you!"

I hesitated; Lewis grabbed me by the arm. " Come on and get yourself immortalised," he said gaily, " since it seems you're so seductive."

" For others," I thought sadly, " and never again for him." I sat down beside him in a painted aeroplane, and I had a hard time forcing a smile. He didn't notice my dresses; for him I no longer had a body, I barely had a face. If only I could have felt that a cataclysm had disfigured me! But it was the same me whom he had loved whom he no longer loved; Dorothy's enthusiasm bore witness to it, and that was why it had upset my whole equilibrium. I was crumbling. I was going to pieces. And I would have to hold myself erect and smile well into the night.

"Lewis, you should keep Evelyn company," Dorothy said. "The sun tires her out. She'd like to sit down in the shade. When she gets back from the toilet, buy her a drink while we go and see the waxworks."

"Oh, no! Not me!" Lewis replied.

"But she needs a man to look after her. She doesn't know Bert and she can't stand Willie."

"And I can't stand Evelyn," Lewis said.

"All right, I'll stay with her," Dorothy said angrily. I made a gesture, but she protested. "No, not you, Anne. Go on, go on—you'll tell me all about it."

As we went off, I asked Lewis, "Why aren't you nicer to Dorothy?"

"She's the one who invited Evelyn. No one asked her to invite her."

I let that pass and became absorbed in the contemplation of murderers frozen in the act of murder standing over their victims frozen in their deaths. Sitting in her hospital bed, a little five-year-old Peruvian was cradling a newborn baby in her arms; Goering was lying in agony on a stretcher, and bodies dressed in German uniforms were swinging from gallows. Behind a barbed wire fence, wax corpses were piled one on top of the other in a huge charnel heap. I looked at them, stupefied. There were Buchenwald and Dachau withdrawing into the murky depths of history, as distant as the Christians being thrown to the lions in the Musée Grévin. When I found myself outside again in the sun's dazzling light, the whole of Europe had vanished somewhere in the outer limits of space. I looked at the women with their bare shoulders, at the men in their bright sports shirts, biting into hot dogs or licking ice-cream cones. No one spoke my language, and I myself had forgotten it. I had lost all my memories, even the memory of my own face: there was no mirror in Lewis's house which I could look into at eye-level, and I had to apply my make-up gropingly in a little hand mirror. I hardly remembered who I was, and I wondered if Paris still existed.

I heard Dorothy saying angrily, "You decide it's time to

leave, and you don't even ask Anne's opinion. It seems they're going to show some old silent films at seven o'clock; and someone told me about an amazing magician . . ."

Her voice pleaded, but all the faces around her remained set.

"Oh, come on, let's go home!" Willie said. "We've got some martinis waiting for us and everyone's hungry."

"Men are so selfish!" she muttered.

I sat down between her and Willie in her old car; she was so disappointed that she remained silent throughout the entire ride. So did I. As we stepped out of the car, she grabbed my arm and said impulsively, "Why don't you stay here for good? You should stay."

"I can't."

"But why not? It's such a shame!"

"I can't."

"At least you'll come back, won't you? Come back in the springtime; it's the loveliest season here."

"I'll try."

"What right does she have to talk to me like this?" I asked myself irritably as I entered the house. Why all that superfluous kindness when Lewis hadn't once asked me, "Will you come back?" I eagerly took the martini Willie handed me. My nerves were raw. I looked with distress at the table covered with sandwich spreads, salads, and cakes. I was in for a long evening! Dorothy had disappeared; she returned, heavily powdered, and wearing a long, shabby, flower-printed gown. Bert, Virginia, Evelyn, and Lewis arrived laughing a few minutes after us. They were all talking together, and I didn't try to follow the conversation; I looked at Lewis, who had regained his cheerfulness, and I wondered, "How much longer before we're alone together?" This was the way I had waited before for Teddy to leave, for Maria to leave. But now, my impatience was silly; away from the others, Lewis would be no closer to me. Bert set a plate of sandwiches on my knees; he was smiling at me, and I heard him asking me, "Were you in Paris on August twenty-fourth in '44?"

"Anne spent the whole war in Paris," Lewis said with a kind of pride.

"What a day!" Bert said. "We thought we were going to find a dead city—and everywhere there were women in bright, flowered dresses with beautiful tanned legs! What a difference from the way we thought of French women over here!"

"Yes," I said, "your reporters were deceived by our good health."

"Oh, a few idiots!" Bert said. "It was easy to understand that the old people and the sick weren't out in the streets. And neither were the deportees and the dead." A dreamy look crept over his heavy face. "All the same, it was an extraordinary day!"

"When I got there," Willie said regretfully, "no one liked us the least bit any more."

"Yes, it didn't take us long to get ourselves hated," Bert said. "We behaved like animals."

"Naturally," Lewis said.

"It could have been prevented. All that was needed was a little discipline . . ."

"Don't you think enough guys were hanged?" Lewis said hotly. "You throw men into a war and then, at the first rape, you hang them!"

"I agree with you," Bert said. "There were too many hangings. But that's just it; it's because the necessary measures weren't taken at once."

"What measures?" Willie asked.

"Oh, if they start hashing over their war now, it's liable to go on all night!" Dorothy said.

The faces of the three warriors were glowing with animation; they were talking volubly, interrupting each other constantly. There was no doubting their sympathy for France, they were not the least bit complacent about their own country; and yet, listening to them, I felt uncomfortable. It was their war they were talking about, a war in which we had been only the somewhat pitiful excuse. Their scruples concerning us were like those a man could feel towards a weak woman or a passive animal. And already they were making wax legends out of our history.

When finally they stopped talking, Evelyn asked me languidly, "And how is Paris now?"

"Invaded by Americans," I replied.

"That doesn't seem to please you," Lewis said. "What a thankless people! We gorge them with powdered milk, we're going to flood them with Coca-Cola and tanks—and they

don't fall on their knees before us!" He began to laugh.
"Greece, China, France; we aid, we aid, it's crazy. We're a
nation of Boy Scouts!"

"You think that's funny, do you?" Dorothy said aggressively. "It's great to have a sense of humour!" She shrugged
her shoulders. "After we've dropped atom bombs on the
whole world, Lewis will amuse us again with a few good
morbid jokes."

Lewis looked at me cheerfully. "Wasn't it a Frenchman
who said that it's better to laugh at things than to cry over
them?"

"It isn't a question of crying or laughing, but of acting,"
Dorothy said.

Lewis's face became serious. "I vote for Wallace, I argue
for him; what more do you want me to do?"

"My God, Dorothy!" Willie said. "Lewis can't create a
real leftist party, nor can any of us."

"And yet," I said, "there are a lot of you who hold the
same views. Isn't there any way you can get together?"

"First of all, there are fewer and fewer of us," Lewis
replied. "And secondly, we're isolated."

"And above all, you find it a lot more comfortable to
snicker than to try to do something," Dorothy said.

I, too, was sometimes irritated by Lewis's placid irony. He
was lucid, critical; he was even often indignant. But he bore
the same intimate relationship to the shortcomings and
blemishes he objected to in America as a patient bears to his
affliction, a tramp to his filth. It was enough to make him
seem to me vaguely a party to them. I suddenly remembered
that he had blamed me for not having adopted his country,
while telling me that he could never settle in mine. That was
really arrogance! "I wouldn't become an American for
anything in the world!" I protested to myself. And while
they continued squabbling, I wondered facetiously where
inside me that angry chauvinist had been hiding all these
years.

Bert drove us home in his car, and once inside the house
Lewis took me affectionately in his arms. "Did you have a
nice day?"

My moods were of interest to no one, and his warm smile
dictated my answer. "Very nice," I said. "How aggressive
Dorothy is!" I added.

"She isn't happy," Lewis said. He reflected a moment. "And neither is Virginia, or Willie, or Evelyn. We're pretty lucky, you and I, to be more or less satisfied with our lot."

"I'm not so satisfied with mine."

"Oh, you have your bad moments, like everyone else. But it isn't chronic."

He was speaking with so much assurance that I could find nothing to say in reply.

"They're all more or less slaves," he resumed. "Of their husbands, their wives, their children. That's their big misfortune."

"Last year," I said, "you told me you hoped to get married one day."

"Sometimes I think about it." He began to laugh. "But stick me in a house with a wife and children and I'd have only one thought: escape."

His cheerful voice gave me courage. "Lewis, do you think we'll ever see each other again?"

His face darkened. "Why not?" he said casually.

"Because we live very far from each other."

"Yes," he said. "We do live far apart."

He walked away and disappeared in the bathroom. It was always that way: as soon as I tried to approach him, he would run off. Doubtless, he was afraid I might demand warmth from him or lies or promises which he was unable to give me. I began undressing. I had known in advance that that little tête-à-tête would be disappointing; I was, however, no less disappointed for having known it. At least I had one small bit of luck: my body was so precisely attuned to Lewis's that it had no trouble matching his indifference. We slept in our twin beds, separated by an icy crevasse, and I didn't even understand the meaning of the word "desire" any more.

I could have wished that my heart were equally compatible. Lewis claimed that to love you had to be all worked up; supposing I stopped working myself up? Lewis was sleeping; I listened to his even breathing, and for the first time I tried to see him with other eyes than my own—with Dorothy's spiteful eyes. It was true that he was selfish. He had made up his mind to extract the most possible pleasure from our affair with the least possible bother, and what I felt didn't matter to him. He had let me come to Chicago without warning me about anything, because it pleased him to see me. And once he had me at his mercy, he promptly gave me notice that he no longer loved me. To top it all off. he wanted me to act as if I were enjoying myself. Really. all he cared about was himself. And why, after all, did he have to defend himself so savagely against regrets, emotions, suffering? There was a good deal of niggardliness in that caution of his. The next morning, I tried to steel myself to the situation. I watched him as he watered the lawn looking thoughtful, and I said to myself, " He's just one man among millions of others. Why should I stubbornly insist on considering him unique?" I heard the mail car arriving. The postman pulled out the little red flag sticking up from the letter box and tossed it inside with the mail. I walked down the gravel path. No letters, but several newspapers and magazines. I would look through them, and then choose a book in the library; I would go for a swim, and in the afternoon I would listen to records. There were a lot of pleasant things I could do without torturing either my head or my heart any more.

" Anne!" Lewis cried out. " Come see! I caught a rainbow." He was watering the lawn and a rainbow was dancing in the spray. " Come quick!" I recognised that urgent, friendly voice, that happy face—a face which was like no other. It was Lewis; it was he and no one else. He had stopped loving me, but he was still the same. Why, then, should I have suddenly thought ill of him? No, I couldn't get off that cheaply. The truth was that I understood him. I, too, hated unhappiness and was loathe to make sacrifices: I could understand his refusing at one and the same time to suffer because of me and to lose me; I could understand his being too busy deciphering his own heart to bother much about what was going on in mine. And then I remembered his voice that day he had gripped my shoulders and said, " I'd marry you to-morrow." At that moment, I had repudiated all rancour, forever. When you really want to stop loving, you stop loving. But you can't want to at will.

And so I went on loving Lewis; it wasn't at all restful. I had only to hear a certain inflection in his voice and, all at once, I would find his whole being again. And then a minute later, I would once more lose him. When he went to spend a day in Chicago, at the end of the week, I felt rather relieved. Twenty-four hours of solitude would be a welcome respite! I walked him to the bus stop and returned slowly to the house along a road bordered by gardens and summer cottages. I sat down on the lawn with a pile of books. It was very hot; not a leaf was stirring; the lake was still. I took Robert's letter from my purse; he had written to me in detail about the Madagascar trial. Henri was writing an article that would appear in the next issue of *Vigilance,* but it wasn't nearly enough; to rouse public opinion, what they needed was a daily or a weekly with a large circulation. They had also thought of organising a protest meeting, but there wasn't enough time. I folded the letter and put it back in my purse. My eyes followed a plane passing overhead; they went by all the time, they could easily take me back to Paris. But to what avail? If I had been with Robert, he would have spoken to me instead of writing, but he would not have been any better off for it. I could do nothing for him, and he wasn't calling me back; I had no reason to leave here. I looked around me: the lawn was well kept, the sky glossy, the squirrels and birds were like domesticatd animals; I had no reason to stay, either. I picked up a book: *The Literature of New England.* A year earlier, I would have been deeply interested in it, but now Lewis's country, his past, had ceased to concern me; all those books scattered on the grass were totally mute. I stretched out. What to do? I had absolutely nothing to do. For what seemed a very long time, I lay there, motionless. And then I was seized with a sudden panic. I had often told myself that there could be no worse fate than to be paralysed, blind and deaf, with a mind that was alive. And that was my fate. In the end, I got up and went into the house. I took a bath, washed my hair, but I had never been able to spend much time on my body. I opened the refrigerator: a pitcher of tomato juice, another filled with orange juice, ready-made salads, cold joints, milk—all I had to do was reach out my hand. And the cupboards were plentifully stocked with canned goods, magic powders, instant rice which had only to be brought to the boil. In a quarter of an hour, I had finished my dinner. There must be an art to killing time, but it's always been completely foreign to me. What to do? I listened to a few records and then turned on the television. I amused myself skipping from channel to channel, jumbling together movies, comedy shows, adventure stories, newscasts, detective dramas, and quiz programmes. But there came a moment when something happened out there, in the world: no matter where I turned the dial the screen remained black. I thought about going to sleep, but for the first time in my life I was afraid of prowlers, thieves, escaped lunatics; I was afraid of sleep and afraid of wakefulness. Now, the lake was roaring, animals were snapping dead branches; in the house, the silence was oppressive. I locked all the doors, took a blanket, and a pillow from my room, and leaving the lights on, lay down on the couch completely dressed. I fell asleep; whereupon a band of thugs came in through the closed windows and butchered me. When I awakened, a bird was singing, another was tapping a tree with its beak. I preferred even my nightmares to reality, and I closed my eyes again; but under my eyelids it was broad daylight. I got up. How empty the house was! How bare the future! There was a time when I would have been deeply moved by the sight of that white bathrobe thrown across a chair, by those old slippers left under the desk. Now, those objects meant nothing to me. They belonged to Lewis, yes, Lewis still existed. But the man who loved me had disappeared without leaving a trace. It was Lewis; it wasn't he. I was in his house, and at a stranger's.

I went out, walked down the gravel path; the letter-box flag had disappeared: the postman had come. I took the mail. There was a letter for me: Myriam and Philip were travelling in Mexico; on their way back, they planned to stop off in Chicago; they were hoping to see me. I hadn't seen them since '46, but Nancy had been in Paris the previous May and I had given her my address in the United States. There was certainly nothing extraordinary about Myriam writing me, and yet I looked at her letter with stupefaction; it brought back a time when Lewis didn't exist for me. How could his absence have become that gaping, all-devouring emptiness? The garden was dead, and my memories as well. I found it impossible to take an interest for even a second in Myriam, in Philip, in anything. The only thing that mattered was that man for whom I was waiting, and I didn't even know who he was. I didn't know who I myself was. I circled the garden, I paced back and forth in the house, I called out, "Lewis! Come back! Help me!" I swallowed whisky and benzedrine—in vain. That unbearable emptiness refused to leave me. I sat down at the bay window, and I watched.

"Lewis!" It was about two in the afternoon when I heard his step on the gravel. I sprang up. He was loaded down with packages: books, records, Chinese tea, a bottle of Chianti. It was as if they were presents, and that day a holiday. I took the bottle from his hands.

"Chianti! What a good idea! Did you have a good time? Did you win at poker? What would you like to eat—a steak? Chicken?"

"I've had lunch," Lewis replied. He set down the packages, took off his shoes, and put on his slippers.

"I was afraid all night without you here. I dreamt that prowlers were beating me to death."

"I suppose you had too much to drink."

He sat down in the arm-chair near the bay window, and I settled myself on the couch. "Now, tell me all about it," he said.

"Nothing very interesting happened," I said.

I had greeted him with the customary ineptitude of women who are no longer loved—too much warmth, too much zeal, too many questions. He spoke to me, but he was obviously just making conversation. Yes, he had played poker, he had neither won nor lost. Teddy was in jail for the usual reason. No, he hadn't seen Martha. He had seen Bert, but they hadn't spoken of anything special. As soon as I asked him for a detail, he became irritated. In the end, he picked up a newspaper and I opened a book which I pretended to read. I hadn't had any lunch, but I couldn't eat.

"But what was I expecting?" I wondered. I had given up the hope of ever finding the past again. What, then, was I counting on? A friendship capable of replacing that lost love? But a love wouldn't mean very much if something else could take its place. No, it was as final as death. Again, I thought, "If at least I held a corpse in my arms!" I wanted to draw close to Lewis, place my hand on his shoulder, ask him, "How could a love like ours have gone up in smoke? Explain it to me." But he would have answered, "There's nothing to explain."

"Wouldn't you like to take a walk on the beach?" I suggested.

"No," he replied without looking up, "I don't feel like it."

Only two hours had gone by. I still had to live through the whole rest of the afternoon, and then the evening, the night, and another day, and still other days. How would I kill them? If only there were a cinema nearby, or a real country-side with woods and meadows where I could have walked myself to exhaustion. But those straight roads bordered by gardens were like a prison yard. I poured myself a drink. The sun was shining, and yet there wasn't enough strength in its light to keep things at a distance; they were crushing me; the print of my book stuck to my eyes and blinded me. Reading was out of the question. I tried to think of Paris, of Robert, of the past, the future. Impossible. I was im-prisoned in that moment, bound hand and foot, an iron collar around my neck. The weight of my body was stifling me, my breath was poisoning the air. It was myself whom I wanted to escape, and it was that, precisely, which would never be granted me again. "I'm willing to give up making love," I thought, "to wear the clothes of an old woman, to have white hair. But never again to be able to get out of myself—what torture!" My hand touched the bottle, moved away from it. I had grown too used to alcohol; it played havoc with my stomach without numbing or warming me. What would happen? Something had to happen. This motionless torture couldn't continue into eternity. Lewis was still reading—and suddenly everything came clear to me. It wasn't the same man! The man who used to love me had disappeared, and Lewis had, too. How could I have been so completely fooled! Lewis! I remembered him so well! He used to say, "You've got such a pretty little head, all round . . . Do you have any idea how much I love you?" He had given me a flower, he had asked, "Do they eat flowers in France?" What had become of him? And who had condemned me to that funereal tête-à-tête with an impostor? Suddenly, I heard the echo of a hateful memory: a yawn.

"For God's sake, don't yawn!" I said, bursting into tears.

"For God's sake, don't cry!" he said.

I threw myself full length on the couch. I was plummeting through space; orange discs were spinning before my eyes, and I was falling into darkness.

"When you start crying, I feel like leaving and never coming back," Lewis said angrily.

I heard him leaving the room; I was exasperating him, I was losing him for good. I should have stopped. For a moment I struggled. And then I sank to the bottom. From very far off, I heard the sound of steps; Lewis was walking in the basement, he was watering the garden, he was coming back into the house. I continued to cry.

"Haven't you finished yet?"

I didn't answer. I was exhausted, but I was still crying. It's astounding the quantity of tears a woman's eyes can hold. Lewis sat down at his desk, the typewriter began clacking. "He wouldn't let a dog suffer," I thought. "And I'm crying because of him and he won't make a move." I clenched my teeth. I had promised myself never to hate him, that man who had opened his heart to me without reserve. "But it isn't he any more," I repeated to myself. My teeth were chattering; I was on the very edge of hysterics. I made an effort which rent me from head to foot; I opened my eyes, I stared at the wall.

"What do you want me to do?" I shouted. "I'm here, shut in, shut in with you. I can't go and lie down in a ditch."

"My God!" he said in a somewhat more friendly voice. "How you make yourself suffer!"

"It's you," I said. "You don't even try to help me."

"What can you do about a woman who cries?"

"No matter who else it was, you'd try to help."

"I hate to see you lose your head."

"Do you think I do it on purpose? Do you think it's easy to live with someone you love and who doesn't love you?"

He remained seated in his chair, he didn't attempt to flee any more, but I knew he wouldn't speak the words we needed to conclude that scene; it was up to me to contrive an ending. I tossed out words at random: "I'm here only for you; all I have is you! When I feel I'm being a burden on you, what can I do?"

"There's no reason to burst into tears because I don't feel like talking just when you get an urge to," he said. "Do I have to give in to your every whim?"

"Oh, you're being completely unfair!" I said, wiping my eyes. "It was you who invited me to spend the summer here; you told me you were happy I was here. You shouldn't be so hostile."

"I'm not hostile. When you start to cry, I feel like leaving, that's all."

"I don't cry that often," I said. I twisted my handkerchief in my hands. "You may not be aware of it, but there are times when you act as if I'm an enemy, as if you mistrusted me. And that's horrible."

Lewis smiled. "I do mistrust you a bit," he said.

"You have no right to!" I said. "I know perfectly well you don't love me. I'll never again ask you for anything that resembles love. I'm doing my best to make us get along together."

"Yes, you're very nice," Lewis said. "But that's just it," he added. "That's why I mistrust you." His voice rose a little. "Your niceness is the most dangerous trap of all! That's how you got me last year. It seems ridiculous to defend yourself against someone who isn't attacking you. So you don't defend yourself. And then when you're alone once more, you find your heart's all upside-down again. No, I don't want any repetition of that."

I got up. I took a few steps around the room, trying to calm myself. Reproaching me for being nice—that, that really was the limit!

"I can't be disagreeable on purpose!" I said. "You're really not making things easy for me," I added. "If that's the way it is, I see only one solution. I'll leave."

"But I don't want you to leave!" Lewis said. He shrugged his shoulders. "Things aren't easy for me either."

"I know," I said.

I really couldn't get angry at him. He had hoped to keep me with him forever, and I had refused. If to-day his moods were capricious and his desires incoherent, I should not have let myself be surprised by this. You inevitably contradict yourself when you're forced to want something other than what you really want.

"I don't want to leave," I said. "Only you mustn't start hating me."

He smiled. "We haven't come to that!"

"A litle while ago, you would have let me die where I was without lifting a finger."

"That's true," he said. "I couldn't have lifted a finger. But it wasn't my fault: I was paralysed."

I went over to him. For once, we had begun to speak out to each other. I wanted to take advantage of this opportunity.

"You're wrong to mistrust me," I said. "There's one thing you must know: I don't hold it against you, I've never held it against you that you no longer love me. There's no reason for it to be unpleasant for you to think about what I think of you. There's nothing in me that could be unpleasant to you."

I cut myself off short; he was looking at me with a slightly worried look. He was afraid of words; so was I. I had seen too many women try to calm the regrets of their flesh with words: I had known too many who had dismally suceeded in leading back to their beds a man benumbed by words. It's a horrible thing, a woman who labours to lead a man's hands to her body by appealing to his mind.

I added only, "We're friends, Lewis."

"Of course!" He put his arm around me and whispered, "I'm sorry I was so hard."

"I'm sorry I was so silly."

"Yes! What a silly little fool! You did have a good idea though. Why didn't you go and lie down in a ditch?"

"Because you wouldn't have come to look for me."

He laughed. "The day after to-morrow, I'd have notified the police."

"You'd win either way," I said. "It isn't fair. I could never make myself suffer for two whole days, or try to make you suffer for even an hour."

"I know. There isn't much meanness in that poor heart of yours. And not much wisdom in that head!"

"That's why you have to be nice to me."

"I'll try," he said, giving me a playful hug.

After that, there was less distance between us. When we would go for walks on the beach, when we would lie in the sun, or in the evening, when we were listening to records, Lewis would talk to me without restraint. Our understanding was coming to life again. He was no longer afraid to take me in his arms, to kiss me; we even made love two or three times. When I felt his mouth find mine again, my heart began beating wildly: a kiss of desire is so much like a kiss of love! But my body would quickly regain its composure. It was only a matter of a brief conjugal coition, an act so insignificant that it's difficult to understand how the great concepts of pleasure and sin could ever be associated with it.

The days passed without too much difficulty; it was mostly the nights that were troublesome. Dorothy had made me a present of a stock of little yellow capsules; she had a collection of pills, powders, lozenges, and capsules for every purpose. I would swallow two or three of the sedatives before going to bed, but I slept and I had bad dreams. And soon I began to suffer from a new malady: in a month, in two weeks, in ten days, I would leave. Would I ever return? Would I ever see Lewis again? He himself probably didn't know the answer; he wasn't very good at forecasting the state of his heart.

We decided to spend the last week in Chicago. One evening, Myriam called me up from Denver to ask if we could see each other. I told her yes, and Lewis and I agreed that I would go to Chicago a day before he did; we would meet at the old flat about midnight of the following day. At the time, it all seemed very simple. But the morning I was to leave, I could feel my heart failing me. We were strolling along the beach; the lake was such a hard green that it seemed almost as if you could walk on its waves. Dead butterflies were lying on the sand; the cottages were all closed for the winter, except the fishermen's shack, where nets had been laid out to dry alongside a black boat. "This is the last time I'll ever see the lake," I thought. "The last time in my life." I looked intently at everything; I didn't want to forget. But to keep the past alive, it has to be fed with regrets and tears. How was I to hold on to my memories and protect my heart?

Abruptly, I said, " I'm going to ring up my friends and tell them I'm not coming."

" Why?" Lewis asked. " What a silly idea!"

" I'd rather stay here an extra day."

" But you were looking forward to seeing them," Lewis said reproachfully, as if nothing in the world were more foreign to him than a sudden change of mind.

" I don't feel like it any more," I said.

He shrugged his shoulders. " I think you're silly."

I didn't make the call. If Lewis thought it silly of me to stay, then it was indeed silly. Seeing me one day more or less meant hardly anything to him. What, then, would I get out of lingering an extra day on that beach? I said my good-byes to everyone. "You'll come back?" Dorothy asked, and I replied, "Yes." I packed my suitcases, entrusted them to Lewis, and took only a little overnight bag with me. When he closed the door of the house behind us, he asked me, "Don't you want to say good-bye to the pond?" I shook my head and began walking towards the bus stop. If he had loved me, leaving him for twenty-four hours would hardly have been a tragedy. But it was too cold inside me; I needed his presence to warm me. I had made myself an uncomfortable nest in that house, but at least it was a nest; I made the best of it. I was afraid of venturing out into the open air.

The bus drew up. Lewis gave my cheek a perfunctory kiss. "Have a nice time!" And the door slammed, he disappeared. Soon, another door would slam; he would disappear forever. How, far away from him, would I bear that certainty? Evening was falling when I settled down in the train; the sky was the colour of a tea rose, and I understood then how breathing in the fragrance of a rose could make one faint. We crossed the flatlands. And then the train entered the outskirts of Chicago. I recognised the black brick façades with their wooden stairs and porches; it was, reproduced in thousands of copies, the house of my love, which was no longer my house.

I got off at the station. The windows of the buildings were lighting up; the neon signs were beginning to glow. The headlights, the gaudy shop windows, the roar of the traffic made my head spin; I stopped alongside the river. Its draw-bridges were raised; a cargo ship with black smokestacks was solemnly splitting the acquiescing city in two. Slowly, I walked down towards the lake along the river's dark waters, in which captive fires were glittering. Those transparent stones, that painted sky, those waters from which rose the lights and clamour of a submerged city—it wasn't a dream dreamed by someone else. It was human, teeming, real, a city of the earth in which I, a flesh-and-blood I, was walking. How beautiful it was under its silvery brocade! I looked at it wide-eyed, and something stirred timidly in my heart. We think that it is love that gives the world all its brilliance, but the world, too, swells love with its riches. Love was dead, yet the earth was still there, intact, with its secret songs, its smells, its tenderness. I felt strangely moved, like the convalescent who discovers that during his illness the sun hasn't gone out.

Neither Myriam nor Philip knew Chicago, but they had managed to pick out the city's most sophisticated restaurant to meet me in. Crossing the resplendent lobby, I stopped in front of a mirror; it was the first time in many weeks I had had a full-length view of myself. I had put up my hair, put on my city make-up, I had exhumed my Indian blouse; its colours were still as precious as they were in Chichicastenango; and as for me, I hadn't aged, I wasn't disfigured; seeing my reflection again wasn't at all unpleasant. I sat down at the bar and, while drinking a martini, I remembered with surprise that waiting could be restful and solitude pleasant.

" Anne, darling!" Myriam said, kissing me on the cheek. Under her ebony-and-silver hair, she seemed younger and more resolute than ever. Philip's handshake was full of ineffable innuendoes. He had put on a little bit of weight, but he had kept his adolescent charm and his haughty elegance. We talked disjointedly of France, of Nancy's marriage, of Mexico. And then we went to beg for our table in a vast room dripping with crystal chandeliers and presided over by a haughty maître d'hôtel. It was—God only knows through what whim!—the exact replica of a room—the Pump Room at Bath—where the elegant eighteenth-century English went to take the waters. Negro waiters disguised as Indian maharajahs were brandishing skewers on which chunks of flaming lamb were impaled; others, costumed as eighteenth-century lackeys, were parading giant fish.

" What a masquerade!" I said.

" I love these silly places," Philip said, smiling his subtle smile. They finally conceded him the table he had reserved, and he scrupulously composed our menus. When we began talking, I was surprised to find out that we agreed on almost nothing. They had read Lewis's book; they did not think it was written tightly enough. In Mexico, the bullfights had sickened them; on the other hand, the Indian villages in Honduras and Guatemala seemed to them poetic Edens.

" Poetic for the tourist!" I said. "But didn't you see all those blind children, and the women with their swollen bellies? A strange sort of paradise!"

"You mustn't judge the Indians according to our standards," Philip said.

"When you're starving to death, you're starving to death; it's the same for everyone."

Philip raised his eyebrows. "How strange!" he said. "Europeans accuse Americans of being materialistic; but you give much more importance than we do to the material aspects of life."

"Perhaps one has to have enjoyed American comforts to understand how very little comfort matters," Myriam said.

She was devouring her *canard aux cerises* with quiet detachment. Her electric-blue dress revealed beautiful, ripe shoulders. She was certainly capable of sleeping in a caravan and of following, for a while, a carefully planned vegetarian diet.

"It isn't a question of comfort," I said a little too impatiently. "Being deprived of the basic necessities, that matters. Nothing else matters."

Philip smiled at me. "What's necessary for some isn't necessary for others. You know better than I do how subjective a thing happiness is." Allowing me no time to answer, he added, "We're very tempted to spend a year or two in Honduras and work there in peace and quiet. I'm sure we have a great deal to learn from those old civilisations."

"I really don't see what," I said. "Inasmuch as you object to certain things that are going on now in the United States, it would be far better to try to do something about them."

"You, too? Have you also become a victim of that psychosis?" Philip said. "Action—it's the obsession of every French writer! It betrays some strange complexes—because they know perfectly well they'll never change a thing."

"All the American intellectuals plead impotence," I said. "That's what seems like a strange complex. You won't have any right to complain the day the United States become completely fascist, or the day it starts a war."

Myriam was about to put a croquette of wild rice in her mouth, but she let her fork fall back on her plate. "You talk like a Communist, Anne," she said sharply.

"The United States doesn't want war, Anne," Philip said,

giving me a look heavy with reproach. "You can assure your French friends of that. If we're actively preparing for one, it's precisely to avoid having to wage it. And we shall never become fascists."

"That isn't what you were saying two years ago," I said. "You thought then that American democracy was seriously threatened."

Philip's face became very grave. "What I've learned since then is that it isn't possible to defend democracy with democratic methods. The Soviet Union's fanaticism is forcing us into a balancing stiffness of policies; that leads to excesses which I'm the first to deplore. But they don't imply that we've chosen fascism. They express the universal tragedy of the modern world."

I studied him in astonishment. Two years before, we had understood each other quite well; at that time he firmly asserted the independence of his mind. And he had let himself be convinced with such ease by the official propaganda! Lewis, no doubt, was right when he said to me, "There are fewer and fewer of us."

"In other words," I said, "you feel the State Department's present policy is dictated by the situation?"

"Even if a different one could be imagined, dear Anne," he said gently, "it isn't I who would be capable of forcing in upon them. No, if one wishes to escape all complicity with this distressing age, the only solution is to withdraw to some remote corner and live there apart from the world."

They wanted to continue leading their comfortable, care-free, æsthete's life; no argument would dent their genteel egotism. I decided to let it drop. "I believe we could discuss the matter all night without convincing each other," I said. "These discussions leading to nothing are really a waste of time."

"Especially when we've been deprived of you for so long and when we're so happy to see you again!" Philip said with a smile. He began talking about a new American poet.

"Anne, we're putting ourselves in your hands to-night. I'm sure you're an admirable guide," Philip said as we left the restaurant.

We got in the car, and I took them to the lakeside. Philip gave it his approval. "It's the loveliest skyline in the United States, lovelier than New York's." On the other hand, it was established that the burlesque shows were inferior to Boston's, the cheap saloons less picturesque than San Francisco's. Those comparisons astonished me. To what could they be compared, those places Lewis had one night plucked from nothingness? Did they, then, have their geographical place? The fact was that, through my memories, I discovered the way to them easily. The Club Delisa belonged to a now-defunct past, was situated nowhere on earth. And yet there it was, at the intersection of two streets. And both streets had names, both were printed on maps.

"Excellent atmosphere!" Philip said with a satisfied air. And while watching the jugglers, the dancers, the acrobats, I wondered what would have happened if, two years earlier, he had said to me on the telephone, "I'll be down." Certainly, we would have had a few beautiful nights together, but I wouldn't have liked him for long; I would never have really loved him. It seemed strange indeed that chance could have chosen for me with such certainty. No doubt it wasn't by chance that Philip had preferred a week-end in Cape Cod to me, that out of deference to his mother he hadn't joined me in my room. Had he been more passionate, more courageous, he would also have thought, felt, and lived differently; he would have been someone else. Nevertheless, slightly different circumstances could have thrown me into his arms, could have deprived me of Lewis. The thought revolted me. Our affair had cost me dearly in tears; and yet I would not have agreed to rip it from my past for anything in the world. And suddenly, it was a consolation to think that even ended, doomed, it would continue to live in me forever.

When we left the club, Philip drove us back to the lake. The tall buildings had dissolved in the early morning's haze. He stopped the car alongside the planetarium and we went down the steps of the promontory to hear at closer range the lapping of the blue waters. How new they looked under that slate-coloured sky! "I, too," I said to myself hopefully, "my life, too, is going to begin again. Once again it will be a life, my own life." The following afternoon, I guided Myriam and Philip through parks and market places, along streets and avenues which quite plainly belonged to an earth-bound city, a city in which I knew my way about without guidance. If the world had been given back to me, the future was no longer completely impossible.

And yet, at dusk, when the red car sped off towards New York, I was reluctant to go back to the apartment; I was afraid of the empty room and of the mourning in my heart. I went to a film, and then I walked along the streets. Never before had I strolled alone at night through Chicago; under its spangled veils, the city had lost its hostile air, but I didn't know what to do with it. I was wandering aimlessly through a party to which I hadn't been invited, and my eyes filled. I bit my lip. No, I didn't want to cry. Really. I wasn't crying, I told myself; it was the night lights that trembled inside of me, and their glitter was condensing in salty drops on the edge of my lashes—because I was there, because I would never return, because the world is too rich, too poor, the past too heavy, too light, because I couldn't turn that too-beautiful hour into happiness, because my love had died and I would survive it.

I took a cab. I found myself once more at the corner of the alley lined with ash cans; in the darkness, my foot bumped against the first step of the stairway. A red crown was glowing on top of the gas tank, and in the distance a train whistled. I opened the door; a light was on, but Lewis was sleeping. I undressed, turned out the light, and slipped into that bed where I had cried so much. Where had I found all those tears? Why? Suddenly, there was nothing any more that was worth even a single sob. I crushed my body against the wall; I hadn't slept in Lewis's warmth for so long that I felt as if a stranger had granted me, out of pity, a piece of his bed.

He stirred, he reached out his hand. " You're back? What time is it? "

" Midnight. I didn't want to get here before you."

" Oh, I was here at ten o'clock." His voice sounded wide awake. " How sad this house is, isn't it? "

" Yes. A funeral parlour."

" An abandoned funeral parlour," he said. " It's full of ghosts: the little whore, the madwoman, the pickpocket—all those people I'll never see again. They won't come out there. I like the house in Parker very much, but it's too sensible. Here . . ."

" Here there was a sort of magic," I said.

" Magic? I don't know. But, at least, people dropped in, things happened."

Lying on his back in the darkness, he conjured up aloud the days and nights spent in that room, and I felt a tug at my heart. His life had seemed poetic to me, as the Indians' had to Philip. But for him, what an austere existence it had been! How many weeks, how many months without a friendly encounter, without an adventure, without a presence! How he must have wanted a woman, a woman completely his! For a moment, he had thought he had escaped solitude; he had dared to wish for something other than security. And he had been duped, he had suffered, he had recovered. I ran my hand over my face; from now on, my eyes would stay dry. I understood only too well he had been unable to afford the luxuries of regret, of waiting; I didn't want to be a thorn in his life. I didn't even have the right to a single regret; I was left without complaint. I was left with absolutely nothing.

Suddenly, he turned on the light and smiled at me. "Anne, you didn't have too bad a summer, did you?"

I hesitated. "It wasn't the best one of my life."

"I know," he said, "I know. And there are many things I'm sorry about. There were times when you thought I felt superior or hostile. That was not so. But sometimes I get a knot in my chest. I'd let everybody in the world die, and die myself, rather than budge an inch."

"I know too," I said. "I suppose it all goes very far back. It must have come from your having had such a hard youth, and probably from your childhood, too."

"No! You aren't going to start psycho-analysing me!" he said, laughing. But he was already on the defensive.

"You needn't worry about that," I said. "But I remember a night two years ago, when we were at the Club Delisa and I wanted to give you back my ring and leave for New York. Afterwards, you said to me, 'I couldn't get myself to say a single word.'"

"I said that? What a memory you have!"

"Yes, I've got a good memory," I said. "It doesn't help. Don't you remember that that night we made love without a word? You looked almost hostile, and I said, 'Do you at least feel a little friendship for me?' You backed up against the wall and you answered, 'Friendship? Why, I love you!'"

I had mimicked his half-mocking voice and Lewis burst out laughing. "It seems absurd!"

"That's what you said, and that's the way you said it."

Staring at the ceiling, he murmured, "Maybe I still love you."

A few weeks earlier, I would have clutched eagerly at that sentence, I would have tried to nurture it into a hope. But it evoked no echo in me. It was natural that Lewis should question himself about his feelings, and one can always play with words; but there could be no doubt that our affair was over. He knew it, and so did I.

During those last days, we spoke neither of the past, nor of the future, nor of our feelings. Lewis was there and I was near him: that was enough. Since we asked for nothing, nothing was denied us; it was almost impossible to believe ourselves filled to overflowing. And perhaps we were.

The night of my departure, I said, "Lewis, I don't know if I'll ever stop loving you; but I do know that all my life you'll be in my heart."

He held me against him. "And you in mine, all my life."

Would we ever see each other again? I didn't want to question myself any more. Lewis accompanied me to the airport. He kissed me quickly when he left me in front of the ticket windows, and I swept everything from my mind. Just before boarding the plane, a messenger handed me a cardboard box in which lay, under a shroud of silky paper, a huge orchid. When I arrived in Paris, it still hadn't faded.

CHAPTER ELEVEN

A BEE WAS buzzing around around the ash tray. Henri raised his head and breathed in the sweet smell of the phlox. Once more, his hand glided over the paper and finished recopying a page of the rough draft. He enjoyed these mornings in the shade of the linden tree. Perhaps it was because he had nothing else to do but write that a book seemed to him an important thing. And then, he was happy that Dubreuilh had liked his novel; this short story would surely please him, too. Henri had a feeling that, for once, he had done exactly what he had set out to do. It's a pleasant feeling to be satisfied with oneself.

Nadine's face appeared at one of the upstairs windows, between a pair of blue shutters. "How studious you look! Like a schoolboy doing his homework."

Henri smiled. Actually, he did feel the clear, happy conscience of a schoolboy who had just finished his lessons. " Is Maria awake?" he asked.

" Yes, we're coming down," Nadine replied.

He set his papers in order. Noon. If he wanted to avoid Charlier and Méricaud, it was time to leave. They were coming again to urge Dubreuilh to undertake that weekly, and Henri was weary of repeating, " I don't want to get mixed up in it."

"Here we are!" Nadine said.

In one hand, she was carrying a shopping bag, and in the other a contraption of which she was very proud: something between a suitcase and a cradle. Henri took hold of it.

"Careful! Don't disturb her!" Nadine said.

Henri smiled at Maria. He was still full of astonishment at having produced from nothingness a brand-new little girl, a blue-eyed, dark-haired little girl who was his. She stared confidently into space as he set her down in the back of the car.

"Let's get out of here fast!" he said.

Nadine sat down at the wheel; she loved to drive.

"I'll stop at the station first and buy the papers."

" If you really want to."

" Of course I want to. Especially since it's Thursday."

L'Enclume came out on Thursdays, as well as *L'Espoir-Magazine,* which had merged with *Les Beaux Jours.* Nadine didn't want to miss such excellent opportunities to become indignant.

They bought a pile of newspapers and magazines and drove off towards the woods. Nadine never spoke while she was driving ; she was much too intent on the task at hand. Henri looked affectionately at her stubborn profile. He found her touching when she steeped herself in something with that intense concentration. It was this quality above all—her fierce willingness—that had moved him when he began seeing her again. " I've changed, you know," she had said to him the first day. Actually, she hadn't changed very much ; but she had realised that something inside her was out of joint and she was trying to set herself straight. He had wanted to help her. He had told himself that if he could make her happy he would free her of that confused resentment which was poisoning her life. Since she had wanted so much to be married to him, he had decided to marry her ; he was fond enough of her to risk it. Strange girl! She always had to wrest from you by main force what you were quite willing to give her. Henri was certain that, to force his hand, she had manœuvred her pregnancy by cheating on the dates. And afterwards, of course, she had convinced herself that by confronting him with an accomplished fact, she had merely helped make him aware of his true desires. He studied her, perplexed. She was a storehouse of self-deceptions, but she was also perspicacious. Certainly, deep down inside, she had her doubts that he had acted of his own free will. To a great extent, that was why he hadn't succeeded in making her really happy ; she knew he didn't really love her and she held it against him. " Maybe it would be better to explain to her that I always felt free because I was never fooled," Henri said to himself. But learning that he had known all along what she had been up to would painfully humiliate Nadine ; she would become convinced that Henri despised her and had only taken pity on her. Nothing could have hurt her more ; she hated to be judged, but she also hated to be showered with overgenerous gifts No, it would do no good to tell her the truth.

Nadine stopped the car alongside the pond. " It's really a

nice spot," she said. " During the week, no one's ever here."

" It'll be wonderful in the water," Henri said.

She checked to see if Maria was all right, and they undressed. Under her linen dress, Nadine was wearing a green, very brief Bikini bathing suit. Her legs had grown more slender, and her breasts were as young as ever.

Henri said cheerfully, " You're a pretty little wench!"

" You're not so bad yourself," she said, laughing.

They ran down to the pond. Nadine swam with her head sticking straight up in the water, majestically, as if she were bearing it on a tray. He liked her face. " I'm fond of her," he said to himself. " I m even very fond of her. Why isn't it quite love?" Something in Nadine chilled him: her suspiciousness, her grudges, her deceitfulness, the hostile solitude in which she took refuge. But perhaps if he had loved her more, she would have become more open, more expansive, more agreeable. It was a vicious circle: love can't be served up to order, nor can confidence. Neither one could come first.

They swam for a long time and then stretched out in the sun. Nadine pulled a package of sandwiches out of the shopping bag. Henri took one.

" You know," he said after a moment, " I've been thinking over what you told me yesterday about Sézenac. I just can't bring myself to believe it. Is Vincent sure it was really Sézenac?"

" Absolutely sure," Nadine replied. " It took him a year, but he finally found some people and made them talk. Sézenac was working the border-crossing swindle. God only knows how many Jews he betrayed to the Germans! There's no doubt he's the one."

" But why?" Henri asked.

He could hear Chancel's enthusiastic voice: " I bring you my best friend." He could see that hard, pure, handsome face that immediately inspired confidence.

" For the money, I suppose," Nadine said. " No one suspected it, but he must have been a drug addict even then."

" And why did he take drugs?"

" That I don't know," Nadine replied.

" Where is he now?"

" Vincent would love to know! He threw him out last year when he found out he was a stool pigeon. Since then, he's lost trace of him. But he'll find him again," she added.

Henri bit into his sandwich. He wasn't anxious for Sézenac to be found. Dubreuilh had promised him that, if necessary, he would swear he had known Mercier very well, and between the two of them they would surely be able to pull it off. But all the same, it would be far better if that business never came up again.

"What are you thinking about?" Nadine asked.

"Sézenac."

He hadn't told Nadine about the Mercier affair. She would never, of course, have betrayed a secret, but somehow it was difficult to confide in her; she displayed too much curiosity and showed too little sympathy. And you needed a great deal of sympathy to stomach that incident. Despite Anne's and Dubreuilh's indulgence, Henri could never think of it without feeling uncomfortable. Anyhow, he had got what he wanted. Josette hadn't killed herself; she had become a much-talked-about starlet; every week her picture appeared in one magazine or another.

"Sézenac will be found," Nadine repeated.

She unfolded a newspaper; Henri picked one up, too. As long as he was in France, he couldn't avoid looking through them; and yet, he would have willingly done without them. "American Strangle Hold on Europe . . . R.P.F. Triumph . . . Wholesale Return of Collaborators . . . Communist Blunder "—it was rather depressing. In Berlin, things weren't getting any better; war could very well break out any day. Henri lay back and closed his eyes. In Porto Venere, he wouldn't open a single paper. What for? Since you can't prevent anything, you might just as well spend your remaining days completely free of care. "That shocks Dubreuilh. But he thinks it's reasonable to live as if you were never going to die. It amounts to the same thing," Henri said to himself. "What's the good of preparing yourself? No matter what you do, you're never really ready. And then again, you're always ready enough."

"It's unbelievable the fuss they're making over that miserable book of Volange's!" Nadine said.

"Naturally. At the moment, the whole press is on the right," Henri said.

"Even on the right, they aren't all idiots."

"But they need a masterpiece so badly!" Henri said.

Volange's book was a padded trifle. But he had launched a rather ingenious slogan: "The integration of evil." To have been a collaborator was to have drunk at the fecund springs of error; a lynching in the South was sin, therefore redemption; blessed be America for all her crimes, and long live the Marshall Plan! Our civilisation is guilty—that is its highest claim to glory. And wanting to bring about a more just world—that was a glaring error!

"Listen, dear heart, when your novel comes out, are they ever going to let you have it!" Nadine said.

"I can well imagine!" Henri said. He yawned. "Ah, it's no fun any more! I know in advance exactly what Volange is going to write. And Lenoir, too. Even the others, the ones who claim they're impartial, I can tell you what they're going to say."

"What?" Nadine asked.

"They'll criticise me for having written neither *War and Peace* nor *La Princesse de Clèves*. Mind you, the libraries are filled with all the books I didn't write," he added cheerfully, "but it's always those two they throw up to you."

"When is Mauvanes planning to bring it out?"

"In two months, at the end of September."

"Just a short time before we leave," Nadine said. She stretched out on the ground. "I wish we were there already."

"So do I," Henri said.

It wouldn't have been nice to leave Dubreuilh alone; he could understand Nadine's wanting to wait for her mother to get back before taking off. And besides, Henri liked it a lot at St. Martin. But he would like it even better in Italy. That house on the sea, among the crags and pine trees, was exactly the kind of place he had often dreamed of, never quite believing in it, when he used to say to himself, "Drop everything, leave for the Midi, write."

"We'll take a good gramophone with us, and piles of records," Nadine said.

"And lots of books," Henri added. "We'll make a good life for ourselves there, you'll see."

Nadine raised herself on an elbow. "It's funny. We're going to move into Pimienta's house in Italy, and he's coming to live in Paris. Langstone doesn't ever want to set foot in America again . . ."

"All three of us are in the same boat," Henri said.

"Writers who engaged in politics and who got fed up with it. Living in a foreign country is the best way of burning one's bridges."

"I was the one who had the idea of taking that house," Nadine said, looking pleased with herself.

"You were the one," Henri smiled. "You do manage to have a good idea every now and then."

Nadine's face darkened. For a moment, she stared angrily at the horizon, and then she abruptly got up. "I'm going to give Maria her bottle."

Henri followed her with his eyes. What exactly had she been thinking of just then? One thing was certain: she found it difficult to resign herself to the prospect of being nothing but a housewife. She sat down on a tree trunk, Maria in her arms. She gave the baby her bottle with authority, with patience; she made it a point of honour of being a competent mother, she had acquired both a solid background in child care and a lot of hygienic gadgets. But never had Henri caught a look of real affection in her eyes while she was tending Maria. Yes, that was what made it difficult to love her: even with her own baby she kept her distance; she still remained shut in herself.

"Are you going for another swim?" she asked.

"Yes."

They went back into the water for a few minutes, dried themselves, got dressed, and then Nadine took the wheel again.

"I hope they've already left," Henri said when the car drew up before the iron gate.

"I'll go and see," Nadine said.

Maria was sleeping. Henri carried her into the house and set her down on a chest in the foyer. Nadine glued her ear to the door of the study and then pushed it open. "Are you alone?"

"Yes. Come in, come on in," Dubreuilh called out.

"I'm going upstairs to put the baby to bed," Nadine said.

Henri went into the study and smiled. "It's a shame you weren't able to come with us. The water was fine."

"I'll go one of these days," Dubreuilh said. He picked up a slip of paper from his desk. "I have a message for you. A certain Jean Patureau, a brother of the lawyer you know, called up and asked that you call him back as soon as possible. His brother sent him some information from Madagascar which he wants to pass on to you."

"Why does he want to see me particularly?" Henri asked.

"Because of those articles you wrote last year, I suppose," Dubreuilh replied. "You're the only one who broke the story." Dubreuilh handed Henri a slip of paper. "If the fellow can give you the facts about what's brewing down there, you still have enough time for an article for *Vigilance*, if we hold up the next issue a bit."

"I'll ring him in a bit," Henri said.

"Méricaud was telling me that what they're doing there is completely without precedent: trying the accused on the spot," Dubreuilh said. "In all similar cases, the trials were held in France."

Henri sat down. "Did your luncheon go well?"

"Poor Charlier is falling apart more and more," Dubreuilh said. "It's sad to grow old."

"Did they bring up the weekly again?"

"That's what they came for. It seems that Manheim insists on seeing me."

"It's really funny," Henri said. "When we needed money, we could never find any. And now that we're not asking anybody for anything, here's this character chasing after you begging you to take the lot."

Manheim was the son of a wealthy banker who had died in a concentration camp; he himself had been deported and afterwards had spent three years in a Swiss sanatorium. He had written a book there, a very bad one, but full of good intentions. Now he had decided to establish a big leftist weekly, and he had made up his mind that he wanted Dubreuilh to edit it.

"I'm going to see him," Dubreuilh said.

"And what are you going to tell him?" Henri asked. He smiled. "Are you beginning to be tempted?"

"You've got to admit that it's tempting," Dubreuilh replied. "Besides the Communist sheets, there isn't a single leftist weekly. If we could really have a magazine with a big circulation and pictures, articles, everything, it would be well worth while."

Henri shrugged his shoulders. "Do you have any idea of

the work it takes to build up a big successful weekly? It's a far cry from *Vigilance*. You've got to work on it night and day, especially the first year."

"I know," Dubreuilh said. He sought Henri's eyes. "That's why I can't think of accepting unless you go along, too."

"You know very well that I'm leaving for Italy," Henri said, a little impatiently. "But if this thing really interests you, you won't have any trouble finding associates," he added.

Dubreuilh shook his head. "I have absolutely no experience in journalism," he said. "If I went into this thing, I'd need a specialist at my side. And you know how things like that work; in actual fact, he'd be the one who would have the guiding hand in everything. I'd have to be able to trust him as I trust myself. And you're the only one."

"Even if I weren't leaving, I'd never take on a job like that," Henri said.

"That's too bad," Dubreuilh said reproachfully. "Because it's just the kind of job we could handle well. We might have turned out something really good."

"And then what?" Henri said. "We're in an even tighter squeeze than we were last year. What possible influence could we exert? None."

"Nevertheless there are still certain things we could do," Dubreuilh said. "America wants to arm Europe: there's a point on which we could organise some resistance. And for that, a magazine would be damned helpful."

Henri began to laugh. "What it adds up to is that you're only looking for an opportunity to get back into politics again. What an iron constitution!"

"Who has an iron constitution?" Nadine asked as she entered the study.

"Your father. He still hasn't had his fill of politics. He wants to give it another try."

"People have to do something to keep busy," Nadine said. She kneeled in front of the record cabinet and began going through the records. "Yes," Henri thought, "Dubreuilh is bored; that's why he wants to get back into the thick of things."

"I've never been happier than I have been since I gave up

politics," Henri said. "I wouldn't get involved in it again for anything in the world."

"I think that that kind of stagnation is pretty rotten," Dubreuilh said. "The left completely dispersed, the Communist Party isolated! Some attempt ought to be made to get together again."

"Are you thinking of a new S.R.L.?" Henri asked incredulously.

"No, above all not that!" Dubreuilh replied. He shrugged his shoulders. "I'm not thinking of anything specific. All I'm saying is that we're in a lousy mess and I wish we could get out of it."

There was a silence. Henri recalled a very similar scene: Dubreuilh was pressuring him, he was defending himself, and he was thinking that soon he would be far from Paris, elsewhere. But in those days, he still believed he had obligations. To-day, he was sufficiently convinced of his impotence to feel absolutely free. "Whether I say yes or whether I say no," Henri thought, "isn't going to affect the fate of humanity. It will only affect the way I tie my own fate to his. Dubreuilh keeps confusing them in his mind. He's concerned about it, not I. At any rate, it concerns only him, only me. Nothing else is at stake."

"May I put a record on?" Nadine asked.

"Of course," Dubreuilh replied.

Henri got up. "I'm going to work."

"Don't forget to ring up that fellow," Dubreuilh said.

"I won't forget," Henri said.

He crossed the hall and picked up the telephone. The voice at the other end of the line seemed filled at once with bewilderment, importance, and diffidence. One felt that its owner had just received an imperious message from the gods which he had to deliver immediately and at all cost. Pompously, he said, "My brother writes: 'No one is lifting a finger, but I'm sure Henri Perron would do something.'" And Henri thought, "It looks as if I can't get out of writing an article." He made an appointment to see Patureau the next day in Paris and then went back to the table under the linden tree. That was why he was so anxious to leave for Italy: here he still received too many letters, too many visits, too many phone calls. He spread out his papers in front of him.

Nadine was sitting on the window sill, listening to the César Franck quartet; the bees were buzzing around the cluster of phlox; and an ox-cart, creaking with age, was going down the road. "What peace!" Henri said to himself. Why were they forcing him to get involved in something that was happening in Tananarive? Horrible things are constantly happening on earth; but a person doesn't live all over the world, and dwelling endlessly on distant misfortunes, which you can't do anything about, is nothing but a form of morbid self-indulgence. "This is where I live, and here there is peace," he thought. He looked at Nadine. She was quietly relaxed in a way that was quite unusual for her. She, who had so much trouble concentrating on a book, could listen for hours to music she liked, and at those times one could feel a stillness in her that was close to happiness. "I've got to make her happy," Henri said to himself. "There must be a way of breaking that vicious circle." Making someone happy: that was concrete, that was solid, and if you really put your heart in it, it could keep you pretty well absorbed. Looking after Nadine, raising Maria, writing his books—it wasn't quite the life he had once hoped for. There was a time when he believed that happiness was one way of mastering the world, while actually it was closer to being a way of protecting yourself against it. Nevertheless, it was good to hear that music, to look at the house, at the linden tree, at his manuscript there on the table, saying to himself as he did so, "I am happy."

Henri's article on Madagascar appeared on the tenth of August. He had written it with intense emotion. Illegal execution of the star witness, attempts made on the lawyers' lives, tortures inflicted on the accused in order to extract false confessions from them—the truth was even more monstrous than he had imagined. And it wasn't just in Tananarive that those things were happening; it was here, in France, as well. Everyone was guilty. Guilty the Assembly and the Senate which had voted the suspension of immunity; guilty the government, the High Court, and the President of the Republic; guilty the newspapers which remained silent and the millions of citizens who accepted that silence. "Now, at least, there are a few thousand who know," he said to himself when he had the issue of *Vigilance* in his hands. But regretfully, he thought, "It isn't a hell of a lot." He had studied that affair so closely, had taken it so much to heart, that it began to concern him personally. Each morning, he would look through the papers for the small news items devoted to the trial and he would think about them all day long. He had a good deal of trouble finishing his story. Now, when he wrote in the shade of the linden tree, the smell of the phlox and the distant sounds from the village didn't have the same savour as before.

He was working one morning, absent-mindedly, when the bell rang at the gate. He crossed the garden to open it: it was Lachaume.

" You!" he said.

" Yes. I'd like to talk to you," Lachaume said calmly. " You don't look very happy to see me, but at least you can let me in," he added. " You'll be interested in what I have to tell you."

Lachaume had aged during those eighteen months, and there were deep circles under his eyes.

" What do you want to talk to me about?"

" The Madagascan affair."

Henri opened the gate. " What business could you possibly have with a dirty fascist?"

" Oh, drop it!" Lachaume said. " You know how politics are. When I wrote that article, I had to execute you. But that's an old story."

" I have a good memory," Henri said.

Lachaume looked pained. " Hold a grudge against me if you must! Although you really ought to understand," he said with a sigh. " But just now it isn't a question of either you or me; there are human lives to be saved. You could at least listen to me for five minutes."

" I'm listening," Henri said, motioning him to one of the wicker chairs. As a matter of fact, he no longer felt any anger towards Lachaume; that whole past was much too far from him now.

" You've just written a very wonderful article; I'd even call it an overpowering article," Lachaume said determinedly.

Henri shrugged his shoulders. " Unfortunately, it hasn't overpowered very many."

" Yes, that's the whole trouble," Lachaume said. He looked Henri in the eyes. " If you were offered the chance to exert a broader influence, I don't suppose you'd turn it down, would you?"

"What do you have in mind?" Henri asked.

"In a word, here it is. We're organising a committee for the defence of the Madagascans. It would have been a lot better if some other group had taken the initiative rather than we. But the petit-bourgeois idealists don't always have a very sensitive conscience; at times, they're able to stomach damned near anything without flinching. The fact remains that no one is lifting a finger."

"Until now, you haven't done very much either," Henri said.

"We couldn't," Lachaume replied quickly. "The whole business was cooked up in order to liquidate the M.D.R.M. Through the Madagascan representatives, they're aiming at the Party. If we make too much noise, it'll only turn against them."

"All right," Henri said. "What then?"

"Well, I got the idea of a committee in which there'd be two or three Communists and a majority of non-Communists. When I read your article, I said to myself that no one was better qualified than you to act as chairman." Lachaume looked at Henri questioningly. "The Party isn't against the idea. But before making you an official offer, Lafaurie wants to be sure you'll accept."

Henri remained silent. Fascist, traitor, squealer, bastard— they had accused him of being capable of every crime in the book. And now they were coming to him with out- stretched hands. It gave him a little feeling of triumph, a rather agreeable feeling.

"Who exactly is going to be on the committee?" he asked.

"Anyone of any importance who's willing to join up," Lachaume replied. "They aren't legion." He shrugged his shoulders. "They're all so damned frightened of compromis- ing themselves! They'd rather let twenty innocent people be tortured to death than have anything to do with us. If you took the thing in hand, it would change everything," he added urgently. "You, they'd follow."

Henri hesitated. "Why don't you ask Dubreuilh instead? His name carries more weight than mine, and he's sure to say yes."

"We could certainly use Dubreuilh," Lachaume replied.

"But it's your name that has to go on top. Dubreuilh is too close to us. Above all, this committee mustn't look as if it's Communist-inspired. Otherwise, it's done for, right from the start. With you, there's no uncertainty."

"I see," Henri said curtly. "In so far as I'm a social traitor, I can be useful to you."

"Useful to us?" Lachaume said in an irritated voice. "It's the accused you can be useful to! What the hell do you think? What have we got to gain in this business? You haven't any idea," he continued, looking at Henri reproachfully. "Every day—this morning again—we get heart-breaking letters and telegrams from Madagascar. 'Speak out! Alert public opinion! Tell the people in France what's going on here!' And our hands are tied! What else can we do, except try to work by indirection?"

Henri smiled; he was touched by Lachaume's vehemence. Yes, he was quite capable of carrying out a piece of very dirty work, but not of accepting calmly the torture and wholesale massacre of innocent people.

"What do you expect?" Henri said in a conciliatory tone. "Everything is so jumbled up with you people—political lies and true feelings—that it's hard to know what you're up to."

"If all of you wouldn't start right off by accusing us of Machiavellism, you'd know a lot better what we're up to," Lachaume said. "You always seem to believe that the Party works only for itself! Do you remember in '46 when we intervened in behalf of Cristino Garcia? Afterwards, they blamed us for having made his execution inevitable. Now we're keeping our mouths shut. And then you come and tell me: 'You're not doing very much.'"

"Calm down," Henri said. "You seem to have got pretty touchy."

"You just can't imagine! That distrust we run into everywhere! After a while it becomes exasperating."

Henri felt like answering, "It's your own fault." But he said nothing; he felt he had no right to assume an attitude of facile superiority. To tell the truth, he no longer bore any grudge against Lachaume. One day in the Bar Rouge, Lachaume had told him, "I'd swallow anything rather than leave the Party." He felt his own person didn't count for much alongside what was at stake. Why then should he have accorded any more value to Henri's? Of course, under those conditions friendship was no longer possible. But there was no reason why they couldn't work together.

"Listen," he said, "I'd like nothing better than to work with you. I don't believe we have much chance of succeeding—but at least we can try."

Lachaume's face lit up. "Then I can tell Lafaurie you'll accept?"

"Yes. But give me an idea of what you have in mind."

"We'll work it out together," Lachaume said.

"Well, that's it!" Henri said to himself. "It's the same old story: every time you do something decent, it leads to new duties." The editorials he wrote in '47 had led to the article for *Vigilance*, which in turn brought on the task of organising this committee. Once again, he was hooked. "But not for long," he said to himself.

"You ought to go to bed," Nadine said scoldingly. "You look exhausted."

"The plane trip tired me out," Anne replied apologetically. "And then there's that difference in time—I slept very badly last night."

The study had a festive air. Anne had returned the day before, and Nadine had gathered all the flowers from the garden and had filled the house with them. But no one was very gay. Anne had aged markedly and she was drinking far too much whisky. Dubreuilh, who had been so wound-up the past few weeks, seemed worried—no doubt because of Anne. And Nadine, who was knitting something in scarlet, looked rather sullen. Henri's story had cast an even darker shadow over the evening.

"Then it's all over?" Anne asked. "There's absolutely no hope left of saving these men?"

"I see none at all," Henri replied.

"It was a foregone conclusion that the Assembly would bury the whole thing," Dubreuilh said.

"Nevertheless, if you had been at the session, you would have been amazed," Henri said. "I thought I was hardened to that kind of thing; but there were moments when I felt like killing."

"Yes, they were pretty strong," Dubreuilh said.

"I'm not surprised by politicians acting that way," Anne

said. "What I can't seem to understand is why there was so little reaction from people on the whole."

"No, in this matter, there wasn't much reaction," Henri said.

Gérard Patureau and the other lawyers had come to Paris, determined to move heaven and earth. The Committee had helped them all it could, but at every turn they ran into a wall of widespread indifference.

Anne looked at Dubreuilh. "Don't you find this discouraging?"

"Not at all," he replied. "All it proves is that you can't improvise political action. We started off at zero, so obviously . . ."

Dubreuilh had joined the Committee but had given it very little of his time. The thing that had interested him in that affair was that he had re-established political contacts. He had joined a movement called "Fighter for Freedom"; he had taken part in one of their meetings, and in a few days he was going to speak at another. He didn't insist on Henri's following him, and he didn't bring up the subject of the weekly again, but from time to time he let a more or less veiled reproach slip out.

"Improvised or not, action of whatever kind is bound to lead nowhere, the way things are to-day," Henri said.

"That's what you say," Dubreuilh protested. "If we had had an established group behind us, a paper, funds, we might have succeeded in stirring up public opinion."

"I'm not so sure about that," Henri said.

"At any rate, you'd better realise one thing: if we want to stand any chance at all of achieving our goal when the next opportunity comes along, we've got to prepare for it in advance."

"For me, there isn't going to be any next opportunity," Henri said.

"Come now!" Dubreuilh said. "You really make me laugh when you say that it's all over between politics and you. You're like me. You've had too much of it to give it up altogether. You'll be hooked again."

"No, I won't—because I'm taking shelter," Henri said gaily.

Dubreuilh's eyes lit up. "I'll make you a bet: you won't stay a year in Italy."

"I'll take that bet," Nadine said quickly. She turned to her mother. "What do you think?"

"I don't know," Anne replied. "It depends upon how you like it there."

"How can you possibly expect us not to like it? You saw the picture of the house. Isn't it pretty?"

"It looks lovely," Anne replied. Suddenly, she stood up. "Excuse me. I'm completely exhausted."

"I'll go up with you," Dubreuilh said.

"Try to get some sleep to-night," Nadine said, giving her mother a kiss. "Really, you look awful."

"I'll sleep," Anne said.

When she had closed the door, Henri sought Nadine's eyes. "Anne does look worn out," he said.

"Worn out and grim," Nadine said maliciously. "If she misses her America so much, she should have stayed there."

"Didn't she tell you how it went over there?"

"Of course not! She's much too secretive," Nadine replied. "Besides, no one ever tells me anything," she added.

Henri studied her with curiosity. "You have a strange relationship with your mother."

"Why strange?" Nadine said, annoyed. "I'm very fond of her, but she often gets on my nerves. I suppose it's the same with her. There's really nothing unusual about it; that's the way family relationships are."

Henri didn't pursue the issue. But he had always been aware of the fact that, while those two women would have given their lives for each other, there was, nevertheless, quite a bit of friction between them; Nadine became much more aggressive and much more stubborn when her mother was present. In the days that followed, Anne made an effort to appear cheerful, and Nadine loosened up. But one still had the feeling that a storm could break out at any moment.

Looking out of his window one morning, Henri saw them leaving the garden arm in arm, laughing happily together. When they again crossed the lawn two hours later, Anne carrying a loaf of bread under her arm, Nadine the newspapers, they looked as if they had had an argument. It was lunchtime. Henri arranged his papers, washed his hands, and went down to the living-room. Anne was sitting on the edge of a chair, wool-gathering; Dubreuilh was reading

L'Espoir-Magazine, and Nadine, standing beside him, was watching him intently.

"Hallo! What's up?" Henri asked, giving everyone a smile.

"This!" Nadine said, pointing to the newspaper. "I hope you're going to smash Lambert's face in," she added sharply.

"Oh, it's begun, eh? Lambert's dragging me through the mud?" Henri asked with a smile.

"If it were you alone he was dragging!"

"Here," Dubreuilh said, handing the paper to Henri.

It was titled "Self-Portraits." Lambert began by once more deploring the evil influence exerted by Dubreuilh: it was his fault if, after a brilliant start, Henri had lost all talent. Next, Lambert gave a summary of Henri's novel with the help of distorted quotes coupled together so as to make them seem ludicrous. Under the pretext of revealing the keys of a novel that had none, he related a lot of half-truths, about the private lives of Dubreuilh, Anne, Nadine and Henri, half-truths chosen in a way to make them appear both detestable and ridiculous.

"What a bastard!" Henri said. "I remember that conversation we once had on our attitudes towards money. And this is what he twisted it into! This filthy paragraph on ' the hypocrisy of the moneyed leftists!' What a bastard!" he repeated.

"You aren't going to let him get away with it, are you?" Nadine asked.

Henri glanced at Dubreuilh. "I'd love to smash his face in, and it wouldn't be very difficult. But what would we gain by it? A scandal, reverberations in all the newspapers, another article even worse than this one . . ."

"Punch him hard enough, and he'll shut up," Nadine said.

"Certainly not," Dubreuilh said. "All he wants is to be talked about. He'd jump at the opportunity. I'm in favour of Henri's letting it drop," he concluded.

"Yes? And whenever he gets the urge, what's to stop him from writing another article, and going even further?" Nadine said. "If he knows he has nothing to fear, you can be sure he won't be bashful."

"That's the way it is when you get mixed up in writing," Henri said. "Everyone has the right to spit on you; in fact, a lot of people even consider it a duty."

"I don't write," Nadine said. "No one has the right to spit on *me*."

"Yes, at first it upsets you," Anne said. "But you'll see; you'll get used to it." She got up. "How about having lunch?'

They sat down at the table in silence. Nadine speared a slice of sausage on the serving platter, and her face relaxed. "It irritates me to think he's going to triumph in peace," she said in a puzzled voice.

"He isn't triumphing as much as all that," Henri said. "What he wanted to write were personal sketches and novels. And apart from his articles, Volange hasn't published anything of his since that famous short story which was so lousy."

Nadine turned to Anne. "Did you hear what he had the gall to write last week?"

"No."

"He stated that the Pétainists had loved France in their own way and that they're closer to the Gaullists than a separatist who fought in the Resistance. No one else has gone that far yet!" Nadine said, looking pleased. "Ah, the old friends are really turning sour!" she added. "Did you read what Julien had to say about Volange's book?"

"Robert showed it to me," Anne replied. "Julien! Who would have believed it!"

"It isn't so surprising," Dubreuilh said. "After all, what other course can an anarchist take nowadays? On the left, no one's amused by their little destructive games."

"I don't see why an anarchist inevitably has to become a Gaullist," Nadine said.

She always took any explanation for an excuse, and often she would refuse to understand in order not to spoil the pleasure of venting her indignation. There was a silence. Those four-sided conversations had never been easy; now they were less so than ever. Henri began talking to Anne about a novel which she had brought back from the United States and which he had just finished reading. Dubreuilh was thinking of something else. So was Nadine. Everyone felt relieved when the meal was over.

"May I take the car?" Nadine asked, getting up from the table. "If someone's willing to look after Maria, I'd love to go for a drive."

"I'll look after her," Anne volunteered.

"Aren't you going to take me along?" Henri asked, smiling.

"First of all, you don't really want to go," Nadine replied. "And secondly, I'd rather be alone," she added with a smile.

"All right, I won't insist!" Henri said. He kissed her. "Have a nice drive—and be careful."

He had no desire to go for a drive, but neither did he feel very much like working. Dubreuilh had thought highly of his first short story, and the one he now wanted to write was constantly on his mind. But he felt a little at sea these days. He was no longer in France, and not yet in Italy; to all intents and purposes, the trial in Tananarive was over, since the accused refused to defend themselves, and the verdict itself a foregone conclusion; Dubreuilh's activities irritated him, and yet he vaguely envied him the joys he appeared to be deriving from them. He picked up a book. Thank heavens, his days, his hours were no longer filled to overflowing; there was no need for him to push himself. He would wait until he was settled in Porto Venere to begin his new story.

About seven o'clock, Anne called him in to have an *apéritif*—a little rite she had established. Dubreuilh was still writing when Henri entered the study. He pushed aside his papers. "Well, that's done, at least."

"What is it?" Henri asked.

"An outline of the talk I'm going to give on Friday in Lyon."

Henri smiled. "You certainly have a lot of courage. Nancy, Lyon! What dismal cities!"

"Yes, Nancy is dismal," Dubreuilh said. "And yet, I have pleasant memories of the evening I spent there."

"I'm beginning to suspect you of being just a litle eccentric," Henri said.

"Maybe," Dubreuilh said. He smiled. "I don't know how to explain it to you. After the meeting, we went to a bistro to have some sauerkraut and sausages and drink some beer. There was nothing unusual about the place; I barely knew the men who were with me, and we talked very little. But we had done something together, something with which we were satisfied. It was a good feeling."

"I know. I've had that feeling," Henri said. He had had such moments in the war, during the Resistance, at the newspaper the first year. "But I never had it with the S.R.L.," he added.

"Neither did I," Dubreuilh said. He took the martini Anne handed him and drank a sip. "We weren't modest enough. To have those little moments of happiness, you've got to work in the actual present."

"Look," Henri said. "Wanting to prevent war doesn't seem to me so modest!"

"It's modest because we aren't organising in terms of a lot of preconceived ideas we'd like to impose upon the world," Dubreuilh said. "The S.R.L. had a constructive programme and it was necessarily utopian. What I am doing now is much more like what I was doing in '36. We're trying to defend ourselves against a given danger by employing whatever means are at hand. That's far more realistic."

"It's realistic if it serves some purpose," Henri remarked.

"It can serve a purpose," Dubreuilh said.

There was a silence. "What exactly is going on in his head?" Henri wondered. He had too readily accepted Nadine's point of view: "He gets excited because he's bored." But that bit of cynicism didn't take care of things at all. He had learned that Dubreuilh couldn't blindly be taken seriously; that, however, didn't give him the right to consider the man an impetuous fool.

"There's one thing I don't understand," Henri said. "You were saying last year that you, personally, couldn't swallow what you called 'the new humanism.' And here you are walking hand in hand with the Communists, right down the line. What bothered you then doesn't bother you any more?"

"You know," Dubreuilh said, "that humanism I spoke about is nothing more or less than the expression of the world of to-day. You can no more reject it than you can reject the world. You can sulk about it, that's all."

"That's what he thinks of me," Henri thought. "I'm sulking." Until the day he died, Dubreuilh would continue looking upon his own past and the pasts of others with a superior air. "Well, I was the one who went looking for it," Henri said to himself. He wanted to understand Dubreuilh and not defend himself against him. There was no point in defending himself: he knew he was safe.

He smiled. "What made you stop sulking?"

"Because one day I felt as if I belonged back in the thick

of things," Dubreuilh replied. "Oh, it's quite simple," he went on. "Last year, I would say to myself, 'Everything is evil; even the least of evils is still too hard to swallow so that I can think of it as a good thing.' But the situation grew even graver. The worst evil became so menacing that my reservations in regard to Communism and the Soviet Union seemed to me very secondary." Dubreuilh looked directly at Henri. "What surprises me is that you didn't feel that as I did."

Henri shrugged his shoulders. "I've known quite a few Communists, and this past month I've worked with La-chaume. I understand their point of view very well. But I just don't take to them; I'll never take to them."

"It's not a question of joining the Party," Dubreuilh said. "But you don't have to agree with them about everything to wage a common fight against America and against war."

"You're more dedicated than I am," Henri said. "I'm not going to sacrifice the life I want to lead to a cause I only half believe in."

"Oh, don't give me that kind of argument!" Dubreuilh said. "It makes me think of Volange when he says: 'Man doesn't deserve to have any interest taken in him.'"

"That isn't the same thing at all," Henri said sharply.

"It's closer than you think," Dubreuilh said. He looked at Henri questioningly. "You are convinced, aren't you, that as between Russia and the United States you must choose Russia?"

"Of course."

"All right! That's quite enough! There's one thing that you must realise," he said heatedly, "and that is that accept-ance is always a matter of choice, love always a matter of preference. If you wait until you meet absolute perfection before getting involved, you'll never love anyone and never do anything."

"Without demanding perfection, you can nevertheless come to the conclusion that things are pretty rotten, and not feel like getting mixed up in them," Henri said.

"Rotten in relation to what?" Dubreuilh asked.

"In relation to what they could be."

"You mean to certain concepts you have in your head," Dubreuilh said. He shrugged his shoulders. "The Soviet Union as it should be, revolution without tears—those are all

pure concepts, that is to say: nothing. Obviously, compared
to the concept, reality is always wrong; as soon as a concept
is embodied, it becomes deformed. But the superiority of the
Soviet Union over all other possible socialisms is that it
exists."

Henri looked questioningly at Dubreuilh. "If what exists
is always right, there's nothing left to do but fold your arms
and sit back."

"Not at all. Reality isn't frozen," Dubreuilh said. "It
has possibilities, a future. But to act on it—and even to
think about it—you've got to get inside it and stop playing
around with little dreams."

"You know, I have very few dreams," Henri said.

"When someone says, 'Things are rotten,' or, as I was
saying last year, 'Everything is evil,' it can mean only that
he's dreaming secretly of some absolute good." He looked
Henri in the eyes. "We don't always realise it, but it takes a
hell of a lot of arrogance to place your dreams above everything else. When you're modest, you begin to understand
that, on the one hand, there's reality, and on the other,
nothing. And I know of no worse error than preferring
emptiness to fullness," he added.

Henri turned to Anne, who was silently drinking a second
martini. "What do you think about it?"

"Personally, I've always had trouble considering a lesser
evil a good thing," she replied. "But that's because I believed
too long in God. I think Robert is right."

"Maybe," Henri said.

"I speak as one who knows," Dubreuilh said. "I also
tried to justify my inclinations in terms of the unworthiness
of the world."

Henri refilled his glass. Wasn't Dubreuilh actually attempting to justify his present inclinations in terms of theories?
"But if you take that tack, then it's also through inclination
that I'm trying to belittle what he's saying," he thought. He
decided to concede the point to him, at least until the conversation was over.

"All the same, your way of seeing things seems rather
pessimistic to me," he said.

"There again, it's only pessimistic in relation to the ideas
I used to conjure up," Dubreuilh said, "ideas which were
much too rosy. History isn't rosy. But since you can't escape

it, you've got to seek the best way of living in it. In my opinion, abstention isn't the answer."

Henri wanted to question him further, but there was a sound of steps in the hall, and then Nadine opened the door.

"Hallo, you drunkards," she said gaily. "You can drink to my health—I deserve a toast of honour!" She looked at them triumphantly. "Guess what I did?"

"What?" Henri said.

"I went to Paris and took our revenge. I slapped Lambert." There was a brief silence.

"Where did you run into him? How did it happen?" Henri asked.

"Well, I went up to *L'Espoir*," Nadine said proudly, "and I walked right into the editorial room. They were all there— Samazelle, Volange, Lambert, and a lot of new ones with nasty-looking faces. It seemed strange to see them there." Nadine began to laugh. "Lambert looked flabbergasted. He started to mumble something, but I cut him off. 'There's an old debt I owe you,' I said to him. 'I'm glad you've given me the opportunity to pay you back.' And I hit him right in the face."

"What did he do?" Henri asked.

"Oh, he played it dignified," Nadine replied. "He put on a big show of pained self-righteousness. I got out of there fast."

"Did he ask why I don't run my own errands? That's what I would have said in his place," Henri said. He didn't want to scold Nadine, but he was very displeased.

"I didn't listen to what he said," Nadine replied. She looked defiantly from one to the other. "Well? Aren't you going to congratulate me?"

"No," Dubreuilh replied. "I don't think what you just did was clever at all."

"Well, I think it was very clever," Nadine said. "I saw Vincent as I was leaving and he told me I was quite a girl," she added spitefully.

"If what you want is publicity, you certainly did the right thing," Dubreuilh said. "The papers are going to eat it up."

"I don't give a damn about the papers," Nadine said.

"This seems to prove that you do give a damn!"

They glared at each other angrily for a moment.

"If you like being covered with muck, that's your business," Nadine said angrily. "As for me, I don't like it at all." She turned to Henri. "It's all your fault," she said sharply. "Why did you have to go telling everyone all about us?"

"Look," Henri said, "I didn't write about us. You know very well that all the characters were made up."

"Nonsense. There are dozens of things in your novel that apply to Father and you. And I very clearly recognised three lines of mine," she said.

"They're spoken by people who have no connection with you," Henri said. He shrugged his shoulders. "Of course, I tried to depict present-day people, men and women who are in somewhat the same situation as ours. But there are thousands of people like that; neither your father nor I is specifically portrayed. On the contrary, in most respects my characters don't resemble us at all."

"I didn't protest until now because you would have told me I was just making a fuss over nothing again," Nadine said bitterly. "But do you think it's pleasant? I talk to you unsuspectingly, I believe we're friends, and all the while you're observing, you're taking notes in your head. And then, bang! one fine day you see it all written down in black and white, words that were spoken to be forgotten, gestures that didn't count. I call that an abuse of confidence!"

"You can't write a novel without picking up little things around you," Henri said.

"Maybe, but then people shouldn't associate with writers," Nadine said furiously.

Henri smiled at her. "You certainly must have been born under an evil star!"

"Go ahead! Make fun of me now," she said, growing very red.

"I'm not making fun of you," Henri said. He put his arm around Nadine's shoulder. "Look, let's not turn this thing into a minor tragedy."

"You're the ones who are making a tragedy of it!" Nadine said. "Ah, you look just great, the three of you, looking at me as if you were judges!"

"Don't be foolish, no one's judging you," Anne said in a conciliatory voice. She sought Dubreuilh's eyes. "All the same, it's satisfying to think that Lambert got a good slap in the face."

Dubreuilh didn't answer. Henri tried to change the subject. "You saw Vincent? What's he doing these days?"

"What would you like him to be doing?" she said offensively.

"Is he still with the radio?"

"Yes." Nadine hesitated. "I had something very interesting to tell you, but I don't feel like it any more."

"Go on, let's hear it!" Henri said.

"Vincent has located Sézenac!" Nadine said. "In a little hotel in the Batignolles section. As soon as he got the address, he went over and knocked on Sézenac's door; he wanted to let him know what was on his mind. Sézenac refused to open the door. So Vincent decided to wait for him in front of the hotel, and while he stood guard there Sézenac got away by a back entrance. For three days now, he hasn't shown his face—not at the hotel, nor his regular restaurant, or any of the bars where he gets his dope. Nowhere." Triumphantly, she added, "Isn't that an admission of guilt? If he had nothing on his conscience, he wouldn't be hiding."

"That depends on what Vincent said to him through the door," Henri said. "Even if he were innocent, he could have got scared."

"I disagree. An innocent man would have tried to explain himself," Nadine said. She turned to her mother and added, aggressively, "You don't seem to be very interested —even though you knew Sézenac."

"Yes," Anne said, "I had him down as a confirmed addict. When you reach that stage, you're capable of anything."

There was a heavy silence. Anxiously, Henri thought, "Sooner or later, Vincent is going to find Sézenac again. And then what?" If Sézenac talked and if Lambert were furious enough with Henri to confirm his story, what would happen? Anne and Dubreuilh were probably asking themselves the same question.

"Well, if that's all the effect it has on you, I'd have done better to keep it to myself," Nadine said resentfully.

"Not at all," Henri said. "It's rather a strange story; that's why we're mulling it over."

"Don't bother to be polite!" Nadine said. "You're grown-ups and I'm just a child. What I find interesting doesn't interest you. It's only natural." She walked to the door. "I'm going up and take a look at Maria."

She sulked all through the rest of the evening. "Living here all together like this is no good for her," Henri thought. "It'll be a lot better in Italy." And with a slight feeling of anguish, he said to himself. "Only ten more days." Everything was set. Nadine and Maria were going by train in a sleeping car and he would precede them in the car. Just ten days. At moments, he could already feel a warm wind on his face, a wind smelling of salt and resin, and a surge of happiness would swell his heart. But at other moments, he had a feeling of regret that bordered on resentment—as if he were being sent into exile against his will.

All the next day, Henri kept thinking about the conversation he had had with Dubreuilh, a conversation that had continued late into the night. The only question, Dubreuilh declared, was to choose, among existing things, those you preferred. It wasn't a question of resignation; you resign yourself when, between two real things, you accept the one which is worth less. But there was nothing above humanity, even such as it was. Yes, on certain levels, Henri agreed. Preferring emptiness to fullness was what he had blamed Paula for; she had clung steadfastly to old myths instead of taking him as he was. Conversely, he had never sought "the ideal woman" in Nadine; he had chosen to live with her in spite of knowing her faults. It was especially when you thought of books and works of art that Dubreuilh's attitude seemed justified. The books you want to write are never written, and you can amuse yourself by seeing a defeat in every masterpiece. And yet, we don't dream of a superterrestrial art; the works we prefer command our absolute love. On the political level, however, Henri felt less convinced—because evil intervenes there. And it isn't always just a lesser good; it can be the absolutes of misery, of death. But then again, if you attach importance to misery, to death, to individual men, it isn't enough to say to yourself, "Anyhow, it's a sad business," to feel authorised to wash your hands of it. It is essential that it be more or less sad. Evening was falling and Henri was musing under the linden tree when Anne appeared in the doorway.

"Henri!" she called to him in a calm but urgent voice, and
he thought, with a touch of annoyance, "More trouble with
Nadine."

He walked to the house. "Yes?" he said.

Dubreuilh was sitting beside the fireplace and Nadine was
standing in front of him, an obstinate look on her face, her
hands dug into the pockets of her slacks.

"Sézenac just showed up," Anne said.

"Sézenac?"

"He claims someone's after him—to kill him. He's been
hiding for five days, but he couldn't hold out any longer.
Five days without drugs—he's at the end of his tether." She
pointed to the door leading to the dining-room. "He's in
there, lying on the couch, sick as a dog. I'm going to give him
a shot."

She was holding a hypodermic syringe in her hand and
there was a box of pharmaceuticals on the table.

"You'll give him a shot after he's talked," Nadine said in
a merciless voice. "He was hoping Mother would be chump
enough to help him without asking any questions," she
added. "But no luck—I happened to be here."

"Did he talk?" Henri asked.

"He's going to talk," Nadine said. She walked briskly to
the door and opened it. In an almost friendly voice, she
called out, "Sézenac!"

Henri stood motionless in the doorway next to Anne as
Nadine went over to the couch. Sézenac didn't move; he was
lying on his back, he was moaning, his hands were opening
and closing spasmodically. "Hurry!" he said. "Hurry!"

"You're going to get your shot," Nadine said. "Look!
Mother has brought you some morphine."

Sézenac turned his head; his face was dripping with
sweat.

"Only first you're going to answer some questions," Nadine
said. "What year did you begin working for the Gestapo?"

"I'm going to die," Sézenac said. Tears were streaming
down his cheeks and he was kicking at empty air. It was an
almost intolerable scene, and Henri wished that Anne would
put an end to it immediately. But she seemed paralysed.

Nadine stepped closer to the couch. "Answer and you'll
get your shot," she said. She leaned over Sézenac. "Answer
or it will go hard on you. What year?"

"Never," he gasped. He kicked the air once more and sank back on the couch, inert. There was a bit of white foam at the corner of his mouth.

Henri took a step towards Nadine. "Leave him alone."

"No, I want him to talk," she said violently. "He'll talk or he'll die. Do you hear?" she asked, turning to Sézenac. "If you don't talk, we'll let you die."

Anne and Dubreuilh stood rooted to the floor; it was true that if one wanted to know what to believe about Sézenac now if ever was the time to question him. And it was better to know.

Nadine grabbed Sézenac by the hair. "We know you denounced Jews, lots of Jews. When did you begin? Talk!"

She shook his head, and he groaned, "You're hurting me!"

"Answer! How many Jews did you denounce?" Nadine said.

He whimpered in pain. "I helped them," he said. "I helped them escape."

Nadine let him drop. "You didn't help them; you denounced them! How many did you denounce?"

Sézenac began sobbing into the pillow.

"You denounced them! Admit it!" Nadine said.

"Just one from time to time, to save the others. I had to," Sézenac said. He raised himself and looked around him with a dazed expression. "You're unfair! I saved them. I saved many of them."

"It's just the opposite," Nadine said. "You saved one out of twenty so that it would bring you customers. And you denounced the others. How many did you denounce?"

"I don't know," Sézenac said. Suddenly he cried out, "Don't let me die!"

"Oh, that's enough!" Anne said, walking over to the couch. She leaned over Sézenac and pushed up his sleeve.

Nadine turned to Henri. "Are you convinced?"

"Yes," he said. "And yet," he added, "I still can't bring myself to believe it."

Often he had seen Sézenac, his eyes glassy, his palms damp; and he was seeing him now, prostrate on that couch. But all that couldn't blot out the image of the young hero in his red neckerchief, strutting from barricade to barricade with a huge rifle on his shoulder.

They returned to the study and sat down, and Henri asked, " Well, what are we going to do?"

" There can't be any question about that," Nadine said. " He deserves a bullet in the head."

" Are you the one who's going to shoot him?" Dubreuilh said.

" No, but I'm going to call the police," Nadine said, reaching for the telephone.

" The police! Do you realise what you're saying!" Dubreuilh said.

" You'd turn someone in to the police?" Henri asked.

" Hell! You don't think I'm going to have any qualms about a man who denounced dozens of Jews to the Gestapo!" Nadine said.

" Hang up that telephone and sit down," Dubreuilh said impatiently. " Calling the police is out of the question. That said, we've got to decide on what to do. We can't nurse him, shelter him and calmly send him back to his charming trade."

" That's being logical!" Nadine said angrily. She stood, her back pressed hard against the wall, glaring at the others.

There was a silence. Four years earlier, everything would have been simple. When action is a living reality, when you believe in certain objectives, the verdict is inevitable: a traitor is something you shoot down. But what to do with a traitor out of the past when you no longer have any hope?

" Let's keep him here two or three days—long enough to get him back on his feet," Anne said. " He's really very sick. And then we can ship him off to some distant colony— French West Africa, for example. We know some people there. He'd never come back; he's too afraid of getting himself killed."

" And what will he do there? After all, we aren't going to give him letters of recommendation," Dubreuilh said.

" And why not? While you're at it, you might as well give him an allowance too," Nadine said, her voice trembling with anger.

" You know, he'll never break himself of the habit; he's a complete wreck," Anne said. " Whatever we decide, the life he has ahead of him is quite horrible enough."

Nadine stamped her foot. " He isn't going to get away with it that easy!"

" There are so many others who got away with it," Henri said.

"That's no reason." She looked at Henri suspiciously. "Would you by any chance be afraid of him?"

" Me?"

" He seems to have something on you."

" He thinks that Henri belongs to Vincent's gang," Dubreuilh said.

" It's not that," Nadine said. "You heard him. He said to me, ' If I talk, your husband's in for the same trouble I am.' "

Henri smiled. " Do you think I was a double agent?"

" I don't know what to think," she replied. " No one ever tells me anything. Oh, I don't give a damn," she added. " You can keep your secrets. But I want Sézenac to pay! You do realise what's he's done, don't you?"

" We realise," Anne said. " But what good will it do to make him pay for it? You can't bring the dead back to life."

" You talk like Lambert! You may not be able to bring them back to life, but that's no reason to forget them. We aren't dead ; we can still think of them and not kiss the feet of their murderers."

" But we have forgotten them," Anne said sharply. " Maybe it isn't our fault, but it means we no longer have any rights on the past."

" I haven't forgotten anything," Nadine said. " Not I."

" You're no different. You have your life, you have a little girl ; you have forgotten. And if you're so set on having Sézenac punished, it's because you want to prove the opposite to yourself. And that is being dishonest."

" Refusing to take part in your little schemes is being dishonest?" Nadine said. She walked to the door. " Well, I call your scruples cowardice!" she shouted. She slammed the door behind her.

" I understand her," Anne said. " When I think of Diego, I understand her." She got up. " I'm going to put up a bed for him in the cottage. He's sleeping ; all you'll have to do is carry him over . . ." She left the room quickly, and Henri had the feeling that she was on the verge of tears.

" There was a time when I would have been capable of killing him myself," Henri said. " To-day it would make no sense. And yet it is shameful to help someone like that to go on living," he added.

" Yes, any solution will necessarily be a bad one," Dubreuilh said. He looked over at Sézenac. " The only time problems are capable of solution is when they don't arise. If we were still active, there would be no problem. Only now we're on the outside, so our decision will necessarily be arbitrary." He stood up. " Let's put him to bed."

Sézenac was sleeping. With his eyes closed, there were traces of his former good looks on his peaceful face. He wasn't heavy. They carried him over to the cottage and set him down fully dressed on the bed. Anne spread a blanket over his legs.

" Someone who's sleeping always seems so harmless," she murmured.

" He may not be as harmless as all that," Henri said. " He must have a lot on Vincent and his pals. And the way things are now, there are a lot of people around who'd gladly whitewash a former Gestapo agent in order to jump on some former Maquisards."

" Don't you think that if Sézenac had something on him Vincent would already have been in trouble?" Anne asked.

" Listen," Dubreuilh said, " while you're taking care of him, why not try to pump him? Drug addicts talk easily; we might find out what he's got on his chest." He thought for a moment. " I think that, after all, the best solution will be to ship him off," he said.

" Why did he have to come here!" Anne said.

She seemed so overwrought that Henri felt he had best leave her alone with Dubreuilh. He went up to his room, explaining that he had lost his appetite and would have a bite with Nadine a little later.

He leaned his elbows on the window sill. In the distance, he could see the dark mass of a hill and, close up, the cottage in which Sézenac was lying. He recalled another night, a joyous Christmas Eve, when Sézenac was sprawled out on a rug in Paula's apartment. They had been laughing happily together, congratulating each other on the victory, shouting, " Long live America!" with Preston and drinking to the Soviet Union. And Sézenac was a traitor, helpful America was preparing to subjugate Europe, and as for what was going

on in Russia it was better not to look too closely. Emptied
of the promises it had never held, the past was now nothing
but a booby trap. The headlights of a car dug a wide, bright
trench in the side of the black hill. For a long time, Henri
remained motionless, watching those beams of light winding
their way through the night. Sézenac was sleeping, and his
crimes with him. Nadine was wandering about the countryside; he had no desire to have it out with her. He went to
bed without waiting for her to return.

Through a confused dream, Henri suddenly thought he
heard a strange sound, the sound of hail. He opened his eyes.
A ray of light was filtering under the door; Nadine had
returned and was lying awake, still full of wrath. But the
sound hadn't come from Nadine's room. There was a rain
of pebbles against the window panes. "Sézenac," Henri
thought, jumping out of bed. He opened the window and
leaned out. It was Vincent. Quickly, he put on his clothes
and went down to the garden.

"What the hell are you doing here?"

Vincent was sitting on the green wooden bench against the
wall of the house. His face was calm, but his left foot was
tapping the ground with a convulsive movement; his trouser
leg was trembling.

"I need your help. Do you have your car here?"

"Yes. Why?"

"I just killed Sézenac. We've got to get him out of here."
Stupefied, Henri looked at Vincent. "You killed him?"

"There was nothing to it," Vincent said. "He was sleeping. I used my silencer, it didn't make a sound." He was
speaking in a clear fast voice. "Only the bastard wouldn't
burn," he added.

"Burn?"

"We swiped some phosphorus tablets from the Krauts
during the Resistance. They usually work very well, but
maybe they're too old now—although I did take care to
keep them dry. I waited three hours and all they did was
make a little hole in his belly. It's getting late; we'll haul
him off in the car."

"Why did you do it?" Henri murmured. He sat down on
the bench. He knew that Vincent was capable of killing,
that he had killed. But that was abstract knowledge; until
now, Vincent was a murderer without victims; his habit,

like drinking or drug addiction, was harmful to no one but himself. And now he had gone into the cottage, a gun in his hand, had placed the barrel against a living temple, and Sézenac was dead. For three hours, Vincent had sat up with a friend he had just shot, a friend who refused to burn.

"We should have shipped him off to some jungle and he'd have never come back!" Henri said.

"Not a chance!" Vincent said. His leg had stopped trembling, but his voice seemed less sure. "Sézenac! A denouncer! Can you imagine that! What was the matter with us? Chancel who used to say, 'That's my little brother.' And me, poor fool! If I hadn't been on my guard because of the dope business, he'd have squealed on me to the cops. And I did things for him I never did for anyone else. Even if I had been sure it would cost me my life, I'd have treated myself to his."

"How did you know he was here?"

"I picked up his trail," Vincent replied vaguely. "I came by bike," he added. "I'd have stuffed the remains in a sack, tied a rock to it, and tossed it all in the river. I could easily have managed it alone. I just can't understand why he didn't burn," he repeated in perplexity. He thought for a moment in silence and then stood up. "We'd better hurry."

"What do you intend doing?"

"We'll take him for a bath, a little eternal bath. I found just the place for it."

Henri didn't budge. He felt as if he were being asked to kill Sézenac with his own hands.

"What's the matter?" Vincent asked. "We can't leave him here, can we? If you don't want to give me a hand, all right. Just lend me the car and I'll try to manage it without you."

"I'll help you," Henri said. "But I ask you one thing in return; promise me you'll leave that gang."

"What I just did, I did on my own," Vincent replied. "And as for my gang, I repeat what I told you once before: you have nothing better to offer me. All those bastards who are showing up again—what are you doing to stop them? Nothing. So just let us look out for ourselves."

"That's no way of looking out for yourself."

"You have none better to suggest. Come or don't come," Vincent added, "but make up your mind."

" All right," Henri said. " I'll come."

It wasn't the moment to hold a discussion. And besides, he didn't really know what it was he was talking about; nothing seemed real. A little breeze was playing with the branches of the linden tree and the smell of fading roses was drifting up towards the blue-shuttered house; it was one of those nights like all other nights, in which nothing happens. He followed Vincent into the cottage, and it was the everyday world that collapsed into nothingness. The smell was unmistakable: thick, overwhelming, the smell that fills a kitchen when a chicken is being singed. Henri looked at the bed and stifled a cry. A Negro! The face of the man lying on the white sheet was totally black.

" It's the phosphorus," Vincent said. He threw back the sheet. " Look at that."

The little hole in his temple was stopped with cotton: not a trace of blood. Vincent was meticulous. The body with its protruding ribs was the colour of burned bread, and the phosphorus had dug a deep furrow in the middle of the abdomen. There was no connection between Sézenac and that black, lifeless object.

" How about the clothes?" Henri asked.

" I'll take care of that; I'll stick them in my saddlebags." He grabbed hold of the corpse under the arms. " Watch out he doesn't break in half; it would make quite a mess," he said in the competent voice of a nurse. Henri took the corpse by the feet, and they carried it to the garage.

" Wait till I get my stuff," Vincent said.

He had hidden his bicycle behind a bush; he brought back a length of rope and a sack weighted down with a rock.

" He won't fit in the sack, but I'll manage," Vincent said. He placed the rock wrapped in the sack against Sézenac's body, binding it firmly with several turns of rope which he made fast with a running knot. " This way, he's sure to go to the bottom," he said with satisfaction.

They set the thing down on the rear seat and covered it with a blanket. The house seemed asleep; only Nadine's window was lit. Did she suspect something? They pushed the car out to the road, and Henri did his best to start it up quietly. The village, too, seemed asleep, but there were surely insomniacs about listening to every sound.

"Did he denounce many Jews?" Henri asked. Justice hardly entered into this thing, but he needed to convince himself of Sézenac's crimes.

"Hundreds. It was wholesale work, that border-crossing business. The bastard! When I think he almost got away from me!" Vincent said. "And it was my own fault; I did a stupid thing. When I picked up his trail, I ran right over to his hotel, like a fool. I'd have killed him there in his room —which wouldn't have been very clever. He refused to open up, and then he slipped through my fingers. But I got him, all the same!"

He continued talking, stammering occasionally, as the car drove along the sleeping road. It was hard to believe, under that silent sky, that there were men in every part of the world who were dying, killing, and that this story was real.

"Why did he work with the Gestapo?" Henri asked.

"He needed the cash," Vincent replied. "I thought he started taking dope only after Chancel died, after everything began turning rotten. But no, it goes 'way back. Poor Chancel! He used to say that Sézenac liked to live danger-ously, and he admired him for that. He never suspected that what it added up to was dope and cash at any price."

"But why did he take dope? He seemed like a decent sort of guy—good background, respectable family."

"He was a black sheep," Vincent said puritanically. "A black sheep who turned into a bastard." He fell silent, and after a moment, pointed ahead. "There's the bridge."

The road was deserted, the river deserted. In a matter of seconds, they tossed the thing that was once Sézenac over the parapet. There was a splash, an eddy, a few ripples, and once more an innocent river, a deserted road, the sky, silence. "I'll never really know who it was who was just swallowed up," Henri said to himself. The thought disturbed him, as if he at least owed Sézenac a formal funeral oration.

"Thanks a lot," Vincent said when they got back into the car.

"Keep your thanks," Henri said. "I helped you because I had to. But I'm against these killings—more than ever."

"A bastard less is a bastard less," Vincent said.

"I can understand your wanting to settle Sézenac's account," Henri said. "But don't tell me you have genuine reasons for killing men you don't even know. You, too, have found a kind of dope there, a mania."

"You're wrong," Vincent said. "I don't like to kill. I'm not a sadist, I hate blood. There were guys in the Maquis who got a big thrill out of shooting down the Militiamen. They'd slice them to bits with their sub-machine guns. I hated that. I'm a normal guy, and you damned well know it!"

"There must be something wrong," Henri said. "It isn't normal to kill for the sake of killing."

"I don't kill for the sake of killing, but only to make sure that certain bastards die."

"And why are you so bent on seeing them dead?"

"It's normal to want somebody you really hate to die. If you didn't, you'd be warped." He shrugged his shoulders. "It's a lot of bunk, those stories about killers being sex perverts, and all that crap. I don't say there aren't one or two nuts in the gang, but the wildest bunch are the good solid family men who screw to their heart's content, and without any nonsense."

For a moment, they drove along in silence.

"You see," Vincent said, "you've got to know what side you're on."

"No need to kill for that," Henri said.

"You've got to get your feet wet."

"When a man like Gérard Patureau goes off to defend the Madagascans at the risk of getting himself lynched, he's wetting his feet, and it means something. I advise you to wet your feet doing something useful."

"What can you do that's useful when we're all going to die in the next war? You can settle accounts, that's all."

"There may not be any war."

"You know damned well there will! We're caught like rats in a trap!" Vincent said. They arrived in front of the garden, and Vincent added, "Listen, if anything ever comes up, you know nothing, saw nothing, heard nothing. Sézenac disappeared, and you thought he just took off. If they tell you I talked, you can be sure and certain that it's a bluff. Deny everything."

"If anything comes up, I won't let you down," Henri said. "And now, get the hell out of here quietly."

"I'm getting the hell out."

Henri put the car in the garage; when he came out again, Vincent had disappeared. It was possible to believe that Sézenac had indeed vanished into thin air, that Vincent had never set foot in St. Martin, that nothing had happened.

But something had happened. In the greyness of the early morning, they were sitting in the living-room, all three of them, Anne and Dubreuilh wrapped in bathrobes and Nadine fully dressed. She was crying; she raised her head and asked in a frenzied voice, "Where were you?"

He sat down beside her and put his arm around her shoulders. "Why are you crying?"

"It's my fault!" Nadine moaned.

"What's your fault?"

"I was the one who called up Vincent. I called him from the café. If only I wasn't overheard!"

Anne quickly said, "She only wanted Vincent to denounce Sézenac to the police."

"I begged him not to come," Nadine said. "But nothing doing. I waited for him out on the road; I was afraid. He swore to me he just wanted to talk to Sézenac, and then he sent me back to my room. Quite a while later, he threw some pebbles at my window and asked me which one was yours. What happened?" she asked in a terrorised voice.

"Sézenac's at the bottom of a river with a big rock around his neck," Henri replied. "It'll be a long time before he's found."

"Oh, my God!" Nadine began to weep again and her sobs shook her whole sturdy body.

"Sézenac deserved a bullet in the head, you said so yourself," Dubreuilh said. "And I honestly believe that's the best thing that could have happened to him."

"He was living, and now he's dead!" Nadine said. "It's so horrible!"

They let her weep without saying anything. Finally, she raised her head. "What's going to happen now?"

"Nothing at all."

"Suppose someone finds him?"

"No one will find him," Henri replied.

"They're going to start worrying about his disappearance. Who knows if he didn't tell his girl or his friends he was coming here? Maybe someone in the village noticed Vincent's comings and goings, and yours. And suppose there's another spy in Vincent's crowd and he guesses the whole thing?"

"Calm down. If the worst happens, I can take care of myself."

"You're an accomplice to a murder."

"I'm sure that with a good lawyer I'd be acquitted," Henri said.

"No, it isn't that sure!" Nadine said.

She was weeping in an access of remorse that filled Henri with consternation. It was to spite her parents and himself that she had gone into the telephone booth. Was it really impossible to rid her of that stubborn resentment of which she herself was the first victim? How unhappy she made herself!

"They'll put you in prison for years!" she said.

"Of course not!" Henri said. He took Nadine by the arm. "Come and lie down. You haven't slept all night."

"I won't be able to sleep."

"You're going to try. And so am I."

They climbed the stairs and went into Henri's room. Nadine wiped her eyes and noisily blew her nose. "You hate me, don't you?"

"You're out of your mind!" Henri said. "You know what I think," he added. "I think it's you who hates everyone a little. I don't care about the others, but you mustn't hate me—because I love you. Get that in your head: I love you."

"No, you don't, you don't really love me," Nadine said. "And you're right, too. I'm not a very lovable kind of person."

"Sit down here," Henri said. He sat down beside her and placed his hand on hers. He felt very much like being alone, but he couldn't leave Nadine to her remorse. And he himself had a vague feeling of remorse, because he hadn't succeeded in winning her confidence. "Look at me," he said.

She turned her face to him, a pitiful face with rings under the eyes, and suddenly he felt a great surge of affection for her. Yes, the thing you prefer to all others, you love, and he was fonder of her than anything else in the world. He loved her, and he had to convince her of it.

"You really believe I don't love you? You're serious about it?"

Nadine shrugged her shoulders. " Why should you love me? What have I got to give you? I'm not even pretty."

"Oh, for God's stake, drop those idiotic complexes!" Henri said. " I like you the way you are. And what you have to give me is yourself. And since I love you, that's all I ask of you."

Nadine looked up at him disconsolately. " If only I could believe it."

" Try."

" No," she replied, "I know myself too well."

" I know you pretty well, too."

" Exactly."

" I know you and I think only well of you. So?"

" So that means you don't know me at all."

Henri laughed. " Now there's what I call a wonderful piece of reasoning!"

" I'm rotten!" Nadine said. " I'm always doing rotten things."

" You know that isn't true. Last night you were furious, and it's understandable. You didn't foresee what would happen. So stop eating yourself up over it."

" You're nice," Nadine said. " But I don't deserve it." She began crying again. " Why am I like that? I disgust myself."

" That's very wrong of you," Henri said tenderly.

" I disgust myself!" she repeated.

" You mustn't darling," Henri said. " Don't you see, everything would be so much better if your mind weren't made up that no one loves you. You hold a grudge against people because of their supposed indifference, so from time to time, in reprisal, you lie to them or play a nasty trick on them. But it never really amounts to much, and it doesn't stem from a very black soul."

Nadine shook her head. " You don't know what I'm capable of."

Henri smiled. " I know very well."

" No, you don't," she said in such a desperate voice that Henri took her in his arms.

" Listen," he said, " if you have something on your conscience, you'd do best to tell me about it. It will seem less terrible once you've said it."

" I can't," Nadine said. " It's too rotten."

" Don't tell me about it if you don't want to," Henri said.
" But if it's what I think it really isn't very serious."

Nadine looked at him, worried. " What do you think it is?"

" Is it something that concerns you and me?"

" Yes," she replied without taking her eyes off him. Her
lips were trembling.

" You became pregnant on purpose? Is that what's tormenting you?"

Nadine lowered her head. " How did you guess?"

" You must have cheated; that was the only explanation."

" You knew it all along!" she said. " Don't tell me I don't
disgust you!"

" But look here, Nadine; you'd never have let me marry
you if I hadn't honestly wanted to; you'd never have black-
mailed me. It was just a little game you were playing with
yourself."

With a pleading look, she raised her eyes to him. " No, I
would never have blackmailed you."

" I know that. For one reason or another, you must have
been angry with me, so you arranged that little business. It
gave you pleasure to force a situation on me I hadn't wanted.
But you were risking much more than I, because you never
seriously intended to force my hand."

" All the same, it *was* rotten!" Nadine said.

" Not really. It was mostly useless. A little sooner or a
little later, we would have got married and had a child."

" Do you really mean that?" Nadine asked.

" Of course. We got married because we wanted to, both
of us. And the fact that I suspected you actually wanted
what happened to you made me feel under less of an obligation to you."

Nadine hesitated. " Yes, I suppose that if the prospect of
living with me had really displeased you, you wouldn't have
married me," she said.

" Put just a little more effort into it," Henri said gaily,
" and try to understand that if I didn't love you, it certainly
would have displeased me."

" That's something else again," Nadine said. " You can
enjoy living with someone without being in love."

" Not I," Henri said. " Look, why don't you want to
believe I love you?" he added a little impatiently.

"It isn't my fault," Nadine said with a sigh. "I'm suspicious."

"You haven't always been," Henri said. "You weren't with Diego."

Nadine stiffened. "That was different."

"In what way?"

"Diego belonged to me."

"No more than I do," Henri said with spirit. "The difference is that he was a child. But he would have grown up. And if you weren't convinced beforehand that every adult is a judge, therefore an enemy, my age wouldn't bother you."

"With you it will never be the way it was with Diego," Nadine said firmly.

"No two loves are alike," Henri said. "But why make comparisons? Obviously, if you seek something in our relationship other than what it is, you won't find it."

"I'll never forget Diego," Nadine said.

"Don't forget him. But don't use your memories against me. That's what you're doing," he added. "For a lot of reasons, you've got a grudge against your present life. So you take refuge in the past; and in the name of the past, you assume a superior attitude over everything that happens to you."

Nadine looked up at him hesitantly. "Yes, I do cling to my past," she said.

"And I can well understand that," Henri said. "But there's one thing you've got to recognise: it isn't because you have very vivid memories that you're always approaching life with a chip on your shoulder. It's the reverse: you call upon those memories to justify your temperament."

Nadine remained silent a moment. Thoughtfully, she bit her lower lip. "Why do I have a chip on my shoulder?"

"Out of resentment, out of distrust. It's a vicious circle," Henri replied. "You start by doubting my love, which gives you a reason to bear me a grudge; and then, as if to punish me, you distrust me all the more and you become sulky. But think a moment," he said emphatically. "If I love you, I deserve your confidence, and you're being unfair in not giving it to me."

Nadine shrugged her shoulders dejectedly. "If it's a vicious circle, you can't break it."

"You can," Henri said. "If you want to, you can." He held her against him. "Make up your mind to give me your confidence, even without being sure I deserve it. I know you dread the thought of being had, but at least it's better than being unfair. And you'll see," he added, "I'll deserve it."

"You think I'm unfair to you?" Nadine asked.

"Yes. You're unfair when you blame me for not being Diego, unfair when you look upon me as a judge when I'm a man who loves you."

"I don't want to be unfair," Nadine said in a troubled voice. "I don't want to."

Henri smiled. "Then don't. If you'd just co-operate a little, I'd end up by convincing you," he said, giving her a kiss.

She threw her arms around his neck. "Forgive me," she said.

"I've nothing to forgive you for. Come," he added. "Now, you're going to try and get some sleep. We'll talk it all over again to-morrow."

He helped put her to bed, tucked her in, and went back to his room. Never had he talked so frankly with Nadine, and it seemed to him as if something had given way in her. He had to persevere. "And then what?" he said to himself with a sigh. To make her happy, he himself would have to be happy. That morning, he had absolutely no idea of what that word might mean.

The next day and the day after, the newspapers carried no mention of Sézenac's disappearance. Henri thought he could still smell an odour of burnt flesh around the cottage, and he was unable to blot from his mind the image of Sézenac's bloated face, his gashed belly. But that nightmare was already overshadowed by another anxiety: the Big Three had just broken with Moscow and the situation between East and West was so tense that war seemed imminent. That afternoon, Henri and Nadine drove Dubreuilh to the Gare de Lyon; like everyone else, he, too, was sombre. From afar, Henri watched him shaking hands inside the station. "He must think it's rather ridiculous to be going off to-day of all days, to defend the peace with speeches," Henri said to himself. And yet, when Dubreuilh started walking towards the platforms accompanied by three other men, Henri felt a sort of regret as he followed them with his eyes. He had the feeling of being excluded.

"What now?" Nadine asked.

"First, we'll go and pick up your tickets, and then we'll get the permit for the car."

"We're going to leave anyhow?"

"Yes," Henri replied. "If we see that the situation is getting worse, we'll put off our departure. But maybe things will ease up. We've set a date; for the time being, we'll stick to it."

They did some shopping, bought some records, stopped off at *Vigilance*, and then went to see Lachaume at *L'Enclume*. The Communists had decided to take the Madagascan affair in hand, officially, as soon as the verdict was handed down. The political committee would issue a statement, petitions would be circulated, meetings organised. Lachaume was trying hard to seem optimistic, but he knew perfectly well that nothing would be achieved. As for the international situation, he wasn't at all cheerful, either. Henri took Nadine to the cinema. On their way back to St. Martin, as they drove along the highway, through a late afternoon drizzle, she pestered him with questions he was unable to answer. "If they want to mobilise you, what will you do? What will it be like if the Russians occupy Paris? What's going to become of us if America wins?" Dinner was gloomy and, immediately afterwards, Anne went up to her room; Henri remained in the study with Nadine. She took two bulging envelopes and her sleeping-car tickets from her purse.

"Do you want to see your post?"

"Yes, let me have it."

Nadine handed him one of the envelopes and then examined her ticket. "Can you imagine! I'm going to travel in a sleeping car! I'll be ashamed."

"Aren't you happy? You always wanted so much to travel by sleeping car."

"When I used to go third class, I envied the people in the sleeping cars. But I don't like to think that I'm the one who's going to be envied now," Nadine said. She put her ticket back into her purse. "Now that I've actually got the ticket in my hands, going away seems terribly real to me."

"Why do you say ' terribly '?"

"Going away is always a little terrible, isn't it?"

"The thing that bothers me is the uncertainty," Henri said. "I'd like to be sure we'll be able to leave."

"You know, maybe we should have pushed back the date a little," Nadine said. "Are you sure you don't mind not taking part in that meeting Lachaume was talking about?"

"Now that the Communists are going to go all out, there won't be any need for me any more," Henri said. "If we start putting off our departure, there's no point at which we can stop," he added sharply. "On the fourteenth, a new trial begins. And when the Madagascan affair is over with, there'll be other things coming up. We must make it a clear break."

"Well, that's your business," Nadine said.

She began going through the press clippings, and Henri opened a letter, a very amiable letter from a young man. There were a lot of amiable letters, and usually they pleased him. But that night, without quite knowing why, it irritated him to think that in the eyes of certain people he passed for a splendid specimen of humanity. The clock struck ten. Dubreuilh was speaking out against war, but Henri suddenly wished he were in his place. He had often said to himself, "War is like death: there's no use preparing for it." But when an aeroplane starts into a nose-dive, it's better to be the pilot who's trying to pull out of it than a terrorised passenger. Doing something, even though it were only speaking, was better than sitting by himself in a corner with that dark weight on his heart. Henri pictured the hall filled with people, their faces upturned towards Dubreuilh, Dubreuilh bent towards them, throwing out words. There was no room in them for fear, for anguish; together, they were hoping. After it was over, Dubreuilh would go to a bistro, a very ordinary bistro, and eat sausages and drink wine. No one would have very much to say, but they would feel good. Henri lit a cigarette. You don't prevent a war with words. But speaking was not necessarily a way of changing history; it was also a certain way of living it. In the silence of that study, given over to his innermost nightmares, Henri felt he was living it poorly.

"The last issue got a good press," Nadine said. "They say a lot of nice things about your story."

"Yes, it's doing all right, that monthly," Henri replied indifferently.

"The only thing wrong with it is that it's a monthly," Nadine said. "Obviously, for day-to-day news, it would be another matter if we had a weekly."

"Why doesn't your father accept the offer?" Henri asked. "He's dying to do it. The people in his movement would be delighted, and the Communists look on the project with a very favourable eye. What's holding him back?"

"You know very well," Nadine replied. "He doesn't want to get involved in it without you."

"That's ridiculous," Henri said. "He can find all the associates he wants."

"It wouldn't be the same thing," Nadine said with animation. "He needs someone he could trust with his eyes closed. He's changed, you know," she added. "It must be his age. He no longer thinks that there's nothing in the world he cannot do."

"All the same, I think he'll end up by accepting," Henri said. "Everyone's pushing him."

Nadine sought Henri's eyes. "If we weren't leaving for Italy, would you have liked to take a hand in it?"

"To get away from that kind of thing is precisely why we're leaving," Henri replied.

"Not I," she said. "I'm leaving so that I can live in the sun in a lovely place."

"There's that, too, of course," Henri said.

Nadine reached for the letters. "May I read them?"

"If you like."

He began thumbing through the press clippings, but without conviction. He would no longer have anything to do with *Vigilance*; all that didn't concern him any more.

"It's nice, this letter from the college boy," Nadine said.

Henri smiled. "The one who says my life serves him as an example?"

"One follows whatever examples one can," Nadine said with a smile. "Seriously, though," she added, "he's got a pretty good way of looking at things."

"Yes. This idea of a total man is idiotic. Actually I'm just a petit-bourgeois writer who steers his course more or less well—and usually rather less well—between his obligations and his desires. That's all."

Nadine's face darkened. "And I, what am I?"

Henri shrugged his shoulders. "The truth is it's best not to concern yourself with what you are, because there's nothing you can do about it."

Nadine looked at him uncertainly. "Well, what else do you want me to be concerned with?"

Henri fell silent. And he, once he was in Italy, with what would he concern himself? He would begin again to take a deep interest in writing; therefore, he would no longer be tempted to question himself as a writer. Good. But being a writer doesn't solve everything. He didn't very well see how he could avoid thinking about himself.

"You have Maria, you have your life, you have things that interest you," he replied weakly.

"I also have lots of time," Nadine said. "In Porto Venere, we'll have a tremendous amount of time."

Henri studied her for a moment. "Does that frighten you?"

"I don't know," she replied. "All I know is that before I had this ticket in my pocket, I never really believed we would leave. Did you believe it?"

"Naturally."

"It isn't natural," Nadine said in a slightly aggressive voice. "You talk, you exchange letters, you make preparations—but as long as you haven't actually boarded the train, it might all very well be nothing but a game." She paused a moment and then added, "Are you at least sure that you want to leave?"

"Why do you ask that?"

"Just a feeling I have," she replied.

"You think I'm afraid of being bored with you?"

"No. You've told me fifty times already that I don't bore you, and I've decided to believe you," she said in a serious voice. "I'm thinking of, well, of the whole thing . . ."

"What whole thing?" Henri asked.

He was a little annoyed. That was just like Nadine: she wanted things, and more greedily than anyone else, but when she got them she lost her head. It was she who had had the idea of that house, and she seemed so set on going that not for a moment had Henri ever questioned the project. And suddenly, she left him standing alone before a future that could no longer be taken for granted.

" You say you won't read the newspapers any more—but you'll read them," Nadine said. " It's going to seem strange when we receive *Vigilance,* or that weekly, if it ever comes out."

" Listen," Henri said, " when you leave like this for a long time, there's always a bad moment to go through. But that's no reason to suddenly change all your plans."

" It would be silly to leave only so as not to change our plans," Nadine said soberly.

" Didn't you hear what your father was saying the other day? If I stayed, everything would begin all over again ; it would be the same as it was before, when you used to scold me for not taking any time off to live."

" I used to say a lot of stupid things," Nadine said.

" This year, I've taken time off and I've been very happy," Henri said. " I'm leaving for Italy so that it will go on like this."

Nadine looked at him hesitantly. " If you really think you'll be happy there . . ."

Henri didn't answer. Happy. The fact was the word no longer had any meaning. You can never possess the world, and protecting yourself against it is out of the question, too. You're in it, that's all. In Porto Venere, as in Paris, the whole earth would be present around him, with its miseries, its crimes, its injustices. He could spend the rest of his life fleeing and he would never find a refuge. He would read the papers, he would listen to the radio, he would receive letters. All he could gain would be that he could say to himself, " There's nothing I can do." Suddenly, something exploded inside his chest. No. The solitude that was suffocating him that evening, that mute impotence, that wasn't what he wanted. No. He would never consent to say to himself for the rest of his life, " Everything is happening without me." Nadine had seen through him: not for a moment had he really chosen that exile. He suddenly realised that for days he had been suffering the thought with dread.

" Would you be happy if we stayed here?" he asked.

" I'd be happy anywhere, if you were," she replied with ardour.

" You wanted to live in the sun, in a beautiful place."

" Yes." Nadine hesitated. " You know, people who dream of paradise, when they're actually faced with the prospect, they aren't in so much of a hurry to go any more," she said.

"In other words, you'd be sorry to leave?"

Nadine looked at him seriously. "I ask only one thing of you: do what you want to do. I suppose I'm just as selfish as I always was," she added, "but I'm less nearsighted. If I thought I'd forced you into something, it would poison my existence."

"I really don't know what I want any more," Henri said. He got up and put one of the records they had just bought on the gramophone. If he didn't leave, he wouldn't often find the time to listen to them. He looked around him. If he didn't leave, he knew what would be awaiting him. This time he was forewarned. "At least, I'll avoid certain traps," he said to himself. And then he thought, with resignation, "But I'll fall into others."

"Shall we listen to a little music?" he asked. "We don't have to decide anything to-night."

But he knew he had already decided.

CHAPTER TWELVE

DID I have a presentiment I would come to this? When I took that vial from Paula's purse, I had intended to throw it away, and I hid it in the bottom of my glove box. I need only go up to my room, I need only make a single move, and I'll be done with it. That thought gives me a feeling of reassurance. I press my cheek against the warm grass; I say softly, "I want to die." The tenseness in my throat disappears, I suddenly feel very calm.

It isn't because of Lewis. It's been two weeks since the huge orchid faded, since I threw it away—the end of an unresolved affair. Even in Chicago, I was beginning to get over it; I would get over it, I couldn't help but get over it. It isn't because of those men who are being murdered almost everywhere in the world, nor because of the war hanging over us: whether you're killed or whether you die doesn't make very much difference. And everyone dies, at about the same age, at about forty. No, none of that moves me; if things move me, I would feel alive, I wouldn't want to stop being alive. But once more, as on that day when I was fifteen, when I cried out in fear, death is stalking me. I am no longer fifteen. I no longer have the strength to flee. To escape a few days of waiting, the condemned man hangs himself in his cell. And I'm supposed to wait patiently for years! What for? I'm tired. Death seems much less terrible when you're tired. If I could die of the longing I have for death, I should take advantage of it.

It's been going on like this for two weeks now, since the moment I arrived in Paris. Robert was waiting for me at the Gare des Invalides. He didn't see me right away. He was pacing the sidewalk with the little steps of an old man, and suddenly I thought, "He's old!" He smiled at me; his eyes were as young as ever, but his face was beginning to crumble; it will go on crumbling until the day it decomposes. Since then, I haven't stopped thinking: "He's good for ten or fifteen years, twenty years, perhaps. Twenty years

is so little time! And then he'll die. He'll die before me."
There are nights when I awaken with a start and say to
myself, "He'll die before me." He was talking with Henri
this morning, they were saying they would have to start all
over again, that one always started all over again, that one
can't do otherwise; they were making plans, they were arguing. And I was looking at his teeth; it's the only constant
thing in a body—the teeth, where the skeleton bares itself.
I was looking at Robert's skeleton and I was saying to
myself, "He's waiting for his hour." The hour would come.
We're allowed to linger a while, some more, some less, but
none of us are ever spared. I shall see Robert stretched out
on a bed, his skin waxen, a false smile on his lips; I'll be
alone before his body. What lies, those peaceful monuments
of stone sleeping side by side in their crypts, and those
couples entwined on their funeral urns! They can mix our
ashes together as much as they want to, but they won't unite
our deaths. For twenty years, I believed we were living
together; but no, each of us is alone, imprisoned in his
body, with his arteries hardening under his withering skin,
with his liver, his kidneys, wearing out and his blood turning
pale, with his death which ripens noiselessly inside him and
which separates him from everyone else.

I know what Robert would tell me; he's told it to me
before: "I'm not a reprieved corpse. I'm a living man." He
had convinced me. But that's the truth by which the living
live. At that time, I was playing with the idea of death—
with the idea only, for I still belonged to this world. To-day,
it's another matter. I'm not playing any more. Death is here.
It's masking the blue of the sky, it has swallowed the past and
devoured the future. The earth is frozen over; nothingness
has reclaimed it. A bad dream is still floating through
eternity, a bubble which I shall burst.

I raise myself on my elbow, I look at the house, the linden
tree, the cradle in which Maria is sleeping. It's a day like
any other, and in appearance the sky is blue. But what a
desert! Everything is still. Perhaps that stillness is only the
silence in my heart. There is no more love in me, for anyone,
for anything, I used to think, "The world is vast inexhaustible; a single existence is hardly enough to drink your fill
of it." And now, I look at it with indifference; it's nothing
but a huge place of exile. What do I care about the distant

galaxies and the billions of men who will forever not know me! I have only my life; it alone counts. And now it doesn't count any more. I can see nothing left for me to do on earth. My profession? What a joke! How could I presume to stop a woman from crying, compel a man to sleep? Nadine loves Henri; I'm no longer important to her. Robert has been happy with me as he would have been with someone else, or none. *Give him paper, time, and he lacks for nothing.* He'll miss me, of course; but he isn't given to sorrowing, and besides, he too will soon be under the earth. Lewis had needed me; I had thought, "It's too late to start, too late to start over again"; I gave myself reasons, all my reasons have left me; he doesn't need me any more. I listen attentively: not a call, anywhere. Nothing protects me against that little vial waiting for me in the bottom of my glove box.

I sat up. I looked at Maria. On her inscrutable little face I again see my death. One day she'll be as old as I am, and I'll no longer be here. She sleeps, she breathes; she's very real. She's the reality of the future and of oblivion. It will be autumn; she'll be walking in this garden, perhaps, or somewhere else. If by chance she should speak my name, no one will answer—and my silence will be lost in the universal silence. But she won't even speak it; my absence will be so complete that no one will be aware of it. The thought of that emptiness makes me dizzy.

And yet I remember that life, sometimes, was as wonderful as a fair, and sleep as tender as a smile. In Goa, we slept on the terrace of the hotel; at dawn, the wind rushed into the mosquito netting and the bed pitched like a boat; off Aegina, it was on the bridge of a ship smelling of tar, and a plump orange moon was rising behind the island; the sky and the earth were blending together in the waters of the Mississippi, the hammock was swinging gently in the patio where the frogs were croaking, and I could see the constellations jostling one another above my head. I have slept in the sand of dunes, in the hay of barns, on moss, on pine needles, under tents, in the Delphic stadium and the Epidaurus theatre with the sky as my roof, on the floors of waiting-rooms, on wooden window seats, in old canopied beds, in big country beds stuffed with down, and on balconies, on benches, on roof tops. I have also slept in men's arms.

Enough! Every memory awakens another agony. How many of the dead I carry within me! Dead is the child who believed in paradise, dead the girl who thought immortal the books, the ideas, and the man she loved, dead the young woman who walked overwhelmed through a world promised to happiness, dead the woman in love who would wake up laughing in Lewis's arms. They're as dead as Diego, as dead as Lewis's love. And they have no tombs either; that is why the peacefulness of hell is forbidden them. They still remember, feebly; and moaning, they call out for sleep. Take pity on them. Let us bury them all at once.

I walked towards the house, I slipped noiselessly past Robert's window. He is sitting at his desk; he is working. How close he is! How far away! I need only to call him and he'll smile at me. And then what? He would smile from a distance—an impassable distance. Between his life and my death, there is no road. I went up to my room; I opened the glove box. I took out the vial. The death that's in me I hold in my hand—a small brownish vial. Suddenly death no longer threatens me; he is dependent on me. I lay down on the bed, gripping the vial, and I closed my eyes.

I was cold, and yet I was bathed in sweat. I was afraid. Someone was going to poison me. It was I; it was no longer I. It was pitch black; everything was very far away. My fingers tightened around the vial. I was afraid. But with all my soul I wanted to conquer fear. I will conquer it. I will drink. If not, everything will begin again. I don't want it to. Everything will begin again; once more, I'll find my thoughts in order, always in the same order, and things as well, and people, Maria in her cradle, Diego nowhere, Robert peacefully heading towards his death, Lewis towards oblivion, I towards reason, which maintains order: the past behind, the future ahead, invisible, light distinct from darkness, this world emerging victoriously from nothingness, and my heart precisely in the place where it's beating, neither in Chicago, nor beside Robert's corpse, but in its cage under my ribs. Everything will begin again. I will tell myself, "It's just that I was feeling very depressed." The facts that nail me to this bed, I will explain away as depression. No! I've denied enough, forgotten enough, fled enough, lied enough. Once, one single time and forever, I want to make truth triumph.

Death has won; death is now the only truth. A single move and that truth will become eternal.

I opened my eyes; it was daytime. But there was no longer any difference between night and day. I was floating on silence, a great religious silence, the same silence I knew when I used to lie on my eiderdown pillow, waiting for an angel to carry me off. The garden, the rooms were silent. I, too. I was no longer afraid. Everything consented to my death. I consented to it. My heart is no longer beating for anyone; it's as if it were no longer beating at all, it's as if everyone else in the world had already fallen to dust.

Sounds rose from the garden—steps, voices. But they did not disturb the silence. I could see, and I was blind; I could hear, and I was deaf. Nadine said very loudly in an irritated voice, " Mother shouldn't have left Maria alone." The words passed over my head without grazing me; their words could no longer reach me. Suddenly, there was a feeble echo in me, a little gnawing sound. " Did something happen?" Maria alone on the lawn: a cat might have scratched her, a dog bitten her. No, they were laughing in the garden, but the silence didn't close in again. The echo repeated, " I shouldn't have done it." And I imagined Nadine's voice, intense and indignant, saying, " You shouldn't have done it! You had no right to do it! " The blood rushed to my face and something living burned my heart. " I have no right to do it!" The burning awakened me. I sat up, looked dully at the walls; I was holding the vial in my hand, the room was empty, but I was no longer alone. They would come into the room; I would see nothing, but they would see me. How could I have not thought of it? I can't impose my corpse and everything that would come after that on their hearts: Robert bending over this bed, Lewis in his house in Parker with the words dancing before his eyes, Nadine sobbing furiously. I can't. I stood up, I took a few steps, I fell into a chair in front of my dressing-table. It's strange. I would die alone; yet it's the others who would live my death.

For a long time, I sat before the mirror, looking at my face, the face of a survivor. The lips would have become blue, the nostrils pinched. But not for me: for them. My death does not belong to me. The vial is still here, within reach of my hand; death is still present. But the living are even more so. At least as long as Robert lives, I won't be able to escape them. I put the vial away. Condemned to death; but also condemned to live! how long! ten years? twenty years? I had said, "Twenty years is so little time." Now ten years seems endless to me—a long black tunnel.

"A.en't you coming down?"

Nadine has knocked, has come in; she is standing beside me. I can feel myself turning pale. She would have come in, would have seen me on the bed, my body convulsed—how horrible!

"What's wrong with you? Are you sick?" she asks in a worried voice.

"I had a headache. I came up to take some aspirin."

My voice issues effortlessly from my mouth; it seems normal to me.

"And you left Maria alone," Nadine says, scolding.

"I would have gone straight back down, but I heard you. So I decided to stay here and rest a moment." I add, "I feel much better."

Nadine looks at me suspiciously, but all she suspects is that I'm pining over a love affair.

"Really? Are you sure?"

"The aspirin helped." I get up to escape that inquisitor's look. "Let's go down."

Henri handed me a cocktail. He was looking over some papers with Robert, who cheerfully began explaining things to me. I asked myself in bewilderment, "How could I ever have been such a fool? How could I have failed to think of the endless remorse I was preparing for him?" No, it wasn't just foolishness. For a moment, I had really passed over to the other side, there where nothing counts any more, where everything is equal to nothing.

"Are you listening to me?" Robert asked. He smiled at me. "Where are you?"

"Here," I replied.

I am here. They are living. they speak to me, I'm alive. Once more, I've jumped feet first into life. Words are entering my ears; little by little, they take on meaning. Here are the estimates for the weekly and the layouts Henri suggests. Do I have an idea for a name? None of the ones they've thought of so far are suitable. I try to think of a name. I say to myself that, since they were strong enough to wrest me from death, perhaps they will know how to help me to live again. They will surely know. Either one founders in apathy, or the earth becomes repeopled. I didn't founder. Since my heart continues to beat, it will have to beat for something, for someone. Since I'm not deaf, I'll once more hear people calling to me. Who knows? Perhaps one day I'll be happy again. Who knows?

THE END

Simone de Beauvoir

She Came to Stay

The passionately eloquent and ironic novel she wrote as an act of revenge against the woman who so nearly destroyed her life with the philosopher Sartre. 'A writer whose tears for her characters freeze as they drop.'   *Sunday Times*

The Mandarins

'A magnificent satire by the author of *The Second Sex*. *The Mandarins* gives us a brilliant survey of the post-war French intellectual . . . a dazzling panorama.'   *New Statesman*

'A superb document . . . a remarkable novel.'   *Sunday Times*

The Woman Destroyed

'Simone de Beauvoir shares with other women novelists the ability to write about emotion in terms of direct experience. What is almost unique, and supremely valuable, in her work is the capacity to retain a crucial detachment towards her material. The women at the centre of *The Woman Destroyed* all suffer the pains of growing older and of being betrayed by husbands and children.'   *Sunday Times*

When Things of the Spirit Come First

The five women at the centre of this novel are all enmeshed in the moral and social demands of middle-class society. Even those among them who try to be rebels themselves are hobbled by their upbringing and their self-deception. 'It is because of women like Simone De Beauvoir that the prejudice and repression of which she writes no longer has such effect.'

Over 21

FLAMINGO

André Brink

One of South Africa's leading Afrikaner Writers

Looking on Darkness

'A novel of stature that explores our cancerous condition more persistently than any other novel has done before, and without benefit of anaesthetic.' *Alan Paton*

An Instant in the Wind

'It is difficult to see how any South African novelist will be able to surpass the honesty of this novel.'
World Literature Today

Rumours of Rain

'It both enriches our understanding and increases our knowledge of the world we live in.' *Spectator*

A Dry White Season

Winner of the Martin Luther King Memorial Prize, 1980.

'The revolt of the reasonable . . . far more deadly than any amount of shouting from the housetops.' *Guardian*

A Chain of Voices

This novel transforms a political statement into a compelling and moving artistic achievement.

'A triumph.' *The Times*

The Wall of the Plague

'Particularly powerful and affecting . . . subtle and suggestive.' *Literary Review*

FLAMINGO

Russian Novels

The First Circle Alexander Solzhenitsyn

The unforgettable novel of Stalin's post-war Terror.

'An unqualified masterpiece – this immense epic of the dark side of Soviet life.' *Observer*

'At once classic and contemporary . . . future generations will read it with wonder and awe.' *New York Times*

The White Guard Mikhail Bulgakov

'A powerful reverie . . . the city is so vivid to the eye that it is the real hero of the book.' *V. S. Pritchett, New Statesman*

'Set in Kiev in 1918 . . . the tumultuous atmosphere of the Ukrainian capital in revolution and civil war is brilliantly evoked.' *Daily Telegraph*

The Master and Margarita Mikhail Bulgakov

'This fantasy entirely captures me. Wildly funny as it often is, the maddest jokes have an ominous tone.' *Guardian*

'A dazzling translation from the uncut, smuggled original.' *Sunday Telegraph*

Doctor Zhivago Boris Pasternak

'One of the great events in man's literary and moral history.' *New Yorker*

'Pasternak has written one of the great books, courageous, tender, tragic, humble.' *The Times*

FLAMINGO

Anthony Powell

A Dance to the Music of Time

'The most significant work of fiction produced in England since the last war.' *Clive James*

FLAMINGO

FLAMINGO

Flamingo is a quality imprint publishing both fiction and non-fiction. Below are some recent titles.

Fiction

☐ Life and Fate *Vasily Grossman* £5.95
☐ Shadows on Our Skin *Jennifer Johnston* £2.95
☐ Sent For You Yesterday *John Edgar Wideman* £2.95
☐ The Lover *Marguerite Duras* £2.95
☐ Hiding Place *John Edgar Wideman* £2.95
☐ Black Snow *Mikhail Bulgakov* £2.95
☐ A Perfect Peace *Amos Oz* £3.95
☐ Damballah *John Edgar Wideman* £2.95

Non-fiction

☐ Myths and Memories *Gilbert Adair* £3.50
☐ Surviving the Holocaust *Bruno Bettelheim* £3.50
☐ Cappaghglass *Peter Somerville-Large* £3.95
☐ Pictures from the Water Trade *John David Morley* £3.50
☐ Love Lessons *Joan Wyndham* £2.95
☐ In the Freud Archives *Janet Malcolm* £3.50
☐ My Last Breath *Luis Buñuel* £3.50

You can buy Flamingo paperbacks at your local bookshop or newsagent. Or you can order them from Fontana Paperbacks, Cash Sales Department, Box 29, Douglas, Isle of Man. Please send a cheque, postal or money order (not currency) worth the purchase price plus 15p per book (maximum postal charge is £3.00 for orders within the UK).

NAME (Block letters) _____

ADDRESS_____

_____

_____